THE HALVA-MAKER

Reem Bassiouney

The Halva-Maker (Novel)

The Trilogy of the Fatimids

Originally published as *'Al-Halawani'*

Translated by:Roger Allen

© 2024 Dar Arab For Publishing and Translation LTD.

United Kingdom
60 Blakes Quay
Gas Works Road
RG1 3EN
Reading
United Kingdom
info@dararab.co.uk
www.dararab.co.uk

First Edition 2024
ISBN 978-1-78871-102-9

Copyrights © dararab 2024

دار عرب للنشر والترجمة
DAR ARAB FOR PUBLISHING & TRANSLATION

Text Edited: Marcia Lynx Qualey
Cover & Text Design: Nasser Al Badri

REEM BASSIOUNEY

THE
HALVA-MAKER

THE TRILOGY OF THE FATIMIDS
(SICILIAN, ARMENIAN, KURDISH)

A NOVEL

TRANSLATED BY ROGER ALLEN

Table of Contents

DEDICATION 7
THE FIRST STORY
CHAPTER ONE 17
CHAPTER TWO 35
CHAPTER THREE 47
CHAPTER FOUR 97
 BOOK TWO
CHAPTER FIVE 113
CHAPTER SIX..139
CHAPTER SEVEN 149
CHAPTER EIGHT..161
THE SECOND STORY
BOOK ONE
CHAPTER ONE 175
CHAPTER TWO 191
CHAPTER THREE 223
CHAPTER FOUR...233
BOOK TWO
CHAPTER FIVE 243
CHAPTER SIX..253
BOOK THREE
CHAPTER SEVEN 297
CHAPTER EIGHT..311
CHAPTER NINE 335
CHAPTER TEN 351
CHAPTER ELEVEN 359
CHAPTER TWELVE..369
CHAPTER THIRTEEN...383
CHAPTER FOURTEEN..387
CHAPTER FIFTEEN...391

CHAPTER SIXTEEN 403

BOOK FOUR

CHAPTER SEVENTEEN..................413

CHAPTER EIGHTEEN..................431

CHAPTER NINETEEN..................441

CHAPTER TWENTY..................453

THE THIRD STORY

BOOK ONE

CHAPTER ONE..................469

CHAPTER TWO..................481

CHAPTER THREE..................493

CHAPTER FOUR..................507

CHAPTER FIVE..................533

CHAPTER SIX..................545

BOOK TWO

CHAPTER SEVEN..................597

CHAPTER EIGHT..................603

CHAPTER NINE..................613

BOOK THREE

CHAPTER TEN..................637

CHAPTER ELEVEN..................643

CHAPTER TWELVE..................649

CHAPTER THIRTEEN..................671

CHAPTER FOURTEEN..................687

CHAPTER FIFTEEN..................697

CHAPTER SIXTEEN..................707

CHAPTER SEVENTEEN..................725

LIST OF CHARACTERS (in order of appearance)..................739

A LIST OF FATIMID HALVA..................743

EGYPT: DYNASTIC CHART..................745

TIMELINE..................747

THE HALVA-MAKER: AFTERWORD..................751

DEDICATION

My dear beautiful mother, this novel is the last work you read before you departed to a better place. With me, you loved Badr al-Jamali, the Supreme Master; with me, you walked through the Cairo streets with the Sicilian and travelled to universes with Ibrahim and Rashida. Thank you for making the best halva in the land of Egypt.

I don't want this novel to be the last work you will read in your better place. I hear your voice all around me and want to assure you that your presence in our lives—yours and my father's—is a continuing one and an affectionate counsellor. Every single day, you both teach us lessons more profound and powerful than in the past.

I dedicate this novel to you both.

Mother, you taught me courage and adherence to the flash of lightning.

Father, you are the one who taught me to trust that I could achieve the goal, no matter how often the demons of heaven and earth fought me.

You are far, yet your love is never far from the heart.

You are absent, yet ever present in the heart.

Ibn al-Farid, 12-13th century poet

For Nur ad-din Muhammad Khidr
and Ahmad Rif`at Bassiouney

"It is said that, when Joseph—prayers and blessings be upon him!—entered Egypt and took up residence there, he said: 'O God, I am a stranger here. Make this land beloved to me and every stranger.' Joseph's prayer was answered. No stranger ever entered Egypt without relishing his residence there."

Imam Jalal ad-din as-Suyuti,

Husn al-muhadara fi akhbar Misr wa-al-Qahira

"Courage is a moment when man chooses to butt against the demons of heaven and earth on his own. There is neither hesitation nor misgiving. He casts all caution into the river's depths and cleaves solely to the lightning flash."

Bahnas, the Pyramid Witch

2016 CE / 1437 AH

"Crazy `Amm `Abdo is the Doughnut-man"—or, anyhow, that's what the people in Cairo's Bab al-Bahr district used to call him. He had perfected the art of conversation and yet would speak only to those who wanted to listen. He would make doughnuts for people who really valued them and could never complete a sentence without cursing the world and everything in it. Before I met him, I had already heard a good deal about him. They said that no one could make sweet pastries like `Amm `Abdo in the whole of Cairo, and maybe even the world. In his younger days, he would only moisten kunafa with sherbet after he had smoked a cigarette packed with Afghan hashish, all in order to retrieve glorious memories. The first time I met `Amm `Abdo, I deliberately wore loose-fitting clothes and listened with a patient humility. He opened his fingers very precisely, and bits of dough dropped into the hot oil. They crystalised in seconds and assumed a symmetrical circular shape and a solid, stable identity. I stared at the pieces of dough as they slipped from his fingers. He looked away, spat, and cursed the oil. Then he bent over with a frown, grabbed hold of his foot, and, using his fingers, pulled out a nail that had been bothering him. That done, he plunged his hand back into the dough. I restrained myself so I would not lose my temper or scold him. Instead, I gave him a smile.

"Do you know who I am, `Amm `Abdo?" I asked.

"No, I don't," he replied without a moment's thought.

He looked skinny. His thin white hair was dishevelled, and his shirt (which was also white) sagged from a long life spent covering his skin.

"I've come to see you," I told him gently, "specially to ask you..."

He stuck his fingers in the oil and brought out a piece of doughnut.

"Taste this first," he said, handing it to me.

I took it and put it in my mouth without thinking. It burned my mouth, so I spat it out, nervously, then put it back in my mouth.

"Forgive me, `Amm `Abdo," I told him gently, "I've come to ask you about your life."

"If you write a pack of lies," he replied without the slightest surprise, "then there's nothing about my life to interest you. But if your accounts tell the truth, then I'll talk to you."

"My accounts are truthful," I said. "Talk to me."

He went on opening his fingers and rolling the dough between his hands.

"Do you know," he asked me "who has tasted my sweet pastries?"

"Who?" I asked, without thinking. "A minister, or—"

"Salah ad-din the Ayyubid," he interrupted eagerly.

I pressed down on my chest so as not to gasp.

"`Amm `Abdo," I replied, "Salah ad-din died over a thousand years ago."

"Go on, say it," he went on, just as eagerly, "don't be shy. `Amm `Abdo's crazy. His name's Yusuf, Salah ad-din Yusuf ibn Ayyub. His given name's Yusuf. He couldn't resist doughnuts. Who built Misr?"

"What do you mean by that?" I asked, swallowing hard. "Egypt or Cairo?"

He laughed out loud.

"Who built Cairo?" he asked.

"Jawhar the Sicilian," I replied, remembering my history classes.

"You know a lot," he told me, as though I were his five-year-old daughter.

"People say that Jawhar the Sicilian was a halva-maker, and so the builder of Cairo was one, too. Don't believe them. Jawhar the Sicilian was an army general, but I know about the halva-maker who managed to vanquish the fires started by Al-Hakim bi-Amr Allah. Then Badr al-Jamali learned to relish the taste of sugar and tempted Salah ad-din with sweet pastries."

"But ` Amm ` Abdo, Al-Hakim bi-Amr Allah was a Fatimid and Salah ad-din was an Ayyubid. Now we're in the era of—"

"It's an era with no name, my daughter. As I told you, if you've come only to complain, then leave now. But, if you've come to listen, then do so without interrupting. What I'm going to tell you is true. Humanity has only just a few stories left. The day will come when you'll be saying that ` Amm ` Abdo told you this and that. Some people might not believe you, but you'll keep on telling the stories and overcome every fear, just as Ja`far did."

"God grant you long life!" I whispered sympathetically. "Who is this Ja`far?"

"The only one who was never afraid of the Armenian. But Ja`far the Sicilian..."

"Tell me all about it slowly and forgive my ignorance. Start at the beginning."

"Do you have enough time to listen?"

"Yes, I do."

"What do you know about halva?" he asked with no preliminaries.

"It's full of honey and sugar."

He stopped abruptly, as though I had slapped or dishonoured him.

"You don't know a thing about it," he said. "I'll teach you to open your heart to what's beautiful. We can only observe beauty when our hearts are opened. There are tales and legends about halva."

I opened my eyes wide, like a child seeing colours for the very first time, hearing birdcalls and hanging suspended with the rain in the thick foliage of trees. He spoke slowly, as though he wanted me to memorise his words.

"I'm going to tell you about the Sicilian, the Armenian, and the Kurd," he said, "and the confectioner as well. I'll tell you what they said. Some of the words will emerge only from the soul, and they'll linger in the memory. You know about Jawhar the Sicilian and what he said, don't you?"

"Yes, I do know about him," I replied eagerly. "But I don't know what he said."

"Everyone loves their home and the land where they grew up," he said. "That's the way people and countries are. But sometimes—actually rarely—your foot will tread on a land where you did not grow up, and yet it will draw you in so much that you'll get stuck in its mud like someone bewitched. Then you'll adopt it as your homeland and make its territory into a home, just like a doughnut when it sticks to your fingers and the sweet taste lingers in your mouth. Of the past, all we remember are smells and tastes. Homeland has a smell that lingers inside your mouth. Anyone who savours that sweetness never forgets it. When that taste lingers, if indeed it does, it's something amazing. You'll go to war for its sake, as though your roots keep on growing inside its belly. Not every land is destined for settlement, and yet, once you discover the land where you're going to take the plunge, you'll never escape its grasp. In Egypt, my daughter, there was an Egyptian who wanted to run away and emigrate, and there was a Sicilian who built walls and settled down. But that Sicilian never would have learned anything about Egypt had it not been for the confectioner and what he heard from halva."

It seemed to me that the lump of hashish that ʿAmm ʿAbdo had swallowed was going to do away with his mind.

"ʿAmm ʿAbdo," I asked him in amazement, "can halva talk?"

This time, he gave me an angry look, as though I was his ten-year-old daughter who had forgotten her multiplication tables.

"I don't smoke hashish anymore," he went on. "I used to smoke it as a way of forgetting that halva can talk. They were forever looking over my shoulder and criticising, and I hate criticism. Yes, O learned researcher, they can talk, just as walls can— as buildings rue the loss of passion and walls seek help from the sheer crush of humanity. Yes, they can talk, like sails, mosques, and city walls."

"But ʿAmm ʿAbdo, those are buildings constructed for eternity. But doughnuts and maulid treats—"

I was shocked by the abrupt way he interrupted me.

"Those are buildings intended to remind us that there's an eternity in another world. Doughnuts have the nectar of paradise and the savour of that other world. If you listened to them and gave them the chance, they would talk to you. I listen and talk to them every day. Then what happens to them? Don't they toy with your heart, even if it's only for a little while?"

"What do doughnuts tell you?"

"They tell me that you haven't come in quest of the story, but only in search of honey in bitter times. What are you really doing here? Are you just a passer-by who'll forget everything?"

"I swear I won't forget."

"Swear that you'll believe the halva even if it's short-lived. Nothing can rival their beauty. They'll talk to you about the Sicilian, the Armenian, and the Kurd, because all three men spoke to them."

I swallowed hard and looked all around me.

"Who did they speak to, ʿAmm ʿAbdo?" I asked.

"All three men told their stories to the doughnut balls," he replied. "Now leave if you think I'm crazy."

"I believe you, and...I believe the halva, too."

THE FIRST STORY

THE SICILIAN

BOOK ONE: 1019 CE, 410 AH

"Every time has a state and men," Jawhar the Sicilian

CHAPTER ONE

Jawhar, son of Husain ibn Jawhar the Sicilian, narrated as follows:

For just a moment, I hesitated, as though I was expecting someone to ask for help before I went in through the lofty gate. I looked at the smooth brick wall. I heard the call for help, or rather, I did not hear it; it took the form of a gesture, the shaikh tapping me on the shoulder. He pointed to the city gate. I understood what he was asking, but I did not hear his voice or see his face. His face and body were completely wrapped in scruffy, torn clothing.

"Shaikh," I told him, "only people with needs or prestige enter Cairo. How can I take you through the gates?"

The shaikh gestured again, his eyes imploring from behind the threadbare rag that covered his face. Our eyes met. I scrutinised the shaikh, his bent body, his appearance, and his hands that he had covered with strips of white cloth. I stretched out my hand and grabbed the shaikh's.

"Your eyes are pleading for help," I said gently. "Why does the shaikh want to enter the city, or rather, why do you want to do so?"

Before the shaikh could say anything, I ripped the cloth from his hand and brought it up to my nose.

"The scent of jasmine is on your hands, Sundus," I said. "You're no good at lying or trickery, my wife who's tried to dupe me. So why have you come here today?"

"I want to go into the city," she whispered pleadingly.

"The guards would slaughter you if you did."

"If I go in with you, dressed as an elderly shaikh, no one's going to slaughter me."

"I'm not going to ask you why you want to see the city," I said. "You won't tell the truth. You're not the first nor the last person who's wanted to enter the city but been unable to do so. It doesn't belong to you. It belongs to the Banu Ubaid, just the Fatimids."

"Amir Jawhar," she whispered. "you're in charge of the city. You know it. It was built with your own blood and your grandfather's. You're the one who decides who can enter."

"Are you out of your mind? Those words of yours will bring death."

Sundus unwound the cloth from her hand, raised it, put it over my heart, and slowly tugged.

"Please, Jawhar," she said, "take me with you into Cairo. You'll have everything you want."

"Stop playing games with me, woman," he shot back. "Did you really think I wouldn't recognise you? You can cover your face all you want, but your hand shows who you are."

"I'm your wife," she said softly.

"You're an unmitigated disaster in dark times. Deceit doesn't make a marriage or a home. I've kept you as a wife so you won't be exposed to scandal."

She removed her hand.

"I beg you," she whispered, drawing closer, "show me Cairo and all its wonders. All the dust in Fustat has given me chest infections."

"Sundus," I told her firmly. "go back home. Beware of even trying to see me again!"

"I want to go into the city and wander around the Bab al-Bahr district. I want to stay with you all day."

"Leave now!" I yelled, pushing her away.

"How can you've failed to notice my existence all these years? I used to follow you with my eyes..."

She drew closer and removed her face-covering, well aware of my confusion.

"Today," she whispered in my ear, "I've split your heart in two. There's no escape."

I opened my mouth.

"Clutch the air in your hand," she went on, "then open it. Where's beauty? You once held it in your hand, but then it vanished over the horizon. Beauty is tentative. It's delicate, like the heart's membrane, dispersed through motes in the air before restoring your sight as life and time."

Our eyes met again.

"Take me to Cairo's parks, grandson of the heroic commander!" she insisted. "Show me the palace flower gardens and cleanse my vision of sorrow's dust."

This time, when she stretched out her hand, I took it and entered the city with her. I was born here and planned to die here, lingering in an unending paradise. It is a paradise for the Caliph; decent people may enter, and sinners and rebels can leave. This paradise is Cairo.

I married my wife, Sundus, four years ago in hard times. Ever since I discovered her deceit, I have not touched her. These are times of darkness and poverty. Poverty is a particularly cruel torment when it follows prosperity, and loneliness is the worst possible affliction when it afflicts a heart that was previously well-regarded and powerful. That is what happens when the Caliph is annoyed. I realise now that the Caliph's anger brings with it the darkness of graves, hellfire, and the impotence of the hoopoe standing before Solomon. Nothing concerns me now other than gaining the Caliph's favour. I do not hate him because he killed my father. The Caliph has the right to kill and crush whomever he pleases. He is Al-Hakim bi-Amr Allah. Even though my father was cautious, his end nevertheless came, and I have learned the lesson. I have learned that life is short; you have to grab opportunity and enjoy life's pleasures. I have also learned that trickery is a necessity, and that justice, like the mercy that is one of the attributes of God, is not something enjoyed by human beings. When I suffered the Caliph's wrath, I was forced to live among the people in Fustat and then to flee to Disuq. I ate vegetables and forgot all about the taste of poultry. I sniffed the air of poverty, almost forgetting that I was actually an Amir. Even women in Fustat have a different flavour than the ones in Cairo. Fustat prostitutes had sad eyes and faces as grey as dust, while Cairo's call girls radiate good health and plenty from every pore. People obey the Caliph's instructions to the letter apart from closing brothels. They have remained secretly open, offering some joy to defeated hearts like mine.

God be praised that the Caliph's heart has softened towards the Sicilian Jawhar, which is me. Today I'm praying even though I don't pray a lot. Today I'm praising God and thanking His Caliph to the fullest possible extent. I've entered Cairo with an eager heart, ready to use my sword and slaughter enemies. I've entered the city, looking at the palace and parks and smiling in satisfaction. I'm Amir Jawhar, son of Husain, son of Jawhar the Sicilian. My grandfather is Jawhar the Sicilian who conquered Egypt and built the city of Cairo. However annoyed the Caliph may be, he will never be able to erase the past or ignore the existence of walls and cities. I shall return to the Fatimid army and serve the Banu Ubaid just as my grandfather and father did. I shall return as an Amir and recall a past that is not all that distant. My father was the ruler and commander, and my grandfather was the builder and donor to livelihoods and armies. Today, I shall remember who I am. The commanding general, Mas'ud ibn Thabit, has asked to meet me. He tells me that the Caliph has forgiven me. Today, I'm returning to my father's palace in Cairo.

"Never trust a king," and "Never accept a pledge from a minister." So said my mother Lamya, daughter of Hamdoon. She was like an Indian sword, sharp and keen, not suited for this age or any other. Her father had been Amir of Sijilmasa in Morocco. Defeated by Jawhar the Sicilian, he had converted to Shi'a, but not in his heart. He had forced his daughter to be married to Jawhar the Sicilian's son, Al-Husain ibn Jawhar. She had agreed and had fulfilled her obligations to her husband until he was killed at the hands of Al-Hakim bi-Amr Allah. She had grieved, but she hadn't lost her pride. However, not for a single day did she understand me or sympathise with my plight. Her heart was still Sunni, whereas mine was Shi'i. Even when it comes to mother and son, hearts have never been in harmony. How could

I not trust a king when my life was in his hands? How could I not accept a minister's pledge when humiliation had followed opulence, wracking my soul with every affliction? So then, let my mother remain immaculate; I shall remain a human being.

The army commander, General Mas`ud ibn Thabit, wanted to see me today.

I sat down in front of him, anxiously awaiting his words, while my heart longed for release.

"Your father was a beloved friend and brother," Mas`ud said. "Let's allow the past to rest in peace. The topic is always distressing and painful. Let's think instead about what's to come. The Caliph wants you to be an army general. He's keeping his pledge to your father, Jawhar."

"The Caliph is always generous, may God aid and protect him!" I replied with a smile. "We're indebted to him for our life and death, my Lord."

Mas`ud gave me a doubtful look.

"What I mean," I continued quickly, "is that, if he commanded us now to die for his sake, I would be the very first to respond."

"Carrying out the Caliph's orders is an obligation, Jawhar; it's like fasting and prayer. You don't have the luxury of choice."

"Indeed it's an obligation," I replied firmly.

"God forgives us occasional slips. You drink some wine, then pray. That's okay. His mercy is all encompassing. However, the Caliph is occasionally involved with idiots and frequently with swindlers. Egyptians need some discipline."

I gave him a quizzical look.

"What I admire about you," Mas`ud went on, "is your understanding of the essence of life. You seize opportunities, you chase pleasure, you realise that a night spent in a Byzantine call girl's arms is worth fifty years in Fustat, and that an unruly horse, once trained, can give you as much pleasure as sex and sometimes more. Stop drinking wine so the Caliph won't slaughter you."

"Done as of now," I replied firmly.

"What happened in Fustat was a major crime, an unforgivable sin. What do you think about someone who slaps his own father, then spits in his face? If you were an army general, what would you do with him?"

"He deserves no punishment but death."

"You understand me, Jawhar. I'm going to open up a brand new track for you. Together, we'll begin anew. We'll forget the complexities of the past and contemplate the present and its successes. Today, I'm going to choose a hundred soldiers, Turks and Maghrebis, who'll be under our command. I'll also be giving you three gorgeous slave girls—one of them's good at poetry, the second at dancing, and the third...well, never mind. The Caliph wants to be sure of your loyalty."

"If matters were in my hands," I replied bluntly, "I'd use your sword to cut off some of my fingers. But then I wouldn't be able to fight for the Caliph."

"Don't promise more than you can deliver," Mas`ud replied with a smile. "The Caliph doesn't like to be praised. As you already know, he stays away from worldly pleasures, horses, and women."

"I'm not promising more than I can deliver," I told him eagerly. "My life's at his command, and my neck and limbs are enslaved to him."

"Jawhar," Mas`ud went on with a smile, "your next conflict is with the populace. I want Fustat's flames to reach all the way to the Abbasids in Iraq. When a child pierces his father's eyes, he's killed. So what can you say about someone who denounces the Caliph himself? You're not like your father or grandfather. You'll be better than them and more famous, too: Jawhar, son of Husain, son of Jawhar the Sicilian. People in Sicily will talk about him and do their best to please him. Egyptians will tremble as they speak about him with awe. So, General, confirm your loyalty, and you'll be able to live in Egypt with no trouble. Move your mother to Cairo and accept your soldiers and slave girls. Return to the palace from which you were ejected years ago."

"It's Cairo, city of kings."

But something happened. I clutched my heart, feeling a pain in my chest that suggested either death or magic. I realised that Sundus had put a spell on me—Sundus, the wife that I neither chose nor wanted. She had betrayed me and made me think that she was spectacularly beautiful. They say that people touched by fire fall flat on their face. It was when I was part of the common rabble that I was married to her. It had been a moment of despair. I spotted her eyes in the Disuq market in the Nile Delta. Along with my mother, she was avoiding people's sarcastic and sympathetic glances. The wind blew the veil off half of her face, and, in that moment, I knew the meaning of beauty. I forgot everything I knew. I asked to be married to her with no preliminaries. At that moment, I was a weakling, having totally forgotten that I was the son of Husain, son of Jawhar the Sicilian, and the world with all its splendour was at my disposal. I wanted a beautiful wife. I went to see her mother, and she turned out to be a fatherless girl about whom no one had any information, neither where she was living, nor what was the source of her wealth. People said that she had a house in Fustat. I did not ask, nor did I care. No sooner had I asked to be married to her than her mother welcomed the idea and accepted with no conditions; the beautiful girl did not cost me a single dinar. At the time, I thought that the world could sometimes bring some joy to the wretched; I would no longer need to save a dinar every night to enjoy a prostitute's services. I failed to realise that the world is just like kings; it can trick you without warning and remove light from your eyes with neither fault nor mercy. On our wedding night, I learned the truth: she was angry and resisted. She left the room, headed for her mother's room, and screamed at the top of her voice. Her mother lowered her head and begged me to keep her in my house, as a slave girl or blameless individual in need of sanctuary. I insisted on sending her back, but my mother refused. Ever since my father died, she has always opposed me, blocking my wishes like a wall constructed of Pyramid stones. My mother Lamya was unafraid of kings, even though they had robbed her of everything she owned. I wonder, when you wake up and find yourself surrounded by desert after being the owner of lush gardens, do you obey the king's commands or rebel against him? I saw my father dying under the Caliph's feet. I had never seen the Caliph. I shivered, but did not weep or swear to take revenge. The desert wastes had been toppled. Today, I can remember. The soldier entered his general's quarters, my father. He was the general, or rather the senior general. The soldier raised his sword.

"Lift your head, Sir," he said without the slightest hesitation. "I don't want to kill you when you can't see me."

I'll tell you about the Sicilian. It was Jawhar the Sicilian who built the city of Cairo. His son, Husain the Sicilian, was my father.

My father raised his head and smiled sadly.

"I've tried," he said. "As you know, I've tried. Years have gone by, and still I've tried. I wonder, why is the Caliph killing me today? Is it because my loyalty reminds him of his own weakness, or rather that people's love for me is more dangerous than a hyena's jaws?"

"I didn't hear anything, Sir," the soldier whispered slowly. "I don't want to see the stake kill my commander."

With that, he raised his sword and killed my father right in front of me. Once the blood had seeped out of his veins, I watched as the soldier stuck the sword into my father's neck. He was trying to sever the head from the body and was having trouble pulling it out. I swear that I saw the body twitch for a moment, whether rejecting, submitting, or rejoicing—I have no idea.

My mother held her breath, tears pouring silently down her cheeks. She put her hand over my eyes; I was seventeen at the time. As she removed her hand, I could see the soldier was having a hard time severing a stubborn sinew at the edge of my father's neck. At the time, I had no idea whether I wanted the soldier to finish his task as quickly as possible or spend a long time on it so my father's body would not be taken from me. Maybe someone else would take revenge; maybe the prime of my youth had misled me, and now things and people all looked the same; maybe my mother was expecting me to explode with fury, yell at the soldier, and curse the Caliph.

Wake up, Lamya! Didn't the king believe that he could grant life and death? Didn't he kill in front of Abraham the Prophet? Those who oppose kings perish for sure. It was at that moment that I knew for certain that life is short and can end at any moment. Beauty and pleasure are both whiffs of paradise that we gather in our hands and spend eternity invoking and extolling.

That day, I left our house and my mother's tears. I quaffed wine till I was drunk—I Jawhar, son of Husain, son of Jawhar the Sicilian. I told the bar owner that my grandfather had built Cairo; he had used soft brick to make the walls, and at some point, they were bound to collapse.

"Today, my father was killed," I went on with a laugh, "slaughtered like a sheep. Do you know him, Husain son of Jawhar? He never mounted his steed for fear of arousing the jealousy of the Caliph, Al-Hakim bi-Amr Allah. He ignored the admiring looks from soldiers and commoners— Al-Husain ibn Jawhar, who gathered around him Turkish soldiers from every region. He instructed them not to make a fuss about him and not to address him when he was mounted on his steed. He told them to look only at the Caliph and to obey only him. With my own eyes, I saw him quiver whenever an Egyptian praised him, for fear that Al-Hakim bi-Amr Allah would be jealous. However, caution is no defence against fate. We spent only a few days in the folds of the barren desert, then they vanished. Do not promise me paradise or the reward for someone wronged. Do not ask me why my father was killed. What crime had my grandfather committed, to be banished by Mu`izz li-Din Allah for fear of his influence? He died in his own house, without even a single horse. My grandfather, Jawhar the Sicilian, was the one who said: 'Every time has a state and men.' This is my time and my state. So let us live together for two or three days, then die. Wine servant, I want the most beautiful slave girl in all Egypt. Tell her that Jawhar, son of Husain, son of Jawhar the Sicilian, wants to forget his own father's death and his mother's copious tears in her arms. Tell her also that Jawhar wants to clutch the halva in his hands and enjoy the taste of sugar and the passion of lovers. Today, we celebrate the end of fear; today, we celebrate the Caliph's power. We pray for him. He has said that he can grant both life and death. But it is death that he grants, not life. Inevitably, death is coming.

All that was in the past. Now here I am, returning to Cairo as an Amir, son and grandson of Amirs. I've ordered the soldiers to bring our possessions to Cairo. I've tried to postpone a meeting with my mother, but such moments inevitably come to pass, like the rebuke of the Angel of Death and the mosque's shaikh.

"Come and join us in our palace," I told her, avoiding her stare.

"So, my son," she spat back in fury, "what compromises have you made that the Caliph, your father's killer, is happy with you again? Jawhar, has Mas'ud castrated you as a way of assuring your loyalty? These are times of betrayal and weakness. What about your father and grandfather? They died as real men, and you will, too."

"Dear mother, how I wish your heart would soften toward your son, with everything he's been through."

"You have no mother. What Mas'ud has demanded of you is a fit of sheer madness, and madness is harsher than any number of wars. Caution is one of the hallmarks of intelligent people. Violence, on the other hand, is characteristic of people who are weak and submissive. Even if you killed everyone in Cairo and Fustat, you'd never enter Cairo or enjoy its parks. Ah, my dear husband Husain, woe is me! Al-Hakim bi-Amr Allah has slain you twice over: the first time when he failed to keep his promise and slew you as you defended him, and the second when he killed all pride in your own son's heart, leading him to obey his father's killer and to idolise monarchs and generals."

I took out my father's red coat and blue turban decorated with gold and stared at them for an hour or more. Something had happened to change the Caliph's attitude towards Husain ibn Jawhar. My mother says it was things that the common people were saying in the Fustat market. Husain had been avoiding riding his horse for fear of making the Caliph angry. Some merchants and craftsmen came out to greet the Army Commander.

"Supreme Commander," they said, "God has sent you to us as helper and provider."

"No," he responded immediately, "it's the Caliph whom He's sent as helper and provider."

They all looked at each other.

"May God prolong your life, Supreme Commander," they continued, "so that you can defend the Egyptian people."

At that moment, my father swallowed hard, as though someone had thrust a sword into his heart. He rushed back to his palace, looking fearfully over his shoulder.

"Get your things ready," he told his wife Lamya. "We're leaving today. We can't stay here. The Caliph's angry with us."

She did not believe her husband.

"He's decorated and honoured you," she said. "Even when you refused to ride your horse and declined titles, he still insisted on giving you gold and horses. He appointed you Supreme Commander. He realises how loyal you are. This is our country; we have no other."

He kept on insisting as he gathered up his belongings.

"There's no time to talk," he yelled at his children.

My father fled and took me and my brothers with him. He left Cairo and Fustat, but he did not leave Egypt entirely. He even took my sister and her husband, who was a judge. So what happened then? Al-Hakim bi-Amr Allah learned that his Supreme Commander had fled, which puzzled and alarmed him. He had people search for him, but failed to find him. However, he granted him a pledge of safety. Three days later, Al-Husain returned to Cairo with his children to stand before the Caliph. The Caliph forgave him and gave him gold and silver and a pledge of safety for himself and his children: 'No harm shall touch the son of Jawhar the Sicilian, general and general's son.'

Husain returned to his own house, his feelings a mixture of reassurance and alarm. He woke up that night with a start.

"What's the matter with you, man?!" Lamya asked. "You've fought armies and won. So why are you so afraid? Yes, he's the Caliph, but life's in God's hands."

"I swear that I'm scared for you and the children."

"Life's in God's hands. Fear won't change fate; actually, it'll bring it sooner."

Three days later, the Caliph summoned Husain son of Jawhar and his children.

I remember and smile in anger and despair. What really makes me angry is that the Caliph's swordsman was a lousy executioner. Why did he have to wield his sword over and over again in order to sever the limbs and sinews? What transpired was even stranger than the fables of the ancients!

My elder brother, `Abdallah, went back to the house and collected his belongings.

"It'll be our turn next," he told his mother and wife and brothers. "That's for certain. We must escape. There's no hope for us here. The Caliph's men keep slandering us. I'm more afraid of them than the Caliph himself."

After my father was killed, I made my way by night, as I've already mentioned, to a covered boat on the Nile. It already had everything a man could want—tasty dishes, wine, and women. Al-Hakim bi-Amr Allah could not find it; he did not even know about its existence. It had been made ready specially for Amirs in the days of Tamim, the son of Al-Mu`izz li-Din Allah, whom his father had excluded from the caliphate because of his shameless behaviour and wonderful poetry. Had he ever become Caliph, the entire world would have flourished. Every sun would have shone, and the beauties would have come down to the river. Ah yes, the beauties of Fustat when they come down to the boat at night!

While my brother and mother were talking, I was pouring all my anger and sorrow into a slave girl. My mother kept looking for me and worrying about me. My elder brother `Abdallah, meanwhile, kept to himself.

"The Caliph's killed my father," he told our mother. "And now he's offered us a pledge of safety. He can't be trusted. We have to leave for Syria or Iraq, anywhere that Al-Hakim bi-Amr Allah's hand can't reach. Come on, Mother, night-time travel is faster; and these days it's safer, too."

"I'm not leaving without my son Jawhar," she insisted.

"Leave him! This is like Resurrection Day: either we flee now, or we'll be killed tomorrow. Do you want to see your three children killed in front of you? Flee with us, daughter of Hamdoon, and preserve what you have left."

"I'm not leaving without my son," she said again. "Look for your brother."

"Mother, I've a wife and sons who'll be killed before my very eyes. There's no time to search for him. Where's he gone in the depths of night? He's either getting drunk or looking for women. That's the way he's been since he was a boy: attack and revenge."

"You and your brothers can leave," she said calmly. "Leave me here. I'm not going without my son."

"We're your children, too."

"You'll all be safe outside Egypt. We'll stay here and look for a safe haven. Some day, we'll meet again."

"Mother..."

There was not much time. My brothers fled, heading for Syria or Iraq. I returned three days later—three days in the life of Egypt that were like the whole of eternity. Everything exploded, then settled down again. Planets shifted, then the sun settled beyond the heavens, angry and depressed at its companions on the stupid earth. Should I laugh or cry?

I came back three days later to discover that Al-Hakim bi-Amr Allah had ordered the arrest of my brothers. He set aside three hundred thousand dinars for the person who found them. One of his men found and killed them. This time, the slaughter was swift, and their heads were sent to the Caliph. I returned from three days of buffoonery to find my brothers' heads as a reminder of those who fled in fear and those were willing to take risks. My laughter only increased as I witnessed my mother's terrifying silence and stony eyes. I laughed and laughed as she stared at me in silence, without either blaming me or criticising my shameless behaviour and postponement of my eventual fate. Lamya, your eyes are forever finding fault, as sharp as any sword. What kind of woman are you? Have you regretted not going with the others, or have you praised God, because one of the brothers is still alive? Al-Hakim bi-Amr Allah has given me a pledge of security. He said that I did not run away. People who are scared have inevitably committed a sin. Prophets are never afraid, and pious men suffer patiently without running away. I have learned the lesson. It is fear that rattles the Caliph and kindles his doubts. So then, it is fear. It is life, like a piece of powdered halva, made over several hours and swallowed in mere seconds; once swallowed, there is nothing left; a life like foam at sea, with no goal or benefit; a life with the bitter taste of colocynth and the flash of mirage. These are times that we spend split between passion and panic. Anyone who emerges may be cured, but those who linger suffer fatigue and chronic illness, with no hope of a cure. Anyone who can escape the dark shadows is happy; that much is certain. However, those who remain in the deep, narrow corridor of slander will find the fires burning until his tastes change and soften.

Ah Lamya! Why such bitterness, Hamdoon's daughter? You've never rejoiced at my safety or told me, to my face, that I'm a traitor. I'm still alive.

O Caliph, you have slain the best of men and kept alive a disloyal buffoon who is motivated by his bodily desires, like the predatory birds that soar alone, craving only absolute freedom and a gorgeous, tattooed slave girl who makes love and sings to perfection. O Caliph, sometimes people with no fear possess no soul to be afraid with and no chest to breathe.

That is what happened, an inevitable past. Now, we work with the Caliph and swear fealty to him. If the jinn confront you with his cruelty, then go ahead: acknowledge him and follow him so he will not wipe you off the face of the earth. As part of that acknowledgment, do your best to pluck the pleasures that life offers. It is just a clutch of ephemeral pleasures, no more.

If only my mother realised that, before all else, she is bringing my own end that much closer. If only she knew that, if I do not obey the Caliph's commands, she is planning for me to die. As I confirm my loyalty today, the Caliph may perhaps grant me a little time for enjoyment. That is not a lot to ask. When it comes to heaven and hell, God is the most merciful and powerful.

Here in the Bab al-Bahr district, paradise emerges, grows, and innovates. Whereas heaven's paradise is far out of reach, paradise on earth is once again in my arms; its sweet perfume has reached my nose and tongue. Cairo, how I long to see it once again! I stroll through its parks, which flower both summer and winter. I feast my eyes on the stone palaces and the gold that never loses its sheen nor sees its source dry up. In my imagination, I have pictured the Caliph's palace and its fountain quaffing golden water, then spraying it time and again. How wonderful opulence is, and how content are sultans! Once we close the city gates, it becomes a place for people who deserve paradise, not for those who commit sins and are punished with hellfire. If God's paradise were a monopoly for the good and desperate, then Cairo would be the monopoly of those with authority and prestige, for those who construct a paradise for themselves on earth because they are not sure whether the heavenly paradise will open its doors to them.

My eyes closed, I let out a happy sigh. Cairo's breezes were all intoxication, pulsing with plenty and eternity: bird meat, brocade, and fashion; slave girls' bodies untouched by the sun and unacquainted with winter; a swing rising but never falling. Here dwell joy, beauty, and a sweet life. Now I have returned to Cairo and my palace...

I opened my eyes.

Instead of trees reaching to the heavens, I found black stones controlling past and present. The lovely slave girls vanished from in front of me, to be replaced by fire-breathing beasts. The gold turned into bitter colocynth, and the straight paths were replaced by poisonous snakes and scorpions. I clutched my heart as it defaulted and lost its way. This was the Devil's doing, the work of Sundus, my treacherous and deceitful wife. She was eager to get her revenge because I had neglected her for years. She was the one who has cleft my heart in two today. Only death and fire could overcome magic. My heart no longer yearns for Cairo, nor do my eyes gaze on its splendours. I have eradicated my deceitful heart. Death is an effective punishment for anyone who wishes to put an end to Jawhar's happiness and well-being.

I frowned and started training my soldiers. Next morning, I was going to attack Fustat. People in that city know that the Caliph's army is on the way. They realize their crime and are anticipating punishment. People are saying: 'You're getting ready to fight. When people prepare to fight the Caliph's army, Cairo's fountains will inevitably spout their blood, and it will be their heads that decorate the walls rather than windows. The people of Fustat need to be punished; that's certain, and their crimes are no longer forgivable. Tomorrow, everything will be over.'

Fine, so let me remember. I am Jawhar. I grew up and was raised in Caliphs' palaces amid Cairo's parks. I am Jawhar, grandson of General Jawhar the Sicilian. He was the one who entered Egypt with the Banu Ubaid army. But for him, the Banu Ubaid would not exist. They had tried to enter Egypt many times and had failed; that is, until Al-Mu'izz li-Din Allah sought the help of Jawhar, the general who had spent his entire life fighting and knew only loyalty and hard work.

Alas for my mother and her ever-sharp sword. She does not know a lot of rulers. Once, my grandfather had said that 'every time has a state and men.'

My grandfather Jawhar knew. He conquered Egypt for Al-Mu'izz li-Din Allah and built Cairo and the Al-Azhar Mosque. For four years, he ruled in Al-Mu'izz's place, as Caliph or almost. Egyptians loved him and admired his shrewd judgement and power. Then Al-Mu'izz arrived, and Jawhar handed Egypt over to him. He then disappeared from view, that being the lot of states and men; there is room for only one man. When the general's light beams bright, it blinds people's vision, and they are confused. In that case, the general can either disappear or be punished for his success and magic image. For countries and people, success is the biggest mistake of all, one that no Caliph can forgive.

Do you know my grandfather? Come, then, I will tell you about him. He was someone for whom doors were open and entire armies bowed in awe and reverence in the face of his prestige.

The Caliph Al-Mu'izz stayed in Tunisia and dispatched his general, fully confident that the Sicilian would not be defeated.

"By God," he told his assembly one day, "if Jawhar goes on his own to conquer Egypt, then he will certainly enter it in robes without any war, settle in the ruins of Ibn Tulun, and build a city called 'the powerful,' or Al-Qahira, to conquer the world."

That is my grandfather, the man of times past who read and learned. As a boy, he crossed the Mediterranean from Sicily on a boat with slave traders. In front of him, he could see the desert stretching away into the distance. He left valley and family behind. The Caliph housed him in his palace and brought him up in an atmosphere of obedience and religion. Sicily was now far away, but it never left his heart. Years later, he went back to Sicily to search for his family. He found his mother and brothers, but not his home, which had been lost to the greed and whims of rulers. Then he came here, to Egypt. Here, he made plans for the Caliph's palace; here, he designed a home and country for himself. He constructed walls, inhaling Cairo's air and blending it with the moist breezes of Sicily and the dewy droplets of the island's trees. Closing his eyes, my grandfather could envisage the beauty of abode and safety; and safety has a beauty that does not last. His loyalty to the Caliph was proverbial. He ruled and showed justice. He instituted the Shi`i call to prayer and added to it: 'Hail to the best of deeds.' On the walls, he wrote: 'Muhammad is the Prophet of God and Ali is the Guardian of God.' He behaved justly, and the people adored him. Powerful men who are just have a special magic, like that of the ancients. He told his son Husain about the trees in Sicily, which were like the ones growing in Cairo, and the wooden horse he had inherited from his father—all that remained of an old home in the country he no longer knew.

When Jawhar the Sicilian was almost eighty, he went to see the Caliph Al-`Aziz bi-Allah, son of Al-Mu`izz li-Din Allah. He emerged from the Caliph's residence on foot, while the generals were riding on horseback. The Caliph let out a huge, heart-rending sigh and wept over the status of the man who had commanded armies, who was walking on foot while his juniors were all mounted on horses. My grandfather Jawhar calmed the Caliph down.

"Abu 'Ammar," he said, "I used to possess something yet more reliable. 'Every time has a state and men.' Do we really want to detract from our own state and that of others? Here I am today, walking in front of a new commander. These are a people who have honoured us and honoured others through us. That acknowledged, I can only say: 'May God bring my time to an end soon. I'm almost eighty.'"

Oh, my grandfather, if only you could witness these times today: the populace in revolt and the loss of prestige! Oh, Grandfather, why did you build a wall around the city that has now expelled your grandson and the entire population of Egypt?

Al-Husain ibn Jawhar learned the lesson and preferred that the bright gleam of his courage not be evident to the masses. For that reason, Al-Hakim bi-Amr Allah, grandson of Al-Mu`izz li-Din Allah, killed him, but the Caliph did so even though he meant to be cautious. Thus does the people's love turn into revenge and pestilence, leading to inevitable destruction, whether through delusion or betrayal. To tell you the truth, I possess neither my mother's pride nor my father's sincerity.

CHAPTER TWO

My mother Lamya, spoke to me. Normally, she did not bother about anyone or speak to me a lot. But now, she started talking to me with a childlike enthusiasm, her brows knit and her eyes wide. I wonder, Lamya, what were you like as a girl? Did you really love Al-Husain ibn Jawhar, or did you simply accept living with him? Why is it that I never see any signs of affection in your eyes? How is it that you were never jealous of his other wives and slave girls? Lamya told me about my own wife whom I don't know; I parted company with her on the very first day, leaving her in a room in my small house in Disuq. Today, she entered Cairo as she had wanted; she will be living in Jawhar's palace. I do not plan to see her or check on her wellbeing. How can anyone who has entered paradise mar its beauty with Sundus?

Lamya checked on the slave girls, just as she did with all the beings that entered her house, anxious to be sure of their health and loyalty. For a moment, Sundus watched her from afar, but then she walked over to her.

"My lady," she asked, "let me choose a slave girl for my husband."

The look that Lamya gave her was a blend of shock and sympathy.

"Sundus," she replied, "a reasonable wife is a blessing from God. You know, when I was a girl of your age, I may have been even more jealous and impetuous than you are, but now I've learned and understood. Marriage, Sundus, is not simply a contract between a man and woman, nor is it a few hours of lustful passion spent in bed. Marriage involves sincerity and warm companionship. Take your face veil off. Your face doesn't scare me, my daughter, nor does my body shudder from fire."

"Forgive me, my lady," Sundus said calmly.

"No, don't say 'my lady.' Say Aunt, or Mother.'"

"I've wanted to talk to you for some time, Aunt," Sundus went on calmly. "I've wanted to explain to you what happened."

"I'm listening."

"I didn't plan to deceive the Amir; I just wanted to accompany him. I swear to you that, ever since I was fourteen, I've realised my destiny and been happy with it. Unlike other girls, I don't have dreams, nor do I desire a man. What I was looking for was protection and kindness."

Lamya stared at her.

"Explain what you mean," she said.

"Aunt, I want to accompany Jawhar with my veil on," Sundus replied, "so I don't hurt his eyes; no more than that. With the fire, all hopes vanished."

Lamya moved closer.

"Did the fire burn your femininity?" she asked.

Sundus swallowed hard.

"No, it didn't," she replied, "but it's surrounded by fire. There's no escape."

"Have you never longed for a man? How old are you? You must be at least twenty-one. Women your age have at least five children."

"I swear to you that I feel no love for men," Sundus replied firmly. "All I want is a house where I can live in safety after the deaths of my mother and father."

With that, she looked at the slave girls, and her eyes met those of one of the girls who seemed to be the most beautiful and intelligent. When Lamya asked the girl if she could sing, the girl started to croon in a sweet voice.

"She's just right for Jawhar," Sundus said. "She's beautiful, and her face augurs well, God willing."

"I'll tell him that you were the one who chose her for him," Lamya said enthusiastically.

Sundus smiled behind her veil.

"Let me dress her in finery," Sundus said, "and teach her how to make the Amir happy."

With that, she stepped back, leaving the room and bowing slightly to Lamya as she did so.

For me, it is enough that moments of trial always occur in bright colours and with a pungent smell that never leaves the memory nor slips out of our hands like moments of pleasure. My wife has her own story to tell. In the past, people had said that Sundus was the most beautiful girl, when she was ten and still had a little girl's body. She would rush around the fields and defeat the bitter-orange trees in every battle. She would talk to the ants in their nests and devour rose-petals mixed with honey. Sundus. When she was just fourteen, one man after another had come to ask for her hand, but her heart belonged to one man only: Mahmood, her neighbour. Every time he set eyes on her, he would shiver bashfully. She would lower her head and run back to the house. One day, he whispered to her that she was the most beautiful girl he had ever seen, and he wanted to be married to her. She loved him with her young heart, which would take the plunge with no fears or obstacles. He asked her father for her hand. Then, everything happened, and life changed as it always does between morning and night. The flames of cruel fire put an end to everything that her mother had been planning for so many years. That is all I know about Sundus. At the time, I had no idea how the fires had afflicted her.

She says that she can remember; how can she forget? The colour, the smell, the flames singeing her cheek, followed by the stench of burning flesh. Then the pricks of a cold dagger as the fires enveloped her and seized her body as an abode and dwelling. It spread and invaded with knowing spontaneity, as though her body were now a residence, a property, from face to arm, arm to thigh, thigh to foot. People started screaming, but not her. She does not remember screaming. All she recalls is a sigh emerging from her ribs that reached her spine. The screams were her mother's, as she pushed her to the floor and started slapping at the flames with her hands, the way a child does with floodwaters. People clustered around the two of them, uttering prayers and rubbing their hands in despair. Then they threw covers over her body— half her body, half her face, half her arm, half her chest, half her thigh. From then on, she owned half a life, but life refused to acknowledge the division and would not agree to negotiation. Sundus gave nothing; with half a body, she disappeared from view and wept in her room for years, while her mother grieved her own failures. Mahmood disappeared and never made another appearance. He rid himself of her with all the fluidity of cascading water during a flood. Her mother took her from one shaikh to another, one monk to another, until they advised her to go to see the Pyramid Witch. They told her that, for over a thousand years, the Witch had lived in the Pyramid; no one knew if she had died or if someone had taken her place. Was she training another orphan to practice witchcraft, giving her both the training and the name? Or was she still alive? Even witches have to die. Her name is "Bahnas," and it has been the same for a hundred years: grandmother, daughter, and granddaughter. She understands curses and sorrows, possessing the insight of one who has abandoned the world and the courage of one who is certain of God's existence. Sundus's mother rushed to see her, and, after Sundus had tried to kill herself more than once, she left her daughter with the Witch for a whole year.

Years later, she learned about the final conversation between Sundus and the Witch.

"Sundus," the Witch said.

Sundus removed her face veil and stared at her for a moment.

"So, Witch," she asked aggressively, "do you feel sorry for me or do fires scare you? Even you must be frightened of fire. They say that burning is punishment. What have I done that God should punish me like this?"

"Yes, my girl," the Witch replied calmly. "I'm afraid of real fires that bear no resemblance to the fires that have changed your features. Those fires are a mirage. Bodies change, whether we like it or not. Your Lord does not punish those whom He loves. To the contrary, He keeps certain aspects of beauty hidden so that an even brighter and more copious beauty will emerge."

"You have no idea how much I've suffered. Don't lecture me."

"Everyone beautiful suffers."

"What beauty are you talking about? Everyone suffers when people hurt them with words about their ugliness."

"Those who want to please people spend their entire lives being belittled. Look inside yourself for a force that God has given you to confront adversity. When tribulation strikes, there comes the time for giving. But don't imagine that this involves money, children, finery, vanity, and beauty. However beautiful the body, it will always cheat and turn on its owner. Giving implies stability. With that acceptance, potential is doubled; it provides you with a whiff of its magnanimity and bestows its mercy."

"Why has it afflicted me? Why choose me?"

"That's between the two of you. The Witch cannot reveal what is not clear to her."

"Will I wake up to find myself rid of any evidence of burns on my body?"

"You may wake up to realise that the body is transitory, departing either today or tomorrow. Its very sweetness is mixed with life's deceit, its maturity with the vicissitudes of time. Perhaps you'll understand that beauty resides in what is everlasting, not in skin and flesh. Wait in patience for a day when you'll appreciate your own strength and potential."

The Witch kept her for a whole year inside the Pyramid's darkness.

Then I asked for her hand in marriage. Her mother spoke to her, and, as she said, she resisted the idea. However, her mother was dying and insisted that she be married to me.

"He'll reject me as soon as he finds out. Are you trying to deceive him? How can I take my face veil off? Tell me how!"

"This is a world where all is madness. The expert is someone who can toy with the world the way it toys with us. Be patient."

How did Sundus come to be married to me? No one knows for certain. When certain people found out the truth, they said she was a miracle. Others claimed it was God's punishment on the grandson of Jawhat the Sicilian, the Shi`i who had brought the Banu Ubaid into Egypt. But, when her mother left for Disuq in the Nile Delta, she kept her daughter's condition a secret and claimed that her daughter was the most beautiful girl in Egypt. She made the acquaintance of Lamya, Jawhar's mother, and learned about their family history and the way they had fled from the Caliph's brutality. Sundus's mother told Lamya that her daughter was the most beautiful girl in the whole of Egypt. She adamantly refused to let anyone see her daughter, and so, like an idiot, I fell into Sundus's mother's trap.

I found out on our wedding night. She took off her face veil, and I stayed riveted to the spot without saying a word.

"It was stupid," she said, in a quavering voice. "Forgive me."

"What's stupidity got to do with outright deception?"

"Don't expose me."

"How could you be so bold?" I asked bluntly. "Husain, Jawhar's son, married to someone like you?"

She swallowed her words.

"A noble person like yourself will never expose me," she said. "It's not in my hands..."

"To the contrary, you've deceived me and my mother."

I left the room and did not return. Year after year went by—four years. I neither set eyes on her nor asked about her. My mother and I would leave her some money, then forget about her.

Our sorrows only intensified, and times of hope passed by. Two year later, her mother died, still insisting that what had happened was correct and that the person who had been married to her daughter had gained all the world's blessings.

She only rarely left her room, lingering with the poetry that she would recite so as not to lose her mind. Then Lamya, daughter of Hamdoon, announced that they would be going to Cairo.

Sundus never lied nor dreamed of a knight on horseback. Her dreams were all flames and groans. She had no desire for a man's touch or a body's attention. Her body was an eternal curse; indeed, she loathed any touch or any shocked or sympathetic glance. It seemed that all she wanted of me was companionship. As far as she was concerned, bodies were a perfidious curse, causing nothing but pain. She hated her body, all bodies, all touch and kisses. Bodily contact frightened her as sin scares a monk. I left the room and did not go back. Year after year went by—fur years. I neither set eyes on her nor asked about her. Along with my mother, I would leave her some money, then forget about her.

Sorrow only intensified, and times of hope passed by. Two years later, her mother died, still insisting that what had happened was correct and that the person who had been married to her daughter had gained all the world's blessings.

Sundus never lied or dreamed of a knight on horseback. Her dreams were all flames and groans. She had no desire for a man's touch or a body's attention. Her body was an eternal curse; indeed she loathed any touch or any sympathetic or shocked glance. It seemed that all she wanted of me was companionship. As far as she was concerned, bodies were a perfidious curse, causing nothing but pain. She hated her body, all bodies, all touches and kisses. Bodily contact scared her as much as sin scares a monk.

She wanted to see me, wanting me to stop and listen. What made her look for me was her desire for friendship. She was now even more keen on Laila, the slave girl she had chosen for me. She had started thinking about how to teach and train her. If the girl was good at poetry, then that was best. She was beautiful, but she could do with some embellishment and careful attention. She would do that today, she said. She was extremely fond of Laila and encouraged her to make love to me, so frequently that I began to have my doubts and be aware whenever she was around. Who knows, maybe all these stories were just fairy tales; perhaps Sundus was a spy sent to kill me.

I looked into her eyes as she drank her fill of the greenery. Sundus let out a sigh at the grandeur of the palace. Maybe she was feeling sorry for me and realised the scope of my defeat. How could someone who had lived in these lovely parks be happy to live in Fustat, even Disuq? How could someone who had been born an Amir be content to live among the plebs and common people? At sunset, she set off running as fast as she could through the bitter-orange trees and then plunged her face into the ground like a bird in search of seeds. She inhaled the scent of life amid the roses and black mud. Here, she took off her face veil. No child would ever be scared of her, and no woman would ever pity her. Here, no one would be put off by her appearance, nor would she encounter censorious looks because she was still alive.

"What are you doing here?" I asked her bluntly.

"I was enjoying the park, my lord," she replied, quickly putting her face veil back on.

"My mother's told me everything you've done," I said, looking straight at her. "But I don't believe it. You're just a snake, or even more dangerous. Words may be gentle, but the heart's a drawn sword."

"You're wiser than I," she said.

"My mother says that it's companionship you want. Why should I be a companion to a woman I don't want?"

"The same way a brother is with his sister."

"You're not my sister, and I didn't grow up with you. Take off your face veil when you're with me. Burns don't shock me."

She took off her veil without any objections. I looked closely at the burn marks.

"Laila," I said.

"She has a spontaneity and knowledge that I've never seen in a slave girl before," she replied eagerly. "She's beautiful, my lord."

"Yes, she is."

"Is she what you've been wanting? Has she pleased you? Has she satisfied your bodily needs? I realise that you want a lot. The day will come when you get everything you want."

"What about you?" I asked with a smile.

"What about me, my lord?"

"What did you want when you were married to me? You certainly didn't expect me to have sex with you, nor that I would desire you. So what did you want? I know you were engaged to a man before me. After the fire, he abandoned you. But I still don't know how you came to be burned."

She did not respond.

I grabbed her hand, opened her palm, and ran my fingers over it. Still, she remained silent.

"Can you feel that?" I asked.

She shook her head. I put my hand on her shoulder, lowered her blouse, and ran my fingers over her naked shoulder—the one that had not been brushed by the flames.

"What do you feel?" I asked.

"Nothing," she replied firmly.

I moved my hand further down, until it touched her breasts. Her gaze was still fixed on mine.

"What about now?" I asked.

She shook her head. I was puzzled.

"I don't know a lot about fire," I said, "but the body lives on. You must feel *something*, or is it that you don't care about men? Have you pressed your body against that of any man who's not your former beloved?"

"I don't care about bodies," she said firmly, ignoring my hand.

"There's nothing more important than bodies," I retorted with a chuckle. "They control us and dominate us. We're eager to sate them with women, money, food, water, and fruit. The eye demands greenery, the stomach demands meat, and the nose asks for sweet smells that promise pleasure. Even the hand and fingers want silver and gold. We're totally controlled by predators, Sundus. Bodies are what govern this entire world. Some of us try to train them, others simply spoil them, and many of us are enslaved by them."

"That's because your body is complete and beautiful. I know things that other people don't."

"You're wise, Sundus."

I took my hand out of her blouse.

"I wonder," I said. "Will you be like a brother or sister to me? Do you prefer women to men?

"I don't like men or women," she replied. "I don't like bodies, either."

"The heart's love begins with the body. Hearts don't speak, hug, or dissolve into tears. The body does all those things. Why are you lying? You told me that you loved me. Like the wife of an amir, you must be suppressing your jealousy. You tell yourself that Laila's a slave girl, and you're free."

She was shocked.

"I do love you," she replied. "Of course, I love you. Forgive me, my lord. You don't understand what I mean by those words. When I said I *love*, I mean that I want to stay with you in the same house. I want to see you and talk to you occasionally; that's all. I know my place and have for some time now. I'm used to it."

"For you, then, love means sharing your beloved's company?"

"Staying with him, that's all. Laila's my sister. I love her, too. With all my heart, I hope she gives you a child."

"Do you know the Caliph?" I asked, rubbing my hands together. "His heart's as muddled as yours. He loves and hates; he's jealous one moment, then generous the next. He builds schools, then destroys them. He gives the Christians prominence, then humiliates them. After hanging someone by the neck, he forgives him once he's dead. Yes indeed, his heart's as muddled as yours. But he's the Caliph, and the Caliph is all-knowing."

"Sometimes," I rambled on "I get the impression that his mind is distracted. It was my grandfather who said: "'Every time has a state and men.' But I'm inclined to say that 'every time has its lunatics and leaders.'"

She looked shocked, and I pretended to get serious again.

"What's the matter with you?" I asked. "Are you going to tell the Caliph that I've accused him of madness? Or do you believe that keeping him happy is God's work?"

"Your bitter feelings do not stem from anyone else; they're signs of a confused soul."

"What do you know about souls?"

She did not respond, but put her face veil back on.

"The days to come," she said with a smile, "will bring you successes."

Like fires, wars do not make a noise, nor do they have a familiar pattern. But people who have smelled the reek of fire can recognise it from afar. She kept an eye on me as I trained my soldiers. I expected her to betray me. Her loyalty was to Fustat, the site of the fire, not to me or some beloved whose death she feared. Fustat. She had lived there as a fourteen-year-old, then what happened had happened, and she had moved to Disuq with her mother.

However, what the people of Fustat have done to the Caliph Al-Hakim bi-Amr Allah will not be easily forgotten. These days, all is chaos and shame, plus a good deal of both fear and shock. What are the abstemious Caliph's intentions for the people? By now, they have heard the news—words and whispers exchanged in private. Throw the book at people in Fustat: women must stay indoors; shoe-manufacture is banned; grapes are banned; honey is banned. Stop all work in Egypt and throw it all in the Nile so it is not turned into wine. Sometimes, he tells people to work only at night. Then he tells Christians and Jews to wear different clothing. He will kill one scholar and give another presents. Mulukhiyya and taro are both banned. Ramadan night-time prayers are first banned, then permitted. The Caliph has a good heart; that's for certain. First there's a ban, then comes permission. Even so, what happened in Fustat was completely different. When the Caliph went out on his donkey, wearing his white sackcloth, to check on the people's circumstances, he saw an extremely beautiful woman in front of him, fully decorated with jewellery and kohl. In her hand, she held a piece of paper to give to the Caliph. The Caliph approached her in a fury and chided the woman for leaving her house and showing her face. He grabbed the piece of paper to read it. What he read was a curse on him and his family, and things that were even worse. It was as though the Egyptian people were accusing him of insanity and tyranny. Yelling at the top of his voice, he drew his sword and plunged it into the woman's chest. With that, the statue that had been so carefully and skilfully crafted collapsed; the woman's statue fell apart in front of him. The children's laughter continued until their elders disappeared inside their houses. The Caliph clutched the piece of paper in his fingers and ordered his general Mas`ood to return to Cairo.

"What am I to do with people who cheat with their scales?" he asked on the way back. "How many vendors in Fustat do that? Do you remember the wheat crisis?"

"Yes, my lord, I do."

"The punishment will suit the crime. If we hadn't been decisive, the entire country would have suffered hunger. I saved them, but they're infidels. They've no respect for Caliphs and true believers. They want only wine and prostitution."

"My lord," Mas`ood said in a quavering voice, "if you gave me orders..."

"I will when the time is right."

I do not know why I could picture her reaction and fear. Actually, I do not know why I was at all bothered about her. Fustat on fire loomed in her eyes, just as her own burning did. That is how I saw her on that day.

CHAPTER THREE

Victory in the Fustat war will happen, and yet they will not be attacking any fortresses or ripping out gates by their roots. No swords will stave off arrows, and no cavaliers will deftly plunge their swords into people's hearts. The Amir's instructions are clear. Now I'm an Amir with soldiers, and soon I'll be part of the Amiriyya and one of Al-Hakim's own generals.

General Mas`ood ibn Thabit did not tell them until the conflict was over. Even so, he told them to use their swords on the entire populace and to burn Fustat down with neither mercy nor pause. No mercy on those who skewered their father's eyes or who scoffed at the Caliph's wisdom.

I used to be familiar with Fustat. I would often stroll through its streets, sad at times, and drunk at many others. In my imagination today, I can see it as gloomy, full of refuse, infested with lice and cockroaches, assaulting my body and tearing me to pieces. Poverty and destitution, misery and curses. Here are subjects of wrath and lunatics. People of Fustat, your end has come by fire, burning by earth and sky. Your sad days are at an end, as are your coarse laughter, your dark taverns, and your unveiled women. You men, have a laugh before you cry. Lock the doors of your houses against the sunlight, and you will encounter the bitterest of colds.

The Caliph's soldiers swore that they would burn everything, setting fire to woodpiles, grain, leftover food, and deceitful tongues. They would plunge their swords into anyone who raised their hands, whether in quest of peace or war. Today women belong to the soldiers; all girls are captives. The entire country needs to be punished. Standing at a distance, I watched as the noise of the fire blended with the hissing of snakes and the shouts of men before women. One man raised a knife, another a hammer, and still another a cane; they launched a simultaneous assault on the soldiers, yelling words that I could not make out. I raised my hands, instructing the soldiers to fight them. They struck the man with the cane, disembowelled the man raising the knife, and set the man with the hammer on fire. They kept dragging girls out, sometimes hurling them into the flames, but more often seizing them in anticipation of pleasurable moments later on. The stench of the fires was pleasant as well, suggesting both erasure and cleansing. Once the fires died down, there was not a single dirty street, no cloak soiled by animal dung, and no human waste. How beautiful fires are, and how swift, as rigorous as my grandfather, as courageous as my father, as fiery as my mother, and as cruel as me! I kept curtly addressing my own heartbeats.

Jawhar, where do you stand in relation to the one who built and constructed? They have left, my friend, and no one recalls their history. They say that the Caliph built Cairo and founded the Al-Azhar. The Caliph! Who remembers Jawhar the Sicilian now? Even the Sicilians do not recognise him. He is buried in Egypt, and yet you do not do him justice.

Nighttime. Today, the Egyptians put up a courageous fight, but, as I expected, the soldiers won. It was time to gather up the spoils and enjoy the lovely girls. I told my soldiers to relax. The fighting would continue tomorrow. This was a powerful victory like the one that the Banu Ubaid had enjoyed in Tunisia. How hard it is to fight the populace, and how bitter the treachery of those who are not skilled fighters. I told my soldiers to be cautious, and they erected their tents outside the city. However, the Egyptians would be attacking either today or tomorrow. The Fatimid army was divided between myself, the amirs, and Commander-in-chief General Mas`ood ibn Thabit himself. I had hundreds of soldiers under my command. Anyone who killed realised that he had overcome fear. I have killed, but I have not killed my father's killer. I did not wish to do that.

The women gathered in the house, waiting for the Amir. They had heard about the fighting in Fustat and the fires. No one knew when it would end or why it had started. People said that the Caliph had ordered Fustat burned after Egyptians had scoffed at him. Al-Hakim bi-Amr Allah was reported to have scaled the mountain and watched Fustat burn with tears in his eyes. He asked the people around him who was doing this and who was fighting whom. When they explained it to him, he simply rubbed his hands together.

"To God alone belongs the power and might," he said tearfully. "O Lord, lift the torment from this country."

But the fire was even faster than Solomon's jinn. It destroyed houses before you could look around.

When I entered my house, my white shirt and trousers were still blood-soaked, and drops of blood fell from my sword-blade. Laila grabbed herself around the neck and let out a scream. She hurried over and gave me a hug.

"Thank God you're safe, my lord," she said. "Without you, I've no life!"

My mother did not say anything. She stared straight at me, but I looked away. She looked at Sundus, who lowered her head.

"Laila," she said gently, "get a bath ready and stay with him. He needs you today."

Laila bowed and kissed my hand.

"My heart's with him every day," she said.

I stretched out on the bed, and the slave girls brought me food, halva, and bowls of water. I sat there with Laila behind me, rubbing my neck, massaging my joints, and whispering how much she loved me. I closed my eyes, utterly exhausted.

"I feel sorry for you, Amir," my mother said dryly. "Killing people is tiring work, and fires are soul-destroying."

I ignored her.

"Rub him here," she told Laila. "That's where his old wound is."

"How did you get this wound, my lord?" Laila asked. "I'm not going to leave you today, even if you ask me. You've come back safe and sound."

I looked at Sundus.

"Come on," I told her. "Recite some poetry for us."

Laila's hand was gently massaging my shoulder.

Sundus recited these lines:

Within my three prisons I find myself confined,

Ask not about the murky message:

My faulty vision, confinement in my house,

And soul encased in an evil body.

"Why are you quoting that miserable poet now? Forget about the Abbasids and their poets. All they can talk about is their own problems. They can only talk about the hues of death."

"Forgive me, my lord," Sundus said, looking at my mother. "I love Al-Ma'arri's poetry. Like him, I feel that I'm a prisoner. My prison's even worse than his. My eye is unwatered by vision; the only escape from prison is death. There's no end to the malice of a perfidious body."

"I don't understand what you're saying, and I don't like your poetry. What I wanted was poetry about love and happiness. Now you've made me gloomy."

"I wanted to tell you the truth, my lord," she replied rapidly. "Sometimes poetic truth can give the heart some pleasure, even if it's sad."

Laila ran her fingers over my hair and chin, then kissed me on the cheek.

"Tell them all to leave," she whispered. "I want you now."

At that moment, I longed for her as well, wanting to plunge into her beauty. But Sundus was standing there in front of me, like sin itself. There was no blame in her expression; instead, there was grief enough to crush the heart.

"I want you even more," I whispered to Laila. "It'll happen, but wait a while..."

I gave Sundus an angry look.

"Do you think I'm a prisoner like you?" I asked.

"Even more so."

"Beware! You managed to bewitch me years ago. You stole a part of me and bewitched me. Which part did you take? An eyelash or a dust-filled breath that makes the chest rattle?"

"In you, I discovered a part of myself."

I forced a smile.

"Do you see?" I asked Laila. "Do you think my wife has a heart like ours? Is she jealous of you, Laila, or simply against me?"

"Laila's my sister," Sundus responded calmly. "I give her advice about you every day. That evil body can neither speak nor collapse, my lord."

"Now you're conversing with me, word by word."

Laila kissed my ear.

"Send them away," she whispered. "My longing for you is wider than oceans."

I raised my hand for everyone to leave, but raised it again to tell Sundus to stay. I looked at Sundus, then went over to Laila and kissed her hard, as the fires of passion flared and overtook me. However, relaxation approached and played dirty tricks.

"Why are you keeping her here with us?" Laila asked.

"To punish her."

"Why are you punishing her, my darling? She's good."

"She's the worst—a nasty, evil person. Ever since she placed her hand on my chest, she's taken away any sense of peace from my heart."

"I don't understand, my lord."

I hugged her hard. Sundus gave me a fixed, emotionless stare. I moved away from Laila.

"I want you to come back in a little while," I told her.

She nodded and left quietly.

Hours later, just before dawn, I asked Laila to summon Sundus.

"She's an angel, my lord," Laila said. "Believe me, I want you to be nice to her and show her some sympathy. I love her like a sister."

Sundus came into the room. I was standing on the balcony, wearing only my trousers.

"Take your face veil off," I told her without even looking at her. "I've told you before that fire has no effect on me."

She slowly removed her veil, her gaze fixed on my back. She could see the signs of my lovemaking with Laila. She smiled, maybe because she realised that she alone could tell the difference between marks of love and swords in action, and yet she knew nothing about passionate love.

"Laila really loves you," she said eagerly.

"My heart is attached to her," I said, still looking up at the stars. "She has all the spontaneity and crazy impetuosity of children. It is as though she was created specially for this moment. Today, Fustat has burned—the Caliph's orders. But something else happened that I did not expect...it was as though people in Fustat were aware that our soldiers were coming. I wonder, how could anyone other than a woman in an amir's household know about something like that? Could we say that one of those women knew about it, but did not inform the people in Fustat? Amirs' womenfolk are not Egyptians, and their slave girls are not Copts. There are very few Egyptians in Cairo, very few indeed. Halva-makers, bean and lentil merchants, butchers, drapery storeowners. They are all chosen with extreme care; they have to be close to the Caliph himself. That is why they will never know anything about the onset of war, even assuming they know how to talk, but..."

She remained silent. I looked at her slowly, checking the burn scars on her cheeks.

"Take off your dress," I told her. "I want to see the burn scar I don't remember."

For just a moment, she stared at me.

"Are you scared?" I asked defiantly.

She grabbed hold of her dress with a shaking hand and ripped it off her body. She stood in front of me, with a body that was half sound and half crumpled by fire.

"Have you seen enough, my lord?" she asked, eyes closed.

"Today in Fustat," I replied decisively, "I've burned many bodies. How were you burned, Sundus?"

She opened her eyes with a shudder.

"How did you feel today, my lord," she asked, "as you burned bodies? I would like to remind you that burns are not like other wounds. It doesn't kill, it doesn't fade. To the contrary, it lingers on the body and in the heart, inflicting hellish torture, making no distinction between good and evil. My lord, nothing is crueller than burning."

"Do you suffer?"

"In the distant past, yes," she replied, swallowing hard. "But not now."

"What did the Witch teach you? You seem different from others. No weakness seems to penetrate your innards and no passion can melt your body."

"Humans are weak by nature," she said. "There are moments when they lose their composure and act unconsciously."

"They act unconsciously," he repeated. "Do you know the penalty for treason?"

"Burning."

"No, not burning. Death."

"That's release and bliss."

"Do you think that your past has made you as rigid as iron, or even more cruel?"

"No one in Egypt is as rigid as me."

"Help me put on my fighting armour. Bring me the swords. Those same swords are going to kill everyone who scoffs at the Caliph and thinks he's capable of everything. Will you do it?"

"I obey your commands, my lord."

She grabbed the shirt and moved closer to me. I opened my arms and put them into the sleeves.

I held her hand, turned toward her, and put my nose close to her neck.

"Even your soul has a different smell," I said. "Does the smell of burning linger throughout life?"

"Yes, it does," she replied, seemingly unmoved by my touch.

I moved even closer and kissed her shoulder.

"Do you feel anything today?" I asked.

She shook her head.

"That's a lot better."

Would that I had been able to delve inside her and extract the magic or to take an awl to her limbs, but I could not.

The second day was even more savage and cruel than the first. Catapults hurled unquenchable balls of fire on stores and houses. Egyptians no longer had much to fear, either for or about. There arose cries of sorrow for what had been lost and anger over what was still to come. My eyes embraced the city's colonnades. On horseback, I entered the narrow streets and assortment of houses amid the fallen stones. I saw severed limbs scattered around and blood not flowing like water but rather cascading like stone chunks from gaps in marble and soft clay. A head lost its way, and another was chased by a friend in the hope of picking it up. One woman tugged at her hair and rolled her head in the sand; another was on her knees, weeping in front of the soldiers. Had the Egyptians been punished enough, I wondered, or not? The fire that was doing its work on their houses was not following the Caliph's instructions; it was moving quickly and efficiently, eradicating all rebellion and sarcasm. So, let Egyptians have their laugh now; why are they not laughing? He smiled, unbothered. What utter futility! Some years earlier, he had seen his own father's head in a soldier's hands as he tried to sever the very last sinew from the body. He had wanted the soldier to get it over with quickly; he'd prayed to God that he would do so. Today, all heads could be severed. There was no longer a precious person to be worried about.

What on earth were Egyptians doing, fighting with piercing stone swords and mercilessly slaying the Caliph's soldiers? What kind of disloyalty was it to attack the Caliph's soldiers and insult the Caliph himself? They were eager to live depraved lives and loved brothels and casual sex. They would be furious with anyone who stopped them boozing or tried to keep women safe. What kind of mob were they, and what punishment did they deserve?

Today, I gave orders to the soldiers to leave nothing standing in Fustat. I wanted to smell ashes in the air for the next year or two. I have no idea what hit me, or why I so relished the taste of blood and the stench of death.

Moments flashed by like years and regulated time. The world lost its colours, and I dearly wished for my soul to re-establish itself in my body, that same soul that had roamed, aimless and helpless, amidst the glowing embers.

Today, I will console myself with the populace's total subjection and punishment. It is a world like a sword that has spotted a gorgeous girl, killing before ripping bodies apart and chopping off limbs, while she toys with the mouth and kisses the lips. If only my mother had realised—if only she knew how savage killing and warmongering can be! Here I am now, raising my hand to order the soldiers to massacre people. Is that not true religious initiative? Here I am, confronting the crafty and deceitful ways in which

Egyptian corpses are defying the Caliph's soldiers. Is it not exhausting and tiresome? I have only had a few hours' sleep. I am expecting gifts and realise that my own end is not too far off. Today, no one can feel safe; only burning brings security.

I entered a narrow street, searching for a man who for two days had been hurling burning logs at the soldiers and running away. He was fast and thin with neatly trimmed hair, an olive complexion, and bulging eyes like a fox's.

"I want him alive," I said, surrounded by my soldiers.

I took off some of my heavy armour, grabbed my sword, and ran between the houses, with the olive-skinned spectre appearing, then disappearing. He tossed burning logs from the roofs of houses and stores, cursing and swearing without fear or restraint. When I heard the voice, I recognised its scent.

"I want him alive," I yelled in a pique of fury, "I want that thieving scum alive!"

I scrambled up on to the scruffy roof and disturbed the birds that screamed in surprise. I would stay there until the man appeared. He wanted me, too: Amir Jawhar. I remembered my father teaching me how to throw spears, ride horses, and wield a sword.

"Jawhar," he told me proudly, "you're no different from your grandfather. Of all your brothers, you're the best at wielding a sword and throwing spears. You're the amir horseman. Remember your heritage and grandfather. If not for you, the pride of the Banu Ubaid would not have survived. Your grandfather built the city and Al-Azhar Mosque. Your Sicilian grandfather left his own city and came here with a commission from destiny to settle and be buried in Cairo."

I was fourteen at the time. I have no idea how I came to forget my father's words or why I suddenly recalled them today. One day in the distant past, I got drunk on wine in Bulaq. My father met me at dawn. He gave me a sad look. I was staggering left and right.

"Forgive me, Father," I said without even thinking.

"Don't ask me to forgive you," he replied, head lowered. "You're the Sicilian's son. You may need some time, but eventually you'll realise who you are."

"My brothers are well prepared for authority," I said. "Look on me as if I were Tamam ibn al-Mu`izz bi-Din Alleh. I like his poetry."

"I've met him and know him well, my son," my father replied. "He's a fine man, even though the world has led him slightly astray."

"No patience, no forgiveness."

It was bitter feelings for myself and not my father that made me repeat that phrase. 'No patience, no forgiveness.' All that was in the past. Today, I am waiting for the thin man, the salamander, to appear. I've named him 'salamander' because he can transform himself amid the fires and not get burned.

I sensed his approach, sneaking into my chest like blood.

"No patience, no forgiveness," I repeated to myself with a smile.

I realised that the person I was looking for was behind me—the man with the thin body and bulging eyes, moving like a fox and running away like a mouse. The salamander. I stayed silent, using my sword to draw in the sand. I was looking at Fustat as it collapsed, burned, and screamed.

The olive-skinned man raised his sword. I turned toward him, shoved him, and had him on the ground in seconds, my sword aimed at his neck. I heard him gasp and noticed the shock in his large, bulging eyes. He dropped his sword.

"Amir," he shouted, "don't kill me, I beg you!"

The sword stuck in my hands, and I swear that I had never hesitated to kill someone before. I opened my mouth to curse the man and his people, but he grabbed a stone from beside me and smashed my hand with it as hard as he could. He twisted away like a snake and yelled at the top of his voice. Chickens panicked, and ducks and geese started running around in circles.

There was general chaos. Before things became clearer, the salamander man had disappeared. Twisting and moving with incredible speed, he was the man who had wounded the hand of Amir Jawhar, son of Husain, son of Jawhar the Sicilian. He had to be killed.

The man had driven me crazy. I grabbed hold of my hand; the chunk of brick had penetrated to the bone. As I climbed down from the roof, I chided myself for letting the man get away. How could I be the son of General Husain and be defeated by the salamander, the thin man? In just a few seconds, he had escaped; in a single moment, I was going to kill him.

The incident with that man weighed heavily on me. I asked the soldiers to discover his identity. After a while, I had the information. They said he was a halva-maker in Fustat, renowned for his pastries stuffed with cheese and nuts. I asked where his store was, what he owned and did not own, about his life and name. None of the soldiers knew his name, but everyone knew about his store in the halva-makers' market in Fustat. It was still standing; it had not been burned or destroyed. I allowed myself a smile. Tomorrow, I would burn the store down, then the halva, and finally the halva-maker. I felt a buried hatred for people in Fustat and for Sundus. I was convinced that she was the one who had warned the Egyptians about the attack. She was the traitorous spy. Was killing permissible after fire? What could I do with her? Should I send her away? I already had. Should I put her in prison? She had done that to herself as well. Should I kill her? The fires had already killed her body. All I could do was loathe her, and I was not capable of even that.

"I've broken your heart," she had said. "And there's no escape from that."

Have I told you about Lamya, my mother? No, I have not told you anything about her and her incredible vigour, which is something to rival the savagery of an eagle ripping apart a mouse. She stolidly endured the deaths of her son and husband without complaint. There were no tears of grief. She was much stronger and more vicious than me.

"What are those bloodstains on your clothes, my son?" she asked me.

I looked at her for a moment without responding.

"I really don't know," she worried, "if they'd slaughtered you along with your father right in front of me, would my heart have stayed calm, or would it have erupted in flames?"

"Slaughter's coming for sure," I replied with a bitter smile. "Just wait a while."

"It'll never come," she replied without thinking, her gaze still fixed on my eyes. "Not as long as you bow and scrape to Al-Hakim bi-Amr Allah. How many men have you killed in Fustat?"

I sighed as I looked at the blood on my fingers, where the thin man had crushed the bone.

"Everyone in Fustat's a traitor," I said, worried about my finger bone. "They're insurgents by nature. Just look at what they've done to your son. This finger will be useless from now on."

She prodded my chest.

"That heart in there won't be of any use from now on," she said bluntly.

"Egyptians aren't going to help you, Lamya," I shot back.

"Who's expecting any help from humanity?" she asked decisively. "They're all stupid."

Pursing my lips, I looked at my wife, who was staring distractedly at the floor. She left the room, and I told the slave girls to prepare the water for a bath. The slaughter's coming, Mother, and it is your destiny to watch your husband and son being slaughtered before your very eyes.

That is what I told myself. I saw her tears falling, something I had never seen before.

There is a sense of support in being surrounded by slave girls. I can choose one that I like and feel that I have entered paradise and settled there. They want to make me happy and give me passionate looks, as though they want an hour of sex with me, no more. I stretched out on my back and closed my eyes. We had to forget everything that was happening. It could neither be analysed nor anticipated. The slave girl ran her hand over my back and whispered amorous words. The images in my mind were all scrambled. There was Sundus, her face aglow and unsullied by dust, then the halva-maker begging for help, then plunging his dagger into my chest. Blood was everywhere—but there, too, was Sundus's face, still glowing with the light of paradise, devoid of both fear and greed. How could I imagine paradise without slave girls and wine? Why was the thin halva-maker plunging his dagger into my chest?

The slave girl held my hand and washed the wound. She kissed my hand.

"Does it hurt, my lord?" she asked.

I did not answer. This is Cairo, a city that compensates for what has been lost. I was expelled from it, but then returned in triumph. I wonder, if I met the Caliph Al-Hakim, would I be awed by him? If I obeyed all his commands, would I be saved? Was this the kind of fear that makes trees lose their colours, that can turn branches into serpents that inject poison into every honey vessel, and that makes the slave girl's hand unsatisfying and incapable of staunching a wound?

Inevitably, my actions today were sheer madness, the opening gesture to perdition. I won't think about it. I'll just go to sleep. I need to sleep.

Today, I told my soldiers not to leave a single house standing. My fury was uncontrollable and took over everything. As the soldiers entered the streets, I was thinking about that halva-maker. I asked where his store was and eventually located it. Everything was displayed with care. For just a moment I stared at it, before telling my soldiers to knock it down and burn it. There was an array of basandud cakes stuck to each other in hollow circles, which made it difficult to be satisfied with just one, or to separate one from the other. The smell of almonds and pistachio blended in with the bright colours that decorated them. To the right, khushkananaj sweetcakes had been placed one on top the other, like new moons high in the sky. I have no idea why the tower of them did not collapse. Cream had been mixed with sugar, almonds, and pistachio until I could picture a hundred feast days for every new moon that rises, a hundred prohibited months. But I was going to kill him for certain even if he resorted to prohibited months. I looked inside the store where fanayid, sugar-cane halva, was on display—indoors, so that it would not be spoiled by the Fustat sunshine. They were made of sugar, eggs, rose petals, and almonds. They would melt in your fingers before you could even get them into your mouth; the scent would warm your nostrils and fire your craving for more. Then my eyes fell on some 'needa,' as it's called by the locals. I already knew he was a thief; 'needa' is a sweet found only in Cairo. They do not make it in Fustat; they are not allowed to. But here it was inside his store. I could almost smell it: wheat with cream and sugar, blended with all the delicate care of a palace fountain. I could also see some of the sweets called Zainab's fingers and judge's morsels. I could see pendants shaped like animals and roses. What perfect skill this halva-maker possessed! What was to be the fate of these types of sweets?

I told the soldiers to take the halva out first, then burn the store. Those types of halva were all vestiges of the past, just like Egyptian temples—made with creativity and care, just like the statues of the ancients and the drawings inside their tombs. They had to be preserved. I personally do not like halva, but the soldiers crave them even more than they do women.

Once they had wolfed down the halva, they started burning the store. They tossed fireballs inside and grabbed the women. Each chose the most beautiful one for himself. For my part, I brandished my sword at everyone, killing and hacking, my heart neither sated nor settled. The halva-maker was bound to appear; he had to. Anyone who had laid out his store with such care and built his own house beside it could not stay silent while it was being destroyed. Wails of grief arose, and it was not just the women. No one had ever heard men wailing like that, the noise sounding like someone with a raffia rope around their neck—not a little unsettling. As the bloody scene unfolded, there appeared a column of men from the mountains dressed in white gallabiyyas. They were holding up copies of the Qur'an, weeping loudly, and pleading with verses from the Qur'an. I could tell that they were shareefs, descendants of the Prophet: 'Salaam, greetings of peace, a word from the Merciful Lord,' and again, 'Salaam, greetings of peace, a word from the Merciful Lord.'

The soldiers moved away, scared of killing them while they were carrying copies of the Qur'an. The Egyptians stopped fighting; some sat down, others remained standing. They thrust the Qur'ans in the soldiers' faces and wept.

The soldiers hesitated, and that made me choke with fury, although I had no idea why. It was then that I spotted him: the sweet seller, the salamander. Today, he had come running from the far end of the street, holding up a copy of the Qur'an. He raised it in the air.

"Stop," he pleaded. "In the Lord's name, stop!"

I raised my sword and pointed it at the halva-maker's neck. His hand trembled, and he almost dropped the Qur'an.

"I implore you by God to stop," he whispered. "I implore you by God's holy book."

I ran my sword over his neck and then his chest. I thrust the tip eagerly between his ribs until blood flowed. He groaned in pain, but still clutched the Qur'an.

"There can be no pact with Egyptians," I said, withdrawing my sword.

The Egyptians kept repeating the same phrase: "Salaam, greetings of peace, a word from the Merciful Lord."

The soldiers lowered their weapons. One of them came over to me.

"Amir," he asked, "why are we fighting Egyptians?"

"What kind of question is that," I asked angrily. "The Caliph's orders."

"Yes, I know," he replied. "But Egyptians want peace."

My eyes met the halva-maker's. His had a magic gleam to them, along with a false sense of loss. I knew that look well, but I had no idea why I spoke the words I did.

"Stop," I yelled loudly. "Stop fighting!"

No sooner did people hear that than they sank to the ground in prayers to God. The group of shareefs who had come from the mountain heights approached me.

"My Lord Amir," one of them told me in loud tones, "these people are

Egyptians. They share family and marriage ties to the soldiers. Treat them kindly and forgive them—may God have mercy on you!"

I swallowed hard.

"Shareef Shaikh ` Ali," I replied, "don't try to intercede on behalf of people who have rebelled against the Caliph. He may get angry with you."

"By Him who made the earth a cover and the heavens a structure," the Shareef Shaikh ` Ali ibn Hasan replied, "do not destroy what God has commanded us to build. Amir, you're the same age as my own son."

"These are the Caliph's orders," I replied angrily.

The shaikh nodded.

"I'll speak to him," he told me calmly. "Till then, grant the Egyptians some peace. Your own grandfather built, and he destroyed nothing."

"Yes," I replied loudly. "My grandfather did build things, but then his name was forever buried. My father—"

"The one who builds is never lost, even if his career has been somewhat forgotten. Soldiers offer protection; they don't launch attacks."

"Don't interfere in my work, Shaikh," I told him firmly. "I have my job, and you have yours."

Before the Shaikh could respond, the halva-maker shouted:

"The Ubaid are still attacking, Shaikh. They haven't stopped fighting. They have our women."

With that, he fell to his knees and grabbed my hand.

"If you want to kill me," he said, "go ahead. But tell the Ubaid to stop fighting."

I withdrew my hand.

"You can change like a chameleon," I said. "Yesterday, you were out to kill me, but today you're begging me to help you!"

"I'd beg the Devil if I could," the halva-maker replied instantly, tears still falling. "The Ubaid are massacring Egyptians."

I raised my hand and slapped him across the face.

"Be polite when you're addressing your Amir," I said. "Which devil are you talking about?"

I could see hatred in the halva-maker's eyes.

"Forgive me, Amir," he said, suppressing his fury. "Please help us. You're our people, you sons of the great leader."

I turned to address the Shareef Shaikh ʿAli.

"I've ordered my soldiers to stop fighting," I told him. "But a section of the Ubaid army is not under my authority. Their commander is Masʿood ibn Thabit."

I signalled to my own soldiers.

"Stop fighting the Egyptians," I yelled. "Stop and stay where you are. That's an order from your Amir."

"Amir Jawhar," the Shareef Shaikh said hurriedly, "he's the son of the general whom Egyptians admire, Husain, son of the Sicilian."

"But what did Egyptians do to save him? Tell me, Shaikh, how did the Egyptian people's love help him? That same love hastened his end."

"My son," the Shaikh replied gently, "the Caliph did not order Egyptians to be killed. I personally saw him atop the hills, looking down on Fustat with tears in his eyes."

I gave a mocking smile.

"Don't ask me to do things that I can't," I told him.

"No," the Shaikh responded, "you can do what I'm asking. In your eyes, I can detect the distraction of someone who is merciful and the hesitation of someone confronting tyranny."

"I'm going to withdraw my troops from Fustat," I declared firmly. "That's all I can do. In so doing, I'll already have contravened the orders of the commanding general and the Caliph himself."

Before the Shaikh could say anything else, I mounted my horse and took my troops away. I chuckled to myself as I recalled his words: hesitant, devout, distracted, merciful! Those shareefs inhabited a cloister unvisited by the rest of humanity! *Shareef Shaikh 'Ali, you can stay on your mountain so you won't soil your white gallabiyya with the stench of people scared of the stake.*

I looked at the slave girl whose hair covered the whole of her naked body. Spreadeagled across the bed, she seemed both elated and tired, half-asleep and half-awake, closed off from the entire world apart from the Amir's bedchamber. I was not seeing her; what I was seeing was Sundus's burned face. I shouted for her and told the slave girl to bring her.

When Sundus arrived, she looked at me like a mother scolding a child who has not performed the Friday prayers. She pursed her lips with a sigh, not expecting me to be having sex with a new slave girl. From hour to hour and day to day, I was forgetting about Laila.

"I want you to recite some of your poetry for me," I said. "Or else tell me a story about the prisoner."

"What about Laila?" she asked, looking at the slave girl.

"What's Laila got to do with what happens in my bedroom?"

"Laila loves you."

"That's her problem. I never asked her to love me. All I ever promised her was a few hours of pleasure."

"Send the slave girl away," she said, "so I can talk to you."

"The slave girl stays; her place is here with me. And you're going to talk."

"Take off your face veil," I went on. "I've told you before that the burn marks don't scare me or make me feel sorry for you."

"I don't want to hurt your slave girl or give her heart, as meek as a sparrow's, a shock."

I looked at my slave girl.

"Do burn scars scare you?" I asked her. "My wife's face is disfigured by burns."

"If they don't scare you, my lord," she said, half-awake, "then they don't scare me."

I went over to Sundus and removed the veil.

"You've betrayed your husband," I said. "You warned the people in Fustat. Who knows, maybe you're acquainted with the halva-maker. Do you know him?"

She stared at my shoulder, then looked at the wound on my hand.

"Sometimes, fate will imprison us by force," she said. "But other times, we'll choose prison voluntarily."

"When does man choose to lose his freedom?"

"When he realises that freedom involves defeat and humiliation."

"When can he escape from that prison?"

"When he turns into an eagle. Eagles stick to themselves, trusting neither birds nor humans."

"You're talking riddles and magic. Come over here."

She came over.

"I can send the slave girl away," I told her suddenly. "And you can sleep in my arms."

She looked shocked.

"Don't misunderstand me," I went on. "Don't let hope toy with your heart. Today, I'm feeling a strange kind of sympathy toward you—I don't know why. It's as though you're a child who's lost its parents in the desert and fallen into my lap in search of safety."

Before she could respond, I pushed the slave girl away.

"Go back to your room," I told her.

She stood up at once and left the room in seconds. Now, I grabbed Sundus's arm.

"Come to my chest," I told her.

She did not move, so I hugged her hard, put an arm around her waist, and rubbed my cheek against hers with its burns.

"All humanity needs affectionate caresses," I said. "The whole of humanity."

"What does my lord know about affection," she asked, "now that he's burned Fustat?"

"Do you need to sleep on my chest, Sundus?" I asked. "Tell me the truth. For me to want you the way a man usually wants a woman is impossible. But getting you to sleep on my chest is certainly possible. I don't hate you, nor do your burn scars distress me. But I do have one condition."

"What's that?"

"Stop practicing your magic. Ever since you touched my chest, the world's not been the same. Things that used to make me happy now make me upset. Things that used to quench my thirst now suck water out of my stomach. Everything's confused."

"I don't have any magic."

"I've said that you're part of me."

"You were correct."

"You people in Egypt are good at magic. I'm Sicilian, and I know nothing about your ancient learning. Talk to me about the spirit's prison."

"There's no escaping it."

"What about the soul's prison?"

"You can be rid of it by seeking forgiveness and purifying your inner self of greed."

"And the heart's prison?"

"We stay there, forever bound in contentment, neither rebelling nor seeking freedom. Passion is a disease, one we accept and to which we submit."

"The eye's prison?

"It finishes with magic's end and the destruction of all hate's symbols. Then, all vision's doors are open before us."

"Everything you say is profound."

"People like myself can boast only of their intelligence."

She lay down on my bed, and I carried her to me.

"You're a traitor," I told her, moving my mouth close to her ear. "You want me to die. You prefer the people of Fustat to your own husband."

She calmly slipped out of my arms and stood up.

"My lord needs to get some sleep," she said. "He has a lot of killing to do tomorrow."

"Talk to me. Your words are always different; they make me happy. Tell me about your poets, the tunes on the lute and dulcimer in your hand. How can such beauty emerge from..."

She smiled knowingly and sat down beside me. Her eyes left no signs of love on my body. She started talking, about love and pride, the wars of our ancestors, cities and walls...

I closed my eyes like a child. She took up the lute and started playing as she recited some poetry for me. It seemed I started talking to her while I was half-awake—about my mother, my father, slave-girls, and wine—about slaughter, burning, and generals' orders.

"I can tell you anything," I said. "You're nothing to me. Your opinions are of no interest, and..."

She said nothing. I found myself having doubts about Sundus's heart. I felt like ripping it out of her to check on it, already aware of every single speck of its blood and every desire that controlled it.

"If you longed for anyone else," I told her angrily, "I'd slaughter you myself, put your head in front of me, and recite it some poetry. Don't you say that the body is an untruthful, echoing vessel. If that were the case, I'd have to plunge my sword into your heart. Tell me what it's doing and how it is that I now see you as beautiful. Sundus, what does the body have to do with the heart?"

She looked at me.

"The body is slave to the heart, Amir," she said. "It obeys it and moves it the same way that you move your spear tips."

"So then, the body's as important as the heart."

"The body's like the spear. Without it, you cannot win. But the heart is like the spear tip; without it, you can't do anything."

"How can you speak such wisdom? You're just a woman, no more..."

Would that buckets of blood could relieve the sickly heart, and that gorgeous slave girls could sate the living body! Were I to dispense with the love of life and embrace death, I would be saved. I have become intimate with death. I have killed and slaughtered. On every occasion, I have seen my father's head refuse to be liberated from death's butchery. I have called out to it at night and missed it by day. Death: a sword strike that butchers, a waft of traitorous air that throttles. O Angel of Death, why have you spared me, yet not spared me? You have saved the body and taken the soul. Were you a genuine companion, you would not have obscured all vision and robbed trees of all their leaves. Why don't you come and finish what you have started? Are you like me, scared of endings? Or is it that you hate futile beginnings that emerge amid the entrails of wild beasts and are spat out by foxes at magical moments? Oh, for times that were all prisons! Air was in short supply, and people fought to breathe. Resurrection Day appeared, but did not come close. So man fled from his brother man with no account or reason. Why do you seize pure spirits and leave satanic ones in place? Why do you relieve some and torture others? Take me to you: I am not bothered by fire; all that scares me is the wrath of rulers.

"It was jealousy." A word—or three words, actually—do you know them all? Did Al-Hakim feel jealous of my father, then kill him? I jeer and mock you, I scoff at your impotence in the face of rulers, your hesitation in dealing with tyrants. Very well, O monarch of death, continue seizing the souls of the innocent. I shall continue to confront you and criticise you every single day, every hour, every noon, every dusk. I shall blame you whenever I witness a fire that is not hell or torture that is not a blaze. Where are you today, Monarch? Come to me, indeed accompany me, embrace me hard. Remind me that my heart was split in two the moment my father died. My own impotence still corrupts my body like the plague. Embrace me, O Monarch of Death, and finish your task. Why do you hesitate? I have known you to be both powerful and learned. Or do you prefer to embrace those who are loyal to you? If it is loyalty that you prefer, then you have no place in this land or these times. Plunge your spear into my belly and do not hesitate. My soul is dangling between earth and sky, awaiting mercy and fearing the encounter. Woe to a time when light and colours have disappeared, along with all scents, sweet tastes, and lovely vistas.

Why is the_Monarch of_Death torturing me day and night? Will he be merciful and seize my soul? Will he free my imprisoned body from the endless darkness that will not let me finish?

Here I am, suspended by my feet, hovering in the clouds, sometimes facing the sky, but most of the time towards the earth's depths. Ah me, suffering that my mother neither knows nor understands. She views the world in two colours, when there are none. She sees trees with wings, while they are stuck in the ground, sickly and foot-tied, just like me. But she does not hover in the sky or leave the dark soil. O Lamya, why don't you know or feel? What connects you now to that woman who would dry the child's tears with a frown?

"Men never cry," she would insist. "They don't ask for sympathy, they're never scared, and they don't beg. Just say what you want and take it without a word."

How can you have wanted me to speak and not speak? To want something, and not say so? To take something, when my hands are in fetters and my feet are bound? What is the matter with you, Lamya? Do you not know the Monarch of Death? Or has treachery never impacted you or made its way toward you? You can cry or not. You will witness my death and know tears. As long as I want to see your tears, I want them to be tears of love and affection, not defiance and knowledge. Ah Lamya, I shall be looking down on you from the heavens. I will smile when you cry over your loss, your heart tied to the Monarch. Like me, you will beg him to let you meet your beloveds. The day will surely come when you can feel and know. I was here, and you were not. I loved you and criticised you. Forgive me, Mother! I never rose to the rank of son; I was always shame and disgrace. Once we are separated, the truth will be revealed. Life always misleads and deceives. It is death that throws back the covers and makes rocks split into two or more pieces. Be patient for a while, daughter of Hamdoon. Did your father not teach you that commanders are never afraid? They accompany the monarch and converse with him. That is what I willingly do now. I am keeping him company, and without fear.

I heard a knock at the door. It was almost midnight. I got dressed and left the room. I had told the slave girls not to open any doors; people could not be trusted.

I asked who was knocking. It was him—the halva-maker. I had been expecting him, although I had no idea why.

"What's brought you here?" I asked angrily.

"My lord, despair led prophets to part the waters of the sea. I'm a poor servant; all I can do is to cling to you."

"I've saved your life, true enough. I could have killed you, but I didn't. But don't test my patience, or else I'll kill you on the spot. Make sure you don't slink into my house again."

"I've brought you a present, my lord. I want to express my gratitude."

I stared at him without saying a word. He came in and closed the door.

The light from the lamp mingled with the pale face. To me, the halva-maker looked like a jinn come from hell, his head surrounded by fiery streaks. His thin layer of hair kept stiffening, then collapsing. I swear that his hair completely filled my room, and I had no idea how to be rid of it for the rest of my life.

From his pocket, the halva-maker produced a statue of coloured sugar, shaped like a combination of fox and mouse. The eyes were red, the tail yellow, and the body grey.

"This is for you, my lord," the halva-maker said, holding out his hand. "It's a gift to sweeten your mouth and your days. Sugar can always sweeten tense times, solve riddles, and lift curses. People who say that salt is a blessing have lied to you. Sugar is the only blessing. It's like beautiful eyes and paradise fruit, with a pure honeyed taste and the sea's foam. It's yours in profound gratitude."

I grabbed it and turned it over.

"What kind of madness is this?" I asked.

"It's what you can see, my lord."

"What I see is a mouse."

"I see it as a fox."

"You've come here to mock me. You're crazy, that's for sure. Get out of my house and take your mouse with you."

The halva-maker shuddered and burst into tears. He seized the sweet from me and bit off the animal's head, the sound of his tears traveling all the way to Fustat.

I looked at him aghast and not a little curious.

"You've finished me, Sicilian," he said between sobs. "You've taken everything. Now that you've finished me, you can sleep safe and sound in your house with your slave girls."

I grabbed my sword but stayed where I was.

He started eating the animal's leg, chewing it with his mouth open, while tears poured from eyes, nose, and mouth.

"If you killed me, I could find some rest," he said. "Come on then, kill me now. I've come here so you can finish your task. Sicilian Amir, you've come to my country to burn, not to build. I built my store with my dreams, and now you've burned it. When something is built on dreams, it is difficult to rebuild once it's destroyed. However, I've brought you some of the ashes."

He plunged his hand back into his pocket, brought out some ashes, and used his fingers to spread them around.

"Do you imagine I'm scared of your sword?" he asked. "Do you think I've come to thank you for sparing my life? Yes, I wanted to kill you, but I didn't. Do you know why, Sicilian? Because I found part of me in you."

I opened my mouth to put an end to this madness and brandished my sword.

"We both wanted to die," the halva-maker went on. "Kill me, then yourself, and it'll be over."

"What kind of lunatic are you?"

The halva-maker, still tearful, took the animal's stomach, scrunched it in his hands, and started licking it with his tongue.

"If you'd just put an end to my dream, I could have forgiven you. But you've put an end to every kind of longing on this earth. You've taken from me all honour and respect, my wife, and my son."

"What nonsense is this? I don't know either your wife or son."

The halva-maker burst into laughter, spitting the sugar out of his mouth.

"Sicilian," he said, "I've only known you to be intelligent. You've ordered your soldiers to have fun with Egyptian women. They captured my wife and son. Yes, they took my nursing son along with his mother. What's left for a man when they marry off his daughters and wife? Do you know? Have you thought about it?"

"The Caliph's orders."

"I don't know him. He seems to change as one day follows the next. One day he's kind, the next everything's prohibited; cruel one day, merciful the next; building schools one day, knocking them down the next. He kills the shaikh, then weeps over his grave. I don't know him, just as I don't know the times we're in. But I do know you. You've finished me off, finished the man inside me, finished the halva-maker represented by my body. I've nothing left. I made that animal amid the ashes of my home and store. What pleasure did you feel today, destroying everything and kidnapping women?"

"Get out of my house before I kill you."

"You won't do that. You've discovered a bit of me inside yourself. I've come to strike a deal with you, Sicilian,"

"Call me 'my Lord Amir.'"

"I'm talking to the Sicilian, not the Amir. I'll kill you."

"What did you just say?"

"I'll kill you, and you'll kill me. If you want."

"Have you lost your mind?"

"You love death as much as I do. You can't kill yourself. I kill you, and you kill me."

Before I could say anything, the halva-maker grabbed me and held on to my hand.

"I want my wife and son back," he pleaded, bits of the halva still falling from his mouth onto my arm. "I can't just leave them to the soldiers. They took both of them away right in front of me, and I couldn't resist. They lifted my arms, put a dagger to my neck, but didn't kill me. If only they had! Before my very eyes, they dragged my wife away and stripped her. As she screamed, they picked her up and took her away. As I stood there, as helpless as a mouse, they ripped her upper garments. She'll never let them touch her. I know her; Mariam would never let them. When she resisted, they must have killed her. The Caliph's soldiers—actually, your own soldiers, Amir—stripped her right in front of me. Do you realise how much I loathe you? Even so, I'm begging you to give me back my wife and son."

"Get out of my house before I slaughter you."

"You won't do that; you'll never do that. I'm part of you. Think about what I've said. Forgive me for eating the fox and mouse, so profound is my grief. I'd brought it to you as a gift, General Amir, you who've burned Fustat to the ground and ordered his soldiers to kidnap Egyptian women. The Ubaids are still massacring Egyptians, Amir. Withdraw your soldiers and those of Mas`ood ibn Thabit. You're still devastating the land."

"Beware! They're the Caliph's orders."

"He ordered your father to be killed. You've ignored all his instructions. I wonder, did you imagine that he could restore your father to life if you made him happy? He kills people, Amir; he doesn't bring them back to life."

As the halva-maker rapidly disappeared from my presence, he repeated: 'He kills people, he doesn't bring them back to life.'

"Wait!" I yelled without thinking. "I never told my soldiers to kidnap women. Who kidnapped your wife?"

He didn't respond. And I did not see him as he left.

I clutched my neck as though the halva-maker had beheaded me, but not completely. I could envisage my father and the soldier freeing the final sinew from his body. I wonder, do eyes keep hovering in the permanent void? A desolate world like the ancient pots that children find in the Fustat desert. Does the halva-maker feel sorry for me? Of course not. People who can be cruel are cruel; those who spill blood can do nothing else. What is really troubling me is the way I am deliberately selling all my limbs. I can no longer feel either elation or pain. Laila no longer sates my bodily needs, nor does the foreign slave girl or any slave girl, for that matter. Once I've exhausted my energy on her, my mind starts playing games. My heart does not race, nor does my body relax. It's as though I've satisfied my needs but no more. Now, the deed that previously used to help me transcend a life of ease has turned into something with no effect. No beauty can help me relax, no plunge inside the world's beautiful women can quiet the moaning that creeps through my body like an insect and feeds on the polluted blood. Who on earth can witness his father's death without rebelling or even objecting? The body is sated, but not grateful; it eats, but does not recognise meat's taste, the smooth texture of bones, or the welcome savour of fresh milk. Then what? What makes the earth tolerable? Now, sex with women has no taste. Only wine is left. I'll start drinking till the glass itself begs me for mercy. But even wine no longer lets you forget and helps to console. You have started banging your head and arousing nostalgia. Death is distant, life is long, and time, like the Caliph, keeps on deceiving.

I went out at dawn. Don't ask me how or why I came up with that idea. I wasn't thinking, nor had I learned how to analyse my actions. Now, it was the heart in motion, giving instructions. I gathered my soldiers and ordered them to fight the soldiers of my commander, Mas'ood ibn Thabit, in Fustat. All the soldiers, the Turks and Sicilians under my command, would be fighting the Ubaid troops. Amir Jawhar will be rebelling against his commanding officer. They will keep fighting until the Ubaid troops stop making Egyptians suffer. That is what I will be doing without even thinking about it. The Shareef Shaikh 'Ali appears in front of me, carrying a copy of the Qur'an, and the Egyptians' words still haunt me even though I am half dead: 'Salaam, greetings of peace, a word from the Merciful Lord.' A merciful Lord? O Lord, where is Your mercy toward me? Why don't You help me? So then, put an end to what remains, rip out the rebellious vein from my neck, and hasten the slaughter. The world has been blended with stars and planets. Life has turned into seas in the sky, and death a revival of rulers' frivolity. O

Lord, pity Your recalcitrant servant; Your mercy encompasses everything. I am not asking for Your forgiveness; I have never sinned, or perhaps a little. But today, it is Your sympathy I want.

The soldiers did not argue with me. I rode my horse out from Cairo to Fustat, with the soldiers behind me. We heard shouts coming from Cairo's gates. I made the horse gallop until our soldiers started attacking Mas`ood ibn Thabit's forces, sword against sword, spear against spear. All Egyptians froze in place. They stopped pleading for help and started putting out the flames. They paid no attention to the armies fighting each other.

People say that the Caliph climbed up the mountain and looked down on Fustat as it burned. He asked what was happening, and his retainers told him that the army was split. Soldiers under the command of Jawhar, son of Husain the Sicilian, were fighting Mas`ood ibn Thabit's troops to stop the damage being done to Egyptians. The Caliph asked about the army generals, then ordered Mas`ood to take charge, gave him fulsome praise, and told him to keep fighting the rebellious forces. He asked to have a meeting with the commander of the Turkish forces. I did not trust him, so I did not go. I may have been scared or unable to confront him because of a bitter feeling that I had. I do not know exactly. I sent one of my men to meet the Caliph on the Muqattam Hills, and he came hurrying back invoking prayers for the Caliph. He told me that the Caliph had ordered him to attack Mas`ood's forces. I looked around me and turned. If the Caliph had truly held a meeting with Mas`ood, why did he not order him to put an end to the Egyptians' suffering? Had he ordered Mas`ood to attack the Turks? Had he ordered us to attack Mas`ood's forces? Did he want the entire army to attack itself? Or was it that we did not understand the Caliph's mission? Or that he was not with us and listening to us? Perhaps he did not realise or appreciate what was happening. Even so, the general swore that the Caliph had tears in his eyes, as he pitied what the people of Fustat were going through. My overriding priority now was to save the people of Fustat from my own commander and his army. I fought on with all the strength I could muster.

Then I spotted him—the halva-maker. He was walking behind me, following me all the way.

"You promised to find my wife," he repeated. "You promised to help me, you promised—"

"Get out of my sight," I interrupted. "We're at war."

"I realise that you're defending us, but that's not enough. You promised—"

"I didn't promise you anything. I don't want to know you."

He disappeared from view, but did not leave me.

I hurried back to my house in Cairo, leaving my soldiers to fight my commander's soldiers. I told them not to stop, whatever happened. On the way back, my horse's hooves threw dirt into my eyes, and I kept seeing the image of the halva-maker. Like the zephyr from the East, his loathing for me made me somewhat happy, but also concerned me a little. Even so, I thought about him all day. I could see the sugar spilling from his mouth and the tears he shed like a mutilated beast. I am amazed at my ability to inflict such misery on my fellow humans. I used to tell myself that I was just following orders and not coming up with new types of torture and burning. But now, it seems that I can top even the Caliph when it comes to burning bones and chopping off limbs. How proud I am, halva-maker, when I observe your suffering, and yet how sorry I feel, too. I did not choose to destroy your life, and you did not choose me as a pivot point in your entire life.

I stopped by the gate, out of breath, and dismounted. I was about to go inside, but stopped. I was not expecting what I saw.

I saw my wife Sundus, with her hands plunged into a bowl of dough. Do not ask me how I ended up in the baking room today; I have no idea. However, she had made up her mind to spend the night there. Over time, I had forgotten what her face looked like. She was now inured to shocked and sympathetic glances, as though it was all natural and anything else would be an attack on the Caliph. I appreciated the prison walls with which she surrounded herself, their duration as long as life itself. She had accepted her situation and lived with it. But today, she had been burned again. Do not ask why today in particular. I saw her right in front of me today, looking at the huge bowl full of dough. She took the cover off, and it was fresh dough, carefully prepared to be cooked at dawn. She plunged her hands into the dough, took some of it out, and put it over her left cheek, where the burn-scars were. Then, gazing at her face, she went over to a ewer full of water. The dough covered the burn-scars, but the heart remained as dry as apricots and dates. She smiled. If she stayed here for the rest of her life, she would relax and feel safe. I heard her whisper to herself: "He's come to close the prison door on me and shut out whatever light is left. Anyone whose gift is tribulation also provides the means to tolerate it; those who touch skin will inevitably penetrate the depths and not gnaw at the chest."

She squeezed the dough with her hand, then took another look at her face in the water ewer. Tears welled up in her eyes, but they did not fall. Spontaneously, she put some dough on her cheek again, then lay down beside the bowl of dough, her refuge and saviour, and closed her eyes.

"Wake up, Sundus!" she yelled to herself, although I heard it, too. "You know who you are... so what's led you astray and befuddled you?"

"You're talking to yourself," I said.

She looked to see where the voice was coming from and stared at me without batting an eyelash. I raised my hand and put it on her cheek.

"What's brought you here?" I asked gently. "No, don't tell me; you needn't reply. Don't tell me why you've spread dough over your cheek. Do you know that the Caliph has forbidden Egyptians from using their feet to knead dough? Our Caliph has good intentions. Have you ever seen him, Sundus?"

She sat up, then stood and headed for the door.

"Where are you going?" I asked, grabbing her hand.

"I don't know," she replied bashfully. "I was feeling tired, and I must have put some dough on my cheek without realising it. I used my hand to wipe—"

"Sit down," I interrupted. "Let's have an honest chat. Honesty only emerges at night, as does fear. Tell me, Sundus, have you started feeling like other human beings? Do you have desires and cravings? We think that the body is the traitor, but it's the heart that always betrays. Fustat is on fire."

She looked shocked and was about to stand up. I pulled her to my chest.

"Has a man ever hugged you before?" I asked. "Of course not, nor will it ever happen. You realise that, so you've bottled the pain up inside you. Hardship is always on is way, and you wait for it with constant satisfaction. What has happened to contentment inside you?"

No sooner had she put her head on my chest than she closed her eyes in pain. I put my arm around her waist and ran it over her back and shoulder.

"Do you want to hug me?" I whispered. "Put you hand on my neck and chest. Do what you want."

Her body pulsed with life and arousal. She hesitated, then put her fingers around my neck. I gently grasped her fingers and kissed them slowly.

"You're a traitor," I told her. "I know. Tell me what you want. Would you like me to touch you? Do you want to experience a man's caress and touch?"

She opened her mouth in surprise.

"You warned the people in Fustat that the army was coming," I went on, forgetting all about the halva-maker. "Who did you talk to? Do you have family in Fustat? Don't be scared. I'm not going to punish you, I've already decided that."

She tried to move, but I hugged her hard, and her chest melted into mine. Her body shuddered, her limbs quivered, and her whole being shifted. Her eyes closed, she put her arms around my neck. Moving her hand slowly, she rubbed my shoulder and arm. Grabbing my hand and squeezing my fingers, she sighed deeply as she brought her mouth close to my neck and brushed it past my temple and ear. She donned the garb of the devout worshipper and found within me a sea of mercy and a river of pity mingled with affection. Before this, had I deliberately hurt or punished her? What had happened today? Had I now realised how much I had wronged and punished her when, with all her human frailty and weakness, she had collapsed in front of me?

I brought my mouth close to her cheek, which still covered in dough. I used my finger to wipe some of it off.

"There," I said.

"I don't understand."

"There's nothing to understand. You know that there's nothing that requires understanding."

For a while, she rested in my arms—a moment that lasted as long as life itself with its harsh, gloomy days; a moment like vain hope, a crazed heart, and pure honey slipping between the fingers for a few seconds, then slowly seeping away into the void.

"There can't be anything between us," I said, without knowing why. "You realise that. What I like about you is that you know and acknowledge it."

Did I realise that those words would penetrate to her very heart and split it in two? Doesn't the heart only die once, like the body? Hadn't she realised that for some time? Why such murderous desire? How can love turn into delusion and despair? She had suppressed all hope and throttled it. The same hope had blended with stupidity and naiveté. But she certainly knew that, too. *The Amir doesn't want her. How can he when she's...?*

"Thank you, my lord!" she said, reassembling the parts of her distracted self.

She tried to wriggle out of my arms.

"Don't leave me," I said immediately. "Not now, and not today!"

"But I'm choking," she said.

"Sometimes shortness of breath revives you," I said. "I need to talk to you. You've no sense of loyalty, Sundus, and no love in your heart."

"That's not true," she replied. "I was overwhelmed when I watched the flames destroying everything and gnawing at people's hearts. Fire makes me fear for you. It's never satisfied with the things it's burned, my lord. You have an army, soldiers, weapons, and supplies. All the people in Fustat has is a knife or hammer. They're not used to fighting, and they don't know how."

"No, you know nothing about them. But never mind! I've said that I forgive you."

I let her go and looked at her face.

"Why are you looking at me like that?" she asked. "How utterly ashamed I feel as I spoil the beauty of everything around me. But it's God's will. And that's beautiful, my lord, even if the eye perceives it as being as ugly as hellfire. I wonder, do you regard me as a bit of soup coated in flour? Do you want to taste it because it's been around for a while? It was sheer curiosity that made Adam leave the Garden of Eden. For me, you're a spirit, not a body. I've learned how to plumb the depths and see what lies beneath flesh and soft skin."

I moved closer and cupped my hands around her face.

"What do you see?" I asked gently.

"I see you as the graceful trees of paradise, the sweet waters of cascading rivers, the soft fingers of a newborn baby. Jawhar, I see you..."

I kissed her neck, and she sighed. My kiss went on and spread.

"What is it that you see?"

"You endow everything around you with beauty, Sicilian."

"You have only a single eye with which to see me. Love has led you astray. It has enveloped you, so you can no longer see."

"I can no longer see, but I still have my vision."

I kissed her lips gently.

"I pity you," I whispered. "I realise that I'm burned just like you. You may actually be better than me; your heart's not burned."

"Intense passion is the devil's doing," she replied, as though she had not heard what I had just said. "It's a trial, just like money and power. Tempting and misleading."

"Your kisses have a different taste to them. How can that be?"

"Maybe because I'm part of you."

"Don't say things like that. I don't understand you. You're saying that I endow everything around me with beauty. Isn't that right?"

She swallowed.

"Yes, I am," she replied.

"I've burned Fustat, I've killed men and women, and I've orphaned children. How can you see beauty, Sundus? No, don't say anything. You're going to tell me that I was compelled—the Caliph's orders. I was out to save myself and restore my former prestige. You'll say—"

She put her finger over my mouth.

"I see you," she replied. "And you don't see yourself."

I gave her a full-fledged kiss on the lips, and she choked. I ran my hands over the burn-scars on her face and shoulder, and then her arms. I took off her dress and ran my hands over the burn-scars on her stomach. My kisses went on and on until she pushed me away.

"I beg you," she pleaded with tears in her eyes.

"What are you afraid of?"

"My own self. Imprisoned passion testing the heart. Someone like me," she went on, breathing hard, "can't have sex with the likes of you."

"When you put your hand on my heart," I asked spontaneously, "what did you do to me?"

"I was searching for your inner self," she replied with an innocent look. "I don't know if I found it."

"What demon is controlling you, woman?"

I closed my eyes to avoid seeing what troubled me. But the only thing that appeared in my mind's eye was a cluster of snakes, drawing near, then receding, biting my fingers, then spreading poison across the havens of existence, as it made its way—with its grey hue and slimy feel—to plaster itself against my face and neck. I opened my mouth to breathe, but I could not. I opened my eyes in the hopes of catching my breath, and the ugly image disappeared. Raising my hand, I ran it over her face where the burn-scars were. Now I could breathe easily, and my brain stopped working, or almost. I have no idea what came over me. I could smell the stench of fire in the folds of her soul. She picked up her dress and headed for the door.

"You know," I whispered. "Your magic won't work. But wait…Sundus…"

She turned and looked at me. Her tears were mixing with the dough. It looked just like the dough that I used to see in my mother's kitchen years ago, when she was making Judge's Pastry.

"If you want to try passion with a man and satisfying the body's needs," I told her, without even thinking, "then come over here. I'll wait for you. Once. From today on, we'll agree: don't expect anything more than bodily enjoyment and satisfaction. You deserve that at least once."

She looked at me, her mouth agape, then left the room at a run.

The Fustat battle continued. Every night, I came home at dusk. I waited for her, but she did not come.

I was expecting her to throw herself into my arms, kiss my feet, and beg me to give her a taste of paradise's honey. But she did not. As day followed day, she disappeared completely from view. I felt angry and in despair. I asked myself why I was so bothered about someone like her. I persuaded myself that it must be magic that was making every single day seem the same. All I could see was night's curtains descending, keeping beloveds apart. I asked Laila to summon Sundus, but she did not respond. I found myself going to Sundus's room and opening the door, while trying to keep my temper in check.

"I was expecting you to come," I told her angrily.

"My lord Amir," she said. "Perhaps you've misunderstood me. You don't realise what I need."

"Yes, I do," I replied scornfully. "Women love to adorn their bodily desires with fancy talk about passion and caresses. What is it you want to hear me say?"

She was about to get up from her place on the bed, but I told her not to do it.

"Don't lie to me," I said. "Do you need to talk? Tell me who burned you."

She just stared at the pattern on the rug in front of her.

"Why do you think the burning was deliberate?" she asked.

"Everything's deliberate," I said. "So is all pain. Today I'm yours, to talk, to ask, to touch, to ask for help, to love."

"And what do you require in return, my lord?" she asked.

"I have all the energy of the destitute. You have lots of it."

"To what do I owe this generosity, Amir?"

"We all have our moments of generosity. Think about it."

I widened my eyes again and kept looking at her, as if I were a child that has lost both sight and hearing, but can now see again. I looked at her burn-scars, the wrinkles in her neck, her blurry eye that perhaps did not see very well, and her other eye, fully open and stunningly beautiful, that kept staring at my face. Lifting my hand, I ran it over the burn-scars, then her face and neck. I lowered her dress a little and rubbed her arm.

"I wonder," I asked her, "did you ever imagine that Jawhar, son of Husain the Sicilian, would ever be married to you, a woman with features shaped by fire? What about a woman who's pearly white and jasmine scented? Today all the women in Cairo are under my authority."

"I know," she stuttered.

"So, lady of demons and magic, what were you after? Was it before or after the burning that the devil got to you?"

She kept her tears inside, and none fell. I neither noticed nor cared; or that is how it felt to me.

"Your treachery and your father's both deserve death. But then, you're dead whether I punish you or not. As you know, I watched my own father being beheaded right in front of me."

"They slaughtered your heart," she whispered in a barely audible voice. "Your heart can no longer feel or show regret. Your words slaughter and burn just like your swords and men."

I grabbed her arm.

"I no longer know my own self," I said. "I don't see the things around me. Tell me what you've done."

"I've split your chest in two," she replied calmly, "and searched for you inside."

"Have you found me?"

"I'm still searching."

"How is it that I see you like the full moon?"

"Don't ask me about what you're seeing. My eyes aren't like yours."

"It feels as though I'm fond of you and desire you. Is that possible?"

"Don't ask me about your heart. It's not like mine."

"What have you discovered inside my chest now that you've split it open?"

"I've found part of me and part of you."

"I've met a man who's distressed me. He was out to kill me, but I couldn't kill him. I wonder, have I lost my mind? He was a pathetic halva-maker with bulging eyes. I could have killed him, but I wasn't able to do it. That worries me a lot. I didn't do it, even though I could have. Tell your devil that toying with Jawhar's mind is a crime. His revenge will be coming."

I moved close, cupped my hands around her face, and gently kissed her burned cheek.

"How is it," I whispered, "that I can see you only as a light from the heavens? All beauty around me fades away, and I can see it only in your face. Do you love me, Sundus?"

She did not respond; there was no passion in her look. Her passivity annoyed me. Even so, I kept my frustration to myself.

"Where's all the beauty around me?" I asked.

Moving closer to me, she whispered:

"Use your eyes to traverse this world,

You will see beauty in the fleeting grains of sand,

The sea's glistening spume,

The sighs of distance and groans of separation—

Days—that slip through our fingers like glory and prancing horses,

Twisting, fading,

Twisting, then vanishing,

Slipping through your hand like a fisherman's catch,

Days—like the shape and taste of halva in a child's mouth,

Passion's gleam in the eyes of men,

Smiles of pleasure in the eyes of the poor,

Resigned looks in the face of destiny.

If you wish to recognise beauty, then search far and wide for everything that slips from your hands—like water—or let the beauty of evanescence envelop you. Don't despair. Sugar is but one of the particles of paradise.

Taste, smell, and use your eyes. What remains was not created for this world."

Our eyes met.

"Those are different words indeed," I said. "I have not heard the like before, neither in poetry nor prose. I don't understand them. What do you mean by the sweetness of sugar and the few days that escape from us? What's the point of days and sugar, Sundus?"

"Doesn't sugar's taste stay in your mouth for just a few seconds, Amir? Even so, we all still love it."

I stretched out my hand and held her forearm.

"I'd like you to taste another type of sweetness," I said. "Let me give you some sugar..."

She held my hand and looked at me for a moment, then took her hand away.

"I'm grateful for your generosity," she said. "But you've dislodged the knife inside me and ignited wars inside my peaceful, submissive heart. I'm afraid that I'd hate myself if I savoured love at your hands. By now, I've accepted its state and grown used to its wounds. Do you realise? The burning body is a journey just like those of loss and death. You begin with disbelief coupled with anger and aversion to pleasures, then hatred of everyone who loves us, then..."

"Then what?"

"Even worse than the burning is having to live with it. My face may have faded, but I can still remember it. Do you understand what I mean?"

"Who is he? Who did this to you? Is he still alive?"

"Yes, he is."

"Why didn't your father kill him?"

She let out a shockingly sad cackle.

"Not everyone's like you, Amir," she said. "The sword doesn't put an end to all conflicts, only the easiest and least complicated."

I ran my hand over her burned cheek, but I had no idea whether or not she could feel it. She closed her eyes.

"You're cruel," she muttered. "I had put up gates as big as your grandfather's around my heart. I changed course and for years did my best to be content. Now you've made me resort to putting dough on my face to hide the scars as though I'm stupid."

I rubbed her neck.

"Are you attracted to me?" I whispered. "Did you want to hear what Laila was telling you? That's only natural; you needn't blame yourself."

She clasped my fingers, brought them up to her mouth, and kissed them slowly.

"When you sleep with Laila," she told him firmly, "then forget about her the next day, and choose a slave girl the day after, you really hurt the poor girl. But she still manages to move beyond it. If you slept with me, then forgot about it, you would be mistreating my soul, which I've kept safe for years. My suitor rejected me without a word, and the next day, people spat at me and hissed in my face. One day, my mother hid me away, and on another, the Pyramid Witch cured me with her words and treatment. The day I met you, my heart decided to put me through yet another trial, and I fell in love with the Amir. That was the day of my end."

"You've opened your heart to me."

"It feels as though I see you as a lone wanderer through the forests, one who deprives his tongue of water so that it's burned, just like my body."

I put my mouth close to her chin and kissed it. I desired her more than any other woman before, as if I were a teenager, although I've no idea why.

She stood up slowly and moved away.

"Shall I call Laila for you, my lord," she asked as she opened the door, "or do you prefer another slave girl? Sundus has nothing to do with men."

"You've just said that you adore me," I snarled.

"If my lord wishes to stay in the room," she said, "then I'm leaving."

I pursed my lips in anger and tried to get closer to her, but she pushed me away roughly.

"You're going to come," I told her, "either tonight or tomorrow. It was curiosity that expelled Adam from Eden."

She shook her head vigorously and left the room. I was left suspended between heaven and earth. To me, she seemed like a star orbiting around me, walking beside me at night, and tracking me without ever drawing near.

But it seemed that I knew her as she knew me. Before dawn, there was a tap on the door. With a smile of victory, I got up, opened the door, and looked at her. She fell to the floor in front of me and covered her face with her hands. She did not cry, but kept sobbing in pain.

"Turn out the lights," she stuttered in defeat.

With that, I laughed, grabbed her hand, and pulled her beside me.

"Take your clothes off," I said. "There's no need to have them on when you're with me. Calm down! What's frightening you? That I'll do something you don't want? Today, Sundus, the Amir is at your command. What do you want?"

"We'll make an agreement today," she replied with a sigh, covering her face. "It'll happen just once, and then we'll forget about it tomorrow and never speak of it again."

At that moment, I felt a kind of sympathy that I had never felt before, even with my slaughtered father and wounded mother. The sensation was fused with outpouring of love and affection. I closed my eyes and snuffed out the candle.

"In the dark," I told her, "all your burn scars and sufferings disappear. But for me, the darkness aggravates my wounds."

I pushed her until she was underneath my body.

"Tell your demon," I said, as I kissed her affectionately, "to thwart this passion, this weakness, this..."

She shuddered and sat up.

"Who did this to me?" she asked. "I haven't forgiven him, I can't. And I wonder: Is that a sin?"

I had not been listening carefully to her words.

"What do you say to my kissing every part of you?" I asked. "Do you agree?"

"Today I hate myself," she replied, "and don't admit it. I want to die."

"Why such crazy talk?"

When I ran my hand over her shoulder, she recoiled in shock.

"You can have feelings just like us. Stop blaming yourself. Today, let your body take control."

She did not object or argue. Even so, her tremors and fears presented an obstacle that I could recognise and knew how to overcome.

"Calm down, Sundus," I told her firmly. "I can't see you in the dark, and I know nothing about you."

"Come on then," she replied impatiently. "Kiss me and do whatever you want."

"I'm only going to do what you want," I told her as I held her hand with a smile. "In fact, I'm not going to do anything until you calm down. I'll just hold your hand."

We stayed that way for an hour or more. I've no idea who gave me the patience and why I wanted to make her relax. She stopped shaking, and I moved closer. Our breaths blended, and she was on the point of kissing me. I moved away a little.

"Your hand's still shaking," I whispered.

She swallowed hard.

"Don't hate me," she said in despair.

I kissed her hard.

"Me hate you?" I said. "That'll never happen."

As she closed her eyes, her body throbbed with life. But I'm going to talk about what happened to me that day. I heard passionate sighs reverberating in the folds of her soul, even though she didn't say a word. She begged me to stop, but I did not. Eventually, she was scattered all around me like so many corpses and bones. What happened to me that day was not simply enjoyment between a man and woman, nor was it mere moments of rapture that come to an end whatever else remains.

I clutched my heart and looked at her. I could no longer see the burn scars on her face; in fact, I could not see her face at all. What I did see was a vast expanse of open land. My heart started beating so fast that the death rattle almost did away with me. I heaved and sighed, then closed my eyes. I moved away from her and stood up. She did not move, but pulled the sheet up to her chest, covered her body, and lowered her head.

"You're right," she said. "I know exactly what you're going to say. But please don't say it. If you want me to leave the house and not come back, I'll do it. If you want me to disappear for the rest of my life, I'll do that too. If..."

I gestured for her to stop talking. Sitting on the edge of the bed, I covered my face. I made love to her, my own wife. I ran my fingers over the painful spots, of which there were many that marred the beauty she had once had. I wonder, does pain actually erase beauty or enhance it?

Something about the rest of my life had changed. It was magic; that much was obvious. But I could almost swear that, throughout my life and ever since I started having sex with women at the age of fifteen and right up to today, I had never trembled in a woman's arms, nor had my limbs rushed to confide in the awe of the dark and the moon's radiant glow. My heart almost stopped. There came a moment of union. I felt like shouting, but suppressed it. What was it about Sundus? Was she a magician, I wonder? She was behaving like one: hesitating, stopping, freezing her limbs. But then, gasps of desire flared like lamps. Closing her eyes, she let me do what I wanted.

"Please don't scoff at my body," she whispered. "I beg you to be kind to me."

She moved slowly away, trying to put her clothes back on. I looked at her suddenly and was shocked.

"What are you doing?" I asked.

"I'm leaving you on your own, Sir, so you can forget the ugliness you've just seen."

"By the God whom I worship, I've never seen such beauty in a human being. I swear that, if you leave my bed, I'm going to kill you with my own hands. You're going to stay here in my arms night and day. Do you understand?"

"No, I don't, my lord."

I grabbed her wrist hard and pulled her toward me.

"Kiss me, Sundus."

She looked confused as she opened her mouth.

"Kiss me," I said again.

"Please don't make fun of me."

"Enough nonsense. Do what I tell you. Kiss me."

I moved closer and touched her lips slowly, as though I were tasting halva that I was afraid might run out, then delving deeper, but only managing to grab a single piece. I grasped her arm and put it on my shoulder.

"What's the matter with you?" I asked her between kisses. "Are you shunning me?"

"I'm scared?"

"What's frightening you?"

"What's going to happen once the night is over."

"What about the next day for the two of us?"

"You're scratching old wounds and delving into things I've kept hidden for years."

"This isn't time for talk. Come into my arms. Do you want me? Do you like my caresses?"

She buried her head in my chest.

"You're wonderful, Amir," she sighed. "You don't need someone like me to tell you."

"I want to hear it from you."

"You've aroused things that were long forgotten. It saddens me to have been defeated today. Now I've lost the entire victory that I'd won against my ugly body."

"Your body's not ugly."

"It's disloyal. Believe me."

"It's alive, pulsating with passion. Enough talk. Tomorrow, I'll go back to killing. Today, I don't need any wine as long as you're in my arms. Tomorrow I may die, Sundus, but today I'm alive for the very first time."

"That's how men tell lies in lustful moments."

"To the contrary, that's when the truth emerges..."

I silenced her with a passionate kiss. For hours, there was no conversation between us. What happened and what I felt scrambled the wounds and demolished my mind.

"Sundus," I told her between kisses, "you can suck out both breath and mind. I've never been so alive before."

She neither sighed nor whispered her love and passion. Even so, I could feel her presence in the very depths of my heart.

Once I had finished, she pulled her legs up to her chest like a foetus.

"Can you let me go now?" she asked.

I hugged her to my chest.

"No," I replied, "that's impossible."

I kissed her scarred cheek and ran my hand over her damaged arm.

"Ah!" she yelled out in pain, as though the fire had burned her only today or the day before.

"What's hurting you?" I asked.

"Your presence."

"There's no avoiding that."

"As I've told you, you're invading my world like Byzantine armies."

"No, I'm conquering your country and staying there."

"I don't want to hate you."

"The lover never hates."

"You don't know anything about love."

"Teach me then! What do poets have to say about love?"

"There's no power in love, and no mercy in separation."

I smothered her in kisses.

"There's one kind of flame that can penetrate the skin," I said, "and another that can penetrate the heart. If only flames would stop at penetrating the skin. If only they did not torture the heart like hellfire. How much of me is in your heart, and you in mine? From today onward, you're the only one who'll be staying in my room. Make sure you don't defy me, make very sure!"

After a while, I stood up, got dressed, and headed for the door.

"If you go to Laila," she said quickly, "I won't get angry."

I gave her a mocking glance.

"I expected you to give me leave," I said. "I'm grateful for your generosity... and lies."

However, in spite of all my attempts and threats in the days that followed, Sundus locked her door and did not let me touch her again. My own heart dismissed all other women.

CHAPTER FOUR

My soldiers kept fighting Mas`ood's forces, Muslim against Muslim, man against man, commander against commander. No copies of the Qur'an were raised in the air, and no shareef shaikhs intervened to put a stop to the fighting. Armies at war are all about desires: if only they were just about money and women, rather than blood and slaves. But why am I so angry? Am I afraid of blood? My soldiers are dying—too bad! So are Mas`ood's soldiers. What am I defending? The Egyptian people? Why am I defending them? I don't care about them; I've burned and humiliated them. Why, these days, do I act without conscious thought? Ever since I saw the halva-maker and the world, nothing has been the same. My hand has been operating without any instructions from my brain. My eyes see things I do not expect. My memory toys with what time remains. I have started chiding myself every day even though I do not recognise myself. I have always assumed that the Day of Resurrection would bear witness to my arms and legs; my tongue would utter things that I did not want to hear. So then, has the Day of Resurrection arrived, or is it the Caliph's instructions? What is happening to me? What will be the end of this nonsense?

I can hurt myself later, but, for the time being, my tongue can do the talking—a word or two, then the Caliph can kill me. I looked at the soldier who was parrying the arrows. Spurring my horse, I headed toward Cairo.

"Keep fighting Mas`ood's forces," I said.

Taking half my men with me, I headed for Cairo!

I was following the Caliph's orders, fighting for the Caliph and for the Egyptian people. I was using the Caliph's army to fight the Caliph's army. When mountains split and the moon folds on itself, we know that it's the end. For four days, war had been burning Egypt's face. Four whole days, which passed like four years—like the years when my deceitful wife went away. I dug into my horse's flanks and stopped by the Cairo Gate, Bab al-Bahr... Here, she had put her hand on my heart. This place marked the beginning. My grandfather had arrived, had enthusiastically started constructing the city, and had worked conscientiously for someone who only valued and cared about his own interests and self-esteem. Very well then, Caliph, Al-Mansoor, Al-Hakim, do your slaughtering; I am no longer afraid. Torture as much as you want. How I long for you to sever my limbs so that the groans of heart and spirit can be released. That will be the very best moment in my entire life, past and present. Where are you now, Lamya, daughter of Hamdoon, to witness your son's courage and suicide? Now that the day I've longed for has finally arrived.

Cairo opened its gates to me, showing me due respect and smiling in my face.

"Jawhar, come and take a look at what the Sicilian is doing today. He's bolder than you are, but perhaps less courageous."

I headed for the Caliph's palace, well aware that some paths—from Fustat to Cairo, for example—are as extensive as sorrow and old age. They are like someone who, in spite of everything, actually knows nothing.

Mas'ood and I glared at each other, and he could see the madness in my gaze.

"The Caliph has no time for you, Jawhar," he told me, both aware and frightened.

"With my soldiers," I replied firmly, "I'm going to bring down Cairo on your head. I'm going to see the Caliph this very instant."

I did not wait. The guards let me go in.

I entered the chamber—Al-Mansoor ibn Al-'Aziz bi-Allah Nizar ibn al-Mu'izz bi-Din Allah, the Caliph Al-Hakim bi-Amr Allah! He was dressed in wool and roaming a world different from ours. His eyes were searching the stars and circling the walls. He did not look at me.

With my eyes focused on the Caliph's head, I did not kiss the ground in front of him or show obeisance in his presence. In my imagination, I could see my father's body, with the head on the ground beside it. I had to thank the soldier who had anxiously grabbed my father's head, put it in a big cloth, and carried it away like precious gold or cultured pearls. At the time, I had laughed, and that made me cry. What price for human heads?

"Greetings to the Caliph of the Faithful!" I declared solemnly.

"Speak, son of Husain," the Caliph replied quietly, without looking at me.

"My Lord remembers me?"

"The Caliph knows everything. Have you come to intercede on behalf of the Egyptians, of the Kutama and Turkish forces, or Ubaidi forces? I am so upset at what is happening."

"I've left five hundred troops behind me," I declared, "and another two thousand, with a further ten thousand behind them. That's a huge army of Muslims, my Lord, an army that has no idea why it's been at war for four days. It started as a fight against the Egyptians, but now it's turned into a fight between Ubaidi forces and Mas`ood's army."

The Caliph looked at Mas`ood.

"How that saddens me, Mas`ood," he said.

"By your merciful heart and mighty generosity, my Lord," Mas`ood responded immediately, "the people fighting deserve—"

"Muslim is fighting Muslim," I interrupted forcefully. "They're raping women, stealing and burning. I don't know of any crime that the Egyptian people have committed that can justify this action. If they had, my lord—"

"Be polite!" Mas`ood said. "You've lost your mind. You're addressing..."

Al-Hakim raised his hand to tell Mas`ood to remain silent. He then signalled to me to keep speaking. Without thinking about the consequences, I went on:

"If the fighting doesn't stop, my men, along with the Turks and Kutama, will enter Cairo and burn it. This total destruction of the country has no precedent. Cairo will burn just as Fustat has. The Caliph's palace will see the same kind of destruction that has overwhelmed the Egyptian people."

Jawhar could almost swear that everyone inside the palace was struck dumb. All the guards wet their pants for fear of what was to come. Even the Caliph himself seemed overcome. The Caliph sat down slowly, and Mas`ood bent over and kissed the floor at his feet.

"We all deserve to die," Mas`ood panted. "Behead me first, before him. My Lord, I had no idea he was so crazy. I was following your orders. You told me to enrol him in the army. Forgive me, you who are so forgiving, and have mercy, you who show mercy."

I felt things careening ahead, giving me a sense of elation far above life and death.

"It is God who is forgiving and merciful," I said. "God who gives life before death."

With that, the guards approached. One of them slapped me, another punched me in the stomach, and a third was about to behead me.

Al-Hakim raised his hand to tell them to stop. He signalled to me to go over to him.

Tears dripped from my nose, and I allowed myself a victorious smile. I've won today, halva-maker. I don't need you in order to kill myself.

"Do you intend to burn Cairo, son of Husain?" Al-Hakim asked me calmly. "Burn my palace?"

"There can be no palace without an army," I insisted, still pursuing my reckless adventure, "and no Caliph without walls. I have a thousand men— or, more like twenty thousand, a hundred thousand. My men are waiting now for me to return or not. If I don't return, they'll know what to do."

"I'll cut out his tongue," Mas`ood said immediately. "They're going to commit an atrocity. He deserves a year's worth of torture before he dies, right now, in front of the people sitting here."

"Jawhar, son of Husain son of Jawhar the Sicilian," the Caliph asked calmly, "where's that loyal commander and brother who came to bless the

Caliph with his peaceful intentions? Why are you punishing him now?"

"According to his own words, my Lord," Mas`ood said immediately.

Al-Hakim gave him an uncomprehending look and stared into his eyes.

"Has he said something?" he asked in amazement. "Has he said something to annoy the Caliph or make him jealous?"

Al-Hakim looked all around him.

"Have you heard anything, men?" he asked. "Has Jawhar said something? Hasn't he kissed the ground in front of me and asked for blessings and security?"

"Yes, he has," they all replied in unison.

"Have you heard anything else, Mas`ood?" Al-Hakim asked.

"No, my Lord," Mas`ood stuttered quickly.

"What did Jawhar say?"

"He was asking for blessings and security."

"That's much better. I was thinking that you'd lost your mind, Mas`ood. If that had happened, I would have been forced to punish you until you recovered it, or else I'd have to remove it from your throat."

"I only wish to please you, my Lord," Mas`ood pleaded.

"Order the guards to bring my donkey. I want to go to Fustat now."

Wearing his white turban and sack-cloth clothing, the Caliph stopped, but did not dismount from his donkey. The two sides stopped fighting. He raised his hand to Mas`ood's troops and ordered them to stop, then to the Turkish and Kutama soldiers, ordering them to stop as well.

"Egyptians," he said in a loud voice.

People gathered around him, some of them shuddering, others looking sad and defeated. Many bore only the vestiges of body and soul. They kissed the ground at his feet. He swore that he had never given orders for Egypt to be burned. Soldiers lowered their heads. He then promised Egyptians security. The shareef shaikhs approached him, among them Shaikh ʿAli.

"The soldiers have sold off the women as slave girls, my Lord," the Shaikh told him. "They're your people and daughters of your community. Are you happy to see that happen to daughters of the Egyptian people?"

"Shareef," the Caliph replied emotionally, "you know me and realise that I'm far from happy about that. I was already scared about women falling into disrepute, so I gave instructions that they were to stay inside the house. But they eagerly went ahead with their debauched behaviour. What is the Caliph supposed to do about people who can only be happy when they tip the scales and scoff at what God has ordained and forbidden? But, needless to say, I don't want to see them involved in any scandal."

"I realise that, my Lord," the Shaikh replied. "That's why I'm asking you in front of everyone to order the release of the women."

The halva-maker ran from the edge of Fustat to the place where the Caliph was standing.

"My wife and son," he yelled at the top of his voice, "my wife and son! My Lord Al-Hakim bi-Amr Allah, rescue them from the soldiers' clutches."

Al-Hakim looked all around him.

"I seem to be hearing someone's voice. Did any of you hear someone? Are the Egyptian people asking the Caliph for help today?"

A terrifying silence ensued. Even the halva-maker stopped speaking.

"Tell me, General Masʿood," the Caliph asked, "what's happened to Egypt?"

"Fire has consumed a third of Fustat and destroyed half of it."

"I'm begging you, my Lord," the Shaikh said, "to restore the women to their families."

"Shareef," the Caliph replied in all innocence, "I appreciate how worried you are. The whole thing is simple: they can buy them back from the soldiers."

"My Lord, the soldiers have taken Egypt's very essence as slave-girls."

"Every husband should buy back his wife, and every father his daughter. Are you listening, people of Fustat? Buy your women back from the soldiers."

Silence prevailed. The Caliph turned around and rode off on his donkey.

"May God inscribe for you what He has decreed for the Egyptian people," he whispered to me. "God never wastes the funds of believers. Today, you should acknowledge the fires of ignominy."

With that, he lowered his head and made off toward the mountains. The fighting stopped, but hearts were still on fire.

I saw the halva-maker hovering around me and heard what he had said. He looked straight at me.

"The Caliph Al-Hakim bi-Amr Allah yielded before the grandson of Jawhar the Sicilian. He cringed, but no one in Egypt is going to believe that, and no one dares tell the truth. I alone realise what happened, because truth in despair is like no other. Give me back my wife and son. You can do it. People say that one of the Caliph's aides has claimed that he is God's shadow on earth, killed by people in the `Amr ibn al-`As Mosque. Do you know why the people are so afraid of him? Al-Hakim is powerful and acts without ever considering the consequences. He knows no fear, just like you. I know what happened between the two of you."

I smiled, victorious and proud.

There, in the distance, I spotted Amir Mas`ood's face. I realised that what I had done, and the risks I had taken, would have consequences. Only those who are subject to the judgement of the Just and Merciful One can escape such punishment. But I had not been expecting what was being concocted for me. Mas`ood waved a hand to call me over. I rode my horse slowly toward him, with my soldiers behind me.

"You defied your Amir," he said, "and did not follow his instructions."

He did not even mention the major crime, as though he did not dare pronounce the Caliph's name. In his eyes, I could detect a blue gleam, like suppressed breath and bodily demise.

"Are you defending the people of Fustat, Sicilian?" he asked me politely. "You're defying the Caliph's orders for the sake of the people in Fustat. No matter! I'd like the people of Fustat to remember you for your nobility and courage. I forgive you, Jawhar."

With a laugh, he signalled his soldiers to follow him. I looked all around me. The halva-maker had vanished—I had no idea when he'd left, nor where the soldiers had gone. I rushed back to my palace, unsure whether I should stay in Cairo and await punishment or flee. I seemed fated to escape, because my father had been a general and so had my grandfather. If I had been the halva-maker, for example, the world would still have adjusted, even though I had lost all my beloved friends, which is what had happened to him.

When I entered the house, I looked for my mother. I noticed how the slave girls were staring and winking. I stood by the entrance to the women's quarters and listened. They were poking fun at Sundus. I assumed that had happened every day since she was a girl, since I knew that it was typical of human beings. However, this time I witnessed a scene that aroused in me a kind of pity I had not realised I possessed. Now Jawhar, weak-willed between night and day, had turned into Jawhar, the Egyptian people's saviour and protector of his scarred wife. Do not ask me how I had changed, because I do not know.

Ever since Sundus was a child, she had grown used to people's unkindness and cruelty. However, when it came from inside a house where she was living, where she was belittled and in despair, that was an even worse punishment for a sin that she had not in fact committed. Laila gave the slave girls a smile, then went over to Sundus. She grabbed the edge of her face-veil to rip it off, but Sundus kept hold of it.

"Let them see what you really look like!" Laila shouted.

Laila tugged hard, but she could not pull it off. She signalled to one of the slave girls, and they both pulled. For the first time ever, Sundus's face was exposed. Women screamed in shock.

"This ugly woman is causing hatred between the Amir and me," Laila said. "Can you believe it? Evil emerges from—"

"You're addressing your mistress," Sundus told her forcefully.

"How can anyone's mistress have a face like yours?" Laila asked. "You're the devil in human form."

"No, the devil's the one who makes fun of God's own creation and will."

"God only sets the worst people on fire," Laila said immediately. "It's your punishment for something you did."

"If trial is a punishment," Sundus told her, "then why did God makes His prophets suffer? What did Job do to merit God's trial?"

As she headed for the door, she saw me standing there and stopped.

"Now all of us have seen your face, my lady," Laila went on. "Go and tell the Amir that all his slave girls now realise that you're not a suitable wife for him."

Without a second thought, I grabbed my wife's hand as she struggled to put her face-veil back on. I took the veil off.

"This is my wife," I told Laila, "and she's the mistress of this house and of all its slave girls, too. When she gives orders, you obey. If I hear her raise a complaint against any one of you, you'll be whipped on the spot."

I faced Laila.

"What do you see?" I demanded.

"My Lord..." she replied with a shudder.

"Bow down in front of me and kiss your mistress's hand. Then tell me what a lovely face she has."

Without even thinking, she leaned down and tried to kiss Sundus's hand.

"There's no need for..." Sundus started, quickly withdrawing her hand.

"Don't disobey my orders," I interrupted. "Laila, bend down and kiss Sundus's hand, then tell her how lovely her face is because it belongs to the Amir's wife."

"Forgive me, my Lady," Laila said, kissing her hand. "You have a lovely face."

"Today, your mistress will be transferring her belongings to my room," I said. "From now on, you're all at her command. If she complains about any one of you, that girl will see how I'll deal with her."

I took her hand and left the room. Sundus was upset.

"There was no need for that," she said. "I've been used to it for some time. Their nasty words don't affect me or pierce my heart."

"Well, they affect me."

"Because you weren't burned by fire, my Lord."

I was still looking for my mother.

"Tomorrow, I'll be burning with fire," I said. "Don't be upset."

"But I'm not going to transfer to your room," she insisted. "Your words are still ringing in my ears. You told me that I wasn't a suitable wife for you. All you wanted was a single night. I was just doing what you told me."

I gave her an angry look and was about to raise my hand to slap her. She gave me a powerful glare, and I stopped.

"Don't you dare defy me!" I said.

"That won't happen," she replied.

"Defy me?"

"Transfer to your room."

She held my hand so I wouldn't slap her. I closed my eyes to keep my anger in check and left the room.

I wandered around Giza, sometimes looking at the grass and, at others, at the desert. While I was searching for her, my eyes blended with the waters of the blessed Nile. Everyone in Egypt who is in trouble goes to see her: Bahnas, the Pyramid Witch. All of us are aware that she emerges as one witch after another, taking the name and features of the grandmother, with wide eyes and a luminous countenance that dazzles all those who get to see it.

I knocked on her door inside the Great Pyramid and started searching for her in the darkness. She was behind me.

"I've been expecting you, Sicilian," she said with a smile. "How are you?"

As I looked at her, I almost stopped breathing.

"How do you know me?" I asked.

"Make your request and don't ask questions."

"I've come to ask you to nullify a piece of magic imposed on me by a girl called Sundus and a halva-maker."

"Don't give orders to the Pyramid Witch, Sicilian. Offer greetings to the ancestors and thank them, first of all, for preserving the land and gold..."

"They're not my ancestors, Witch."

She scoffed.

"Greet the ancestors," she repeated. "They're yours, whether you like it or not. Your body's going to nourish the soil just like your father's and grandfather's. Sea and moon are bound to each other. Sometimes the waters ebb, at others they swell. There are times when things will seem placid and compliant, while at others they will penetrate to the very depths. That's the way we are on this earth, like the sea in relation to the moon. We're drawn to it and obey its commands. Now Egypt has you in its charge, my son. Since the moment you arrived here as a warrior, and until its sands cover you, you're confirming your own lineage in the country's depths."

"I've made a complete mess of things, as though I'm afflicted with an incurable madness. I've defied the Caliph even though I don't like Egyptians; and, of course, I don't love Sundus, either. Why on earth do I long for a girl like her when I can have my pick of any woman in the country? And the halva-maker—my God! He's the curse personified! They're all sorcerers. As you well know, Egyptians have been good at magic forever."

"Who are you?

"I'm the son of Lamya from the Maghreb and Husain the Sicilian."

"Where did Husain the Sicilian die?"

"Here. The Egyptian people deserted him."

"He placed burdens on them that were too heavy."

"Cowards!"

"And even so, you've defied the Caliph."

"Because they've bewitched me. I've lost my mind."

"Remember."

"Remember what?"

"The worst forms of madness only impact the wise. It's only prophets and saints who are subjected to the worst kinds of injustice."

"Dear Witch."

"Call me Bahnas. We've become good friends now."

"What do I have to do with saints? I've killed countless men, and it's been wrong."

"So, you know then?"

"Know what?"

"Sometimes, Sicilian, the difference between wrongdoer and wronged imposes a heavy burden on the shoulders of mere transients. It's the kind of heroism you hear about in stories. Don't question fate about its actions. God knows things that we don't."

"I don't understand what you're saying."

"One man kills hundreds, with mercy in his heart. Another prays and fasts, while his heart is as impenetrable as a rock or even worse. When the eye can see and what the heart conceals cannot be evaluated by human beings."

"I've come here to nullify the magic. You can have whatever you want."

"I need you to realise that, amid all the madness and treachery, courage can sometimes show itself. Its gleam is more priceless than any gold or emeralds, a moment when a man decides to take on the demons of heaven and earth on his own—no hesitation, no mutterings, tossing all caution into the river's depths and cleaving only to the flash of lightning."

"I was saying—"

"Follow the halva-maker, and you'll come to know everything."

"But Witch—"

"You're searching for a kind of beauty that melts in your mouth like sugar. No one in Egypt is lovelier than Sundus. She has a part of you."

"You're talking just like her."

"No, you idiot, she's talking like me."

"I've come to you in search of a cure."

"First of all, you need to know what the illness is."

"What am I to do?"

"Follow the halva-maker, and you'll get there."

"Get to what?"

"Yourself."

"I'm the Sicilian."

"We'll meet again in a while and talk."

BOOK TWO

Those who saw me witnessed flame and water.

How incredible is the meeting of fire and water!

Tamim ibn Al-Mu'izz li-Din Allah, the Fatimid

CHAPTER FIVE

I did not have long to wait before Mas'ood carried out his punishment
and revenge. Just two days later, I saw soldiers at my door. Mas'ood stripped
me of my rank and soldiers as punishment for defying him. He ordered that
I be banished from Cairo to Fustat. My mother asked no questions and did
not seem shocked. Even when Mas'ood gave her permission to stay in the
city, she neither rejoiced nor objected. I bade her farewell, and Sundus as
well. But Sundus said she was coming with me.

I gave her a despairing look but did not object. I took my wife's hand and
mounted my horse. I told the slave girls that they could either stay or leave.
I manumitted them all; there was no reason for them to be punished along
with me. I made my way to the Cairo Gate, Bab an-Nasr, and looked at it
for a moment. Beyond it was a life different from the one that I had always
wanted. All the palaces, parks, beautiful flowers, and lemon tress that I had
dreamed of as a child—they were all behind me now. I was going to the place
where the common people lived; indeed, where they were dying. Just a few
days earlier I had burned them with my own hands. Is this not a period of
sheer madness? First, I burned them, then I helped them, then I defied the
Caliph for their sake. I can see that I have no idea who I am. My father told
me about my grandfather: Jawhar the Sicilian always remembered his home
country, the lemon trees and mountains that could cover and enfold the sea,
then swell and withdraw. I remember grandfather Jawhar. He kept a wooden
horse decorated with subtle porcelain pieces that his father had given him
one day. At the time, he did not realise that his father would be going away;
all that would be left of Sicily, his original homeland, was that wooden horse
and the porcelain around its belly and head. I have never seen the horse, but I
heard the story from my father. Husain used to talk about his father a lot; he
regarded him as a gigantic knight who could tame wild beasts and finish off
the Phoenix. I never saw my grandfather or witnessed his wars and victories,
but today I am still thinking about that wooden horse. I wonder where it is.
Does my mother know anything about it? Cairo, O Cairo, city of palaces
and the Prophet's holy family, here I am leaving you once again, a fugitive
with no refuge. O city, have you no feelings? Why do you favour the rich

and sympathise with amirs, and yet you are not sensitive to the sufferings of your founder's grandson? Do you not feel any sense of obligation? And what about you, Jawhar the Sicilian? I wonder, did you realise that the walls you built of soft clay and the solid gates you constructed would be closed to the Egyptian people and your own grandson? Come back, Sicilian, come back and tell people that I deserve to live in the city built with my blood and lineage.

As I entered the outskirts of Fustat, I could not see in front of me. It was a world consisting of stories from the past and just a few attempts from the present, in the face of which we stand baffled. If only I knew who I am! No matter. It feels as though I'm hearing Laila's mocking whispers about Sundus all over again. I heard them, then they turned into screams. When I looked around me, I could see a whole crowd of people clustered around my horse and surrounded by ruins. They grabbed my horse—was it to celebrate my arrival or something else? I had no idea. Maybe they realised that I had saved them. Sundus's screams made me try to resist, but it was pointless. They threw my horse to the ground, and my head crashed into Fustat's stony soil. Blood coursed over my face, and I could taste it in my mouth. It was then that I heard people yelling:

"This is the amir who ordered Fustat to be torched. He's the one who sent our children away and flogged our women. He's Jawfar, that's his name— Jawhar. It's not enough just to kill him..."

Mas`ood had spread his hatred throughout the city! If only I could cut out his tongue with my own hand. In my imagination, I could hear him speaking to me.

"You're challenging the Caliph because of these people!" he was saying. "Just look what they're going to do to you! And what I'm going to do to you... There will be few words, but they're going to destroy you as though you tore down houses and killed children."

I could hear women keening all around me, and the horizon disappeared. I could not see either Sundus or the horse; all I could think about was Mas`ood and the halva-maker. Mas`ood's revenge had been even more original and clever than expected. Pouring poison into people's ears and completely inverting realities. All wounded and charred people could think about was whom to blame. I had now become the culprit rather than the victim. All this really happened, I swear to you. Mas`ood's soldiers started making up stories about the Amir, who ordered his troops to burn Fustat. Some of them asked questions and had their doubts, saying that they had seen Jawhar fighting Mas`ood's soldiers and defying them. But the reply that came was:

"That was just a dream. Your imagination's come up with those things. The devil's leading you astray. Who was it who arrived and put a stop to the fighting? The Caliph! Why was the army at war with itself? For the spoils, that's all. Nobody cares about Fustat and its people. The Caliph was the only one who took pity on their situation and wept for them. He stopped plunderers from robbing the city."

He was there, the halva-maker, atop the mountain; I could almost see him chuckling at my fate. I tried to stand up, but a hundred or more men pounced on me. They started tugging me and tying my limbs with ropes so they could drag me around the city till I was dead. Even the children were throwing stones at me. I was semi-conscious. I will tell you what I heard, but not what I saw, because I did not see anything. Flames came close; an old woman had them alongside my head, but someone else told her to be patient till they could drag me around Fustat before ripping me apart. For someone like me, being gradually peeled was the best way to be killed; they actually said that. I will tell you about the peeling process. Earth entered my chest, and my eyes lost their ability to distinguish colours. I kept them closed for fear of what I might see and not see. My skin split open, and Fustat's dust made its way inside. There was not a single spot on my entire body that was not split open, with blood pouring out. My blood poured out like a highly organised colony of ants.

The horse that was carrying me drew to a halt, and one of them turned me over on my face, raised his hand, and punched me, once, twice, ten times, on the nose. I heard it crack and realised what had happened.

Then they took off Sundus's face veil. For just a moment, people stared at her in shock and concern. As they stared at her, she spoke to the halva-maker who was standing at a distance, gleefully observing the proceedings.

"Halva-maker," Sundus said, "save my husband. Now you know who I am.

Look at me, ʿAbdallah, and you'll realise who I am."

As the halva-maker approached, people went on hitting me and dragging me through the streets. When he looked at her, his eyes widened in shock and fear.

"Save my husband," Sundus said again.

He swallowed hard.

"He deserves to die," he replied in a quavering tone.

"Save my husband. That's what I'm asking."

He neither hesitated nor argued. He yelled at the people to stop. Chasing after the horse that was carrying me, he tried cutting through the rope, but a man stopped him and gave him a cuff. He told the man that he had to save the Sicilian because he was the one to take revenge. He was intending to kill the Sicilian, but not now.

After a whole hour of argument, during which the halva-maker was beaten as well, he managed to rescue my body from the mass of people and put it on his donkey.

"I'm going to kill the Sicilian," he said. "I have the honour of doing that. Leave him to me."

My eyes met those of my wife, but neither of us spoke.

After several days, it seems that I eventually woke up, not knowing exactly what had transpired. All I can remember is that the wounds all over my body ached; it felt as though my ribs and bones were being burned by fire. When I felt my nose, it seemed to me somewhere other than its usual place. A woman was muttering softly as she stroked my hair. It was not my mother, and Laila did not know how to sing or show any affection like common people. No, it was Sundus. I opened my eyes and looked at her without actually seeing her. Her entire face looked like a mass of fragments, and, in its place, there was an angelic light; it was surrounded by the weak light of yellow candles.

"My whole body aches," I told her without thinking.

She ran her hand over my arm and stomach.

"Forget about your body," she said, "and the pain will lessen. Just think that you're alive."

"The halva-maker..." I said weakly.

She did not respond. I closed my eyes.

"He's the one responsible for you being burned a while ago," I insisted. "You never told me, but I know. Tell me now. Perhaps your stories will let me forget the pain. Come over here and attach your body to my back so that you can give me some of your magic."

She did what I asked with no objection. She wrapped her arms around my stomach. I let out a groan, and she paused. She moved away, but I pulled her back and put my hand on hers so she would stay where she was and never move.

"You've saved me," I repeated, "again."

"When was the first time?"

"When you put your hand on my heart."

"Are you raving, Amir?"

"I'm not an amir anymore. Say 'my husband' or 'Sicilian.' This country is rejecting me like a filthy mouse. Egyptians can't be trusted. It's power that moves them and fear that blots their vision."

"They've all suffered, Amir. Such suffering leads to distraction."

"I don't know them. I'm going to look for some other country. Maybe in Sicily, where my grandfather came from."

"You've killed them, and they've killed you. You've burned them, and they've burned you. Sometimes lovers will hurt each other even more that the most dogged of enemies. Even so, the love survives even if the beloveds mangle each other. The first thing is to move on and save yourself."

"You're crazy! There's no love left in this country. I was burned in Fustat like a piece of firewood. If I leave, you're coming with me."

"How will it help you to have someone like me with you?"

"Is my nose smashed?"

"A bit. Your face is not as handsome as it was, Sicilian. Your nose was like those Roman statues we find underneath our houses—straight and sturdy. It's no longer in its proper place, but you're still handsome."

She gave a bitter smile and moved her hand close to my mouth. I kissed it and kept it on my lips.

"You told the halva-maker that I was going to fight in Fustat," I said, "even though he had burned you. You kept hovering around him the way flies hover around spiders, hopelessly searching for release, for their memories to be erased. How did he burn you? You're going to tell me."

She put her mouth close to my ear and kissed my cheek.

"You've commiserated with me," she whispered. "And you've revived something that I've kept suppressed for years. I don't know: am I to be tortured with your love for the rest of my days, or shall I die and find peace?"

"Where am I?"

"On the mountain, in a ruined house far away from the nob."

"I want to go back to my country."

"This is your country."

"This is the Caliph's country. I have nothing to do with it."

"Caliphs come and are soon gone, like winter nights. The people are always there, just like the Sahara pyramids."

"Or else they're killed by the Caliphs."

"Even if they were to kill thousands, there would still be thousands left. Those who remain have ownership. That belongs first to God, then to the country's people."

"You're talking like the Witch. Talk to me. My body aches all over."

She ran her hands over my entire body so as to eliminate all pain and every instance of cruelty and degradation.

"Don't stop," I whispered, my eyes closed.

"I was fourteen, and I had come from Disuq with my father and mother to visit a close friend of my father, `Abdallah the halva-maker. They had grown up together in Cairo before my father left for Disuq. I had heard about `Abdallah's behaviour. He liked wine and could never get enough. His wife had suffered and lost hope of reforming him. However, my father valued and respected him. I don't know why—perhaps because his father was a halva-maker who was senior commander for Jawhar the Sicilian. I never asked my father. `Abdallah was the best of halva-makers. At the time, his wife offered us kunafa.

"I don't eat halva," I said without thinking.

His wife gave me a pleading look.

"`Abdallah's sweets are not like any others," she said. "Try some kunafa."

She insisted, but I still refused.

"I don't like halva," I replied firmly.

"Somehow, he heard—or else his wife told him—that I did not like the halva he had made and had not eaten any.

"At night, the halva-maker went out to Bulaq as usual to drink wine and have fun with the prostitutes. His wife complained to my mother and wept. She then went off to go to sleep, and my mother slept in a room beside hers. I had a stomach-ache, so I moved away from my mother so as not to wake her up. I went to the room with the oven and slept there. At dawn or even earlier, `Abdallah came in, totally drunk. He started talking to me rapidly, asking if I liked halva. Still half-asleep, I stood up, intending to go back to my mother's room. He started lighting the oven and boasting about his craft and skills. I asked him to let me go back to my room, but I think that he either did not realise who I was or else he actually did know and was furious because I had spurned his halva."

"I know," he said, staring at me. "You're the Caliph's daughter. Wait till you've tasted my halva."

"I realised that he was drunk and out of his mind. I was in a total panic, with no idea what I should do, so I sat down. I could not decide whether to stay or leave. He kept cursing as he clumsily tried to light the oven. The flames grew larger and larger, and his crazy behaviour terrified me. I stood up to leave."

"Stay here and taste my halva," he said as he moved toward me.

"When I grabbed the door, he seized my hand."

"Stay here," he insisted.

"I burst into tears and said that I wanted to go back to my mother. He was holding the torch in his other hand."

"Have you tried `Abdallah's halva before?" he asked, trying to convince me.

"Then he lost his balance and dropped the lighted torch. He grabbed my hand. I tripped, and the burning torch landed on my face, and...'

She had been talking very fast, but now she fell silent.

"Then what happened?" I asked.

She swallowed hard and started crying.

"I don't remember," she said.

"Did he try to assault you?"

"No, he was drunk and totally obsessed with his halva. He didn't know who I was. I was scared, but he didn't try to rape me. He had killed me in mere seconds, then left me to roam the world with no refuge."

"What did your father do?"

"I don't remember. I watched him crying and begging for forgiveness. It wasn't supposed to happen. That's what he said, but I didn't forgive him. I started waiting for news of him and following him like a lame dog trailing behind the owner of a field, even from afar. Then I sent him a message, saying that you were planning to attack Fustat. I don't know why."

"Have you forgiven him?"

"I can't."

"Did you want to be avenged?"

"I don't like revenge. Imprison the soul or let it roam free, I don't know. He killed me, Amir."

I turned to look at her, aching all over.

"Your love totally enfolds me," I said, giving her a big hug.

"Now you're raving."

"I've looked at you with an eye different from all others."

She wept silently for an hour or more.

"But he's suffering too," I said. "He's lost everything."

"Don't sneer or rejoice at his sorrows."

"Even though you won't forgive him?"

"I orbit around him, as he does me. When I uncovered my face, he recognised me. I knew he would. When I asked him to rescue you, he had no choice but to obey my instructions. He's never forgotten and can't live in peace. I haven't forgotten either, and I can't live at all. It's true: I sent him a message about what was going to happen in Fustat. I didn't know anyone else, and I was frightened about what might happen to me in the city."

I sat up and kept her head against my chest.

"We'll go to Sicily," I told her. "Let's forget all about the halva-maker, Fustat, and Cairo, and start a new life."

"I have no life, Amir."

"What if I told you I want no one but you?"

"I'd say you were spouting death's ravings."

"How can I convince you?"

"I don't need you to do that. Let's save ourselves first, or save you at least."

"Did you fall in love with me because I was so handsome?"

"I don't know."

"I fell in love with you because I discovered part of myself in you."

"All men can see is shells. It's women who search for the kernel."

"Here is a man unlike all other men. Don't leave my side tonight."

At night, the wounds ached and the groans reverberated. I closed my eyes and tried to go to sleep with Sundus hugging my back. I held her hand.

"Sundus," I muttered between groans, "where does all this pain come from?"

"My darling," she whispered as she kissed my shoulder.

I kissed her hand with a smile.

"You've never called me that before," I said. "Dull my pain for me. I'm going to die, Sundus. You realise that..."

Kissing my back, she proceeded to wrap her arms around my waist hard enough to squeeze me. Turning into a magician, she enveloped me in spells, breathed her magic formulae over me, and encircled my wounds. It felt as though she were exploiting the body's weakness and taking control. I watched her as she shifted my body and lay me submissively on my back. As the pain gradually diminished, I felt a longing for her as though my body were still alert and healthy. But she was the one who was in charge, plunging my body into hers as she quivered and sighed.

"How I yearn for you!" she said forcefully.

As I closed my eyes, the pain I felt was mingled with a kind of rapture that I had never experienced before.

"You're lying," I mumbled.

"No, I'm not," she replied gently as she kissed my neck.

She put my hand over her heart that was pounding like a catapult about to be fired. She sighed, and her breaths quickened. We then wrapped ourselves in the embers of a fire that never burns or leaves any traces. I was granted entry to heaven before my own death, and then returned to earth. She clutched my shoulder as though to cling to her passion so that it could not slip away through her limbs.

"I love you," I said.

"You're raving again..."

As I closed my eyes, she collapsed beside me panting, held my hand, and kissed it.

"Thank you, Amir," she said, "for bodily pleasure."

I fell into a deep slumber or left the world; I don't know which. How had I managed to rouse my body in her arms? I've no idea. When I was so wounded, how could I have made love to her so that we met each other in paradise? I don't know. What I do know is that we were linked with the stars, fused together, then returned to earth. I am certain that, this time, she pulsed with life, pleasure, and rapture in my arms.

Next morning, I opened my eyes, sat up, and called for her, but she did not reply. Fighting off the pain, I slowly got out of bed and shouted her name again, but there was still no reply. I went out of the small house and looked all around me. I felt like a lost child wandering through a mountain of fire. I shouted for the halva-maker, but he did not respond. I stumbled and leaned my hand against the wall of the house. I went back to look for a dagger or some other weapon so I could leave this prison. It was then that I saw him.

I gave him a defiant stare.

"The criminal in person," I said. "So, halva-maker, is there to be compensation? Or has that girl's life been wasted in vain because a drunk man made a stupid mistake?"

"You're no better than me," he replied, staring at me. "In fact, you're worse. The crime that I committed by mistake is not as bad as the one you've committed deliberately. I wonder, have you any idea how many women you've burned, how many children you've orphaned, how many—"

"Quit blaming me, man," I interrupted. "You're no better than me; you're worse. Where is she? What have you done with her?"

"She's gone away," he replied with a sarcastic grin.

I grabbed his collar in despair and threw him to the ground. I piled on top of him, my strength failing me as I did so.

"I'll kill you," I panted. "Where's my wife?"

"Don't ask me. She left. She took her things and left."

"If you don't tell me where you've hidden her," I said, grabbing him by the neck, "I'm going to kill you."

"By my own son's life," he replied, "I don't know where she is. But I've saved your life, and you have to help me. If I take you out to the people of Fustat, they'll tear your guts apart. If you stay hidden here in an old house on the mountain, I'll never find enough money to feed you."

"You expect me to help you get flour," I answered with a cackle, "drink wine and consort with loose women? I'm with you on the latter, but not the former."

"Don't make fun of me, Sicilian."

"I'm not going to stay here. Don't worry. I'll leave in a day or so, once I've found out where you've hidden her."

"Where do you plan to go?"

"That's none of your business."

"People told the wolf to leave its lair. It looked all around, then went back disappointed. It said this was a new lair. The other forest animals scoffed.

'When it comes to love, place your heart wherever you like.

'Love is only for the very first beloved.

'However many homes on earth the young man comes to know,

'He always yearns for the very first!'

"Cairo's my very first home, but now I can't live there. I'm not from Fustat, either, nor am I one of the common people in Egypt."

He looked at me and at the state of my wounds.

"You've two choices," he said. "You can stay with me and help me look for my wife and son; or you can run away as you've done before."

"I didn't run away, you fool. If it weren't for me, you and others like you wouldn't still be alive. I'm the one who defied the Caliph."

"I'm talking about the past, when you ran away to Disuq with your mother and lived like brigands."

"You realise that I'm going to leave.

"No, you'll stay."

"I'm going to find her, then I'll leave."

"She's left you on purpose, Amir," he said, moving closer. "She collected her things and left because she doesn't want you to find her."

I stood up slowly and slapped him. I discovered that, even though I was weak, I could still overpower him, or indeed strangle him on the spot. I grabbed him by the neck and squeezed as hard as I could, until his tongue was lolling out of his mouth and he was pleading and trying to shout.

"Tell me where she is," I said.

I looked into his eyes as the spirit vaulted in the mountain air. I realised that he actually did not know. Feeling utterly despondent, I looked all around me for some way out. But found none. I fell to the ground, threatening and longing for her but with no idea where she was. Had she left of her own free will, or had she been forced?

I donned a face veil and left the house. Day after day, I walked on my wounded feet all around Fustat and Giza, looking for her and calling for her. I even went to see the Pyramid Witch.

"These days," she told me with a smile, "every lover keeps coming here with ragged clothes and shattered hearts. They're all saying, Sicilian, that you burned Fustat."

"But I didn't burn it, Bahnas. I saved it."

"But I don't know who you are. Do you know who you are?"

"I'm searching."

"Where?"

"Everywhere."

"When we lose something, we search in all kinds of strange places. Yet what we regard as being far away turns out to be wrapped within the folds of familiar limbs."

"You're speaking in riddles. I don't understand that language."

"I thought you only understood the language of feelings, but you've shocked me by knowing the language of beauty."

"So there's no hope for me. If I don't find her, I'm going to lose my mind."

But I did not find her. I walked around the alleys in Disuq and Fustat in search of her neighbours and relatives, but without success. If someone had kidnapped her, I would have found out. I went to Cairo in disguise and complained to my mother about what she had done. She listened and rubbed my shoulder.

"God will compensate you," she told me.

Exhausted, I went back to the mountain, feeling as though I had made a tour of the entire world. I lay my despairing frame down on the ground and went to sleep.

He slunk into my room at night and whispered in my ear that he loathed me and would never forgive me for destroying his entire life. He said that he could change people's hearts and tell them the truth. Everyone knew him; they enjoyed his halva and realised what he had suffered at the hands of the Caliph's soldiers. But he was never going to do that. I pretended to be asleep so as not to kill him, but he went on. He told me how Egyptian attitudes towards me had changed. Now I was the source of all their troubles and suffering. Mas`ood had spread poison along with the special kind of halva that the halva-maker had concocted. He had distributed them to the Egyptian people as a way of consoling them for the loss of sons, houses, and city. It was as though he were entirely innocent of their loss of both blood and respect. He told them all that he had wept. He had begged me to stop burning the city. I had defied my commander's instructions, and instead had plundered, burned, and kidnapped women. His men had started telling all sorts of stories about Jawhar, who was kidnapping women and doing things to them in the street, right in front of their families. They claimed that it was all Jawhar's idea and plan; the Caliph had nothing to do with the burning of Fustat. Jawhar is full of hatred, they went on, because Egyptians did not treat his father fairly. He was out for revenge. The actual truth of things now started to float down the river and break up into separate pieces. To see was to doubt. Everyone felt bitter and sank into despair. At this point, killing Jawhar became the primary goal, the full moon that had yet to appear. No one breathed a word about what had happened between the Caliph and Jawhar;

even birds did not chirp the information to one another. But 'Abdallah the halva-maker knew.

"Look for my wife," he whispered in my ear. "If you find her, I'll help you."

When I stood up, the halva-maker shivered and moved away. I stared at him.

"You're acting as though you're innocent, man," I said. "I wonder, has the people's memory erased all the crimes they've committed? Your wife's surely in a better situation than mine. Anyone who's shaped by fire suffers forever, you drunkard. Here you are, toying with the concept of innocence and mixing sweet and sour."

I saw him before me, white-faced, as though the blood had drained from his body. He opened his mouth, and I saw water dripping from his teeth or eyes—I don't know which. At that moment, I thought he was going to die. Then he disappeared.

I went out to look for him and found him silently making halva. It looked as though, whenever he felt sad or his mind wandered off somewhere, he would make halva. I watched him in silence. He would rub the date-paste in his hands, then add almonds and sesame seeds, soaking them in saffron, adding poppy seeds and sugar, and coating them in musk and rose-water. Lighting the fire, he would put some sesame oil in a bowl and toss the sweets known as 'judge's morsels' into it. Adding corn starch and peeled and crushed pistachio to the mixture, he would mould them into dinar shapes. Once he had finished, he would sprinkle cloves, saffron, aloes, and musk on the individual pieces.

He said things that I will never forget as long as I live. His eyes bulged still further, so much so that I pictured them as twin frogs leaping over the water in front of me.

"Every plant has a meaning and soul," he told me. "Every animal has its own scent, which reveals its life: happy or miserable; deprived or wealthy; killed deceitfully or honourably. Butter has a smell that comes from a cow; if it was downtrodden or sad, then you can taste that feeling in your throat. But halva has no taste without sesame oil, from tiny sesame seeds. Does halva look as splendid as caliphs do? Of course not. But it's more important than caliphs and amirs. Without it. the Fatimids would not be in Egypt. When Egyptians stop planting sesame, it'll mark the end for the Ubaidis. Remember these words of mine, Amir. Plants are just like human beings; when you probe their depths, you emerge either with something good or bad. If you crush sesame, it gives you oil that you can use for many things, just like an honest woman who is ready to give in difficult times before things turn easier. But, like people, each type of halva has its own range, power, vessel, and appointed time, when all its qualities, good and bad, come together. However, when those qualities *do* come together, there are some of us who seem as sweet as the moon in the sky, whereas others resemble a red devil with a bitter taste and a poison that hurts but does not kill. Just like the human heart, halva is a blend of plants, each with its own scope and power. Through the Virgin Mary's suffering and her heart blended with good, your own wife, Amir, has been ordered by God to eat dates as she seeks help against pain, fear, and hope. Dates on their own can provide energy and courage, but, if they're mixed with other healthy plants, they become even more effective and taste even sweeter. Just as you grind wheat, I grind pistachios and almonds with sugar. Some souls have brilliant colours to them, and you never tire of sitting with them even if time comes to an end. When sugar is mixed with pistachios and almonds, you'll never forget the taste. Then I'll add ground dates and rosewater. And then, there comes the amir, the amir of all spices. Without it, no dish can be eaten, and no heart can flourish and win. There can be no halva without saffron; it gives both colour and vigour to halva as a whole. Just take a look at the sweet dough, my lord. What do you see?"

"Pastry dough."

"No, a heart with all its debauchery and piety. We all consist of just four elements, no more: water, fire, earth, and air, all of them in proportion. If there's too much water, then it drowns in its own scruples. Too much fire, and it's burned by its own hatred and greed. A surfeit of air leads humanity to pause and fear the consequences. Too much earth, and it's like sesame oil: without it there's no halva to eat and no life on earth. That said, too much of it crushes the heart and buries it in a pit of sorrow. Here, right in front of you is some halva dough, the like of which you have never eaten before. But, before I give it to you, I'm going to add some musk. Noses can smell and mouths can taste before the eye ever sees or the ear hears anything. When you eat this halva, you will pray for me.

"Just like humanity itself, it can take many long hours to make this halva, but you can eat it in seconds. Like building and destruction, you need years to construct the cavalier, but, when war comes, it can finish him off overnight. But don't despair. In hours of craft lies every kind of pleasure. When you've finished making halva, you have to eat it. Every soul has its particular power and scope. Do you realise what it is that distinguishes 'Abdallah the halva-maker's halva? It's that, while he's making it, he is fully aware of the soul that inhabits every creature."

In a defiant gesture I put my hand on my waist.

"Have you finished?" I asked.

"I saw you, Amir," he replied, not looking at me. "I wanted you to hear those words. Now I'm going to tell you about my father and your grandfather."

I had already heard the story of my grandfather's relationship to halva, although I did not know the finer details. In my imagination, my grandfather was a blend of soft clay, the Al-Azhar mosque, and doughnuts. Sometimes, I would see him warming doughnuts in the halva-makers' market; at others, he would be carrying clay to build a city and mosque; at still others, I would see him entering Cairo with his sword held high, strutting with all the arrogance of the mighty. I heard how important halva was to the Ubaidis. During every festival, every Ramadan, all Egyptians would be eating the Caliph's halva. I already knew that, but I was not bothered about its origins. Then he started telling me about it, as though the entire world was waiting for judge's morsels and nothing else. Everyone would be sitting quietly, enjoying each other's company in the moonlight.

I gave him a defiant look.

"I used to know your father and grandfather," he told me enthusiastically. "We had a pact, different from the one your grandfather made with the Egyptians. Your grandfather was an unusual man. You realise that, don't you? And yet he died like an ordinary person.

"All deaths are the same, my lord Amir," he went on. "What's important are the stories that we tell about significant people. They're what survives. The general was a truly great man. He was one of my father's friends. Did you know that?"

I raised my eyebrows in a mocking gesture.

"Don't you believe me?" he went on. "My father told me about the great general Jawhar. We know the story from beginning to end. You never hear such stories in royal palaces; I myself have heard them from the common people. You'll never hear the truth from viziers and sultans. Forgive me for speaking so frankly. Jawhar was like a magic piece of gold; any time you rubbed it, it would double in size. My father says that the ancestors of old used to worship gold; they would depict everything they wanted to preserve: people, clothes, food, even their enemies. They loved drawing pictures and gold. Your grandfather was like magic gold, a fighter and soldier. Ever since he had arrived from Sicily, he had devoted himself to fighting. Soldiers have their own morals and compacts, Amir, especially when they're young and in training. My father would regularly repeat words that spread like puffs of air throughout the Egyptian territories. They were spoken by the Caliph, who let Jawhar establish his regime while he remained safe and sound in Tunis. Years earlier, the Caliph Al-Mu'izz li-din Allah declared: 'If Jawhar leaves on his own, he'll conquer Egypt without any fighting, settle in Ibn Tulun's ruins, and build a city that will conquer the world.' Jawhar did indeed come, conquering first Egypt and then Damascus, then building the city of Cairo for his Caliph, not for us—but no matter! However, Amir, soldiers are not like the Caliph. Do you know why? They deal with the populace every single day and get to know them. The worldly-wise commander will enter the country and study its people just as he would study linguistics. Jawhar knew everything about the Egyptian people even before he arrived. Once he had entered the country, he assembled the people and religious scholars and gave them a pledge of security, with freedom of religious belief and livelihood. Are you aware, Amir, of how much Egyptians value their freedom? Even so, commanders still have some tricks up their sleeves that can change people's minds. When General Jawhar built the Al-Azhar Mosque, it was for the Shi'a, even though it was an enormous structure built in a very short time. It was a city and mosque constructed for the Fatimid amirs, not for us. I've already told you that your grandfather was not just any old commander; he realised that Egyptians value freedom—yes indeed, but they are also observant, even though they may look dreamy and distracted. He came to see my father in the khan; yes, that's right, the indomitable commander came to see my father, the halva-maker, in his shop. I was only eight years old at the time, but I can still remember. He arrived all of a sudden, accompanied by a group of men wearing light, white garments. At first, my father could not believe that the person who had come into his store was Jawhar. As the commander was speaking, my father's eyes opened wide in sheer amazement. Do you know what your grandfather said, Amir? I did not hear it at the time, but I know because my father told me about it later, a hundred times every day.

"'Halva-maker,' he said, 'I'm bringing good things to the Egyptian people. They may not appreciate what I've built so far, because it's not for them. And yet it may well become theirs in the future. Who knows? I wish to express my admiration for you and to confirm the pledge between us. I'm going to offer a repast for a hundred days; every day, Egyptians will be able to eat bread and meat. That way, they will come to trust me more and realise the difference between the descendants of Fatima Zahra and the Ikhshidids. However, today, halva-maker, I've come here to inscribe my name on your hearts. I want you to make a type of halva more wonderful than any other that people have ever eaten. This shouldn't be like the halva the Abbasids eat in Baghdad. No, I want this halva to be delicious for amirs and the poor alike, like the halva of paradise that makes no distinction between sultans and slaves. It should have a musky smell and the savour of heaven above. When I invite all Egyptians to try it, they will realise the genuineness of my intentions and my softness of heart. Halva is life's ornament, halva-maker, just like wealth and children. Without it, life has no colour, and it is only sugar that manages to counter the tribulations that we have to endure. If you can make for me a different kind of halva for this noble month, I'll give you all kinds of gifts until the Caliph arrives.'

"'Till the Caliph arrives?' my father asked.

"'Your name has been frequently mentioned in all the palaces,' he replied. 'You'll be transferred to Cairo and become the Caliph's halva-maker.'

"'I can't leave Fustat, my Lord. Let me think about the halva. I'll create something very special.'

"That night, my father did not get any sleep. He started wandering around the parks at night, chatting to the flowers and bees. Eyes closed, he swallowed some honey as he usually did. He picked a red flower that was widely admired.

"'I want the halva to be like this flower,' he told himself, "one that people will pick because they can enjoy its colour, touch, and nectar. When they eventually swallow it, it will give them a rapturous feeling such as lovers have when they meet. With doughnuts, it was the sugar and wheat that made no distinction between amirs and poor folk. When the two are blended together, they satisfy both the hunger of the poor and the cravings of the amir. Apply wheat dough to a blend of sugar, pistachio, and almonds, and even the most miserable of people will break out in a smile, however hard their lot in life. It's the element of surprise in the stuffing of doughnuts, Amir, that is the very secret of existence. My father's doughnuts are unlike any others—hand-picked flowers in the hands of lovers that you would swallow the way a hungry child wolfs down the bread of life. My father's the only one who knows the secret. You blend the sugar with bees' honey, pistachio, and hazelnut, then add musk, smoke the mixture in aloes and ambergris, and insert it all into the doughnuts. You boil them in sesame oil. The oil is made in a particular way that involves a long history—I'll tell you about it shortly. When the general tasted those doughnuts, he beamed with pleasure, gave my father gifts, and asked him to prepare a thousand pots full of this new kind of halva. He provided my father with lots of sugar. At this, the entire Egyptian population was happy and gave Jawhar the Sicilian a genuine welcome.""

The halva-maker and I were together the whole day.

"Neither of us has a wife," he told me with a scoff. "We've ended up together—the lion and gazelle, hunter and prey. The trap-setter has fallen into the trap. Ah well, so what now, son of the commander of all commanders? Make halva with me!"

I have told you that I left no stone unturned in my search for Sundus; I even went into Cairo once or twice in disguise. My beard and hair grew long, and my broken nose gave me a coarse, troubled look. The Egyptians took pity on me; some of them were disgusted by my clothes, while others asked me to pray for them. They forgot all about Jawhar, who had brought so much destruction. On the city's outskirts, I heard about what had happened to one of the Caliph's closest commanders, a man called Ghabn. The Caliph gave orders that his left hand should be amputated; his right had already been cut off three years earlier. However, after both his right and left hands had been taken, the Caliph proceeded to send him gold, doctors, and costly clothes. Three weeks later, the Caliph ordered that the man's tongue be cut out. He had heard that the man's words and deeds had been harmful. I have no idea why I burst into laughter as I was sitting by Bab al-Bahr and listening to the story of that unfortunate commander. The men simply shrugged their shoulders and assumed I was out of my mind. I wanted to pay a visit to my mother. Ever since the Egyptians had dragged me through the streets and brought me low, I'd had only one opportunity to do so.

I stopped in front of the palace gate and covered my face. I looked at the flowers covering the walls and the bright green making its effortless way into the garden. No guards were posted at my father's and mother's palace. I went looking for my mother. She came out and stared at me for a moment. Needless to say, she recognised me without my needing to take off my face-covering.

"My dear son," she said, showing some affection for the first time since I was born. "How are you?"

She moved toward me.

"I'm afraid to get too close to you in these clothes," I replied hesitantly.

She grasped my hand and pulled me close to her bosom.

"I swear to God," she said, "I've never felt you as clean and pure as you are today, nor have I been so proud to have you as a son."

How could Lamya's praise so warm the heart when I was this age, I wondered. I had no idea. I just sat on the floor and looked all around me.

"You know that I can't find Sundus," I said.

She looked surprised.

"Yes, my son, I know," she replied. "You told me last time."

"I don't know whether she was forced to go or went of her own accord. I can't find her and have no idea where to look."

"I sense a kind of impotent wandering in your gaze," she told me emotionally. "Stand in front of me like a man. She's just a woman, no more. If she's left you willingly, then forget about her. She doesn't deserve you."

I opened my mouth to explain things, but closed it again. I stroked her hand.

"I give thanks to God that you're well," I told her as I stood up. "I'll come to see you soon if I can and am still alive."

"Don't take any risks for her sake," she replied immediately. "Promise me that."

She stood up, went to her room, and came back with an old wrapper. When she opened it, it proved to be the wooden horse that my father had taken from his father, Jawhar the Sicilian—all that was left of his childhood and youth in Sicily. She unwrapped it eagerly and looked at its superb filigree decorations.

"I've never seen anything so beautiful, Jawhar," she said. "Your father gave it to me, but not to his second wife or any of his slave girls. It was just for me. Your father said that Jawhar the Sicilian received it as a gift from his own father before he was captured, sold, and transferred to the Fatimid Caliph, Al-Mansoor bi-Llah. Your father maintains that your grandfather used to sleep with this horse beside him all his life, even when he was really old. When Husain sensed that he was in danger, he gave it to me for safekeeping. He told me that it was all that was left of his father. I objected and pointed out that the entire city of Cairo, the Al-Azhar Mosque, and city walls were all remnants of his father. He replied that all those things were remnants of the army commander, but the horse was all that remained of the child. I want to preserve the father and child, not the army commander. History will keep his memory alive. Today, Jawhar, I'm giving you this horse to look after and remember that the heart of your father as a child resided in Sicily with his own father, and yet he was passionate about the city that he himself had built. Never for a single day did he want to leave it. He lived in it and died there. For years, he disappeared from view, but there's one person who's never forgotten. Do you understand me, my son?"

"Jawhar's mother," I replied with a bitter smile, "do you really think I deserve it?"

"Yes, my son, you do deserve it today, because you're the bravest man in all of Egypt."

"You're a Sunni at heart. You've never changed, have you?"

"Let's forget about these sectarian ideas that divide us. Instead, let's remember that life's struggles are endless, and humanity's evil is ephemeral."

"You've suffered a lot, mother."

"No more than the Egyptians have."

"They don't know you and aren't bothered about our fate."

"They can recognise sorrow in people's eyes and engage with it with all the intensity of someone who loses a beloved, then goes back."

"I don't understand you."

"Stay alive; you're the only one I have left. Don't mistreat those people who have suffered and lost. They're victims just like us, or even worse."

I nodded and left through the palace gate. I wandered through the crowded Cairo streets. There was no animal dung or refuse in Cairo; no dirty walls and burned houses. Every palace was surrounded by pomegranate, quince, and orange trees. Fruits were plentiful, and sugar would invite its lover to taste. The buildings were lofty, a reminder to those who entered that this was the land of noble Caliphs. The streets were comfortable to walk in, soothing hearts that were tormented by fiery passion. Cairo was distant from the blessed Nile, and yet its fountains could reach almost as far as Ifriqiya. What a wonderful city, and yet I'm afraid of you! There's no place for me here. Today I'm Sicilian—Egyptian—crazy —a loser—incapable—yet able to laugh at the vicissitudes of fate and master of time's perfidy. Today, I'm the Egyptian who can only enter your gates after suffering hardship, enduring a wrong whose origins remain unknown, with little initiative and little knowledge. I wonder, who orders hands to be amputated: the Caliph or his aides? Who is cruel and perfidious? Who makes the days as treacherous as snakes spitting poison without cause or risk? You city, what is this madness that has afflicted you? What destiny awaits your citizens? How I yearn for you and the childhood I spent in you! How I fear your transformation and intolerance. In your eyes, there is neither fault nor pity! Even rapacious beasts attack only when they are either hungry or threatened, and yet you, Cairo, attack for no reason. You slaughter wantonly and offer phony cures. You, like sins—you grasp me and stick. I was both dream and lesson. At your hands, I learned that we love what is most evil within us and loathe everything good. I no longer have a place either here or in Fustat. Today, I'm wandering hither and yon in the streets, and no one looks at me because I'm just as weak as they are. When I burned things, I was weak; when I was greedy, I was weak. Hours and minutes are all confused. I've spent an entire age enjoying what's to come without using a mind to organise or a heart to yearn. That's enough, city of Caliphs. Enough and more.

The halva-maker was also still looking for his wife. He had asked about her with every army division and in every section of the city. He discovered that his wife was currently in the hands of a Turkish soldier who had been under my command. He was delighted when he came back to see me.

"Go to him," I told him firmly, "and tell him that I order him to give you the slave girl, meaning your wife. I'll give him a thousand dinars for her. He'll agree."

"But you're no longer his commander."

"He still knows I'm his commander even though Mas'ood has denied it. Go!"

The halva-maker went back to the soldier. He told me what transpired. He asked to see Mariam just once. The soldier agreed to this, and he also agreed to sell her.

"Have you touched her?" the halva-maker asked hesitantly.

The soldier gave him an angry look.

"She's my slave," he replied. "But I haven't touched her. She has a suckling baby. I don't like that."

He heaved a sigh of relief, then asked to see her. She came in, head lowered, with the baby. Among the things that the halva-maker told me was that she wept and blamed him for an hour or more. She told him he was the lousiest husband in all of Egypt, and he was to blame for what had happened. He tried to explain that it was not his fault that the soldiers had burned Fustat. She didn't understand. He begged her to give him just one day.

"So, now you've made sure that he hasn't touched me," she replied astutely. "If only he had, 'Abdallah! If only I'd stayed with him as a slave girl, so I wouldn't have to go back to your ruckus and the frivolous way you handle yourself and me."

"I swear," he begged, sinking to the floor at her feet.

"Don't swear anything," she interrupted. "Your vows are worth nothing."

He kissed his baby, swaying between heaven and earth, and left her. Then he came to see me and told me everything.

"What's she planning? Does Mariam really hate me that much? Does she fancy the young soldier?"

"Don't believe women," I replied with a smile. "They've tongues like scorpions, ready to sting anyone indiscriminately. You've been humiliating her all your life, and she wanted to pay you back."

I went to see my mother in disguise. I gave the halva-maker some of the money and gold I had taken from my palace.

"Give it to the soldier," I told him confidently, "so he'll give you back your wife. Then I don't want to see your face ever again."

Two hours later, he took the money and left, quivering in fear at the thought of the way the soldier and Mariam had changed, and at the perfidy of time. His fear was justified.

CHAPTER SIX

The Pyramid Witch says that you cannot compel the soul to see the east wind blow or to listen to the sound of clouds. You have to open your heart in order to experience those things. For me, Sundus has become all my hopes; I have no idea when or how. The world had all the sweetness of judge's morsels halva; the moon was like a semolina cookie stuffed with almonds and honey. Now hope had turned feeble like strands of clothing. I had strained every muscle in my attempt to find her, but had not succeeded.

"When you're ready to welcome her," Bahnas, the Pyramid Witch told me, "she'll come to you. But she'll only come back to someone from whose breast we have removed evil and greed."

I yelled in outrage and swore to punish her. Then I surrendered and started chatting to her like one of the poets. The Mawlid was approaching. I kept looking at the wooden horse and imagining my grandfather, the great cavalier, training his horse and riding it through the various quarters of life...

The Mawlid is a major event for which people make halva.

I spoke to the wooden horse or my grandfather, I don't know which.

"If you saw Sundus," I said, "you'd recognise her. Not because of the burns on her face, but because she has the soul of a bird, the lightness of the breeze, and the sweet taste of honey. You would recognise her."

As I turned the horse over in my hands, I recalled what my father had told me.

"In Sicily," he said, "the sea is linked to the mountains. But the mountains are not like the ones in Egypt. Grasses grow there, and valleys extend all around the sea, beyond and around the mountains. People say that there's a fire that ignites every time, just like in curses, but that it always brings plentiful benefits—in Sicily."

How can I go back to a place where I wasn't born? Yes, it still lingers in my heart, but, alas, I only know this land, one that has rejected and humiliated me. I've kept talking to it like a wounded soldier in case it might take pity on me. That's this land.

The horse had some delicate filigree on it, created by a very skilled carpenter. I held the wood in my hand and tried to make an empty horse into which I could stuff halva. With my eyes closed, I could see her as a bride, with brilliant colours, just like a king and princess. This was her own horse, with a cavalier riding on it who was her husband. Sundus, the most beautiful woman I had ever seen, who had penetrated to my inner heart and was part of me. She saw things that I had never seen, the unmatched courage of the supreme commander who had died a while ago. That's what she had said.

From the wood, I fashioned a shape for the rider, another for the horse, and still another for the bride dressed in all her finery. I carved all kinds of shapes into the wood. I wonder: How are you, Sundus?

Was it all just a fancy? Had she died, perhaps? I started weeping, but carried on carving wooden shapes. As soon as I had finished, I made a mix of sugar, water, and starch and put it inside the shapes to gel.

When the halva-maker arrived, he looked at me for a second, and then started decorating the bride with colours and brocaded leaves.

A halva bride, and a halva horse and rider. I have made them for you, two or three days before the Mawlid.

My mother... I reached the Bab al-Bahr and almost went through, but I did not. Her words kept ringing in my ears. Not what she'd said about the horse, but about my wife. For the very first time, she was being a bit malicious. She had sympathised with her and loved her, so how could she now say such nasty things about her when she had saved my life? Unless she knew something about her that I had not heard or wanted to keep something hidden from me? So she was pretending to hate her and stand with me against her, keeping something hidden...

What had the Pyramid Witch said?

"When we lose something, we search in all kinds of strange places, whereas what we regard as being far away turns out to be wrapped within the folds of familiar limbs."

I rushed back to the palace and opened the door. My mother shrieked.

"Where is she?" I asked in a fury.

She looked totally shocked.

"What's the matter with you, my son?" she asked.

I snuffed out a burning coal strong enough to burn down the whole of Fustat again.

"I'm going to slaughter her," I said. "I'm going to search for her in every single room. If you don't tell me now, you're going to witness her demise."

"My son," she pleaded, swallowing hard. "I promised her, I swore to her."

"How could you have lied to me?"

"My son?"

"Where is she?"

I left her and prepared to go inside the palace.

"Be gentle with her, Jawhar," she said. "She came to me and did not run away. She wanted me to protect her and to stay with me. I promised her I wouldn't tell you."

I stopped her, then drew my sword from beneath my scruffy clothes and charged through all the rooms in the palace. Eventually, I came across a locked door.

I banged on the door.

"Open the door," I yelled, "or else I'm going to smash it down on your head!"

After waiting a moment, I was about to plunge the sword into the centre of the door so as not to impale either myself or her. She opened the door and stared at the sword pointed straight at her.

"Welcome, dear husband," she said calmly, with a smile.

I threw the sword aside and pushed her back into the room.

"How dare you?!" I yelled. "Who do you think you are? You..."

"I don't deserve the Amir," she said, sitting on the floor in front of me.

I took a deep breath to squelch my anger, so she would not see how weak and feeble I felt.

"I'm not going to ask you why," I said. "We won't talk about the past. You're going to come with me now without any comment."

She covered her head with her hands and stayed where she was. I sank to the floor in front of her.

"I've no idea when or how to keep my anger under control," I told her affectionately. "It just spread in my soul. Why did you leave me? I was scared for you, and terrible thoughts toyed with me and made me suffer."

She picked up her face-veil to put it on.

"No suffering comes close to the suffering that you've caused me," she responded calmly.

I grabbed the face-veil from her hand.

"Make sure you don't cover your face when you're with me," I told her.

She groaned and started to cry. The entire room started to tremble and almost collapsed.

"I was content with myself," she said, covering her face with her hand. "I learned to accept my fate and live with it. But then you insisted on spreading the wounds and blowing the pain out of my heart. Sicilian, no one in all

Egypt is a cruel as you are. Even if you slaughter me, I'm not going back with you. I've started to hate myself and loathe my body. I've started wanting to change fate and rewrite it, to run time backwards so I don't meet the halva-maker and you. Leave me alone and go away! When you have sex with one of your slave girls, you'll be burning the rest of my body. I can't face any more burning."

If she had stuck a sword in my guts, I could not have been more shocked. But in her eyes, I could see a certainty that disturbed me. She did not want to come back to me, and I was not as good with words as she was.

"You're coming back with me now," I told her firmly. "I'm taking you by force, and you won't be able to run away again."

I grabbed her hand and tried to pull her up.

"Come along!" I told her, keeping my shame to myself.

She stayed on the floor, so I grabbed her hand again.

"I'm going to take you," I said, "whether you like it or not."

"If you force me," she replied firmly, "I'm going to kill myself."

I looked all around me in despair.

"If you're scared of adventure," I told her, "then you're a coward. You've no internal strength, as you claim. You're afraid I'm going to hurt you, and that makes things twice as bad, as I'm well aware. I don't know my own self; I don't know how you'll behave. I never expected to fall in love with you, or that I'd help the halva-maker and stand before the Caliph, that my heart would be torn apart in front of you and stand firm in the face of death like a tent peg. Would that I knew, would that I could promise you something! All I know is that my life has no purpose, but I want to stay alive so I can protect you from all evil. Do you understand?"

She lowered her head, and I moved closer. My fingers wiped the tears from her face, and then I gave her cheek a long, slow kiss. My lips roamed over her face, as I kissed her mouth, then her nose, and then her eye.

"This won't work," she said, her eyes closed.

I hugged her hard.

"I've missed you," I whispered.

"You're so cruel, Sicilian," she said in despair.

"Give me one chance."

"How have you changed?"

"Because you're part of me, you've split my heart in two, no escape! I've seen what I'd never seen before. I can't live without you."

She paused and shuddered. For just a moment, her resources flagged. She gave me a passionate kiss, then moved away again.

"I swear to you," she said, making things abundantly clear, "that if you take me by force, I'm going to kill myself."

I gave her an angry look, then picked her up in my arms while she put up some pointless resistance. I took her out of the room and the palace, with my mother yelling after me that I should not hurl myself into perdition.

I walked with her through Cairo's parks.

"People will say that the poor man has stolen the princess from the palace," I said. "Will you walk beside me so they don't kill me?"

"Fine," she said, "I'll come with you. But you won't be seeing me. You'll give me a place where I can be on my own. You'll promise not to force me."

"As you wish," I answered firmly.

She walked beside me.

"Where are we going?" she asked after a while. "This isn't the mountain road."

"The mountain's no use," I replied. "We need somewhere further away.

The days to come are going to witness turmoil like that in the Caliph's heart."

She did not speak. We took a carriage to Alexandria, and she did not say a single word to me all the way there. She had enough strength and resolve to turn any young man's hair grey. Her strength scared me, as did the beauty hidden inside her.

When I reached Alexandria, she did not break her oath. Entering a room in the small wooden house, she locked the door. I tried once affectionately, and a second time nastily, but she refused to open her heart or look at me. I was utterly miserable and thought about visiting the Pyramid Witch. However, I preferred to talk to the halva-maker and ask him for help. Who knows, maybe I would die as she hoped.

The halva-maker offered the money to the soldier.

"I don't have a slave girl to give you," he replied, looking disappointed.

"My son?" the halva-maker asked.

"I know nothing about the two of them."

He grabbed the soldier by the lapels, but the man pushed him away.

"I've told you I know nothing about the two of them," he said. "Get out of here before I kill you."

He roamed the earth like someone damned. He looked all around him as he kept questioning people. He knocked on palace doors and begged passers-by to help him, but no one did. Egyptians stared at him, sometimes in sympathy, at others in disgust. They asked him to leave, and he came tottering back to me. By now, I had almost completely recovered. He told me what had happened.

"That despicable woman, Mariam!" he yelled. "She's seduced him. She asked him to let her stay."

"If she'd wanted to stay before," I replied slowly, "she would have done so.

But he wouldn't have agreed to give her to you."

"She's the one behind it."

"Maybe she's being driven by all the faults and crimes of generals. If only you could beg her to forgive you."

"How merciful you are, Sicilian!"

"Sit down and tell me what he said exactly."

He told me, and I repeated the words once or twice.

"Maybe someone else encouraged him not to give her to you or took her away from him. Maybe someone more powerful than him. Maybe...who is there who knows you?"

"Everyone in Egypt."

"Who knows that you rescued me?"

"Everyone in Egypt."

"But they don't know where I am."

"Nobody has asked about your fate. Within days, they'd forgotten about you."

"But some people are interested."

"I don't know what you're driving at."

"Mas`ood ibn Thabit. He's poisoned Egyptians' ears. He's out to kill me, and you saved me. You're enemy number one."

"I don't have any enemies," he replied sadly. "All I want is my wife and son. I saved you for Sun..."

He paused.

"Go on," I said. "Say her name. Why did you stop?"

"We've both of us lost our wives," he replied in despair. "Even your wife can't stand you."

"Both of us will get our wives back. My wife left me on purpose, and she has come back but doesn't want to be with me. Your wife left you against her will, so you're better off. Send a woman to Mas`ood's palace with some fabrics, a well-known hairdresser. Give her half the gold and ask her to find out if Mariam is in Mas`ood ibn Thabit's harem. If she tells you the truth, give her more."

"If she's there," he asked painfully," how am I supposed to kidnap her from the Commander-in-chief's palace?"

"Leave that to me."

"You're just a feeble fugitive."

"I'm Jawhar son of Husain, you idiot."

Everything is happening so quickly. My decision and plan is taking shape the way a piece of "judge's morsel" halva browns on the fire. You neither recognise nor expect any other shape.

My assumption proved correct. Within a few days, we learned that Mas`ood ibn Thabit had taken Mariam in order to get his revenge on the halva-maker and also on me. Anyone offering aid to the Sicilian would be destroyed. It was a message that Mas`ood ib Thabit was sending to all Egyptians, as they would all see when the halva-maker lost his mind, after realising that his wife was in the commander's arms.

No one was safe in Egyptian territory; even someone simply walking on his own could be eliminated. Those who followed 'the straight path' would be deserted by loved ones. I sent my mother a message, telling her to come alone in the dead of night; the halva-maker would be waiting for her at the city gates. It was risky for her to stay in Cairo; the sea was broad, and the sands would hide every refugee and anyone in need of concealment. We settled in a wooden house close to the shore near Kum al-Nadura and the Mosque of a Thousand Columns, close enough to the sea that the winter waves would almost demolish our home, but the waves were still more merciful than the ruling authorities and their aides. I left my wife and mother there in God's care and went back with the halva-maker as I had promised. The two women took new names: my mother became Zainab, and my wife Jamila. They both discovered some people whose hearts had kindly feelings for them, and they started making and selling halva.

I had promised the halva-maker that I would rescue his wife and son and then not set eyes on him for the rest of my life. There are times when he reminds me of my sins and weaknesses. Even more often, he reminds me of friendships and home; he reminds me that I am stuck here with no home in Egypt, even though I may occasionally disappear into the sands or seafoam.

CHAPTER SEVEN

"Do you think she really wants him?" the halva-maker asked me in confusion. "Does she really want to live with Mas'ood ibn Thabit? Has she forgotten our relationship?"

"What kind of relationship was that, man?" I scoffed.

"You don't know anything about love. It can forgive what happens after and what comes before."

"So, if she's in love with Mas'ood, then maybe you can wait!"

"Anything but that!" he replied, giving me a furious look.

"Love, halva-maker, is just like a sword," I said. "There's no response to its decisions and no mediation in its killing. It will never forgive."

"How can you get into Mas'ood's palace? Even if you did, could you free my wife and son? Who do you think you are?"

"I'm the grandson of Jawhar the Sicilian. Let me think of a plan. I need you to make me an animal—a fox perhaps, or maybe a salamander. It should be made of sugar, and big enough to fill a large dish with my father's gold sword concealed inside. We'll carry the dish together and go to the palace on the Mawlid celebration—God being with us.

"Why are you helping me?"

"Don't' ask me that, because I don't know. Even so, I pity you and myself."

"Even if you help me, I'll never forgive you."

"Perhaps you don't know your own self, halva-maker," I said. "Just look. Can you make some halva horses and dolls to sell at the Mawlid? That'll convince people that we're both halva-makers."

"Sicilian, this is a new tradition. We're selling blackberries, but we've never made halva horses or decorated dolls like the ones we're making for your wife."

"It's a new tradition devised by the Sicilian."

The halva-maker gave me a smile.

"What did your wife do," he asked derisively, "when you gave them to her?"

"She looked at them, smiled, and closed her door."

"Our fate is in God's hands. For the very first time, we're selling the Mawlid doll in Egypt."

The Caliph left the palace, wearing a white woollen garment, a cloth turban, and modest Arab shoes. As he went on his way with his white sunshield, commanders kissed the ground at his feet. He stopped by the Ahmad ibn Tulun Mosque to talk to the populace, mix with them, and listen to their complaints. As he listened to them until sunset, he was patient, tolerant, and abstemious with those around him, sympathising and showing them affection. They all forgot everything that had passed; today was a festival. The Prophet's intercession had inevitably helped ease the removal of distress and the establishment of a sense of security. I was standing by the city gates, holding a large tray with a brightly coloured fox on it made of sugar and covered with musk and almonds. Its aroma was enough to make wine with no vendor and slave girls with no customer.

I stood by the gates, waiting for people to crowd around while they waited for halva and dinars. The guards pointed out beyond the gates, and everyone dashed out like on the Day of Resurrection. Gold trays with gilded towels on them were distributed, covered with stuffed dates, fancy desserts with various scents, gilded napkins, and minted dinars.

The halva-maker and I stayed by the Cairo gate.

"We've brought a present for the commander," he told the guard in a friendly manner.

The guard gave him a dubious look. The halva-maker assured him that he was a regular provider of halva to palaces. He took out some warm kunafa and a piece of Mawlid doughnut and invited the guards to taste. They did, and with mumbles and sighs they escorted us to the commander's palace.

Next, Mas`ood's palace guards had a taste of `Abdallah's halva. Eventually, the halva-maker sat down.

"Tell me about the harem..."

The guard gave him another dubious look.

"I hear there's a new Egyptian slave girl," he added quickly. "The commander's chosen her for himself. She's called Mariam."

The guard swallowed hard.

"Leave the halva and get out!" he told them in no uncertain terms.

"You know me. How many times have I come here before?"

"But I don't know your companion."

"He's a stranger who needs work. He doesn't have a weapon."

"He looks like a soldier."

"I'll send him away if you like."

The guard hesitated.

"How do you know about Mariam?" he asked. "Nobody knows about her."

I could see the trepidation in the halva-maker's eyes. Our gazes met. At that moment, he was telling himself that Mariam was living in luxury in the commander's palace. She had forgotten about the husband who could not stop drinking or keep company with his own wife. How many times had he beaten her and made fun of her? And yet she had taken it all stoically. How often had he not even been aware of the sorrow she felt at the death of one of their children? Even so, he used to hug her and cry in her arms. She had often given him protection and showed all the patience of prophets. He adored her, and she held the reins of his inner self. Mariam would never betray him.

The guard told us to leave, but I assured him that we were waiting to give the commander the gift in person.

He stuck to his guns, and so did we. We sat down in front of the palace until the guard changed. At night, one of the slave girls come out to the garden. I rushed over and called out to her from the trees. She turned around and came over. I put the gold in her hand.

"Where's Mariam?" I asked. "Can you take me to the harem?"

She looked surprised. She moved closer and pushed me back into the trees.

"She's dead," she said. "Don't you know?"

"How did she die?" I asked, swallowing hard.

"Once or twice, she refused to have sex with my master. When he tried forcing her, she used a dagger to kill herself, saying that she could not go on living with such disaster and dishonour."

I did not ask how she had used the dagger, nor did I have any doubt about the truth of the story. I knew truth from falsehood, but I had never loathed the truth as much as I did that day.

"I want her son," I whispered to her. "I'll give you anything."

"No one here wants him. He's sick and almost dying. He's going to die tonight, but I can't carry him out. They'd slaughter me."

I let her go back to the harem and returned to the halva-maker. Sitting down beside him, I put my hand on my cheek.

"Did you find a way to get into the harem?" he asked me.

"We'll wait for Mas'ood to come," I whispered. "He's the one we need."

"It's my wife and son I want," he repeated. "I've nothing to do with Mas'ood."

"When you see him," I insisted, "give him the tray. Leave the rest to me. Then take your son and leave. Don't wait for your wife; she's not coming."

"Mariam doesn't want me?"

"We'll talk soon. Take your son and go to Alexandria. If I'm still alive, I'll join you there. If I don't live, then take care of my mother and Sundus. Actually, take care of them, because I'm not going to make it. Do you understand?"

"What about my wife?"

"If I tell you she's dead, will you burst into tears and leave your son to die as well?"

He swallowed hard, but said nothing. He did not ask anything for fear of what he might hear.

At midnight, the commander returned to his palace on horseback, surrounded by his soldiers. No sooner had he dismounted than the halva-maker went up to him and begged him to accept his gift. The soldiers looked confused. Mas`ood went over to the gigantic halva statue and looked at it admiringly. I was standing right beside him, but he paid me no attention. My face covered, I moved behind him in seconds and grabbed the statue. He stopped me, and the guard hit me on the head, but I hurled my whole body at the statue and took out the sword I had concealed under my clothes—my father's gold sword. The soldiers were confused, and the general was about to escape. I grabbed his coat and pulled him toward me as hard as I could. I gave him a shove, and he fell to the ground.

"Move away, all of you," I yelled as loudly as I could, with the edge of my sword on his neck, "or else I'm going to kill him!"

"The Sicilian," he mumbled, his voice shaking. "If only I'd killed you myself, and not left you for the Egyptians."

I moved the sword closer to his neck.

"If I kill you now," I said, "I'll feel at peace about the Egyptians."

"And you'll die with me."

"Bring the halva-maker's son now!" I ordered the soldiers.

Mas'ood tried to move, but I kept my sword on his neck. He ordered his soldiers to bring the halva-maker's son.

"Let me leave with his son," I yelled.

He pursed his lips in anger.

"Not till I've told him how passionate his wife was in my arms," he said.

The halva-maker lowered his head.

"That's right, Mas'ood," I responded, looking at the soldiers. "She adored your arms so much that she killed herself to be rid of them."

"Everything you're doing is futile," he said. "You and I are both carrying out the Caliph's orders. Neither of us has any mercy in our hearts. Don't try to claim you're better than me. Egyptians don't deserve any sacrifice. What did they do to you? Do you remember?"

"To tell you the truth, I haven't done anything for the Egyptians or for the halva-maker. I've been doing it all for the sake of a part of my heart that's giving me instructions. I don't know what's driving me on or giving me courage."

The halva-maker held his son, and the soldiers opened the gates.

"I'll know what happens," I said. "If the halva-maker isn't able to get out of Cairo, then the general's not going to escape!"

I waited for a while. Who knows, the soldiers might yet catch up with him and kill him. Maybe....maybe. I was just a night-stalker moving in the dead of night, hoping for the stars to shine bright.

"Leave me alone, you coward!" Mas'ood yelled. "If you kill me, I'll rip you apart and scatter you all across the mountain."

"Let's fight, man to man!" I told him, my voice full of hate.

"That's not going to happen."

"So, men, your commander isn't strong enough to fight Jawhar!" I scoffed. "Listen to him!"

He moved, then gave his soldier a mocking look.

"Of course, I'll fight you!" he yelled angrily.

I tossed him one of the soldiers' swords and grabbed his hand to pull him up. I fought him as hard as I could. He was vicious and aged; I was driven by feelings in my own heart that I would never understand. I was out of breath, and so was he. I was sure I knew how it would all end: if I killed him, then the soldiers would kill me; if he killed me, I would die along with my humiliation and shame. Even so, Mas'ood had to die. I had given him the honour of dying in a fight, something he did not deserve. He turned to the soldiers and signalled that they should interfere. I did not have much time left. He must have realised that, sooner or later, I was going to win. I plunged my sword into his guts and made sure he was going to die. He let out a yell and went over to his soldiers. They all raised their swords and pointed them at my body.

In the distance, I spotted a light; my father was smiling at me and raising his gold sword. How wonderful my father's smile, dream, and patience were! Yet as his smile faded away, I was left in this predicament.

"Leave him!" one of the soldiers yelled. "The Caliph will decide what to do with him."

They subjected me to a ferocious beating and then left me in a gloomy prison. I thought that I would not make it until morning. But I found a doctor coming into my cell and asking if I felt all right. He staunched my wounds and treated me kindly.

"You're free," he told me calmly. "The Caliph has forgiven you. He says that Mas'ood deserved to die."

"Why has he forgiven me?" I asked, swallowing hard.

"You don't question the Caliph's actions," he replied. "He found some good in you."

"He knows me."

"Yes, he does. You're Jawhar, the Sicilian's son."

I was not sure whether I was dreaming or had died and been resurrected.

Everything was a jumble for me. After a month, I was feeling much better. The soldiers told me to leave, so, with a shrug, I exited the prison. "To God alone belongs the power and strength," I said, and then again, "To God alone belongs the power and strength."

I rushed to the wooden house on the seashore in Alexandria. My mind was preoccupied with the fate of the halva-maker, Sundus, and my mother. What had the halva-maker done, I wondered, when he found out that his wife had died? Had he made do with his son? Had he calmed down, or sworn to kill me? Was I not the one responsible for all these catastrophes? And yet, I'd had no specific intention. I had been motivated by the commander's hand, just like the pawn on the chessboard, or, at least, that is what I was hoping he would think. I forgot that I had deliberately burned down his store, and that hatred had seared my heart against him not all that long ago. They had been just a few moments that were now at an end, and yet I had thrown a black garment over his entire world, throttling him without destroying his soul.

I banged weakly on the door. I was tired of rulers and commanders, the changing moods of people, the destruction of the soul, and my prolonged absence from my own wife, the only woman I had ever loved. But today, there could be no approaching her, no possibility of finding a way to her heart.

My mother opened the door, hugged me in despair, and started crying.

"You're a wonderful son," she said. "You're all that's left to me in the world."

Just then, my eyes met Sundus's, and she was wearing no face veil. Holding the door to her room, she stared at me as though to confirm that I was really alive. Then she came over to me, swallowing hard, her head lowered.

"Thank God, you're well!" she said.

Her coldness made me angry.

"Where's the halva-maker?" I asked brusquely.

As she looked at me, I would swear that I saw her hugging me with her eyes. Love was cascading from her every pore. But she did not move.

I learned that the halva-maker's spirit was about to crack. He was isolated in his own room, and my mother was putting food by the door because she had been very worried about the chronic illness that had almost taken his infant son's life. The little boy had recovered, but the father had not.

I had killed any number of people since I had been made an amir again. I really had no idea whether the Caliph had ordered me to kill them, or whether he actually knew nothing about them. But the halva-maker's plight tore at my heart, as though it were my own brothers and father that had been killed. I sank to the floor in front of him.

"Your wife," I told him eagerly, "remained faithful to the point of death; her love for you was such that she was willing to neglect her own soul. Your son is fine. She's fine, too; she has to be fine, now that she's far removed from all the intrigues, conspiracies, popular squabbles, and changes in rulers. Today, no drought can affect her, and no fear can dominate her body. Do you hear me?"

I saw his eyes searching, although I had no idea for what. Then I guessed. I found myself searching for Sundus. I called her name as loudly as I could, and she came in, shaking. She looked at him without saying a single word, then burst into tears.

"Forgive him," I said forcefully.

She looked down, but did not say anything.

"The man's dying," I said, clasping her shoulder. "What kind of heart do you have? People who kill by mistake always pay an indemnity. You're still alive, woman. Forgive him!"

"I'm sorry for you, halva-maker," she muttered clearly. "I'm aware of the pain of loss and the terror of separation. But I don't forgive you; I never will. I pray that God may forgive you. He is merciful, but I'm not. There's little mercy on earth. The sweet taste of sugar fades away when confronted with the evil and corruption in people's hearts."

I gave her a frightened look. Her persistence was enough to make mountains shake in respect and rivers ripple at her power.

"Sundus," I chided her.

"Sundus will never be untrue to herself," she replied, wiping away her tears, "or hypocritical."

I had been saving up all kinds of stories to tell the halva-maker. I was anxious to hear how he had looked after his son, saving his life while he was dying. What did he think of this wife, to whom he had given only a few drops of affection, while she had given him her entire life? I wanted to talk to him and to complain about Sundus's power and dignity. It felt as though her sufferings had afforded the rest of her life the awesome aspect of angels and the perseverance of jinn confronting Solomon, even if he were dead. Sometimes, he was scared of her temper. She would never forget about things quickly, if ever.

"Mariam loved you," I told him. "That's a victory. Mas`ood is dead."

He gave me a smile and held out his fingers.

"I forgive you," he whispered, holding my hand. "Not only that..."

I was confused.

"Not only that?" I asked.

He closed his eyes.

"Perhaps you think you're my friend," I went on, "and find a part of your own self in me. Halva-maker, salamander, you who have exhausted rulers and commanders...don't you dare die now. Not before we've had a chance to talk, halva-maker.

As I left the room, my heart was filled with anger at everything. I looked at Sundus, who was cradling the baby in her arms.

"Can I speak to you, Amir?" she asked.

I looked at her for a moment, then went into her room, as she walked behind me. She put the baby down on her bed.

"If you'll allow me," she said, "I'll take care of him."

"Is that what you want?" I asked, feeling frustrated.

She moved a bit closer, then slipped behind me and started hugging my back. She kissed me on the neck.

"There's no longer any point," she whispered in a sorrowful tone. "Distance, fear, fasting, praying, and asking for forgiveness, none of them work. I haven't kept my oath."

I closed my eyes. I had so missed the smell of her. I did not move.

"When I found the doll and horse," she went on, running her face over my neck, "and discovered that you'd gone, my heart almost escaped my body and chased after you. I love you so much that I'm willing to risk even my own self. I thought I would never see you again and..."

I turned and hugged her so hard that her ribs groaned. I said nothing. Today, she was all mine, loving and feeling the stabs of passion and agonies of emotion. After a while, she let out a sigh as I kept hugging her.

"How I've missed you!" I whispered. "Did I have to create the doll and horse to make you happy?"

"You made them with your heart, Amir from Sicily!"

CHAPTER EIGHT

I am not sure: do I want to forget or remember what happened afterwards? I am someone who has spent an age riding horses with gilded saddles, but who has now started mixing sugar and flour, peeling pistachios and almonds, and copying the halva-maker. Yes indeed, all that has happened in spite of me. I light the firewood and wait for my wife to bring the sesame oil.

I have started working all day around the fireplace. At sunset, I set off for the sea, like a caged lion roaring in agony, waving a sword in my hand and blaming the passage of days. It was a sword of pure gold that Al-Hakim bi-amr Allah gave my father, Husain ibn Jawhar, when he named him Supreme Commander. He dressed my father in a red brocade coat, pearls, and a blue turban flecked with gold; that was a few months before he had my father slaughtered. I used to laugh at myself and my family as I searched for a horse amid the sands without ever finding it. What a sea, perched between cities that raged with suffering people, but had neither a ripple nor pity. It reminded me of the Pyramid Witch. Tell me, Bahnas, where are you today? You told me to follow the halva-maker. Today I have no idea whether I learned from him how to make halva or about the beauty of life, the tenderness of hearts, and the vision of rulers. I was surprised to find myself sticking to life for Sundus's sake and pitying her to the extent of actual affection. I wanted light-heartedness and frivolity not to be a sign of my love for her, and yet I would wait for darkness to fall to take her in my arms every day and tell her about my preoccupations. She would always listen closely, then stroke my heart as though to comfort my soul. I have never seen anyone so beautiful—I swear.

Everything in Egypt is changing with the change of the Coptic months. Every day brings us a new situation. Did I say 'we'? I forgot to tell you, my friend, that, amid the tumult of my war with myself—that is, my war just to stay alive, and my war to save those I love and do not love, I've forgotten to leave Egypt. That is right, I've forgotten. It's not possible to forget a beloved, even amid the conflagration of changing times. The Arabs say that love is for the first beloved, and I say that love is for an abode where I've tried to forget. While I pined for pleasures, it was the profound beauty inside it that aroused me. Do not ask me how; I have no idea, and I cannot explain my actions. I am a soldier and an émigré, and it as if I have come from a land I do not know to one that I barely know. In summary, I can say that I prefer to stay in Egypt, a place where my father and grandfather are buried.

I always used to talk about the months of the year in Coptic, moving from Tut with its wisdom, to the storms of Amshir and the cold of Tuba, without yet culling the harvest. I didn't bypass Baramuda, with all its goodness, but passed through Ba'una and travelled from East to West, as I anticipated the valley and the queen of the river. My wife still counts off the days in Coptic and refers to the Coptic months. That is all she knows of that language, but, for my part, I know that the Pyramid Witch holds the secret of the language and the ancients. For that reason, her knowledge is different from ours.

The Caliph Al-Hakim bi-Amr Allah is searching for Jawhar. He intends to amputate both his hands and cut out his tongue. However, he will still treat him and take care of his affairs. He has committed an unforgivable crime. Have any of you seen Jawhar, son of Husain, son of Jawhar the Sicilian? Where is his mother? The Caliph has ordered that, in order to honour her late husband, she is to be married to his general. Once Jawhar's hands have been amputated and his tongue cut out, people of Egypt, he will be handed over to his mother's care. Anyone who can find Jawhar will receive a reward. He was keeping company with a halva-maker. Where is that halva-maker?

I laughed; don't ask me why. I went back to Sundus and asked her which month we were in. Jawhar no longer exists; there is only the halva-maker. The person who died was a greedy vagrant, someone who wanted to keep company with commanders and live inside the bulging chest of the city of caliphs. He died and has not risen again. He left his soul, shameless and sinful, to blend with that of the halva-maker. One of them disappeared, and the other remained, seeking forgiveness. Having abandoned the sword, he now lives by dough; after burning the city, he now sticks to firewood.

"That's all we have left," I told Sundus as she slept beside me.

She nodded.

"Do you love the soldier more than the halva-maker?" I asked her.

"It's the Sicilian I love," she replied with conviction.

"'Abdallah the halva-maker's son is entrusted to me," I said.

"He's my son, too."

"That's what I expected you to say."

She seemed tense.

"He's a Sunni, Jawhar," she muttered.

"He is," I replied with a smile, "and so are you."

"Does that annoy you, Sicilian?" she asked.

"No, it doesn't. As long as we're worshipping the same deity, let's put disagreements aside. History is full of treachery, and treachery makes no distinction between religious schools and faiths."

Months went by, and the Caliph found neither me nor my mother. He married my father's wife to one of his generals. Gradually the halva-maker grew inside me like the fig tree that can grow without water or attention. I found myself getting really good at assessing and decorating halva. I heard that the Caliph had started going into the mountains on his own to communicate with the stars. He had styled himself a man of learning, traveling with a servant behind him who would be carrying medicine, sword, and paper in a satchel slung over his shoulder. People said that the Caliph had his fill of caliphal luxuries and started living like a monk. He only greeted his armed forces on festival days. One day, he went out through the city gates, looked at it for an unusually long time, and stared down at the Ahmad ibn Tulun Mosque from the mountain. Al-Hakim had built his own mosque in Cairo to rival that of Ibn Tulun, but people in Cairo still preferred Ibn Tulun's mosque. People say that he stared long and hard at the Ibn Tulun Mosque, then disappeared. People say that he was killed; that he preferred the ascetic life and devotion; and that he was possessed by the Sufi spirit, just as I was by the halva-maker's spirit. Like the Coptic month, he came to his end, and the new month arrived. My mother emerged overjoyed.

"Now we can go back to our house and Cairo." she announced. "The Caliph's dead. His successor is his son, Az-Zahir li-i`zaz din Allah. I've heard that it was his sister who killed him, either her or a Maghrebi general named Saif ad-din Husain ibn `Ali ibn Dawwas. No one knows exactly."

"That's all past and over," I declared.

I said nothing more, and she did not ask.

At the beginning of the Coptic month Abib, they finally found me.

Guards surrounded the halva-maker's store and demanded to talk to the halva-maker. When I went out, I was afflicted by the lethargy that had recently come over me in the face of all the guards, governors, wars, and slogans. A man looked at me. He seemed to be either a Maghrebi general or perhaps someone from the Kutama tribe. He stepped closer.

"Are you the halva-maker?" he whispered.

"Yes, I am," I replied calmly.

"You look like a soldier," he said, glancing at my arms and shoulders, "not a halva-maker."

"Don't let appearances deceive you, my Lord," I replied with a smile. "We've learned from the Caliph that someone who looks devout is in fact the devil personified, while someone dressed in sinful garb may actually be somewhat devout in his heart."

"Are you making fun of the Caliph?"

"I wouldn't dare."

I stayed silent, and Sundus crept behind me and held my hand. For the first time in my life, I could sense some fear in her bodily scent—Sundus, who was never scared or shaken. I felt like laughing, but I did not out of respect for the general.

He stared at me.

"I've brought you a letter, Jawhar," he said. "It's from Saif ad-din ibn `Ali ibn Dawwas. I know who you are. It isn't right for the son of the Commander-in-chief to become a halva-maker, or for the line of the man who built Cairo and the Al-Azhar Mosque to disappear."

I did not speak. Sundus held onto my arm. I looked at her.

"Go back to your room," I told her.

But she did not go. I could hear her staggered breathing. She was in her final month, about to give birth. I did not know whether the baby inside her could sense what was going on all round her.

"Al-Hakim bi-amr Allah went out to the mountain," the man said, "and didn't come back. Today there is general amnesty. The new Caliph is correcting his father's mistakes, and they are many..."

"I know nothing."

"There's been widespread inflation, and Egyptians have died."

"I make halva."

"Your grandfather was Egyptian..."

"He used to make halva."

"No, he didn't. You're spouting nonsense, man. I'm telling you: Al-Hakim's regime's over. I've come here today to ask you to acknowledge your lineage and name and return to Cairo, head held high. Saif ad-din ibn `Ali ibn Dawwas needs you there. By God's decree, Al-Hakim's regime is at an end. You've nothing to fear any longer, either you or your mother."

For a moment, there was silence.

"Go back to the general," I told him calmly, "and tell him that you found only the halva-maker."

"What you're doing is ridiculous, almost insane. I know who you are."

"This is the halva-maker's country."

"Sicilian!"

"The Sicilian's a halva-maker, general."

"Things are stable now. Forget the past. All those mistakes are going to be corrected by the new Caliph."

"With rulers, there's never stability, and there's no life without the past. That said, I can provide the general, the Caliph, and all Egyptians with halva."

"You're going to regret it," the general said with a shrug.

"Would you like to have a taste of the Sicilian's sugared doughnut?"

"Insanity's a disease that's spreading in this country!"

"Egyptians are waiting for delicious treats on festival days. Don't stop those traditions—the mawlid doll and the cavalier on horseback. That's a tradition that I invented. I, the halva-maker."

"Think about it. I'm offering you a way of honouring your parents."

"I already have it."

"With dough and sugar, man?!"

"That's right, general."

"Listen, man," he said sorrowfully. "You're the grandson of the man who built the city of Cairo, with all its people!"

"Originally, he was a halva-maker," I replied confidently.

1437AH / 2016CE

Months before my daughter's wedding, I had gone to see `Amm `Abdo the halva-maker. She had asked for different kinds of halva, some with foreign names. But my daughter was determined that her wedding was going to be traditional, and she was looking for types of halva about which I knew nothing. She said they dated from the Fatimid period. I was worried about her craziness and the scandal that would ensue, but I found myself heading for a halva-maker with multiple stories so I could understand what was drawing her to popular types of halva. It made me feel unexpectedly sad. I learned things I had not anticipated and began to feel anxious—and I'm not the type to shed tears. My daughter may have realised things that I had not; how hard it is for parents when their children realise things before they do!

"So what happened to the Sicilian?" I asked impatiently.

`Amm `Abdo the halva-maker told me that the man who built Cairo was originally a halva-maker. Maybe, if you asked people, they wouldn't know the origins of the word 'halva-maker'. If they did know, they would tell you that the halva-maker was the man who built Cairo. They would claim that he was Jawhar the Sicilian, Cairo's builder. People believe wrongly that, before Jawhar the Sicilian built Cairo, he was a halva-maker. He was not, nor was his father. He was a warrior, kidnapped from Sicily before his fate was decided.

"Do you understand me, my daughter? You need to understand. The person who thought up the mawlid halva and overcame grief through his genius and craftsmanship was Jawhar, the son of Husain, the son of Jawhar the Sicilian, thus the grandson of Jawhar the Sicilian. As I've told you, he made halva in an era when everything was confused. Loss and grief were widespread. The communal pact disappeared and was replaced by something else. While Cairo remained, its walls, which had been built by his grandfather, were demolished. However, halva made with sugar thrived, generation after generation, conveying a sense of victory after so many defeats and of satisfaction after impotence. What the halva-maker made, after being both an amir and general, has lived on, while, whether today or tomorrow, the violence of the city's rulers has vanished. The sweet taste of sugar remains to remind us of the things that deserve to remain in this world, even if tyranny spreads. Dazzled looks in the eyes of children need to be tolerated year after year. Do you understand? Inevitably, you don't. The man who built Cairo was a halva-maker. But Cairo was not built by Jawhar the Sicilian, whose city walls separated the populace from the Fatimids. No, Cairo was built by the man who made the doll and cavalier. A few of those walls that separate and protect may still survive, but the sweet taste of sugar is definitely still there in your mouth. Or don't you eat sugary things? Make sure that you're not like today's girls who are scared of sugar or long for Western candy. Anyone who does not grind his teeth while chewing the horse's head has never eaten real halva."

I suppressed my sorrow and lack of initiative. I had probed as far as I could.

"You'll be coming back tomorrow," he said, "and you'll see for yourself the wooden horse, something you've inherited from my grandfather."

"Which grandfather?"

"I have a grandfather who's Armenian, another who's Sicilian, and many other ancestors who are Egyptian, Shi`i, Sunni, and Christian. If you like American cheesecake, don't come back tomorrow."

"No," I replied firmly, "I'll come. Will you tell me about Saladin?"

"Patience is the gateway to relief. First, I'll tell you about the Armenian."

THE SECOND STORY

THE ARMENIAN

My people and I, I see them rent asunder by doctrines,

Even though relationships were what originally formed us.

I am a stranger, and, wherever I cast my eye,

My family is alone, while around me my men are in cliques.

I have gained experience of both days and people,

And practiced until experience has taught me.

Abu Firas al-Hamdani, Abbasid poet.

"You promised to show me the wooden horse," I told ʿAmm ʿAbdo the madman impatiently, "and tell me about the Armenian. But, for seven days now, you've been making types of halva about which I know nothing. You haven't told me anything."

He was mixing saffron with flour and sugar.

"I hoped you'd learn," he replied. "But you didn't open your heart to the basandud cakes and doughnuts."

"They're just bits of halva," I said with a sigh.

"Tell me, Madam," he said, "what did the Sicilian halva-maker say? Do you remember? 'Just like humanity itself, it can take many long hours to make this halva, but you can eat it in seconds. Like building and destruction, you need years to construct the cavalier, but, when war comes, it can finish him off overnight. But don't despair. In hours of craft lies every kind of pleasure. When you've finished making halva, you have to eat it. Every soul has its particular power and scope. Do you know what distinguishes ʿAbdallah the halva-maker's halva? It's that, while he is making it, he is fully the soul that inhabits every creature.'"

"Do you think ʿAbdallah the halva-maker is your grandfather?" I asked immediately.

"He is my grandfather," he replied. "But not of my thoughts. When I'm governed by thoughts, I lose my mind. Telling the story can bring about a cure. When you listen to the story, you too are cured of your heedlessness."

"Tell me about the Armenian and reassure me about the Sicilian."

"Are you still asking about the Sicilian?" ʿAmm Abduh asked. "He's still making halva in Fustat for people in Cairo and all over Egypt. The most important ingredients that distinguish Fatimid halva are musk, saffron, and sugar, which are blended carefully with flour and sesame oil. It's a kind of halva that is only worthwhile when it's mixed with all the other amounts. It's like Egypt; whenever anything different is added to it, it's mixed in with the ingredients and gives its sweetness a wonderful taste and colour. Like sesame oil, the Sicilian will add fat to the mixture and stimulate the appetite. From the wooden horse that he inherited from his Sicilian grandfather, he will make an Egyptian horse, one with no strength, and a doll like the statues of the ancients with moonlike features and the sun's gleam.

So here, my daughter, you can see perfect craft, and a struggle to earn a living, a country like no other. You mix the sesame oil with sugar and flour, then add saffron, which gives it a bright yellow colour. Like the saffron, the Armenian came from a distant land, as did the Sicilian. He was blended in life's container; his soul was thus purified, and his heart shattered from a thousand years of bodily exertion. Like saffron, the halva is no good without the Armenian. If you try eating it without colour, you find out what you've missed and not savoured.

BOOK ONE

Damascus 460AH / 1067CE

There are times, Sicilian, when destiny will toss onto the shoulders of passers-by a heavy load—the kind of heroic deed you have heard about in stories. Do not question destiny about its deeds. God knows things that we do not.

Bahnas, the Pyramid Witch

CHAPTER ONE

Ever since the Governor of Damascus hosted us in his palace, life has not been the same. The palace has little gold. It's all shades of monochrome, with no decoration, alcoves, or pillars. What governor could possibly stay in such a place? You long for Fustat, days of wealth, and halva stuffed with honey, sesame oil, pistachio, and almonds. But most of all you long for the maulid doll. The Maulid is tomorrow, and today you'll only be making the actual maulid doll, with its colourful decoration. You will put a crown of coloured leaves on it. How much you are missing colours! Ever since they left Egypt, colours have disappeared.

She had stayed up till dawn, making the doll as her father had taught her as a young girl. She had sucked the vestiges of the dough off her fingers and sat down to look with pride at what her hands had crafted. All her sisters and relatives would be envious. People would say that Furoon is making halva while the Egyptians are dying of hunger. Her father managed to escape to Damascus with all his money, leaving her uncle and the rest of the family to plagues, drought, and cannibals. Things had turned much harder and become the norm until life itself was a luxury and death was inevitable. Was not death always inevitable? Now that life itself had become something to endure reluctantly, the simple act of staying alive had turned into a luxury. So then, she would keep her doll hidden from people; today no one could find any sugar, water, or even colours and utensils. Furoon was always sensitive, and she worried about what people were feeling, not least because she had stolen the sugar from the Amir's kitchen. She would have to think about what her father, sister, brother, and uncle might say...

How she longed for Egypt and its blessed River Nile! How scared she felt about going back, knowing nothing about today's Egypt or daring to confront the feelings of regret, loss, and sorrow. She put her doll far away from the lamps. The cold weather in Syria would help keep the doll fresh for as long as possible. She slept for an hour or two, then woke up to the sound of whispers and laughter. She looked all around her like someone who has just been arrested and is about to die. She found the doll in her sister's hands, pushing it toward her other sister's hands.

"Please don't break it!" she yelled, stretching out her hand.

"What's the matter with you, Furoon?" her sister asked, obviously out to annoy her. "Gentle Furoon with her tender heart, always thinking about her family; Furoon, who hates tyranny and death. But here she is, secretly eating halva, toying with it, and making a doll when there's widespread drought and hardship."

She stayed silent, summoning her reserves of courage, and lowered her head in shame.

"I'm going to tell Father and the whole house," her sister went on. "You're greedy. Where did you get the sugar? Did you steal it? Your family in Cairo is dying of hunger. Kind and generous Furoon, the girl who cried when we came here because we were leaving the family in dire straits, is now making and eating halva when death is all around."

"I haven't made it for myself," she said immediately, "I haven't."

"You're lying," her two sisters replied. "You were eating it just now, on your own."

"I swear I didn't make it for myself."

She muttered an apology, and God is merciful. But her two sisters, who were many years older than her, were cruelty personified.

Her sister turned the doll over in her hands.

"So who did you make it for?" she asked, with the doll still in her hands. "Which man deserves such a prize?"

She looked all around her, pleading for help from someone for her troubled mind. Her sister asked the same question again.

"I made them for the Governor of Damascus, the Amir," she said. "He's the one who's invited us. Don't destroy them. Give them to my father to give to him."

"Your father," her sister scoffed. "Of course, he's *your* father! He always favours you over us. You'll make a deal with him, and then you eat the halva by yourself. We don't even know the governor; we've never set eyes on him."

She apologised again.

"I swear I made them for him," she said.

"You're lying," her sister yelled. "You're a hypocrite, the devil's own daughter who'll go straight to hell! You pretend to be so innocent, but you're evil personified. If you've really made them for the Governor Amir, then go now and take them to him while we watch. Are you going to swear you've not tasted sugar? Go on then, swear."

"I'll go and give them to him," she shot back, pursing her lips. "Do you think I'm scared? I'm not!"

"But he won't receive you, poor girl. You're nothing. Give me the doll to give to him. If I ask my husband to give them to him..."

"No!" Furoon replied firmly. "I said that I made them for him, and I'll be the one to give them to him. Give me back the doll, or else I'm going to tell my father and the governor."

The two sisters looked baffled

"Fine!" they both said. "Go on and defy us, Furoon. Go and see him then, and we'll follow you. If you start eating them on the way, be ready to be spanked the way we did when you were little. Do you remember?"

"Get out of my room," she replied, hiding her fear. "I need to get dressed."

Furoon walked along the long corridor with her two sisters behind her as she had expected. It truly was just like entering a prison, where she would be either killed or tortured. She stopped by the Amir's door and asked the guards to let her greet him and give him a present from the Sicilian's family, `Ali the halva-maker, her father, whom the Amir was hosting along with his family. He was the son of `Abdallah, the halva-maker who had been a friend of Jawhar, son of Husain the Sicilian. `Abdallah had saved his life, and so

Jawhar son of Husain had taken care of his son, `Ali, and married him to his daughter, `Azeeza. `Azeeza's much-travelled mother was the granddaughter of Jawhar the Sicilian. But the Amir knew that, of course. The guard was astonished and told her to leave, but she insisted on meeting the Amir herself.

"You do realise, don't you," her sister whispered in her ear, "that the Amir's going to kill you as soon as he sets eyes on you. You're bothering him on a workday just to give him a doll doughnut. If I were the Amir, I'd flay you alive."

She suppressed her fears and waited for the guard to return. He gestured to her to go inside. She blushed, and her hands started shaking so much that she was worried she might demolish the doll before she had given it to him. She had to fret. If her two sisters found out that she had stolen sugar from the Amir's house the day before...O my God, if the Amir found out! She was a thief, that's all. In a rash moment, she had wanted to bring back the days of yore. Now here she was, in front of the Amir. She held out her shaking hand and looked up.

He raised an eyebrow, expecting her to say something. Now, she swore a solemn oath that was no lie, namely that never in her entire life had she seen a more handsome man. His square face, pointed nose, rugged jaw, and eyes... Those honey-coloured eyes were a whole sea of honey, the very best kinds of clover-flavoured honey. She plunged into them before she remembered why it was she had come and what she was planning to do. He looked forty, or maybe late thirties.

"Young lady," he said with a frown. "Have you come here just to stare at me?"

She stretched out her hand. But first, she looked all around her to make sure her sisters could not see her, and discovered that they had disappeared before she had entered the room. In fact, the entire universe seemed to have vanished.

"I've come to give you a present, my Lord," she said. "And to thank you for your kindness to us. My Lord, I'm the daughter of `Ali, the Sicilian-Egyptian halva-maker. I've come..."

Before she could finish, the doll fell out of her hands and smashed into tiny pieces on the palace floor right before their eyes.

"Forgive me!" she said sadly as she bent down. "It was a doll for the Maulid. I came..."

Pausing for a moment, she took a piece of it, and, without even realising what she was doing, she put it in her mouth and swallowed it. She stood up again.

"My Lord," she said, wiping her mouth, "I'm ready to be punished. I brought you a gift, but then..."

He gestured for her to sit down and examined her as though she were a horse that had just lost its homeland and family.

"Are you the daughter of `Ali, the husband of the Sicilian woman from Fustat?"

"Yes."

"What did you make for me?"

"A bride-doll."

"Do you make people in Egypt, then eat them?"

"No, my Lord, it's from halva, just halva."

"In prosperous times it's halva, but, when poverty is widespread, you eat the living and the dead. What's your name?"

"Furoon."

"What kind of name is that?"

She hesitated, her eyes still riveted on his face.

"I don't know," she replied. "I was the youngest of my sisters. When my mother gave birth to me, she was making halva in the *furn*, so they called me Furoon."

"But the plural of the Arabic word *furn* is *afraan*. Why didn't they call you Afraan?"

"She wasn't thinking too clearly at the time," she replied with a spontaneous grin. "Sooner or later, you're going to find out: I stole some sugar from your kitchen yesterday. But I made the doll for you, not for me. How we all long for halva, my Lord. Did you know that, since we came here to Damascus, my father has stopped making halva out of sympathy for our family in Egypt?"

"You've a lot to say," he told her with a frown. "Take off your veil."

With a shaking hand, she removed her veil and looked down.

"Don't torture me," she said. "I can't stand that. Don't cut my hand off. I made it for you."

"Do you have any other instructions to give the Governor?"

She shook her head. Her mouth fell open, as she could not explain the shock she was feeling. She was terrified at the way her heart was racing, and her eyelids would not stop blinking.

"Do you like halva, Furoon?"

Before she could answer, he gestured to the guard, and they brought in a tray full of the sweets called judge's morsels, as well as fresh kunafa. With another gesture, he ordered them all to leave. The only people left in the room were him and her.

"Guests have to be properly treated," he told her. "Go ahead and eat."

Eyes popping, she stared at the tray of halva and did not even think. She plunged her hand into the tray and shifted the sweets from tray to mouth without stopping for perhaps a whole hour, while he watched her silently. The last time she had tasted halva had been three years earlier, and she was now eighteen years old. Three whole years without a single grain of sugar.

He watched her in silence, his chin resting on his hand. When she'd had enough, she burst into tears as she sucked the sugar off her fingers.

"Forgive me, Father," she said. "Forgive me, my family still in Egypt! I realise that I don't deserve to be alive, I realise, my Lord..."

"Yes, Furoon," he said mockingly, "keep talking. I want to spend two hours of my time listening to you talking about your tragedy with sugar and to leave the populace and army outside."

"Forgive me, my Lord," she replied bashfully, "I forgot who I am."

She fell silent.

"Have you had enough halva?" he asked her deliberately.

She nodded enthusiastically.

"I'm not forgetting my rights here," he went on. "You've stolen sugar, and then you claimed that you were making a doll-bride for me to eat because apparently you people in Egypt eat women. I didn't get the doll, and you haven't paid for the sugar."

"I'm at your command, my Lord."

She stood up and did her best to look away from his face, but she could not do it.

"Today," he instructed her, "you'll go to the kitchen and make me another halva doll. I'll be waiting for you."

"When?" she asked at once.

"When what?"

"When will you see me again?"

"When you finish making the doll."

"I can finish today."

"No, I can't do it today. Tomorrow perhaps, or the day after. You'll know."

"How will I know?"

"Come on, daughter of `Ali the halva-maker," he replied impatiently. "Leave my presence now. Why are you so bold? Are all Egyptian girls like you?"

"But I've never seen any man as handsome as you," she muttered to herself.

"What was that you said?" he asked.

"I beg your pardon, my Lord," she replied, rushing for the door. "I'll start making the doll for you to eat."

Passion always involves circumstances, vicissitudes, and a cryptic sense of offense against the heart. Giving itself as a gift to another heart is never easy. God is aware that the heart is a stern critic, oppressive and brutal, but no match for the brutality of passion. As she buried her head in the pillow, she could see him all around her in the moonlight, in the confines of the old house, in the smell of burnt sugar and boiling honey. The pupils of his eyes harboured the entire world, everything she did not know, but wanted to find out. She could not rouse herself, and she had no desire to confront her world.

Even though Furoon was eighteen years old, she had never been married. In her country, people were eating babies and fighting each other over corpses and dead animals. Wars, destruction, and plague were all gnawing at the living, then turned to the dead and erasing their life and history. She realised that it was probably impossible to go back, but how she missed Egypt! And now she was in love, choosing something that she could not hope to achieve. Her arms were short, while the full moon was in the heavens. How many women longed for him? A man that handsome was bound to have slain lovers and killed virgins with his looks alone. Now here she was, like other girls, rhapsodising about his beauty. For her to be in love with him was perfectly normal. How many girls had done the same? If she did not love him for his beauty, then she did for his rigor, his sword, his status, and his prestige. Ah, Badr, what have you done to my heart? If only you realised how my heart is racing after a single meeting!

Hafsa, her brother's wife and her tutor on religion and learning, called her. She was shocked.

"You haven't read the Qur'an today," she told Furoon, "and you didn't go to your lesson. What's the matter with you, Furoon? Have you forgotten who you are?"

"I'm afraid of offending God," she replied shyly, turning to face Hafsa.

"His mercy is wide enough for everything. As you know, He willingly accepts those who sin and disobey."

She shuddered, and tears welled in her eyes.

"Hug me, Hafsa," she said, opening her arms.

"What's the matter with you?" Hafsa asked, giving her a hug.

"First tell me honestly," she pleaded, "am I beautiful?"

"By God," Hafsa replied, looking straight at her, "I've never seen any girl as beautiful as you in all of Egypt and Syria. You have a face like an angel. If it weren't for the famine, you'd have been married by the time you were thirteen. Your mother, Sundus, is grandmother to all of us. She was just as beautiful before she was burned. If the sea set eyes on you, it would lower its waves in honour of your beauty. Ever since you were a little girl, your beauty has been dazzling people."

"Is passionate love a sin?" Furoon asked, her hand over her heart.

"Your Lord is the Lord of hearts, my daughter," Hafsa replied. "You've always been like the daughter that I've never had. Passionate love is not a sin."

"But what about love for a different kind of man?"

"Different how?"

"I believe I'm in love with Badr, son of ʿAbdallah al-Jamali, the owner of this palace."

Hafsa froze in place and moved away from Furoon.

"Are you out of your mind?" Hafsa asked.

"You've just said that the heart is God's creation. He knows that I've no choice when it comes to the one I love."

"You've admired his good looks. But that's not love."

"I've started following his footsteps. I go out at night and look up at the moon, hoping that it'll shine brightly, to remind me of him. I hide behind trees and look around, in case I see his shadow at dawn. Whenever I see him, Hafsa, my entire body starts convulsing and all my joints open up."

"This is serious, and a calamity for us. Control yourself, Furoon. You've no hope. The Amir Badr al-Jamali is not of the same religion as us and knows nothing about our country. To tell you the truth, I've heard my father-in-law say bad things about him. He doesn't trust him."

"But he's been kind, opening his house to us."

"Governance involves a lot of things that are crazy and illogical. Like magic, you can't anticipate it or realise how risky it is."

"Hafsa, ever since I was born, I have never suffered this way or felt so happy. If I dream about him, if...do you think my dreams are sinful?"

"Remember, I've taught you hadith and jurisprudence because you asked me. You wanted to teach women and raise their status. That's a loftier goal than love, nobler and more lasting. Suppress this passion in your heart; it's hopeless. Badr al-Jamali has seventy slave-girls, Furoon, of every colour and from every land. He has not just one son, but three. He'll never look at you or bother about you. I hear he's merciless and harsh, attacking enemies in seconds and shedding blood. Forget him. If you want to be married, there are suitable men for you in Syria. I'll talk to your brother today."

"Don't do that, I beg you. I don't want to be married. I'll go to the lessons and suppress the love in my heart."

Furoon does not remember her mother, but she does know Hafsa's scent and hugs. When her mother ʿAzeeza died, she was only six years old. Hafsa took her to her own room and hugged her. She told Furoon that, from then on, she would be her daughter. Hafsa never had any children, and her brother did not try to marry. He was afraid of tyranny. Hafsa was the daughter of a legist shaikh; she had learned about prophetic hadith and memorised God's book. He would never find a woman as loyal as her. Furoon's father, ʿAli, never remarried after her mother's death. He devoted his attention to the workshops of Jawhar, who had brought him up, and the halva stores that, as he had pledged to Jawhar, would be more important to him than his own children and would remain a central part of the history of the Sicilian and his family. He would tell his children about their grandfather, Jawhar the Sicilian, who had built Cairo, conquered Egypt, and constructed the Al-Azhar Mosque. He would go on to tell them about Jawhar, the grandson, son of the martyred Husain, son of Jawhar the Sicilian, who had been treacherously killed. That was Jawhar, who had made his wife a doll out of halva and a cavalier on horseback, wearing a sword and turban. He had crafted the two pieces for her to let her know that there was still some sweetness left in the world and that the taste of sugar, even if it were just a little inside the mouth, would always help mitigate the pain and ugliness that emerged from the heart, but not the body. ʿAli urged his son to remarry, but he refused. With his daughters, their husbands, and his youngest daughter, Furoon, he fled the country to escape certain death. Even so, he never forgot the pledge he had made to himself, to preserve the way halva was made in Egypt. At one point, ʿAli was halva-maker for the Caliph. After that, he occupied the same position with Ibn Hamdan, the Caliph's minister. When the situation became dire, the minister Ibn Hamdan advised him to take his money and escape. He also advised him to stay in the palace of Badr al-Jamali, the Governor of Damascus, even though for some time Badr had been an enemy of Ibn Hamdan. The two men were rivals and competitors. At first, ʿAli could not understand why his friend had advised him to stay in the Governor's palace or why the Governor had agreed to let him stay in his residence, even though he was aware of ʿAli's friendship with Ibn Hamdan. ʿAli had no idea about the chicanery and brute force of rulers. What Ibn Hamdan wanted was a spy inside Badr al-Jamali's palace, and what Badr needed was someone inside his house to spy on Ibn Hamdan. Between the two men, ʿAli became someone to be carefully watched. Badr al-Jamali did not meet him, even after the family had moved into his residence. The only member of the halva-maker's family whom he'd met was Furoon.

An aspect of God's greatness is that He will listen without laying blame, even when the words emerge like death-throes: foolish, genuine, or hurtful.

"O Lord," she whispered to Him, "is my love for him punishment for stealing sugar? But he has not punished me for something I did in a foolish moment. Actually, maybe it's a work-based punishment. I stole the sugar, and my heart was lost. But he has forgiven me for stealing the sugar. Will You never forgive me and wrest my love for him from my heart? Why do I need to struggle for the rest of my life? Are You tormenting one of Your servants, a girl who has only wished well for the people around her? If his intentions toward me are good, then make him draw close, change his religious affiliation, and sacrifice everything for my sake. Make him appreciate the value of learning and religious scholars, showing his fear of God in the way he treats his subjects and distances himself from wars and conspiracies. Don't make him like my father. As you well know, my Lord God, my father is greedy and can only envision halva factories and a Sicilian family name. He never looks at things that are more significant and further in the future. We only have a short life, and money is a temptation, like lineage and children. But he does not realise. Do not make him like my father, Lord. Change him so that I can either be married to him or push him away. Why do I have to fall in love with a soldier who was an Armenian Mamluk and then became an amir, one of the Imam Caliph's supporters? Of all the men on earth, why did You select the Shi'ite Badr for me? Why did You make him so handsome? Those eyes of his...those lashes that provoke sin...Push him away from me, Lord. There's no avoiding struggle.

"You have saved me, Lord; I realise that. I was on the edge of a fiery pit. After my mother's death, You rescued me and did not desert me. Instead, You sent a sister-in-law just like my mother, the daughter of a pious shaikh who knows mercy and works with God's holy book. You also sent me a brother to be like a father to me, to take care of me like the children he never had. I realise that You made them both clasp me to their shoulders in order to rescue me from my two elder sisters who do not care about me. You have given me a mother in Hafsa and an affectionate and courageous uncle in Jawhar the Sicilian in Alexandria. He is still making halva and looking after the first Jawhar store. Then there's my father—I love him and blame him. I love him and realise that he is concerned about us. But I still blame him for running away. I wanted to die in Egypt, even if it was from hunger. My uncle, Abu l-Qaasim, did not run away. My father says that I am naïve, inexperienced, and stupid. I have never known hunger or suffered any hardship. O Lord, sometimes I am more afraid of my father than I am of You. You are my beloved and friend. Your punishment is light, and Your knowledge is enormous. Do You know what is in my heart? Should I feel ashamed of this new passion or embrace it? How can I rest my head on a flame that sears the brow like bitter cold? Help me to see and understand.

Forgive me for falling short or following my desires."

She took three days to make a perfect doll with passion. She asked to see him to give it to him, but she was not permitted. The guard told her that he was busy; he would give the doll to his master. She refused and insisted that the guard tell his master that Furoon wanted to give it to him in person, as she had promised. The guard went in, then came back and said that the governor was busy. She came back the next day, and the same thing happened. Two days, then three.

"Why haven't you told him?" she asked the guard impatiently. "It's part of your job to tell him."

"I have told him," the guard replied angrily. "As I've told you, he doesn't have time."

In despair, she took the doll and handed it over to the guard. Returning to her room, she talked to her Lord.

"Have you pushed him away from me, Lord?" she asked. "So quickly? Can't I see him once or twice more, and then You can push him away?"

Every night she slunk out to see him, sitting on his own after midnight in his palace garden. She hid behind a tree, and no sooner did she set eyes on him than her heart recovered and endured.

Badr ibn `Abdallah al-Jamali. Hafsa, her brother's wife, her intimate friend and tutor, now told her everything about him. He was Armenian, and Jamal ad-daula ibn `Ammaar had bought him as a young boy. People say that he was kidnapped from slavers during a raid and brought up as a Muslim and soldier. He was courageous and honest, but also vicious and stubborn. No one ever knows, Furoon, what is going on inside his mind. When he was not yet eighteen, he was married to a lady chosen for him by Jamal ad-daula. Once he was manumitted, he became one of those closest to Jamal ad-daula. His former wife, Amina Khatun, was the daughter of one of his soldiers. The marriage lasted for ten years. She bore him three sons and a daughter, and then they both decided to get divorced. That does not happen very often, Furoon, but he's cruel. People say that his relationship with his wife was insipid and cold; she did not love him, nor he her. However, that's common in their milieu.

Marriage is always a matter of convenience. But why has he never been married to anyone else and kept her in his care? People suggest that he grew up in a different kind of environment and was affected by it. Over there, a man is only married to a single woman, but he claims that he's being honest with himself. He doesn't want to tie his ex-wife's fate to his. She was married to another man, but he died. She has stayed unmarried, and her house is not far from the palace. Even so, Furoon, the honesty that he claims has not stopped him from purchasing beautiful slave girls, one after another. Your father doesn't like him, Furoon, as you well know. Your father's an ally of the minister Ibn Hamdan and the Shareef Abu Taher. They both belong to our sect, Furoon. They pray for the Abbasid Caliph, but not the Fatimid Imam who's caused us this catastrophe, leaving country and family behind. Your father's right.

"But he still eats at Badr al-Jamali's house," Furoon said defiantly, "and sleeps in his palace."

"That's different, my daughter. Understand me. You're young and don't understand. Do you notice that Badr has never received your father even once? He invited him to his palace when he found out that your father was an ally of Shareef Abu Taher. He wanted to keep an eye on him because he realised that the Sicilian's family was one of the most important in Cairo and Fustat. If the family emigrated to Syria, then he would have to keep them in his house, but out of fear, not charity. It's been a year or more, Furoon, since Badr lost his position in Damascus. The amirs opposed him because he's so cruel, as I've told you. The way he treats them is harsh and unbefitting an amir. He has no understanding of the Syrian people and their instinct for freedom and exuberance. He's a stranger here, Furoon, with a strange temperament that no one understands. Instead of a single guard, he has three that he keeps around him at all times. Do you understand why it's impossible for there to be anything between the two of you? It all stands in your way, my daughter!"

"Hafsa, what's my father planning?"

"Your father wants to preserve his country and factories. For him, the family name is more important than all rulers combined."

"What I mean is that, if he's an ally of Shareef Abu Taher and the minister Ibn Hamdan, does he intend to damage the Amir somehow...?"

Hafsa put her hand over Furoon's mouth.

"Make sure you don't say that in front of anyone," she told Furoon. "You can be certain that Badr could kill your father today with no mercy. Stop dreaming, my daughter. Don't dream that he's looking at you, because you're an enemy, and he knows that. Badr's one of the few men in Syria who's still loyal to the Fatimid Imam and Caliph, Al-Mustansir. Even in Egypt itself, prayers for him have often been cut off in favour of the Abbasid Caliph in Baghdad. Badr's betting on the loser, and your father's putting his money on the winner. Do you understand?"

"Hafsa, you've taught me that life is a matter of illusion, that the game of maisir is forbidden, and that filth is the devil's doing. So why is my father busying his mind with profits or defeat?"

"Maybe for the same reason that you're busying your mind with a hopeless passion and neglecting your studies."

"I swear to you I'm not neglecting them. I've memorised ten hadiths. Do you want to hear them?"

"My daughter," she replied with a smile. "You're basically my daughter—you realise that, don't you? In you, I can see a scholar who'll teach others and help women around her. Don't disappoint me. How about your prayers? Are you thinking about anything but God?"

"I know He's merciful," she replied, swallowing hard. "I'm doing my best."

"'The human heart incites evil' [Qur'an, Sura 12 (Yusuf), v. 53]. Watch yourself, Furoon!"

Furoon wanted to feel free and to have Hafsa's strength, but she could not. She loved sugar and, had she been able, would have consumed a lot of it. Now she adores Badr al-Jamali, and dearly wishes to immerse herself in his love until time comes to an end.

CHAPTER TWO

No one knows if Badr al-Jamali is aware of the plots being hatched all around him. His close friend and secretary, ` Abd al-Wahhab, asked him to be lenient and generous with the soldiers. Ever since the famine in Egypt, they had become used to receiving generous rewards. But Badr al-Jamali had refused. He surrounded himself with a few trustworthy soldiers, to defend his palace against attacks of the sort that had happened before. He also realised that ` Ali, the son of the Sicilian, was an enemy lurking inside his own palace. Every day, ` Ali would go through his things, searching for letters and listening in on his conversations. He had no desire to meet him.

Ibn Hamdan and Abu Taher had made a pact with Haidar, some Bedouin tribes in Syria, and ` Ali the halva-maker. Their intent was to do away with Badr al-Jamali, either by killing him or severing his limbs, which was always more effective. Ibn Hamdan collected all the money left in the Egyptian treasury—four thousand dinars—and sent it all to Abu Taher, asking him to purchase some men. War was coming, and Badr would eventually leave Damascus, never to return.

` Ali, the son of the Sicilian halva-maker, had made halva for palaces, ministers, and the Caliph himself: Sicilian kunafa, Sicilian doughnuts, and halva dolls that the treasures of all the Fatimids could not rival. The secret ingredients in halva could addle the brain even more than wine, and knowledge of the right proportions made the halva-maker the supreme arbiter in matters of destinies and desires. Ever since the start of the Sicilian family's era, their passion for halva had involved them in the governance of Egypt and linked them to the rulers by marriage. Throughout his life, ` Ali had been eager to remain chief halva-maker in every Islamic dominion. But then, years of hardship had arrived, and the flour era came to an end. A few pounds of flour cost as much as a few pounds of gold. People sweated for a few grains of bread and completely forgot how sugar tasted. When the crisis first started, he took all his gold and property with him and fled to Syria, but he met Ibn Hamdan in Egypt while he was escaping the brutal behaviour of Badr al-Jamali. In a time of both despair and hope, the two of them made plans. `Ali the halva-maker would return to Egypt and make halva for monarchs, but, when he returned, the Caliph Al-Mustansir was not going to be the Imam. Who could confirm the lineage of the Ubaidis? The Abbasids had often cast doubts on their origins. `Ali convinced himself that that was the case. When `Ali returned to Egypt, he would find Shareef Abu Taher as Imam and Caliph. His lineage was well-established and reliable. People in Damascus had been calling him Commander of the Faithful. How much he had suffered at the hands of Badr al-Jamali, his brutality and jealousy! Some friendships can change people's fates, only solidifying at night and in times of trouble. Now the halva-maker's goal was tied to that of Ibn Hamdan and Abu Taher, namely getting rid of the Caliph and his powerful henchman, Badr al-Jamali. That was not going to be easy. Badr was brutal and merciless, embracing his gains like a scorpion about to sting. The halva-seller would go to Badr al-Jamali's palace. He was still Al-Mustansir's halva-maker and friend. Once there, he would send word to Ibn Hamdan in Egypt and Abu Taher in Damascus about what was happening within the palace walls. He might even try to get close to Badr and find out about his intentions. But no one could get close to Badr or understand his ambitions and goals. Furoon knew nothing about her father's plans, nor about how he had collected his money and treasures and left Egypt before everything crashed. She had no idea that he was conspiring against the man she loved. All she knew about Ibn Hamdan was that he was responsible for all the disasters plaguing Egypt: he had laid siege to its people and imposed heavy taxes on them in order to pay for his soldiers and their retinue; he had squeezed them so hard that they had started eating each other. Some people were even begging for the plague to come and bring things to a decent end. Then, they would not have to sell their daughters in the market in order to get a single loaf of bread.

There was a lot that Furoon did not know. She had heard about alarms and drought. She knew that, these days in Egypt, a drink of water was worth the whole world. Women were throwing jewellery away because it was worth nothing compared with a sip of water. Men were selling old corpses in the markets as though they were expensive meat. She did not realise the full extent of the disaster and terror that had struck the people who were left behind. However, `Ali was safe and sound, making plans to become the right-hand man of the new Caliph, aspiring to Solomon's dominion, but in a country that had gone through seven years of famine without any Joseph or discernment on the Pharaoh's part. Furoon was reading and learning things, but she still did not understand what was happening all around her—for lack of experience perhaps, or out of purity of heart. On the other hand, Badr al-Jamali was well aware and kept watching, but then pretended not to know. He let her father send letters; in fact, he dictated to his soldiers what they should say in 'Ali's presence. If Ibn Hamdan wanted to play games, then let him start, and he—Badr—would put an end to it. That is how authority becomes a game between the greedy and the fearful, and the world is a bauble in their hands. The aspirations of some come through kindness and protection for fear of punishment, while others crave an imperishable dominion in an ephemeral land; for such a person, they fear the power of a rival who might strike at any moment.

Furoon had arrived and given the game a jolt. Badr could tell truth from falsehood, and the girl longed for him in a different way. Ah, how cruel time was being to 'Ali the halva-maker, with his naïve daughter falling in love with his enemy. He kept watching and understanding, seeing how her eyes followed him even though he refused to meet her. He had no doubts about her intentions; ever since he was a boy, he had learned that the eye's glances can penetrate to the very core and extract what is buried in the ground. Her eyes were telling the truth, as innocent as those of a frightened gazelle.

He heard a slave girl singing in a room nearby:

No sword can do to me what you are doing;

No enemy encounter can equal one with you.

If an enemy arrow pierces my liver,

It could not do me more harm than those eyes of yours.

"Who's singing those lines?" he asked his servant.

"A slave girl, my Lord."

"Who's the poet?"

For a moment, the servant felt awkward and said nothing.

"Al-Mutanabbi," he said, "an Abbasid poet. In the past, he was court poet for Sayf ad-Dawla in Aleppo. He died a while ago."

"I don't want to hear his poetry in my palace," he insisted. "Tell her to stop. No court poet of Sayf ad-Dawla can have his poetry recited in the house of the marshal of the Caliph Imam's armies."

"As you command, my Lord."

However, those lines of poetry did not leave his ears. He heard their echo all night.

She repeated the poetry in the moonlight and committed it to memory:

For travellers, night-time adopts various elongated forms,

For lovers, night is always long.

To me appears the crescent moon that I do not desire,

While they hide from me a *badr* to whom there is no path.

Poetry may have the same effect as magic. The moon, or Badr, did in fact appear, even if the path was somewhat obscure. As on every night, he came out to look at the stars. She could not tell whether he was conversing with God or aspiring to achieve starry heights. Did he nurse within him the vanity of the lunar crescent, fully convinced that it would turn into the full moon, or did he have instead the ascetic spirit of the believer who will converse only with his Lord? How could the Armenian mamluk exert his authority over night and day like this? Were these the clouds of the east wind, passing slowly by and then disappearing, or was this the lover's certainty that the heart had finally found its rendezvous and abode? Today was not like other days. She heard his voice. He was still looking up at the stars, but he spoke to her in a loud voice.

"Furoon," he said, "why don't you show yourself to me? Are you going to hide behind the trees forever?"

She gasped. She had no idea whether her imagination had now taken charge or reality had been transformed. She stayed where she was, too frightened to run back to her room, in case he caught up with her there.

If she showed herself now, he would know everything. While she did not move, her heart was pounding, and her cheeks turned bright scarlet.

When he called out again, she was sure that it was indeed him and not a dream.

"Come on out of there," he said, looking straight at the tree.

She closed her eyes, struggling to think of what she could say now. Then she moved slowly and showed herself.

"How are you?" he asked.

She sighed in relief. She had been worried that he would ask her what she was doing there or whether she was following in his footsteps, but he did not.

"I'm well, my Lord," she replied quickly. "I thank you for your generosity. I just wanted to make sure, my Lord, that the doll I made for you had truly reached you."

He looked straight into her eyes, and she turned away bashfully.

"Are you asking me that question because you don't trust my men," he asked her, "or because you wanted to give me the doll in person? Perhaps you wanted to explain something about it to me that I don't know. Or perhaps you wanted to tell me why she has her hand placed defiantly on her waist and is so colourfully decorated. Then again, maybe you wanted to warn me not to cave in and eat it before the Maulid festival."

"Please slow down, my Lord," she replied without thinking. "I can't possibly come up with conversation the way you can, nor can I respond to your questions."

"Forgive me," he told her gently, his eyes still fixed on hers, "I'll never eat the doll. I pity her that fate."

"I'm amazed, my Lord. You're an amir and a warrior, and yet you feel sympathy for a halva doll."

"In times of conflict and tyranny, I fight and kill. But all that poor little girl did was to fall into your hands. You fashioned her and gave her as a sacrificial victim to an amir! You sacrifice a virgin girl every year so the river will stay within its banks and yield. I wonder, hasn't the river always provided for that very reason?"

"My Lord knows a great deal about Egypt."

"I haven't visited in years, but I still read about it. I started as soon as the halva-maker came to my house. Every night, you follow my footsteps. If I did not have some insight, I would say that your father has asked you to spy on the amir on behalf of the minister Ibn Hamdan. But I can claim to have certain information."

She lowered her head, hoping that he would not go on.

"You're innocent of the spying charge, Furoon," he said. "The heart has no caliph and no sultan. I'm afraid of it because it has neither curb, nor commander, nor teacher. Do you realise that? From my teacher, I learned how to fight and control. But he didn't teach me anything about the soul's love and desires. I only learned about that later..."

"My Lord is wise," she said, hoping to change the subject. "He knows everything."

"Not everything," he replied. "Just some things. Tell me, Furoon, have you liked the halva in our house?"

She did not reply. That surprised him.

"Haven't you liked it?" he asked.

"I only like halva," she replied, "if I've made it myself. But I've missed it. It's like eating after a long journey, when you eat slowly and can tell which food is sweet, excellent, and bad."

"Your relationship with halva is peculiar, like that between lover and beloved. Maybe that's because you're the halva-maker's daughter."

"Forgive me, my Lord," she said suddenly, staring at the ground. "I've been taking your valuable time. Will you allow me to leave?"

"Yes, I will," he replied, "provided that I can see you, and that you'll tell me why you prefer Egyptian halva even though you're in Syria. There's no halva to rival what's made in Syria. Or is it perhaps that you prefer eating only doll doughnuts?"

She did not respond, suppressing a smile as she kept her throbbing heart in check.

"So," he said again, "you'll come tomorrow and hide behind the tree."

She shuddered.

"Let me leave, my Lord," she said.

"No, I won't let you. You've wasted my time, and that's the end of it. I want to know more about the doll and about you."

"Why is the Governor of Damascus so concerned about the halva-maker's daughter?"

"Maybe because the doll is not like other dolls. It's brightly coloured, defiant, and pure-hearted. As you know, purity of heart is something strange for me. There's no evil, rancour, jealousy, or envy. No, it's as if your heart dangles outside your breast, accessible to passers-by, common folk, riffraff, and commanders alike. I've never seen anything like it. How did you get that way?"

She closed her eyes so he would not see how delighted she was by his words. If this was a dream, then it would certainly linger in her memory, its hues clustering in the recesses of her soul and folds of her breast.

"Furoon," he said calmly.

"I don't know, Amir," she replied. "You can see and know things that we don't. Maybe the halva doll was always kept in a box and never came out. It wasn't polluted by the atmosphere or touched by human hands. That's why it seems different. Who knows? Purity has to be tested in dirty water first, and honesty needs to be examined in the company of hypocrites. Those procedures are difficult to implement, my Lord."

"You know how to counter me, one word with another. You're studying jurisprudence and hadith. What do you want to become? Like the religious shaikhs and missionaries?"

"I want to benefit the women around me. Some of them are so ignorant of the fundamentals of religion!"

"What is the foundation of religion, Furoon?"

"Godliness."

"And what is that?"

"The soul's avoidance of whims, my Lord."

That made him smile. It was the first time she had seen him do so, and it dissolved what was left of her own will.

"May I leave now?" she asked immediately.

"Godliness is difficult, Furoon," he replied, as though he had not heard her. "It has to be accompanied by humility and sacrifice."

"You're right, my Lord. You know as much about religion as I do, and more."

"Are those words part of your humility?

"If my Lord will allow me," she stuttered as she hurried back to her room.

The presence of sugar inside the palace of the Amir of Damascus added to the house's warmth. In its presence there lay both purpose and tranquillity. She went into the Amir's kitchen and asked if she could make him some rose halva. Inside his palace, rose petals had a different feel. The man's aura did not reside in his retinue and palace, nor in the sword he wielded, nor in his brilliant embroidered uniform. No, it resided in his eyes, his certain looks, and his confidence in his own identity and person. She cut the rose petals slowly and put them in a bowl full of water. After adding some starch, she left it to boil, expecting eventually to add some musk and sesame oil. Once it had turned bright red, she added sesame oil and sat by the bowl while it cooled, her hand resting on her cheek while her heart focused on the Amir's eyes, hair, and trim beard. She did not notice that the same person who had gained control of her life had entered the kitchen until she heard all the cooks moving around and bowing down to him. She just stood there, staring at him, without noticing or realising what she was doing, as though she had been touched by magic or jinn. They looked at each other.

"What are you making?" he asked her.

Everyone else still had their heads bowed.

"Rose halva," she replied. "Would you like to taste some, my Lord?"

"When you've finished making it," he replied. "I want to watch the halva-maker's daughter making it. Go on, finish it."

As she held the bowl in her shaking hand, her cheeks were on fire and her hands were quivering. When he was around, her heart beat faster.

After a while, he raised his hand to signal everyone else to leave. They left in minutes, as she was holding the sesame oil and putting it in the bowl again.

"Now you've put the sesame oil in," he told her quickly, "all that's left is the musk. You need two okas of musk."

He moved closer, grabbed the musk between his hands, and threw it slowly onto the halva.

"Anyone making halva," he said, "remembers the description and doesn't put double of anything on it. Like governance, making halva demands perfection."

"My Lord knows about rose halva," she said, avoiding his eyes, "and is aware of the exact amount of musk."

"Your Lord remembers the quantity of everything," he replied with a smile. "Someone like me is not going to put double quantity on anything. If he did, Furoon, he'd lose his head."

He took the bowl and put it in front of her.

"You try it first," he said gently.

"Furoon can't harm the Amir," she said. "If you still have your doubts about me, my Lord..."

"Why shouldn't I have doubts about you, halva-maker's daughter?" he asked her with a smile.

She put the halva in her mouth.

"If only I could be as accomplished as my Lord!" she stuttered. "He's so capable with accounts and memory."

"You don't need that, Furoon. It's only for those who have no other resort."

He leaned over and put his hand atop hers. As he took the bowl from her, it would have dropped out of her hand if he had not held on to it.

"Let go of the bowl," he said gently, "and look at me."

She swallowed hard and removed her hand from the bowl. She said nothing as she looked into his eyes. A tense silence followed, marked by feelings that were difficult to describe.

"What is it the halva-maker's daughter wants from the Governor of Damascus?" he asked all of a sudden.

His blunt question shocked her. She had no idea how to respond and stayed silent.

"Forgive me," she said. "I surprised you and wasted your time."

"Why haven't you been married so far, Furoon?" he asked, as he tasted the halva. "A lot of men must have been asking to be married to a pretty girl like you."

As she lowered her hand, she felt embarrassed.

"Famine and drought have meant that my father's been scared marrying me in Egypt," she replied.

"Or perhaps your father wants you to be married to a man who doesn't work as a halva-maker," he said. "'Ali the halva-maker is interested in governance, but the fate of a daughter whose father aspires to such authority is gloomy and miserable."

She looked at him, and their eyes met. She had no idea what his intentions were, but she was the happiest person alive. She squeezed her mind, struggling to come up with something useful to say.

"My Lord," she said, "I can teach one of your slave girls or your wife how to make halva. It would be an honour for me to teach your wife or daughter."

"My daughter doesn't like halva," he replied with a smile. "And I don't have a wife. But I'll think about it."

"About what?"

"About slave girls. I'll choose one or two for you to teach how to make halva."

"I'm at your command, my Lord," she said with a frown.

"You're bold, Furoon!" he said, moving his face closer to hers.

"Sometimes," she replied, "my heart runs ahead of my mind."

"But you're good at making halva," he said, "even if you've forgotten the proportions. Take care of yourself. This is a cruel and selfish era."

"I will, my Lord."

He held out his hand, and she hesitated.

"Do you refuse the Amir's hand?" he asked.

She grabbed his hand quickly, leaned over, brought it close to her mouth, and kissed it.

"May God preserve the Amir of Damascus!" she said.

He did not pull his hand away from hers, and she removed hers slowly. For a moment, he looked at the spot where she had kissed it.

"We've talked a lot," he said, "but you haven't told me what you want. You follow my footsteps and spend the night talking to all the stars in the firmament. Then you make halva inside my palace. What is it you want, I wonder."

"If my presence annoys you, my Lord..." she said.

"Your presence is the best thing that's happened in this palace for ages," he interrupted.

She felt confused as she stared at him, doing her best to find a safe place in her heart to store his words.

"My Lord," she asked, "did you say a moment ago that that I'm pretty?"

"Yes, I did," he replied firmly, looking into her eyes.

"Did you also say that you like having me here in the palace?"

"Are you repeating everything I say? If you were working as a secretary to the Governor of Damascus, you'd certainly be very good at your job!"

"It's just that I wasn't expecting to hear such words."

"The most wonderful things in the world," he replied with another smile, "are things we are neither anticipating nor expecting. I'll see you tomorrow, pretty Furoon!"

Night assumed a brilliant white hue, its gleam enticing both to the quarter's head and the country's ruler. At night, she waits for Badr, the moon, to appear and snuff out some of passion's blaze. He does not appear every day, but, when he does, he can suppress ugliness, drought, wars involving amirs, the stench of eaten corpses, and the smell of wheat blended with death. How can a man be so splendid and innocent when he is an army general and governor? She saw in him a sincerity that he also saw in her. And, if what he saw was spontaneity and beauty, then she saw power, justice, and the ability of endure and win in troubled times.

"Tell me about Egypt, Furoon," he asked her one day as he was surveying the horizon.

She frowned, and all smiles vanished.

"There are two Egypts," she began. "There's the one I saw in my childhood, a bride with a multi-coloured crown on her head, and then there's the other Egypt, the one I left behind. I do not know it, my Lord. Amirs and an army squabble and fight each other until they manage to erase everything and replace it with rubble. Famine, plague, evil and hatred are everywhere. I've seen my country in difficult times, and they do not elicit the best in people. Quite the opposite. If I'm going to see so much desolation, I've no desire to see Egypt again. Let Egypt remain in my heart, a halva doll, rather than be replaced by black decay burying its head like cockroaches and locusts. Ah, my Lord, why did you remind me? If only there existed amirs who could reconcile their feelings and concern themselves with something more important than fighting—Turks fighting slaves, Maghrebis fighting Turks and Egyptians. I can no longer recognise them, fighting each other without mercy, my Lord, for gold and wheat."

"So stop talking about things that make you so unhappy," he said, looking straight at her. "I've grown accustomed to having you here, halva-maker's daughter. If I were married to you, I wonder, would I be putting an end to you and your happiness."

She opened her eyes. Her heart pulsed to a joyous song, but she said nothing. He held her hand in his. She looked into his eyes that she loved so much, but she could not say a word.

He put his hand on the embroidered turban she was wearing and pulled it off.

"I want to see your hair," he said.

She stood there, unable to move. He ran his fingers through her curly hair.

"I wonder," he said. "In your religious community, do you regard me as an unbeliever or pretender?"

"Heaven forbid I say any such thing, my Lord," she replied immediately. "You're a Muslim like me."

He smiled, held her hand again, and pulled it closer to him. Passion now raged till she thought that winter winds had arrived with their chill and frost. He took off his turban and wrapped it around her back.

She stayed silent, trying her best to summon her courage. He put his hand on her cheek.

"You're still young," he said, "but you're stubborn. Do you love the Amir, master of this palace, or the soldier carrying his sword? Love is like clouds, passing slowly overhead, then vanishing."

She felt embarrassed and slowly removed her hand.

"No," she said. "Love's like the crescent moon. It only disappears for a while, then returns and grows."

He moved closer till she could feel his breath on her lips. Feeling frightened, she closed her eyes and shuddered.

"Will my Lord permit me to return to my room?" she asked.

He pulled her toward him and pressed her head to his chest.

"You know more about love than I do, halva-maker's daughter," he whispered.

He put his arm round her waist, but did not pull her any closer. Not for a second did he forget that he was the Amir.

"I'm used to seeing you every night," he told her gently. "And, when I do, I can forget all the worries, intrigues, and fighting. How do you do it, I wonder?"

She had no idea how to respond, and she did not. She was wandering in a haze of rapture and certainty, sure now that what she was feeling was not weakness. Maybe the Amir, who was so aware and perceptive, was actually looking at the halva-maker's daughter. This was the age of miracles. If Egypt, which had been a paradise on the banks of the blessed Nile, had now turned into a rotten piece of halva, if that were true, then perhaps God wanted to console the Egyptian girl just once and compensate her for the loss of her family and homeland. She wanted to race through the Damascus streets, greeting every passer-by and hugging every sick and downtrodden person. Time had now adjusted itself, and the heart had been sincere. She moved away from him bashfully and leaned against the palace wall so she would not fall over.

"Forgive me, my Lord," she said.

"Have you fallen in love with me, Furoon?" he asked, staring into her eyes. "Is that why you've been following me?"

She blushed in embarrassment and did not respond.

"When the Amir asks you a question, Furoon," he insisted, "you have to answer."

"My grandmother Sundus," she stuttered, swallowing hard, "says that love is a feeling of reassurance and comfort, as though you're talking to your soul with no barriers or tricks."

"No barriers or tricks," he repeated, holding her hand. "Your grandmother doesn't know a lot about our world, Furoon. The entire world is a series of fortresses built like barriers of deceit. Evidently, she didn't tell you to build fortresses around your heart to protect you from trickery."

The agony of love she was feeling was mixed with a scary—no, a terrifying love.

"I love you," she said. "And I realise that the same love has brought me to an end."

"Why has your love for a man like me brought you to an end?" he asked, clasping her hand.

"I can't reach you."

"If I lifted you up, you'd be taller than me."

"You've all the girls on earth at your beck and call. I have only one heart."

"Everyone has just one heart, even if they do control the earth. Our marriage won't be easy. If you think it'll be easy, you're wrong. There are all kinds of plot, and difference is the means to destruction."

"I've asked God for guidance multiple times, seeking the right path," she said sorrowfully. "I realise that love is one of the sentiments of paradise."

"We aren't in paradise. Even so, we can do our best to protect ourselves against intrigue."

At night, she sniffed his coat passionately, then hugged it to herself. She was on the point of putting it on her bed and squeezing it while she slept. But then she decided against it, because it might be seen as sinful. She kissed it cautiously and then hid it from view.

She revealed her secret to Hafsa, telling her about everything that had transpired between the two of them, apart from the fact that he had hugged her and kissed her forehead.

"Why are you hurling yourself into perdition?" she asked as gently as she could. "If you were married to a man like your brother, you would at least have control of his heart. But do you really want to be one of the Amir's women, Furoon? You realise that amirs are never satisfied with just one woman. He'll be spending his life with slave girls and in marriages to other women. You'll be alone in your room, waiting for him to look at you and remember you. He also has four sons, and, needless to say, they control his heart. I've heard that his eldest son, Sha'baan, whom he had before he was yet twenty years old, is his entire life. Who will you be, halva-maker's daughter, when faced with Sha'baan, the Amir's son? Who's to say that he won't be looking for a wife from his own lineage? And then remember, my daughter, that he's not like us. He's used to war. He left both family and homeland. People like him cannot be trusted. You need to understand, Furoon, that the heart can regularly lead you astray. And bear in mind that Amina Khatun, his former wife, is still living in a house next to his. Do you think he's doing this just for his children's sake or out of affection for an old love? My daughter, this is risky, and it's end for your heart. If you could be married to a man who would be loyal to you alone, then why would you choose a man with slave girls?"

She did not respond.

"Is he going to get rid of all his slave girls for your sake?" Hafsa asked. "Have you asked him to do that?"

"No."

"So are you agreeing to stay in the harem until one day he remembers that you exist?"

Once again, she did not respond.

"What do we have to do with amirs?" Hafsa asked. "You're my daughter, and I don't want this for you. What if he gets bored with you after a while? Have you thought of that? After one year or twenty, he'll find someone younger than you and fall in love all over again. You're so innocent and inexperienced. He's a fighter; he's had sex with hundreds of women and knows things about women that you don't, Furoon. Don't cast your gaze on the river's edge, or you'll drown. If it's the Amir's power and prestige you love, then you're going to suffer."

"I swear to you that he's the one I love."

"That's a mere fancy that's taken control of you. My dear daughter, you need to wake up before you die of your sorrow. I don't accept this marriage, and I don't trust Badr al-Jamali."

"Badr al-Jamali's the only man I want," she replied firmly.

When they took Badr son of `Abdallah out of his country, he did not complain or cry like other children. At the time, he was eleven years old. He fixed his gaze on the mountains coated in white snow in case he never saw them again. He kept in his memory vestiges of his family during this raid. He and his younger sister had been playing with a wooden sword in a narrow courtyard. Just then, he heard his mother scream. The sword fell from his hand, and he rushed indoors to find his mother lying motionless on the floor. How had she died so quickly? He noticed that her eyes were closed and blood was pouring out around her face. Then he heard his sister scream as a man carried her out of the house. He stretched out his hand, but a steel sword—not a wooden one—poked him the stomach. It did not injure him; it was just a warning of what was to come. His sister disappeared. This was his first encounter with weakness, and he swore it would also be his last. He did not feel sad; the dominant emotion was anger. He did not loathe the killer as much as he did his own father, who had deserted them years ago. All that remained of his country were the mountains and the bread that his mother used to bury in the ground like a sorceress, so that it would emerge like a thin leaf, ablaze and full of smoke. Sometimes, he would long for that bread and ask his slave girls to bake it. But it never turned out like the bread of those mountains; it was not as soft, and the slave girls were not sorceresses like his mother. Sometimes, when his heart was on fire, he would take on the pain and grow accustomed to it, with no resistance or pleas for help. He was like someone who had lost his arm, but did not cry because he could not feel it. Year after year, he would swear to search for his sister and rescue her. When he did his weapons training, when his owner manumitted him, when he became Amir and ruler, he would search for her and all that remained of his previous life and weakness. He dispatched soldiers all over the earth, all in vain. It was all fated. Inevitable. Was she now serving an amir or a poor man, he wondered. Was she working in a brothel or singing in bars? He kept that weakness always in front of him, and engraved it like Kufic script so as to remember it. Badr would never be weak again. Yes indeed. When Jamal ad-daula ibn ʿAmmar purchased him, he was thinking about his sister, Susie. He would rescue her the way cavaliers did. He would keep her as the lady in his palace, in charge of everything. Had he not wanted to be a soldier ever since he was a boy? He would carry out his master Jamal ad-daula ibn ʿAmmar's orders efficiently and to the letter, even if it involved hard days of training and non-stop work.

One day, he and a friend were watching the soldier who was their trainer.

"One day, I'm going to be like that soldier," his friend said.

"One day," Badr responded, "I'm going to be like the Governor of Tripoli."

His friend looked stunned and ran over to Jamal ad-daula to complain about Badr and denounce him.

When Jamal ad-daula came over to Badr, the boy lowered his head and remained silent.

"Do you want to be like me, Badr?" Jamal ad-daula he asked. "How can that be, when you're just a mamluk, nothing more?"

"Dreams have neither cover nor limits, my lord," Badr replied. "It's just that there's someone who's very dear to me. I've vowed to rescue that person from weakness. To do that, I need power."

"Who's that?"

"One of my sisters."

"Badr," his instructor told him firmly, "don't addle your brain with impossible dreams. You're never going to find your sister. Remember that destinies are never secure. What's happened to your sister might well have happened to mine as well, if the Abbasids had defeated me. We live in a world teetering between success and failure. Those who fail pay the price, while those who succeed get all the spoils. But then, times change, and conclusions are subverted. Do you understand? Now you need to regard all the women around you as part of the world's finery, a source of peace after exhaustion, a prize. Don't place your life into a woman's hands, or else it'll seep through her fingers like water through a fisherman's fingers. You're seventeen years old now, and it's time for you to make love to a beautiful slave girl. Which of them would you prefer?"

Badr remained silent.

"In that case, Badr," Jamal ad-daula said, "I'll choose one with a lovely voice and give her to you. But how can I do that when you're still a slave? First, I'll manumit you, and then I'll give her to you."

He had been waiting for this particular day ever since he had become one of Jamal ad-daula's mamluks.

"Even if you set me free," Badr said with a smile, "you're still my master. I shall sacrifice my entire life to your cause."

"I wouldn't be giving you your freedom if I didn't know how loyal and ambitious you were. The Ubaidis are surrounded by dangers. Their dynasty will fail either today or tomorrow, in which case the first people to lose will be you and me."

"Heaven forbid!"

"Are you afraid of losing?"

"Nothing else scares me."

"Neither death nor loss of family scares you...I can understand. Even so, the things that do scare you will always happen. Beware of a love that humbles a woman or position. Free yourself of fear, my son, so you don't have to kneel to the world."

"I hear and obey, my lord and teacher!"

However, the Armenian mamluk did fall in love, in spite of himself and the self-control he exercised when dealing with others. Love always involves excess: in gentleness, wishes, fears, and the heart's natural instinct for affection. Furoon's sincerity would pour forth and drown any hypocrisy around it; her spontaneity could overtop the vicissitudes of embryonic souls in the heavens at dusk. How beautiful this girl was, and how difficult it was to submit to the sweet savour of a passion mixed with wine, not water. When it came to losing your mind and roiling your entire being, she had no idea what effect she was having on him. For his part, he did not reveal a single one of his thoughts.

He started looking forward to their nightly encounter in his palace garden. He no longer enjoyed slave girls and stopped inviting them to his room. Having sex with a gorgeous slave girl no longer satisfied his desire or extinguished the fire of his passion. Fulfilment consisted in holding Furoon's hand in all innocence, like a young boy who has just achieved maturity, has no experience, and does not dare to venture any further. The mere touch of Furoon's hand gave him something far more powerful than sex with slave girls: a fresh feeling of joy. He had not felt like this before, nor had he laughed when tripping over a cat in his garden or watching a lazy butterfly at night sleeping on a flower. But now, he had started to laugh and look at everything around him as though he were in a totally different world, filled with beauty and goodness. Day after day, he would meet her, and she would gaze at him with her pleading eyes, hoping to spend the rest of her days in his warm embrace.

When she met him today with her flashing eyes, her face was red from shyness. She wanted to throw herself into his arms, but she did not. She grabbed the wall so as not to fall and looked up at the moon in the heavens, which were turning black despite the moon's gleam. He moved over and stood next to her, his eyes matching the moon in the sky. He raised his hand and put it on her shoulder.

"Your father wants to leave the palace," he told her. "Tomorrow."

Her whole body shivered. She did not know whether to remove his hand or leave it there forever.

"My Lord," she replied, eyes closed.

"Call me Badr."

"If you'll allow me," she replied hesitantly, "you're all-powerful and I'm all-weak."

"You're going to be mine. Don't worry. I know what's going through your mind. Your father will agree, even though he loathes me..."

"God forbid! I don't believe my father would hate someone who's been so generous in hosting us."

"You may not know all that much about the world, Furoon," he replied decisively. "But you're intelligent enough. This Caliphate involves two men. There are two of them, and the Caliph cannot rely on two men. It's like a virgin girl who marries only one man. Do you know who those two men are?"

"Minister Nasir ibn Hamdan," she replied hesitantly, "and the Caliph Al-Mustansir."

He smiled, but did not react.

"I understand what you mean... My father says..."

She fell silent.

"Your father says," he said, "that there are two men around the Ubaidi family squabbling over power and influence. One is the Turk, Nasir ad-daula ibn Hamdan, and the other is the Armenian, Badr al-Jamali, who is not in Egypt but nearby, a mere inch or so away. Nasir ad-daula ibn Hamdan is in Egypt, and he's toying with it like a dimwit playing with kittens. He's destroyed it and won't stop until the very last Egyptian has been killed. Even so, your father still favours him and cooperates with him. I ask myself, is your father working for his own benefit, for that of his religious affiliation, or for his store and factory, rather than for the interests of Egypt as a whole? People keep saying that the halva-maker makes halva for Ibn Hamdan's household even though he's living in Damascus."

Hiding her annoyance at the truth of what he was saying and her own sense of shame at her father's loyalties, she did not respond.

"But why should we bother about rulers?" he asked. "Instead, let's talk about you, Furoon. How come you're not scared of the army officer? Where do you get such a bold heart?"

Closing her eyes, she sniffed the fresh air. She put her hand on top of his, which was still clasping her shoulder.

"If only I didn't realise," she said, "how much I'm going to suffer waiting for you, as I nurse my hopes amid doubt and despair and rest my head on the pillow at night, searching for you as though you're my entire life, while you hold your own life in your hands. Badr may not be my Amir, but he's the monarch of my heart, Amir."

"Here you are, reciting poetry! For twenty years or more, I've been listening to poetry, but, when it's you reciting, it has a different hue, one I don't recognise, one that relentlessly penetrates to the very core. Once we are married, what do you expect?"

"Nothing," she replied immediately. "Just being beside you and around you will be enough, and, of course, worshipping God. I want to spend my time helping people, distributing money, handing out food, then..."

"Then what?" he asked, running his hand over her hair.

"Do you want Egypt, Badr?" she asked abruptly.

He was shocked by her brazen question. Just a few seconds earlier, she had seemed so pliant and loyal.

"Why are you asking?" he demanded seriously.

"Sometimes I get the impression that you see it in me. You listen to my accent and look into my eyes..."

"Is there anyone who doesn't want Egypt? It's as though you're asking a man if he wants prestige and gold. As it is, Furoon, I've no desire for it as long as Ibn Hamdan is a minister there."

"Not as long as Ibn Hamdan is a minister there? What does that mean? Do you plan to remove him, or—?

"If I didn't know you," he interrupted, "I would think that your father's hired you to spy on his behalf."

"I won't swear to you," she replied, looking straight at him. "But I... Forgive my boldness. Sometimes I forget who you are and think of you as—"

"As your beloved," he interrupted, moving closer.

He put his hands around her head and kissed her forehead.

"And soon, your husband as well," he said. "Once we're married, halva-maker's daughter, you'll be able to ask me multiple times whether I want Egypt and see it in you."

He had visited Egypt for the first time with his teacher when he was thirteen years old. The reason why his very soul joined itself to that country was not just its wealth and the blue and green emeralds that lay hidden in the folds of its mountains, but also its ancient temples and pyramids. He had run his fingers over the writing on the temple walls.

"This is the language of birds," he'd said timorously. "I used to dream of learning it."

"People say this country grows jewels amid its rocks," his companion had said at the time. "If you smash the ancient rocks, you find gold. Dig into the ground amid the rocks, and you'll find emeralds."

He stared at the piece of emerald in his companion's hand.

"Where did you find that?" he asked.

"Here by the walls."

"Give it to me," he said, stretching out his hand. "I'll give you whatever you want. I'd like to keep it."

"Are you tying your heart to gold or emeralds?" his companion asked, giving him a dubious look. "Fine then; you can buy it for five dinars."

Badr looked down for a moment.

"Agreed," he said.

"That's more than you own," the boy replied, looking amazed.

"No, it's not. For the past year, I've been saving all my money. Just give me a chance. We can go to my house, and I'll give it to you today."

When they returned, he gave his companion the money, carefully counting out every single dirham. He took the emerald and clutched it proudly to his chest.

"This is a country where people settle down for good," he told his companion. "They don't just pass through."

"Egypt always tempts men with its treasures. And yet, like time itself, it evolves."

"This is a wealth that never disappears, an earthly paradise imitating the one beyond: the River Nile in flood, a valley thick with innumerable trees, and wheat enough to cover the earth's surface and more. I realise why the

Imam chooses it."

"Just wait till you see the beautiful palaces in Cairo."

He rolled the uncut emerald in his hands. Tomorrow, he would clean it and either make a necklet or ring out of it or else keep it close to hand. He was drawn to it, as though it possessed his mother's warmth and his sister's innocence. Susie, I wonder where you are. If you had died right in front of me, I would have eventually found some peace. But I keep hearing screams and feeling the pain of humiliation after a fall. Forgive me my weakness, daughter of my own mother! Born amid increasing population and ever expanding territory, how am I supposed to find you? I've followed trade routes, to no avail.

Hearing a knock on the door, he stood up. It was his teacher, and he lowered his head.

"How was your day in Egypt?" the teacher asked.

"Wonderful, Sir," he replied with a bow.

"Give me the emerald," Jamal ad-daula said, holding out his hand.

Badr looked at him and, without a word, handed him the emerald.

"If you had hesitated," Jamal ad-daula told him, "I would have cut off your head. Mamluks own nothing; they care only about fighting. Do you understand?"

"Yes, I do."

"Today, I want you to clean all the caravan's horses and get them ready. No sleep until you've finished the job on your own. Tomorrow, you won't be visiting Cairo with us. You're going to stay here till we leave. Don't leave the house. Do you hear me?"

"Yes, I hear you."

Ever since, Badr had failed to comprehend what had happened. Yes indeed, he had lost the emerald, but why such sorrow? Had he not already lost his mother, sister, and homeland? For the first time, and against his will, tears welled in his eyes. Then, with his head lowered, a solitary tear left him down and fell onto his cheek.

Jamal ad-daula looked at him.

"Are you crying like a woman, Badr?" he asked angrily. "Over an emerald? Or is it over Cairo? Maybe you're not fit to be a fighter?"

"I'm not crying, my lord," he replied quickly, wiping away the tear. "The Cairo dust hurts my eyes."

"You're a liar as well," Jamal ad-daula said, slapping him across the face.

Grabbing his hand, he punched Badr hard in the stomach.

"That'll give you something to cry about, boy," he said. "Or rather, *child*."

His guts were on fire, but he stood ramrod straight.

"I beg your forgiveness, my Lord," he said.

"Whatever you want badly, you'll lose with no mercy. You'll be forcibly deprived of whatever it is you desire. Forget about your desires, boy; fighters don't have any. The glint and dark colour of emeralds have their particular magic, and that can easily take away your vision and perception. You'll be wandering around like madmen chasing after money, a boy, a woman, and a sultan. Make use of the most expensive thing you own to establish a tent and residence."

He had no idea exactly why Jamal ad-daula was punishing him this way, but he carried out his orders without the slightest hesitation. He worked nonstop for eight hours. Once he had finished, he went to tell his master.

"That's the kind of will I want from you," Jamal ad-daula told him.

When he went back to his room, he burst into tears. It was not just that he really wanted the emerald. It had now taken over his life, and he had forgotten everything else. He did not know whether he was the sword-wielding cavalier who had rode steadily, then stumbled over puny grains of sand or whether that the emerald would glint with colours of a rare purity that he did not recognise.

Days of innocence did not last for very long. Certainly innocence found no home with the Governor of Damascus. Now, his son Sha`baan, came in to see him. Badr looked at his son proudly, recognising his mother's eyes. As long as the boy was a part of him, then his family was here, and his homeland was in his pocket. Badr said something in his own language.

"My father and lord," Sha`baan said, looking straight at him. "I don't understand."

"I know. I was saying how proud I am of you and your bravery."

"I must learn your language."

"There's no need.

"Do you miss her, Father?"

"I talk to her along with a few soldiers."

"No, I mean your country. Do you miss it?"

"The soldier's country is the one he defends," he answered with a smile. "Not the one where he was born."

"So which is your country, Father? Damascus? Syria?"

He did not reply.

"The army's mutiny is dangerous," Badr said seriously.

"I'm dealing with them, my Lord," Sha`baan answered quickly.

"How?"

"A combination of leniency and toughness."

"You can't handle mutinies leniently," Badr said.

"My Lord..."

"You can't be lenient with soldiers. You need resolve and firmness; death to every rebellious traitor and deceitful agitator. Any soldier who mutinies over money does not know the true meaning of military service. He has to be killed immediately. Bear in mind, Sha`baan, that there's intrigue all around you; don't trust anyone. There was a day when we left Damascus to escape from the Seljuqs and revolution. But today, we treat anyone who even thinks about mutiny brutally and without the slightest mercy."

For Furoon, the bliss did not last long. Before Badr had the chance to ask her father for her hand or to simply order him to do it, her father made up his mind to leave Badr al-Jamali's household, along with his entire family, and to move outside Damascus. The decision frightened her, not only because it would distance her from the only man she desired, but also because she did not trust what her father was proposing, and she thought it might endanger her very soul. She moved without a word of farewell, but she also waited for her father to speak to her about Badr's request for her hand. It happened two weeks after they had moved. He sat down beside her.

"Why is the army commander asking to be married to the halva-maker's daughter?" he asked with a frown. "Has he seen you?"

She did not like telling lies, so she swallowed hard and said nothing.

"Maybe he's seen you," her father went on, controlling his temper. "Perhaps you encouraged him and want to be married to him. This calamity is much worse than anything before. Do you want him, Furoon?"

She hugged herself, but said nothing.

"The Armenian mamluk slave may be crown among amirs and army commanders," her father said, "but he's not going to be married to my daughter. Needless to say, he's ordering, not asking. But he doesn't know the Sicilian's family, or who `Ali, son of the halva-maker and Sicilian, truly is."

Father," she pleaded, "He's not an enemy. He's opened his palace to us."

"He did that in spite of himself, because the Caliph told him to do so. Your father's the personal halva-maker of the Caliph Al-Mustansir. The Caliph may be able to change his ministers and amirs, but it's far more difficult to change his halva-maker. Badr doesn't like Nasir ad-daula ibn Hamdan, Al-Mustansir's minister. They've been enemies for some time. Today or tomorrow, Damascus will fall into Seljuq hands."

"Father," she said, "I know nothing about wars."

"Is love what you know about? If I had to choose between my sons and preserving the inheritance left to me by Jawhar, son of Husain, I'd choose the Sicilian and the halva-maker. If you're so keen to be married to Badr, I shall disown you on the Day of Resurrection. Is that what you want?"

"No," she replied at once.

"You'll be married to whomever your father chooses. Amir Hamza, associate of Shareef Abu Taher Haidar, belongs to our religious community. And you claim to be so knowledgeable and devout! Or are you in love with that apostate Shi`i man?"

Unwittingly she let out a scream.

"Father," she said, "I don't want to be married, but I'll die before I'm married to that man."

"Why? Because he's your beloved's enemy?"

He grabbed her neck as though he were planning to strangle her.

"Badr is ordering me to marry you to him. But, if Damascus burns, that'll never happen. I'll kill you before he even touches you."

So Furoon wrote Badr a letter, saying: My father will not accept our marriage. I want you to know that, if everything changes, if sun and moon disappear, if we are separated, my love for you remains hidden inside me and in every drop of blood—not because you're an amir or the handsomest man I've ever seen. I know of no reason or method for love. I love you, Amir, and hoped to rest my head on your chest just once before we left. Perhaps you think I'm just a child playing games, tempted by the glitter of gold and sword. But one day, you'll discover that Furoon falls in love only once. But then, Amir, love has no impact in this world; it's lighter than a feather, just like air and wind.

Furoon locked the door of her room. She stopped eating and drinking and spent her nights praying and conversing with God:

"O God, if You are angry with me for being in love with him, You're the one who planted his love in my heart. Do not let me lose my way between hatred and wars."

Hafsa came to see her every day, urging her to eat something, but she refused. She told Furoon that this world of ours was not for the fulfilment of hopes but the endurance of trials. Furoon listened patiently.

"Persuade my father not to marry me to Abu Taher's colleague," she said, "and I'll eat something."

"Furoon..."

"I've repented of love now. Tell him I don't want to be married to Badr al-Jamali; I just want him to leave me alone. I beg you. It's no part of religion to force his daughter to be married."

After a day or two, Badr's response was brought by one of his slave girls. She entered Furoon's room as though she were coming on behalf of one of her girlfriends. When she slunk into the room, Hafsa, who was well aware of who she was, allowed her to stay. Furoon sat down wearily, took the letter, and read it. Badr wrote that he could take her away today in spite of her father and the entire world, if she agreed. He was going to give her time to think about it, but she would have to decide in a day or so. He would come and take her away.

She recalled her father's words: "You're not my daughter. You want to humiliate your father. You like the idea of seeing him humbled by the Governor of Damascus, the same way that Egypt is being humiliated by an Imam who's not of the same sect and knows nothing about the country. But, through God's will, the minister Ibn Hamdan and Shareef Abu Taher will rid the country of them."

She looked at the slave girl.

"How is the Amir going to rescue me?" she asked.

"He can do anything," she replied forcefully. "All he needs to know is that you are still committed. Let him arrange things."

She thought for a while. They had left Damascus under an escort provided by Shareef Abu Taher's aides, as though they were Al-Jamali's enemies. If Al-Jamali wanted to take her away, was he going to kidnap her? Would he humiliate her father? Arrest him? Badr probably had as much power as Ibn Hamdan. She now found herself in the middle, between men who would kill her and her father. Furoon had no power of her own. Would she be happy to see her father humiliated?

With a quivering hand, she wrote him just three or four words: "I can't. You'll stay with me, but I don't have your courage, Badr."

She handed the note to the slave-girl, then threw herself on her bed without tears or a single word. She also sent a letter to her father: "God 'does not charge any soul except to its capacity' [Qur'an Sura 2 [Al-Baqara], v. 233], but you intend to charge me with what I cannot bear. I shall never be married to Amir Hamza."

CHAPTER THREE

Badr al-Jamali did not believe her letter, or perhaps at first he did his best not to believe it. It had not occurred to him that someone who had followed him around with such rugged determination could not defy her own father. So, should he despise her today or feel sorry for her? She was not yet twenty years old and was surrounded by people who hated Badr al-Jamali. Was that enough of an excuse, halva-maker's daughter? Badr's heart only pulsed for Furoon. He lusted after other women and enjoyed them all, but then the halva-maker's daughter had arrived with her peculiar accent, her stammer, her innocence, and the supreme sincerity of her desire to penetrate to his very core. He was abundantly aware that passionate love had no cause; like death itself, it provides no preliminaries or warnings. Like death, it can change times, wreck plans, and disperse all sense of security from within the folds of fortresses. For the first time, his secretary, ʿAbd al-Wahhab, gave him a sympathetic look.

"Love can pass over the eye," he said, "and give it a gleam like shining stars. But can't you find another girl apart from the halva-maker's daughter? People are saying that the Governor of Damascus, commander of the Imam and Caliph's armed forces, is in love with a girl who does not belong to the Imam's sect. I'm talking to you like a brother, my Lord, as you've taught me."

"Since when has Badr al-Jamali been bothered about what the common people and amirs have to say? You've known me since I was young. You know that I didn't chose my destiny, wars, or being an amir, even if I'd wished it. But I've chosen Furoon."

"I know you, my lord, and I realise that you have an iron will. However, love's the only thing that can melt iron. Don't grieve if she can't be yours, and don't let bitterness control your heart. The world never gives us what we want. Still, I realise that you'll never surrender. If you'd been expelled from Damascus and come back two years later, you'd still carve out a place for yourself amid the Seljuq ranks. Nothing can stand in your way. I've known you for ages; you're harder on yourself than on other people. My only hope, my Lord, is that you won't take out that instinct of yours on the girl so she comes to be scared of you. Don't punish her because she doesn't have your courage. Men and women are not alike."

"Shareef Ab Taher Haidar is out to finish me off gradually," Badr said, as though he had not heard what his secretary had just been saying. "Firstly, he's stirring up the Seljuqs against me, then he wants to marry the halva-maker's daughter to an amir who's one of his aides. I don't trust our soldiers, ʿAbd al-wahhab. They're few in number, and their resolve is weak."

"They're just a strong as you are."

"It's nothing to do with strength. What my men fight for is money. As far as they're concerned, I'm not as generous as either Abu Taher Haidar or Ibn Hamdan."

"If you were as generous as Ibn Hamdan, you would have destroyed Damascus by now, the way he's destroyed Egypt. People are saying that Egyptians are dying because they can't find anywhere to hide their wealth. Ibn Hamdan has destroyed Egypt with his greed and wars. He has goaded the amirs into rebellion. He's no longer just Al-Mustansir's minister; he's the country's actual ruler. I've just one request, my Lord."

"Tell me."

"If you could be just a bit more lenient with the soldiers, it would be better for us. Money's like soil: it can bury intrigues before they even start."

"I'm not like Ibn Hamdan; I don't buy loyalty."

"As you well know, my Lord, power isn't all about truth."

"If I had to purchase any soldier's loyalty, it would be better for me to die at his hands. If the army rebels, I'll fight them. I prefer to confront them rather than purchase their loyalty. I'll fight along with my son, Shaʿbaan. Badr never submits to amirs, nor does he buy security; he's the one who gives it. I swear that I'll fight the soldiers myself, and my son, Shaʿbaan, will take his own soldiers, find Shareef Abu Taher, and kill him, and then kill Ibn Hamdan as well, even if that means going to Egypt."

"As you command, my Lord," `Abd al-wahhab said. "You know more than me."

He could not believe Furoon's letter. Perhaps she had written it because she did not trust the slave girl, or else her father had threatened to kill her. He sent spies and a whole series of slave girls, but every time the same answer came back: 'I don't have your courage, Badr.'"

He received the Imam and Caliph Al-Mustansir's letter while he was quelling the rebellion in Damascus. It was an army rebellion, not a popular one: sword against sword, cavalier against cavalier, one religious community against another, one ambition against another. He read the letter. The Caliph was complaining about the way he was being impeded by his minister Ibn Hamdan. He had taken away everything of his: the gold, horses, and men. If only he had helped the Egyptians; instead, he had helped destroy them. The Caliph wrote.

Now, my only hope is with my God to whom I pray.

To Him belong the grace and favour.

My grandfather is a prophet; my Imam is my father;

I speak of God's unity and justice.

He summoned `Abd al-wahhab.

"Send a message back to the Caliph," Badr told him. "Tell him that Badr al-Jamali is his man and his supporter. Damascus is in danger, but Badr will be fighting with his son to secure it for the Caliph."

Egypt's tragedy had started years earlier, and it showed no sign of coming to an end. It seemed as though the country would be going through seven fallow years, and then seven more. The war had started among different divisions of the army: one group calling itself Ubaidis, another the Turks. The Caliph's mother was an Ubaidi and favoured her own family over the Turks. For that reason, the Turkish troops had set out with their swords to kill Ubaidi soldiers in every part of Egypt. This war between different contingents of the army carried on, and then the Maghrebis and Kitama tribe joined in as well.

The whole situation was exploited by corrupt and greedy people, merchants, Bedouin, and Egyptians. Wheat disappeared from markets, produce was in short supply, and highwaymen and vagabonds controlled the fates of people in both the south and Delta. They imposed taxes and demolished both lands and roads. They spread like locusts and destroyed all produce. Peasants fled into the desert, women were humiliated, and children starved. Then Ibn Hamdan arrived, escaping from Badr al-Jamali. He was a Turkish Amir, a Sunni, seeking refuge with the Fatimid Caliph Al-Mustansir, and that he offer him protection from Badr al-Jamali. He promised Shareef Abu Taher that he would become the Caliph and also promised the Sunni Caliph in Baghdad that he would cite his name from mosque pulpits throughout Egypt. In fact, he did that in the south and in Alexandria, and he also joined the robbers in their plunder. He lavished the wealth of Egyptians on his own soldiers. There was widespread chaos, and amid such chaos, fear. Everything was buried: people with wheat decided to hide it; people with animals decided to hide them; and people with gold buried it. The entire population of Egypt starved, and no wheat emerged from its hiding place. Gold was now worthless. As the chaos spread, corruption saturated people's hearts and spread abroad. Anyone who was not willing to sacrifice his own honour, money, and decency was like a man with no backbone. Canals were demolished, bridges knocked down, and roads destroyed. Between night and day, Egypt turned into a country of miracles begging for help, with people eating each other. An Abbasid Caliph in Baghdad heard that a Turkish Amir in Egypt was citing his name in Egyptian mosques, and a Fatimid Caliph amid the pillars of what was left of his palace in Cairo was well aware that there were very few men around him, and the number of people praying for him was even smaller. He had already lost parts of Syria to the Seljuqs and amirs; only Badr al-Jamali remained loyal to him, although he did not know why. It was as if Badr did not belong in this world; a mamluk trained to be loyal. From time to time, he would ask him for help, and, far more often, he would be praying to his Lord as he clung to a caliphate that was collapsing and slipping through his fingers.

No one knows for sure whether Badr realised the full extent of the danger to Damascus and yet thought he could confront it, or whether he did not appreciate the power that Shareef Abu Taher had to mobilise the tribes against the Governor of Damascus. Every revolt comes as a surprise. This was not just a revolt against the men of Damascus; it was civil strike and burning fire.

The day that Damascus burned was one to change destinies and sear people's hearts. The citizens of Damascus and their soldiers rebelled against Badr al-Jamali. They claimed that his strictness was not helping them, but rather shackling them. His stinginess with his soldiers showed that he was not loyal to the Imam. They said that the Armenian was intent only on his own interests and those of his Armenian soldiers. He wanted to occupy Muslim territory. They had a lot to say: Who says that Badr was originally a Muslim? Was he not kidnapped when he was twelve years old? Islam was not the faith into which he was born. He claims to be a Muslim so as to earn people's affection and stir up controversies. Badr is the cause of all our disasters, the only governor who hasn't yet been defeated or made a pact with the Turkish amirs. If his allegiance was to the Caliph Al-Mustansir, then he's gone astray. Who's responsible for all these intrigues? The Caliph Al-Mustansir. He has allowed his mother Rasad to interfere in affairs of state. She is appointing judges and ministers from among people of her own background and despises the Turks. She is the one responsible for the wars between Ubaidis, Turks, Maghrebis, and people from other factions in Egypt, a war involving Egyptians' bodies and inner selves. It had never happened before, that a people would attack its own, and yet it had happened in Egypt. When the Ubaidis and Maghrebis faded away and the Turks seized the reins of power, Rasad the Caliph's mother set out to destroy the entire country. Who is the Imam? A weak Caliph who cannot even rein in the mule he is riding? A Caliph who inspires no awe? How can the Imam inspire awe when he has not been feeding the people and resolving their disputes? People have said that Badr al-Jamali is responsible for all these catastrophes. Who brought the Armenians into the picture? Why give him a role? Does the Caliph trust his loyalty? Badr has only come to preserve himself and his sons. He is training his son to fight as though Egypt were his own country: Sha'baan, not yet twenty years old, has now become a very competent commander, while his other son, Ahmad, is following the same path. Badr is working on a state within a state. Getting rid of Badr is more important than getting rid of the Caliph. That involves weakening him, not killing him. Weakness is a disease with no cure, whereas death has one: resurrection and eternity. The cure for weakness does not lie in human hands.

On the day Damascus burned, when Badr al-Jamali's forces clashed with the Seljuks on one side and the supporters of Shareef Abu Taher on the other, defeat was inevitable. He did not have men as courageous as the Seljuk soldiers, nor could he rid his tents of the scourge of rebellion. Ah, Badr, such weakness! Today, your palace is surrounded by ten thousand men. If you do not escape, it will be burned to the ground. Run away and abandon Damascus, this time forever.

The blaze reached the Umayyad Mosque. He came out fighting defiantly and searching for soldiers with braver hearts. But all he found was shame.

"Defeat, my lord," `Abd al-wahhab told Badr sympathetically, "does not always attach to those who are not in the right. It often involves people who quest for justice."

"I'll only ever leave Damascus as a corpse," Badr replied. "I came on orders from the Muslim Caliph."

"Muslims have two Caliphs, not one. We can't fight the Seljuqs or an army out to defend ideas that don't alleviate people's hunger."

"I've never known defeat all my life, and I won't acknowledge it today. I returned to Damascus to stay. Where is Sha`baan? Why didn't he come with you?"

`Abd al-wahhab lowered his head.

"If I didn't realise how important I am to you," he replied humbly, "I would not have come. You've been a brother to me even when I've been working at your command."

He looked into his eyes. Badr's face paled, then turned bluish. His soul stopped breathing even though his body continued to do so. His eyes quivered.

"Has my son been hit?" he asked. "Is he in danger? Tell me the truth. Where is he?"

Not waiting for a response, he charged out of the palace into the Damascus streets, which were filled with the smell of incense. He ran past vendors peddling their wares and women strolling around in search of gold and silk. The Amir kept on running, as though he had no idea where he would be going from today onward and till the end of time. His heart had shattered and his veins had frozen.

"My lord Amir," `Abd al-wahhab shouted as he panted after him, "Sha`baan has been martyred today."

"You mean he's been hit."

"No, martyred. If you'll allow me, he's in the palace. If we go back..."

His joints froze and his feet refused to move. He could neither go back nor continue. He stayed still and, for the first time ever, felt scared. Weakness can shock like a ravenous beast, paralyze like the curse of the ancients, and weaken bones like years of a long life. If only tears would fall so we could come to terms with the truth and submit to it. But they did not.

`Abd al-wahhab put his hand on Badr's shoulder.

"I beg you, my Lord," he said. "Please let us return to the palace. Your entire family is in danger. This time, you won't be leaving Damascus safe and sound as you've done in the past."

"I've had no peace ever since I was born," Badr said.

"Your other children, my Lord—"

"Where's Sha`baan?"

"If we gather what's most valuable and escape from here—"

"Where's my son?"

"If—"

"You said he's in the palace."

"Yes."

"Where was he hit? I want to see."

He did not hear the screams of Amina Khatun, Sha`baan's mother and his former wife, nor did they have any effect on him. He brushed his hands over his son's face and kissed his lips. The boy was still and at peace, leaving the eternal concern to his father, like Adam when he emerged from Eden, and Cain's weakness and sorrow after killing his brother Abel. He heard Khatun's voice. Before, she had neither loved him nor hated him. But that day, she loathed him.

"My son!" she screamed, slapping her face and covering her head with dirt. "The primary joy in my life! You've caused his death. Your delusion is going to kill everyone else, too. Your Caliph and palace can both go to hell! If you're that weak, then surrender to the Seljuqs and don't hurl your son, who's not yet twenty, to perdition. Now he's dead, Badr, and you're still alive. He's dead, and you're alive."

She screamed as loud as she could, and women took her out of the room. He did not react, but a sense of guilt remained with him for the rest of his life. He was still alive, even though his life was full of misery and troubles.

The stench of burning needs a clear nose that is not already smelling the reek of death. He could neither inhale the smell of flames nor extinguish the fires of separation that invaded his heart and lingered. `Abd al-wahhab grabbed him by the arm.

"All the children are safe," he said. "They've left the palace. Come on, my Lord. Soldiers loyal to Shareef Abu Tahir and his own forces are burning down the palace. You're going to die inside. You've already spent hours here. Please permit me, my brother, my Lord."

Still, Badr clung to his dead son.

"We'll move him far from the fires," he said. "His lovely face must survive, as pure and radiant as sunlight."

He carried his son outside and, with heartfelt grief, put him on his horse. Along with the rest of his family, he fled to the edge of Damascus.

It may have been two days before he realised what had happened and what his new destiny was to be. The only people with him were a few men, his parents, and his daughter. Amina Khatun may have stayed with him to remind him of his own crime or else to urge him to get himself killed—he was not sure.

Furoon's words soon loomed in front of him, but then all trace of them vanished. At that point, he laughed at himself and the world.

"I don't have your courage, Amir," she had said.

What kind of courage was the halva-maker's daughter talking about? Had he not just abandoned Damascus in defeat? Was his palace and part of the Umayyad Mosque not on fire? Was not everything he loved being destroyed? The halva-maker's daughter had done the right thing. She had chosen the winner. That is the way it is with women and the world; they latch on to the winner till he is defeated, then they despise him like so many mosquitoes.

Why had the light dimmed and colours faded? How could this day have become so utterly impossible? Eyes closed, he spent his time feeling a mixture of anger and sorrow and seeing the image of his son. Every day, he would pray to God to let him die in conflict, to die as Sha`baan had, his chest pierced by a sword, ripping apart the pulsating heart that now looked down to blame and castigate him for not realising how grave the danger was and not winning the battle. Not only that, he'd not put any distance between his children and wars and betrayals; he had dared to fall in love, and he had forgotten that he was a mere mamluk, slave to his Caliph, his gold, children, position, and religious community. A mere boy with no name and no destiny.

Susie, lovely sister! Where are you? Your destiny must be better than mine. I remember now: my name was Aram; how could I ever forget? I've become Badr, and I've completely forgotten about the mountains and ice. Then Sha`baan arrived and gave life an emerald hue that it has now lost. Today, he remembers his original name, one that no one has used in years. It was Jamal ad-daula who had named him 'Badr son of `Abdallah.' But he misses the name Aram. Aram, a boy unsoiled by a sin that now haunts him the way a hyena will chase its foul, shit-encrusted tail. Ah, sin and its foul stench! Does he dare stay alive? Carrying on? How was it that he could cry when his teacher took away that piece of emerald, and yet he could not cry over the death of his own son? Had his tears all dried up? Or was it that, like the fates, he had been caught up in the curse of different names? Sha`baan had come from his own stock, even though he did not speak his father's native language and had never heard his original name. When he died, would the angels call him Badr or Aram, he wondered. He could remember his mother, too, drowning in blood. Why could he still see her talking to him, with blood all around her? He had asked her then what his name meant, and she replied that it meant safety and peace.

Today, he praises God that Jamal ad-daula changed his name. His first one did not suit his days or nights.

Two months earlier, he had assumed that the world was granting him peace. The Armenian was madly in love like a teenager, giving no thought to his status or rank. He was in love with the halva-maker's daughter. He wanted to hold her in his arms and laughed with her as he sought serenity. Fires of passion had seared his bones, and now he longed for her like an innocent boy who has never killed anyone or had sex with hundreds of women. At the time, he must have realised that, ever since the day of his birth, his destiny had not been in his own hands. When he stood there helpless before the people who had killed his mother and stolen his sister, he was actually seeing his future life in front of him, with all of it blood, impotence, and sorrow.

Months later, he heard the news: Furoon had been married to Amir Hamza, the ally of Shareef Abu Taher and Ibn Hamdan. Did he expect something different? He did not pay much attention to the news, but the rage inside him would not allow him to breathe until his son's killer was dead. And yet, death brought relief; the dead were secure and peaceful. He would think about it. Even more important, he would think about the loyal men who had not run away when the fighting started or abandoned their commander to the Seljuk hyenas.

CHAPTER FOUR

Her screams reached all the way to Acre, till people assumed that she had lost her mind. As she wept and slapped her cheeks, Hafsa kept trying to clasp her hand.

"This is wrong, my daughter," Hafsa said gently. "You're hurting yourself."

"I told him I'd never be married to Hamza," she replied. "But he's married me to him against my will. That's what's wrong. I'm going to argue with him and then run away."

"He's you father, Furoon. Do you want to cause him a scandal? It's your destiny, my daughter. All of us have to surrender and endure our destinies. You need to endure your own sufferings. Maybe he'll turn out to be a good husband."

"No!" she yelled. "I'll never do it!"

"If you want to cause your father a scandal, then go ahead. I don't approve. But you're devout, and you're required to obey your father."

"You're lying. You can obey your father when it doesn't offend God. But forcing me to be married is wrong. You don't know anything; none of you do. If only I'd gone away with him and left this hell behind! I hate you all. Ever since I was born, my life with you has been nothing but suffering."

Amir Hamza was at least twenty-five years older than her and had three wives, two daughters, and a son. Why did he want her?

Hafsa listened patiently to what Furoon had to say, then handed her the new clothes to put on.

"When you've calmed down," she told Furoon, "go out to your husband. I'll leave the door open. If you want to run away and join Badr, then go ahead. I'll help you. But just imagine your father's expression when he faces his men."

Having lit the flame in Furoon's heart, Hafsa left. Furoon collected her possessions and gold and headed for the door.

"My darling," she whispered to herself, "my only darling."

Slinking in, she listened as her father was telling Shareef Abu Taher about her.

"She's a good girl," he was saying. "God has given me good recompense in her. She'll be a wife who will obey her husband and stick to her pledge."

That made her even more furious. As she eyed him from behind the door, her eyes were dim and fretful. It sounded as though her father had no faith in her. That gave her a bit of a chill.

"It's what you deserve, Father," she told herself. "I don't love you, with all your cruelty and egotism. You don't care about me, you..."

She dug her nails into her face and dropped the bag of clothes.

"Still, I can't do this to you," she told herself in a suppressed scream.

Her hand shaking, she took out Badr's coat, kissed it, and pulled it close to her chest before she burst into tears. After drying her tears, she put on a face veil to hide the wounds that covered it, then went out to her father.

When she was left alone with her husband, whom she refused to look at, even though he was right in front of her, he took off his clothes.

"Welcome to your husband's home, Furoon," he told her.

When she removed her face veil, he came over, looking shocked.

"Who did that to you?" he asked, rubbing his hand over her cheek. "What about those wounds? Did you do that to yourself?"

"We need to talk, Amir," she replied, removing his hand.

"Why talk on our wedding day?" he asked. "We can postpone talk about the wounds till the wedding has been consummated. For now, I can say that I've never seen anyone as beautiful as you. Those eyes of yours send out arrows of passion. Those lips..."

He put his hand on her lips.

"We have to talk," she insisted.

He gave her a dubious look.

"It's for your sake, Amir," she went on. "We're going to talk specifically for your sake. Then I shall obey you as my husband."

Did she tell the truth or a lie? She had no idea. She told her husband that having sex with him was impossible; a Sicilian jinn had fallen in love with her and taken possession of her soul. Anyone else who touched her would be killed or lose his manhood. She gave him a detailed description of the jinn and what she had seen. If he intended to take the risk, he might well lose something he would never get back. She screamed and cried like a madwoman. That both frightened and troubled him. At first, he did not believe her, but then she put all her gold in front of him.

"You can have all this," she told him insistently, "but you can't touch me. It's everything that I've inherited from my mother and all the gold that you have given my father. I'll stay here in your house, taking care of you and your children. But don't risk our lives."

He had heard about her love for Badr, and for him alone. Raising his hand, he slapped her hard.

"You're a tart," he said, "nothing more. You're scared I'm going to expose you in front of your father. Well, I'm going to do it."

When he moved closer to her, she invoked the jinn's help and said some words in Coptic that she had learned from her grandmother. Those words and her call for help spooked him. Egyptian magic had been famous for ages. If he lost his manhood because of the halva-maker's daughter, he would be losing everything. She told him hysterically about the Pyramid Witch, how she had met the witch along with her grandmother and asked for a cure for the jinn's love. The Witch had told her that any man who touched her would either die or lose his manhood. Hamza left her that night and went to one of his other wives. Each month, Furoon used her own money, which her father was giving her, to buy him a slave girl. Furoon started working in his household, taking care of his daughters. She would obey all his instructions, and he would not ask her to do anything that she could not handle. Sometimes, he would come into her room unexpectedly, and she would scream, slap herself, scratch her face, and yell to the jinn to come to her aid. Hamza was not convinced that she truly was mad, or that the jinn story was true, but he was afraid to talk to her father about it. Magic can affect people differently, and people are scared of witches even if they are madly in love.

After a year, people started asking why Furoon had not had a baby. People said that she was barren. She was hated by everyone around her. She tried to spend most of her time with Hafsa and her brother, and, a year later, she moved in with them. She was now separated from her husband, but she continued to provide him with money every month, everything her brother and father gave her or that she earned from selling halva. She gave up all hope of ever seeing Badr and did her best to carry on living, her one hope being that her body would remain her own and not Hamza's or any other man's. She was like the mother who has lost everything and has no alternative but to work night and day, paying the cost of her son's life; in this case, Hamza was just like that son. At the start of every month, he would come to see her brother, and, if he did not get enough money to satisfy him, he would grab her, drag her away, and try to hit her. Her brother would stop him and give him more money. Her entire goal in life became keeping herself just for Badr, making halva, and working night and day to keep herself for herself.

She explained the situation to Hafsa and told her bitterly that she had not given herself to her husband, adding that, "God does not charge any soul except to its capacity." She asked Hafsa if she had committed a sin by behaving that way.

"I don't know, my daughter," Hafsa replied after a moment's silence. "But God knows, hears, and sees. He never asks us to do anything beyond our capabilities. His mercy covers everything."

She calmed down and relaxed. She loathed Hamza for his cruelty and for the fact that he could force her to have sex with him. His very existence was a threat to her soul and made her anxious.

At night in Hafsa's house, she went over to the closet and, with shaking hands, took out Badr's coat that she had kept.

"Would it annoy you, Lord," she whispered, clutching it to her chest, "if I kissed his coat just once and lay my head on it as a pillow? I'm the very worst of women, but I can't help it. I've no control over my heart, nor can I curb the gale inside my breast."

"Badr," she muttered as she clasped the coat passionately. "You're my only love."

She pushed the coat away and put it back in the closet. The next morning, Hamza banged on her door and dragged her off to his house.

"Hamza's not someone to be controlled by a woman!" he yelled in her face. "Everyone in the house needs to be told the truth about you."

"Hamza's household," he told the entire family once he had brought them together, "I want you all to know that Furoon is a liar. She doesn't deserve to live. I'm only keeping her as a wife in order to humiliate her, that's all."

Head bowed, she prayed to God that he would stay away from her, but he did not. He pushed her into a room, locked the door, and took off his coat. She gave him a shocked look.

"If you killed me now," she told him forcefully, "it will never happen."

Her entire body was shivering.

"I'm giving you one last chance," he said, "before I kill you with my bare hands."

"Let me go back to my brother's house," she replied breathlessly. "You can have everything you want."

"You're what I want," he said. "Today, I'll find out if you've been lying. I've brought someone who can reveal your lies. When she does, I'm going to kill you in front of your own father."

She did not understand what he meant, but then he opened the door and summoned an old woman, who slowly walked in.

"Leave me with her," the woman said.

She was carrying a thick stick.

"I've come to expel the jinn from your body," she said in a monotone.

The old woman beat her with the stick for an hour or more. Furoon bore it all, groaning but neither talking nor pleading. When the woman stopped, she pursed her lips and looked at Furoon.

"You're lying to your husband," she said. "The jinn's in your heart, not your body."

"You can have whatever you want," Furoon told the woman after a moment's pause. "Tell him that you've failed."

"I never fail," the woman replied triumphantly. "But this time, I'm prepared to fail."

Furoon took off her earrings and put them in the woman's hand. The old woman left and told Hamza that Furoon's entire body was possessed by the jinn. Killing her was the only way to get rid of it.

"Kill her then," he muttered. "Then we'll be done with her."

He went over to Furoon and looked into her eyes.

"Even before I was married to you, I knew everything. Do you realise what I liked about you, halva-maker's daughter? That Badr wants you and can't have you as long as I'm alive. Badr's aflame with the fires of intrigue that I've kindled. You're the devil incarnate. Anyone who's in love with the Armenian is a devil."

Then, with a shrug, he left. Furoon slunk out, went back to Hafsa's house, and wept in her arms.

"Hafsa," she said, "I don't deserve to be your daughter. My heart is evil.

I utterly loathe Hamza, and I can't forgive the father who gave me life. My bitter feelings are big enough to reach all the way to India."

Hafsa patted her shoulder.

"Pray and ask for forgiveness," she said. "God knows best what is in your heart."

"It grieves me, Hafsa, that I can't talk to God with a clean heart. It's full of malice and hatred."

"As long as you're aware of sin, you're fine. Your heart can resist the anger inside you."

But the sin of hatred was easier to deal with than the unruly image that kept returning to her very single day: Badr in her arms. She longed for his embrace like a singing girl, even though she was someone else's wife. She would remind herself that she was indeed married to another man. She would wake in the middle of the night, having dreamt that she was kissing Badr. She would beg God for forgiveness, pray, and weep as she bowed down in prayer to her God:

"O Lord, forgive me for my dreams, or punish me for them in this world, not the next. My heart is weak; there is no good in it. O Lord, it is the devil who portrays passion to me as a paradise and love as achievement. O Lord, Your mercy is all encompassing."

She searched for Badr's coat in the closet. Today, she was going to use it as a pillow without any shame. But she did not find it. Frantically, she searched for it.

"Has anyone opened the closet?" she called anxiously to Hafsa.

"What are you looking for, my daughter?" Hafsa replied.

Without saying anything, she simply pointed at the closet.

"I burned it, Furoon," Hafsa told her firmly. "It's not right, my daughter. That coat of his will torture you even more when you're married to another man."

"I'm not married to any man," Furoon yelled without even thinking. "How can you do such a thing? Why did you do it? Why do you hate me so much? If only I could die and be rid of all of you! This family can go to hell. I hate you all—my father, you, my husband, the whole lot of you. Now you take away the only thing I have left. Why? Where did you learn to be so unkind?"

Hafsa did not respond. She just listened with a frown. Furoon sobbed, wiped away her tears, and buried her face in the pillow.

"Why can't I die?" she asked. "This life has gone on too long, too long..."

"Forgive me," she said, turning to face Hafsa. "I no longer know my own self."

BOOK TWO

Acre 1073 CE / 466 AH

Her tears mixed with blood, she speaks.

She runs, her breaths raised on high,

Ask not to greet me, she said.

Your absence leaves me just spirit, not body.

Tamim ibn Al-Mu'izz, Fatimid poet

CHAPTER FIVE

The best plan might be to rip all passion out of the heart. Once you are accustomed to the pain, the world, with all its problems and joys, becomes one and the same. He retired to Acre or sought refuge there. Time now became long. He was no longer involved with revolts by greedy soldiers, their eyes empty of gold, unsated and unfed; by tribes unwilling to accept his strict regime and firm control over everything; and by spies and conspiracies hatching plots against him. In Damascus, he had spent his time stopping attacks and doing his best to stay upright. Here in Acre, there was lots of time for planning and reckoning with the truth—acknowledging what was and what had been. He had lost his son and his beloved. His son was now at peace with his Lord, allowing him to avoid seeing how much savagery his father had witnessed in a world that neither tolerated the truthful nor pitied the virtuous. It would also bring relief from days when he would turn his head and ask himself whether it was his own heart that was deceiving him, or whether it was his father, his wife, a slave girl, or servant; a relief from embellishments that managed to gleam and burn at the same time.

Ah, Sha`baan, I greet you! And yet, I am asking for mercy for myself, not for you. That same groan emerges from my heart and almost floods the entire horizon with tears. But someone like me never cries, someone created to destroy the enemy like a rugged sword; when it buckles, we get rid of it. When you meet God, tell Him that Badr can never buckle, but his heart is dead in his hands. God is merciful and will listen to you. I do not know if He will hear my prayer, but I will try. How trivial and stupid love is, like stagnant water in bitter cold. It was a tale like the ones about girls plying their trade in boats on the Nile before Al-Hakim bi-Amr Allah came to power. Those girls would say that girls, too, have passions, as a way of justifying the dirhams they earned, and they would claim to be in love in order to improve their business. How can a burning heart fall in love? What can you expect from the girl? Can she attack her own father for the sake of an Armenian? Fine, in moments of closeness, he can scoff at his own naivete. In the future, he can steer clear of such idiocies so as not to see himself the way he does today, ashamed of his own weakness and stupidity. The girl was married to Hamza,

Abu Taher's ally. For just a moment, he laughed out loud, then he stopped, stood up, and went out.

His two sons came in to see him. Ahmad was twelve, and Muhammad was five or six. After kissing his father's hand, Ahmad sat down, looking gloomy.

"Father," he asked, "am I going to be killed like my brother?"

"That will never happen," he replied immediately. "I swear to you that I'll die before anyone touches you."

"My mother says," Ahmad went on fearfully, "that, as long as the wars continue, I'll be killed."

After a moment's pause, he asked the boy: "Do you trust your father?"

"Sha`baan was my friend and companion," Ahmad went on hesitantly. "I miss him a lot. I don't want to die."

Badr stretched out his hand, intending to give his son a hug and tell him that he would be the one to die first. But he changed his mind.

"Soldiers don't say such things," he told Ahmad firmly. "Death's not in our own hands. Like life itself, it's part of our destiny. Raise your head. You're just as strong as your father. One day, you'll be an army commander."

With a nod of his head, he obeyed his father. Grabbing his brother's hand, he left the room.

He took a long look at the soldiers: the same uniform, the same posture, eyes fixed on the horizon, a hard stare into the unknown. They neither knew nor cared about their goals. These soldiers were different from Al-Mustansir's; they were part of his family, spoke its language, and knew its bread and mountains. He had been training them for five years, always reminding them of the goal and teacher; that teacher was not the Imam, but rather Badr, son of `Abdallah who, like them, had come here for a task known only to God. These were men who would not be frightened by Abu Taher or Ibn Hamdan. He understood why Ibn Hamdan was afraid of him and had set Abu Taher and the Seljuqs on him in order to remind him of his own weakness. He also realised that having two men involved in a single caliphate was illegitimate and as inconceivable as having a phoenix with a man's head on it. But Ibn Hamdan had been killing people in Egypt.

He inspected his soldiers, his gaze tracked by the eyes of his own son, who was standing enthusiastically among them, agleam like the honest, courageous fighter he was, always full of life. Sometimes when he looked around, he would see in his son's face, glances, gestures, and movements the faces of these young men and hear his cheerful voice. Regretfully he would repeat the words of the poet, Ibn ar-Rumi:

May God do battle with the fates and

Their deliberate assaults on our hearts' beloveds.

I am amazed that my heart has not been rent asunder for him,

Even if it is harder than solid rock.

Bereft of him, I have abandoned all joy;

Now I have become an abstainer from life's pleasures.

Should someone offer a lover a gift,

Mine would be to glimpse your spectre in my dreams.

Peace be upon you, a greeting from me

And from every rain cloud with its thunder and lightning!

"My Lord," `Abd al-wahhab said gently.

"My friend," Badr replied, "it's as though you can read my mind!"

"No one knows you as well as I do."

"Sometimes poets will tell the truth when, like us, they've had a taste of treachery. But Abbasid poets speak the truth only when they experience pain. Tell me, how are things in Egypt?"

"Are you asking a question or complaining?"

"We're waiting for a letter from the Caliph. Times are not the same now; they've lost their colour, as dry as the river Nile. The stench is as foul as that of the country's many corpses and has the same savour as the plague that is ravaging its very innards."

"Anyone who set eyes on you would think that you're strong, but that strength owes as much to hatred as to love."

"Whoever killed my son has to be punished."

"You never said he'd be killed."

"For me, the killing was never a punishment, `Abd al-wahhab. It's all a mercy!"

For a moment, `Abd al-wahhab looked down.

"You don't mention the halva-maker's daughter anymore," he said hesitantly. "Does her spectre haunt you, my son?"

For a moment, he said nothing.

"Badr never forgives deceit," he finally said. "I don't even remember her."

"But Badr is fully aware," `Abd al-wahhab went on, "that, at the time, he was Governor of Damascus and was close to forty years old. The girl was just eighteen, and she had never witnessed war nor spoken to soldiers. Tell me, Badr, how is a girl supposed to stand in front of her parents and change her religion? Don't ask anyone to take on more than they can bear. There's no mercy in that."

"I have no mercy," he replied without thinking. "I've never learned it. This is an era of power and justice, not mercy and forgiveness."

"How can you have erased your love for her from your heart? You have an iron will."

"She's not worth talking about."

`Abd al-wahhab looked at him carefully.

"There's something I need to talk about," he said. "The presence of Armenian Christians in the army may well incite rebellion. People will say that Badr is more sympathetic to his ancestors' religion. I have to be frank with you, my son. Unrest in this country is a hot issue. It's a major priority that..."

"`Abd al-wahhab," Badr interrupted, "not for a single day have I denied that my parents and entire family were Christians. That's who I am, and I'll never be anyone else. I welcome into my army with open arms anyone who's loyal, and I'm not bothered about either his religion or sect. Isn't that part of Islam's calling? Justice for everyone? Dear man, commanders can take me as a model to emulate."

"I understand you, my Lord," `Abd al-wahhab replied. "But I'm still afraid of what the populace is saying."

"Don't be afraid. Didn't you know that the populace is more intelligent than either commanders or the people in authority?"

Aram, the Armenian, now looked all around him. He dispatched some of his men to search for his cousin and his former residence. They found a family member, but he knew nothing about Susie. If she had died, that would be a better fate than imprisonment and slavery. Was anyone else in the family still alive? Was there no other trace of the former house than the person who was currently living there? But Badr no longer acknowledged Aram and did his best to forget about Susie.

Amina Khatun took up residence in her former husband's palace. He wanted to have her beside him so he could protect her, his daughter, and two sons: Al-Awhad and Al-Afdal. They both needed their mother's care. He had not set eyes on her for five years and still had no desire to see her. Her words may well have been true, but there are times when speaking the truth can be more painful than the death of children. Amina Khatun could live in peace where she was, far away from him. Five whole years, following in the footsteps of Abu Taher and the Seljuqs. The day would come when he would recapture Damascus, but, for now, using Acre as a headquarters gave him the opportunity to assemble an army. Five whole years of dreaming—not about his son, Sha'baan, but instead about Abu Taher, his son's killer. How he planned to attack him, and how to make sure that he was not killed. For five years now, seven amirs had conspired against him, including Abu Taher and Hamza, Furoon's husband. Was it not an irony of history that the only girl he really desired was married to his enemy? Was she plotting with her husband today, he wondered, to put an end to Badr? Had she given birth to sons and daughters who would fight Badr? That's why women's hearts were even smaller than those of pigeons winging their way around the country—no loyalty, no charity. This way was better. For a man like him, love was just another weak spot, another defeat. He had a task to perform, indeed many tasks, and he intended to finish them—no more, no less. After that, life could come to an end, with no regrets over a heart that had loved and been sacrificed; or had weakened, then been expunged so as to quell the passion and retreat the same way as the Amir had retreated from Damascus. In a time of deceit and treachery, let all loves go up in flames! He was tougher on his own heart than on hers. There were many other women. His palace was full of beautiful women who were accomplished poets, reciters, singers, musicians, and also passionate lovers. However, between him and all women there existed a stone fortress as solid as the very Pyramids, imperishable and unbreakable. For years, the same fortress had kept him apart from other people, ever since he had watched his family being killed. Leaving his house had frozen his veins and stopped innocent blood from flowing. Life still afforded its pleasures. But instead of providing satisfaction, it kept on toying with him, day after day, year after year. Now the time had come to take on Abu Taher and his supporters. He would spend the night plotting his revenge. Once that was done, he could relax and sleep, and then meet Amina Khatun.

Here is a slave girl unlike any other: spectacularly beautiful and intelligent enough to handle any kind of trickery amirs might use. She is what he needs. He has lavished money on her, but not touched her. He has treated her like an amir and then asked her to do something for which, if she manages to bring it off, he will not only set her free but also give her ten thousand dinars. Year after year, he has been collecting money and making preparations for this day. He wants her to go to the secret place where Abu Taher is hiding outside Damascus. Once there, she is to give a letter to Abu Hazim, the tribal leader, along with twelve thousand dinars. In the letter, she is going to ask for just one thing, that Abu Taher is to be handed over to the soldiers who are accompanying her—no more, no less. However, the slave girl must first make sure that Abu Hazim is going to be loyal to her. If he does not actually fall in love with her, then maybe he will double-cross her. Who knows? If her intelligence does not work, then she will perish and so will he.

He is going to hunt down his enemies, one by one. He has made that decision. Five years of work. He will start with his son's killer, then Ibn Hamdan, then ʿAli the halva-maker. He has decided to leave ʿAli till last, because they have a lot to say to each other.

The slave girl managed to carry out her task to the letter. A month later, the glad tidings arrived that the soldiers had brought Abu Taher. The girl had succeeded. If ever there was a pleasurable moment in his entire life, then it was now and today. He went to Amina Khatun's room and, without any explanation, asked her to come with him.

Once inside his prison in Acre, he descended the stairs. It had not been used for some time, and it was gloomy and dilapidated. Men would arrive, then disappear. He had not done a lot of damage here, but others had. Any number of screams had damaged the steps, and tears had accumulated like stale water on cave walls. Today, he wanted the prison to be lit up, a lot of light. He was going to set a lot of people free. That day, Amina Khatun could not understand her former husband; she did not love him, but still she followed his footsteps, eager to find out what he was planning and hoping that her guess was correct. Removing his coat, Badr opened the cell door on Abu Taher. Their eyes met.

"How can he be Commander of the Faithful?" he asked calmly, raising his head.

"If you so much as touch me," Abu Taher replied in a quavering tone, "the people of Acre will rise up against you the same way the people of Damascus did before. You've no hope, Badr."

He looked at Amina.

"What do you think, Shaʿbaan's mother?" he asked her sarcastically. "The Commander of the Faithful who killed your son, Khatun, is now threatening me. I wonder, is his army outside the door, waiting to pounce on me? Or is he going to burn down Acre the way he did Damascus?"

Tears in her eyes, Khatun just stayed where she was.

"When I send you to hellfire, God willing," Badr said bluntly, "Ibn Hamdan will be joining you there. Then Muslim lands will be purged of greed and corruption."

"As if you're a Muslim like us, you Mamluk renegade!" Abu Taher shot back.

"You're still brave, even when you're in prison. Let's leave it to God to decide who's a Muslim. But I promise you, I *can* dispatch you to hellfire."

"Let's start afresh," Abu Taher said, his tone suddenly pleading. "I'm not to blame for your son's death. It was war."

"And who started it?"

"I don't know. It started, and that was that. Let's start from scratch, Badr. Don't kill me so the populace will hate you even more than they already do. You've no friends. Look on me as a friend, and—"

Badr went over to him and grabbed his lapels.

"Don't you understand, Abu Taher?" he said. "When I flay your skin, you're going to die of the excruciating pain after several days, but I still won't have punished you enough. Like the body, the skin is cold and disloyal. On the other hand, when you flay the heart, there are no sighs or blood, just groans and flames."

Abu Taher pleaded with him and kissed the ground at his feet. He made promises and wept, but Badr ignored him.

"I want him to be flayed alive in front of Sha'baan's mother," he told them.

"My Lord," Amina Khatun said immediately.

"Console your heart, if you can," Badr told her.

"There's no consolation for the heart, Badr," she replied. "As you well know."

The soldiers started flaying Abu Taher's feet, and the screams started.

"I want to leave this place, Badr," she said at once. "Stop it."

Their eyes met.

"You can leave," he told her, opening the door.

"It's as though I don't even know you," she stuttered.

"Or perhaps it's that you don't appreciate the extent of my own weakness and the death of my soul."

After years of anxiety, he could sleep, calmly and peacefully, as he awaited the morrow, when Ibn Hamdan would meet his end. It is not hard to understand human beings. Greed and fear always prevail, and betrayal is an intrinsic feature of greed and the bane of fear. Ibn Hamdan could only ever be killed by the people closest to him. He wrote a letter to the husband of Ibn Hamdan's daughter, who was the Turkish Amir Ildakiz. The letter was full of requests for help. He told him that Al-Mustansir was asking him to rid Egypt of Ibn Hamdan. He had totally destroyed the country, provoked rebellion, and waged battles in Cairo, Alexandria, Fustat, and Damietta. No one was safe from Ibn Hamdan, even in Upper Egypt. He would only stop when people abandoned their homes and started selling them for bread and water. He would neither stop nor have any sense of the weight of the destruction he had wrought. Corruption was widespread, and whole properties had been destroyed. Egypt—the nation that Arabs regarded as a slice of paradise, with its green hue—had now turned into a wasteland. No peasants were farming or even staying with their land. The whole country had been destroyed.

Badr had started his plan some time ago. He had befriended Ildakiz the Turk, who was married to Ibn Hamdan's daughter. He kept sending him gifts and messages. In his letters, he wrote: The rescue of Egypt from the tyranny of Ibn Hamdan lies in the hands of Ildakiz the Turk. That is a command from the Caliph. If he killed Ibn Hamdan, he would become his minister. People loved and respected him. Badr realised that he was married to Ibn

Hamdan's daughter, but truth outweighed any marital bond. Did not God demand of us to tell the truth, even if it did not favour those close to us? Beyond that, Ibn Hamdan's coffers were still full, and his son-in-law would be the inheritor and also ruler of Egypt. He might even be like Joseph the prophet, Egypt's saviour, and save the country from plague, famine, and hardship.

He waited for the response, although he already knew what it would be. One month later, Ibn Hamdan was killed in his house by his son-in-law, Ildakiz, as he sat there peacefully in his own home, the Egyptians dying of hunger. Amir Ildakiz went to the Caliph to give him the good news and demand money. The Caliph Al-Mustansir was astonished and told him that he had not asked him to kill Ibn Hamdan and did not want any bloodshed. There was already more than enough killing in the country. But Ildakiz was not convinced and brought his soldiers in to take the emeralds and gold that Al-Mustansir still possessed. It was not a lot, and so he also took the very last horse the man had ridden. With that, he left and became minister of Egypt, as Badr had promised him, and as he himself had wanted all his life.

CHAPTER SIX

In Damascus, Hamza rushed to Hafsa's house, dragged his wife out without a word, and assembled all his children, men before women.

"Now that the miserable Armenian has killed Abu Taher and Ibn Hamdan," he told them gloomily, "he's planning to kill me, too."

Hafsa swallowed hard, but said nothing. He looked into her eyes.

"I wonder," he said in front of his children. "If he comes to my house, who'll be the betrayer and who'll put up a fight?"

"Father," the children all responded at once, "we'll sacrifice ourselves for you."

"And what about you, Furoon?" he asked, shaking her.

"Hamza," she replied quietly, "we'll all be your ransom."

"Say it, my wife. 'Whatever happens, I'll be faithful to you.' Go on, say it."

She looked at his children's expressions, realising how much they hated and distrusted her.

"I shall do only what pleases God," she said.

"My husband...'"

"My husband..."

"You're unfaithful," he yelled, as he slapped her face. "My children need to know the truth about you. Have you told your lover where to find me?"

He remained silent. He grabbed his sword, raised it, and set it against her neck.

"If I killed you now, I'd be burning his heart and yours. But I'm going to wait a while..."

After talking to his children for an hour or more, he ran out of the house.

Following Ibn Hamdan's death, arresting Hamza proved easier than expected. Badr sent soldiers to Damascus, and they brought him back. Indeed, it did not take long before he found Hamza standing in front of him in irons and begging for mercy. For a moment, he stared at this man who was Furoon's husband. Was she searching for him with those gentle eyes of hers, he wondered, and praying to God that Badr would treat him mercifully? He smiled as he looked at the man.

"Cut off his head now," he ordered his soldiers. "Then I want you to sell his daughters and wives in the Acre market in front of the populace. Tell people that this is the fate of people who plot against Badr al-Jamali. You can sell his horses for a dinar and a half. Don't forget: wives for a dinar, horses for a dinar and a half."

Hamza stayed silent, his head lowered.

"You traitor," Badr told him calmly. "What hurts you more: your horses being sold, or your women?"

He had been waiting for this moment for five years. Like all his victories, it had arrived smoothly and easily.

Hamza was different. He'd had sex with Furoon and lived with her. He had been married to her against her will, knowing full well that she wanted Badr. So where was the victory today? Badr moved closer to him.

"How sorry for you I feel today, man," he said. "You're dying today, knowing that your wives are being embraced by ordinary men, and that's what they deserve. Who's going to pay a dinar, I wonder, and who'll be buying Furoon? Have you thought about that?"

Hamza stared at him for just a moment.

"Maybe you need to ask today who it is that she loves," he said. "Has it occurred to you that she'll be sad about her husband? You're out to hurt her because hatred has never left your foreigner's heart."

"And the Arab heart is all affection? What do you say, man: should we have a duel between two men? Whoever wins gets to live and enjoy your wife."

Hamza looked at him as though he did not understand. Badr took off his coat and grabbed his sword.

"Men are never scared of getting old," Badr said, looking at the sword. "But they worry about losing their strength. I practice sword-drill every day. When I lose my ability to fight, I'll die."

Raising his sword, he pointed it at Hamza.

"Let's fight like men," he said.

Hamza went over to him.

"There's something I need to tell you about your beloved," he said. "She's been in the arms of a different man every single night. We don't need to fight about the halva-maker's daughter. She's a slut who's sighed in the arms of every man in Damascus."

Badr's face was blank, but he raised his sword. At that point, the duel was not with Hamza. It was with a sorrow that lurked deep inside him, with not the least hope of a cure; with a world that gave him only what he wanted when he lowered his eyes and forgot; with his longing for those brief moments of passion that they may have shared. When Furoon smiled, lions stopped roaring, and hyenas submitted to rules of mercy and compassion. But all that was in the past; now he neither wanted nor knew her. He heard Hamza panting, then pleading. He was no good at fighting, so was he perhaps better at loving? Had she kissed him out of love, realising that he was going to die? Would she beg Badr to let him live? What was Furoon going to do?

He rammed the sword into Hamza's chest, then looked away.

"Badr's still powerful," he said casually, "and he'll stay that way till the day he dies. Take Hamza's corpse out of the palace and bring me his entire family."

The daughter's screams over her father's death did not stop. Furoon blocked her ears with her hands and closed her eyes. It had been four months since her husband had been killed, and she and his children were prisoners of the Amir. Which amir? Badr al-Jamali. Hamza's daughter shook her.

"That devil killed my father in cold blood," she screamed, "and now he's humiliating all of us. He killed your husband."

"We have God," she replied weakly.

"What are you going to do, Furoon?" she asked.

"We must try to reach my father and brother," she replied at once, "and ask them to protect us."

She had no idea how Badr's soldiers had managed to bring them to Acre, nor could she recall how things had ended up the way they had.

She did not see Badr's face, nor did she analyse her feelings. There was blood all around her, and screams deafened her ears. The fact that she was kept in prison, along with her husband's daughters and other women from the families of Badr al-Jamali's enemies, was a new phenomenon for her, something she had neither anticipated nor knew how to handle. How she had prayed to be able to see him at least once before her life came to an end, and how she had come to despair of ever seeing him again. Now she had no idea how she would face him if he asked to see her, or maybe if he did not. She asked the guard to let her see her brother just once; she begged and offered him money, but he refused. After a whole month in prison, only Hafsa came to see her, looking anxious.

"What have they done with you, my daughter?" she asked.

She did not reply, nor did she cry.

"Ask to speak to him," she told her softly. "He'll listen to you. I can't see him selling you in the markets. What guardian would ever do that?"

"He's done that before," she replied, her eyes fixed on the floor, "punishing his enemies' wives and making them an example for every traitor and enemy. That's their lives, Hafsa. Halva's diverted our attention from the cruelties of this era, and so we know nothing about those woman's lives."

"But you're not just any girl," Hafsa said. "You know what I mean."

Furoon looked at her in amazement.

"If he still has feelings towards you," Hafsa said, "if only just sympathy, he would never be doing this to you."

Furoon swallowed hard, almost choking herself. She closed her eyes without saying a word.

"Ask to see him, and—"

"I'll never plead with him," Furoon stated loud and clear.

"Do you prefer to turn into a slave girl? You, the very best of people?"

Hugging herself, she recited some verses from the Qur'an, but did not respond.

For those four months, she had not asked to see or talk to him. He was the one who invited her and Hamza's two daughters to attend his council.

She remained silent as she awaited the guard's instructions to go into the Amir's chamber.

Was she afraid of Badr? She was shivering like a coward as she rehearsed her defence...over and over again.

As soon as he entered, she closed her eyes. She could remember the smell of his musk-scented coat and the way she had cried and moaned when Hafsa had burned it. For a while, she kept her eyes closed. When she opened them again, she was not sure whether it was love, despair, or raw passion that was overwhelming her.

Their eyes met. He knew those eyes of hers well, when they were angry, affectionate, and in moments of despair and longing. Today, he could not be sure what feelings were raging inside her. He would not be bothered about the past.

She bowed in front of him, her face still covered, and everyone else did the same. He signalled to her to rise, and then sat down, but did not allow them to do so.

"Hamza intended to challenge Amir Badr al-Jamali," he stated. "He has to be an example for others. You all know what happens to the women in the household of a disloyal rebel. Today, his womenfolk are being sold in the Acre markets for a dinar and his horses for a dinar and a half. I wonder, Furoon, how many men will want to buy you. Hamza's wife for sale for just a dinar in Acre's markets. I won't allow the price to be any higher."

She stifled some tears. When she spoke, it was in that hoarse voice that he had heard every day, every moment, every night.

"Amir Badr al-Jamali is all-powerful," she said, "sword in hand and army at his command. However, I beg him to show mercy. Hamza has been killed, my Lord, and his daughters do not deserve to be punished. Do not pile one sin on top of others."

"Listen, slave girl," he replied, "the punishment is not for crimes committed, but for brazen defiance. It is to make clear the power that I possess: to show mercy, to forgive, or to punish. Your husband's been killed because he brought disaster to this land. Killing him and other traitors like him will be my ongoing goal and duty. You'll be an example for others like you."

"Do you really intend to sell the Sicilian's daughter in the Acre markets?" she asked.

"Yes," he replied without looking at her. "Today, this very moment. Her and all the women in Hamza's household. I'm not going to treat his household more mercifully than others."

He bent over to bring his face closer to hers.

"All I know about the Sicilian and his family is that they want all the glory for themselves and degradation for Egyptians."

She remained silent.

"Furoon's not pleading," he asked, looking straight at her, "or asking me for forgiveness?"

"We're asking to be forgiven, my Lord," Hamza's two daughters said. "We're begging you and swearing allegiance to you."

"I want to hear it from Hamza's wife," he replied with a smile. "Then I'll think about it."

She lowered her head, but said nothing. One of Hamza's daughters hit Furoon on the shoulder.

"Come on," she said, full of hatred. "Plead with him. What are you waiting for?"

She pursed her lips, then looked at him.

"The Amir's going to do whatever he wants," she said, "whether we beg or not."

"You've brought disaster on us!" the daughters said. "Sell her, Amir. She's the one who's caused the disaster. We're just children of General Hamza. I beg you to be merciful with us."

Their eyes met, and she felt a pang in her heart.

"I'm asking the Amir," she stuttered, "to be merciful with Hamza's daughters even if he's not going to do so with his wife.

"His wife," Badr repeated.

He moved closer to her.

"Any woman who is married to an amir in the army has to realise that her fate is tied to his. Didn't your father tell you that when you were married to Hamza?"

She did not respond.

"If you said something," he told her all of a sudden, "I might sympathise with your situation—either you or the two of them. I need to know everything about Hamza, his men—who ran away and who stayed. Where's his money?"

Swallowing hard, she put her hand behind her back so he would not see it trembling. She did not speak.

"Is it that you don't know, or that you're deliberately hanging on to what's left? The fact that you're afraid means that you do know. You must realise, don't you, that I can make you talk."

He made a hand gesture, and the soldiers grabbed the two daughters, who groaned and pleaded. But they did not seize Furoon.

She kept her head lowered and her hands behind her back.

"Furoon," he said, moving closer to her, "the girl who makes a doll out of halva and then eats it without compassion, I wonder if you can tell me everything about Hamza. How much does he have in his treasury?"

She swallowed hard and avoided looking at him.

"I don't know, my Lord," she replied.

"You gave him the gold. What did you give him?"

"I don't remember," she replied without thinking.

For a while, he said nothing.

"You don't know the Amir," he went on in a slippery tone. "Have they told you about the way Abu Taher was flayed? Are you familiar with flaying, Furoon? You can feel the skin being stripped from the body. Humans are not like animals, Furoon. Their skin is attached to their heart. Having the skin stripped is sheer hellfire."

"Hellfire," she repeated, still keeping her shaking hands hidden.

He grabbed her hand from behind her back and looked at it.

"So is the halva-maker's daughter scared?" he asked dryly.

If he had been thinking of having her flayed, he would have done it some time ago. If he had wanted to cut her heart out, he would have done it. She did not reply. Looking at him defiantly, she removed her hand.

"I gave Hamza seven and a half rotls of gold," he said.

"My Lord is very good at his job," she replied, "and he well knows that I'm no good at arithmetic. I know nothing about numbers."

"That's a love that's different from all others. A wife who gives her husband gold deserves to be loved by him. But he didn't love you. Instead, he accused you of lechery and being a tart."

She did not respond. She pursed her lips, praying to God that Badr would leave her alone and not carry on setting her on fire. The flesh was ablaze, and it was over.

"I'm going to sell you for a dinar," he said. "You're not worth a penny more."

She did not respond.

"Say something," he shouted, "or else I'm going to kill his two daughters."

"My Lord is always just," she stuttered.

"Are you pleading with me, Furoon," he asked her, "the way Abu Taher did? Maybe I can forgive the two of them, but I'll never forgive you."

She frowned, and then bowed down, clutched his coat, and kissed it.

"My Lord," she choked, "please be merciful with Hamza's children and wives, except for me."

Now, here she was, kissing his coat the way Abu Taher had. But there was all the difference between those two kisses. Was she moving his dead heart or cleaving it in two? He did not know and did not want to know.

"Stand up, Furoon."

"You asked me to beg you," she said as she stood up slowly.

"But you didn't beg. You asked me to show mercy to someone else, not yourself. Is that your pride or courage talking?"

"My certainty," she responded after a pause.

"Certainty about whom?"

She did not reply.

"You're even more malicious than I thought," he yelled at her furiously. "Get out of here before I kill you instead of selling you."

He gave orders to his soldiers, and they grabbed Furoon. She left silently with them.

He then ordered his soldiers to do everything he had decided.

That day, he was in the market in disguise, watching with a childish glee as Furoon and Hamza's daughters were being sold. `Amer, Hamza's son, had managing to flee outside the country, but he would be found sooner or later. He looked at her eyes, eager to see a shattered expression, humiliation, and weakness—yes, especially weakness. He wanted her to have a taste of separation, the torment of remoteness, the darkness of despair. Disloyalty has its price, that is certain. In the past, he had not sought her love or expected it. Then she had invaded his world like the plants of paradise, opening their blooms inside his limbs and at the entryway to his soul. All that was in the past. She had not pleaded for herself or tried to renew the old pact. He was well aware of her pride and loyalty. Was her sorrowful look out of love for her husband, or because of her loss of freedom and her humiliation in front of others?

A man came forward to purchase Furoon. She closed her eyes as though to shut out all sense of what was to come. He paid the dinar and told her to follow him. She did so, her eyes cast down as she walked, her body totally defeated. She neither screamed nor cursed Badr al-Jamali as Hamza's daughters had done. The market ended, and the women were sold. He went back to the palace, the pleasurable smile on his face accompanied by an unrelenting sorrow.

Amid all the bustle of the market—the shouts and men and women—she closed her eyes and moved into a different world. She did not even look at the man who had bought her or bother about anything else. All she could remember was the moment when she had opened her closet and found that Badr's coat had disappeared; how shocked she had been, like a child that has just lost its mother, and how she had come to hate everyone she loved. She put her hand over her heart.

"In anger, Badr," she whispered to herself, "you know neither sorrow nor blame."

After walking for an hour or more, she was panting alongside the men of whoever it was had bought her.

"When will we arrive?" she asked.

No one answered.

"It's Badr," she muttered to herself.

"What did you just say?" the man walking beside her asked.

She did not reply. She stopped abruptly and looked at the man.

"Who are you?" she asked.

"The man who's bought you for a dinar," he replied nonchalantly.

"Where are we going?"

He did not reply.

"Keep walking with no talk," he told her. "Don't stop. You're not healthy enough. How are you going to serve an entire household? Come on, you're certainly not worth more than a dinar."

She walked stoically beside him, panting with exhaustion, until they finally arrived.

As she stood there waiting, her eyes lowered. She was not waiting for the man who had bought her. Her heart had not deceived her before. He opened the door, then sat on the bed.

"Look up and take off the veil," he told her. "I want to see your face."

She raised her head, her heart clearly audible. Then she removed her face-veil and looked at him. Her eyes looked dull, that was for sure. The bloom in her features had been extinguished like fire that has been blown out by winds.

"You've killed my husband, Badr," she mumbled without thinking, "then humiliated me. Why didn't you leave me for some other man to buy?"

"I've killed people who've conspired against me," he replied angrily. "Don't give yourself an importance you don't deserve. Don't speak my name without saying 'Amir.' As long as you can be my property, why should I leave you to another man?"

He had carried out his plan just as he'd wanted. Now she knew who Badr al-Jamali really was. She would find out that, as far as he was concerned, she was nothing—just a body with no soul, a slave girl he had purchased for a single dinar in the market, and worth no more than that. The horse was more expensive and important than her. Today, he would make her realise that he had managed to overcome his love for her years ago and would never forgive disloyalty and cowardice. And cowardice was even more lethal than disloyalty, the greatest sin on earth. He would have sex with her and then toss her where he would never set eyes on her again. Why have sex with her? Maybe because he'd once desired her. Yes, it was just a craving, no more. That would come to an end once he'd had sex with her. She would never again have the kind of effect on him that she'd once had. The past was over, and Furoon was nothing. As he looked at her, he told himself that again: she was nothing, a body he craved, one with which he could quench his thirst and then be done with it. If she could be his own slave girl, how could he let her be sold to someone else? Did she realise, he wondered. Or all the way there had she been anticipating her destiny with another man?

But she had known all along. She did not know how or why, but she was sure that he was the one who was going to buy her, even though she'd had occasional moments of doubt.

He took off his shirt, sat down on the bed, and signalled to her to join him. She sat down, blinking hard, trying her best not to look at him. As she wrung her hands, she felt giddy in both mind and body.

"So, Badr," she mumbled, "did you intend to humiliate me?"

"Yes," he replied firmly.

She could not stop herself looking at him. She noticed the scars on his arms. There was now some grey hair mixed in with the black, but his eyebrows still radiated enough power and resolve to melt stone. She clutched her hands even tighter, not sure whether she wanted to hug him or punch him. In the past, she had imagined him bare-chested in her arms. How many times had she run her hands over his ribs and kissed every part of him in her dreams! She had wanted to apologise, but she could not stop dreaming even when she was married to someone else. Sin can destroy the heart; there is no torture to rival it. Recalling her dreams, she clutched her neck as though she were being strangled.

"Tell me the truth, Furoon," he demanded in the same detached tone, "did you betray your husband? When you were with him, were you thinking about some other man, as he claimed? Did you commit adultery with another man?"

"I did in my imagination," she replied, her quivering fingers fiddling with her gown, "and I realise that's a sin."

"In your imagination, halva-maker's daughter!" he reacted with a scoff. "There's no room for imagination in amirs' lives. Tell me, slave girl, how did you commit adultery in your imagination?"

"I was dreaming of another man," she replied, clutching her gown, "embracing him and running my hand over his chest. I was part of him and he of me. I recognise my sin and ask God to forgive me. He is merciful and all-knowing."

He put his hand on her cheek.

"Who's the unlucky man," he wondered, "who's being toyed with by your imagination?"

"You," she replied after a pause.

His hand froze on her cheek, and furious flashes of anger flew from his eyes.

"Don't you dare!" he said. "I'm going to kill you right now. Don't even try to win me over or toy with me. We're not equals. You're here as a slave girl, just remember that."

He withdrew his hand from her cheek and started breathing slowly. He may have been trying to make up his mind about killing her or about something else. She had no idea, but she was no longer afraid of him.

After a while, he put his hand on her chin, then ran it over her neck. She held his hand, kissed it quickly, and whispered his name. He pulled his hand away.

"Stop it!" he chided.

"What did I do, my Lord?" she asked, hugging herself.

"As I've told you," he replied impatiently, "your tricks won't work with me. I want you here on my bed. I bought you today. Lie on your back and wait for my instructions, slave girl. Furoon, Sicilian's daughter, you're now my slave, at my command."

He could not see what lay beyond her gaze. He pushed her back and moved close. He touched the lines on her forehead.

"When did those lines start to appear?" he asked. "Have you been frowning a lot?"

"You were always a master when it comes to details," she replied in despair. "You never forget anything."

"Stop pretending to be a victim," he told her. "Your fate is a lot better than some other people's."

"I don't even know my fate yet," she replied, holding herself tightly.

He ran his hand over her hair. She closed her eyes, and a tear she had been fighting for years fell.

"Badr," she whispered.

He moved closer and slowly kissed the edge of her mouth.

"Forget everything that happened in the past," he told her. "Now, you're my slave girl. As I've told you, you're paying the price for treachery and desertion. You're going to learn the difference between love and commerce, halva-maker's daughter. I promise you that you're nothing to me, just a body just like any other. I won't remember it or know who you are. I can promise you that, whatever happens, Badr never forgets betrayal. Once this night is over, you'll never set eyes on me again. As far as I'm concerned, you'll be finished."

She stared at him for a moment, her eyes a tissue of suffering. As though she was not listening to him, she chided him.

"Not betrayal," she said. "Accuse me of cowardice if you wish, but not betrayal. If only you knew how much I've wanted to lie with you as your slave girl every single day, every moment. I'm not at your level, Badr; there's no humiliation in that."

That flummoxed him; he had not expected her to acknowledge the situation, nor had he anticipated the weakness and affection in her eyes. If he were willing to confront her blame like this, then maybe he could also handle her affection.

"Don't speak," he told her, as he ran his hand through her hair. "As I've said, forget about those womanly schemes."

Closing his eyes, he slowly kissed her hair. Then he regained his self-control.

"Take off your clothes," he told her angrily. "I want to look at you."

She sat up, put her hand on his cheek, and rubbed it cautiously.

"Here you are with me," she said. "I thought I would never see you again before I died—punishment perhaps for my own fear. I didn't deserve to see you again, but God has been merciful with me."

He no longer knew whether he could control the affection, the love, the passion that had taken possession of him. So, let him recall the past: it was just the halva-maker's daughter's little game, that's all. All she would be doing was giving him pleasure. She was the one who had deserted him and been married to Hamza. Badr never forgave. Once he had quenched his thirst, he would leave the room and never return, no matter what happened. One hour from now. He promised himself to stay no longer than that. He had an iron will and had often stopped himself doing what he wanted, steering himself away from life's pleasures. He recalled the cuff he had received from his teacher those many years ago; how he had snatched the emerald out of his grasp and punished him for wanting it.

"Only do what I tell you to do," he said, moving her hand away. "I don't want to hear a word from you, or for you to touch me without permission. Do you hear me?"

"Yes." She nodded.

He moved closer.

"I've told you to take off your clothes," he whispered in her ear.

She did not respond.

He grabbed hold of her dress and started to remove it from her shoulders. Without even thinking, she seized his hand to stop him. He moved her hand away and felt her entire body shiver.

"What's the matter, Furoon?" he scoffed "Are you afraid? And you ashamed of me?"

"Be kind to me," she whispered, nodding her head.

"Now here you are, begging me," he said. "I thought you'd never plead."

He moved even closer.

"I'm pleading now," she told him gently, "because I'm with my own soul. As my grandmother told my grandfather, you're a part of me."

He did his best not to understand what she was saying or be affected by it.

He slowly took off her dress, and she hurriedly grabbed a coat to cover her body and shield her embarrassment. She pursed her lips in regret and blamed herself for dreams of the past, which made her incapable of keeping her pact with a husband who had been foisted on her. Badr was in total command of her.

He put his hand on her cheek and raised an eyebrow.

"Anyone touching your hot cheek and seeing the way your whole body is shaking," he said mockingly, "would assume that you're a virgin. Didn't you take your clothes off for your husband, Furoon?"

She muttered something that he did not hear.

"You're beautiful," he said dryly as he ran his hand over her neck and shoulder. "That's certainly true and can't be denied. But slave girls are never shy, Furoon."

If he was trying to hurt her, he did not succeed. His body was rebelling, remembering desire. He grabbed her hand, which still clutched the coat, and pulled it away.

"Open your eyes," he said as he looked at her. "Don't pretend to be so indifferent. I want you to be alert and aware of who I am."

"I know who you are," she replied, still feeling the pain of an endless passion.

"I'm your owner," he told her as he drew closer and ran his hand over her body.

"You've been my owner for ages," she repeated, although he did not know what she meant.

If he even thought he was punishing her, he obviously did not know her. He had sworn not to kiss her or melt into her bosom as he had dreamed of doing. He had sworn to have sex with her as though she were a slave girl and then forget her. Every time he tried, he found his lips searching for hers, for her face, for every single part of her. There are times when there is widespread confusion. Yes indeed, he had not been with her for some time, and he had left her when they were very much in love. That was all there was to it. But she was a betrayer and no more; fear and passion sent a single tremor to remind his evil self that Furoon had indeed betrayed and deserted. Furoon had told him that she did not have his strength and courage. Furoon... Why did his mind always vanish into the vast expanse of a dawn that never came?

He was punishing himself, trying to separate body from soul and using his sword to sever his heart's desires. She had never resisted or asked anything from him. Whenever she felt his hand or kissed him, she would close her eyes and heave a sigh as though she wanted to hold the moment in her hands forever, in case it did not last.

If she was feeling guilty because her lover had killed her husband, then the fact that she was with him now had made every other sentiment disappear.

"I've longed for you for a lifetime!' she said as she felt him inside her.

Never in her entire life had she felt so trusting as she did at that moment. All her life, she had dreamed of him and asked to be forgiven. But today, she was his; he owned her. Maybe he would try not to be gentle with her, to be sparing with his kisses, to frown when his expression was kind. He might resist, but that did not bother her. All she wanted was to have him close, close when he was angry, close when he was hateful, close when he was inside her.

He froze in place and turned pale, either from surprise or delight, she did not know which.

"How could that be?" he asked her, totally confused.

"I couldn't do it," she replied without even thinking. "I swear that you're the first man to see me and touch me. Don't leave me and go away."

She kept her pain to herself and wandered through a new and different world. Those touches of his had transformed the whole of life. This was a love about which no one had ever written.

His entire plan now came crashing down in front of him and dissipated like so much dust. Furoon was no betrayer; Furoon, the halva-maker's daughter, was a spout of sincerity and love. Now, he needed to keep his mind; that he had to do. When he had finished having sex with her, he lay flat on his back and pulled her to his chest.

"What about your husband?" he asked her. "He didn't touch you for five whole years? You were a virgin? How could that be?"

"Will you allow me?" she asked, as though she had not been listening.

"Allow you to do what?"

"To kiss you and touch you."

He swallowed hard and did his best to sound strong, but failed.

"I hereby allow you," he said.

She gave his chest a passionate kiss, then wrapped him in her arms, and put her head on his stomach. She had defeated him. The hand that had carried his sword was paralyzed in a moment. Years of blame and scattered days of hatred all vanished.

"You could have come with me," he whispered as he stroked her hair. "You refused. Do you remember?"

"You wanted to hear me beg," she replied, her heart pounding. "I'm doing it now. Please forgive me because I'm not as brave as you. Every day, every moment, I've regretted being so far away from you, realising that I might never see you again as long as I live. I regretted it and wanted to die. I couldn't cause a scandal for my father, and I couldn't belong to anyone but you. If it weren't for my faith, I would have killed myself. You're my soul, my entire existence; you're..."

"Don't say any more," he told her, closing his eyes. "Don't talk about love; I don't like hearing it."

"But I love you," she replied at once, tears pouring nonstop. "I swear that I could never have belonged to anyone else, even if they had cut up my body. Do you realise how much I've suffered?"

Her hand was still shaking as she wiped away her tears. His strategy for domination had completely collapsed.

"Don't cry," he said gently. "Please don't cry."

"For five long years," she said, lowering her head, "I've been dying every single day, knowing I wouldn't see you again for the rest of my life. The heart mourns in silence and cracks like parched land. And now, do you plan to punish me? The mere appearance of your face before me is reward enough, my Lord. Punishment would mean being far away from you. Maybe you're planning to do that in order to punish me. I hope you aren't."

He put his hands around her face and gave her a passionate kiss, something he had been dreaming of doing for years, a kiss that melted souls and joined one heart to another. Such was their fervour that breathing became heavier amid the sweet savour of so much passion. This was not like the very first time. He had loved her the way he dreamed of doing: gently, softly, perfectly. He could listen to her sighs as she whispered his name and felt her hands running over his wounds, pouring a magic potion to protect them from all treason and intrigue. This time, the passion was so intense that he lost all reason, and his fortresses collapsed in the face of her total giving of herself, something he had neither anticipated nor recognised. Had he been dreaming? Had Furoon really been married? How had that happened? Had Hamza never touched her? How could any man leave a woman like Furoon untouched? She had an iron will. This was a girl like no other woman on earth. What had she endured in order to keep herself apart from Hamza? If there was one single person who could make him lose his mind, it was Furoon. Maybe he already had. Perhaps the effects of love had erased his memory, so he no longer knew why he was staying in Acre or what was going to happen next. If only he had been satisfied, or had snuffed out his passion. But instead he had increased it, with the groans of deep-seated wounds.

Furoon nestled in his arms in total submission, her hand clasping his arm as though she were worried he might leave her again. Neither of them slept; this night, there would be no sleep, as the moon first shone bright, then dodged around a cloudy sky. At dawn, he covered her in his coat and carried her out on the balcony. He sat down and set her on his knee. She gave him a hug, put her head on his shoulder, and closed her eyes. Love was a wine, its flavour like no other. This was paradise, and it had arrived with no forewarning. He had been out for revenge and had hoped to humiliate her. From one day to the next, she had managed to put an end to all that and to extinguish his anger.

She stared up at the moon in the sky: was it a new moon, a *badr*, or was it full? How could it become full in just an hour? Then she turned to look at him.

"Badr," she said, planting a kiss on his head, "you're the moon both on earth and in the heavens."

He said nothing. Putting her arms around his neck, she settled into his chest.

"Ah, the loss and longing," she sighed. "Ah, the separation of two bodies and souls. They took away my life when I was so away from you. I hated all of life, and I was afraid that my heart would be soiled and learn how to hate. I've missed you, oh, how I've missed you!"

She clasped his shoulder and kissed his chest. Looking at him, she rubbed her cheek against his throat.

Did he shudder? Did all his defences collapse in the face of her honesty and passion?

"I've longed for you," she whispered. "I wanted you like a slave girl. I chided and punished my heart, but that only made it even more stubborn. You've taken charge, Badr. For years, you've been the master. Every night, I could see you in my imagination; I pictured myself in your arms and asked to be forgiven for my sin."

At that point, he could not speak. He was afraid of the words he might use.

"There'll be time for us to talk to each other," he said, kissing her all over her cheeks. "But not today."

"Promise me: you're going to stay with me today," she replied, kissing him on the chin. "We'll forget the entire world and stay here. Can you do that?"

"Yes, I can," he declared firmly. "We'll forget the world. We have days, years, an eternity ahead of us. This time, no one's going to take you away from me."

"The world never gives," she said, clasping his hand and kissing his palm. "It only afflicts and takes. It's never been generous with me."

He could not come up with a response. He was now in a different universe; she had taken him into her world, then aroused both wounds and hopes. Love now had a different flavour, lingering in the limbs, invigorating the sickly heart, and preserving the soul in the midst of demons and hellfire. Ah, Furoon, if only you knew... And yet, for certain, she had surprised him and brought the vestiges of his days crashing down. He opened his mouth, but the words had a hard time emerging.

"Furoon," he managed to say, "you've addled my mind. When you're in my arms, I no longer know who I am."

"Are you angry with me?" she asked, somewhat worried. "You're still angry with me. I swear that I've regretted every single day I've spent without you. I'm ready to stay here as your slave girl if you'll keep me with you, but—"

"There's no 'but' about it," he made abundantly clear. "You're staying with me."

"People will say: She killed her husband so she could be with her lover. Why did you kill him, Badr?"

"Because he helped kill my son. Isn't that reason enough? Badr al-Jamali is not merely a lover."

As though Furoon were anticipating his reply, she let out a deep sigh. Yes, he was right. He was not the lover; he was the beloved.

"My father, my brothers, all of Egypt and Syria," she said, "He'll never allow anyone to—"

"All that's mine," he replied. "You're mine before anything else. You belong to me."

"Don't cast yourself into perdition."

"But your husband. How could he leave you a virgin for five whole years?"

She moved away, hesitant, and clutched herself.

"As I've told you," she said, "I couldn't do it. Is that what's making you angry? Are you like everyone else, thinking that I did wrong?"

"Are you out of your mind?" he asked, pulling her towards him. "This is the happiest day of my life. Angry with you? No, I'm not; maybe I'm angry with myself. Didn't he force you? Hamza is not a man of mercy."

"We had an agreement."

"What did you give him in return?"

"Everything except myself. I couldn't do that."

"Now I've understood. You gave him your gold."

If she had been out to torture him, she had succeeded. He hugged her even harder till she almost stopped breathing. He plunged inside her once again, wanting her to be a part of him, never outside his emotional core. She sighed, and he was not sure whether it was out of pain, an excess of passion, or a combination of both.

"Do you want me as much as I want you?" she whispered after a while. "Do you love me as much as I love you? No, don't say anything. I'm afraid of what you might say. I've been a coward, but I've never been a liar. You can try me for cowardice, but not for betrayal. That, I've never done."

He could not respond; his mind was a confused muddle, and his heart was overjoyed. He imagined that he was not even on the earth.

"Your coat that I kept," she went on, brushing his cheek with her lips. "I used to clutch it in my suffering, but they took even that away from me. At that point, Badr, I wanted to kill myself. It was as though that coat was you, and I had to cling to anything connected with you, absolutely anything that would reassure me about this world. Without you, I was a stranger, alone. I want to tell you this. I realise that I'm just one among hundreds of women in your palace, but that's enough for me; it's what I deserve."

"From today on," he told her spontaneously, "everything is yours. Furoon, you're the mistress of this palace, of all Acre."

"Men have no patience with passion, I realise that. You're not like me. Today I'm one of your slave girls. I love you. I swear that I've no idea what came over me today and made me behave this way, exchanging kisses and seducing you like a slave girl, even though I've only ever kissed you in my imagination and have never kissed anyone else."

"Do you trust me? he asked her suddenly.

"Yes, I do," she replied immediately. "I can see part of you in me."

"Five long years of weakness," he told himself, but not her. "Do you understand, do you even know what weakness is? It involves me brandishing my sword and controlling armies, and yet standing helpless before a woman I love, unable to be married to her or have her as my own. Ever since I was born, drew breath, and fate unspooled, it's been years of torture waiting for this special moment. Sometimes, it was all I desired. The passion never faded, and I was not satisfied with my lot."

She did not wake up, nor could she ask anything of him. As she had wished for a lifetime, her ribs were blended with his. All suffering melted away, slipping through the folds of time; even treachery burned in the flames. She had found a place here, in the depths of his chest, where all bright planets and fixed stars were to be found. Night came and then was over without her knowing either what was to come or what had passed. Time stopped, and everything froze in place. How could this happen when the heart was filled, and mouth was firmly placed on mouth, flesh acknowledged its twin, and the wandering spirit had found a place of refuge? He leaned his back against the balcony wall to look up at the stars. Her head was securely in place, as she ran her fingers over the wounds on his chest, something she did every day.

"If only I could stay like this forever!" she whispered.

"You're going to stay here with me," he replied resolutely.

She opened her mouth, but he put his arm around her waist.

"Be careful!" he told her. "I need you to be strong. Enough of weakness! You're not the Furoon who's not yet eighteen years old, nor are you subject to your father's dictates. You're here in my palace, and you belong to me. Today you're mine, and tomorrow you'll be my wife."

Five days went by, making up for five fallow years, and they were all good. He did not leave Furoon's room; the food was delivered there. He told his soldiers he was busy; he did not wish to meet anyone or see a single soul. For all those five days, he could not recall leaving her even once. They were just like two children, never tiring of the other's company and desiring no one else in a wide world that was loftier than their every capacity.

"I'm scared for you, my darling," she said abruptly.

"My darling!" he repeated.

She grabbed his hand and kissed it.

"If you bought me, that might be possible," she said. "But, if you want to be married to me, then my father will have to agree, and so will the Caliph. Are you willing to be married to a woman from a religious community other than your own, Amir?"

"Badr will do as he pleases," he replied. "Yes, I'll do it."

For a moment, there was silence. Her head was still buried in his chest.

"Do you recognise suffering?" she asked. "Have you had a taste of it? Have you ever spent a night when you've ingested a poison that neither kills nor goes away? Have you spent a morning that sears your limbs? Leaving you would mark my end and disappearance. Night after night, I conjure up your face before me and feel your touch. Badr, I close my eyes to see your face…"

He hugged her so tightly that she cried out in pain.

"Did you forget about me?" she asked. "Tell me the truth."

"Did I forget you?" he repeated, after taking a deep breath. "Did a single day go by without me hating you, loving you, desiring you, and wanting to kill you? While the universe has failed to put an end to me, you've crushed me and weakened me at a time when my power has extended to encompass heaven and earth. You're the only one whose arrow has pierced my heart, and I can't even rip it out for fear of losing it. You're the one who has illuminated the whole earth in front of me. Have I had sex with women before you? Probably. I was a mamluk. The Governor of Tripoli bought me. I was tied to greed and power. Then your passion arrived and made me rebel against all rulers and ties. Your passion is unlike any other. The touch that a man gives a woman he loves brings both freedom and power. I love you."

She was so thrilled that she almost fainted.

"Handsomest man of all," she said, "let me love you today the way I've wanted to do in my dreams."

She threw herself down on their bed, resting her head on the sheet to remind her of his presence and scent. He had promised her not to be late and to stay with her for the remaining nights of their lives. She smiled, her body revived, and was celebrated by his kisses and touches. Stretching out, she buried her head in the pillow again. Today, she would make him some pistachio-flavored kunafa by hand; she was eager for him to taste different types of halva. With her usual sincerity, she had told him everything that had happened ever since she had scratched her face with her nails, hoping to set fire to the days till she could be alone with her husband. As he listened to her, he hugged her tightly and kept her head on his chest until morning. Neither of them slept or moved.

"I no longer hate anyone, Badr," she told him. "I'm not angry at my father, and I love every person. I forgive everyone who has humiliated me and hope that anyone I've hurt will forgive me. I ask God to be merciful with Hamza and I pray for him."

He gave her a chiding look.

"You're the one," she said, "who's restored my soul."

The palace of Badr al-Jamali, Amir and Army Commander, was in shock. The Amir's eyes did not normally gleam with pleasure, nor did he ask so eagerly about everyone inside the palace. He was not in the habit of finishing his day as quickly as possible so he could go back to his room. His story with Furoon was known to everyone, including Amina Khatun. She was not jealous, but he still baffled her. Never for a day had she imagined that Badr could be in love. Badr al-Jamali had started smiling, even laughing. When he joked with them, they would give him a frightened look, and then listen as he laughed; they would all then pray to God that Furoon would stay with him for the rest of his life. Here was a man who had handed over the reins to feelings that toyed and flirted with him. His laughter encouraged the slave girls to try to get close to him whereas before they had been too scared. But he never even saw them. He saw only Furoon. Faced with her, fortresses collapsed and cities opened their gates.

Amina Khatun heard the slave girls whispering to each other and saw Furoon for herself. She watched from a distance as Furoon made halva expertly and hummed love songs to herself. Then she saw her walking around the garden, looking for animals to feed. She looked on in amazement as Furoon picked up a tiny kitten that had lost its mother, held it lovingly to herself, and put her mouth on the kitten's, all the while whispering to it that it would stay with her forever. Amina simply shrugged as she realised how crazy Badr actually was, and the way this slave girl—who was actually not a slave girl at all, but rather mistress of the palace—behaved. Her word was now law, with everyone around her listening and harkening. Every night, she would put down some milk for the cat, but it would refuse to drink without her help. So Furoon did help it, then put it on her bed and covered it. When Badr came in, she went over to him with her usual passion, helped him take off his coat, and gave him a big hug. When he saw the cat on his bed, he stopped and looked at Furoon.

"It's a kitten with no mother," she told him affectionately. "I found it in your palace garden, Amir. I'd like to take care of it. Just look at it; it's tiny and weak and needs your protection."

He stared into her eyes as though he did not understand.

"Take it out of the room, Furoon," he told her. "Give it to one of the slave girls to look after."

"I'm afraid for it," she replied, kissing his mouth. "They'll let it die. I don't like death, Badr, particularly when it involves the weak. You're protecting the country, so protect animals as well. Leave the kitten with me, just for today."

"Furoon," he replied, stroking her face, "this is the Amir's room."

"Just look at it shivering," she said sadly, holding the kitten. "It'll die of cold outside the room. I want to warm it up a bit. I know what fear and a lack of security feels like."

Unable to resist her, he shrugged, fully aware of the things she had been through.

Next morning, `Abd al-wahhab had a little joke.

"I've heard," he said, "that Amir Badr al-Jamali is raising a kitten in his room."

"We need a bit of insanity, man!" Badr replied with a laugh.

"Yes indeed," `Abd al-wahhab replied, completely understanding. "How wonderful and delightfully crazy love can be! If only it never ended! I swear that, ever since I've known you, I've never seen you so happy or the glint in your eyes so like a young man's."

"Hey now," Badr replied, pretending to be angry. "I'm still young, even though I've some grey hairs. Badr will never get old."

"Badr al-Jamali will never get old," `Abd al-wahhab said craftily. "But Badr the lover is more sincere and cheerful."

Badr felt awkward and faked a frown, as he did his best to change the subject.

"You deserve your good fortune, my lord," his secretary told him. "To be passionately in love is a weakness, but to share such passion with your lover is one of God's miracles for us here on earth."

"She is indeed a miracle," Badr replied firmly.

He was anticipating a visit from her father, and the halva-maker came. Badr left him waiting outside the palace for an entire day and did not inform his daughter that her father had come. Then he let him into the palace. Her father brought his son Muhammad with him. With their heads lowered, they both felt humiliated. Badr and her father exchanged glances.

"Amir," her father said, "the Sicilian's daughter cannot be a slave girl. I've come to ask for mediation."

"How so?" Badr asked with a smile.

"My lord," Furoon's father said gently, "if you wished to be married to Furoon, that would be a great honour for us. But you can't keep her as a slave girl."

"If I wanted to be married to your daughter, halva-maker," Badr replied, "I would do so. But I don't."

"Amir," her brother said, "I know you to be a man of justice. Why punish my sister when she had nothing to do with the measures her husband took?"

"What punishment is it to be the Amir's slave girl? That's a great honour."

"My lord," Muhammad replied at once. "Once, you wanted to be married to her, but circumstances at the time did not permit it."

'That was in the past," Badr said, looking at her father. "Today, she's my property."

"Amirs are not supposed to humiliate their people, my Lord," `Ali said. "I've known you to be an amir and army commander who appreciates the value of the Egyptian people."

"I do appreciate them."

"So why enslave them?"

"'Ali, you're the one who's enslaved them, not me. You abandoned your country out of sheer greed, only bothering about your own interests. You're the one who aided corruption and corrupt people, as though the polluted water would stop and never inundate your house. At the time, you didn't realise that anyone who lets polluted water linger will foul his neighbour's house as well, further extending the decay so that it thrives amid the rotten planks for the rest of its life. 'Ali, you're the one who entered my palace to spy on me. Where's your partner today? He's dead, but here you are, coming to ask and beg me to be married to your daughter. I've wanted to arrest you for some time, and now you've come of your own accord."

Silence and fear prevailed.

"We ask the Amir to forgive us," Muhammad said. "My father may have behaved badly, but our family does have certain customs and codes of behaviour. We've pledged ourselves to continue our grandfather's craft whatever may happen."

"But where's that craft today, Muhammad?

"We haven't been able to keep it going. These are times when some people have lost their way on the path toward the truth. Like many others, we've lost ours. In deadly moments, everyone holds on to his wheat and holds his breath."

"Then both wheat and breaths are lost."

"My Lord," Muhammad said, "I've come here on behalf of my father and sister to ask you to intercede and to be reassured that she is safe and well."

"She's fine!" Badr replied angrily. "I won't put your father in prison because he's her father. But I don't want to see him in front of me ever again."

"Amir, we've come here so you won't humiliate us in front of everyone. Furoon isn't a slave girl."

"Today, she's become my slave girl. As I've told you already, I did want to be married to her, but you refused. You're not welcome in my palace. If you want to see Furoon, that'll only be with my permission. I will allow you to leave the palace today without going to prison, but today only."

He did not tell her about her father's visit. When she asked him about her brother and father, he told her that he had confirmed that they were both well. She was preoccupied with the kitten and something else as well. A month after she had come to his palace and taken up residence there, she spoke to him.

"You've given me gold and money," she told him gently.

"You deserve everything," he replied.

"What should I do with them?

"Are you crazy, Furoon? Never in my entire life have I heard anyone ask such a question. Won't people be asking themselves what they can do without money, not with it?"

"I've one favour to ask of you. I want you to let me do it. I want to go out tomorrow."

He looked at her, doing his best to understand.

"I want to purchase Hamza's daughters, Badr," she went on. "I'll use my own money, if you'll let me, whatever the cost. I don't want to haggle over their humiliation while I'm enjoying being with you here."

"That'll never happen," he replied firmly. "They're an example to others. Don't you dare ever interfere in my affairs or ask for anything to do with the Amir's business."

"I swear never to do that," she replied, holding his hand. "I don't want them saying that I had their father killed so I could have my beloved to myself. I don't want them maligning me, Badr. Every night, I fall asleep feeling guilty. I want the whole world to feel as happy as I do."

"Furoon," he told her firmly, "keep your ideas about the world to yourself."

"You sold them, and I want to buy them. That has nothing to do with you. You gave me the money, and all I want to do is to buy them. That's only just, Amir. If someone else bought them and set them free, that would be permissible, wouldn't it?"

She kept at him all night and placed the money in front of him. She kissed him passionately and reminded him of the days of separation and sorrow until he finally agreed. He did not take the money from her, but purchased the daughters himself and set them free. He did it only for her, and he was not happy or satisfied about it. He was afraid that she was having too much influence over him with her gentleness and naiveté. But, at the same time, he realised the weight of guilt that would not leave her. When he saw the glint in her eyes and her childlike joy, he had no regrets.

"Are you ever going to ask me to set you free?" he asked her with a smile.

"That's impossible," she replied, putting her arms around his neck.

"You'll never ask me to be married to you either?" he asked. "Why haven't you asked?"

She did not respond.

"I trust you, Badr," she replied after a while, looking into his eyes. "Do what you think is right and won't cause you any harm. All I want is to be with you."

"You're not like anyone else. How did that happen?"

"Being in love with you is the best thing that's ever happened to me. Staying with you is a bounty from my Lord."

He held her hand and kissed it.

"I don't know," he said, "whether the bounty is your love for me or mine for you."

But the sheer rapture of love and the expressions of delight and satisfaction in Furoon's eyes had no effect on Hafsa. When Badr gave Furoon permission to visit her father and brother's house, she brought a lot of gifts with her. Her father didn't have much to say to her, and she was not sure whether he was blaming her or feeling sorry for her. But Hafsa talked nonstop.

"Wake up!" she said. "You're melting away into his existence. When a girl does that with a man, it's the end for her. You have to understand!"

"I'm not doing anything to annoy God," Furoon replied. "If God is not angry with me, I really don't care. It's war, and Badr has won."

"Yes, and you're one of the spoils of that war, Furoon! You're the daughter of the halva-maker to caliphs, so how can you possibly become a slave to a renegade? Use your mind! Or has he taken it away?"

Furoon did not respond.

"He doesn't want to be married to a Sunni woman," Hafsa went on, "so he won't lose his value for the Caliph and his people. That's the way they've been from the start, living inside the walls of their city. We know nothing about them. They keep making promises and pledges, and then they've imposed the new call to prayer on us after promising us freedom of belief. Thanks be to God that some cities in Egypt have gone back to the old one. Badr will either force you to convert to his faith or else keep you as a slave girl. What'll happen, Furoon, if you have a baby? Do you think he'll make his son a Sunni? Why are you being so naïve? Demand your freedom and leave him."

"Out of the question," Furoon replied firmly.

"In that case, ask him to be married to you while you keep your own faith. If he refuses, then demand your freedom. Wake up, my daughter. Days of love are just as short as those of youth and beauty."

She did not respond as she pondered the issues involved. She had made up her mind that, whatever happened, nothing would keep them apart as long as she lived. Hafsa had no idea, no notion of the nights she had spent just wanting to touch him and clasp him to her chest, if only once; nights when she was afraid that a husband whom she loathed would assault her and shackle her body; nights when she would pray to God to relieve her of the weight of separation and loss. Night and day, she would pray, begging God for mercy: either by wrenching his love from her heart, or else pouring some water over its blazing flames. Hafsa knew none of that. Why should Furoon be bothered about different faiths? What did she have to do with caliphs?

When her father came to see her, she wanted to forgive him, to forgive him for all the deprivation and humiliation. Perhaps she had done that already; she was not sure. But she had missed him. He looked into her eyes, but she did not look back.

"Praise be to God, Father," she said, 'that you are well."

He looked down for a while, then their eyes met. She looked away.

"You're angry with me," he said. "You think I abandoned you and sold you to Hamza, but you don't realise the sacrifices I'd been making for this family. My father died before I ever set eyes on him. But the Sicilian raised me and married me to his daughter. He told me about the halva-maker, my father. I made this family my primary focus, doing my best to rescue it from hardship and misery. At the time, I wasn't worried about myself, but about something more important. Do you understand? What was it that brought us so much hardship? Was it wars involving Imam Al-Mustansir's army and his followers? No, it was Badr al-Jamali, who's taken my daughter as one of his slaves."

She did not respond.

"Do you understand what I'm saying?" he asked angrily.

She still did not respond.

"Run away," her father told her firmly. "My daughter isn't a slave. Are you happy being one of the Armenian's slave girls?"

She swallowed hard.

"It's fate," she replied, head lowered. "He took all the wives who conspired against him and sold them in the markets. Praise be to God, he didn't sell me to a man I didn't know. It's all fate, Father. As long as I don't do anything to anger God, I don't care."

"Are you scared of Badr?" her father asked, looking at the soldier who had accompanied her. "Tell me the truth."

She did not reply.

"You're the Sicilian's daughter," he told her firmly, "the granddaughter of General Jawhar, the Sicilian who built Cairo and the Al-Azhar Mosque. Are you out of your mind? Today you're staying here and not coming back. If he took you, it was against your will. You're his slave in spite of yourself."

"I..." she stammered.

"You what?"

"I won't leave Badr for the rest of my life."

Raising his hand, he slapped her hard, while the soldier watched in consternation.

"My Lord won't be happy about that," the soldier told her father.

"My Lord won't interfere between father and daughter," he replied.

She clutched her inflamed cheek, but said nothing.

"Tomorrow, he'll have had enough of you," her father told her, "and he'll toss you in with the servants. You'll be washing his wife's feet, halva-maker's daughter, and cleaning out the animal dung."

She said nothing.

"I realise that you're going to him," he said once again. "But don't give yourself to him. If you do, you're betraying your family and your origins."

When she came back from her journey, he was waiting for her. He could see how unhappy she was, something he had been expecting. The soldier had told him everything. Today, he had no idea what he was expecting of her. Would she obey her father? If she did, he was not sure that he could blame her. He went over to her and lifted her chin. He could see the sorrow in her eyes.

"I missed you," he said as he kissed her.

"Me too!" she replied without hesitation.

She gave herself to him with the same spirit of sincerity and generosity. He may have sensed her suppressed sorrow, and yet she was still as generous as angels and as pure as people in heaven above.

"Is there anything you want to ask of me?" he asked as she went to sleep in his arms.

"No," she replied emphatically, burying her head in his chest "I have everything I want."

"This chest of yours," she said as she pounded on the spot where his heart was. "It's all I need."

She had plunged a dagger into the depths of his heart. Closing his eyes, for the very first time he lost all ability to focus. He found himself wandering in another world, an innocent one where all was serene. He had never known such fidelity or heard of it before, having had a taste of betrayal before he was even weaned, and having enjoyed the taste of blood, even delighted in shedding it.

"Your father slapped you," he said with a frown.

"He's my father, Badr," she replied bashfully.

"I won't let him do that again. From now on, you'll only meet him when I'm there."

At Hafsa's house, Furoon's husband's two daughters came to thank her. She avoided their glances, although she did not know why, and lowered her gaze. She waited for them to say something. One of the daughters gave her a suspicious look.

"It's strange, my father's wife," she said, "that the Army Commander should decide to buy you, when we were both standing right there in front of him. But it was you he chose, as though he had known you earlier and you him."

Furoon said nothing.

"Praise be to God," Hafsa said nervously, "that you're both well, and that `Amer, Hamza's son, managed to escape and leave Syria. My daughter, we didn't want to see anything bad happen to your family."

Hamza's daughter stared at Furoon.

"I wonder," she suggested to Hafsa, her eyes still glued to Furoon, "if my father was killed because his wife conspired against him. If that's true, then will my brother not take his revenge? He certainly should. If the Army Commander can locate my brother, he'll certainly kill him. We've no idea where he is. We want to live in peace, but it saddens me that my father's wife pretends to be so devout and religious, reading the Qur'an and praying at night, when she's my father's wife but clearly belongs to another man. What does the Sharia law have to say about that, Hafsa?"

"Have faith in God, my daughter. That's not appropriate talk."

Furoon still remained silent, but feelings of guilt began to squeeze her veins. What kind of sin had she committed by being married to one man while her heart belonged to another? To marry a man and yet not give him his legitimate rights? She had just been following her own desires. Her love for Badr had dominated her the same way that her love for halva had before. It had led her to flee Egypt.

Hafsa asked her politely to let them leave. Their conversation had no point. The two girls suddenly looked scared and left. They had decided to leave Acre that day, but they could not do so until they had managed to share their thoughts with Furoon.

"They're right, Hafsa," Furoon said sadly.

Hafsa was stunned.

"You didn't kill your husband, Furoon," she replied.

"But it didn't make me sad, either. If only I'd felt sad or pitied him. My relationship with Badr overwhelmed all other feelings."

"That love's going to destroy you, Furoon. As I've told you before, I would prefer that you made education and religious law your primary focus. But you only follow your heart. I wonder how low you will sink for Badr's sake. Would you kill someone for him?"

"Don't say that. Believe me, Badr's an angel. I'm the only one who really knows him. He seems hard, but he's really affectionate and generous."

"You see him as Badr in the heavens, whereas he's a soldier on earth."

`Abd al-wahhab could not help noticing how alert and eager his master was. Life had been restored to his limbs, and he was enjoying food and smelling flowers again. One day, he put the Caliph's letter in front of Badr.

"The Egyptians are forgetting all about the exiled foreigner and filling the devastation with friendship and sociability."

Badr smiled, but did not react.

"My son," `Abd al-wahhab went on, "the woman who's changed you befriends birds and animals. Every day at dawn, she talks to them, keeps an eye on them, and gives them things to eat. She picks up seeds and follows the tracks of doves and sparrows."

"I know," Badr replied.

"If it was a kind of star or angel you'd brought to our palace, you'd have been right. The two of you are completely different, Badr, but she makes you happy."

He smiled again, but did not respond.

"What's happened to that Badr," `Abd al-wahhab chided, "who would neither forgive nor show any mercy? The man who ripped her love from his heart? Do you recognise that man?"

"The girl was just eighteen years old," Badr replied affectionately. "I swear that, if I'd been in her place, I couldn't have put up with what she has. She's just like an angel. Her innocence injects regret into every kind of sin. She's—"

"People say," `Abd al-wahhab interrupted with a scoff, "that Jawhar the Sicilian proclaimed that every era has its own regime and men. Now I'm suggesting that every era has a woman who manages to change these men. She can evoke a sympathy, the reach of which he does not even realise. Felicitations on the happiness that you richly deserve! You were expecting the letter, and today it's arrived."

"From the Caliph Al-Mustansir?" Badr asked him, giving him an expectant look.

"Yes," `Abd al-wahhab replied.

"Read it to me."

"Here's what the Caliph and Imam Al-Mustansir has written:

'If I am to be devoured, then you are the one to do it.

Come to my aid before I am torn apart.

Al-Mustansir bi-Allah Abu Tamim Ma`ad ibn Az-Zahir'."

"We need to get to Egypt before the year's out," he told `Abd al-wahhab with a smile.

"That's what you've wanted from the start."

"But there's a right time for everything. Patience is the key to resolution. Send a message back to the Caliph, saying that Badr al-Jamali will come to Egypt, but only with his own army. And before he sets foot on Egyptian soil, the Caliph must arrest Ildakiz."

"That's impossible, my son. He's a Caliph who's been stripped of everything he owns."

"I don't want to enter Egypt to punish people, but to build. People will be saying that Badr's entered the country to replace the Minister Asad ad-daula Ildakiz. Badr's more important than any minister of state. If I arrest Ildakiz, I'll be provoking all kinds of intrigue among the amirs even before I arrive. Egypt's already a veritable beehive of intrigue; it doesn't need any more. Send the Caliph some soldiers to provide support and tell him that he has to arrest the minister, because Badr intends to provide support and to seek peace and security with all the amirs and troops. He does not aspire to any office, nor does he need a ministerial appointment.

That day, Badr gave Furoon a shock by coming early. He asked her to get ready, then held her hand and took her out of the room. They sat in front of the palace's resident judge.

"Will you agree to be married to me, Furoon?" he asked her all of a sudden. "Or will I be forced to keep you against your will?"

"Why, Badr?" she asked softly, not understanding what he meant.

Turning to the judge, he gave her name in full. The judge asked about her religious affiliation. She said nothing, scared about what her beloved might say. Would he change his own affiliation, she wondered, so that he could be married to her? But he did not. He told the judge what her affiliation was. Once the judge had completed the proceedings, Badr grabbed her hand and took her into the palace garden.

"I love you," she told him, clutching his arm.

"You didn't ask any questions, as though you trust me, even though I've never trusted anyone my whole life. I was waiting for some sense of purpose."

He did not tell her the purpose; even love has its limits. Would he tell her that he wanted to humiliate her father first and see him plead and beg? If he had done that, she would've found it hard to forgive him. She let go of his hand and looked at some birds constructing a nest in one of the trees.

"How can we get them some food?" she asked. "Today, I want to talk to you about my friends here in the garden. Do you know that, when I was a little girl and missed my mother, I used to talk to the birds? They would stop and listen to me. Who did you talk to, Badr, when you missed your mother?"

"I talked to my sword," he replied, looking into her eyes. "I swore to kill whoever had killed her in front of me."

"Killing isn't always the solution."

"I know. I learned that after a while. I want to tell you something."

She looked at him in alarm.

"I'm traveling to Egypt soon," he said.

"Am I going with you?" she asked, her heart doing a leap.

"No, you'll stay here. I don't know how the amirs are going to receive me. I've no idea how many soldiers are left, or indeed how many Egyptians."

"I'm going with you," she stated firmly.

"Furoon, sometimes you need to remember who I am."

"You're my Amir and my husband, everything I possess. I'll die before I let you go alone. I beg you not to leave me behind. Are you frightened for me?"

Their eyes met.

"Badr al-Jamali is never frightened. If I can't protect you, how am I supposed to save the Caliph's regime and the whole of Egypt?"

She clutched his arm again and put her head on his shoulder.

"Egypt!" she said. "All my dreams are coming to pass. The man I love and the country denied me. If you allowed me, I'll bring Hafsa with me, the woman who raised me. Is it paradise, I wonder, where I'm living? Or is it that God is compensating me for all the years of suffering and worry? He is indeed merciful."

"He is indeed merciful," Badr repeated.

"But we're not at His mercy."

"No, we're not."

BOOK THREE

EGYPT 1073 CE / 466 AH

Regard the structure of the twin pyramids and look:

Between them the amazing Sphinx,

Like twin camel-litters on a journey,

For two beloveds separated by a guardian.

The water of the Nile like tears beneath them,

The sound of the wind around them like a lament.

Zafir al-Haddad al-Skandari, Fatimid poet

CHAPTER SEVEN

There are times when fate will simply ignore us, while at others, it will provide us with benefits and even give us what we dream of as an act of revenge or favour. Badr al-Jamali did not know for sure, but he was absolutely convinced that, if he did not move to Egypt as quickly as possible, he might well lose the opportunity he had been waiting for all his life. Sailors advised him to wait. The winter gales were powerful, and this was not the time to travel. Even so, he insisted. At this point, subduing winds was easier than subduing ambitious people in Egypt. He asked Furoon to stay in Acre, but he did not get his way. She told him that, if he had decided to take the risk, then she would go with him, no matter the misery and suffering involved. He had not told anyone where they were going. He loaded the Armenian soldiers on the boat without telling them anything. Before he left, he sent some men ahead to Damietta, urging its elders to meet him. He was coming as a friend; he neither wanted to hurt anyone nor desired a position. His aim in coming was to reconcile people's hearts so that he could put an end to intrigue. Doing that was much harder and riskier than chopping off heads. But he would be patient; patience was crucial, as was making decisions between anger and compassion. It was compassion that was the mark of great people.

When he reached Damietta, he had a few thousand men with him. He was welcomed, albeit guardedly, by Sulaiman al-Luwati, elder of the Luwata tribe. Why had the Armenian come there when there was general devastation? Why had he brought his army with him if he was not looking for a position? No one ever simply visits the country with his army, brandishing swords and spears. However, when Badr entered the city, he told his soldiers to leave their weapons outside his tent. He gave the elder lots of gifts and asked him how things were in Egypt. He told the elder that he had visited the country as a child, and now God had given him a friend and brother, namely Sulaiman al-Luwati. Badr said that he was aware of how weak the Caliph was and how corrupt the country's affairs were. He sympathised with the Egyptian people, whose suffering had led to such devastation. Sulaiman listened cautiously.

"Have you come to help the Caliph or his mother?" he asked Badr. "In our country, Amir, it is a woman who's in charge, in accordance with her whims and cunning. Are you aware that Rasad, the Caliph's mother, has her own private office? She appoints and fires ministers. You'll need to get the Caliph's mother to agree first. Have you ever met her?"

"No, I haven't," Badr replied slowly.

"Don't believe what you hear about Egypt. Damietta's on the Nile delta, and it's doing fine. Yes, some people have died, and peasants have abandoned their lands and run away. That's happened. But there's something you don't know about the Egyptian people."

"What's that?"

"They're a Nile—a river that never dries up. Squeeze them, and they'll produce a treasure trove of money. Peasants come to me, swearing, begging, and pleading. They'll kiss my feet and say they have no food. But then, if I threaten to take their wife as a slave, suddenly they can come up with a whole pile of gold. They're liars; don't believe them. They're dying of hunger, and yet they go to sleep lying on top of their treasures. I'm here as ruler of the entire country. Your Caliph, who can't control his own mother, has no authority over me."

"You're right," Badr said quietly.

"Aren't you one of the Caliph's followers? And yet, today you're criticising him?"

"No, I'm not criticising him, brother, but you're still right. I want to stroll along the roads and look at the gardens and palm trees by the sea and river. People say that heaven will be just like Damietta, with its sea, river, palm trees, and roses."

"Don't look for any roses here, Amir. They're all in the Caliph's mother's suite."

"You'll like staying here, Amir," he went on, laughing loudly.

"Call me Badr. You've been very kind to me, as well as to my wife and my men. You're a fine man. I'd like you to visit me in Acre soon, so I can repay your hospitality."

"If you stay in Acre and the Seljuks don't take it, I'll certainly pay you a visit. We're happy to have you stay with us, Badr, as long as you're not here to spy or plunder. Look on Damietta as your own country. How long will you be staying?"

"I don't want to be a burden, Brother. Maybe a month, but we'll put up our own tents and cook our own food."

In Damietta, he saw things he had not expected. As he walked through the fields, he found them completely destroyed. Sulaiman's servant was accompanying them, and Badr asked the man about those fields.

"The peasants ran away," he said. "They're scared of my master, Sulaiman. They're all hiding in burrows like mice. But he finds them; he always manages to find them."

"How do people eat?"

"In Cairo and Fustat, they don't eat, and in the Delta there's hardly enough. We don't need to eat; what we need is gold. Then we can buy things to eat, even if it's from outside Egypt. My master Sulaiman controls the whole of Egypt. Those peasants need someone to control them. We go for them at night, and they manage to produce huge amounts of gold, then claim that they're hungry. They have cattle, chickens, and livestock that they keep hidden from our men, but we find them. You have to be firm with peasants. Peasants with no master are like sheep with no shepherd. You can't butcher them or profit from their wool."

Badr looked at the half-destroyed mosque.

"Do you pray in that mosque?" he asked.

"Yes, but people who come to pray have to pay first."

"Who decides the rate?"

"My master Sulaiman."

"The Caliph doesn't appoint anyone around here?"

"The Turkish amirs cooperate with us, Amir."

The man winked.

"Yes, I understand," Badr replied.

"They're like you, Amir," Sulaiman went on. "They want the best for us supporters of the country."

"Where to do the peasants flee to?"

"The desert. They eat lizards. When the majority of them disappear, then they come to offer their obeisance to my master Sulaiman. They're well aware that they're nothing without his protection. Don't imagine that there's a police chief in Egypt. Do you even know his name? I can't remember the names of ministers. All Egypt has is powerful men who protect the weak—at a price."

"You're right. I've perceived only good in your master. What about fish?"

"The fish are all ours. Fishermen go out fishing with our permission and come back with fish."

"What do they get in return?"

"Protection, as I've told you."

"But don't they starve?"

"They buy fish from us. If they hide some of the catch, we find out. The penalty is that their limbs be cut off and their women sold."

When Badr reached Cairo, he left his wife and soldiers before he took his sword, donned a turban, covered his face, and headed for Fustat along with his secretary, 'Abd al-wahhab. He deliberately did not look at things on the way, and instead walked on foot right through the rubble of Al-Qata'i,

Fustat, and Cairo. What he observed was different from anything he had heard described, fouler than any killing or slaughter he had witnessed. Even Badr was deeply affected. Fustat reminded him of his mother as she had tried to remain upright after a soldier had stabbed her in the heart. She had grabbed the edge of the wall, then groaned in front of him as she uttered some words from the Gospel. He had not heard what she said, but he had watched as her eyes turned to stone, filled with dust. How could eyes get so full of dust like that? How could a country where he had lived—which he remembered as a beautiful dream—now resemble his own mother's glazed eyes? He walked through the rubble of ruined houses with no inhabitants or beggars, seeing the vestiges of a life full of warmth: a child's torn clothing, a cooking pot blackened by much use, a bottle of water, a black pillow soiled with blood, then fire, and then plague, that had shrivelled. An old man was using it to wipe off a dirty chunk of bread that he began, reluctantly, to eat. When he walked through Al-Qata'i, Ahmad ibn Tulun's city, Badr looked at the chamberlain whom the Sultan had sent to accompany him.

"Where's the city that Ahmad ibn Tulun built?" he asked.

"It used to be here," the chamberlain replied, pointing in that direction. "But we've constructed a wall between here and Cairo so we can shield the Caliph's eyes from the ugly view. Desolation is all that's left of the city."

The chamberlain now pointed at Fustat. Badr spotted some people still living there despite all the hardship. They were mostly young, with more men than women. Some of them were working silently, breaking up rocks or selling debris. He kept walking in search of somewhere to eat and stretched out his hand to passers-by. There was a spot for merchants who had been wealthy at one point; they were now keeping their stores under lock and key for fear of thieves, and hoarding gold and pearls inside. They would trade secretly in flour, grain, cattle, and chickens. Their houses were firmly locked, and they never showed themselves in public. A shabbily dressed old man caught his attention; he was sitting on top of the ruins of a house and drinking an Egyptian drink made of limes and quince. Badr had no idea how he had come to encounter such famine. The man was barefoot, his clothes were tattered, and his hands showed signs of old, festering wounds. Badr went over to him.

"Why are you sitting here, old man?" he asked.

"I like sitting in the open air," the man replied without looked at Badr, "and watching all this nonsense."

"Is this your house?"

"Maybe."

"Is it or isn't it your house?"

"Don't ask me unanswerable questions. Who are you?"

"A passer-by, perhaps."

"What do you mean, 'perhaps'?"

"Don't you ask me any unanswerable questions either, old man! Give me your hand, I want to help you."

The old man waved his hand away.

"Get away from me," he said. "Nothing good ever comes from rulers, nor do their men offer any help."

"What makes you think I'm one of them?"

"Every single day, an amir comes to see me, saying that he's eager to help me. When I hold out my hand, he puts me in prison. Prison's better for you, he says. You can eat and drink. You don't need to breathe the air or beg for food. Do you want to put me in prison, too, so I won't upset the Caliph with the way I look?"

"No, I'd like to stay with you for a while. I want you to walk with me," Badr told him, holding out his hand. "You can tell me what's happened in the city, and I'll give you a dinar!"

The chamberlain gave him a shocked look.

"That's not right, my Lord," he said. "The lunatic's lying to you."

"Come on, let's go," Badr said, ignoring the chamberlain.

He took the dinar out of his pocket and put it where the man could see it. The old man leapt to his feet and cautiously followed Badr.

"What do you want to know?" he asked. "I can tell you."

"I'm going to walk around all the streets with you today and tomorrow."

"Which side of the walls?"

"Which walls?"

"The ones that the ministers have built so as not to upset the Caliph. Look! Here's a wall by Ahmad ibn Tulun's mosque to block the view of the destruction inside his city, which was called Al-Qata'i. It seems that its location was doomed, with one destruction after another. Behind it lies a life you would not recognise. Another wall here blocks the Caliph's view of Fustat and its living-dead inhabitants. Cairo's still a ruin without Al-Qata'i and Fustat. Do you know, man, what saddens me? The utter stupidity of the Caliph's men. If they've stopped him from observing the debris in Fustat, how can they stop him looking at the debris behind his own residence? People have left and gone away, and his capital city, Cairo, that he's kept closed and locked away from its own people, is just as sad to see as Fustat or even worse. Do you know how many Egyptians have fled with their possessions, and how many others have stayed here and been killed?"

"I want to see what's behind the walls."

He opened his eyes and covered his nose with a handkerchief. The foul stench made his eyes water. All his life, he had never seen such a gruesomely dark colour: black discoloured by grey dominated the area behind the wall where Fustat and Al-Qata'i had been, something that the chamberlain did not want anyone to see. Corpses littered the streets, some of them half-eaten, others with severed or fractured limbs. Worms were living a life of plenty; lots to eat and pleasant company. He watched as girls no older than thirteen sold their bodies on the debris. No one spoke as he watched a completely naked girl being straddled by an old man; she was removing bits of glass from the debris so that she could lie back without being wounded, except in her soul. Another girl seized Badr's hand; he looked at her, but said nothing. She took off her filthy dress, and her breasts were visible right before his eyes. A young man who was competing with her for customers came up and snatched Badr's hand as well. The chamberlain bashfully pushed both of them away.

"Now you know how it is that disaster has struck this land," he said. "Do you see this obscene behaviour? We tell the shaikhs about it every single day, but it's useless."

Never in his life had he seen holes in the ground before. He had not realised that some people lived underground, digging holes to hide from cruelty and greed and decorating them with worm-infested mud, yellowing tree-branches, fresh urine, and animal droppings. The first time Badr had felt such nausea was when he saw his mother dying in front of him. Now, he emptied his stomach in a panic and looked at the mosque as though it could be a source of safety.

"Is that Ahmad ibn Tulun's mosque?" he asked.

"Yes, my Lord," the chamberlain replied. "But its walls are cracked, and the main gate is almost destroyed. It's a Sunni mosque."

"Let's go there."

Inside the mosque, he found refuge, as though it were paradise after the hell he had seen outside. The mosque seemed deserted, with no prayers being performed and no shaikh looking after it. He looked up at the crenulations atop the walls. He was stunned by their beauty and did not understand their purpose, but it was enough to give his chest a jolt and instil a sense of dread in his heart. He walked around the covered courtyard as though compelled, not free to choose. How many gates did this mosque have? It went on forever, built to last, constructed to remind all comers that spaciousness is hope, light is life, and the moon in the heavens must be free to roam amid the stars until it reaches its goal. He looked at the wooden crossbars on the gates with their leafy decorations. Where would the beggar and student be venturing through that gate? Where would his own vagrant soul find rest? He headed over to the mihrab. All of a sudden, he fell to the ground in prayer and put a hand over his face. The chamberlain looked at him in surprise, and the old man laughed.

"Welcome to Egypt, Brother," he said.

The crazy old man kept laughing, and Badr continued to pray, neither seeing nor hearing anything. The chamberlain spoke to one of Badr's soldiers.

"Are you going to let your master pray without a prayer rug?" he asked. "To pray on the stone floor?"

"Shall I bring you a prayer rug, my Lord?" the soldier asked, approaching Badr.

Badr was on his knees, praying, and did not reply. Once he had finished, he gestured to the soldier. The soldier approached.

"The chamberlain," he whispered in the soldier's ear.

"Yes, my Lord, what do you want with the chamberlain?"

"Tell him to go back to the Caliph. I've seen enough for today. I'm going to stay here for a while."

"As you command, my Lord. What about the crazy old man?"

"Let him stay with me for a while. His company's useful."

Ahmad ibn Tulun. Had the man not been chasing him for a while? How much he regretted the fate of his city. And yet, those crenulations in the mosque's turrets lingered in his imagination. He felt drawn to Ibn Tulun's mosque the same way water is attracted to the moon. He felt sorry for the state of the gate through which he had entered and the cracks in the walls. The very first thing he would do would be to repair what Ahmad had built and construct a pulpit in his mosque for Badr al-Jamali. Each one was part of the other. The crenulations were intertwined in endless rows. All sorts of people would come here: those who had wishes, those with increasing worries, those whose lives were lost, those who loved themselves. Ahmad, can you hear me, I wonder. I can see you in the mihrab, sitting there listening to the preacher, walking along your city's streets, and holding banquets and meals for the poor. I can see you; indeed, I can feel you, as though you're my brother, or we share the same blood. You! When you fall ill, I can hear

Egyptians praying for you from the top of the Muqattam Hills, every one of them climbing up there with his Holy Book: Muslims with the Qur'an, Christians with the Gospel, and Jews with the Torah, all united in their love for you. What did you do with the Egyptian people? What is your link to the ancestors? This is a country that confuses you and takes away your ability to control your own desires. You wander like someone possessed and defend it like a lion. Ah, Egypt! Everyone who comes here falls into the pit. I no longer know: do I love you or fear you, or both at once?

"My Lord," the soldier asked.

"This is what we wanted," Badr replied, looking at him. "We've seen what I wanted to see. Tonight, we're going to the Pyramid plateau."

"But, my Lord, that's dangerous at night. Jinn come out, and witches do their dance."

"Then they're all welcome to join us!"

He stared at the Pyramid for a moment, then at the small opening. He pounded on the stone, then headed cautiously inside on his own.

"Pyramid Witch," he said confidently, "I'm here. I've come."

She now appeared with her dark black hair and huge, gleaming round eyes. He was not afraid, but nevertheless, he was stunned.

"Welcome to the Armenian!" she said in a sweet voice. "Have you come here to look for a homeland, man? This one is far more difficult than any other. It gives only to those people who are willing to give themselves, just like the ancients' priests."

"Do you know where I'm from?"

"I've been expecting you. Bahnas knows everything."

"Why have you been expecting me?"

"To warn you about the curse of the mighty..."

"Don't predict some fresh sorrow for me. I've had more than enough."

"When you arrived," she replied with a smile, "you didn't come to the Pyramids first. You went to Ahmad's mosque..."

"Who's Ahmad?"

"Ahmad ibn Tulun. Why did you visit his mosque?"

He looked at her but did not respond.

"No matter!" she said. "Ahmad preserved the land and gold. He's become one of the ancient kings."

"I've come to see you in search of tranquillity."

"If you want me to reassure you about the future, that's not in my hands. If you want me to tell you whether this country can be your homeland or whether you're just passing through, I can give you an answer after a while..."

"You know the language of birds. Tell me, what is the curse that has descended on this country?"

"The ancients say that this is a land that gives only to those in love and embraces those who strive. Striving is the hardest struggle of all; it's all about toil and distress. May God come to your aid! There are some men born in this land who are not part of it, and there are others who are drawn to it the way the moon draws the sea at night, so they become part of it. It can separate good from evil, honest people from hypocrites."

"I was thinking about the moon and the sea. How is it you're talking about them now as though you could read my thoughts?"

"You've asked me about Egypt, Armenian. This is an era of multiple conspiracies and different religious groups. You know that, Badr, and, deep down, you understand. I hope that God will so illuminate your visage that you can see how misguided and stupid human beings are. They always assume that they possess the truth and own the keys to eternity. Do you know why? Because they're weak, as weak as gnats or even more so. The keys to eternity belong with the Creator; the keys to truth, with God. What we know is merely a set of husks. Our knowledge of the world is just like our knowledge of the language of birds. We do our best to solve the riddle of names and pronounce the letters so as to open the gates of paradise, but reaching paradise demands a crossing of twelve barriers or more. That's what the ancients tell us. They understood the world's travails, and that eternal life was not to be the destiny of every human being, but only for some. Some people's memories are enshrined in this world and the next, while others simply disappear in both. Which group do you belong in, I wonder?"

"What do the ancients have to say about discord?"

"Discord is a capacity superior to all other human traits. It engenders chaos. There is no cure for it; it is like hellfire, relentless as it eats away entire civilizations and buildings, eradicating them. The ancients had a god of chaos named Set. Do you know why? Because, just like good, chaos is powerful and influential. However, whereas good is as clear as air, discord has a gleam to it, like red rubies. Do you know what the monarch who built this pyramid had to say? He said: 'I'm the monarch. I built the pyramids. I completed the project in six years. Let anyone who comes after me and claims to be like me try to destroy it in six hundred.' He realised that destruction is much easier than building. My grandmother spoke those very same words to Ahmad ibn Tulun, and now I'm saying them to you. But not all buildings are like the pyramids, Badr. Even the Umayyad Mosque in Damascus was lost to fire. How many buildings are destroyed because of the whims of a ruler or rebel!"

"How do you know about the burning of the Umayyad mosque when you're here in the Pyramid?"

"I grieve the destruction of the mosque because it implies defeat and death. Death that is followed by rebirth is victory. But death by discord has no rebirth. Do you admire Ahmad?"

"You mean Ahmad ibn Tulun? I admire his unique mosque, and his career is extraordinary, a series of triumphs. However, I might have a concern I haven't encountered before."

"I knew Ahmad ibn Tulun. We had a long-standing friendship. If you admire him, then we can lay out a similar path for you."

"Is that a threat or a blessing?"

"Leaders always mirror the people they admire, the same way humans are reborn."

"Are you a Muslim?"

"Don't ask me about my faith, Badr. You're far too important to fall into the pit and cleverer than your peers. Proceed with caution. No one can know where discord will come from or who will set intrigue in motion. Those are lands fractured by different religious communities, each with its own set of factions."

"Pyramid Witch..."

"Call me Bahnas. We're friends and colleagues now."

He headed slowly for the door.

"Aram!" she yelled loudly.

He turned round, and their eyes met. He remembered the trusting little boy, and no longer knew whether he wanted him to die or be reborn.

"How did you know my original name?" he asked apprehensively.

"Is that your name? I thought it was Badr."

"I don't understand you."

"Look for him. You may find him."

"Who? Badr or Aram?"

"Both of them. You'll need them both, but you may not find either of them. Proceed on your journey with caution. It is long and difficult."

CHAPTER EIGHT

Her husband dazzled her with his calm demeanour and generous spirit. He would listen to the amirs, talk to them, and tell them stories. Never in her life had she seen a man with such a magic touch. She watched his eyes, smiling at times, but then focusing on something important. His talk was like honey, even sweeter than sugar cubes, all of it wisdom and knowledge. He gathered the amirs together and told them that he had come to Egypt to help reconcile people's hearts. They all complained about the Caliph's weakness. He listened and understood without bringing up details. He asked them to be united in their charitable acts as their religion enjoined them. If they did so, Egypt could have a powerful army: two hundred amirs, each commanding a thousand soldiers. If they were united, all the discord and intrigue could come to an end. They all complained about the straitened circumstances and the underhand dealings of the Caliph and his mother. He told them that he had come to calm the intense hatred both between them and the Egyptian people and between them and the Caliph. Every problem had its solution, and every pestilence its remedy. At first, they listened to him guardedly; they did not know Badr, and those who did had heard about the way he had eliminated Abu Taher. But he swore that he was being totally honest with them. He told them what had happened with Abu Taher and the way he had killed Badr's eldest son, Sha'baan, seared his heart, and conspired against him. He told him that his sole ambition was to see them unified. There was imminent danger at Egypt's gates, just as there was in Syria. Once Syria fell, Egypt was bound to be next. The Seljuqs wanted Egypt; that much was certain. If they did not join forces with Badr al-Jamali, their end would come before his. They were astonished that Badr had not yet had a meeting with the Caliph, neither paying him a visit nor lingering inside his palace. He had decided to rebuild a derelict Cairo palace and reside there. His men helped him move into the new residence that was ready in less than a month. He told them that he was not seeing any police on the streets and had no idea where they were. He had come in peace, he told them, and was extending his hand so that the country could thrive.

As Furoon listened to him, she was utterly delighted. This was what Egypt needed—someone with his kind of wisdom, her beloved. Recently, he had had no time for her; he had not even come to see here in her room. But she understood. She was watching from afar, listening to what he was saying, and looking forward to his hugs once his work was finished.

He hired the very best cooks and halva-makers still living in Egypt to put on a banquet for the amirs. Today, they would all swear an oath together and pledge to stamp out discord and present a united front. Today would be a decisive moment, and he himself invited each of them individually. Some of them may have been enemies who would never agree to a meeting, but he wanted enemies to gather even before friends. Everyone would have his protection. No amir would ever have to argue with another over a parcel of land or the imposition of taxes. Today, they were all friends. On a day when they were all united, the country would begin to see light.

Furoon hurried over to see him. She realised that he was busy, but she needed his help and wanted to talk to him. She asked the guard to let her see him, and he let her in.

As she went in, she was frightened. He was frowning as he looked over some paperwork. He looked up at her and waited for her to say something.

"Forgive me, Amir," she said falteringly, "I know how busy you are."

He nodded and waited.

"I hear you've invited the army commanders to talk to them," she said.

"Yes, tomorrow," he replied, looking down at the brocade on his coat.

"I think it's a wonderful idea, Badr," she went on. "Peace always results in success. Once you've honoured them and reached an agreement with them, war will come to an end, and the people will prosper. Egypt needs a man with your wisdom, someone who knows how to reconcile people's hearts."

"Don't bother yourself with matters of state," he told her with a smile, stroking her hand.

"Those are matters that concern you," she said, "and I'm your wife."

"There's something I need to talk to you about," she went on gently.

He stood up and put his sword in its scabbard.

"Go ahead," he told her, "I'm listening."

"Can I make halva with the other cooks?" she asked. "I promise you won't be eating anything so sweet."

"If halva can put an end to discord, Furoon," he told her, "then let's give it a try. Are you sure that, once they've tasted your halva, they're going to come to an agreement?"

"Yes, I am," she replied confidently.

"Fine then, do what you want."

"Don't get angry with me, Badr. I'm just going to tell you what's on my mind."

"I don't know if I'll get angry or not."

"This is a house where I pray and read God's book. I don't like having wine here, and I don't like that you've invited the amirs to drink wine with you after dinner today."

"You like, you don't like?" he replied, staring at her in amazement. "Don't forget who you're talking to, Furoon. Don't forget—"

"I'm talking to my husband," she stuttered in reply.

"You're addressing the Amir. You're under his command and will obey his orders in silence."

She stayed silent.

"Do you hear?" he asked.

"Yes," she replied.

"You'll hear and carry out orders without any fuss or disagreement. If I want to serve wine to the amirs, I shall do so. Did your father drink wine, Furoon? Tell me!"

She did not reply.

"Don't you dare interfere in things that don't concern you again. I'm doing my best to save this country. Don't change my mood before I even get to meet them. Believe me: meeting and convincing them is far more difficult than conquering Damascus. Now leave!"

She was shocked to see how furious he was, but she left in silence.

As she watched the amirs arrive, she was feeling anxious and a bit guilty as well. Was not Badr the love of her life? Had she not waged war on the world for his sake? Why had she annoyed him? Once the dinner was over, she would apologise and hoped he would accept it. Amirs would be drinking wine, whether or not he offered it to them. The issues involving amirs were far more serious than bothering about wine. From the window, she listened to the amirs' chatter, watched as her husband's eyes moved swiftly from one amir to the next, and listened to his calm words. How she loved him, and how proud of him she felt! She could not hear everything, but she was able to pick up snatches of what the amirs were saying. They were complaining about each other, about the Caliph, about the general situation, about land, about Egyptians. Badr kept calming them down and assuring them that he had come to help and to work in their interest first and foremost. Egypt's tax revenue was no larger than the smallest piece of Islamic territory. Egypt was full of gold, but every time a new ruler passed by, his horse would fall to the ground in prostration, then trip over a hoard of ancient treasure. Now it had turned into a village of poor people with no food. The chance to change everything lay in their hands.

While his men handed out food and drink, he went on talking. He seemed deeply affected by the occasion. She could see from his expression that he really wanted to convince them all. Some of them started to look convinced, and the drink certainly seemed to help ease their minds. They laughed a lot and seemed happier. While she had been standing by the window, she had forgotten to put food out for the birds as she did every day. Doves in Egypt were shy and easily frightened, just like its people; they did not trust friends or brothers. She made her way quietly into the garden, taking some seeds with her. As she looked at the seeds, she blamed herself: how could she feed the birds seeds when Egyptians could not find any food to eat? Did the halva-maker's daughter think she was so merciful? She whispered to the birds that she had not been out of the house so far. When she did go, she would be feeding people, not birds. I want you all to realise that I will not be coming here every day.

She looked at the dove that would approach, then fly away when she moved her hand. When she did not move, it would come back again. The bird started nervously and swiftly pecking away at the seeds, then a second came, then a third. There were doves all around her. She smiled in pleasure at the world. All of a sudden, the birds all flew away, squawking at the abrupt surprise. Furoon looked at the garden gates. Her husband's soldiers were standing there, holding their swords and lances. She was scared and hid behind the wall, although she did not know why; after all, they were her husband Badr's soldiers. Since when was she afraid of soldiers? Then out of the corner of her eye, she spotted the soldier strangling the amir, then covering his mouth with his hand and plunging the sword into his guts till it emerged out of his back. She may have shuddered, but she could not scream. Everything happened so fast. She put her hand over her mouth, as though she were trying to stem the flow of tears and the stench of slaughter. Every time one of the amirs left her husband Badr's dinner to relieve himself after all the eating and drinking, he would be killed by one of Badr's soldiers—one, two, three. She closed her eyes and let out a silent scream. She could not move or leave her eyes closed. Ten, twenty, thirty. His soldiers were carrying out their task to perfection, quickly and perfectly calmly. The corpses of two hundred amirs were piled up in the palace garden. The soldiers started cutting off the heads of the corpses and collecting them for their Amir, her husband Badr al-Jamali. That day, he had invited all the Egyptian amirs and offered them food and then halva and wine. After they had all offered him security and pledged themselves to his cause, and after he had claimed that he wished to be friends and live in peace with them, he had now killed them all. He had made a lot of claims, till even Furoon had believed him. This was Badr, the man who would kiss her tenderly at night and offer her his arm so she could fall asleep on his chest. Had he not killed her husband and Abu Taher? A blood-letter, that's all. He had come here to slaughter people and plunder. But he had not done so. Was it because there was nothing left to plunder? Did authority demand this amount of bloodshed? 'Everything on top of soil is still soil.' Her thoughts were totally scrambled. The stench of freshly spilled blood was making her sick. She emptied her stomach the way Badr had done when he saw the situation in Egypt. She tried to block her nose or run back to her room to contemplate slowly the end of life and all her dreams.

She turned to go back to her room. Badr was standing in front of her.

"What are you doing here?" he asked indignantly.

She lowered her head, and her voice tricked her just as he had tricked the amirs. She was unable to talk. She gestured to him, and he looked into her eyes.

"I just asked you, Furoon," he said. "What are you doing here?"

She heard him call to his soldiers to collect the heads, because he was planning to take them to the Caliph tonight before dawn.

That was the last sentence she heard. After that, she fainted. Badr carried her back to her room and put some water on her face.

"Wake up, Furoon," he said impatiently. "I don't have time..."

Her mental state seemed to frighten him. Opening her eyes, she recited some Quranic verses: 'Whoever kills a soul, not to compensate for another soul killed or for corruption in the land, shall be as though he has killed all the people together.' [Qur'an, Sura 5 [Al-Ma`ida], v. 32]

At that point, she expected him to lop off her head. He would do it; for him, killing was easier than taking off his clothes or greeting his children. So, let him kill her! When she lost consciousness, her courage only grew and intensified.

"You didn't have to kill them," she said. "They would have been convinced and loyal..."

"Finish the verse," he replied, as though killing the amirs had not affected him in the slightest. "'Whoever gives life to a soul, shall be as though he were giving life to all people.' When you feed the birds, halva-maker's daughter, you need to remember that you left your homeland, fleeing from hunger, plague, corruption, and drought so as to enjoy a good life in Syria. You spared no thought for people dying in Egypt or even thought about them. Lady of faith and morality, you need to recall that, like plague, corruption does not distinguish between good and evil; it affects everyone. It impacted your father, your Amir, your judge, and your shaikh. You're living in another world, inside your own self. All you care about is being well, honest, and good. But if everyone else went to hell, you wouldn't care. You'd weep a few tears, then forget, be married, and have children. God knows, Furoon, who's better, you or me. He knows who kills people, who tries to revive them, and who only cares about herself."

She did not respond. He stood up and left, followed by his soldiers carrying all the heads.

He may have decapitated many people today, but the words he had just spoken to her felt just like a whipping.

Badr did not wait to see the Caliph. Al-Mustansir came in, looking gloomy and crushed.

"You've come to save me, Badr," he said, rubbing his hands together.

"When the Caliph and Imam summons me," Badr replied, "I come. I didn't want to enter your palace without a gift. My men have brought two hundred heads—all the amirs of Egypt. Now, my Lord, my men are going to enter their houses and seize everything of value to be spent on the country. My Lord—"

"How did you do it?" the Caliph asked in amazement.

"The killing part was easy. What comes next is much harder. You don't have any honest men in this country. Corruption affects both rich and poor alike. It takes in religious scholars, judges, merchants, craftsmen, tribes, police, and soldiers. I don't want the remnants of your army; it's not fit for the task ahead. People who've had to live with this corruption must now get rid of it. We need those who begin with us to learn afresh and accustom themselves to a different system. However, anyone inured to the turmoil of poverty and drought must be discarded."

"Do you plan to kill my soldiers, Badr? Will you be replacing them, Amir, with your own?"

"That's already happened, my Lord," Badr responded confidently. "I've replaced every amir that I've killed with one of my own men. I'm taking his house, his slave girls, and all of his property. But I don't want to harm the soldiers. Once we've taken away their weapons and given them what they need, we'll leave them to their own devices. Now that the amirs are dead, they're not safe."

"Your army's not more than a few thousand strong, Badr, as you well know."

"Have you heard of an amir who came here two hundred years ago or more? His name's Ibn Tulun."

Al-Mustansir stared at him, but did not say anything.

"You know who he is, don't you?" Badr asked.

"What do we have to do with Ibn Tulun? We're not followers of the Abbasid Caliph. His regime lasted no more than forty years. Less, perhaps."

"He had an army that included Egyptians."

"What's going through your mind, Badr?"

"For soldiers, my Lord, history is important. For commanders, it's even more important. My soldiers belong to the same community as me, and I trust them. Egyptian soldiers are from their own land too, and they want to see their own interests met, even if a quest for gold and riches has led them astray for a while. In the end, they have no other choice."

"Not all Egyptians belong to our Shi`ite faith. For the whole of our regime, we've never used Egyptians in our army."

"Not all my own soldiers are Muslims by birth, my Lord. I have both Christians and Muslims. Ibn Tulun did the same earlier with the Egyptian army, and he defeated the Abbasid Caliph. That's what we want."

"You're taking a risk. It's dangerous to use Egyptians who belong to a different faith community. Using Armenian Christians in your own army is even riskier."

"Risk is our only option. What more can you lose than what you've already lost? I can either restore this country to the way it was, or I can die in your prison and be buried here. Ever since we were young, we've learned that infected wounds have to be cleaned with a knife, then cauterised. If that doesn't work, then you have to amputate mercilessly. You can then live even though you're missing a limb, but at least you're still alive. Cleansing a wound saves people's lives."

"What are your plans?"

"The difficulties lie ahead. What's happened so far is the easy part. It's saddened me to see the Caliph's capital city in ruins, with houses demolished and skeletons of people who've died of plague and hunger. Why should we be keeping Cairo as a Fatimid monopoly?"

"Badr," the Caliph replied in amazement, "this is the Fatimid city. It was built for them and no one else. The city walls have protected it from ignominy and the common people, as well as from raiders."

"But how can the Caliph and his government keep themselves imprisoned inside a city?" Badr asked. "I've never heard of such a thing. The walls have been destroyed, and half the city's in ruins. We'll ask wealthy Egyptians to divide up destroyed property that they find and build their houses inside Cairo. Then we'll invite people who have fled in fear to come back and populate the country, all of it. The wall around Cairo will remain there to ward off raiders, not Egyptians."

The Caliph looked at him, but said nothing.

"And it's time to kill your Minister in prison," Badr went on.

"I'm afraid that his followers will rebel."

"Here, timing is key. Everything has its moment. The amirs are in front of you; here are their severed heads. The Minister in prison won't find anyone to defend him. Don't worry."

"The Minister's post is yours, Badr."

"I don't want it. What I do want is to be Chief Missionary and Judge. I don't trust any of the sectarian judges."

"But you're an Army Commander, Badr. I've never heard of a soldier serving as missionary, judge, and shaikh."

"If you permit me, my Lord, Badr will be Judge, Missionary, Shaikh, and Army Commander."

"You'll always get what you want. You give the orders, and I'll carry them out. But I'm still afraid of annoying the judges."

"The ones that remain, you mean."

"Badr, are you planning to kill the judges too?"

"Not all of them," he replied with a smile. "Only those who participated in the corruption, and there are many. I have nothing to fear from a man of religion who witnesses desolation, yet neither moves nor feels any dread. All those who were corrupt will be punished, the first among them those who claimed to be virtuous."

"Too much spilled blood soils the Caliphate, Badr. Be merciful."

"Mercy, my Lord, belongs to God. I'm a human being. I'm going to do all I can to save the country. I've encountered it great and prosperous, but then miserable, poor, and sick, as sick as Job with no hope of a miracle.'"

"We've heard some information," Al-Mustansir said hesitantly, "but we don't know how accurate it is. Al-Jamali is married to a Sunni woman who does not follow the Shi'ite Imam."

"Badr al-Jamali is Chief Judge and Missionary," Badr replied with a smile. "He has what he wants and does what he wants. My Lord, as long as he has no intention of bringing women into the government, then allow me to make the first decision since my arrival: we will dissolve the Caliph's

Mother's Council."

Al-Mustansir looked at him, not sure whether to trust Badr or be afraid of him.

"Don't stand in my way, Badr," he said. "I've wanted to help you. Don't devour me the way other people have."

"Badr never betrays anyone, nor will he betray the Imam. As long as I'm alive, this regime will be safe. From this moment, there will no longer be a Caliph's Mother's Council. My Lord, we have enough problems already with men's intrigues. So let's just close an unnecessary door."

Furoon clutched her body and slept on her left side, doing her best to erase the image of the severed heads and the stench of blood that had spread as fast as the Nile waters in flood. She could not face the day, nor the next day, nor the day after that. Day after day he would invite her to his room, and she would refuse. She would rub her eyelids in case the colours would change, but things stayed the same ruby-red as her breaths seared and bled. She could see eyes pleading for help, full of sorrow and wanting just a single chance at life. Why was she so shocked? Maybe she was the one with no foresight or knowledge. With her ignorance and naiveté, she had not seen the truth from the very beginning. Furoon was nothing but a pawn in a game of chess in which the loser gets slaughtered and the winner subjects her to a slow death. Her own win had been the man she loved, and yet he did not seem to be on her side. When her husband had killed and sold his womenfolk in cold blood, she had not shuddered, because her own heart had been passionately in love, hoping and wishing, all because she had adored him without asking herself who he was and what he was doing. She had adored his eyes and face, seeing them as support and refuge, a spirit that existed only in her desperate imagination. Perhaps she was the one who did not exist, who knew nothing about this world, about humans and animals. His words still echoed: *Furoon, the little kitten you've been protecting eats dove chicks without the slightest regret. The slave girl who wept at your feet, praying to God and reciting His verses from the Qur'an, did not want to see her sick mother, but instead planned to run away with her lover after she'd stolen your gold. The things you've done, thinking you were doing good, have turned out to be bad. If you hadn't rescued the kitten, you might well have saved the baby doves.*

"It's all your fault, Furoon," she told herself, completing his statement. "You put an end to anything that's good. As you watch your own husband killing and slaughtering people, you maintain a cowardly silence, neither stopping the killing nor helping the weak. Even if you managed to put a stop to the killing, the husband you've saved will be killing someone else the next day." She was a wheel like the ones on war machines, but with hard, pointed edges, crushing everything it rolled over before vanishing. She was the evil in this world, the iniquity of this heart. Furoon had been foolish and misguided ever since she was born, not thinking about anyone else. She claimed to be religious, yet she knew nothing about religion. He was right. What had she done? Even if she had saved a man or woman, who was going to guarantee that this person was going to save anybody else? He might kill instead and create chaos in the land. This was a land that did not deserve any attention. Brothers killed each other as they watched animals doing the same. Every time she tried to make things better, the world brought its ugly visage closer and revealed itself to her. This was a life with viper's fangs, scorpion's stings, crocodile's eyes, and hyena's nose; it was ugly, with no hope of redemption or release other than death. And what about Badr? Could she face him again? In a year, two years? When? Could she ever see his face without recalling the slaughter and sea of blood? Was she scared of him? If only she was. Perhaps she was ashamed of her naiveté. She held her stomach. What would become of the little baby inside her about which he knew nothing? A chess piece to be killed in a war where his father was the target. Or would he be the one to slay all the fighters? Who would her son be?

Oh, Hafsa, where are you now? Furoon wanted to talk to her about this unknown destiny. One day, she would decide to face him and ask to return to Acre. He had left Amina Khatun there, so he could do the same with her. One day, she hoped to be able to embrace him and ask him to let her forget what she had seen. She wanted to erase the memory of all the treachery and ugliness; she could not do that by herself. One day, she would justify all the killing and turn into someone she did not know. In fact, she no longer knew who she was now, and why she had fallen in love with Badr. Why him?

Two weeks passed, and he no longer asked her to come to his room, nor did he come to hers. She still felt nauseous every time she smelled the stench of blood or dreamed about the river converted into veins that flowed without cease or end. Ever since she had first set eyes on Badr, he had been everything. She hadn't worried about jewellery or clothes. All she wanted in her world was to please God and stay around the only man she loved. Hafsa had told her that that type of love only brings suffering; it only bears fruit when you vanish into it and lose yourself with no chance of regrets. But she could not control her own heart. Between his palms, she could glimpse light; in his throat and gleaming teeth, tenderness. One day, she prayed to God: 'O Lord, if loving him is a sin, then forgive me!' If she had not been married to another man, she might perhaps have been more powerful than him, but she had deserted him before and was not about to do it again. Then, why can we not excuse the ones we love? If we are in love, then we must find sympathy and mercy in the heart of the one we love. Perhaps Badr did not realise that his men were going to slay all the amirs. Maybe it was an order from the Caliph, and Badr had no choice. Who knows? Why stand in judgment on her husband and execute the verdicts? She would have to draw a line between all the blood and Badr. With her, he was always gentle and kind; she had never seen him actually kill someone. Yes, he never killed with his own hand. She would beg God to forgive her every single day; she would give alms and pray to Him to grant her vision and forgiveness. Never again would she stand in front of him as arbiter and judge. Had her heart changed, she wondered, because she was missing him? If it was simply desire that moved her, then everything she had learned was forever lost.

Hafsa's return to Egypt brought Furoon much needed relief from the pain of loss and frenzy of passion. She hugged Hafsa tightly, full of despair. As she spoke to Hafsa, breathlessly, she would blame her husband for what he had done, but then reverse herself and thank him. Hafsa listened patiently.

"Have you spoken to him, Furoon?" she asked.

Once again, she felt nauseous.

"I can't," she replied. "I don't dare."

"Are you afraid of him, Furoon? He's your husband."

She did not respond. She did not know whether she was afraid of his anger, upset that he was avoiding her, or annoyed with herself.

"I need to ask you something," she told Hafsa. "If I don't approve of some of the things he's done, but haven't left him or blamed him, is that wrong?"

"God 'does not charge any soul except to its capacity,'" Hafsa replied, her head lowered. "I have no idea what burden your soul is carrying. Talk to your husband. God knows, it seems to me as though you're bound together like tent ropes holding up a dwelling."

"I miss him, Hafsa," Furoon replied. "But I'm scared of him."

After several days, she asked to see him, but he refused. She told the chamberlain to let her in, but he ignored her. The chamberlain said Badr was busy. Putting her hand on her belly, she remembered that, even if he were angry with her now, it could not go on forever. She would be patient. As day followed day, she slept on her own. Sometimes, she imagined him with some other woman, and her heart would break. She was the one who had pushed him away and issued a verdict, as though she were a judge. After a month, she gave up all hope of his coming. He did not welcome her nor even desire to see her. She closed her eyes, her only company the baby in her womb.

She knelt to read from the Qur'an before praying the evening prayer as she usually did. That day, there were still tears in her eyes. She prayed to God to envelop three souls in His mercy: her unborn child, her husband, and herself. 'God does not charge any soul except to its capacity.' He is always merciful; she ealised that. However, that same soul of hers was not part of the Lord's mercy and gift. Once again, she blamed herself. Had she not dreamed of seeing his face, spent nights as sad as a child wandering aimlessly amid all the poverty and drought? Had she not been at war with the entire universe so that she could get close to him?

She did not notice the moment when he came in, but she heard his voice. She turned to look at him.

"Are you cursing me, Furoon," he asked, "or praying for me?"

She stared hard into his eyes. He held out his hand to help her up. She took it without saying anything. He turned her hand over in his own two hands.

"I was thinking," he said thoughtfully, "that, ever since we've been married, we've said the evening prayer together. Won't it be an honour for you, halva-maker's daughter, to pray the evening prayer with the Supervisor of Muslim Judges and Guardian of Muslim Missionaries, Sword of Islam and Protector of the Imam himself, Badr al-Jamali?"

"Certainly, Amir," she replied immediately. "It will be an honour and a pleasure."

"Sometimes," he continued slowly, his gaze still fixed on her, "I still have my doubts as to whether you're convinced that I belong to the same faith as you. I wonder, Furoon, do you regard me as a Muslim, but one who's gone astray?"

"No, I don't," she replied firmly, holding back her tears. "I've never felt that for a single moment. Who am I to pass judgment on your Islam, Amir? Do you know what Ash-Shafi`i has to say?"

"What's that, lady Shaikh?"

"He said:

'Because my sin was love of Muhammad's family,

   It's a sin for which I seek no repentance.

On the day of my gathering and standing, they are my intercessors,

   When, for observers, issues emerge.

They said: 'You have dissented.' I replied: "I have not."

   Dissent is not my faith or belief.

However, without any doubt, I have been entrusted with the bread of an Imam and Guide.

   If the trustee's love is dissent, then my own dissent is mankind.'"

"You can find the right words so quickly, Furoon, just like legal scholars. I feel as though you may have a role to play."

She looked into his eyes, and there was a lot that she wanted to say. But talking about Ash-Shafi`i and religion was easier than talking about feelings, blame, and anger.

He smiled at her somewhat sadly, although she did not know why.

"I'll lead the prayer for you," he said, "as though we're praying together in the Mosque of `Amr ibn al-`As and the Al-Azhar Mosque, with no difference between them."

"It'll be an honour for me," she replied, bowing her head.

She moved behind him, watching for his words and movements. The sound of his voice melted her heart as he recited the Qur'an. He started with the Fatiha, then moved on to the Sura of the Kingdom. She bowed low behind him, then did the full prostration. His voice was full of sorrow, and she began to cry. She kept her head to the ground. 'Everything on top of soil is still soil.' He stood up again, and recited the Fatiha again, followed by the Sura of Forenoon: 'Your Lord has not forsaken you or hated you...Your Lord will give to you, and you will be content.' She could not tell whether he was a jinn, an angel, a devil arrogantly rebelling against all the angels whose names she did not know, or a spirit to whom God has granted His mercy. When he finished, she was certain: he was a part of her, a portion of her own self. Ever since she had first set eyes on him, that is what he had been and still was. He could be none other than the man she loved, with eyes as pure as honey, lighting up the world without burning it. He was her passion, and God would not sanction any suffering for her. As he stood up, she looked at him, her eyes begging him not to leave.

"Badr," she whispered, as the fever of desire set time itself on fire.

Holding her arm, he slowly pulled her toward him, as though he were hesitant or afraid, either of himself or his feelings—she could not tell which. She put her hand over his heart.

"My grandmother put her hand over my grandfather's heart this way," she told him. "He thought she had bewitched him. She found part of herself in his heart. Don't be angry with me."

"What is there inside a soldier's heart, Furoon, that resembles the heart of a Sufi?" As he asked, he cupped his hands around her face.

"Struggle," she replied without thinking. "Will you stay with me tonight?"

"I've come to see you—"

"After a long time. Wasn't my suffering for years and years enough? Don't make me suffer all over again."

"I didn't want you to suffer. You're the one torturing yourself. Your heart is carrying the sins of humanity as a whole. I'm not a shaikh."

"But you are now the Supreme Master."

"I realise that. For that reason, I have to fight, not fast and go into seclusion. All I know is the sword and the need to save this country if I can. Will you help me?"

"How can the Supreme Master possibly need help from a girl like me?"

"You trust me."

She put her arms around his neck, then kissed his cheek and shoulder.

"I love you," she said.

"There can be no love without trust."

"I fear for you."

"I've told you what I want."

"Give me some time."

"It's an oath you must give now."

"Or else what?"

He said nothing, while she kissed his mouth several times.

"Have you come here to stay with me?" she asked.

"Will you join me every day?"

"Without asking me to change my religious community?"

"I've never asked you to do that. What I want is your trust."

"I always trust you," she replied, leaning her head against his shoulder.

"No questions, no blame, and no critical looks."

"I'll do everything you want."

With that, he picked her up and carried her over to their bed. She closed her eyes.

Sex with him after so many executions was different. Blood was not shed, as it had been every other time. She withdrew from her own body, even when she reached a rapture that erased the memory, unaffected by the soul's departure from the body. Her body wanted him, and her heart was building a wall to prevent any surrender. He knew and understood.

"What's the matter?" he whispered in her ear, once he had finished.

"Nothing," she replied at once.

She tried to kiss his chest, but he pushed her away.

"We need to talk first," he said. "Your mind's far away."

She shuddered, afraid that he was angry and she would lose him again. She could not stop shivering. As he pushed her further away and looked at her, she could not control the way her entire body was shuddering. She was beset by a panic that rivalled the way winds assault fields in winter. Her shivers continued, and she was unable to say anything. She hugged herself and tried desperately to say something.

"Forgive....me..."

The human heart can experience some dreadful conditions: a blend of terror, passion, complete satisfaction, and ongoing blame. She kept moaning, while he stared at her without touching her.

"Close your eyes," he eventually told her as he pulled a cover over her. "Stretch out."

She did what he told her. After a while, her heart rate slowed and her moans diminished.

"I recognise this condition," he told her. "I've seen it before in soldiers, after the first killing or injury. You'll get used to the world and recognise it for yourself."

"Isn't reconciling hearts a better idea, Badr?" she said, holding his hand. "There's strength in unity."

"The corrupt heart cannot support a body. The only cure for corruption is amputation, just as it is with rotting trees. If my own son were corrupt, I'd kill him."

That scared her even more, and she almost had a relapse.

"But you're suffering for my sake," he told her. "Perhaps I should leave you alone for a while."

She interrupted him and threw herself into his arms.

"I'll die if you leave me."

"Then talk to me," he told her firmly. "Tell me what you're thinking. I'm listening. Forget who I am and talk."

She opened her mouth, but could not speak. There were still scratch marks on her face, and they had turned sharp, like pieces of broken glass that shimmer without moving.

"The Supreme Master," she eventually said, her eyes closed, "the Sword of Islam, is also my husband."

He remained silent.

"My lord Amir," she said, summoning all her resources, "I'm scared of blood."

"Then you shouldn't have been married to an army commander," he replied with a scoff. "When a third of the people in this country died, a whole lot of blood flowed. Are you afraid only of the blood on my sword, and not of the blood on all the amirs' swords?"

"Badr," she pleaded, "I can't talk to you as though we're equals. We aren't. I can't parry your words with mine. You'll win every time, but I'm still suffering."

"You're torturing yourself," he said, looking into her eyes. "Don't interfere in my work, Furoon. You've no idea what goes on inside palaces, nor do you know anything about intrigues and plots."

"Well then, don't kill anyone in front of me," she replied without even thinking. "Don't slaughter and behead people inside my house. I can't tolerate that, Amir."

She expected him to hit her the way her husband and father had done before and to chide her for giving him orders when he was the Amir with all the authority in the country. But he did neither.

"Are you giving me orders, Furoon?" he asked quietly. "That's amazing! Do you realise that not even the Caliph would dare give me orders the way you are? For one last time, listen to me."

Stuttering and shivering, she sat down in front of him, her head lowered.

"The lover does not change her beloved," he told her. "She accepts him as he is, loving everything about him. That much I know, without listening to poets and studying ther way you have."

Their eyes met. This was Badr, whom she longed for even when he was with her, the lover who had made her suffer when he was away. She shut her eyes tightly, so as to push away the memory of the slaughter, but she could not do it. Even so, she moved closer to him, rested her head on his chest, and gripped his shoulder.

"I've missed you," she whispered. "Every day, I hoped you'd come."

"You're the one who stayed away," he replied, as he smelled her hair and kissed her.

"I was stupid. From now on, I can't stay away from you. Whatever happens next, that never will."

He hugged her gently, but said nothing.

"Were you so angry with me?" she asked. "If only I had your resolve and determination, I could stop my heart from thinking of you, desiring your arms, and wishing only to listen to your breaths. It's in your arms that I feel a sense of peace, like a slice of paradise itself. How can your arms do that? You're right, Amir. I've never done anything to help people here. When I was a girl, I ran away with my father. But maybe now, I have an obligation to the people who are suffering, to all those who are in need of assistance. Will you allow me to do it?"

"Yes, I will, but not now. Later, when the situation's more secure."

She put her hands around his face and kissed him hard. She had no idea whether he really meant those words, or had merely spoken them in a moment of despair, sorrow, and confusion over what he was telling her. Those same words were enough to restore her spirit. She pushed him back on to their bed and put her arms around him.

"I have only you," she said. "You're my husband, and I love you."

She was in love with him again. If the first time, she had felt confused, scared, and hesitant, this time it involved a mix of emotions: fear of losing him again and the triumph of love's resolution over everything else. When they finished, she was panting, and he was looking at her in a daze. She had poured into their love-making the passion of years and all the ardour of a lover who had never possessed such a beloved.

"Do you realise now that I love you?" she whispered.

"Yes, I do," he replied, pressing her to his chest and breathing hard.

"I swear to you..." she said, as she ran her fingers over his chest.

"What do you swear?"

"That I don't know who you spend your nights with, that I'm not jealous like other women, and I know nothing about slave girls."

"You're not jealous?" he replied with a smile, cupping his hands around her face. "Why don't I believe you? Can Furoon the advocate be lying?"

"She can advocate for herself."

A moment of silence followed.

"Badr," she asked, "which of the girls do you like best? Tell me the truth. I just need to know."

How could he respond without sounding like a love-sick teenager? How could he tell her that he had never savoured real love in his life and that, while he might have had sex with lots of women—hundreds maybe—none had touched his heart. They had passed over his body like wind, joining flesh to flesh for a while, then disappearing. If he told her, she might not understand. In the past, he had heard about generals, amirs, and caliphs who had loved only one woman, even when they were surrounded by many. Some of them had abandoned the world in order to spend a few hours with just one woman. He had heard all that and, at the time, he had laughed. He'd had children and been married. A slave girl might stay with him for a whole week before he got tired of her and tried another one. He was like other men, regarding women like music, as something to refresh the heart after all the toil of killing and the evil of betrayal. Men needed moments of serenity in the arms of a beautiful woman who was good at singing and making love. They all needed such a woman because they realised that, either on that day or the next, a sword would slaughter them, and it would be in the hands of someone close, not a stranger. Betrayal was a characteristic of rulers and their entourages. It might come from ʿAbd al-wahhab or one of his own soldiers; he did not yet know. He gave one soldier authority over another, and it was the same with his confidants. She was the only person in this world that he could trust. Furoon alone was like the ascetics; she reminded him of Ja`far the crazy man, sitting atop piles of debris and craving neither prestige, money, nor power. She was a loyal lover and worshipper and gave of herself unreservedly. Ever since he had found her, she had not asked for anything; he was all she wanted. Was he annoyed with her, he wondered, because she did not like blood? Why? Yes, he had been angry. She had wounded his pride; that had indeed happened. He had made up his mind not to see her, even if she insisted. Yes, that had happened, too. But in his heart of hearts, he was delighted, because he could collect in his twin palms a cluster of sincerity, if only for a little while. She wanted to stay the way she was, unchanged by time, her heart unaffected by the desires of slave girls or the brutality of rulers. There is something about authority that has a negative effect on the mind, a buried sense of power unrivalled by any other feeling, whether wealth or children. Orders are obeyed. When you enter a room, everyone bows in awe and obedience. It is as though you're in paradise, although paradise has no walls or borders. And yet, power on earth is actually weakness. You cannot see the truth, nor can you know what is in people's hearts. Every time power is enhanced, fortresses are constructed around vision and balance is distorted.

She strummed on his chest with her fingers.

"I won't get angry, Badr," she said. "Tell me which girl you really like."

"I haven't looked at them, Furoon. I don't have time."

"And when you *do* have time?"

"I'll never look at them," he replied firmly.

"I'm pregnant," she told him hesitantly.

He stroked her arm, but did not react.

"Does that make you happy?" she asked. "You have sons. You don't need another."

"Having a baby with you makes me happy," he replied, hugging her more tightly.

He was being kind, but he was still prepared to confront her. He had given her a pledge so she would talk, but he had kept his stubborn and rebellious streak hidden from her. He was leading her on, like brilliant colours that can dazzle the eye, but he was also waking her up, like freezing cold water. He was not telling her that he would stay with her every day or promising her he wouldn't get angry again.

"I'd like for you to spend your days with me and for my room to be our room."

"People say that army commanders love power and authority," he replied with a smile as he kissed her hand, "but they don't know a thing about women. I promise to come to see you whenever I can. However, there are nights when I have to be at work, Ja'far's mother."

"Why have you chosen the name Ja'far?"

"I met an old man named Ja'far. I've never met anyone like him before, and I like the name."

"If you're working at night, I want to be around you."

"I can't work if you're around me. I can't concentrate. Come on, go to sleep."

CHAPTER NINE

In Syria, `Amer—son of Hamza, son of `Abdallah—couldn't forget his father's desire to take revenge on Badr al-Jamali. He remembered Furoon, his father's wife, whom Badr had taken as a slave girl and then wife. He pledged himself to eliminate Badr, Furoon, and their offspring. It was time to put an end to Ubaidi rule in Egypt, just as would soon happen in Syria. Once they were defeated in Egypt, the Seljuqs would take over and the Abbasids would be mentioned in the Friday sermon. Badr al-Jamali's fate would mirror that of Abu Taher at Badr's hands: Hamza would personally flay him alive. Every single day that was his dearest wish. Hamza was joined by another man whose father Badr had killed: Turkan, son of Ildakiz, the minister Badr had killed in an Egyptian prison. His son had managed to escape to Syria. How easy was friendship when the goal was a desire for revenge, and how wonderful the clique formed around the plan for elimination! They both went to see Atsiz the Seljuq to ask him to launch an invasion of Egypt. Egypt was now weak and had no minister in charge. A third of its inhabitants had died, and the rest were suffering the effects of hardship, drought, and starvation. Not only that, but the bloodthirsty Badr had killed the army commanders and dismissed the Fatimid soldiers. All he had was a few thousand Armenian troops. This was the moment to attack.

"Whoever owns the Egyptian countryside, owns it all," Turkan said. "So the Seljuqs under the command of Atsiz should invade the countryside to pillage and conquer. They should wait for the right opportunity, which was bound to come. Badr always served as war commander himself and took his soldiers to the Delta and Upper Egypt. He would either be killed or defeated."

They would both make use of the opportunity when Badr was preoccupied with his war and invade the Egyptian countryside. After the defeat, Hamza would sell Furoon to Turkan, flay Badr alive, and kill the man's progeny. But Hamza also planned to ask Turkan to slay Furoon after a while. She was a traitor who had caused her husband's death, and she was not to be trusted. She was one of those hypocrites condemned by God in His book, claiming to be virtuous while her body was covered in sin.

Furoon knew nothing about the hatred people harboured in their hearts. She assumed that her husband's children were forgiving. Did they not know love? Didn't they realise how much she had endured with Hamza? She forgave him, her own father, and the whole of humanity. Once one's goal is achieved, it is easy to forgive. When you are still astray, it is that much harder. She had wanted to forgive while she was still suffering, but, in the past few months, she had come to realise her own human weaknesses.

She watched her husband from the window as he read about Egypt: every town and every village. He sat down beside his men, then drew a map of the country.

"How can we control a country," he asked, "when it has a thousand villages or more?"

"We've known about this, my Lord, since ancient times," `Abd al-wahhab replied.

"We're not living in ancient times," Badr said, "nor do we have the power they had. We'll divide Egypt into twenty-one districts and appoint someone with a clear conscience whom we can trust to govern it. He could well be an Egyptian."

"My Lord," `Abd al-wahhab pointed out gently, "Upper Egypt and the Delta are in Turkish and Bedouin hands. There's widespread destruction."

"I realise that. We're going to clean things up, then build. We have to do the cleaning first. Someone who doesn't know how to keep people protected doesn't deserve to govern this country. I want to see the Chief of Police. He's promised to arrest all the corrupt merchants."

"Yes, he's brought them in today. He wants to execute them."

The Caliph had asked him to appoint Ar-Rafi` as Chief of Police. Badr had agreed, out of respect for the Caliph as Imam. However, he didn't trust the Caliph's men or the choices he made.

"He's the new Chief of Police whom you've appointed for Cairo and Egypt. Has he located all the corrupt merchants? Wasn't that difficult?"

"Yes, it was," `Abd al-wahhab responded cheerfully. "He's not like other men."

When the Police Chief came in, he was followed by fifty men who were bound with ropes, their heads lowered. The Chief announced loudly that he had found people hiding grain and wheat to sell at exorbitant prices. He had ordered them killed on the spot. He spoke enthusiastically about the war on corruption and the importance of the Amir, his abilities, and his openness. As Badr listened to him, his eyes were focused on the merchants.

"My Lord," the Chief of Police told him, "don't show them any pity or mercy through God's religion. They deserve to die."

"I know," Badr replied with a smile.

Raising his hand, he ordered the Chief of Police to leave with the arrested merchants. He summoned `Abd al-wahhab.

"I want you to kill the Chief of Police," Badr told him.

"We're the ones who appointed him," `Abd al-wahhab replied, his mouth agape.

"The Caliph's the one who chose him because he trusts him."

"If we kill him, my Lord, that will be a direct challenge to the Caliph."

"The men he brought in are not merchants. They're prisoners he's threatened and tortured so that they'll play the part of merchants."

`Abd al-wahhab's mouth was still wide open.

"The Amir can tell the difference between merchants and prisoners," Badr told him. "Go to the prison and confirm that. When you have, slay the Chief of Police and carry his head through the markets in Cairo and Egypt. You can tell them the story."

"What about the Caliph?"

"Badr al-Jamali, the Supreme Master and Army Commander, is the one who selects official and government personnel."

He was gaining control of Egypt. Today, it was Fustat and Cairo; tomorrow, he would be cleaning up the Delta and Upper Egypt. He would erase all trace of those people who had destroyed and corrupted. He would begin his war with the Luwati tribe. He was already familiar with it and its chief, Sulaiman al-Luwati. He expected this war to be more vicious than the one against the Seljuqs; it would involve continued existence for him and disappearance for others. He drafted ten thousand soldiers from among the Egyptian youth and promised to reward them. He also had with him seven thousand Armenians, both Muslims and Christians, and to them, too, he promised lots rewardsgold and jewels. Sulaiman al-Luwati still had enough resources to inundate the entire population of Egypt with donations; in the process of coming to the aid of a tyrant, death was an obligation.

Badr announced that he was going to Damietta, this time to fight. After that, he would move on to the rest of the Delta. Men blew the trumpet to proclaim war. As Badr went out at the head of his army, he announced to his men that, if anyone was going to die, he himself would be the first; if they were victorious, they would all share that honour. Sulaiman would fight like all cowards, throttling the weak and enslaving women. For people who regularly stole, war was something despicable. For that reason, this battle had to show its leader's resolve.

Sulaiman al-Luwati came out to face Badr with forty thousand men. Some of them were robbers whom he had hired, and still others were men whom he had cajoled, terrified, and threatened into joining his forces. Some ran away at the very outset, while others fought savagely. The fighting lasted a week or more, and people said that blood flooded the river. It came to an end only when Badr's army killed all of Sulaiman al-Luwati's men, twenty thousand of them, and then Sulaiman al-Luwati himself and his son. Badr's soldiers took thousands of Sulaiman's tribeswomen prisoner. The commanders yelled that this was the fate of the womenfolk of thieves, to be sold in the markets. Corrupt people would be paying the price, either today or tomorrow. The past was over, and the future would bring a new era, with fresh air, not dust. It would bring a safe way of life, with no highway robbers, tyranny, or seizures.

Throughout the conflict, peasants hid inside their houses, unsure about who was fighting whom; was this person who had come to finish off Sulaiman al-Luwati a saviour, a deceiver, or just another raider? They did not trust anyone. Whoever arrived would snatch the few decent possessions they owned from their very mouths, and then either smash it all to pieces or run away. Whoever comes, they all said, is no good; that is for sure. Every single family either locked a door, put tree branches at the entrance to their desert caves, or gathered in a semi-destroyed mosque, where they listened to the noise of death and smelled the stench of men in their death throes.

As he washed his hands and face, he kept repeating the names of the Delta villages, more than a thousand of them; even if he tried, he had no way of remembering them all.

"My Lord," `Abd al-wahhab suggested gently, "you need to take a rest. Do you want to go back to Cairo? Thank God, we've finished them off."

"No, my work is only just beginning."

Blood continued to flow from canals and rivers; there was no end to the silence of the long-suffering and the screams of the defeated. Badr had read enough about the villages and the number of their inhabitants.

"Bring me a peasant spokesman," he ordered `Abd al-wahhab. "Someone who can talk to me."

"My Lord," `Abd al-wahhab replied, "how can I choose just one man?"

"He'll choose you. Ask them to choose someone who can speak for all of them."

`Abd al-wahhab went out and shouted at the men who were waiting in silence. They were there to learn their fate, on the day after blood had penetrated both desert and valleys.

`Abd al-wahhab dragged a tribal shaikh in to see Badr al-Jamali. The man was shaking and giving him dubious looks. Badr told him to sit down.

"Shaikh," Badr asked him, "are you speaking on behalf of the peasants?"

"I'm one of them, my Lord," the Shaikh replied. "But I can't speak for anyone else."

"They know who you are here and respect you."

"Yes, they know me, but they respect only power. I've failed to protect them from harm."

For a moment, Badr remained silent.

"I see you're shaking," he said. "Why are you afraid?"

"Are you really asking me, my Lord? Blood has filled the river, and your army has finished off the entire tribe."

"I was under the impression that the tribe was stealing your money and intimidating you. Or haven't I understood?"

The Shaikh remained silent. Badr signalled that the man should sit beside him.

"Come over here," he said.

"Impossible."

"Why?"

"Forgive me, my Lord. I don't know you or who it is that has sent you. Nobody's bothered about us. The only thing we possess that has aroused an army's greed is our women and children."

"Then let's say that we're here to help you. I've come on orders from the Caliph."

"May God preserve the Caliph!"

Silence prevailed.

"Why are the lands so barren?" Badr asked.

"The owners either died or fled."

"I've never known Egyptians to run away from their lands when there's danger."

"It seems as though you know the Egyptians, even though they don't know you."

"I've learned about them so that they can know me. Answer my question."

"It's not their land, my Lord."

"Do you mean it's tribal land?"

"It belongs to amirs and tribal shaikhs. Peasants till it for nothing, for fear of being hungry or killed. If you till land out of fear, it's not yours."

"Yes, you're right."

"Do you want us to till their land, my Lord, and give us a pledge of security?"

"No," Badr replied firmly. "I want you to till your own land, with a pledge of security."

The man looked confused. "I've never seen any good in soldiers," he replied quietly. "They slaughter people like Bedouin or even worse."

"My soldiers are not like amirs' soldiers," Badr told him. "Now you're telling the truth. Listen to me, Shaikh. I want you to offer the peasants a deal. If they agree, let me know their response."

The man hesitated, still feeling doubtful. "First," he said, "I wanted to ask you to forgive me. I wasn't speaking about your soldiers. I was—"

"Listen to my deal!" Badr interrupted. "You needn't ask for forgiveness."

"Some of these lands belonged to people who've died with heirs," he went on. "Others belong to people who fled from death and scandal at the hands of Sulaiman. All Delta lands belong to peasants. I will consider everyone who builds a house on a piece of land and lives there 'a settler peasant,' and I'll record his name in my archives. As far as I'm concerned, the land will be his to till and harvest, with no taxes for one, two, and three years. The crops can be sold to benefit himself and his family."

The shaikh gaped in sheer amazement.

"In the fourth year," Badr continued, "he'll pay me half the taxes, no more. After that, he won't need any more help; he'll be settled and well established, able to buy and sell. For three whole years, he'll be able to sow, reap, and sell without anyone taking a single dirham or dinar from him. These lands belong to the people who settle here and do not run away, not to amirs, tribes, or highway robbers. You will have my protection; no highwaymen will destroy your crops or steal your cattle. There'll be no corruption and no donations to people with power and influence. Today, I'm the one with the power and influence, and I won't tolerate corruption. Tell the peasants that Badr al-Jamali has come here to stay as a settler peasant; he will mercilessly slaughter anyone who steals or spreads corruption in the land. The years of drought are at an end, and the era of plenty has begun."

The shaikh gulped, closed his eyes, then opened them again, as though he could not believe his own ears.

"My Lord," he said.

"Go out and talk to all of them. Don't discriminate between old and young, black and white, rich and poor, Muslim, Christian, and Jew. For me, all peasants are alike, except those who run away and abandon their land. They're not fit for anything. People who don't benefit the populace will find the ground levelled over them. My soldiers will make sure that the lands are fairly distributed among peasants. No powerful forces will have control anymore, leaving only scraps for the weak."

The man now moved backwards, raising his hand to his head to salute Badr. He left and told people exactly what Badr had said. There were whispers and groans. Some people said that it was impossible, a trap set by the amirs. Others asked who Badr was; all they knew about him was that he had slaughtered the amirs in Cairo. Why was he helping them? Since when had a foreigner come to help them? Who was this Badr?

The shaikh confirmed what Badr had said, but they were still dubious.

Badr emerged from his tent, and there was silence.

"Everything the shaikh has just told you is true. We're waiting for the harvest so we can all eat. Get to your fields immediately."

"God preserve Badr al-Jamali," the shaikh said, raising his hand, "and bless us all through him!"

"May God preserve our Lord the Caliph Al-Mustansir," Badr said with a smile. "Badr al-Jamali is Army Commander and Supreme Master!"

Even so, they continued to offer their prayers for him alone. Women ululated, and men kissed one another and exchanged congratulations.

"My Lord," `Abd al-wahhab said, looking at him, "aren't you afraid of making the Caliph jealous?"

"The difficult part's still ahead of us," Badr said, as though he had not heard `Abd al-wahhab's question. "The Delta's always easier than Upper Egypt."

"We can take a break, my Lord."

"There can be no break as long as there's hunger in the air all around us. We'll start by rebuilding destroyed roads, bridges, and canals, so food can get to every part of Egypt.

The news was announced to everyone in Egypt and Syria: Cairo would be opening its gates to all Egyptians. It would be protected by gates different from those Jawhar had built. These gates would be made of stone and would last a thousand years or more, and they would be wide enough to allow anyone who had good intentions and legitimate wealth to pass through. From now on, there would be no taxes on merchants. They could conduct their commerce safely and immediately.

"Today I, Badr al-Jamili, Sword of Islam, hereby invite all Egypt's merchants and men of wealth who have sought refuge in Syria during times of hardship to return. They will have security and protection. Anyone who has closed his store can open it again. Anyone who has been scared of thieves should know that I am offering security without price or fear of those like the Luwata tribe. The Supreme Master is inviting the Egyptian people to trade without either greed or corruption. Today, all previous practices will disappear. People who make contributions to police to divert their attention or pay money so they can sell things for a higher price have no place with us. In commerce, there will be no monopolies or corruption. Badr al-Jamali has already slain twenty thousand crooks, and he plans to slaughter some more. He'll brutalise anyone who plays monopolistic games with merchants and police of every stripe—Turk, Maghrebi, Armenian, and Egyptian. Anyone who wishes to conduct business justly and devoutly has a place in Egypt. Anyone who plans to do it ill should leave and not come back, or else he'll be killed. I won't be showing any sympathy or mercy to people who damage Egypt. The country deserves better than that, and avoidance of doing harm is one of the principles of our faith. I hereby give a pledge of security to all those who live in Egypt. For people who return to Egypt or wish to live here, the ruined houses are a treasure trove. Merchants will have security, but without monopolisation. Egyptians, be aware that I intend to spend every day—night and day—supervising the situation in the country. There are no walls around my palace, nor is there a chamberlain to prevent people with complaints from entering. I shall be walking through the markets in person and making sure that no one is cheating anyone. The era when people could toy with people's property, and rulers and judges could harass them, is over. Today, I've killed a minister and judge who, for seven years, passed judgments on the Egyptians without the slightest clemency or mercy."

The ringing shouts in praise of Badr al-Jamali were loud enough for their echoes to reach all the way to the palace of the Caliph himself. Before a month had passed, people who had fled abroad came back to re-Egyptianise Cairo. Every time a merchant slacked off and went back to his old ways, he recalled the killing of the Minister and Judge, Ibn Abi Kudaina. Badr seemed like a man who was not afraid of tyrannical shaikhs and did not have to rely on judges. Whenever a merchant remembered that, he would step back, ask God for forgiveness, and pray for Badr al-Jamali.

As Furoon gave her husband a hug, her eyes were full of sorrow, but the fact that he was around her overcame her reaction to what she had heard. Her husband had killed twenty thousand men, captured and enslaved their women, and sold them cheap in the markets in order to serve as an example to anyone who dared play corrupt games on this land. Did he have to go to such lengths? Could he not spare the women? She swore that she trusted him and realised that she could not interfere in his actions. How was it she could see things that he could not? How had she managed to discover the gentle, merciful element deep inside him when he was behaving like wild animals defending their turf? She knew what he was going to say: he was defending the oppressed and threatening the oppressor. He was focusing all his attention on Egypt and did not wish to see it in ruins, whatever the cost. He was busy night and day! She had never seen such concentration before: reading, understanding, talking to shaikhs, then banishing people, killing some, and raising the status of just a few others. She could see the doubt in his eyes and sense his carefully calculated moves, as though failure was not an option. If he backed off or forgot something, he would be slaughtered, his children would become slaves, and his wife would be a slave girl to his grimmest foe. Her son had been cradled against her shoulder; now, she handed the baby to his father.

"Ja`far...the Triumphant!" he said.

"Badr," she said, "I'd like to get to know your friend called Ja`far,"

"He's not like anyone else," Badr replied. "He's not greedy and, most important, he's not afraid."

"I'd like to make halva for the whole of Egypt," she said, resting her head against his chest. "What do you think?"

"I'm going to start building a palace in the Bargawan quarter," he said after a pause. "I'll name it 'Ja`far, Palace of the Triumphant.' There, every single Egyptian will get to eat on festivals and seasonal celebrations—not just meat, as under Ahmad ibn Tulun, but halva as well. You'll supervise the making of it. Egypt will once against be the richest land, the land of miracles and magic as it used to be. That's a pledge that I'm making."

"But what about your other children, Badr?" she asked anxiously. "Won't they be angry? Don't name your palace 'Ja`far.'"

"He's my youngest son, and your child."

"Please, I beg you, don't start a fire. Authority has a negative effect on the mind, and jealousy is the way to start a fire."

"I've three sons, Furoon. Ahmad al-Awhad, who'll succeed me. He'll be helped by Muhammad Abu l-Qssim al-Afdal. Ja`far will work in the army. Those are my instructions for my sons."

"I'm thinking about who will succeed you in governing Egypt, Badr. It's the Ubaidi Caliph."

"Treasure doesn't belong to the person who finds it, but the one who preserves it."

The Caliph decorated him with a jewel-encrusted chain, but he substituted ambergris for the gold, because gold was in short supply in Egypt. He also gave Badr the official gown as Chief Judge and dissolved his Mother's Council, as Badr had previously directed. The name Al-Jamali was now on everyone's lips in quarters from Fustat to the farthest reaches of Upper Egypt. Every time he acquired some new title, he became even more worried. Acquiring authority was one thing, but keeping it was an entirely different mattter. As long as Hamza's son`Amer was alive, nothing was stable. How could one man disturb his sleep so much? Every day, `Amer would remember that he was still alive, and the man would keep searching so he could slay him.

Badr insisted on searching for Shaikh Ja`far. His soldiers searched all over Egypt, and they eventually learned that he was living in the Muqattam Hills; he was using a cave as his worship space and never left, whatever the circumstances. Badr still insisted, so they brought him to the Amir's palace against his will. He was carried into the Amir's presence by five men. Once he had entered, Badr dismissed the men and asked Ja`far to sit beside him. He looked weak and skinny, so Badr ordered some food.

"I don't eat rulers' food," Shaikh Ja`far said. "I drink only lime juice with quince. Do you plan to put me in prison, Amir?"

"Certainly not. I want to raise your status."

"I've nothing to do with rulers. People who can see only themselves, and no one else, and are as treacherous as lions. That's the monarch exactly, whenever he's feeling upset about something."

"I'll never behave treacherously with you, Ja`far."

"Because you imagine I've no power. Even so, you admire my courage and madness."

"I always admire the truth. I'd like to learn from you."

"You drag me here to your palace against my will and then ask me to teach you? It's as though you're forcing the angels to admit you to paradise or else you'll kill them."

"Do you see yourself as being like the angels, Ja`far? Are you saying I'm deluded?"

"No, I was just giving you an example. Your sword doesn't scare me, Badr."

"Have you lost your mind? Don't use my name, even if we're friends. Call me 'the Supreme Master'."

Ja`far stared at him in amazement.

"Make sure you don't believe yourself, Armenian," he said. "Do you really imagine that you're 'the Supreme Master'?"

"Who else?"

"God is the only master," Ja`far replied, raising his finger. "No glory is greater than His."

"I realise that. What I mean is 'Supreme Master' here on earth."

"Here too, Badr. If you want to learn, come to see me in the Muqattam Hills. From there, you can see the whole of Egypt. I'd advise you to climb the mountain on your own; it requires patience and self-control. When you reach the top, remember that you are as small as a gnat or even smaller."

"You're making me nervous. If I chopped your head off right now, I could relax."

"Didn't I tell you I've nothing to do with the lives of amirs? You're not a normal man, Badr."

"That's true."

"But the fate of Moses's Pharaoh comes after delusion."

"I'm not deluded. I know my own self and potential, and how much of my own soul I'm giving to this country."

"People say the sands of the Muqattam are blessed," Ja'far went on, as though he had not heard what Badr had just said. "They can cure the sick and give a whiff of paradise. Have you savoured them yet, or put them inside your heart to douse the inferno? Is the world good or evil?"

"It's evil most of time."

"That's because good has no colour, but it can open all doors."

"Talk to me about love."

"Your love for a single woman keeps you awake at night."

"I can't see any other woman. It keeps me awake because she has complete control without even realising it."

"Badr always wants to be in control. Didn't I tell you that delusion's a bane?"

"Whenever she gives," Badr said, as though talking to himself, "I feel feebler and feebler. Whenever I see good pouring out of her inner self, my own strength collapses."

"Do you see in her what you yourself want to be or what you dream of having around you? In her do you see a sister, a mother, a child?"

"I don't know. But the feeling I have when I'm around her upsets me."

"That's when you realise your own burden," Ja'far responded with a smile. "You find out that you can't control your own heart. That's the first step toward achieving the goal. It always involves love. Love His servants, then you'll love Him, too. He exerts control without demanding a lot; He provides protection without imposing taxes; He gives without asking anything in return. He teaches us that mercy is the swiftest path towards Him. In finding an honest woman, you've achieved the goal, man. It's a gift that many people do not receive."

Silence prevailed.

"What's your name, Badr?" Ja`far asked him.

"You idiot, you're saying it."

"Aram, do you remember?"

"How come you knew that name? You and the Pyramid Witch are one and the same."

"Sometimes, God will baffle us with His gifts and decrees. Decrees come from Him, Armenian. Every soul has a purpose. Some of us come to earth, then act like flies to aggravate people, unremembered by anyone. Others arrive like hyenas, recalled by people with fear and disgust. Still others come with an obligation inscribed before they were born."

"Crazy talk from a madman."

"But a madman who knew your name."

Ja`far stretched out his hand and put it over Badr's heart.

"You're searching for a homeland and for a sense of peace," he told Badr. "You'll only find them atop the Muqattam Hills. People will be baffled and ask themselves why Badr al-Jamali built a mosque on top of the hills. Is it a mausoleum, a place of worship, or a place to observe the enemy? Badr, I'm the only one who'll know the answer."

"You're senile! Who's going to build a mosque so far away from everyone? Why should I build a mosque that worshippers can reach only when they're heaving and panting for breath?"

"Because you're Badr. Are you Badr? If you realised that you've been given a charge, then your task would be much easier. From the entire world, God has chosen an Armenian child named Aram. What's that child to do? Save the Egyptian people? Can you imagine any such thing? God Almighty reminds us that, from remotest east to the remotest west, the remotest north to the remotest south, we are all bound together. But we never learn. Instead, we split people up into different faith communities and caliphs, the Abbasid Caliph in Baghdad and the Fatimid Caliph here in Egypt. Seljuqs, Franks, whites, and blacks. But, if we took a look at rocks, we would discover that, whatever country they're in, they all contain sand. Do you still like emeralds?"

Badr stared at him, but said nothing.

"I'm not bothered about caliphs," Ja`far went on. "Religious sects don't concern me either; they're just gloss and boasting. I'm rid of all that stuff. Inside you, there is the ascetic and greedy, the knowledgeable and ignorant, the vain and humble. There is also a heavy burden. Whenever that burden grows heavier, your heart flutters and flies away. I wonder, Badr, are you charged with building things that will last forever, or with rescuing people who deserve to be rescued? The day will come when people won't be concerned about your religious beliefs. That won't matter. People who build survive in memory; people who populate the land are never forgotten even a thousand years or more later. Stay with us."

"I'm with you."

"Stay with us."

"Are you out of your mind? I'm with you."

"Stay with us."

"Stay where?"

"If you want to see me," Ja`far repeated as he ran off, "then come to see me. Otherwise, you'll never hear my voice. Stay with us."

CHAPTER TEN

The war in Upper Egypt was much more brutal. Here, Badr was fighting well-endowed tribes and amirs who had fled from him to the south. This was a fight for survival, not like the one in the Delta. If Badr al-Jamali was defeated, there would be no hope for the Ubaidi Fatimids. Any number of tribes were fighting him: the Juhayna, the Tha`aliba, and the Ja`afra; after them were robbers and soldiers who wanted to see their power restored. Badr had ten thousand Egyptian troops to whom he had promised gifts; the majority were infantry, because he had not had enough time to train them as cavalry. He halted his forces on the outskirts of Toukh and told them to wait; spies informed him that the army facing him consisted of forty thousand men. Having pitched his tent, he calmly and firmly formulated a plan with his soldiers. He was going to strike at night, but, before he did, he would ignite cane branches to frighten their soldiers and, at the same time, to get his revenge on farmers who had appropriated their dues. Above all else, he wanted to illuminate the path for his soldiers. He would be conquering Upper Egypt once again, beginning in Toukh and moving to the south. He was well aware that establishing security in Aswan was going to be difficult, because Kanz ad-daula was there. Badr fully expected him to rebel; all Egypt would get to experience his brutality and endure his perseverance and abuse of power. That was always going to be the case, whenever anyone new arrived—yet that did not apply to Badr, even though he had only been governing Egypt for a few months.

Badr was in the vanguard of his army, riding his mount, raising his sword, and striking with his lance. The fighting lasted for days. He was accompanied by his two sons Ahmad and Muhammad. Ahmad was almost twenty, and Muhammad about eighteen. He had told them to stay with him in his tent and to learn how to fight. He planned for both of them to stay in Egypt for the rest of their lives, governing and administering its affairs after his death.

By the tenth day, he had reached Aswan. As he had anticipated, Kanz ad-daula did rebel and came out to confront him. Badr asked the Egyptians not to get involved. He spoke in every town and village, telling them that he had not come to Upper Egypt to fight them, but rather to protect them. This was a war that had nothing to do with them. He gave them the same promises he had given in the Delta. His reputation had already spread far and wide in Upper Egypt, even before he had arrived. The farmers were hoping to get lands with no monopolies involved, lands that they could till in safety. They had all heard how powerful and fair the Amir was. They could not believe that there could be an amir, whether foreign or Arab, who could put a stop to monopolistic exploitation. But he had managed to do that in the north, so it had to be true. This was no halva cavalier, like the one that Jawhar the Sicilian's grandchildren had made; no, this was a man just like them, someone interested in their welfare—and that was something to which they were not accustomed. Before Badr left his tent to meet the wreckers and highwaymen in Aswan, he spoke to his two sons.

"When you two become generals, you Ahmad and you Muhammad," he told them, "you'll need to fight in the vanguard of your forces. What's the use of a general who stays inside his tent and urges his troops to fight?"

His sons nodded in agreement, and he left the tent. This was a fight involving highway robbers. They came from everywhere, hid in the trees, and emerged from houses. The fighting had exhausted the soldiers, but they carried on.

"It's their country," Badr yelled, "and they're fighting for their families."

Having aroused their enthusiasm, he went out on a night raid with his soldiers.

Hamza's son ʿAmer had been tracking Badr and knew how the man would fight, when he would emerge, and when he would disappear. He got hold of the robbers and told them that any who could bring him Badr's head would get the year's tax income for all of Egypt. A masked robber tracked Badr and hurled his lance from the top of the hill. He managed to strike Badr's shoulder squarely and hard before he vanished. The soldiers let out a yell, but Badr signaled to them to keep silent. He went back to his tent to wait for the doctor to arrive. The doctor duly arrived shaking. The news spread all over Egypt that Badr had been hit. Some people were thrilled, but many more were very upset. They were expecting the saviour and intrepid cavalier they had seen only in their dreams. He was just like the cavalier whose image hung in halva stores, with his cloak and powerful horse, wearing the monarch's crown, and finishing up inside children's stomachs—the horseman with the sweet taste that melted in the mouths of strivers and thieves. But now, here was this sweet-tasting horseman not surviving to witness the great revival and victory. Some women wept, joined by men, and especially the poor and needy. Badr al-Jamali had been hit, and the wound was serious. The dream was over before the celebration could even start.

Furoon hugged her only son. The door to her room was closed, and the world lost all light. Every single path was sheer delusion. Hafsa came in to see her.

"Furoon," she said, "eat something, my daughter, for your son's sake. Don't be afraid. Soldiers are keeping guard here. He hasn't left you here defenceless."

"I adore him, Hafsa," she whispered sadly. "How can I ever have been angry with him? If he comes back, I swear that I'll do anything he wants. Maybe I've never told him how much I love him. Have I told him?"

"Yes, you have," Hafsa replied. "Every single day. Believe me, my daughter, he knows. He'll be back. During wars, soldiers always get hit."

"I feel as though I've sinned."

"You always feel that way, even though true faith serves to strengthen trust and resolve. Deal with your censorious heart!"

"I want to go to him."

"Are you out of your mind? Go where?"

"Wherever he wants."

While Badr was fighting in Upper Egypt, the army that joined together Atsiz the Seljuq; his ally Turkan, the son of Aamir Ildakiz ,who had been killed by Badr; and `Amer, Hamza's son, had reached the Nile Delta. It was the ideal time to occupy Egypt. The Seljuqs now controlled most of Syria, and, once they had conquered Egypt, it would be an even greater triumph than anyone had anticipated. They ravaged the countryside, killed peasants, took women prisoner, and stole all the crops, wheat, gold, and jewels that the peasants had left. It took just two days for everyone to loathe them. When the news reached the wounded Badr, the doctor was in the process of removing the lance tip from his shoulder. To the sound of his children crying, he bit his lip, thinking to himself that his era had come to an end before it had even begun. He did not have enough men, weapons, and equipment to fight the Seljuqs. He had no choice but to flatter ʿAmer. He knew how to choose the right moment.

"The lance wasn't poisoned, was it?" he asked the doctor.

"No, my lord, thank God!" the doctor replied.

"This is pilgrimage season," he said, looking at ʿAbd al-wahhab. "Men are already on their way. How many men are performing the pilgrimage this year?

"I'll find out, my lord," ʿAbd al-wahhab replied, perplexed at being asked that question at such an ill-starred time.

"I want you to find out today and let me know."

Badr was sitting down and eating when ʿAbd al-wahhab returned.

"Three thousand men, my lord," he said. "They're in Upper Egypt on their way to the Hejaz."

"Then let's bring them."

"My Lord..."

"Bring them. Tell them they're fighting in God's cause and stopping the Seljuqs from entering Egypt. This year, that's better than going on the pilgrimage. How can they go to God's house in Mecca while their own houses and wives fall into Seljuq hands? Tell them that it's the Amir's command. Badr al-Jamali promises them gifts and spoils."

"My Lord, that's totally unprecedented."

"Different times demand different ideas. I want them here within the week. I'm announcing a general call-to-arms. This week, I want more Egyptians in the army. I'll be waiting. When the men arrive, we'll finish what we've started. We'll go and confront Atsiz and his army in the Delta. Some Bedouin tribes have sworn allegiance to us; they can help us at the start. I want you to go looking for tribes that have helped the Seljuqs. You must get them to retract their allegiance. Some of them may regret their previous decision and join us. That's really important; this needs someone who's shrewd."

"Once we've won," Badr went on, standing up and clutching his wound, "we need to start building. I want my name to be linked forever to both victory and construction. We'll start with this country, build a mosque here, and call it the Victory Mosque. Everyone who prays in it will remember us forever."

Badr started building the Victory Mosque in Esna even before he left to confront the Seljuqs in the Delta. He made pacts with some of the Bedouin tribes there, and gave Judge Abu l-Husaini ibn Nasr, a local notable who commanded respect and esteem, the responsibility for completing the mosque's construction.

His sons looked at him in awe.

"My Lord never loses a battle," Muhammad said as he kissed his father's cloak.

"That's because I always invoke sincerity," he replied. "That always provides a solution."

"You've defeated two armies at once, one in Upper Egypt and the other in the Delta."

"In defeating the Seljuqs, we were helped by the Bedouin tribes; Egyptians and pilgrims came to our assistance, too. It's a victory for Egypt and Egyptians. Now Badr's tent poles are firmly established in Egypt and in the hearts of the Egyptian people. And you must realise that this is much harder."

Women wept for joy, and men offered intercessions for him after the official prayers were ended. Everyone in Egypt knew about the Amir. They knew who he was and what he had become in Egypt. They all wanted him to neither be killed nor to leave. Someone like him, who worked for them and wanted the Egyptian people to be successful, had to remain alive.

As soon as she had been told that he had been wounded, Furoon had locked her door, refused to eat, and not spoken to anyone. Ten days had passed with her in this state. Eventually, Hafsa sent word to Badr al-Jamali about his wife's condition. She urged him to reassure his wife, but he did not respond. He had pitched his tent on the outskirts of Fustat and was on the point of returning to Cairo. When the news reached Furoon, she ordered the soldiers to take her to see him. The soldiers were reluctant, but she insisted. They escorted her to his tent. When she entered unexpectedly, he was in the process of talking to his soldiers. She bent down and kissed his cloak.

"How did you manage to get here?" he asked, both furious and baffled. "Are you out of your mind?"

She remained silent, head lowered.

He dismissed the assembly.

"My plan was for you not to punish the soldiers," she told him proudly. "Punish me instead. I'm the one who decided to come to see you, my Lord. I needed reassurance."

"You must carry out my orders," he yelled at her. "Do you hear me? I don't have time to be worried about you, to search for you, or to find out where you've gone. This is not going to happen again. And now, you will leave the way you came."

She looked back at him, shaking her head.

"Not before I check on your wound," she replied.

He grabbed her hand to drag her out of the tent.

"Please, let me stay with you for just a few minutes, no more," she pleaded. "I just want to make sure, then I'll leave."

"No."

She resisted as hard as she could, but she could not stop him from dragging her out of his tent. He summoned his soldiers.

"Take her back," he told them. "And don't listen to anyone but me, or else I'll cut your heads off."

When he came back, she realised that he was furious. She waited. The door burst open.

"That's never going to happen again as long as I live," he yelled at her. "Do you hear me?"

"Yes, I hear you," she replied, looking straight at him.

She moved closer, but he raised his hand to keep her away. When he took off his coat, she could see the wound on his shoulder; it was covered with herbs and linen. She put her hand over her mouth to stop herself from crying out. Then she automatically went over to him and put her arms round his back.

"Thank God, you're safe," she said, as she kissed the wound. "Why did you go yourself; you don't need to do that. If I lost you, what would I do? And—"

"That's crazy, Furoon," he interrupted her. "Wake up! You can't carry on this way, taking no account of the way things are."

"Fine, then," she replied, wrapping her arms around his stomach. "Hold me to account, but not now. I would have died without you."

As he put his hands on her arms and caressed them, his anger subsided.

"I'm going to hold you to account," he said, turning toward her with a phony determination, "for what you did. For coming to see me, and..."

She kissed him so hard, she almost ran out of breath.

"Hold me to account later," she panted. "But not now."

He pushed her onto their bed and immersed himself in her flaming passion. He was tired; tired of thinking, tired of dangers, tired of complex calculations. How could her bosom soak up all the hatred and evil that enveloped him? How could a woman's bosom reach out and encircle all the scorpions lurking under rocks; the devilish, blood-sucking mosquitoes; wild beasts with mouths wide open, always asking for more? Such an ability always brings with it concern, and that concern is as heavy as the rocks on the back of a child who is still only a baby. The baby cries for milk, and the burden never lessens or disappears. Her generous spirit is hard to explain: she gives of herself without hesitation or precondition, continually whispering words of love and passion, even when he says nothing in response. At climactic moments, her eyelids flicker. When she gives herself to him, she turns into a thin piece of sweet halva that he can either crush in his hands or else keep for himself. She is fully aware of his power over her; she has no control over that. He closed his eyes, and she moved away. She looked at him and stroked his face, neck, and chest.

"I love you," she said.

"That won't exempt you from punishment," he replied with a smile, his eyes still closed. "Everything you've done—"

"I know," she interrupted him. "I just needed to tell you how much I love you. I was afraid for you, and perhaps you don't realise that."

"But I do realise," he replied with a smile.

He pulled her toward him and wrapped his arms around her.

"The punishment's going to last a long time," he told her. "Today, tomorrow, and the day after... It's been a long time without you."

CHAPTER ELEVEN

It was in Damascus that Badr al-Jamali's war was at its most vicious. It did not involve swords. His aim was to get rid of the enemies whom he knew, and the others whom he did not. Of them all, Turkan was the easiest to get to, the most obvious and genuine of enemies. What really worried him were the ones like ʿAmer son of Hamza, who possessed all the potential venom of poisoned snakes. He did not fully appreciate the extent of the man's bitterness and the poison he had stored inside him before the Seljuq army attack.

Ever since Hamza had decided to be married to Furoon, his son ʿAmer had realised misfortune had reached his household. At the time, his mother had rued the decision. She said that Furoon was really in love with Badr al-Jamali. Everyone in Damascus knew the story. The Armenian had asked her father for her hand, and he had refused because he realised that Ibn Hamdan was on his side and Hamza wanted her for himself. ʿAmer's mother told her son that Furoon was a lecherous devil; she would finish off his father. His mother was right. He did not believe the scenario in the markets where Furoon had been sold; the real plan, he realised, was to humiliate his two sisters, not Furoon. She had thrown herself into her lover's arms and completely forgotten his father, her husband. He had humiliated his two sisters, and she had pretended to be virtue personified, rescuing his sisters. He had sworn a solemn oath that he would humiliate Badr al-Jamali. Simply killing him was not enough; humiliation was much more satisfying than killing. Soldiers embraced the act of killing and longed for it, but they all feared humiliation as much as hellfire itself. He had ingratiated himself with the Seljuqs and been married to the daughter of Seljuq Amir Tutush's brother. He had assured the man that victory was always on their side. However, the Seljuq army had just suffered an ignominious defeat at the hands of Egyptians, some of whom had been on their way to perform the pilgrimage to Mecca. That demanded a change of plans and direction. Even so, finishing off Badr al-Jamali was a good enough reason for staying alive. If Egypt and the Ubaidi Fatimid dynasty was destroyed, that would never bother him. To soothe his burning soul, the entire country could go to hell. If Egypt continued to suffer hardship, it would be that much better and easier to finish off Badr. But the Armenian who had clearly mastered the magic arts of Sicilian jinn could finish the country off in months. No matter. There was still a lot left to life, and patience could produce miracles. Only when 'Amer son of Hamza had taken his revenge could he sleep and relax.

Badr al-Jamali had refused the post of Chief Minister once or twice. The Army Commander did not need to be Chief Minister as well, but, at the same time, he could not stand the thought of someone else serving as 'Minister of Sword and Pen'. He himself was the one who could do it, who was available, who had no aspirations, and did not accept gifts. Egypt had totally preoccupied him, and yet he had not taken control of the reins of its government. The Caliph now appointed him 'Minister of Sword and Pen', and he became the first minister to hold the position of Chief Judge. He donned the official cloak and chain that was supposed to be inlaid with gold, but was actually coated with ambergris because of the lack of gold in Egypt. Two years earlier, Badr had come to Egypt in secret and extended his control over the country, but now the Caliph had just placed the entire country in the hands of the Army Commander. He would be the one appointing missionaries and judges. Shaikhs started to recite the noble Qur'an in his presence. One of them looked at him and then started reciting a verse from Surat Al 'Imran [Sura 3, v. 123]: 'God came to your aid at Badr...' Badr raised his hand, asking the shaikh to stop reciting that particular verse.

"God Almighty has spoken the truth," Badr said. "That verse has its rightful place, and so does your not completing it."

But everyone present was familiar with the verse and finished it off, albeit not out loud: 'And God came to your aid at Badr when you were weak. So fear God. Perhaps you will be grateful.'

"What's happened thus far has been easy," Badr said. "Now the reconstruction and fortification of Egypt begins. That'll be much harder than fighting wars. May God come to our aid!"

"All Egypt stands with you, my Lord," his men and army personnel said. "People say you help the poor and weak."

"Let God do us some good!"

It was a great day in every region of Egypt. Today, the Armenian had come to stay. He had become Egyptian and mingled his blood with the country's sands, his own self with its destiny, and his very soul with the sugar-cane stalks and sweet Nile waters. He was aware and understood. When he stood in his place, Egypt as a whole awaited his vision and commendation, placing their every hope in his hands, everything lost and remaining, everything to come in the future. Every mother with a child, every man anxious to protect his daughter: today they were all looking to Badr. They gathered sugar cubes and strewed them in his path.

"Army Commander," they all shouted, "Army Commander!"

He smiled in pleasure, his eyes fixed on the Muqattam Hills. Today he could envision himself being as powerful and solid as the mountains, albeit not as high. Success had the taste of honey and the crispness of doughnuts dipped in sesame oil. Some people bowed, while others invoked his name in prayer. Children ran after him, hoping to catch a glimpse of his face and shouting his name.

He built his palace in the Burjuwan quarter and decided to plot a new map for Egypt full of roses, new buildings, gold, and emeralds—lots of emeralds.

"Everything you desire intensely you'll lose bitterly. Everything you long for will be taken from you by force."

He frowned as he remembered the words of his teacher. From Jamal ad-daula, he had learned about power, but his teacher had been lying and vicious. He would prove to his teacher that he could have everything he wanted. No one could deprive the Army Commander of anything by force. From today, he would collect emeralds from all over the world; he wanted a thousand pieces.

"Do you see, teacher? The things you brutally seized, I'm giving back."

Being married to the Governor of Acre had been feasible, but being married to the ruler of Egypt was much harder. Furoon could not understand why she did not feel at ease, even when she really wanted him to succeed in providing help and security to Egypt. She was worried about what was to come. She was never going to ask who he was spending his nights with, or which women were hovering around her husband and chasing after him. She was supposed to reconcile herself to this situation, but she could not. Ever since she had fallen so passionately in love with him, selfishness had always won the day and self-love had overwhelmed body and soul. Who was she? Not a king's daughter or a caliph's sister. So who was she? Badr al-Jamali's wife. Why was that not enough? Not only that, but why did the title scare her?

He had allowed her to teach in the Ahmad ibn Tulun Mosque on the condition that she did not tell anyone who she actually was. All the time, she would be surrounded by soldiers in civilian clothes. When she was teaching in the mosque, she felt more relaxed; Furoon started to feel that she deserved to be alive. Even so, selfishness was a sickness that needed treatment. So she hurried to see Hafsa, her teacher, and told her about the troubling thoughts she was having.

"Are you angry because he's so successful?" Hafsa asked her with her usual patience.

"No, that's what I want to happen. I'm scared of his power and control."

"You're scared for the Egyptians?"

"No, for myself."

"Come out of yourself, Furoon. I know it's hard, but give it a try..."

"I can't Hafsa," she replied. "Don't you understand? He loves himself, and I love myself. He's dominated by ambition, and I'm... I don't know what dominates me."

"Love of him, of teaching, of your family. You're Jawhar the Sicilian's granddaughter; don't forget that. Badr al-Jamali may well be Army Commander, but so was your grandfather. Badr al-Jamali may be a commander the Egyptians love, but Jawhar the Sicilian built Cairo and the Al-Azhar Mosque and entered Egypt. But for him, the Ubaidi Fatimids would have no place in this country."

"People are saying," Furoon went on, as though she had not been listening to Hafsa, "that Badr is cursing the Prophet's Companions in mosques."

"Do you believe them?"

"No, I don't. How could he curse the Companions when his wife is a Sunni Muslim? He's better than me, Hafsa. He helps people. I'm just..."

"There's no competition between husband and wife, Furoon. They're both a single spirit."

"He's certainly my spirit. But he'll have a lot of other spirits around him."

"Don't you know your own husband? No general exists who makes Egypt his total focus and then has affairs with women. I've never heard of such a thing. Army commanders are very abstemious when it comes to women, wine, and luxuries."

"Then who's he collecting the emeralds for? I've no idea."

"Why don't you ask him?"

"I don't dare."

"Furoon, make sure that you don't let your worries erect barriers between you and him."

Today, she made him kunafa. She got some semolina, mixed it in her hands, then used her fingers to mix it with butter. After adding honey, she rolled the mix into disc shapes and put them to one side. She took some flour, doused it in sesame oil and water, and made that too into disc-shapes. Then she trimmed their edges and baked them. She read a large segment of the Qur'an, dearly wishing to calm her soul. Passion still predominated over everything else. At this point, she would talk to him only two days a week. Sometimes, he would be outside Cairo, and at others, he would not finish work until dawn. However, what soothed her was that he would always come to her room, even if it was after dawn. If she was asleep, he would take her in his arms and fall asleep. He would then leave again before she even saw him. Sometimes, he would arrive at midnight and drown her in his passionate love without saying a word. Then he would take her in his arms and fall asleep. At those moments, she'd be aware he was exhausted, seeking solace inside her and neither needing her to say anything nor wishing her to miss the joy of ecstasy and moments of sheer rapture. She would clasp his shoulder, groan in a surfeit of love, and fall asleep again. However, he had told her today that he wanted to eat dinner with her. She could remember the nights he had spent with her in Acre on the palace balcony, chatting to the moon, planets, and stars. How wonderful it was to have him around her! She put down the halva, then suddenly stopped and clutched her heart. Why had he told her that he wanted to talk to her? Maybe to tell her that he was going to be married? Yes, that must be it. She clutched her neck and had a coughing fit.

She went out on to the balcony to catch her breath, but it did not work.

"O Lord," she sobbed, praying to God, "help me to be patient and endure. I realise that it's his right, but I can't stand it. O God, rid me of jealousy and hatred! Calm my heart in Your presence."

She was not aware that he was there, looking at her, till he folded his arms and stood right behind her.

"Halva-maker's daughter," he told me. "Every time I come in here, I see you praying to God. I dearly hope that you're not asking him to give you patience with me and to enable you to stand having sex with me."

She gave him a shocked look, lowered her head, bowed, and kissed his coat.

"Oh no, my Lord," she replied. "That's out of the question. Forgive me. I was deep in prayer. Then..."

He grabbed her arms and held her tight.

"'My Lord'?" he said. "I'm flattered, Furoon, but I much prefer 'Badr'."

She gave him a despairing look, then seized his hand and brought it close to her mouth.

"Badr, my darling," she said.

As she slowly kissed his hand, he was still gazing into her eyes.

"I support everything you're doing, my husband," she told him. "Everything. I realise that you haven't come here to tell me anything. You have absolute freedom, but I want you to know that, as long as you're happy, I'll never be angry or sad."

He gave her a mocking smile and sat down.

"You're lying," he said, pulling his hand away. "I'm used to you being honest, and your expression is full of anger and sorrow. I wonder, Furoon, what's going through your mind? You always manage to surprise me with your ideas. Are you supposing, for example, that I've come here to tell you that I'm going to be married to the Caliph's daughter?"

She put her hand over her heart, and unsolicited tears fell from her eyes.

"So now your happiness shows itself to me loud and clear; we can clearly see the moon as a full circle!"

"Badr," she said, looking straight at him.

"I've been thinking," he told her, moving closer, "ever since yesterday..."

"Thinking what?" she asked, swallowing hard and relishing his closeness even more than the very first time.

"That it's been ages since I've kissed you the way I want," he replied, running his fingers over her lips.

Their joint breaths mingled, and then he ran his finger over her lower lip as though he were discovering it afresh. His kiss was like no other. Inside her, there was a gush of success, power, triumph, security, and control.

"The nicest aspect of power is choice," he told her softly, after a while. "The Supreme Master has power. Some time ago, he made a choice. That was the moment his eyes fell on a girl who craved the sugar in his house and looked at him with a sincerity and longing that flooded forth like the blessed river. Do you happen to know her?"

"Yes, Master, you have power," she replied, her heart pounding loud enough for him to hear. "What do you plan to do with it? Badr, are you going to get married?"

"No," he replied, hugging her to his chest. "When I do something, I want to do it well. When I set myself a goal, I have to achieve it. I want to stay the most important thing in your life; I don't want you to find some substitute for me and your love for me. If I were to be married, I would be destroying part of your love. I like immersing myself in your heart's passion."

"Do you mean," she asked softly as she kissed his shoulder, "that you'll never be married to anyone else because you want me to love you with all the passion of a cascading river? That's it?"

"And because I'm as good a lover as I am a ruler. Anyone who's a perfect lover is totally absorbed in it."

"How can I love you even more, Amir?"

"When a woman feels secure, she can love. I realise that. So rest assured, Furoon!"

"Did you but know it," she told him, clasping his hands and kissing them passionately. "You've given me back my soul."

"I know it," he said.

"I wanted to spend some time with you," he went on after a while, "because I'm going to be missing you."

"Why?" she asked, her heart sinking.

"It's time for us to get Damascus back," he said. "It's dangerous for Egypt to leave Syria in Seljuq hands. I'll depart in two days' time. I want you to take care of yourself and Ja`far."

"Do you have to go every time and fight in person?" she asked, rubbing her cheek against his shoulder. "You've an army and loyal commanders. Send one of them and stay here."

"Are you assuming that I'm too old to fight, Furoon?"

"No," she replied. "I think you're the handsomest man in the world."

"We're not talking about beauty here, Furoon. It's about strength."

"The strongest man in the world. But I'm scared..."

He covered her mouth with his hand.

"That's not a word I want to hear in the Supreme Master's house," he said.

It was at this point that she realised for the first time what was frightening her husband: it was life itself and the frail and fickle human body. As year follows year, it changes, dries up, and deteriorates. He was still practising his sword-drill every day, as though he were still in his twenties, and without getting either bored or tired. He still loved her with all the desire and passion of a young man. His war was against life itself, not enemies. How she longed for him to win the battle, although she did not know anyone who had done so before.

CHAPTER TWELVE

Furoon made the halva perfectly. She held her son's tiny hand so she could bring it to his two brothers, Ahmad and Muhammad. Her meetings with the two of them were always short, politesse observed and eyes firmly glued to the floor. Now that their father was in Syria, she could build bridges to them the way her husband was doing in Egypt. They were waiting for her in the room. When she came in, they bowed. She put down the halva in front of them.

"I hope you like it!" she said eagerly.

While Ahmad looked like his father, Muhammad resembled his mother, whom she had met in Acre. Muhammad was probably still about fourteen, but Ahmad was now twenty. He was his father's great hope, and she realised that Badr intended for him to succeed his father as ruler. She was neither jealous nor worried and thanked God that her own son could stay far away from all that killing, slaughter, and heavy responsibility.

Muhammad reached out to taste the halva, but Ahmad stopped him. She gave him a shocked look.

"Don't you like halva?" she asked.

"Forgive me, my father's wife," Ahmad replied. "I never eat anything without the Army Commander's permission. He hasn't told us to meet you or accept gifts from you."

"I'm the one who wanted to meet the two of you," she replied gently. "Your brother Ja`far wants to meet you as well."

Ahmad did not look at Ja`far.

"My father's wife, or should I say 'my lady,'" Ahmad replied dryly, "our brother Ja`far is not like us. He's a halva-maker's son, while we are children of amirs."

"Ahmad," she responded after a pause, "Ja`far's grandfather is the man who built Cairo and conquered Egypt. If it weren't for Jawhar the Sicilian, there would be no Badr al-Jamali."

"I'm going to eat the halva," Muhammad said all of a sudden.

With that, he reached out, but Ahmad snatched the halva from his hand and threw it on the floor.

"My father's wife," Ahmad said, "I cannot talk to you, nor do I dare, because I realise that my life and death are both in your hands. But I don't want any halva made by your hands."

"Heaven forbid, Ahmad," she replied immediately. "Your life and death are in God's hands."

"Halva-maker's daughter, your very existence is crippling my father and leading inevitably to his defeat. People are wondering how he can be Chief Missionary when his wife is Sunni, or how he can govern people when he kills his wife's husband so he can be married to her himself."

His words and his sheer effrontery astonished her.

"Your father doesn't need anybody," she replied. "He's 'Minister of Sword and Pen.' No one else can rival his power. Forgive me if I've caused you some anxiety. The Army Commander's decisions are not in my hands."

"I don't believe you. Who recommended that he rebuild the Ahmad ibn Tulun Mosque?"

"May God bless him if he did!"

"Don't pretend to be such an idealist," Ahmad shouted all of a sudden. "You're the cause of all these disasters! Just don't imagine that your son is going to erase all traces of the Army Commander's children. I myself, my brother, and my sister, the Caliph's wife—we all have rights regarding the palace, my father, and Egypt."

"Your father is still alive and prospering. And you are correct: the rights belong to you."

"My lady," Muhammad now interrupted fearfully, "please forgive my brother. He doesn't mean it. Please don't tell my father."

"You're just like my own son," she replied, putting her hand on his head. "God knows, I wish for both of you what I wish for my own son. I've come in search of friendship and to get to know my family."

"Are you going to tell my father?" Muhammad asked.

She shook her head.

"You're as scared of her as the Caliph's soldiers are of your father," Ahmad said, turning to look at his brother. "What kind of amir are you? Of course, she'll tell your father. Don't believe a word she says."

Picking up Ja`far, she headed for the door.

"I'm sorry for disturbing you both," she said, controlling her anger.

As she left, she was feeling a sense of discomfort, but she was not angry with them. She recited the Qur'an and asked God to guide them. She told no one about what had happened. Even so, she prayed to God that her husband would agree to keep Ja`far far removed from anything to do with government authority.

Hafsa knew how east and west, and sun and moon, came together, and how mountains surmount the valleys below. Badr al-Jamali had never before been in love with a girl like Furoon. A man who spends his entire life anticipating betrayal needs to find the most loyal of hearts and to hold on to them. The man who regards the sword as both saviour and pathway is eager to search for the most peace-loving and conciliatory person who involves both self and others. The man who spends his entire life in a quest for power and carving his name on everything needs to resort to a person who eschews the world's goods and has no desire for either power or prestige. The man who regards himself as the hero of all heroes, the victim of all victims, and Supreme Master, will be looking for a woman who sees herself as a saviour of the weak. He was everything that she was not. How could a man with so much endurance, durability, perfection, and will go looking for a woman who would demand a lot and aspire to glory? That would break his heart and cripple his soul. He had gone in search of someone who could soothe that soul like the very angels so that he could count on her aid when the devils gathered in opposition. She kept telling Hafsa that, in her life, only two things predominated: her love for Badr and sugar. She was continually praying to God to forgive her excesses; moderation was the best course. Even so, she would donate everything he gave her to the poor and needy. She wanted to make halva for every household herself. She had convinced her husband not just to set up a communal table for all Egyptians every Friday, but to distribute halva as well. She would personally supervise its preparation. It would hurt her to hear babies, masters, animals, and birds crying. Like honeybees, she would carefully and patiently keep track of beauty's path. Which explains why, when she took her baby son in her arms that day, she told him that she did not want him to be a fighter, but a halva-maker.

Two days later, Muhammad came rushing in to see her. He asked her to forgive him, and she sat him down beside her and gave him some doughnuts.

"I want you to tell my father what happened," he told her bashfully, munching on a doughnut. "Ever since his elder brother, Sha`baan, was killed, Ahmad's been miserable, never smiling."

"Of course I'm never going to tell him," Furoon replied, stroking his shoulder. "I'm not angry with your brother. I want to see a lot of you! Did you enjoy the halva?"

"I loved it; I've never tasted anything so wonderful! Can I come to see Ja`far every so often?"

"Actually, I'd like you to come and take care of him every day. I trust you because you're the son of my precious, beloved husband."

Badr had not been able to enter, encircle, or gain control of Damascus. For that reason, he decided to focus his energy on fortifying the Syrian ports and restoring them to Fatimid control. Meanwhile, `Amer was still alive and bent on taking revenge for his father.

Within the space of just two years, Badr had managed to put an end to hunger in Egypt, brought back its merchants, used his name to make allies out of its poor so that, throughout the country, people assumed that Badr was some kind of shaikh who had used his magic to put an end to corruption. They did not realise that he had taken the sword to crooks, thus creating both friends and foes. Now, however, there was a sense of security in the smile of every single woman who was no longer worried about her honour, every man who no longer had to fear what the morrow held for his children, and every peasant who was now a 'settled farmer', living in a house alongside his own land, which he could now till in the knowledge that its fruits were his. Everyone in need of assistance now had a police chief who would never accept bribes from the powerful, because he feared the Supreme Master and ealised that he would slay wrongdoers without compunction. The strong no longer dominated the weak, and derelict roadways were no longer the haven of robbers. Instead, Al-Jamali had constructed bridges and canals and restored lands. There was general prosperity; once again, Egypt glistened with a fresh, emerald-hued shine. Badr never stopped or tired. He travelled everywhere himself, following every crumbling road and checking on security from farthest north to deepest south. As he travelled and spoke with the people, some of them would recount how they had met the Supreme Master. They would say that his face had shone, and he had handed out food and gifts. They would say that, sometime in the distant future, there would be a Shaikh Badr shrine dedicated to the friend of the weak and supporter of the poor. Some merchants were angry. Greed was still rampant and profitable, but now, life could not proceed without spies checking to make sure that they were not hoarding goods and monopolising commodities.

However, the Supreme Master was the complete opposite of the Caliph in every conceivable way. Cairo's walls loomed over the Caliph, who was imprisoned inside the city from one era and time to the next, unable to leave and lacking any choice in the matter. By contrast, the Supreme Master had a completely free hand, handling all government business as though there were no one else in the land. He would divide up quarters and streets throughout Egypt, review tax assessments for every region, and do the accounting slowly, as though he were an accountant, not the Army Commander. He was possessed by the idea of authority, and he wanted to be treated as a guest in every Egyptian household. Every marriage contract had to pass by him first, and his name had to appear on it. No one could inherit or be married, could be either happy or sad, unless the Supreme Master were with them. Then he started a trip in search of emeralds, with his teacher's words ringing in his ears: 'Everything you desire intensively you'll lose bitterly. Everything you long for will be taken from you by force.'

"You're wrong, Jamal ad-daula. Today, Badr al-Jamali is ruler of Egypt; whoever rules Egypt controls the world and a chunk of paradise. He has no idea what the future may bring, but, whatever that may be, he'll deal with it. His name's there, and he's managed to do things where previous rulers have failed. Come over here, Jawhar the Sicilian, and let me tell you about Badr al-Jamali. You conquered Egypt when others before you had failed. Now here's the Armenian, filling it with people, restoring it, and reviving its original form. Today, Badr has forgotten all about Aram, but he has not forgotten his sister, Susie. From time to time, she will look down on him to remind him of his own weakness. He has never told anyone about her and is no longer looking for her."

On Friday, the muezzin proclaimed: "Greetings to the best of deeds," and, "Greetings to Muhammad and `Ali, the best of mankind." The Caliph had come to the mosque, accompanied by Badr al-Jamali, all decked out in hood and cope; the Caliph walked alongside Badr, surrounded by amirs, ministers, generals and armed young men. Every week, the Caliph prayed in a different mosque: one week, it would be the Al-Azhar Mosque, then the ancient mosque of `Amr ibn al-`As, and then the Mosque of Ahmad ibn Tulun. On this important day, the Caliph had taken on the ritual observances for himself. When he arrived at the mosque, the Chief Judge came in and greeted the Caliph with: 'Greetings to the Commander of the Faithful, the Shareef, Judge, and Preacher, and God's mercy and blessings be upon him! The prayer, may God have mercy on you!'

The Caliph now went up into the pulpit, while the Minister kissed his hands and feet as people watched. Then the Caliph said: "O God, inspire me to offer You thanks for all the blessings that You have bestowed upon me and my father." The Caliph then offered the congregation a homily and finished by saying: "O God, I am Your servant and Your servant's son. By myself, I possess neither harm nor benefit." He then prayed for the armies to be victorious, and said: "Remember God, and He will remember you." Ever since the beginnings of the Ubaidi Fatimid dynasty, these rituals have remained unaltered, with very few exceptions. But, on this particular day, something had changed. The Caliph was walking alongside the Minister of Sword and Pen, the Army Commander.

"My Lord," Badr asked in a ringing tone, "today I would like you to permit me to pray with the people. Last week, you prayed with them in the Al-Azhar Mosque. This week, allow me to pray with them in the Ahmad ibn Tulun Mosque. I've had it repaired and strengthened the structure, courtyard, and walls."

For a moment, the Caliph said nothing.

"You're right, Army Commander," he eventually said. "We'll pray with them today, then revert to the traditions of our forebears. The Caliph is the one to pray with the people, but we can make an exception for Badr al-Jamali, the Caliph's right-hand man."

"I'll pray with them one time," Badr suggested calmly, "and the Caliph will do it with them another time. We can alternate, my Lord. That will be best for you and for me."

Al-Mustansir was quietly furious, and silence prevailed until they reached the Ahmad ibn Tulun Mosque. Once they arrived, Badr al-Jamali went up into the pulpit. He prayed for the Caliph and his grandfather, then recited some verses from Surat al-Ma'ida [The Table, Sura 5. V 8]:

"'O Ye who believe, be upstanding for God, and bear true testimony. Do not allow the hatred of a people to lead you to be unjust. Be just! That is closer to righteousness. Fear God, for He is aware of what you do.' Let a characteristic of Muslim peoples be equal justice for friend and foe alike. This verse was revealed concerning the Jews of Khaybar. Today, I am talking to you about justice and resisting individual desires. I am now presenting myself to you, a servant of God, much in need of the wisdom of God, who wishes the heart to banish desire and to avoid rancour, showing mercy to his servants and treading the earth's surface with neither pride nor hypocrisy. I am the assistant to the Caliph Al-Mustansir, Badr al-Jamali, the Amir of the armed forces. I pray to God that I may repair, not destroy; give and not take; be abstemious with the wealth and property of others; and use justice in making decisions. If I go astray, remind me; if I succumb to desire, set me straight."

The congregation eagerly prayed for him. Shouts were raised in the name of Badr al-Jamali, while the Caliph watched him gloomily. Badr's gaze met that of the Caliph.

"May God bless the pious ancestors," Badr intoned. "The Caliph. His son and grandfather. May He give us of His blessings and grant our armies victory!"

"I find it offensive, Badr," the Caliph said angrily, when they reached the Caliph's palace, "for you to pray with the people, and then for them to pray for you while I am present."

For a moment, there was silence.

"I prayed for the Caliph," Badr responded quietly. "After that, I prayed with them as a servant of God, Chief Missionary and Judge."

"Do you know the background? My father tells me that, when Jawhar the Sicilian conquered Egypt, built the city and the Al-Azhar Mosque, and gave the Egyptians a sense of security, he always refused to pray with the people because he was afraid that they would become attached to him and not to the Caliph once he arrived in Cairo. He even forbade people to pray for him on Fridays. Jawhar the Sicilian realised that every man has a role to play: the Caliph is the Imam, whereas the Minister of the Sword's task is protection."

"Poor General Jawhar the Sicilian!" Badr replied in a calm voice that kept a good deal suppressed. "He watched minor figures riding horses while he walked. Then the Caliph Al-Hakim did not hesitate to kill his son without cause. We can learn from leaders before us, my Lord. For some time now, the sword has been the instrument of choice. Now, from Alexandria to Upper Egypt the whole country loves Badr. Without him, the Caliph would have no protector or saviour. For the Caliph's sake, I've sacrificed a son. I've never betrayed him or plotted the way previous ministers have done."

"I'm chiding you, Badr, specifically because, above all else, you're my friend."

"My Lord, leave things that are beneath the Caliph's dignity to me, and concentrate on what's more important."

"I've handed you the mission, judging, and the Ministry of Sword and

Pen. What have you left for me? Badr, you're the ruler of Egypt."

"It's part of my vision, one that I preserve and maintain. This year, your tax revenues will be three thousand thousand thousand and a hundred thousand dinars. When you first asked me to take over, it was just six hundred thousand."

"I realise that, Badr, and I fully understand."

"Maybe it's your men who are turning you against me, my Lord. If they do, then punish them. Without Badr al-Jamali, there can be no caliphate. When I first arrived, the Caliph did not possess a single mule to go to the Ahmad ibn Tulun Mosque in Cairo to pray with the people. Ibn Hamdan stole everything, as did Atsiz after him. I have brought good things to this country. So don't object if I hear Egyptians praying for me. That's my right, and I will not relinquish it now, nor have I done so before. I feel sorry for the way that Jawhar the Sicilian met such a sad end, but Badr al-Jamali is neither old nor weak. Hold fast to Egypt, and you'll become part of its ribs and veins. That embrace has to last for evermore."

"But I'm the one who's appointed you," Al-Mustansir said, "and I'm the one who invited you here. Don't forget that. As God states in the Qur'an: 'Do not forget kindness between you.'" [Sura 2 (The Cow), v. 237]

"Yes, my Lord," Badr replied with a smile as he bowed to the Caliph. "You did indeed appoint me. I am the one who has preserved your rule for yourself and your successor for a hundred years or more. I have breathed spirit into it."

"Badr, God is the only one who can breathe spirit into the body."

"God selects from among His servants and chooses those who are strong and reliable to preserve spirits. We used to say that the Caliph would always be with me at every celebration and prayer. For Friday prayers, he would be praying at the Al-Azhar Mosque, and I would be praying with them at the Ahmad ibn Tulun Mosque. Justice is the best of deeds, my Lord, as is giving someone with rights their just due."

"You can have what you want, Badr, you can have what you want. But there's something else..."

Badr looked straight at him.

"People are chiding me," the Caliph continued. "I'm the successor to
`Ali—may God honour him as the very best of humanity—and Muhammad
the Prophet—upon him be prayers and blessings! And yet, the Chief
Missionary is married to a Sunni woman. Even worse than that, Badr—and
don't get angry with me—is that you're building churches for the Armenians
in your army; your commanders are both Christians and Muslims. How
can the Chief Muslim Judge possibly do such things? What am I to tell the
people?"

"Do you recall what your grandfather, Al-Mu`izz li-din Allah, said when
he arrived in Egypt and people asked him about his lineage and status? What
did he say? He brandished his sword and told them that this was his lineage.
He then brought out gold and told them that that was his status."

"Army Commander, I don't want to make people angry."

"People won't be angry because Christians are recruited to defend their
land and honour, nor will they be bothered about the Army Commander's
wife. It's tyranny and corruption that makes them angry. Egypt loves Badr
al-Jamali, and it's my hope that the Caliph of the Ubaidi Fatimids will also
love the person whom the people love."

Their eyes met.

"We used to say," Badr continued, "that justice is the key to faith. The
powerful Christian soldier needs to be recruited because he is fully qualified,
quite apart from his religious affiliation. No one dares talk about my wife that
way. Rest assured, my Lord, that, as long as Badr is in charge, the caliphate is
well. If some people hatch plots against him, he'll still win because Egyptians
have him in their hearts."

The Caliph did not respond. Badr left, keeping his anger to himself.

Furoon was still living in a valley apart from all the other valleys in Egypt
and Cairo. Her father had joined all the other merchants who had returned

to Egypt after Badr had promised prosperity if they came back from Syria. Her father spoke to her and asked her to intercede with the Amir so as to exempt him from taxes. Even though he was the father of Badr's wife, she refused to do it. She kept lavishing gifts on everyone in the palace and could not make up her mind about punishments, even for wrongdoers. She felt equal sympathy for both sinners and the oppressed. She would always give in to tears, so much so that Badr felt compelled to bring in an old woman to direct the palace's functions. His wife would always give generously and expect nothing in return, but she had no idea how to give orders or to say no. Along with Hafsa, she started teaching women in the Ahmad ibn Tulun Mosque, and Badr agreed to have her surrounded by guards. For several hours each week, he would spend time listening to reports about the women who attended the sessions, all in order to confirm that no one was exploiting her or trying to betray or get rid of her.

Furoon felt attached to her students, as though they were her own daughters. Even though the babies that she had after Ja`far all died as young children, her inner sense of motherhood extended to the entire world. The young girl who came to see her was scared and confused: how to worship God? She would tell her to worship God the way she wanted. He is not somehow lacking like the rest of humanity, so that He needs to be treated in some special way. No, He is perfect and all-powerful. Wherever you happen to be, look to Him and talk to Him. Make your request to Him, and He will respond. In women's eyes, she often saw suffering and pain and wept for them.

This year, she had become attached to `Aziza in particular, seeing much good in her and an innocent face untarnished as yet by evil. Furoon would listen closely, and sometimes her eyes would glisten with tears as she heard about the girl's troubles and the extent of her suffering. `Aziza lived with a husband who made her suffer, not only with beatings but also with foul language and physical pain. After each lesson, she would whisper to Furoon that maybe she deserved to suffer at her husband's hands—who knows?

"Don't say that," Furoon would tell her, giving her a hug. "No one deserves to suffer that way. Would you like me to talk to your husband?"

"No, my lady," `Aziza replied. "He'll only blame me even more. It's enough for me to be near you and to learn from your knowledge."

Furoon told her husband about `Aziza. Although he was listening, his mind was focused on the emeralds he was collecting. He picked up a piece, examined it, and then handed it to her.

"What do you think?" he asked. "Shall we make a ring or necklace for you?"

"My Lord is very generous with me," she replied bashfully. "All I need is your love."

"Wife of the Supreme Master," he told her. "It's when you're so abstemious about everything that I'm aware of how covetous I am!"

"Why are you so fond of emeralds?"

"It's made up of hard stone and dry sand and comes from the rock's very core."

"It's just like you, my Lord, with the same strength."

"I had none when I was a boy. Now, as a man, I want to collect as much of it as I can. But sometimes, I think it's possessing me. I feel like getting rid of it, and so I collect even more. Let's talk about this girl who's being mistreated by her husband. I don't want you to get too close to anyone. `Amer is still out for revenge, and he's not the only one. There are many others, too."

"Amir," she replied, "I'm surrounded by your soldiers all the time. `Aziza has an affectionate face, but her eyes are full of misery."

He did not hear her. He was thinking about emeralds: getting rid of them or collecting even more—which was best?

Next morning, he instructed his soldiers to look into `Aziza's history; he did not trust her. They told him that everything Furoon had said about her was correct. There was nothing suspicious about her, and neither she nor her husband had any special connections.

He then instructed them to collect emeralds, lots of emeralds, from Egypt and the entire world.

Furoon allowed herself a happy smile as she observed the way that her work in the mosque was transforming women's lives. An illiterate woman was learning how to read God's book and write; a deceitful woman was begging her Lord to forgive her; and even `Aziza had reached an understanding with her husband, thanks to Furoon, and had now given birth to a daughter whom she had named Furoon as a token of her gratitude. She still came to the classes every day. One year later, she presented Furoon with an expensive copy of the Qur'an, telling her that her husband had given her the money to buy it and give it to her because Furoon had changed her life through her mercy and learning. `Aziza gave her a hug and kissed her hand.

"Don't do that!" Furoon told her, pulling her hand away. "God forbid! You're like a sister to me!"

"No, my lady," `Aziza replied shyly, "you've completely transformed my life. I can put up with my husband's mistreatment so I can bring up my daughter, and that's because I now realise that this lower world of ours isn't worth it."

"No, don't put up with mistreatment. I can talk to him."

"Don't do that, my lady!" `Aziza replied in a panic. "Thanks to you, he's a lot better now. I want to always be able to attend your sessions."

"This copy of the Qur'an is very expensive, `Aziza. Can I pay you...?"

"Please allow me the opportunity to express my love," `Aziza pleaded. "Don't break my love, I beg you. Please accept my gift on behalf of my daughter, little Furoon."

Furoon took it with a smile.

"`Aziza, you are best of all those whom I see," Furoon told her. "May God protect you from all evil!"

The next day, Furoon purchased a necklace of pure gold for her. `Aziza wept as she accepted the gift.

`Aziza told her that she had never had any gifts in her life, neither from her husband nor from her father. She had grown up as an orphan and had been prepared to be married to any kind of husband.

CHAPTER THIRTEEN

Egypt's sugar started pouring joy into the hearts of the weak, to such an extent that governors in Syria asked Badr to give them some of the season's sugar, but he refused. He needed to make halva for the Egyptian people every month, every festival, and every feast.

Was there a single title that Badr, son of `Abdallah al-Jamali, did not adopt? Even the Caliph himself had fewer titles than his Minister: Supreme Master, Army Commander, Sword of Islam, Imam's Aide, Chief Muslim Judge, Chief Missionary of Believers, and Minister of Sword and Pen. When he clambered up the Muqattam Hills that day, he was not just looking for Ja`far. He also wanted to gaze down on the cemetery and on the Egyptian people—Muslims, Christians, and Jews—who had died and been buried there, hoping for the mountain's favours and miracles, as well as the others who were still alive, wrestling with themselves, their sons, companions, and kinsfolk. Who was Aram today? He no longer existed, having melted away in the face of Badr al-Jamali's power, rigidity, and, above all, potential.

"Muqattam Hills!" he yelled. "Which of us is more powerful than the other? Me or you? Which rocks can best provide support and elevate the body, mine or yours? Which heart can terrify souls and fill them with dread, mine or yours? You're a wasteland, and I'm a valley; you're weak, and I'm strong; you have no idea who you are and where your homeland lies, while I have chosen my abode and will never leave it."

He heard Ja`far laughing. The man was wearing only a loincloth to cover his nakedness. He came over and stood in front of Badr.

"Today you're Badr," he said, "not Aram. Aram's left you and won't be back."

"That's because I've found myself here," Badr responded confidently.

Ja`far put his hand over his forehead like an umbrella and looked all around him in confusion, making a show of searching among the rocks.

"Where's Badr's soul?" he asked. "Have you located it? I can't find it."

"That's enough jesting, Ja'far," Badr said, unsheathing his sword. "I've come to put an end to your life so as to relieve you of it."

"Or is it rather to relieve yourself of me? The man possessed is upsetting the Amir."

Badr raised his sword and brought it close to Ja'far. As Ja'far stood there, Badr rested the sword's blade against his neck.

"My brother," he said, "I pity you a life spent on the streets. I want to relieve you of it."

"How exactly have you spent your own life, Badr?" Ja'far asked confidently, his eyes piercing Badr's. "I was searching for the truth. What about you?"

"I too have been searching for truth," Badr replied, "and justice and good..."

Badr dug his sword in a bit, and blood oozed out of Ja'far's neck. But he remained standing.

"Aren't you scared of death, crazy man?" he asked.

"Should I be afraid of meeting my Beloved, you idiot?" Ja'far replied. "I've lived my life in order to meet Him, and I've done my best to remain pure so as to join His company."

"Aren't you afraid of my sword?"

"No, Badr, I'm not afraid of you."

"Because you realise that I'll never kill you."

"No, because I have no fear of mortals. I've withdrawn and gained understanding."

"From the mountaintop," Badr said, withdrawing his sword a little. "I feel a unique sense of ease, as though I'm holding the world's collar and shaping it with my hands."

"You have that feeling because you're removed from the world, not holding it."

"Shut up, crazy man!"

"You don't know your own self, Amir. She does."

"Who's she? Who are you talking about?"

"The one you bow down to," Ja`far replied, "as though she's both dwelling and homeland."

"How do you know about her?"

"I know more about you than you know yourself."

"There are times when I find she frightens me."

"You're afraid of what you see, while she sees only husks. But she knows what lingers inside the soul."

"You're a madman. You assume that I'm one of your crazies. Get out of my sight."

"You've come here to see me and test my power," Ja`far said. "Now you realise I'm more powerful than you."

"Perhaps."

"You're preoccupied with the madman and the mountain," Ja`far went on. "Half of you wants to withdraw, while the other half still clings to the fripperies of this world. One half will intercede for the other. I'll leave you here with the rocks. Maybe you'll be able to squeeze some significance from your heart's desires, one part of you resisting the other. Aram's heart longs for deliverance, while the Supreme Master's heart is aware of the body's prison and the world's futility. Lord Badr, from here you can see your own delusion. Badr, as possessed as Ja`far...Badr, drawn to transcendence, to eternity, eager both for the world's goods and for the sweet pleasure of ridding himself of them; wishing to preserve the earthly body like the ancient Egyptians, but hating his own weakness. Search for yourself, Badr. Whoever disappears is present; whoever usurps is absent."

CHAPTER FOURTEEN

At the siege of Damascus, Badr tried to get to `Amer, Hamza's son. He was not bothered about Turkan, and Atsiz had been killed by Tutush. Yet `Amer was impossible to locate; he had bribed his friends and attempts to find him were fruitless. Badr tried sending a pretty slave girl to find him, but that didn't work either. He even sent letters asking the Seljuqs to hand him over in return for whatever they wanted, but without success. They claimed they did not know where he had gone; he would move from one district to another in disguise. Badr was still trying...

`Amer, son of Hamza, kept the poison and sorrow hidden inside him, but he did not despair. Direct conflict with Badr would not work, but there was no avoiding revenge on the Armenian. How bitter poison can be if some of it affects the body! That is what revenge entails. He could remember what his father had told him about the killing of Sha`baan, Badr al-Jamali's son. At the time, his father had been very happy.

"By killing Badr's son, we've made him weaker than ever before. Sons, `Amer, are both support and backbone. They are youth and long life."

"Sons," `Amer repeated.

`Amer was still in Damascus, but Badr could not finish him off. `Amer had vowed that Badr could no longer do that; he wanted to see Badr weakened in front of him, his crushed expression a tissue of sorrow and regret. If he was going to defeat Badr, then he had to locate a spot on his body that was easy to penetrate. Where was that weakness in Badr's body? Heart or limbs? It would be possible to kill his son, but he did not want to do that. There was something else, something even more painful and soul-destroying than a son's death.

A young man named Mas`ood arrived from Syria and asked to have a meeting with Ahmad al-Awhad, Badr al-Jamali's son. Mas`ood claimed to have come to serve Ahmad without compensation; he simply wanted to be the companion of the undefeated hero cavalier, the Governor of Alexandria who was loved by all Alexandrian Sunni Muslims, not because he was Badr al-Jamali's son, but because he was Ahmad. Ahmad was dubious as he listened to the man, and he did not trust him. But Mas'ood proceeded to show his loyalty in everything he did and asked for nothing in return. He started talking to Ahmad a lot, and Ahmad would listen. Mas'ood found the path into Ahmad's heart clear and the doors ajar, just waiting for someone to push them open. Inside, there was greed, anger, egotism, and a craving for predominance. There was also a fear of death, defeat, and his father. Muhammad al-Afdal warned him that Mas'ood had some peculiar traits. Why was he going everywhere with Ahmad? But Ahmad refused to listen.

"My brother," Muhammad warned him, "your father has lots of enemies. Beware of treason; that's even worse than death. 'Amer's still out for revenge on your father."

"Tell the truth, Muhammad," Ahmad replied angrily, "even if it's about our own family. Doesn't 'Amer have the right to want to take revenge on your father? Think about it."

"Have you lost your mind, Ahmad?" Muhammad said, his mouth agape. "If your father heard you say that, he'd kill you on the spot."

"That's what scares me. My father would never hesitate to kill me, his own son. He's madly in love with the halva-maker's daughter. Her son will get everything—everything we've worked for, Muhammad, and everything I've made sacrifices for. You should either grab your rights from your father now, or else find yourself killed tomorrow."

"You've gone mad," Muhammad responded, looking all around him. "Your father's made you Governor of Alexandria."

"Because Ja'far's still too young. If I could, I'd kill him. But I know that he's going to kill me. Eventually, he'll kill me."

"Wake up, Ahmad, before it's too late. You either send Mas'ood away, or I'm going to tell your father."

"Are you passing judgment on me?" Ahmad asked his brother. "You're a coward, and you can't do anything. You're kowtowing to your father like a blind man, like Sha'baan. He behaved that way, but then what? I saw him right in front of me, bathed in blood. Now your father's producing other children, which means Sha'baan was lost for nothing! Do what you like. Do you want to kill me as well? Perhaps you're keen to become a servant of Furoon's son. Go ahead and kill me! But, while you obey your father without any discussion, just bear in mind that your father's besotted with a woman whose children are the ones he's going to love. Tell me: has he been married to anyone else? Tell me: how many slave girls do you have? How many has your father had sex with? Not a single one! The halva-maker's daughter has total control over him. She's a disease, Muhammad, a plague. She'll be finishing off both you and me. Listen to what I'm saying!"

Ahmad did not dare repeat what he'd just said in the privacy of his own room in the presence of the Supreme Master. He would still bow in honour and respect every time he heard his father's name out loud. His father was still placing all his hopes in him: he was his eldest son now and had been appointed Governor of Alexandria. Badr was hoping to bequeath the rule of all Egypt to his son. Alexandria was not the entire country. It had its own sparkle, and the waves of the sea gave it its own feeling of freedom, a sense of omnipotence. The city was unruly and difficult to govern. But Ahmad al-Awhad, Badr al-Jamali's son, had managed to do it. Like his father, he was astute and stubborn. That is precisely what Mas'ood told him.

"Al-Awhad," he repeated in Ahmad's ear, "there's no one like him. Your own father knows it, my Lord. If there were a single person able to outdo the Supreme Master, then it's my Lord Awhad."

"Are you out of your mind?" Ahmad replied in total shock. "I'm going to slay you now!"

"Forgive me for loving and admiring you!"

"This time only!"

Furoon was still bolstering people's hearts and advocating the public good. She started visiting her father—even he could not avoid being fond of the Army Commander. He resumed his business, and it started to flourish again, as he had hoped. As the trend continued, his mood calmed, and he forgave his daughter for her defiance. In fact, he started asking his daughter to intercede and allow some exceptional requests. Furoon never told her husband, but she was still happy that her father was now acknowledging her and showing affection for her baby son, Ja`far. Today she held the hand of `Aziza's daughter as they walked to the Ahmad ibn Tulun Mosque. The little girl kept giving her admiring looks.

"My every hope," `Aziza said, "is that she'll get a small portion of your light and piety."

"She's my daughter," Furoon said, kissing the little girl. "She's as beloved as my own son, Ja`far."

`Aziza bent down and held Furoon's hand.

"Let me kiss your hand," she said. "You've been so kind to me, and after I was humiliated by all others. You raised me up even when my own husband despised and beat me. You've made me remain steadfast till things changed and I gave birth to a daughter."

"God forbid!" Furoon said, pulling her hand away. "You're my sister, `Aziza!"

"No, no, my lady," `Aziza replied, her mouth agape "I don't deserve such an honour."

"I'm sharing my feelings with you. I've known you for years. In you, I've discovered a good, honest soul. I only wish the very best for you."

"My lady," she replied. "All I ask of you is to take care of my daughter in case something bad happens to me. I'm afraid of time and of leaving her on her own."

"Don't say that," Furoon replied at once. "God willing, we'll witness her marriage ceremony together."

With that, Furoon started reciting verses from the Qur'an, while the women listened in awe and love.

CHAPTER FIFTEEN

No one had expected the news of Al-Awhad Ahmad's fortification of Alexandria and declaration of independence from his father's dominions, not even his brother, Al-Afdal Shahanshah Muhammad Abu al-Qasim. Al-Awhad operated in total secrecy, charging his companion, Mas'ood, with everything. Even the Army Commander's spies had not managed to learn about this manoeuvre. War was a matter of surprise and deceit. This was an entirely different conflict. Women pursed their lips, and men stared at each other in dismay. They could not believe that a son would rebel against his own father. When, how, and what did he hope to achieve? Was he perhaps dreaming of victory? To rule the whole of Egypt? But what about the Caliph? What did he think about all of this? Or was it that Egypt was now the property of Badr al-Jamali and his sons? What about the Egyptian people? Who were they going to stand with? Alexandrians don't side with anyone. In this case, they all entered their homes and locked the doors. However, some notables were now following Al-Awhad, and they were joined by merchants who were fed up with Badr al-Jamali's justice and concern for the poor, as well as by some men from times past who had lost their posts and status because of Badr al-Jamali and soldiers who had stayed in their houses after Badr al-Jamali had fired them and created a new army. All these groups wanted to get rid of Badr. Al-Awhad promised them to change everything. He promised to restore the Organisation of the Egyptian Treasury and to monopolise a system that had been in existence for ages. Why had the Army Commander changed it, leading to the destruction of long-standing households using plundered funds? Al-Jamali had his enemies, and they all gathered around his son. Al-Awhad promised them gold and ancient treasures. He wanted to be Supreme Master, Army Commander, Sword of Islam, all of it.

It fell to Badr al-Jamali's other son, Muhammad al-Afdal, to give his father the news; no one else would dare bring the Army Commander such terrible news. Even Al-Afdal was shaking as he told his father what had happened and begged for mercy. Badr al-Jamali remained silent; no one knew whether or not he believed the story. After a while, he gave orders to the soldiers to go to Alexandria with him. All the way there, he said nothing. Eventually,

Al-Afdal tried to talk to him.

"Father," he "pleaded, "I realise that it's Mas'ood, Al-Awhad's new companion, who has totally changed him. We'll kill Mas'ood, my Lord, but Al-Awhad's your own son..."

Badr al-Jamali stopped by the walls of Alexandria.

"Go to your brother," he told Al-Afdal firmly. "Tell him to surrender. I'll forgive him. I've no desire to enter Alexandria and destroy it. People will say that father and son fought each other."

"Yes, Father, you're right," Al-Afdal responded in delight and relief. "You're always merciful. He'll agree. Of course, he'll agree."

"If he does agree," Badr went on," I want him to hand over Mas'ood, his companion."

When Al-Afdal entered, he had no idea whether his brother was going to kill him or let him live. However, he was doing his best to save his household and family. Al-Awhad gave him a cold reception.

"Tell Badr al-Jamali," he said, "that Al-Awhd will neither surrender nor hand over Mas'ood. In fact, he's going to be Chief Minister when I take over the government."

"What you're doing is sheer insanity," Al-Afdal pleaded with his brother. "What are you hoping to gain? You were my father's successor. Why couldn't you wait a while till God's decree was fulfilled?"

"God's decree will never happen, Brother. Badr al-Jamali will be alive, and we'll all be dead. I'm out to save Egypt from his evil and terrible actions."

Al-Afdal Muhammad tried for two whole days, then left, head lowered and empty-handed. Badr fully understood his son's decision. What was strange was the father's intense dream for his errant son, even though he was always cruel with everyone else.

"We're going to besiege Alexandria," he vowed. "They'll get no food, drink, or weapons. We'll just wait..."

"Yes, you're right, my Lord," Al-Afdal said in relief. "I'm sure Al-Awhad will surrender. He just doesn't want to lose face with his colleagues. It's all Mas`ood's influence on him. The day we kill Mas`ood, we'll see Al-Awhad return to his old self."

As days passed, a letter arrived from Furoon. He opened it angrily, knowing full well what she was going to say and not wanting to hear it:

"Be forgiving, Badr. The boy's lost his way. Don't hurt him. It's `Amer; he wants you to shed your own sons' blood. Amir, don't let him take your heart away."

He did not eat a lot or talk to anyone. His face was expressionless. Al-Afdal, meanwhile, was both anxious and desperate, as he tried to send messengers without success. As day followed day, Al-Awhad refused to surrender. Food became scarce in Alexandria, and the water supply ran out. People in Alexandria waited for the war between father and son to come to an end. After a whole month, people started begging Badr al-Jamali to lift the siege so that their sick and children would not keep dying.

"Go and speak to your brother," Badr told Al-Afdal. "Tell him that, if he does not surrender, I'll attack Alexandria with my army before noon tomorrow. If I do, neither he, Mas`ood, nor any of his aides will escape. If he opens the city gates, I will let him live and forgive him."

Al-Afdal rushed into Alexandria and found Al-Awhad poised behind the gates with his army, ready to confront his father. He relayed to him what his father had said.

"If your father enters the city," he told his brother, "you've no hope of winning. You know that."

"Give me till morning to think it over," Al-Awhad replied.

"You stay here," Al-Awhad told his brother, who was about to leave. "If your father brings his army into the city, you'll be the first one killed."

"Do you want to kill your own brother, Ahmad?"

"It'll be your father who's killed you without even knowing. You're going to die before me, and so is the baby Ja'far and your father's slave girl, who's managed to bewitch him and the whole of Egypt."

"God willing," Al-Afdal replied with a sigh, "no one's going to die if you come out and make peace with your father."

"Do you believe him? He's going to flay me alive."

"No, he's sworn in front of the people."

"He's Badr al-Jamali, the man who killed twenty thousand men in cold blood and sold women in the markets. Don't you know him?"

"And you're his son."

"I don't trust him or you."

"I'll stay here with you. Don't desert me. If he's planning to kill you, then he can do it to both of us. What do you think?"

"I'll think about it and ask the men."

At sunrise, Mas'ood suggested that Al-Awhad surrender, provided that Badr al-Jamali solemnly swear not to kill Mas'ood. Al-Awhad agreed and informed his brother of his decision. For just a moment, Al-Afdal looked down.

"It'll be difficult for me to ask that of my father," he said.

"Ask him to pardon everyone who's worked with me."

"It'll be much easier for him to enter Alexandria and kill your entire army than to forgive people who've rebelled against him. Don't ask the impossible."

"That's my condition," Al-Awhad said. "If he agrees, I'll surrender. I'll send one of my soldiers with the message to your father."

"He's your father, too."

"No, he's not. He's an enemy."

Badr al-Jamali listened to the soldier's message. `Abd al-wahhab lowered his head, realising that his Amir and teacher would be slaughtering everyone he encountered that day.

"Tell Al-Awhad," he said calmly, "that I'll agree to pardon everyone who's worked with him, provided they pay fines to the Egyptian treasury."

`Abd al-wahhab heaved a sigh of relief, but he was still confused. Could the beloved son be leading to all these concessions on Badr's part?

"If it were his own son," `Abd al-wahhab told himself, "he would kill him on the spot. However, Badr's heart seemed to have a softer side to it. Too soft, perhaps. No matter!

Alexandria opened its gates to Badr al-Jamali. There was no bloodshed, and he stopped inside the city to search for his two sons. Al-Afdal appeared first, followed by Al-Awhad, who was shaking and frowning. Father's and son's eyes met, and Al-Awhad noticed that his father seemed to be looking sad, although he did not search for a reason.

"Forgive him, Father," Al-Afdal said immediately. "He's asking you for clemency."

"Where do people pray here on Fridays?" he called out, looking round at the soldiers.

"In the Mosque of a Thousand Pillars, my Lord," `Abd al-wahhab replied, "and in another mosque—actually, a derelict mausoleum where they carefully form rows outside in the Attarin district."

"Take me there," Badr said.

He signalled to his two sons to follow him.

He looked at the demolished mud-brick walls and the vestiges of the mausoleum.

"I want you to collect all the money I've agreed to accept as fines on those who participated in the rebellion and use it to rebuild this place. Construct a new mosque for the people of Alexandria. Tell the people here that, when Badr al-Jamali enters a city, he restores and does not demolish; he builds and does not lay waste. Tell them that his name will remain here in Attarin forever. Now, let's go to the Mosque of Thousand Pillars and perform the Friday prayer, asking that the reconstruction of this mosque be completed."

Badr al-Jamali performed the Friday prayer with his two sons.

"Tell your brother that I've removed him as Governor of Alexandria," he told Al-Afdal as he was on the point of leaving the city. "I want him to build a house back in Cairo and to stay there until I've made up my mind about him. Till then, I don't want to set eyes on him so I won't kill him."

"You're responsible for collecting the fines," he said, turning to `Abd al-wahhab. "You'll stay here until the rebuilding of the mosque is complete."

He then whispered in `Abd al-wahhab's ear: "Before I leave Alexandria, search for Mas`ood and bring him to me."

Later, Furoon knocked on his door. When he gave her permission to enter, she went in, curtsied, and kissed his hand.

"Will you allow me to say something, my Lord?" she asked, her head still lowered.

When he nodded, she looked at his face and noticed the lines around his lips and eyes. How had he aged so much between one day and the next? How could all that white hair have appeared in just a month? Years were not equal, and days were not fair. A day without sorrow was an entire lifetime; a day of loss was like a life of suffering. What did you lose today, Badr? Another son? Why did you have to lose one son after another, and that after you saved the sons of many others from certain death? Is it the curse of fate, one wonders, or the curse of kings? Are you fated to govern the earth, but not the people living on it? Is your destiny a combination of blessing and division, Armenian?

When she looked into his eyes, she felt a rush of affection and love. She bent over and kissed his coat and feet.

"My Lord," she said. "I've never begged you before, but I am now..."

She held his hand. He sat down and pulled her down beside him, waiting for her to say something.

"Ever since we were married ten years ago," she said, "I've never asked you for anything, anything at all. All I've wanted was you. All my life, that's all I've wanted."

"Say what it is you want. I've no patience today."

"Don't kill your own son," she said, resting her forehead on his hand. "Don't do it. The entire plot was a huge mistake, and it landed him in the abyss. You realise that. It's all `Amer's doing. He's out to get his revenge on me. I'm the cause of everything that's happened. If you kill him, my Lord, I'll be the one responsible..."

"Go back to your room," he told her forcibly. "This has nothing to do with you."

"Yes, it does!" she insisted, perhaps for the first time ever. "I don't want you to kill him, and I don't want Ja`far to work with you. That'll soothe Al-Awhad's mind."

"How dare you?" he responded in shock.

"I've come here to plead with you, and I'm still doing it. Don't kill Ahmad your son, and keep Ja`far away from blood. He's my only son. The halva-maker, my Lord, he's fighting a war as well..."

He looked at her, but did not respond.

"The halva-maker's fighting every day," she said. "He's turning sugar into beautiful shapes, and thus has an indescribable burden to bear. He's fighting an evil world in order to make something beautiful. How can you make beauty out of greed, brutality, envy, and hatred? Tell me, how?"

"Badr," she went on affectionately, "you used to tell me that governing always involves intrigues. What your young son needs is guidance, not punishment."

He gestured to her to leave.

"If my Lord will permit me to stay here without saying another word, I'll be indebted to him for the rest of my life. Forgive me if I've had a lot to say and craved your mercy. But you're the judge here, and I'm asking the judge to listen to me."

"I've listened, and that's it."

"Now I'm asking the Supreme Master to let me stay with him for a while. The fighting has disturbed me, and I'm afraid of being left alone."

He looked at her for a moment, as though he were expecting her to lie. But her eyes kept wandering unsteadily, and her hands were shaking, as though she had just lost both parents.

She held his hand, sat on the floor, and rested her head on his knees.

"I haven't slept for a week or more," she told him.

She hugged his knees and ran her hand over his leg and ankles, as though to wipe away a feeling of prolonged distress. She looked up at his frowning face and ran her hand over his chest.

"If I could cure your heart of all its pain, Badr," she whispered, "I'd do it, even if it cost me my life."

He did not speak. She ran her hand over his neck, shoulders, and chest as she recited some verses from the Qur'an.

"It is my hope," she said, "that God will protect you from all evil, the evil of power and the temptations of authority."

"You're putting poison in the honey!" he told her with a sarcastic smile.

"No, I'm just telling you the truth. We're all His servants. So let's allow Him to judge us. Were you planning to punish Ahmad al-Awhad? Don't do it. He's just a victim."

He remained silent.

"My grandmother used to say," Furoon went on, "that there was one amir unlike all the others, Ahmad ibn Tulun, who built the mosque in Cairo. You know about him. His son, Al-`Abbas, rebelled against him, but he didn't kill him or put him in prison. There is always mercy in fathers' hearts, even if not in their sons'. Do you understand me, Badr?"

"You were calling me 'my Lord' before. Furoon, my heart is positively flooded with mercy, but I'm afraid that he's going to destroy everything I've built and spread chaos when, just now, a new sense of security has now prevailed. This country demands that sacrifices be made."

"That won't happen because he won't get involved in government. For some time, it's been Al-Afdal Muhammad Abu l-Qasim who's been your right-hand man. If you want, make him your successor."

"And what about Ja`far?" he asked, looking straight at her. "Do you want Badr al-Jamali's son to become a halva-maker?"

"It's a profession, just like constructing buildings and harvesting wheat. Without the halva-maker, soldiers will never witness any beauty. Without builders, my Lord, Chief Judge, Sword of Islam, you wouldn't be leaving memorials to yourself in Alexandria, in Cairo, and in the world's cities. It's your decision, Badr."

How could he get to her? He had no idea. How was he supposed to accept everything she was saying? He did not know. However, when she recited some passages from the Qur'an, he calmed down a little. All night, he let her hold him in her arms without saying a word. Every loss in his life loomed inside his memory, especially the deaths of his mother and eldest son, Sha`baan. Today, it was all even more evil and hideous: he could see his sister calling for help, while his own inability to act shrouded and restrained him. He saw her, and then Aram disappeared. He was always disappearing whenever people were searching for him.

Mas`ood was brought in, hands tied behind him. Under torture, he had revealed that it was `Amer who had charged him with leading Al-Awhad astray in order to rake revenge on Badr al-Jamali. He had promised him the governorship of Egypt under the Seljuq flag. Badr already knew that; what he really wanted to know was `Amer's whereabouts. Mas`ood told him that he was in the city of Tyre. Badr sent some spies there, but the man had left as soon as he heard about Al-Awhad's rebellion. Badr now ordered Mas'ood's execution; his head was to be hung on the walls of Cairo.

"The traitor!" Al-Awhad yelled when he heard the news. "He promised not to kill my men!"

"Ahmad," Al-Afdal reminded him, "he never promised not to kill Mas'ood."

"Fine, defend him!" Ahmad said. "You're his successor now. But he's still a traitor, a blood-letter. When is he going to kill me?"

"Listen, brother, he's forgiven you. Once he's sure of your loyalty, you'll be able to resume your old relationship with him."

"The past will never come back. It never does. He's out to humiliate me by forgiving me and hanging the head of one of my men on the walls."

He dispatched spies and promised them a thousand dinars. He wanted to find out everything about 'Amer, his past and present, his likes, his preferences in food, clothing, and women. Badr was conducting a search for a single man in an entire community, but that man was someone who had yet to attain power; his son and gut feelings had both turned on him. Badr now sent one of his senior generals, named Afzaghin, to follow 'Amer's tracks. Badr sat with him for a whole hour to find out what he had discovered and to ask his advice. Nothing that Afzaghin said gave any clue as to the path 'Amer had taken. Even his younger sisters had not set eyes on him for ten years.

"I've found out something about 'Amer," Afzaghin whispered in Badr's ear, "that no one else knows."

Badr gave him an expectant look.

"His love for women," the general explained, "does not match the number of his wives."

"You mean, he likes boys," Badr said, understanding what was being implied.

"Yes, he likes them soft-skinned and with delicate features. The whole thing's a secret. He likes them young."

For a while, Badr was silent.

"What about his wives?" he asked. "They've Seljuq protection, of course. But, if he prefers boys, then..."

"That's the thread."

"There are countless men like him. What do you suggest, Afzaghin?"

"We need to be patient, my lord."

"No, we need to find something to bring him out of his lair. Let me give it some thought."

'Abd al-wahhab finished his supervision of the reconstruction of the Attarin Mosque in Alexandria. As Badr always did, he had his name carved there, as with every field, every wall, every battlement, and every house. In the year 477 AH / 1048 CE, the following inscription was carved inside the mosque:

In the name of God, the Merciful, the Compassionate: God's mosques are frequented by those who believe in God and the last day, who perform the prayers, bring alms, and fear only God. This mosque has been rebuilt on the order of the Supreme Master, Army Commander, Sword of Islam, Supporter of the Imam, Chief Judge, and Guide of Muslim Missionaries, Abu Najm Badr al-Mustansiri, on the occasion of his presence in the port of Alexandria and his witnessing the dilapidated state of the mosque. Through his enlightened stewardship, he has seen fit to have it reconstructed as a tribute to God Almighty in the month Rabi al-Awwal of the year 477.

CHAPTER SIXTEEN

She knew for certain that sorrow would never leave her husband. Even so, she managed to make him accept his sorrow, even though she herself could not eradicate it entirely. Every night, he would come to her without saying a word and fall asleep. She would put one hand over his heart and the other under his head, as though he were her child. She would run her hands over his hair, whispering prayers and passages from the Qur'an. When he snored, she would hold his hand, kiss it, and place it over her own heart till morning. Amid all the treachery, he started longing for her arms; she possessed his heart totally, just as she had before, but now even more so. These days, he was spending every single night in her arms. She would hum tunes that she had heard from her mother in Coptic. She had no idea what the words meant, but they managed to soothe the troubled soul.

"You're bewitching me, Egyptian girl," he would whisper to her with a gentleness that left his heart only when he was in her arms.

"There's one Badr [moon] in the sky," she would say, as she stroked his hair with her hand, "and another here with me."

He closed his eyes and smiled.

"The Egyptians will never believe," she told him, kissing his head, "that the man who stays in my arms as a lover is the Supreme Master and ruler of Egypt."

"I'm not Egypt's ruler," he said with a smile. "Do the rivers flows beneath me? Moses's Pharaoh said that, and he was destroyed."

"Is that why you don't take the title of 'king'?"

"Kingdom belongs to God alone, Furoon. I have it for a while, and I'll never let it slip from my grasp."

She managed to suppress a laugh, but he understood.

"You don't believe me!" he said. "I wonder what you're thinking? That Badr loves himself, just like a peacock. He rules the Egyptians like the blessed river itself!"

"That's true, too," she replied deliberately. "What amazes me is that the Supreme Master who has all of earth's paradises at his disposal should choose a woman like me—one who can't even give orders to slave girls and who's afraid of falling rain, wounding doves, and weeping hoopoes. I don't have your courage, Badr."

"Even so, she's someone who, for five whole years when she was with Hamza and ten years with Badr, has managed to guard her heart against hatred and loathing. She resisted Hamza's power, tyranny, and trickery. In spite of all his lies, he never touched her. That's a truly remarkable woman, Furoon."

Next morning, she went to the mosque surrounded by guards. The pained expression in `Aziza's eyes alarmed and shocked her. She had hoped to be able to remove the pains of many, but so far, she had not succeeded.

`Aziza rushed over to Furoon with her little girl, her eyes full of tears.

"My lady and saviour," she begged, "save me from my husband. Please, before he kills my daughter. Here, take her..."

Furoon turned toward the girl and stretched out a hand. The guards pointed their weapons at the child.

"Move away," Furoon told them immediately. "She's a friend and sister."

They stayed in place and did not move away. The Army Commander's instructions had been clear, and anyone who did not carry them out would be killed on the spot. Furoon stared at them angrily, then looked over at `Aziza, who was weeping profusely. `Aziza bent down, grabbed the hem of Furoon's skirt, and kissed it.

"My lady," she said, "there's nothing I can do. It's no longer in my hands. Please save me from him. He slammed her head against the ground till she passed out. I'm afraid she's going to die. I can't take this anymore..."

Furoon grabbed her and made her stand up again.

"Calm down," she said, "and don't be afraid. "God is with you and will treat you right. Bring your daughter. I'm not going to send you away; from today, you're going to stay with me."

"He hit me so hard," `Aziza sobbed, "that he broke my ribs. He threatened to burn me alive if I left him. I'm scared. Maybe I need to stay with him. If I hadn't raised a fuss, I could have gone on living in peace. But...he's going to kill my daughter..."

"No," Furoon replied, holding the woman's hand. "There can never be any peace with tyranny, even if it's firmly established and has constructed its own redoubts. Peace and security always involve power accompanied by justice. Leave it to me. Today, you'll come with me to my house."

`Aziza shuddered, then kissed Furoon's hand, which was clasping her daughter's.

"You're the best person I've ever met," she whispered as she kissed Furoon's shoulder. "If only all human beings could be like you, my lady! It's as though you're an angel walking on earth."

Furoon hugged the little girl, who was crying in shock, and gave her a kiss.

"You take her, `Aziza," Furoon said, as she stretched out her hand to the little girl. "She needs a mother."

"If I take her," `Aziza reacted in shock, "he'll kill her."

The girl stopped crying. Furoon was still holding her hand. `Aziza came over to take the little girl.

"You're going to be fine!" Furoon whispered.

"Please forgive me," `Aziza said. "I have delayed your visit to the mosque and the lesson. I was in need of your help, my lady."

There was a suppressed gasp. Mercy always comes with a sharp blade, and `Aziza had spent two whole days sharpening the knife before plunging it into Furoon's heart.

What happened at that moment was like the original flood—a lot of confusion and chaos. Just as Furoon was handing the little girl back to her mother, `Aziza pulled a knife from her dress and plunged it into Furoon. The guards yelled, grabbed `Aziza, and held her neck from behind. They left the knife in place and carried Furoon away as quickly as they could. They were worried about who would be giving the Supreme Master the news and what that person's fate would be.

"God willing," they muttered to each other, "she'll live and intercede for us. She's the one at fault, not us. She told us to move away."

Badr did not need anyone to tell him; he was in the palace when she was brought in. For just a moment, he froze in place, but then he took her from the soldiers, semi-conscious. She saw Badr enveloped in a white cloud, which hovered around him, gleaming with a different light.

"Badr," she told him. "It wasn't the soldiers' fault."

"Don't speak."

Summoning all of Egypt's doctors, he carried her to her room. He did not ask what had happened.

"That knife's poisoned," he declared firmly as he looked at the knife buried in her chest.

The doctor's hand shook as he moved the knife. Furoon screamed in agony, and Badr held her hand. She kept begging them to leave the knife where it was; removing it was far more painful than leaving it where it was. He wiped her forehead and, without even realising it, licked her sweat, as if he wanted to keep its taste and smell inside him. She sat up, but he lay her back down again.

"Do this for my sake," he told her.

"I can't," she replied weakly, "this pain is…"

The doctor covered the wound in herbs and bound it up. Badr stared at the knife.

"It's a poisoned knife, isn't it?" he asked the doctor.

The doctor was scared. For a moment, he hesitated.

"It might be," he replied.

"Don't lie and don't be afraid," Badr yelled at him. "Otherwise, I'll slay you here."

"Yes, my lord, it's poisoned."

His heart sank. He watched as the doctor crept around like a reptile right in front of him.

"So do something!" Badr said.

"My Lord knows more than I do," the doctor replied, shivering with fear. "I've put herbs on the wound and will give her some medicine."

"No, when it comes to medicine, I don't know more than you. Do something, or else I'll kill you now!"

The doctor put some medicine in her mouth. When he had finished, she was pounding her husband's hand with her fingers. He neither spoke nor cared.

"My Lord," the doctor said eventually, "kill me if you wish. God's will is greater than either you or me. I've done everything I can. We need to wait..."

"No, this is the will of Hamza's son, `Amer."

"He's the instrument, my Lord."

"She still alive, man!"

Furoon clutched Badr's hand as hard as she could. He looked at her suddenly.

"Wait till I've finished speaking to him," he told her. "You're only leaving here when the poison is neutralised. Come on!"

The doctor shuddered and, without saying a word, lowered his head.

She tried to move, but she could not. She grabbed his hand again. He seemed to be avoiding her gaze, denying what was happening.

"Ja`far," she whispered.

He looked at her. Then he knelt down,, put his hand on her forehead, and started stroking her hair.

"Didn't I tell you," he said, in a voice full of blame, bitterness, and impotence, "not to trust anyone? Every good deed you do comes back to haunt you. Why?"

She lifted her hand and put it on his cheek.

"You're always doing good," she said. "There's part of me in you. Your face is always so handsome. Come closer."

All his strength gave out, but no tears fell. He had overcome weakness and built walls, but now his prison was weak and gloomy with no hope of redemption. She had managed to put heavy walls on his chest without stealing his breaths.

He lifted her and gave her a hug, inhaling her scent. Then he leaned over, kissed her breast, and savoured her blood. Putting his hand over the wound, he recited some verses from the Qur'an.

"Bring Ja`far here," he whispered to the doctor.

The doctor hurried out of the room, calling for the little boy. He was waiting outside the room, crying. He came inside the room, but did not come close. He was afraid that, if he came too close or stayed too far away, she would die. Furoon waved a hand at him.

"Come over here," his father told him.

The little boy took her hand and clasped it. She looked first at Badr, then at Ja`far. By now, her body looked as though she were fast asleep, as though the poison were dissolving all pain and eradicating the burning agony. As she closed her eyes, one hand grasped her son's, while the other was dangling over her husband's. She seemed to be smiling at both of them at once.

Badr stayed silent, neither weeping nor screaming. He could see the prison bars getting narrower; the entire world was now stranger and more vicious. Who had invented prisons and discovered that prison was an aspect of hellfire? Why are you smiling? Because you've managed to escape this hell? Why are you leaving me in it? I see myself in three prisons:

I see myself in three prisons.

Ask me not about evil news

My loss of vision, lingering at home,

And my heart's abode in a noxious body.

Yes, Furoon, I've lost my vision. My soul lingers inside the heart's prison, and I'm still enveloped in a noxious body. Yes indeed, halva-maker's daughter, that poet knows something about this world of ours!

"It's God's will," the doctor told him, falling to the ground. "It's not our fault, my Lord!"

He remained silent and closed his eyes. He had a picture of her face the very first time she had seen him, and then on the other nights, when he had come to her room in a fury, expecting to take his revenge. How had she managed to overwhelm and inundate him like a generous rainstorm? He stared at her hand in his and lifted it up to give it a slow kiss. Taking a deep breath, he looked at the doctor.

"Why can her hand still clasp mine?" he asked, calm but baffled. "Are you sure she's dead?"

"That can happen, my Lord," the doctor replied, swallowing hard.

He stayed where he was, then put his other hand around hers.

"Where is she?" he asked the guard who was stationed silent by the door.

"Who, my lord?"

"The woman who stabbed her. I want to see her. Is she still alive?"

BOOK FOUR

Assume not that my white hair is from old age,

Rather a flood of what I have stored within me.

A night as dark as the gazelle's eye

I have loved while the morning stars have yet to glow.

Zafir al-Haddad al-Iskandari, Fatimid poet

CHAPTER SEVENTEEN

He looked at her steady eyes and her hands defiantly splayed out over her knees. He sat down in front of her, and the guard heaved her up to bow to the Supreme Master. When the guard forced her, she did so. Badr gestured to him to move away.

"You realise what's awaiting you," he said. "Who forced you?"

"No one did," she replied firmly.

"We'll find that out in good time," he said carelessly. "I can assure you that I'm going to find out. You have a husband who treats you badly. Even so, you carried out his instructions. Was that because you wanted to die? She helped you and trusted you."

"He doesn't mistreat me," she said, still calm. "He teaches me things I haven't learned."

Their eyes met.

"That's why his fate is going to be yours as well. What did he teach you?"

"He says that the Army Commander has never been defeated," she told him, just as assuredly. "He says that neither the Seljuq armies, the Turkish amirs, the combined forces of the Sudanese and Kitama, nor the Abbasid armies have been able to defeat him. He does not know defeat. However, the Prophet Solomon's staff was gnawed by a puny insect [Qur'am, Sura 34 (Saba). v. 14]. Those who cannot be defeated by armies will always lose to the heart, it being the weakest part of a living man's body. That's where the gnawing has to start."

"That's correct," Badr replied with a nod. "They're teaching you well. What else did they teach you?"

"That you're a heretic, Amir, and so is she. Your deaths will bring some peace to the Egyptian people and the whole world. You're a blood-letter, with no mercy in your heart—claiming that hypocrisy is faith and being married to a woman whose husband you've murdered."

The soldier was about to hit her, but Badr gestured to him to stop.

"Aren't you afraid?" he asked her.

"Why should I be? If you torture me and set me on fire, my husband has already done that and more to teach me a lesson. Anyone who's been tortured once is not bothered about it."

"Is is your husband happy with you today?"

"I hope so."

"Why didn't you feel any sympathy for Furoon the way she did for you? Did you have second thoughts? She'd helped you year after year. When did you hatch your plan?"

"I made up my mind from the very beginning," she said after a pause. "From the very first day. She pretended to be so good, but no human being could be that good. The Furoon I saw was not the real one."

"You're wrong," he replied bitterly. "That's exactly how she was, if you only knew. She did indeed have all that mercy and goodness in her."

"But I hate her," she insisted.

"Despicable people will often hate the genuinely noble; vicious people will be scared of mercy. The tyrant will shiver when faced with someone who can forgive. That's the world that Furoon may never have known or else knew even better than me. What about your daughter? Aren't you afraid for her?"

"You can go to Hell!" she shouted. "If my husband's happy with me, that's enough. I've worn him out in order to learn, and now I've learned. He says the girl's not worth anything, and I believe him."

Badr signaled to the guard.

"Once you have found out everything about her and her husband," Badr told him, "bury them both alive and let me know on the day it happens. Put her daughter in a home for orphans. Her husband has to tell you how he met `Amer. If he didn't meet him, who served as messenger between him and `Amer?"

Then what? He had killed `Aziza, and that was over. But what next? Finding `Amer and flaying him alive for days and nights. `So, Amer had managed to get to Egypt and persuade `Aziza's husband or bribe him, just as he had done with his son. Badr had to bow down in respect: `Amer had known how to flay the flesh, sever limbs, and aim for the heart, not the mind. But Badr was not defeated; he was never defeated. If that happened, no one would know or sense it. `Amer was fighting a dirty war, so now it was time for Badr to respond, blow for blow.

Badr looked at her spot on the bed and her blood-soaked dress. He decided to keep it with him all the time. It was all he had left of her: a strand of linen, a lock of her hair, and a scent that gradually disappeared, all of them as ephemeral as human beings. Ah, Furoon! Did you have to be so amazing and proud? He put the dress on his chest, as though he did not recognise death or believe it. How had he managed to keep death away from himself for so many years? Ever since Sha`baan had died, the world had not been the same. And yet, death refused to leave him alone. It was permanently around him, even if he was unaffected by the death of an enemy or pervert. Why?

Ja`far came into the room, his eyes full of tears.

"My mother," he said, putting his head on Badr's chest.

As he rubbed the boy's shoulders, he remembered. He had been about the same age when he saw his mother killed right in front of him. He had not cried. Why was Ja`far crying? If only he could cry as well...

"Fighters don't cry, Ja`far," he told the boy gently. "Death treats us gently, even though it's delayed sometimes or arrives unexpectedly."

The little boy tried wiping his tears away, but they kept falling.

"I can't feel her around me," he whispered. "People keep saying that her spirit's still with us, but I can't feel it."

The little boy stretched out his hand, but then he grabbed it, as though he were trying to hold on to something.

"Where is she?" he asked.

"You know where she is; she's with God. She loved Him and prayed to Him. He's placed her beside Him."

Badr had no idea how to calm a tearful child or to talk about the spirit. He stood up and called for Hafsa. She was sobbing her heart out and mourning Furoon: "My daughter, my beloved!"

She stood up when she saw Badr and wiped away her tears.

"My Lord," she said.

"I need you to look after Ja`far and talk to him," he said. "He really needs you."

"He's my daughter's son," she responded immediately. "Furoon was my daughter, my Lord."

He nodded and was about to leave, but she stopped him.

"Are you all right, my Lord?" she asked, looking straight at him.

"Yes, I'm fine," he replied.

"Permit me, my Lord," she went on. "I realise that our relationship was difficult to understand. But, if you need anything from me, I'm ready to help Ja`far. And you as well."

"What can I possibly need from you?" he asked bitterly. "I'll never need to cry or ask for your guidance."

"Forgive me, my Lord," she replied hurriedly, her head lowered. "That was not my intention. If only sorrow could be measured in tears! People who cry are just like those who scream in pain. If that pain is suppressed, then the illness takes over and the person inevitably dies. I wish you as much good, my Lord, as she herself wished for you with her love. I swear that I know of no other woman who loved a man as much as she did you."

"I know," he replied, avoiding her eyes. "Take care of Ja`far. I still have to get hold of `Amer, who's currently in Syria under Seljuq protection. That is something worth living for."

`Amer, son of Hamza, knew how to fight. He had fought with the sword, and Badr had won—that much was certain. If he stirred up rebellion, the Armenian would stifle it with his sword. But then, if he spoke about religion, inflamed sentiments, and aroused the spirit of jihad, everyone would listen.

"The Armenian's a foreigner," he said. "He hasn't become a Muslim, but is a heretic following other heretics. The Ubaidis have no connection with Fatima; they claim to be related to the Prophet, but then they kill the ones who are."

"How can infidels rule a Muslim country?" he asked Al-Awhad, Badr's son, with tears in his eyes. "They curse the Prophet's companions in their pulpits and alter the words of the call-to-prayer. Badr al-Jamali used monks to build Cairo's walls. They should be demolished, and the Seljuqs should pass through the infidel's walls, which were built by infidels. Badr al-Jamali has constructed churches in Egypt and honored the Armenian Pope. He's recruited Christian soldiers for the Muslim armed forces, as though he's defending a country and homeland, not a religion. So Al-Awhad, let's erase this country of his. If Egypt and its people understand him and really want Muslims and Christians to be equals, then he and every Egyptian who loves him needs to die. You need to understand, Al-Awhad. You have that name, the One, because other people don't understand. If your father's a heretic, Ahmad, then finish him off and restore the Friday sermon's citation to the Abbasid Caliphate in Baghdad. The future belongs to the Abbasids, even if your father has managed to rescue Al-Mustansir. What has Badr al-Jamali managed to do? Has he saved Egypt from hunger and oblivion? What's Egypt? A country like any other. Egypt can die, and the Truth can live on. Why is Egypt so important for Al-Awhad? Will he be succeeding his father as its ruler? That will never happen. His father's still entranced by the halva-maker's daughter even after her death. He prefers her son. Tomorrow, brother will kill brother, and the flames will spread. Al-Awhad will save the country from the blood-letter. Death to Badr al-Jamali, even if it also involves death to Egypt, Syria, and every other country!"

Once Badr al-Jamali had led the Egyptians in prayer at the Ahmad ibn Tulun Mosque, he returned to his palace in the Burjuwan Quarter and sat in the garden, looking at the quince trees. People said that Ahmad ibn Tulun loved quince. What else did Ahmad ibn Tulun like? Why were their destinies so sharply different?

The arrow intended to hit the Supreme Master today came from inside the palace and its garden. He was only aware of it at the very last moment. He did his best to avoid its path, and it passed behind him. It struck his hand a glancing blow, but blood flowed. He heard a cracking sound, although he could not see where the arrow had embedded itself. Within seconds, the entire palace was surrounded by his soldiers, as people shouted that someone had tried to kill the Supreme Master.

Badr's son, Muhammad, rushed over to look at the wound.

"If that arrow's poisoned, Father," he said, "it'll damage your hand."

Badr's heart was not bothering about the arrow. Instead, he was wondering who had tried to kill him.

"Use a knife to open up the hand," he told Muhammad. "Then blood can flow. It's not a serious wound."

Muhammad took out his dagger, opened up his father's hand, and squeezed it so blood started flowing. The doctor arrived with some ointment. Chaos reigned inside the palace, until the Supreme Master ordered everyone to leave.

"Son of Badr al-Jamali," he told Muhammad. "That arrow came from inside the palace."

"My lord, Supreme Master," Abu l-Qasim Muhammad said, leaning over and kissing his father's coat.

For a moment, Badr did not say anything.

"I got the news," he said. "It always reaches me before you. Do you realise that I didn't believe it? If there's a moment when you receive information about your son's death, you'll disbelieve it because you don't want it to be true. For the first time in my life, I've behaved unwisely."

"Sometimes," Muhammad commented gloomily, "betrayal is even worse than killing."

"What could be worse than a son killing his own father?" Badr asked with a bitter smile.

Muhammad's heart gave a shudder, and he kept his head lowered, not saying a word.

Badr thought back to a time when Ahmad used to laugh as he chased clouds and was frightened if a dog barked at him. In Badr's imagination, Ahmad looked fresh and pale-faced, with long hair that covered his eyes. People said that Ahmad ibn Tulun also had a son who rebelled against him in Alexandria, spreading corruption throughout the land, just as Al-Awhad Ahmad had done. Ahmad ibn Tulun had first put his son in prison, then pardoned him. Badr al-Jamali's son had rebelled against him in Alexandria, so Badr had besieged it until Al-Awhad had surrendered. Badr had forgiven him without even putting him in prison. He was a young man whose mind had been stuffed full of fables and lies. People told him that his father did not love him; he was planning to get rid of him; he did not deserve to stay in power forever. He had ruled Egypt for ten years; wasn't that enough? Sometime soon, Ja`far, his son, would be growing up and would take over everything. They told him that, the next day, his father would be ordering that his son Al-Awhad be killed. They told him many things. He listened and obeyed instructions. Then they told him that his father was a heretic who cursed the Prophet's Companions from the pulpits, claiming all the while that he was a missionary and shaikh. His Caliph was just like a piece of halva, and there was no caliphate without the Caliph. They kept on saying these things, and the boy listened. He then betrayed his father, and his father forgave him. How could he not? He himself was an orphan with no family. Then he had had a son of his own; in fact, he had had four children. The first one had been killed in an act of treachery. The second had arrived and decided to betray his own father. His father had forgiven him. A year later, the same son had decided that betrayal was not enough. He told himself that, even though Badr al-Jamali was over sixty years old, he was going to take his armies out and win all his battles. Just like the Pyramid Witch, his body had not aged. Wars had no point, so he should kill Badr, his father, and put an end to the regime of tyranny and bloodshed. He was a father, just like Abraham's father and the Prophet's uncle, Abu Lahab, stoking fires and slaying people without restraint. So, he would kill his father, not just to give himself priority in succession, but also to save Egypt from Badr al-Jamali's brutality. People claim that Egyptians fall in love the way Qais fell for Laila. They are obviously mistaken. Egyptians really love powerful people, but without any discrimination or knowledge. Al-Awhad's mind had been destroyed the way the liver is destroyed by too much wine, rent asunder by jealousy, greed, hatred, and delusion. What does the father have to say today?

Badr looked at his bandaged hand, where the arrow had struck him. Had one of his son's servants done it, he wondered, or was it actually Al-Awhad himself? He did not want to know. With such knowledge comes unbearable pain. The person who had fired the poisoned arrow at him was either his own son or one of his men. Why was he not in tears? Was there an even crueler fate? One son dies, and another goes astray. Why was his heart still longing for Al-Awhad, as though, if he had another encounter with him, he might be able to purge all the poison lurking inside him? He would remind him of the way things used to be, that he was of his own flesh and blood, a piece of his father's heart and soul. Ah, Furoon! Where are you now with your knowledge of humanity? Come here and tell me what you would have to say today. Be forgiving, Badr? Everything on the earth is earth? Halva-maker's daughter, need I overlook my own humiliation, dejection, and weakness?

"Talk to him, Father," Al-Afdal suggested shyly. "Hear what he has to say."

"I'm going to keep him in prison," Badr replied assertively. "I want you to deal with this. Find out what happened. Try to understand how he dared do this and who helped him."

What was he going to say to Al-Afdal? Should he tell him that he could not talk to his brother? Should he tell his son that his strength had been waning: his heart had bled, and blood poured out of his eyelids? That never again would he look into his son's eyes? He had no desire to look at a desolate void when what he was searching for was a source of water. No such water was to be found in desert landscapes or inside decaying rocks. Even so, he still wanted to see his son and to listen to him with his own ears. The heart never tells the truth; maybe his own heart longed for a son whom he had not set eyes on for a year or more.

He asked Al-Afdal to go to the prison. Badr would stand behind the door, listening but not speaking to his son. He needed to understand.

Now, as he stared at his bandaged hand, he listened with a stony expression. The emeralds with which he surrounded himself were just stones like other stones, even if they did not reflect sunlight and were not scratched by other stones. Pain throbbed and pulsed in his brittle veins. He loved emeralds as he had all his life. Today, in his imagination, emeralds blended with the tiny hand of Ahmad al-Awhad, a little boy not yet five years old. The boy had stretched out his hand, eager to accompany his father. Today, that same hand—the one that had wielded a sword—was out for violence.

"My brother," Al-Afdal Muhammad asked his brother, "did you really intend to kill your father? Why? Tell me you didn't do it."

"If I said I didn't," Al-Awhad replied firmly, "you'd kill me yourself. You've come here to kill me. This family is cursed by deluded pride. It has to be eliminated."

"It's your own family, you idiot! He's your father, the one who made you Governor of Alexandria and wanted to have you at his side."

"My father's a blood-shedder. He's going to kill me either today or tomorrow. The only mercy in his heart is reserved for that slave girl he married. One day, he'll be killing you as well, so he can raise her son's status."

"He's the one who appointed you and gave you men. He's the one who taught you."

"He taught me to put an end to his tyranny."

Badr tightened his grip on the bars and pressed the heavy stone against his chest. Still, he remained silent and cast no blame.

"Just take a look at yourself," Al-Afdal said. "Your greed has blinded your vision."

"So I've inherited that greed from him. Why shouldn't he die? He's like a Pyramid scorpion finishing off his young. What he's done is enough. Let him die so everyone can be relieved of his evil. Sha`baan died, and he stayed alive to enjoy his slave girl and her son."

Al-Afdal was stunned. His mouth agape, he looked over to the spot where his father was hiding.

"Maybe he can hear you," he whispered to his brother. "Say something that can work in your favour."

"Badr al-Jamali," Al-Awhad yelled in a fit of madness, "I'm part of your own heart and your own doing. Egypt, you Armenian, deserves to be governed by `Amer, Turkan, the Seljuqs, and everyone who opposes you. Go ahead, kill me! People will say that Al-Jamali killed his own son and buried him in the sand to forget about him, the way hyenas do. Kill me so you can live a long life. You're not tired of life, while I've no desire to stay in a world where Badr al-Jamali lives."

For two days, Badr did not leave his room. He locked the door and refused to allow anyone to visit him. Then Ja`far knocked on the door and asked to come in. Badr let him in.

"My Lord," Ja`far said in a choking voice, "people are saying that my brother's dead."

"I know," Badr replied. He looked at Ja`far, but without really seeing him.

The boy opened his mouth, but then closed it again. He bent down to kiss his father's coat.

"Forgive me," he said, "I forgot to kiss your coat."

Badr did not respond. He was staring off at the horizon. The darkness was intense, and the magic would not come.

The boy remained silent, his expression totally baffled.

"What have they told you?" his father asked. "That I've killed my son? Did they tell you that? If they say that, then tell them that my son's the one who killed me."

Ja`far hugged his father's legs and started crying.

"Father," he said.

Badr put his hand on his son's hair.

"Egypt has to stay safe and secure," he said.

"How did my brother die?" the boy asked.

"You ask questions just like your mother," Badr replied with a bitter smile. "It's as though she's still with us. I don't know, and I haven't asked. Al-Afdal Abu l-Qasim says that he killed himself in prison. Other people say that his friends killed him so he wouldn't reveal their names. Maybe my own followers killed him. It could be Al-Afdal Muhammad, `Abd al-Wahhab, or soldiers. No one has told me anything; it's as though they all realise I would never order that my son be killed. I haven't asked, and I don't want to know. There are times when knowledge can do you wrong and break your heart. It's all strange, Ja`far. If the heart inside my body turns rotten, then I'll rip it out of my chest."

"Is Al-Awhad your heart, my lord?"

"You, him, Sha`baan, Al-Afdal, and my daughter, you're all my heart. A moment's hesitation, and all is lost. The soldier never hesitates. Security for his country is always his primary goal. Now people are saying that my hair's turned white, and young men see me as feeble and senile."

"Heaven forbid, Father!" Ja`far replied at once.

"So, how do you see me, Ja`far?"

When he looked at this father, he saw an old man, but he could also sense the power in his gleaming eyes and alert expression.

"Al-Awhad was out to trample me underfoot, and then put me in a corner somewhere like a piece of stale bread. Badr is neither weak nor humiliated."

478 AH / 1085 CE

He clambered up the mountain on his own, took a seat by the edge, and looked down on the tombs of the ancients, all of them seeking a blessing even in death, as though sands could intercede and rocks show mercy. He grabbed a handful of sand, then stretched out on the ground and closed his eyes. Inside him, there was a fierce longing for death. Every time part of him died, he dearly wanted to link up with his whole heart, which lingered here inside the mountain beneath his head. The sands now appeared to him in the form of an amir dressed in white, never lying or deceiving, but who also never showed his foes any mercy or forgiveness. How many pounds of emeralds had the Army Commander amassed? Green flashed before his eyes, and then he spotted Ja`far, who faded away without a trace. Ja`far appeared all of a sudden, and he could not be sure if the man was real or imaginary.

"What have you done, Badr?" he asked with a disapproving stare. "Why aren't you dead yet? What are you planning to do with all those emeralds?"

Ja`far's laughter had no end, and, every time he laughed, it ripped a chunk out of Badr's liver. He grabbed another handful of sand and slowly spread it over his face, neck, and hair. He closed his eyes.

"Come on then, mountain," he said, "give me your blessing. Swallow me up or turn me to dust. Life no longer has any pleasure; emeralds no longer glisten. I've lost the ability to see colours and flowers. All I can see is your sand. When I bow down to God in prayer, I want to be by myself, and not with other people. Here. Every amir and caliph builds a mosque where people gather from all around Cairo, but I want mine to be up here, high on your blessed mountain. I want it to be only for people who suffer the exhaustion of worship and struggle with fragile bones and an easy life. Today, I am stripped bare. Before you, I remove my titles, my clothes, my lies, and my suffering. Bear me so I may carry on. I have tried my utmost to purge my heart through devotion to you. Is this a feeling of sorrow because of some sin that I have committed, or is it because you have a good opinion of me? If you would tell me, then I could find peace. In the future, people will be asking why Badr built his mosque on the mountaintop. Is it because his beloved resides here, or his treacherous son? Lord, forgive him his betrayal of his father and join me to him as his mother bore him, with a pure heart and without rancour. Will people believe that Badr wanted to meet his Lord on his own and constructed his mosque just to please himself? 'We have assigned phases to the moon till it has returned like aged palm branches.' [Qur'an, Surat Yasin, v. 39] Just as the moon has its different phases, so do I experience days of weakness and strength. O Lord, give the feeble new moon in the heavens the power it needs. With such strength comes phases that can change from moment to moment. Here with You, I can be apart and believe. You listen patiently. Halva-maker's daughter, you were a part of me. Perhaps, in your purity, I discovered a mustard-seed kernel of purity in my own self; in your very genuineness, I may have seen the way I was as a child; in your spirit always longing for God's love, I was in quest of salvation. Furoon, how could you have been so beautiful? Halva-maker's daughter, do you believe me today? There is no good on this earth. We have come here because we are not fit for paradise. You gave people charity, and they slaughtered you. Had you been more cautious in your generosity, you would have lost your spirit. There is no escaping affliction in a world where people shed blood in order to eat, live, and multiply.

I will build my mosque on this site. People will ask: who on earth is going to scramble up the Muqattam Hills to pray here? Here reside the dead, blessed by sands and tales of miracles. Here reside those who have withdrawn and left in search of communion with the fellowship of beauty and stars. So why was the Supreme Master interested in this particular mountain? People said that his beloved wife and son were both buried there. He was now fused with its stones like emeralds.

For the very first time in Egypt, he was proposing to construct a mosque out of stone. He wanted it to remain; it did not need to be as vast as the Ahmad Ibn Tulun Mosque nor to have the crenulations atop the balconies. Ahmad ibn Tulun's structure would survive because the Army Commander wanted it to do so, and he had spent funds to make that happen. One blessed day, with the Lord of the mountain, he was bound to meet Ahmad ibn Tulun.

The Army Commander's mosque was intended for people who suffered in the course of achieving transcendence. It was both mosque and testimony: a testimony to passion and deceit, to blessed success and poisoned defeat. Here resided his heart, along with his beloved wife and son. Here he was as feeble as a gazelle facing wild beasts. Here, he sought his prey like lions, and became both ruler and master.

The minaret would be like no other. At the northwest entrance, it would have two levels. Having climbed to the mountaintop, one would also climb up the minaret in order to look down on Egypt: people who were alive, who had died, who were to come, people both victorious and defeated. What hero would follow him, one wondered, and what sacrifices would he make? Who would adopt this country as a homeland and who would die here because he had led an invasion? The minaret will have a square base, topped by a second octagonal level and the minaret's dome, which will be semi-spherical like the new moon. He would put decorated gargoyles at the base of the minaret to remind visitors who Badr al-Jamali was: someone who improvised, constructed, populated, and saved. The prayer niche would be decorated with stucco filigree topped by Qur'anic verses, with flower-decorated screens at floor level. He wanted to include the Fatiha there, and then, in the square section topped by the dome, verse 39 from Surat Yasin: 'We have assigned phases to the moon till it has returned like aged palm branches.' He would inscribe the name of Muhammad the Prophet of God and 'Ali in a star shape with six points. The star's branches would represent His omnipotence, and its unity would reflect His sovereignty and perfection: God. He envisioned everything in front of him; in his imagination, every detail was there. By the mosque's entrance, he would place a marble plaque in Kufic script to record the building's date: 478 AH. There would be five lines:

"In the name of God, the Merciful, the Compassionate,

The order to construct this blessed mosque came from our Lord and Master, Imam Al-Mustansir, Commander of the Faithful—the prayers of God be upon him, his forefathers, pure Imams, and his noble sons. To the Day of Resurrection, he has given sanction to the Supreme Master, Army Commander, Sword of Islam, Helper of the Imam, Chief Muslim Judge, and Guide of Muslim Missionaries. Through him, God has bolstered the faith, and the Commander of the Faithful has profited from his long service. He has expanded the Imam's power, made his word prevail, and deceived his foes and rivals, all in quest of God's favour."

"Ah, Badr!" he told himself. "You adore beauty and emeralds and stint yourself when it comes to worldly matters. There are times when you don rebellious garb, and others when you prefer the clothes of the sage fool. One moment, you can desire all the world's treasures and attractions and all the world's titles and dominions, but then the next, you can rid yourself of all frippery in a desire to please God. Who are you, Jamali! I wish I knew."

He was sitting on the mountaintop reciting verses from the Qur'an when he heard Ja'far's voice.

"What's the mighty Lord doing up here," Ja'far asked, "in the valley of the weak?"

"I'm pouring all my weakness over the rocks," Badr told him. "In the hope that they can bandage my empty heart."

"You've grown old, Badr, and time's lines have caught up with you."

"If only it was just my body that has aged. But it's my soul as well."

"Why are you praying alone on the mountain, Egyptian?"

"I'm tired of people with all their hypocrisy and avarice. I'm so full that my cup is overflowing with malicious judgment and the curse of power."

"You had only to make a small movement with your eyes, and all humanity would respond. Simply by raising your hand, you could eradicate tyranny. Tap your feet, and they'd bring you things of great value."

"My soul craves a feeble heart and its own satisfaction. I'm searching for my soul. Do you have any idea where it is, man?"

"Did you come here when your body let you down," Ja'far asked, laughing out loud. "Or was it before?"

"My heart and liver both betrayed me. One son after another was lost. Then she left, too. Badr remains standing, like the Pyramids, neither weakened nor fatigued."

"Why are you building the mosque up here in the desert and on top of the mountain, so far removed and among the dead? Come down into the valley, man!

"I don't want it to be a spectacle. I don't like big crowds when it's time for worship."

"What is it you see on the mountain, Badr?"

"I can pray effectively to God only when I'm on my own. It is only with Him that I feel weak. He envelops me..."

"Weakness is a characteristic of prophets; they were all weak and had their moments of defeat. Remember God's words to Noah: 'I am admonishing you, lest you be among the ignorant.' {Qur'an, Sura 11 (Hud), v. 46]

"I'm afraid I'm the one responsible for his death."

"Did you kill him?"

"No, I swear I didn't."

"Did your men kill him?"

"No, but I'm going to kill you on the spot," he reacted in fury. "I did not kill my son, Ja`far. Maybe I killed him without meaning to do it. I've no idea. I keep losing one son after another."

"That's the way war is, man. Didn't your teacher tell you that you're a Mamluk? You don't get to love and feel attachment. Just like me. But you're not like me. You're a Mamluk for rule, and I'm a Mamluk for being ruled. You cling to a son, to finery and power, while I cling to the ultimate in beauty and the summit of power."

"If you were thinking that I was going to give up, Ja`far, then you've gone crazy from staying here too long."

"Badr will never give up," Ja`far replied. "He's learned how to cling to the world even after it's betrayed him. Here on the mountain, he's searching for companionship. But you'll only ever find it with Him. You know that."

Badr fell to the ground, prostrated himself, and rubbed his face in the sand. He could only perform the prayer properly on his own; doing it with other people was governed by humanity. For a moment, he thought about them, not himself.

I'm a part of you, Furoon, and with you I found my soul. Now, here, among the dead in the valley of the weak, I'm alone...my mosque is for Him alone, not for other people. Those who have left and are in search of companionship will come, but no ruler or master will ever come. I have come to You, O Supreme Lord, You who know well my weakness and my lack of initiative. If I have wronged my children, then forgive them before You forgive me. I'm devastated that I failed to reform my own son while I was remaking the entire country. I saved Egypt and plunged it into hell. Is that my fault, I wonder? How many sins have I committed? Merciful One, do not call me to account the way I have done with Egypt's amirs. Rather, hold me responsible as I have done with the peasants. Forgive my mistakes and reduce my faults by half. In fact, I will never argue with You. You know what I don't know. If You wish to punish me, then I have ealised the need; if You wish to teach me, what a hard lesson it will be. But I can neither leave nor show weakness. You are the creator of the heart, and You know what leads it astray. My greed only increases and does not diminish. But I continue to battle tyranny as much as possible. Tell me that I have not sinned with those whom I love, nor have I thrust the ones I have lost into the fire.

"I'm responsible for the deaths of all those I've loved," he said, looking at Ja`far, "Sha`baan, Furoon, and Ahmad al-Awhad."

"You're stupid, Egyptian!" Ja`far responded with a loud laugh, pointing his finger at Badr. "Yes, genuinely stupid!"

Badr now opened his eyes in surprise.

"I can tell you the truth," Ja`far said, "because I'm not scared of you. Go ahead, Badr al-Jamali, go ahead and slay me! Have you given yourself the very power of God, who can seize souls and delay them for two days or more? Do you imagine that you're in control of everything? Is it because you managed to grab the woman you love after killing her husband that you imagine that you can grant life and death? Those are both appointed times and numbered days known only to Him. No, al-Jamali, the people who have died have died because their heart has tasted death on a day known solely to Him. You've no control over life, Badr, and it's not just those you kill who die, even though you've killed a lot of people. Why have you killed so many?"

"Shut up, or else I'll kill you."

"There's the Badr I know! Welcome to the Valley of the Weak! After such a long life, Badr, don't you realise that the Valley of the Weak is not on the mountain; it's all around us. It's our world, you fool! Come on, show me how powerful you are. You'll never kill me because I'm the only one who believes you. Up here, the Mighty Lord is inside my heart, not in front of me. It is He who has control of the heart. Stay here for a day or two to cleanse your polluted soul. I like your mosque. Will you allow me to stay inside it?"

"Are you asking me, when it's one of God's own houses?"

"For the first time, you've said the right thing. Maybe there's hope. There's a soul inside you like the costly emeralds that you collect so insanely, but it's buried under dirt. If you weren't ruler of Egypt, you'd become like me, roaming through the valley and recalling your weakness and strength, your passion and its gifts, your failings and their influence, your pleas for help and the response. Stay here. Welcome to the Valley of the Weak!"

CHAPTER EIGHTEEN

Was the noble lord really out of breath? Had the sword-sparring with his son, Al-Afdal Muhammad Shahanshah, now become too hard? His anger and frustration with his body was endless.

"That's enough for today, my Lord," Al-Afdal said shyly, putting his sword on the ground.

"No, let's finish," Badr said. "Are you feeling sorry for me, boy?"

Young Ja`far suppressed a grin as he watched his father challenging his body the way devout people challenge their own selves. He had often admired his father's prestige, the awe that enveloped him. But never for a moment had he felt close to him. His father had little to say about emotions and memories. Ja`far's heart was devoted to halva, pistachios, walnuts, honey, musk, and saffron. He was in awe of his father, but he also loved him, fully aware that his father loved him, too—and in a remarkably different and complex way.

How could Badr stop his lungs from panting? He had no idea. But he got his breaths under control, then sat down abruptly.

"The time has come to invade the Syrian ports," he said. "Even though we weren't able to get into Damascus, we'll besiege it from all sides till it reverts to us. In less than a month, I'll take the army out. You, Al-Afdal, will be responsible for Egypt till I get back."

Muhammad remained silent, although he really wanted to tell his father that he preferred Badr to stay in Egypt because of his health. Now, even the journey might cause him problems, and the fighting could be even more difficult than in the past. But Al-Afdal did not dare say so.

Badr gave his son a chiding look, no doubt reading his thoughts.

"My Lord, Father and Master," Muhammad said immediately, "I'd like you to send one of your generals. Your role in Egypt is more important and difficult. I'm afraid..."

"What are you so afraid of, boy, son of Badr al-Jamali?"

"The Caliph," Al-Afdal replied, looking all around him. "I'm worried about his anger at the way you're controlling everything and how the people love you. He's only human, and humans can change and get ambitious."

Badr gestured to his son to sit beside him.

"Muhammad," he said, "this country's your homeland. You're fighting for it and staying here. In a little while, you'll be taking over the reins of power from me and using both wisdom and justice. After a long life, when the Caliph returns to his Lord, who will come after him, I wonder?"

"His eldest son, Nizar."

"And what about my grandson, your sister's son?" Badr asked with a smile. "Ahmad? The Caliph has two sons. One is suitable for the position, the other isn't. The suitable one is your sister's son, Ahmad."

"My Lord, how can I make a decision about this?"

"When you're certain you can make such a decision," Badr said assertively, "you'll make it. When you rip the fear out of your chest, you'll prevail. From this day on, I want you with me, dealing with everything."

"I only wish you'd send one of your generals, my Lord," Muhammad pleaded.

"I'll think about it."

For Badr, keeping track of 'Amer ibn Hamza was still a major preoccupation. He sent Afzaghin himself to Damascus to search for 'Amer. Every man has his own weakness, and his own modes of access: treasure, women, men, and administrative power. Now, he knew how to get at 'Amer. All he needed was to hunt him down and draw him in till he could be arrested. He needed a beautiful, utterly innocent boy, and he had to make sure that the boy in question had no evil intent of his own; that the boy wouldn't seek protection with `Amer, for example...

He decided to send his general, Nasir ad-daula al-Juyushi, to take over the ports of Tyre, Sidon, and Byblos, and then to make for Baalbekk and Homs. Nasir ad-daula was one of his most loyal commanders; Badr himself had trained him. As for Badr, he would remain in Egypt; there was a good deal of work and building to be done. Never would he be thinking that he could no longer travel and take his army out to fight at dawn, on maneuvers, chasing, and fighting... No, no, that was all wrong. He was still capable. He kept up his training every day.

Wartime provides the best opportunity for enticement; greed emerges from the depths, and human beings let their masks fall. Rumours spread to the effect that Nasir ad-daula had managed to take a spectacularly beautiful, untouched boy prisoner. The boy was from Sidon, and his family would be asking the Seljuqs, their ruler Tutush, and all his aides for help. `Amer would emerge from his lair to see how beautiful the boy was; that was a risk, but it was all he could do. There would be general chaos, facts would be blurred, and people would be confused. `Amer would reveal his secret weakness. If he appeared, the Army Ccmmander would be willing to pay any price to whoever brought `Amer to him alive.

Badr's general now sent him a message, informing him that he had managed to enter all the ports. The people in Homs had acknowledged his authority. Badr al-Jamali sent him both medals and money. All the while, as day followed day, Badr was expecting to hear from Afzaghin. A week later, the news arrived. `Amer had sent one of his men to purchase the boy from Nasir ad-daula's men. The man had bought the boy and taken him to `Amer's hiding place in Sidon. The men had chased after him and arrested `Amer, who was now on his way to Egypt.

Badr enjoyed a peaceful night's sleep, something he had not done since Furoon's death. His wicked body was still a prison with bars of flame; he couldn't touch them, nor even get close. Life was still a heavy burden, and the rocks still weighed heavily on his chest. But he slept, smiled, and thought of her. He remembered her at that moment when he had seen her again after five years; she was looking at him from behind her veil, her expression full of words, suffering, passion, and confusion. She was as expert a lover as he was a fighter. Inside him, she constructed walls to protect herself the same way he had built actual walls. She erected a special place for worship, another for passion, and still another for fidelity. Then, right in front of him, he spotted Ahmad's hand—his son, a little boy stretching out his hand to clasp his father's. He looked at his own hand and the scar left by the sword blow his son had wielded against him. Ah, those bitter days! How he wished that God in His great mercy would forgive him. When they all met again, he would rip all hatred out of their chests; they would gather on a wall as brothers. That long-delayed encounter, the most wonderful promise of paradise. In paradise, all he wanted was to see them all again—Furoon, Sha`baan, and Ahmad—all joined together, loved ones with no fear or sense of sin. `Amer... confronting you is a victory as well, a paradise after years spent longing to flay you alive!

Inside Badr al-Jamali's prison, `Amer kept his head down. His beard was long and covered in dust. They had taken away all his jewellery and given him a dirty woollen garment to wear. But his eyes paid no attention. He gave the corners of his cell a sweeping glance, as though they had no boundaries. Badr al-Jamali arrived, opened `Amer's cell, and sat down in front of him. He was displaying all the pomp of kings, wearing his most lavish garments encrusted with emeralds and gold, the chain of the Chief Missionary and Chief Muslim Judge. Today, he had deliberately showed himself in his finest guise, while in front of him `Amer looked downtrodden and worthless.

"`Amer, son of Hamza," Badr said. "It is strange that I've spent ten years or more searching for you, and then a young boy not yet ten shows me where you are. Did you crave his body? Isn't the world full of absurdities?"

"Army Commander, I've no idea what crime I've committed or why you've been looking for me."

"For the moment, let's say that your crime is preying on children. What do you think? Isn't that enough to demand death and exposure?"

Their eyes met.

"With proper confirmation, yes," `Amer replied. "But I don't think the Amy Commander has that."

"No, you need to say 'Supreme Master." I want to hear you say that: your Master and Master of Masters."

"But I'm living where you can't enter—Damascus."

"But I found you in Baalbek, where I can enter...."

"You're planning to torture me for an hour, a day, three days, a year—it doesn't matter. Your wound's that much deeper, Amir. Your suffering involves your own offspring and delight."

"I'll torture you for a while, but God's going to punish you for the rest of time. Still, don't panic."

"Here's the heretic telling me what God's going to do! As you've just said, it's a world of absurdity."

"The heretic's telling you, `Amer, that you're in hell, both in this world and the next."

"What have I done, Amir? I'm innocent of any crime. Who grasped your son's hand and compelled him to try to kill his own father? Nobody. Who asked him to listen and respond? If it was things that Mas`ood said, then your son found the instinct in his own heart. Who's the criminal? Was it your son or `Amer, Hamza's son, who mourned his father all his life? Which father is better, and which son is guiltless? When it comes to your wife, I was not the one to ask her to trust all humanity like the angels and move her guards away so she could hug the baby, as though she were amid the pillars of paradise where all is peace and security. It was `Aziza's husband who prompted her to kill your wife. What's strange is that it was your wife who asked her to obey her husband and try to please him. And that's exactly what she did. So, what's my crime? The Seljuq fighting in Egypt have their winners and losers. In war, the enemy is a friend. It is the disloyal friend who is the real enemy."

"Ever since I was a child, `Amer, I've discovered that killing is the easiest of crimes, while intrigue is the worst form of rebellion. The thing that put an end to a third of this country's population was not killing, but infighting. It is not war that erases all traces and usurps authority; it's rebellion. Your own rebellion is as deep as the ocean. Why so much hatred? Is it avenging your father or a feeling of inadequacy? A desire to prove that you're better and more powerful is simply a contest between two men, nothing more. Take away my heart and eyes, and Badr al-Jamali will still be a man who has preserved this country and fought rebellion. `Amer will still be someone who's incited rebellion and assaulted young children. There's an enormous difference between these two men. Such a man, `Amer, will not be defeated so much by the loss of a loved one as by the deficiencies and destruction of his own self. How much I've wanted to keep you here in my prison year after year, so that you can see what I'm doing and what I'm building, how the fruits of agriculture in this country have grown, and how my dreams have reached the very heavens. But I have to kill you. Your presence is a distraction from building and population projects, and from looking after the interests of the Egyptian people. I'm afraid that, if I had you flayed before being killed, God might forgive you some of your sins. So, I'm going to leave you to die of hunger in prison. You're not worth the trouble of being put to death or the money I'd have to give the soldier who would do it. Day after day, you're going to die of hunger and thirst, pleading, hurting, and recalling—or not recalling—your crimes. People like you will never realise and understand."

Badr al-Jamali lived on, inscribing his name on walls and gates and through the tongues of poets and followers. He decided to fortify Cairo and expand it. Ever since he had allowed wealthy Egyptians to make it their home and residence, it had changed. By now, it had expanded to a point beyond the mosque of Al-Hakim bi-Amr Allah. Who could construct gates for Cairo to protect the city against the Seljuqs and all other foes? His son Muhammad suggested that he ask an Egyptian architect for help. They were good at building things. He had used them to construct his mosque, just as Ahmad ibn Tulun had done before him with his mosque. But Badr was not planning to build a mosque. He wanted to construct a barrier like those that monks build between their souls and humanity, a barrier that no one can destroy. He decided to ask three monks from the Syrian city of Ar-Raha to help him. He brought them to Egypt and told them that Jawhar the Sicilian's walls had collapsed, and he wanted to build new gates for Cairo with towers to ward off raiders. He wanted gates that would not collapse the way Jawhar the Sicilian's had. He was eager for the populace to remember his name a thousand years or more in the future. He brought the three monks who were building monasteries in Ar-Raha.

"I want to fortify the city with gates like the ones to monasteries," he told them. "Or they should be even wider, taller, and stronger, so that no one will ever be able to force their way into Cairo, even in a thousand years' time. When Cairo's gates are closed, getting in will be as hard as it is for a sinner to enter paradise."

"What's a monk going to do in war, my Lord?" one of them asked.

Badr placed his hand on the monk's heart.

"You've built walls around your heart," he said. "Envy, malice, and greed have no way in. Then you've constructed walls around your monastery to protect you from the world's evil ways. Now, build new walls around Cairo to protect it from greed. Don't worry yourselves about the contents of our hearts."

He built a new gate and called it 'Glory Gate' instead of the 'Victory Gate,' or Bab an-Nasr, that Jawhar the Sicilian had built. But people did not accept the name change. They still called it Victory Gate, so that it was still possible for victorious armies to enter the city through it. He built a huge square gate topped by an opening with a frieze that circled the gate's twin towers. Most importantly, engraved on it were the names of Al-Mustansir and Badr al-Jamali. At the top of the gate, in Kufic script, was engraved: 'There is no god but God, Muhammad is His prophet, and ` Ali is His friend.' Badr was there and still is. Even though his body let him down, the building will always live on while humanity perishes. The building will never betray him, just as the mosque of Ahmad ibn Tulun has not betrayed him, even long after his death. The Great Pyramid is still there, even if the King has gone. Those ancient peoples knew, and Badr was quick to learn, his spirit joining with the ancients and the architects of the Great Pyramid and Ahmad ibn Tulun's mosque.

He also had the Gate of Conquests, or Bab al-Futuh, built. Its was semi-circular in shape and stood next to the Mosque of Al-Hakim bi-Amr Allah. It brought the mosque within the bounds of Cairo city. Consisting of twin towers, this gate formed a wall between the two of them, with ledges and apertures so that fire and boiling oil could be poured down on anyone trying to launch an assault on the wall. Then he built the Bab Zuweila, again with twin towers. On this gate, he put a chute made of granite so that enemy horses could not get a grip. Having finished the project of the three gates of Cairo, he decided to pay a visit to Bahnas, the Pyramid Witch. She must have already known how proud he was of what he had built, the fact that the project was completed, and that he had managed to rid himself of ʿAmer. But why did he still feel so utterly weak at heart; why did his soul break apart inside him every single day?

She looked at him, her eyes gleaming in the darkness of time.

"So, you've come, Badr," she said. "I've been expecting you. Bahnas is a part of her grandmother, as her grandmother is part of her. She's always here, and she knows what happened in the past. Look at me!"

He looked at her and sank to the floor. She had never seen such suffering in a man's eyes before, not even in Ahmad ibn Tulun's eyes. The bitterness that had afflicted that man had never reached this pitch. She saw darkness in the gleam of his pupils and despair in his limbs. She could sense the prison enclosing his ribs as he carried the bars around on his back every day. She repeated words that her grandmother had used before.

"Your suffering is not like other kinds of affliction. When the heart loses its desire to continue, it hands over the reins to the soul to draw breath. Tell me now: whose weakness is worse, yours or Al-Mustansir's? Whose sorrow is more intense: yours or Ahmad ibn Tulun's?"

"My weakness is indescribable," he replied feebly.

"Army Commander," she told him with a smile, "armies haven't defeated you, and no governor or caliph has stood up to you. Badr al-Jamali is the winner in every conflict."

"My son's defeated me, as has Furoon's death. One son after another, I lose them the way a shaikh drops the scented beads of his rosary. He bends down to search for them and collects them all, only to discover that he has to stay bent over because he can't straighten up again. One of them dies, and the second betrays me and then dies. Should I feel sadder for the one who betrayed me or the one who died guiltless? Furoon was everything lovely around me. With her departure, desolation is all that's left."

"Make your passion pure," she said, repeating words she had used a while ago. "And make your goal your primary focus."

"I have done," he replied weakly.

"In the past," the Witch went on, "I've told Ahmad ibn Tulun that passionate love will always bring defeat. Love of a son will break the heart and rip out veins from the body's depths. Sorrow is for the mighty, and only stalwart hearts can bear the heavy burden. When misery weighs heavy on your heart, realise that you have ascended, as though you're one of the kings of old. Your beloved still resides in your heart. She used to say that you were a part of her, so search for her, Badr, within your own self. Don't let the darkness prevail, or else you'll lose the path toward her. You'll discover that path and recognise it. She's with you now and hasn't leave you the chance to search, because she has always overwhelmed you with her giving. Sometimes, that same giving can paralyze our legs, so we don't need to stand up. But today, you've the chance to get up, follow the path, and search for her inside yourself. Badr al-Jamali, preserver of land and gold, was drawn to her the way waves are drawn to the moon. He became part of her and belonged to her. As I've told you before, there are countries where sons fight for them and love them, because that's where they were born. Many countries are like that, but there's also one country in all creation to which strangers come, immerse themselves in its depths, and are unable to leave. You want to stay here—you, your son, your grandchildren, and all the people whom you've brought from your old homeland. I realise that."

Looking into her eyes, he could see seas and rocks reflected in the light. Inside those eyes, he discovered Furoon floating on the surface and inviting him to jump in with her. She was smiling and relaxed. Keeping his gaze fixed on the Witch's eyes, he put his hand over his heart and stood up.

"Supreme Master, Army Commander, Sword of Islam, Helper of the Imam, Chief Muslim Judge, and Guide of Muslim Missionaries, Abu Najm Badr al-Jamali," she went on, "you are welcomed by the ancients; they offer you greetings. They are not all rulers. Not everyone who built things is a king, not everyone who has fought is an army commander, and not everyone who stayed and left his sons to inherit and become one of the ancients is an Egyptian. However, you're one of them; they've selected you after a hundred years or more, and you'll live on for a thousand years or more. There are some people like pyramids, and the things they've constructed cannot be destroyed. Do you cry sometimes, King?"

"I'm not a king. I don't understand the language of the ancients."

"No, you've become a king. The people of Egypt will decide whether or not you were a king. The language of the ancients is found in the heart, not on the tongue. I asked you if you cry."

"No, never."

"Because you don't want to or because you can't?"

"Perhaps both."

"Once anxiety settles in, it's difficult to dislodge or resist. O King, I pity you as much as I love you."

CHAPTER NINETEEN

The action of Al-Mustansir bi-Allah the Caliph was unforgivable. After twenty years, how had he managed to slide out of the grasp of his powerful hand? How did he dare do it? When Badr entered the Caliph's chambers that day, he neither bowed nor kissed his robe.

"My Lord Caliph has prepared for a celebration of the Prophet's birthday inside his palace," Badr said in fury, "even though the Minister is always the one to make such preparations."

"Doesn't the Caliph have the necessary authority to plan such a celebration, Badr, servant of Al-Mustansir?" Al-Mustansir responded with a smile.

"I resent that you use your servant when serious matters are involved, but then forget him when it's time for celebrations. For twenty years or more, Egyptians have never celebrated such occasions without the Army Commander's involvement."

"Isn't it time to remind them of who is Caliph?"

Badr looked at him, realising full well what he meant and intended.

"My son, Al-Afdal Muhammad, tells me," Badr said, "that, even though he's my deputy, the Caliph does not allow him to attend meetings in the palace when I'm out of the country and involved in an important matter elsewhere. Why is the Caliph and Imam changing the situation with his major support and Army Commander?"

"That has not happened," Al-Mustansir replied. "However, times are changing, and, as General Jawhar the Sicilian put it, each period demands its own government and men. He conquered Egypt and built Cairo and the Al-Azhar Mosque, but then he vanished from view, so as to keep the caliphate in place. If he had stayed in the Caliph's company, people would have started praying for him to become the next caliph. You've been governing Egypt for twenty years now, Badr..."

"There can be no caliph without an army commander," Badr responded calmly, with a wan smile. "For a year or more, my Lord, I've been breathing spirit into your regime. I'm not Jawhar the Sicilian, nor is my son Husain the Sicilian, either. He's not going to die, murdered by the Caliph's order, nor am I about to disappear. If I'd wanted to dismiss the Caliph, I would have already done it."

Al-Mustansir gaped in shock.

"Ibn Hamdan tried his best," Badr continued. "One minister after another conspired against you, but Badr never breaks his pledge. There can be no celebrations in Egypt without the Army Commander, nor can any government decision be made without consulting me and my son, Al-Afdal Abu l-Qasim Muhammad, my successor and supporter. The Caliph is well aware that the country will never tolerate crises; he knows what the Egyptian people want."

"You're threatening and defying me as though I'm not your Caliph. I never expected that, Amir. I've always had your comfort in mind. You've lost a son and wife, and war has worn you out. I thought you needed to relax."

"Badr will never be exhausted by war, nor will fate's vicissitudes crush him. He has grown accustomed to them and knows them well. The Egyptian people shout out my name and expect me to attend every festival and celebration. They know me, my Lord."

"Are you implying that they don't know their Caliph?"

"What I mean is that the Caliph gains power through his Army Commander. I thank you for considering my health, but I'm the one who has to assume the duties and responsibilities. May God continue to preserve and aid the Caliph for us!"

As Badr left the Caliph's audience, he was suppressing his anger. He then told his son, Muhammad Abu l-Qasim, to place some spies inside the palace—lots of them—and to encircle the palace with his soldiers night and day.

Today, he missed her. Ten years after her death, he still yearned for her every single day. One day, he would want to grasp her to his chest, on another to talk to her, and on still another to blame her for trusting humanity. How could you die, Furoon? How could you leave me on my own for the sake of doing good? Why didn't you think of me? Why didn't I stop you? Her spirit hovered over him, her effect as powerful as the taste of sugar to someone who has been longing for it during years of poverty and hunger. Ah, for the sugar in your mouth, halva-maker's daughter! Opening his hand, he stretched out his arms as though to embrace her. Now, the body was playing tricks: sometimes it was old, but other times it was as passionate as a young lover.

"You traitor! If only I could be rid of you, mindless body!"

When he spoke her name, the fires raged inside him, and he desired her as he had the very first time. The entire world flowed out of his sides, and, in her absence, existence turned into a never-ending twilight. He could still smell her scent, see her smiles, hear her voice, and feel her arms around him. Why did he so desire her when he was annoyed? How strange that was! The only path to consolation was in meeting her.

"Furoon," he said aloud, "people are saying that Badr al-Jamali has grown old. They don't realise that, without your presence, my soul has left, so that Badr's body never grows old."

Ja`far could never understand his father. He observed him from a distance and was frightened in his presence. To be sure, he was Supreme Master. Whenever he wore his sparkling, shiny white uniform embellished with pure gold, all eyes were dazzled. The populace would raise their hands in awe and love, praying for him and forgetting about anyone else. They would call out his name as though he were a close friend, and shout phrases about the revered Shaikh, Missionary, and Just Judge. Every festival and Prophet's birthday, Badr would appear in public with the Caliph, his light obliterating all others. Muhammad al-Afdal Shahanshah and Ja`far al-Muzaffar would both prostrate themselves in front of him and kiss both his cloak and that of the Caliph. The populace would keep shouting, as though every single man, woman, and child dearly wanted to embrace and kiss Badr al-Jamali. He liked to make his way through the markets in his magnificent procession. It so happened that, right in front of his eyes, Ja`far witnessed a woman shouting his name and throwing herself at his feet.

"You've saved our children, Army Commander," she told him. "May you enjoy peace and happiness!"

One day, the populace clustered all around him. He signaled to his soldiers to let them be. The people came over and carried him on their backs. Kisses rained down on him from every direction until he was almost throttled, but he was not worried. At this point, the soldiers interfered, and he congratulated them for doing so. He instructed them to give out golden dinars to the people, coins with his name on them. That name could be found in every nook and store in Egypt, on every marriage license, on contracts of purchase and sale, and on money. He had his name carved on buildings and brands: sword of Islam, Supporter of the Imam, Supreme Master, Army Commander, Chief Missionary. If he did not read his name somewhere ten times a day, he would not be able to sleep; it was as though he was using his hand to inscribe his place in the country for all eternity. He told his son that the ancients had behaved that way, and he was following in their path. For that reason, Ja'far was scared of him. He would be cautious when he spoke to his father, not so much because he was the Supreme Master, but rather because he did not understand his father's contradictory personality, avoiding women and entreating God. Ja'far could not figure out why his father wore such expensive clothes and kept purchasing gold and jewelry. He did not understand his father's self-absorption and arrogance and his desire to see his name everywhere and to hear it spoken by every tongue. Was his father Moses's Pharaoh or the Prophet Jacob? Was Badr out to reach as high as the mountains and traverse the earth, or to rrealise his relationship with God, high in the mountains and far removed from people? Ja'far had never been able to understand. And now that his father had invited him to have a talk, he felt scared; even though he was twenty years old, he was quivering. What worried him even more was that his father had invited him to talk in his mosque atop the Muqattam Hills. He had heard about Ahmad al-Awhad's death. Some people said that his father had killed Ahmad, while others maintained that he had killed himself. Yet others said that it was Ahmad's own followers who had killed him, so that he would not reveal their identities. He had not known Ahmad nor wanted Ahmad to know him. Ahmad used to harass him as a boy and chide him over his mother, the halva-maker's daughter. He used to tell Ja'far that he would never become a soldier like this father and elder brother. That is why Ja'far avoided talking to Ahmad and instead relied on Hafsa, whom he considered to be his mother.

She lavished affection on him and treated him generously; as a result, he became very attached to her. Muhammad al-Afdal Shahanshah felt sorry for him, took him on hunting trips, and was as kind as possible.

Badr stood outside the mosque, listening to the Sufi chanting inside:

'You who are my everything, my family.

When I am crushed and humiliated,

I have only my soul. So take it.

It is the least I can offer.'

He did not ask for permission to enter the mosque until the chanting came to an end. Then Ja'far banged on the door and heard his father's voice.

"What's the matter, Ja'far?" he asked. "This is God's house. Come on in, boy."

He went in, bent to kiss his father's hand, and then sat down in front of him, his eyes glued to the floor. Badr now dismissed everyone else. He was wearing plain wool with no jewelry or decorations. Today, he looked just like one of the possessed. His eyes implored the distant horizon, and his white hair and beard radiated both wisdom and asceticism. He was barefoot and had a glazed expression as he chanted out loud. Once he had finished, he looked at his son.

"Are you scared of me, Ja'far?" he asked.

"Who isn't scared of the Supreme Master, my Lord?"

"Your mother," he replied with a smile.

"Pardon?"

"Your mother was never afraid of the Supreme Master. Do you remember her?"

"Yes, I do. I can remember her affection, her gentleness, and her white gown. She was from another world."

"That is absolutely true, from another world. Do you realise how much I miss her?"

His jaw dropped as he heard those unexpected words from his father, and did not say anything.

"The body's a foul prison," Badr went on, as though talking to himself. "It blocks your vision, much like the high walls built to protect cities. We do our best to stay as far from it as possible, and yet we can't. There are times when I really want to feel her just with my soul. And yet I long for her with my body, as though life can't be on an even keel if I can't actually touch her. No matter! Let's talk about you..."

"There are some gorgeous slave girls in our palace, my Lord," Ja`far said, swallowing hard as he did so. "I don't understand why you don't spend your nights with one of them. Father..."

"You don't seem to be understanding what I'm saying. It's Furoon that I long for. If you longed for a star in the heavens, how could you be satisfied with a fig tree? There can be no women for me after her; I don't have time for them."

"Your brother has seven hundred slave girls," Badr added with a smile. "I don't understand how he can do that. He has a powerful brain, and he's clever and honest. I always maintain that a shrewd man does not need a lot of slave girls. Maybe he likes listening to their music or enjoys sipping a glass of water from a lovely soft hand. I don't know. But we're talking about you, Ja`far, not Muhammad. Does it aggravate you that he'll succeed me?"

"No, my Lord," replied without hesitation. "He's a good brother."

"He has good instincts. He understands how to govern. He knows a lot more than you, that's for sure. What about you?"

"What do you mean, what about me?"

"What are your own plans?"

"Whatever you decide, Father."

"No, Ja`far, it's up to you. You're good at swordsmanship and riding horses, but I've lost two sons, and I don't want to lose any more. Your mother wanted Badr al-Jamali's son to be a halva-maker. Can you believe that?"

He shuddered and stared at the floor.

"I've heard that you're good at making halva," Badr said, looking closely at his son. "Hafsa and your mother have taught you."

"But I'm better with a sword, my Lord," he responded at once.

"Ja`far, your heart's with halva-making."

"That's for women, my Lord."

"The halva-maker was a fine man. I'll give it some thought."

Ja`far gave him a shocked look.

"Why are you afraid?" Badr went on. "I've told you I'll think about halva-making. You really want to work with the Sicilian's sons. I know everything."

"Forgive me, Father..."

"Shall I forgive you for keeping it from me?" Badr asked with a smile. "Or shall I forgive you because you're in love with your uncle's daughter, Furoon's brother's child, whom you go to see in Alexandria every so often?"

Ja`far went pale and shuddered, but said nothing.

"I forgive you for both sins," Badr said, rubbing his son's shoulder. "I forgive you for loving the halva-maker's daughter and for loving making halva. I adored your mother when she made it for me."

He had not expected to hear such words from his father, and stayed silent, not knowing what to say.

"Egyptian women are like river horses," Badr said. "They'll never accept sharing their husband with anyone else, and they don't like being too generous. Have you ever watched a river horse? It may look sweet at first, but it's the most aggressive creature on earth if it feels threatened. Are you prepared to deal with that?"

Ja`far gave an enthusiastic nod.

"You'll forsake all the palace's slave girls?" his father asked.

"Yes, without a single thought."

"You'll have what you want," Badr said, signaling to his son to leave. "Now leave me to my solitude."

"Will you consent, my Lord?"

"I'll give it some thought."

"That's kind of you."

Badr looked away to the horizon and repeated Al-Hallaj's words: "When I am crushed and humiliated, I have only my soul. So take it."

O Lord God, my body has grown weak, even if I make it appear strong in front of others. So strengthen my soul and raise it up; it is all I have left. With you here, I am even weaker than an Armenian Mamluk who is not yet twelve, an orphan from strange lands with neither prestige nor money. I am here, so give me a whiff of Your satisfaction with which to complete my days. I can see and feel You all around me, but I can bring You my heart and soul only when I am alone atop the mountain, forsaking all greenery and trees in order to listen to Your voice and feel Your immanence. That is how the Muqattam Hills acted in sacrificing all its trees, so that God would select it to address Moses from beyond. Today, I am like the mountain—desolate, yellow, naked, and thin—here in front of You, broken in body and soul. Take me to You, and allow me to deceive my own heart. If I could, I would remove its garb of arrogance so that it might enjoy Your immanence, but I cannot do that. The world's frippery can satisfy part of my heart, but not all of it. What I cannot control is my appetite for grandeur and the way that power makes its way into my heart. Now, I expect everyone to praise me and recite my name, just as a suckling baby awaits its mother's milk. However hard I try, I cannot be weaned anytime soon. But now, I am seeking refuge with You from my own self and seek Your all-encompassing mercy. Receive me as I am, just as a mother receives her sinful child. Perhaps it may work in my favor that I have never forgotten You, even in the midst of my greed, delusion, and lust for authority. I desired that authority, fully aware as I did so that You are that very authority. I coveted Egypt, knowing full well that You are its Master. Will You forgive the servant who wanted to savour the taste of great men, even knowing that he was not the country's ruler? Now here I am, hoping that my son will take my place, and then my son's son, and that Badr's name will be inscribed on Egypt forevermore. I now aspire to eternity like the kings of old. But may it work in my favour that I realise I am but a servant, and my contrition before You is genuine, not fake. Furoon says that God loves His honest servant, and Badr has never lied to You.

The next day, Ja`far rushed to see his beloved to tell her that his father had agreed to their being wed. After their marriage, he would abandon the sword and devote his energies to halva-making. Together, they could make halva for the entire population of Egypt, as had been the case before. For the very first time, she gave him a kiss, and he returned to the palace, feeling as if the world had adjusted itself and was now on its proper course. His father asked him to come and talk about Upper Egypt and the sugar-cane harvest. Ja`far came in just as eagerly as he had the day before, but he found a completely different man from the previous day. Badr was decked out in his gold-encrusted cloak and a coat covered in the emeralds that he so loved. Ja`far kissed the ground in front of his father and then listened to all his commands.

"Father," he said, "it's the happiest day in my life!"

His father looked at him in surprise.

"I did what we agreed," Ja`far continued. "I talked to Zubaida about marriage and said that you'd agreed."

"When did I tell you I'd agreed?" Badr asked, raising his eyebrows in surprise.

"Yesterday on the mountain," Ja`far replied immediately. "When—"

"Listen, boy," Badr interrupted. "I can remember what I said yesterday. I said I'd think about it."

"Father," Ja`far said, his heart almost collapsing onto his father's coat.

"You can be married to her if you're that keen," Badr said. "However..."

Ja`far remained silent, waiting for what his father would say next.

"However, don't let her dominate you like this. If you needed to be married to the Caliph's daughter, then you'd do it. Bear in mind that you're not just anyone."

Ja`far dearly wanted to tell his father that he was the one who had decided to be married to the halva-maker's daughter, but he did not dare.

"Of course, Father," he replied immediately. "You also promised me yesterday to think about the swordsmanship issue."

"Badr al-Jamali's son will never work as a halva-maker," Badr insisted. "That will never happen, neither in my lifetime nor thereafter. If the halva-maker's daughter is not happy with you, a member of the ruling family, then choose someone else."

"Of course, she'll be happy!" Ja`far replied quickly.

Badr looked deep into his son's eyes.

"It's only palace women who thwart caliphs," he went on. "The day you let your wife dominate you the way Egyptians do, you won't be Badr al-Jamali's son anymore."

"That'll never happen, Father. And I'm well aware of your affection and kindness towards my mother. You truly appreciated her, and sometimes... I mean, you never married another woman."

"That's different. Your mother was not like any other woman."

"Yes, of course," Ja`far replied, suppressing a grin.

He heard poets outside the palace, singing the praises of the prestigious Supreme Master:

What you have given is without precedent,

A pyramid with neither cube nor clatter,

In the quest for glory, you have surpassed them all;

After you, they are all followers.

I swear, Badr: Were all people to resort to you

And seek refuge, they would never lose.

Badr gave a smile and allowed the poet, `Alqa ibn `Abd al-Razzaq al-`Ulaimi, to kiss his hand, then ordered gifts for him.

CHAPTER TWENTY

Her ghost came at night. In his dream, she was blaming him for leaving her alone and then giving him a passionate kiss. She vanished, and he opened his eyes, not knowing whether it was a dream or reality. His head was crushed with pain, making him feel as though the end had finally come; he did not care. When he sat up, he saw her again. He reached out to touch her hand. This body of his was perfidious, but he was the one who was giving voice to the soul. How could the soul touch its companion without the body? He longed to have her body around him and hoped that, just once perhaps, he could embrace her as he had in the past. He could feel her soft limbs inside his chest and then smelled her scent and kissed her all over. Ah, Furoon, why did you come and leave so soon, like an angel or a fresh, gentle breeze? Ah, Furoon, for a love that recognises despair, for the certainty that accompanies departure! You're in paradise; that much is certain. But what's not so certain is whether he will join you there. You used to say, Furoon, that God's mercy is all-encompassing. Today, he needs that in order to carry on. His feet now feel heavy, and his breaths emerge only after a prolonged struggle with the heart. He could see the ghosts of his sons, Sha`baan and Al-Awhad. So, this was the end. The worst thing about loss is that it reveals the weakness of limbs and delicacy of the heart. Now he could not see her and touch her, nor quell the flames of need. Now he was like someone standing between two mountains, waiting for the flood that never came. Badr al-Jamali had not changed, even though he had lived a long life. His brain still functioned like the builders of palaces for ancient monarchs. Even his body had not been crippled by time the way the Caliph's body had. Egyptians still surrounded him, eager to touch his hand or kiss his shoulder. Mothers were still naming their sons Badr, and men still bowed down to him in respect. Life had proceeded, his body had let him down, and his heart could find no rest. He still aspired to the impossible, and now she was as far away as she had been for years. And yet her voice was still ringing in his ears, at that very moment when she had seen him after he had purchased her and come to see her. She had pronounced his name, as though she had achieved her every goal in the world. Ever since, she had turned his entire universe upside down. With her voice ringing in his ears, he closed his eyes. His head was still hurting him, as though the flow of blood in his heart's arteries had stopped. He had no idea how much time had passed when he heard his son, Abu l-Qasim, talking to him.

When he looked at his son, he could not understand. He opened his mouth to say that he felt fine, but could not do it. He cursed his tongue, his mouth, and his entire body. He banged on the wall, and Ja`far grabbed his hand.

"Father," he said, tears in his eyes. "Relax! Everything's fine. The doctor's on his way. He'll be here any minute..."

Badr pointed to his mouth and banged the wall again. The two brothers looked at each other. The doctor arrived and asked them both to leave, but Badr gestured to him to say something.

"My lord Amir," the doctor said. "You seem to be somewhat exhausted."

He was indeed exhausted; that much was certain. It was as if he had completed his final battle after the thrusts had penetrated every single part of his body. He heard the doctor tell Abu l-Qasim that his father had lost the ability to speak. That happened sometimes. The Amir—God preserve him!—was very old, and diseases were talking hold. He should avoid any strain or distress.

Even though the Supreme Master could no longer speak, the country was still his responsibility. He would never give that up until he died, nor would anyone else replace him or find out the particulars of its rule. Egypt was his desire, what he was living for. He started going out to meet his men; he would gesture to his son to speak on his behalf, listen carefully, and write down what he wanted him to say. His soldiers still bowed down to him in loyalty and obedience. He did not seem to be affected by what had happened, nor did his energy diminish or disappear. However, at night, he wanted to hear again the poetry that the Sicilian's grandson had recited many years earlier:

Within my three prisons I find myself confined,

Ask not about the murky message:

My faulty vision, confinement in my house,

And soul encased in an evil body.

Ah me, that evil and treacherous body! It had started playing games with him: sometimes it was losing the ability to speak, and at others it was a burning sensation in his knees. He would clasp them and long to sever them with his sword, at which point he would have an unbearable pain inside his head. What else could he lose, he wondered. Would he wake up the next day to discover that he was a rigid body lying on his bed, alive but motionless? Today, he prayed to God to die; deep inside, he longed for it. Betrayal erases life from the limbs, but bodily betrayal pits one part against another, the way Al-Awhad had betrayed him. He was destined to be betrayed by those sons and bodies that were a part of him. People will say that Badr is sad, but he does not get sad. They will say that Badr is weak, but he is not. If they say that Badr has surrendered his soul to his Lord, at that point he will have won.

As month followed month, the Caliph summoned Badr's son, Al-Afdal Shahanshah Abu l-Qasim, and had words with him.

"Badr al-Jamali's still running the country," the Caliph said, "when he can't even talk. That's not right. How can the Army Commander address his troops when he's like that? He's grown old now and needs to rest."

"My Lord," Abu l-Qasim responded dubiously. "As long as my father's alive, he'll never rest."

"Don't misunderstand me," the Caliph went on. "I've no desire to be rid of him, nor can I. I want you to take his place, Abu l-Qasim, and to take over from this moment on."

"I'll ask him," Abu l-Qasim replied after a moment's pause. "Then I'll give you an answer."

Abu l-Qasim told his father timidly, and his father listened. He looked at his son, then lowered his head, raised his hand, and gestured to him to be careful.

"I understand, Father," Abu l-Qasim said.

Badr shook his head, then asked for paper and pencil.

"You're my successor," he wrote, "but you'll need all my power and more. Al-Mustansir will do his best to lessen your sway. Don't give him the chance. You can take over while I'm still alive, but you'll first consult me about everything, and I mean *everything*. Don't get the idea that Badr doesn't know what's going on around him."

"Everything," Abu l-Qasim replied, bending over and kissing his father's hand.

"God decides what's before and after," Badr told himself, as he put his hand on his son's head. "I'm well aware that I'm not going to last out the year."

Every night since Furoon had died, he had heard her voice echoing in his ears.

"Let me love you today the way I've always wished in my dreams, you handsomest man in all creation."

How was it possible for a woman to belong to paradise while still on earth? Why had destiny willed that he meet Furoon?

No one could take on the Supreme Commander's functions. His energy was not diminished even if his body had let him down, finally submitting. The human body is deceitful from birth till death, but the powerful spirit can subdue and defeat it. Al-Afdal gave Ja`far a confused look. He had no idea how to convince his father that he would need help in climbing the mountain. He was behind his father, almost propping him up, but not succeeding. Badr was leaning heavily on his cane, his breathing audible to every Egyptian. Today, he was expecting them all, eager perhaps to see them for one last time.

"Father," Ja`far told his father gently, "hold my hand. I can scarcely climb this mountain myself."

Badr frowned at him and gestured with his hand as though to say: "Go away, you fool. I know your tricks!"

He could get to his mosque without even opening his eyes. He knew the way, every single rock; he could stumble to it. He could see her right in front of him. All around him were scenes of slaughter, but this scene was not like any slaughter; this wound was like no other. Even though her chest was covered in blood, she was smiling. How could hatred be so scared of having Furoon so close? What had she managed to do with the devil of her own beloved self?

"My beloved," she had whispered to him, "don't kill too many people for my sake."

But today, Furoon, you yourself have been slaughtered. How could he not kill masses of people when death filled every corner of his life? He stretched out his hand to lean on the rock. One more step, and he would reach the summit. The rock split apart in his hand, but he reached the top. He almost fell flat on his face, and Ja`far grabbed him. Badr pushed him away, stood up, and looked straight in front of him. Today was an appointment between him and the people of Egypt, here at his mosque on the mountain. He wanted to meet and know them, remembering them all by heart—every child, man, halva-maker, baker, grocer, fruitmonger, peasant, Bedouin, and soldier in his army. All those faces had now become friends and family, faces that would stay in the memory with life's lines around the eyes and a powerful, sad smile in times of hardship. They had all come, just as they had promised.

Ja`far looked around him, his eyes open wide in amazement. Since the day he was born, he had never witnessed such a gathering. It was like the Day of Resurrection. People covered the entire mountain, and then there were thousands upon thousands more at the base. They all wanted to greet the Supreme Master.

"Do you see what I'm seeing?" Ja`far asked his brother.

"Yes," Al-Afdal replied with a smile. "Don't worry. They love him. Love comes from God."

Badr raised his hand to greet them all. They tossed branches and flowers at him; some of them managed to reach him, others did not. But he saw, yes, he saw flowers scattered to the heavens like heavenly processions. They all shouted his name and then recited the Qur'anic verse: 'God came to your aid at Badr.' {Qur'an, Sura 3 (Al-`Imran), v. 123]

He and the Egyptian people had had this rendezvous for twenty years or more. He had come at the right moment and had not broken his promise.

"The Supreme Master!" they yelled at the top of their voices.

His eyes glazed over a bit, and he could see the crowd that was shouting his name fused together—Sicilian, Armenian, and Egyptian on the mountaintop. Now he could see more clearly: this people would never come to an end, even if his own vision diminished and words were cut off. He could see them all in his heart and watch as clouds spun around them in perfect circles. Some colours might fade, and trees and flowers might vanish, but he could still transform them into a gigantic pile, like the Pyramid rocks that were never-ending, no matter how many foreigners took some away. Amid all the din, he could see the pillars of Ahmad ibn Tulun's mosque visible below the mountain, as obvious to him as the tombs of the ancients, surviving forever just as he would. What would Egyptians be saying about Badr al-Jamali after a year or two, he wondered. Would they still remember? There was a lot that he wanted to tell them. If he had the time, he was eager to sit down with each of them individually, telling them about the sorrow that follows victory, the weakness that results from a son's betrayal, and the passion that follows loss. But they knew; they had to know. Did not Ahmad ibn Tulun talk to them before? Even if they had forgotten, the very pillars of his mosque would remind them—the same destiny, the same sorrow.

"He's our Shaikh," Badr heard some of them shout. "This is his mausoleum. Badr, Shaikh and Scholar. Badr, Supreme Master. Badr, God's gift to us!"

He looked at his mosque and then at the place where her body was buried, while her spirit was ever with him. He looked up into the heavens. She had always waited for the moon to appear so she could compare it with Badr. Furoon...

He looked all around the mountain, and then turned in the direction of the Pyramids. He could not see it from where he was, but he knew that she could hear him, Bahnas, the Pyramid Witch, even if he could no longer speak.

"Pyramid Witch, don't talk to me about love, the way it can inflame wounds and enlighten the spirit. Like the spirits of the ancients, Badr al-

Jamali's spirit will remain, towering on legs as high as the heavens, a body that is both tall and upright, and arms carrying sword and spear. Make sure you do not measure me by age; life will always come to an end, but the heart will never surrender. Today, tomorrow, and thereafter, Bahnas, remember that the lover's heart lives on even if the body dies away.

He turned to gaze down at the Ahmad ibn Tulun mosque...

Ahmad ibn Tulun, your path was easier than mine and your burden was lighter. Tell me what you felt. Ibn Tulun, our destinies have coincided, as though our souls have an appointment to meet! I wonder, what were we searching for: a homeland, the ancients, or to preserve the land and gold? Can you hear me, Ahmad ibn Tulun, Abu al-`Abbas? I'm speaking to you from atop the mountain. My voice is just one of the things that I've lost. If my burden was heavier than yours, my son more wretched than yours, and my life that much harder than yours, was all that because my triumph was greater than yours, I wonder? Now here I am in quest of sword, assistance, and distinction, even in moments when souls are conversing. Forgive me, my friend. We may well have met in the framework of sorrow and love of Egypt. We both took hold of the country, but I grabbed the whole framework. Both of us tried to gather it all in our hands, but I'm the one who lapped it up and swallowed it whole. You and I, we both stared at the Sphinx on the horizon. I wonder, was it looking at us? What is so frightening about this statue? I was just as lofty, and so was the Sicilian, and so were you. Come now, Ibn Tulun, and I'll tell you about the sorrow that accompanies victory, the defeat that accompanies power, and the weakness that accompanies passion. Ah, now the Sicilian is joining us. Welcome to you, Jawhar the Sicilian! Come here and talk to us about time, the state, men...and Egypt!

THE END—GOD BE PRAISED!

ON THE MARGIN OF HISTORY:

Badr al-Jamali ruled Egypt for twenty-one years. When he died, he had left in the country's treasury six thousand thousand dinars, four thousand thousand dirhams, and a lot of jewellery. Following his death, he left a thousand emeralds that he had collected from all over the country.

Badr al-Jamali divided Egypt up into twenty-three provinces or districts, whereas they had previously been divided into more than a thousand villages. His division is still maintained in large part to this day.

Badr al-Jamali bequeathed the minister's post to his son, Al-Afdal Shshanshah Abu l-Qasim (Muhammad). He used his influence to obtain the caliphate for Ahmad, the Caliph Al-Musa`il, his sister's son, grandson of Badr al-Jamali, rather than for the eldest son, Nizar, resulting in the emergence of the renowned Assassins movement.

Al-Afdal Shahanshah ruled Egypt justly and mercifully as Minister of Sword and Pen for twenty-seven years until the Assassins managed to kill him after several attempts. It took forty days to transfer the treasure that he left behind to the caliph's palace.

Ja`far al-Muzaffar, Badr and Furoon's son, lived in the palace in the Al-Burjuwan quarter for several years, helping his brother govern. Then information about him stops. It is most likely that he left the government and went back to Zubaida in Alexandria to devote himself to halva making. He left behind the palace in the quarter.

Badr al-Jamali restored and rebuilt Ahmad ibn Tulun's mosque, it being from the outset a Sunni mosque, not a Shi`i one. He had a mihrab niche built inside it and left his name there.

Badr al-Jamali left his name all over Egypt: the Jamaliyya quarter, Army Commander Street, and the three of Cairo's gates that still bear witness to his era and have his name carved into their stone: Bab al-Futuh, Bab al-Nasr, and Bab Zuweila. We pass through them every single day, and they remind us of what was.

The Juyushi Mosque contains the first Fatimid minaret in its complete, original form. It is the first mosque in Egypt to be built of stone. The reason why Badr al-Jamali chose to build this mosque on the top of the Muqattam Hills, in a place so difficult to reach, is not clear to historians. Unless, that is, Badr al-Jamali had some more profound reason and was indulging in more complex thinking than all subsequent historians have understood.

He restored and built. Every time he waged war, fell in love, or was sad, he built. The ʿAttarin Mosque in Alexandria still has the marble plaque that bears his name. The Emari Mosque in Esna still exists, and the mosque atop the Muqattam Hills continues to bear witness to Egypt as a whole, hovering on high over Cairo and Egypt. It is also perhaps a reminder of the way the crowds came out to salute the man who had saved the country from the drought and hunger that had lasted more than seven years. Egyptians recall the Armenian who adopted the country as his homeland, melted into its sands, and vanished amid its columns, finding a final refuge among the rocks of the Muqattam Hills.

THE THIRD STORY

THE KURD

Make your passion pure, and your goal your primary focus.

Bahnas, the Pyramid Witch

"At last, `Amm `Abdo, you're going to talk about Saladin!"

"It's as though you haven't been following the story all the way through. I'm talking about Egypt, not kings and sultans. I'm telling you about halva and the people who eat it..."

"Did Saladin like halva?"

"Not to begin with."

"What do you mean?"

"Do you know about his relationship with Ibrahim the Sicilian?"

"Badr al-Jamali's grandson, or Jawhar the Sicilian's?"

"Badr al-Jamali, Jawhar the Sicilian, and all Egyptians. The halva-maker. I'll tell you about Ibrahim and Yusuf ibn Ayyub, the man known as Saladin."

"If the Sicilian was the sesame oil," I said, like a student who's memorised the lesson by heart, "and the Armenian was the saffron, and the Egyptian was the flour and sugar, then who was the Kurd?"

"Now you're starting to understand," he replied with a smile. "The Kurd was like musk—the end of one era and the beginning of another. He arrived at a time when no soul was safe from mutilation and no body from contempt. However, he was able to impose his particular scent on the rest of time. Like Badr al-Jamali, he lived as a warrior and died a Sufi. This land of Egypt does not let any of its rulers die in peace. They must savour the bitter taste of victory and the pain of success. Then their features will soften, old age will desert their hearts, and they'll crawl on their knees like one of Pharaoh's priests. My daughter, I've no idea what Egypt would have become without the two of them and without others as well. Maybe you don't understand the secret of Fatimid halva and how important it was. Maybe your daughter has sent you to learn."

BOOK ONE

My daughter, here you can see perfect craftsmanship and careful living.

'Amm 'Abdo, the man possessed.

CHAPTER ONE

562 AH / 1167 CE

Alexandria.

He was behind him, the foreigner whose arrival he had been anticipating and expecting. It was easy to mark him out from people in Alexandria. Neither his clothes, nor his appearance, nor even the way he was walking suggested that he was from here. Ibrahim expected the foreigner to come at dawn; people like him did not sleep a lot. He did not know precisely if the man had a particular task of his own to perform or had been compelled to do something. Ibrahim did not look at him. He dried his body, then put on his trousers and gallabiyya. Swimming in the sea at dawn was a habit he had inherited from his father. Following his father's death, it had become a matter of intimacy and memory. When the sands meshed with the sun and the droplets of water with the stars, then everything seemed possible—even for Ibrahim the halva-maker to carry weapons in face of the Caliph's army.

Ibrahim sat cross-legged on the sand, and the man continued walking until he was standing right in front of him.

"Ibrahim, son of the Sicilian," the man said with a frown, "I've been looking for you, for you alone. And that's been as hard, Brother, as fighting the Crusaders."

"But now you've found me," Ibrahim replied. "You knew when to find me alone. Is that because you want to get rid of me today, or to force me into imminent destruction?"

"You're the grandson of Jawhar the Sicilian, the greatest of all generals. Don't be surprised; we all know of him. Even though he's not from the same sect as me, we must bow down before the great wherever they are."

"Yusuf, I'm just a halva-maker. I'm no good when it comes to fighting wars or government intrigues."

"So, you know my name?"

"You were looking for me, so I was looking for you as well, Yusuf ibn Ayyub, commonly known as Salah ad-din al-Ayyubi. You are a soldier in the Syrian army, the armed forces of your uncle, Asad ad-din Shirkuh. Needless to say, I asked about you and discovered everything. You're my age, or maybe a year or two younger. I think you're not yet thirty. What's brought you to the seaside?"

"If you know my name, then you'll also know what's brought me here."

"We have no weapons, Brother. I'm just a halva-maker with no experience of war. I know nothing about the Minister. I've never set eyes on the Caliph even though I pray for him every day. I can assure you of that."

"I've read about the people of Alexandria," Salah ad-din Yusuf ibn Ayyub said in all seriousness. "And I've come here rather than elsewhere. They have no fear in their hearts, and no adventure can scare them. They will shout in the face of banal futility. It is hard to gain control of their free spirits. Even `Amr ibn al-`As encountered opposition from the city once or twice. However, there's a huge difference between `Amr and the Crusaders. What I want from you today, Brother, is to agree to resist the Crusaders."

"What exactly do you want from the halva-maker?"

"I want the Alexandrians," Salah ad-din Yusuf ibn Ayyub replied. "I want them to support Amir Nur ad-din Mahmud az-Zengi. I'm a soldier in his army and so is my uncle. All he wants is a victory for the Muslim people, no more and no less. Your Minister wants the Crusaders to enter Egypt. Isn't it enough that they've already captured Jerusalem? Which minister in a Muslim country wants his country to suffer what the Crusaders did to Jerusalem: entering the city, shedding blood, and cutting off food supplies? I don't need to tell you. Alexandrians get information from the world over. Have travellers and passers-by told you, Brother, about the way Crusaders have been shedding blood?"

"Egypt isn't Jerusalem."

"For people, days mean different regimes. Halva is no use, Brother, to someone who's lost the sense of taste because the Crusaders have cut out his tongue. I've come here to you with a particular charge, and I've also come in quest of a close, brotherly relationship."

Ibrahim opened his mouth.

"Don't tell me that the Alexandrians don't have weapons," Yusuf ibn Ayyub insisted. "I've seen the weapons market for myself, and it's larger than any I've ever set eyes on. You all own weapons and men. But even before any of that, there's you. You, Ibrahim, own far more than that, since you have the hearts of the citizens of Alexandria. I'm aware of that, too. They all know your father and your history, and they respect you and appreciate everything you do. Help me, and you'll be helping the whole of Egypt, Syria, and Iraq. And, after a while, Jerusalem itself."

"May God do good! Give me the chance to talk to the shaikhs."

"This is about weapons and men," Yusuf replied. "It's also about family connections."

"I've two sisters who've been married for years," Ibrahim said. "What connections are you talking about, Brother?"

"You have a niece living with you now. She hasn't been married yet."

"Do you mean Rashida?" Ibrahim asked apprehensively, his eyes open wide. "I swear to you, I wouldn't want her for the Crusader King himself."

There was silence.

"People have told you that Ibrahim's honest," Ibrahim went on, "and that's why Alexandrians love him. She's not right for you, Brother. If you've come here to join forces, then look for another woman. In my entire life, I've never encountered a woman who can generate so much strife and division as she can. She's a trial for all of us."

"Marriage can be a training, Brother. It can teach the girl."

"Yes indeed, it can teach a girl who wants to improve herself. But not one who relishes sorrow all around her and goes for defeat so that she can be the winner. Forget about her. May God give me the power to see her married to a man who can manage to control the trouble she causes and endure her scourge."

Rashida was an unmitigated disaster that had fallen on Ibrahim's head during a time replete with danger and fierce tempests, with pouring rain like savage winter waves that would often invade the cellars of his house in Kom Waara. When he was a child, he could remember the waves crashing over the rocks and banging into the wood. He would scream, and his father, who had leapt to his feet in anticipation and understanding, would hear him. Winter waves were not dangerous, even when they would leave their traces on the wood and rock. His colour would change, and his heart would fill with ice. He did not know why his father, `Abd al-Hamid, was so concerned when the waves came into the cellars and soaked every house in the port. What was so frightening about the sea's waves? You could anticipate when they would initiate their assault. But, when it came to Rashida, that attack knew no bounds. All this had started some time ago. He had heard the tale from his father, but he could not believe it. His father said that women's jealousy could obscure realities and distort history, but he had lived with evil and adapted to it after a while. The two brothers—`Abd al-Hamid, Ibrahim's father, and `Abd al-Wadud, Rashida's father—had inherited the halva factories and stores belonging to their grandfather, Jawhar, son of Husain, son of Jawhar the Sicilian.

The elder brother had been married to the daughter of a merchant in Cairo. She was spoiled and greedy, but she had managed to take possession of first his heart and then his mind. She proceeded to extend her grip to his entire will; he would not make any decision without first consulting her. Not a single pound of flour could be sold without Kauthar's permission. The festival doughnuts no longer followed the schedule of the birthdays of saints and the Prophet; now they had to follow the desires of Kauthar, `Abd al-Wadud's wife. If she decided that that day was a festival, then the halva-maker would start making doughnuts and distributing halva horses. The entire world was transformed and drawn forcefully to Kauthar. But then it all fell apart. Laila, Ibrahim's mother, said that Kauthar must have bewitched her husband. For ten whole years, she had not given birth, but, ten years after that, she gave birth to her daughter, Rashida. She kept the daughter in a tower constructed of rocks and fixed posts. Rashida now became her father's whole life. The younger brother, `Abd al-Hamid, was angry about the way his brother was being dominated by his wife. He decided to go to Alexandria and sell his share of the stores to his other brother, `Abd al-Wadud, for a very low price. He opened the halva factory in Alexandria in exactly the same place as his grandfather, Jawhar, son of Husain, son of Jawhar the Sicilian. He settled there with his wife and children. He still loved his brother, but `Abd al-Wadud became jealous as `Abd al-Hamid had expected, because he, `Abd al-Hamid, was more independent than necessary, and that did not please Kauthar. So `Abd al-Hamid got angry with his brother and shunned him. When the brothers died, one after the other, the two wives refused to meet, even as part of the farewell for the two brothers. The younger brother, Ibrahim's father, was the first to die. Ibrahim was twenty years old at the time, and after that Ibrahim became the father and head of family. Then the elder brother, Rashida's father, died two years ago.

When `Abd al-Wadud died, his daughter Rashida went out to work just like a man. She totally dominated her mother, Kauthar. The whole world rose up against the two of them and did not subside. She started sowing discord among halva-makers, setting up spies, and turning brother against brother, shattering all unity and stoking fires. She started a fierce clash with `Abd al-Tawwab, her father's assistant, who had been trained by the grandfather in person. He was one of the most loyal halva-makers in Cairo and Egypt as a whole. She started by humiliating and belittling him, then poked fun at him. `Abd al-Tawwab put up with it out of loyalty to her father. Then Rashida decided to be married to Jawwad, the wheat-porter. She announced her engagement and gave Jawwad both authority and power. He proceeded to cause chaos all around him, ordering people about and making decisions. He had an argument with `Abd al-Tawwab and slapped the man hard in front of everyone passing by. `Abd al-Tawwab burst into tears, and every single halva-maker in Egypt came out, planning to kill Jawwad the wheat-porter and his wife Rashida, as well. People asked the men in Rashida's family, her cousins, for help. The eldest was Ibrahim, who was loved by everyone. He was honest and just, and, when rights were at stake, he feared no censure. They all went to Alexandria and asked him to take charge of his niece, Rashida, or else they would kill her. People were no longer living in an era when this kind of annoyance and humiliation would be tolerated. If he could not control her behavior, he should not be annoyed by what they intended to do. For the very first time, Ibrahim heard threats from the halva-makers and violence in their tone of voices. He ordered his men to go to Cairo and bring back Kauthar and her daughter, Rashida. He then threatened the wheat-porter and banished him. This had happened two months earlier, and he had not slept since. Every night, every hour, disasters kept crashing down on his head. He started feeling giddy and longed for a way out. He had never expected one woman to cause so much destruction in just two months, but, like her mother, she was capable of a lot, and perhaps even more. He needed to marry her off quickly, but not to Yusuf ibn Ayyub. He did not deserve that.

Some weeks earlier, Rashida had insisted on meeting the man, but Ibrahim had stopped her coming in. He had put her and her mother in a wing as far removed from his own room as possible. Today, she neither stopped nor hesitated. As soon as the sun appeared, she opened the door to his room; he was still in bed.

"No good can come from injustice, Cousin," she said firmly.

"Have you lost your mind?" he replied, staring at her in shock.

"This could not be avoided," she said, not looking at him directly. "You've refused to see me on several occasions."

"Get out! I'll see you this afternoon. Leave!"

"I'm not moving," she said.

She closed the door, then sat.

"Open the door," he yelled at her. "Didn't your mother teach you anything?"

"Yes, she's taught me a lot. But you're making decisions for me, taking my money, and separating me from my fiancé. That doesn't make anyone happy."

He just looked at her and did not say anything.

"Jawwad is the very best of men," she went on. "He's the one I want as a husband. There's nothing bad, Cousin, about someone being poor. He'll be responsible for my money, not you. If you don't let me go back to Cairo, then I'm going to complain to the Shaikh in the Attarin Mosque, the one in the

Thousand Columns Mosque, and every shaikh in Alexandria."

"Your words frighten me," he said, placing his hand over his heart and stretching out in bed. "You enter my room while I'm still asleep, close the door, and start threatening me. If I put you in prison today, no one would blame me. You're going to stay here, Rashida, until I can find a husband who deserves you. That is all we have to say to each other."

"What right do you have to take my money?"

"Because you're not capable of looking after it," he replied firmly.

Their eyes met.

"Ibrahim, my cousin," she said in a slinky tone, "I'm fully capable of getting my money back and looking after what my father left me. If you don't give me what's rightfully mine, then I'll take it anyway. But I feel sorry for you when I think of what I'm capable of doing."

He looked at her with a laugh. She was a lot shorter than him, a bit plump, and had gentle features. If it were not for the sparks flying out of her eyes, she might even be beautiful in her silken hairnet and white gown embellished with pure silver.

"Do you need any money," he asked sarcastically, "to buy fabrics or silver?"

"I don't need to take any money from you. It's all mine."

"Leave the room, Rashida," he told her, looking down. "Don't do this again. If your wedding's postponed, that may be because people know you. But don't worry, I'll find a husband who deserves you. However, it seems your mother hasn't taught you not to be alone with men and not to enter a man's room."

"You don't need to teach me," she replied defiantly, staring at him without shame. "I can take care of myself."

She stood up and opened the door.

"He who warns is excused..." she said.

With that, she left and slammed the door.

Women hurried to their rooms, and men shuddered. These days, everything was confusion; no one knew who was fighting whom. The Fatimid Caliph, Imam Al-'Adid li-din Allah, was asking King Nur ad-din Zengi from Syria for help to save him from his tyrannical Minister, Shawar, who was himself asking the Crusaders for support. The Egyptian people were as divided as the Fatimid army. Some of them followed Shawar, while others supported the Caliph and Imam, Al-'Adid. Still others supported the Syrian army and King Nur ad-din Zengi and his Commander, Asad ad-din Shirkuh. Minister Shawar's influence increased, and the walls of Cairo tightened around the Caliph and Imam Al-'Adid. He did not leave his palace and could only move when Minister Shawar gave his permission. He did not choose his destiny and had no desire to face defeat, and yet he could see it all around him. Today, Shawar was in charge and committing outrage after outrage. This was not a war between Sunni and Shi'i, nor was it a conflict between the Abbasid Caliph in Baghdad and the Fatimid Caliph in Egypt. This was a war to retain power, and, when that was the case, there was a need to seek powerful help. The Fatimid Caliph Al-'Adid went to see Nur ad-din Zengi to ask him for help in saving him from his Minister Shawar. Those days, there was nothing to be said against seeking help from a probable enemy. Nur ad-din dispatched his General and Kurdish Aamir Asad ad-din Shirkuh to Egypt, and Asad ad-din took with him his young nephew, Salah ad-din Yusuf ibn Ayyub. That was not the first time; they had been visiting Egypt for several years. However, this was not like previous times: the Minister Shawar was now getting help from the Crusaders in order to do battle with the Caliph Al-'Adid and his allies, Nur ad-din, Asad ad-din Shirkuh, and his nephew, Salah ad-din Yusuf ibn Ayyub.

When the Syrian army under the command of Asad ad-din Shirkuh reached Egypt, the General did some research and understood. Alexandria was both the key and the solution. The people there were Shafi'i Sunnis, and their rebellions had always been the most effective. Had they not rebelled against the Abbasids? Had they not overturned every conqueror throughout history? The city's people were just as sturdy, ferocious, and courageous as the waves of the sea. Asad ad-din sent his young nephew Yusuf to the city. He was both a friend and a stranger. He was dispatched to talk to the people and their leaders, and to discover their inclinations and desires. Today, he would go to the Mosque of a Thousand Columns in Kom Waala, and tomorrow he might go to the Attarin Mosque, but he was hesitating...

"If it's Alexandrians you want," Ibrahim told him clearly, "then let's go to the Attarin Mosque."

"It was built by Badr al-Jamali," Yusuf said.

"If your problem is with Islamic sects, Brother, then we won't be able to fight. Alexandrians are Shafi`i Sunnis. But you'll have to be careful when you speak. Egyptian affections are like no other. They adore the Prophet's family, and they revere Badr al-Jamali."

"But..."

"One day, you'll understand. We'll head for the Attarin Mosque and talk to Shaikh Zaidun ibn Qasim. He'll be able to get people to come and talk to you. He's a friend and brother. He remembers that Badr al-Jamali built the mosque in Alexandria even when the city was in revolt. He built and did not destroy. He didn't require that the mosque be for Shi`is and no one else."

Ibrahim had not enjoyed his youth. He'd made do with watching his brothers play, have fun, and occasionally drink wine. Even though his brother Salim was only two years younger than him, he still loved the world and its delights, hoarding enough money to buy slave girls and listen to singing on the shore. His brother Sadiq, who was three years younger, preferred to be married. He had been married before his twentieth birthday, and now he was loyal to his wife and had a number of children. Yusuf ibn Ayyub joined them, but not in his capacity as a Syrian army soldier, but rather as a brother and friend. He started spending his nights in their company: sometimes, he would go to the shore with them, listen to the singing, and drink a little wine. Like them, he was a young man, his expression full of hope, optimism, and a little sorrow, since he had not been born in another era, one that showed more mercy. Ibrahim would watch from a distance, standing by the shore, hands on hips, listening to the men's laughter and jokes. Ever since his father had died, he had not told any jokes, enjoyed a laugh, drunk wine, or listened to the singing of slave girls. He examined Yusuf closely and saw a brother just like his own. People were saying that he was a Kurd, from a country close to Badr al-Jamali's. Maybe that was why he saw in the man a cousin and support.

Next morning, they prayed together, and then had cautious conversations with the people. Shawar's men were filling the mosques, spying on Alexandrians in particular and frightening them. It was much better and safer to meet in Ibrahim's house.

Rashida told her slave girl to offer halva to the assembled company, to listen to the conversation, and to report back exactly what happened. She needed to know everything about her enemy. She had a secret sense of blood pulsing in her limbs as though her body were getting ready for combat. It was a feeling she enjoyed, just like love itself, or maybe even more profound and effective. But then, love was just delusion and humbug, like the Pyramid Witch, neither staying nor building. But Rashida's magic was going to destroy Ibrahim's life. That much was certain.

Zubaida the slave girl entered the room to offer them juices and halva, and she lingered to listen to what the men were saying. She put a glass of juice in front of Yusuf ibn Ayyub. Her heart throbbed, and she looked into his eyes. When he smiled at her, she was glued to the spot and almost burst into tears, so intense was the unexpected feeling. Could a slave girl fall in love? With who? A soldier from Syria? She knew nothing about him.

"Go back to your mistress," Ibrahim told her firmly. "Don't come back here. Send one of my mother's slave girls."

She nodded and ran out of the room. When Rashida asked her what had happened, Zubaida burst into tears.

"Why are you crying?" Rashida asked. "Did Ibrahim tell you off?"

"No, my Lady. But I'll never see the Syrian again."

"Yusuf ibn Ayyub?"

"Yes, he's..."

"Have you lost your mind, Zubaida? Don't let weakness sap your energy and snap your bones as though they're rotting away. Love's a disaster, a disease."

"I don't have your strength and resolve, my lady."

"Those feelings come from the body, not the heart. Believe me; my mother's told me everything. The body's lecherous and misleads the heart. But there's nothing in this world called love. It's all a matter of relationships with benefits of give and take, no more. We glamourise them because we like to lie, and cultivate them because we crave our own advancement. Do you follow me?"

"No, I don't, my lady."

"No matter. Forget about Yusuf ibn Ayyub. Now, tell me what happened in detail."

Voices were raised in mosques, encouraging Alexandrians to rebel against the Fatimid Minister. As Ibrahim put it: even the Caliph himself had resorted to King Nur ad-din Zengi in Syria.

"Alexandrians do not like to be humiliated and tyrannised. Minister Shawar must be removed. If the Crusaders enter Alexandria, then it is all over for Egypt."

CHAPTER TWO

Inside this Alexandrian house, the cramped feeling oozed out of the gaps in the stones. Her lips pursed, Rashida stared sorrowfully at the different areas of the house. How could this house compare with the houses in Cairo, which were well-lit, beautifully decorated, and shimmering with the rivers of paradise and the squares of freedom? This city was not like Cairo, that was certain. She could not recall ever having visited Alexandria. If things went as she was planning and hoping, then this would be the first and last time. Here, the sea seemed to control both people and city. Sometimes, they looked forward to greeting it, but, at others, they were as scared of it as they were of the jinn. Even with that fear, the sea still sent its waters seeping into every room in the house. The sturdy arched wooden door did not allow any air to enter the house, and the three-story stone structure had wooden windows painted a dark colour, its parts carefully constructed so as not to let in even a puff of air during the cold winter or the splashes from rogue waves. Even the courtyard on the third floor was covered with cracked wood and had no fountain or greenery. Here in Alexandria, people loved colours, especially white and blue. They appreciated only hues that glared, just like their other tastes and ethical principles. How often had she heard men shouting and women arguing, with no mashrabiya like the ones in Cairo houses and no delicate colours as reflections of subtlety, coyness, and a generous dose of cunning. The gentle burble of fountains she could recognise and expect; they would always provide a sense of peace and a specific function. But the sea's waves would come crashing in without restraint; sometimes, they would be calm, but, at others, they would invade the house's basement and flood it. And, if it happened to encounter a head leaning out of a window, it would remind that person of its power and control of both land and rocks.

She would not be staying here for very long. Why was Ibrahim himself not begging her to leave and go back to her home and factory in Cairo? She would never forgive herself. That day, when she woke up, she summoned Zubaida, her slave girl, and asked for milk and eggs. She would only wake up early when she was going to work on a secret project; the only time she would eat breakfast was when her project had been successful. This house consisted of twenty rooms. Ibrahim and his sisters lived there, as did Sadiq and his wife; Salim and his younger brother, Husain; his sister, Kamila; and her husband, Sufyan. For some reason unknown to Rashida, he had also invited his sister, Shafiqa, who was married to a Turkish general and lived in Cairo the blessed, the city of the Imam and Caliph. Rashida knew Shafiqa; she had visited her before in Cairo. A calm and peaceable woman, she desired only good for everyone. Rashida would get to know Ibrahim's mother better, even though her own mother, Kauthar, did not like her. She claimed that she was always jealous of her own beauty and wealth. Those people who make plans understand first, and then they know.

Within a month, Rashida had control of the men and women inside the house, except, that is, for Ibrahim. Ibrahim had five siblings, two girls and three boys: Salim, Sadiq, and Husain. Salim and Sadiq were both completely under Ibrahim's thumb. Husain however was different; he was defiant and obstreperous. As the youngest brother, Husain was the one closest to her heart, modest and loyal. But, faced with Ibrahim's domineering attitude, Husain would cave in and fade away. Why did he let Ibrahim dictate everything? Why was Ibrahim the one to decide how much halva to make and what kind, and to come to agreements with the merchants and amirs? Why had Husain's function as brother been reduced to that of a cane to lean on when Ibrahim felt tired, just that and nothing else? Treating the spirit like a cane was a habit of Ibrahim's.

For an hour or two, Rashida explained things to Husain. She gave him some examples of Ibrahim's bullying behaviour towards her and him and planted some doubt in his ear. Who knows, maybe it was greed that motivated Ibrahim. Why did people have such complete trust in a person whose inner self was all piety and debauchery? If Ibrahim had got his hands on her money, then he would certainly steal from his own brother's money as well. But, when she said that, Husain's eyes opened wide in shock. He asked her to stop talking.

"My brother doesn't steal, Rashida," he told her firmly. "My brother bears the burden of responsibility for history and ancient glory, and he defends it. If it weren't for him, we would not have been successful here, and the Sicilian family would not have maintained its dominance of the halva trade in Cairo and all Egypt."

"My brother," Rashida replied, "there are times when good intentions turn into revenge rather than blessing. I'm sure he means well for our family, but that isn't stopping him from controlling money that's in my name. He's also preventing me from being married to a loyal and decent man simply because he thinks the man's greedy. Those are the kinds of decisions that tyrants make, not family members. It also doesn't stop him erasing your very existence, even though, if he gave you the chance, you'd be able to shine. Tell me, Husain, has he ever asked you if, for example, you'd like to open a store in Dimyat? Has he ever asked you to give some thought to a new kind of halva? Just tell me, and don't let your feelings for your brother blind your vision. Leave love to one side and think about yourself. Why haven't you been married till now? No, no, don't say it... I'm sure that you've wanted to get married, but he's refused."

Husain's mouth fell open in shock.

"You've wanted to get married," Rashida went on with a victorious smile, "and he told you she wasn't suitable, that she was poor. Isn't that right?"

"Rashida..."

"Can't you see, Brother? I've told you to open your eyes. Just think about everything he's done to you, everything he's done. I swear to you that I'm not looking for a fight between you and your brother. I just want you to demand your rights. If he refuses, then you'll realise the truth about him."

"He's the best possible brother," Husain responded at once, "and the best friend."

"The human heart always prompts evil. If you get the chance, tell him when he's wrong. Wasn't it the Caliph 'Umar ibn al-Khattab—God be pleased with him!—who said 'Can a woman be right and 'Umar wrong'?"

"Rashida..."

"Ibrahim's someone who can be right and wrong. Brother, do you ever dare say 'no'? Do you dare object? Your brother's hurling us into the abyss, treating Minister Shawar as an enemy. He realises that that's the end for us. He's making friends with the foreigner, Yusuf ibn Ayyub, even though he's operating under the command of the Syrian, Nur ad-din Zengi. Zengi will still be an enemy of the Caliph, even if he pretends to be a friend at the moment. He's Sunni and the Caliph's Shi`i. My brother—"

"I don't understand government matters. I can't tell the difference between Shawar, Zengi, and Caliphs. I'm a halva-maker, just like my ancestors."

"But your brother's hurled you into those issues of government. Defeat is inevitable. One day, you'll realise that I'm right and God has sent me to you because you're the hope for this family. My only hope is that you'll look into your brother's attitude toward helping this Yusuf ibn Ayyub, known as Salah ad-din. Syrian rulers can't be trusted, whether they're Turks or Kurds. You know that, and so do I. Think about it and tell the truth. Your mother's Shi`i, even though you're Sunni like your father."

"My mother obeys my brother, Rashida. He's all she sees."

"Precisely! He's all she sees, even though she has other children. Do you suppose you're less intelligent or rational than he is?"

"You—"

"Don't curse me! You're my brother, and I only want the best for you. Just give it some thought. If what I'm telling you is wrong, then rub it out the way cities are obliterated, as though it had never existed."

Hard work will always produce positive results. She was no longer sleeping, but making plans day and night. She went to see Ibrahim's mother and sat down beside her. She told her that she wanted to go with her to visit the shrine of Sayyida Nafisa; all God's saints were to be found in Cairo and Egypt. She went on to say that Yusuf ibn Ayyub was paying daily visits to her son and urging him as a Sunni to rebel against Minister Shawar. In the end, he would be the one to choose which sect to follow, and there was no way that Yusuf could be loyal to the Fatimid Caliph and Imam. How could Yusuf be loyal to two Caliphs at once—the Caliph in Baghdad and the other in Cairo?"

"But it's the Caliph himself who's asked Amir Nur ad-din Zengi for help," Ibrahim's mother responded gently. "As a result, General Asad ad-din

Shirkuh has been sent here from Syria, along with his young nephew, Yusuf ibn Ayyub. Yusuf's working for the Caliph now; that's why he's come here."

"Which Caliph do you mean, Aunt?"

"The one who's asked him to come here, Imam Al-'Adid. Shawar's a traitor. He's asked the Crusaders to help him, and we all know what they're doing in the country."

"Shawar doesn't want the Crusaders to enter the country, Aunt."

"All this talk is beyond me, my daughter, and I don't understand it. Ibrahim's the one who knows it all."

"Ibrahim's the one who knows it all," Rashida repeated hatefully, and then muttered, "and he's going to drown us all."

"Tell me, Aunt, about his lovely bride," Rashida went on, turning back to Ibrahim's mother. "She's the merchant's daughter called Sayyida, isn't that right? What's she like? Can we meet her? When you go to visit her."

Ibrahim's mother gave her a dubious look.

"I want to give her a gift," Rashida said. "But, if you want to do it on my behalf, then that's fine. Nobody loves me inside this house. In my quarter, I was on my own, and I came here looking for a family. But it's a tough world."

"My daughter," Ibrahim's mother replied, looking confused, "once you get to know Ibrahim, you'll find that he's a good brother and support."

"I'm trying to get to know him, but he's not giving me the chance. For example, have you ever seen him smile at me? Does he treat me like a sister and worry about me? Didn't he separate me from my fiancé? Has he looked for someone else?"

"Look on the bright side, my daughter," Ibrahim's mother replied, stroking her shoulder. "Be patient. These are difficult times for all of us."

She left his mother and went to see first his sister, Shafiqa, and then his other sister, Kamila. She sat with her for hours, gave her jewellery and gold, and became her close friend. Kamila repeated the things she had told her brother and added that her husband, Sufyan, was operating under Ibrahim's orders; he had no will of his own, but was merely following instructions. Rashida kept hovering around them like a bee, buzzing and sprinkling honey all over the house. Along with Shafiqa, she decided to go and visit Ibrahim's fiancée and her mother, all without Ibrahim or his mother knowing about it.

She had heard about Ibrahim's love for Sayyida. He had chosen her out of all other girls, for her intelligence, her piety, and her morals. He had been waiting to find someone who would understand and support him. Everyone liked Sayyida, and, when she visited them with her mother, Ibrahim's eyes gleamed; yes, they gleamed, and Rashida smiled as she recalled the words.

She sat down with them, removed her face veil, and gave them fabrics and gold-embroidered clothes. She then kissed Sayyida twice on the forehead.

"You're beautiful," she told her. "What a wonderful girl my cousin has chosen!"

She left her with Ibrahim's sister and followed Sayyida's mother out of the room to help them get the food ready.

"Aunt," she said. "I need to speak to you about something important. Send the slave girls away."

Sayyida's mother gave her an anxious look and dismissed the slave girls. Rashida then burst into tears, sat on the floor, and grabbed hold of Sayyida's mother's foot.

"On your honour," she pleaded, "I beg you to help me!"

"God forbid, my daughter!"

Sayyida's mother pulled her up off the floor.

"What's happened," she asked Rashida. "You're a wonderful girl."

She sat Rashida down beside her.

"I may have made a terrible mistake," Rashida said, still pretending to be crying hard. "I know I have. I deserve to be flogged and stoned."

"I seek refuge from Satan the accursed!"

"But I still want you to help me. If my mother found out, she'd kill me. You know I was supposed to be married to the wheat-porter."

"My daughter," Sayyida's mother replied cautiously.

She knew already; she knew everything about Rashida. In Alexandria, news travels as quickly and efficiently as the sea-winds. But she pretended not to know.

"If I'm not married to him, Aunt," Rashida went on, wiping away her tears, "it'll be a huge scandal for me. Please save me. You're a mother. Just imagine something like this happening to Sayyida."

Sayyida's mother put her hand over her mouth and let out a gasp.

"I'll talk to Ibrahim," she said. "This is very important."

"If he finds out that I've told you anything, Aunt, he'll kill me."

"What can I do? How could you allow the wheat-porter to fool with the family honour of the Sicilian? What a disaster! Maybe ask Ibrahim to find you a husband."

Rashida sighed and covered her face with her hand.

"It wasn't the wheat-porter who fooled with the family honour of the Sicilian, Aunt," she muttered. "It's Ibrahim. The wheat-porter was going to be married to me to avoid scandal. I've not found anyone else to whom I can be married. It was Ibrahim who did it. He used to visit us in Cairo. He did it in spite of me, Aunt."

"If he finds out I've told you," she said, bursting into tears again, "he's going to kill me."

"If what you're saying is untrue..."

"Can there be any reason for a girl to make such a claim against herself? He'll reject it, he'll reject it altogether! He might kill me. No, he *will* kill me. But I swear to you that that's what he's done. He did it, and he refused to be married to me afterwards. I swear to you that I was going to be married to the wheat-porter. As the Sicilian's daughter, I was afraid and wanted protection. Why did he separate me from the wheat-porter? Why did he do it? Just think, Aunt. Was it because, even after he is married, he wants to have me with him all the time?"

"Kill me," she said after a pause. "That's easier to take than what he wants me to do."

"You're making a life-threatening accusation against the man and disgracing your family for all time. Do you realise that?"

"I know you and your honourable heritage. You'll never betray my secret."

"What do you want me to do?"

"Just persuade him to let me be married to the wheat-porter so I won't be exposed to scandal and can move far away from him. If he is married to Sayyida and stays in the house with us, I've no idea what might happen between us. I'm scared, Aunt, scared of him. All I want is for him to let me be married to the wheat-porter."

"May God do what is best for all of us!" the mother stuttered.

"I beg you not to tell him what has taken place between the two of us. Please keep my story secret. I'm just like your own daughter. Just convince him to let me be married to the wheat-porter."

"May God do what is best for all of us! I don't think Sayyida deserves this. No marriage can be based on lies and God's wrath."

"No, Aunt," Rashida said, suppressing a smile. "He has to be married to Sayyida, or else he's going to kill me. He'll have his doubts and discover that I've told you the truth. If he finds out, he'll slay me. You've no idea what he's done to me. If only you realised how he's clamped my mouth shut and then had his way with my body."

"He won't find out a thing, I promise you. God will do what's good. What a disaster!"

Victory day was a day like no other! Sayyida was beautiful, with a pale complexion, glowing features, hair that reached to her waist, and buttocks to attract any knight. Rashida could just imagine the story between the two of them. Sayyida as Ibrahim's neighbour. He had met her often, and they had smiled at each other. She was no more than sixteen years old, and Ibrahim was the man in charge around here. It was thus easy for all the girls to be in love with him and desire him. When Ibrahim came to ask her family for her hand, she was thrilled and allowed herself a silent scream of joy. A nice girl from a good household would be a good help and support for him. How had he come to fall in love with her, even though he did not seem like someone who loved or hated? She had never seen him smile or cheer, as though he were some pre-Islamic idol. But no matter! Ibrahim was the one who had separated her from her own fiancé, and now she had done the same thing between him and his fiancée. As the proverb has it, 'What's obvious is always worse.' As far as she was concerned, the money he had stolen from her was most important of all. It was not enough for brother and sister to rebel against him. She would get her money back, no matter the cost. It was a trust from her father, and he had given it to her. Ibrahim was not better than her, even though he put on such a show of virtue and honesty with everyone. For her, he was a thief and a tyrant.

She asked Zubaida to prepare some water for her to bathe in so she could wash off all the filth of machinations and plots and rid herself of his evil and tyrannical intentions.

"You seem very happy today, my Lady," Zubaida said as she scrubbed her back with soap.

"It's been a day of victories," Rashida replied. "What do you think of Ibrahim, Zubaida?"

"My Lady," the slave girl replied bashfully, "it's not for someone like me to express an opinion."

"You're beautiful," Rashida told her, looking at her dark skin and regular features. "You should thank God that you haven't fallen into the clutches of an old man who'll suck out your youth. Here with me, you're safe from all men. Had you ever been in love, Zubaida, before you saw this Syrian, Yusuf ibn Ayyub?"

"No, my Lady," Zubaida replied, swallowing hard. "I haven't dared to be so bold."

"Love's like halva; we taste it to make life better: no more, no less. It doesn't really exist, Zubaida. Poets will tell you that it's just like sweet water. You might drink some one day, not realising that the alternative is nothing. When it resists you, your veins dry up and your soul expires. It's all a lie. Water's water, and men are men."

"Ah, what words you speak from the heart, my Lady, mistress of all!"

Rashida looked at her slave girl in surprise.

"Come on," she said, controlling herself. "We've a lot to do today. Get a move on!"

"As you wish, my Lady," Zubaida responded, having forgotten herself for just a moment.

She slept soundly. She was running on the sand and laughing with her nieces. Victory now seemed close. She heard the sad news and wiped away a tear. The engagement between Ibrahim and Sayyida had been called off. As Rashida clasped Ibrahim's mother's shoulder, she wondered why.

"He deserves someone better," Rashida said. "Your son's an honest and noble man. I've never seen the like of him, Praise God that the truth about Sayyida became known before they were married."

Days like today always pulsed with successes! She renounced him, Ibrahim the Sicilian, the halva-maker, the most important man in all of Alexandria. She spat him out, loathing his foul deed. Was he in love with Sayyida, she wondered. Was he heartbroken? Most important, had his arrogance been cut up and scattered beneath the hooves of horses, making him soft, gentle, and lean like bits of kunafa before it is cooked? Ah, Ibrahim, what next? You have challenged Rashida. Anyone who does that can expect to be defeated, just as a boatman anticipates winds. So, son of the Sicilian, I hope your heart will be split in two, like a piece of 'judge' halva in the hands of a child. You have no idea who you are playing with and against whom you have waged war. Victory will follow victory, the same way that rocks keep tumbling during stormy weather. She had heard about the argument between Husain and Ibrahim, took Zubaida's place, and listened to the mother crying the previous night. She was talking about her younger son, who blew up in her face and told her that she loved only Ibrahim and never defended anyone except him, even if he was the one leading the entire family into the abyss. What was strange was that, on the very same night, her daughter had come in to complain about her brother. She said that Ibrahim was not giving her husband an adequate salary, even though she had a share in the stores and factories. She went on to say that she did not dare talk to him about it. The net was tightening around him. She was dearly hoping that he understood that Rashida was winning; when Rashida wanted something, all fate's lions bowed down before her.

"My Lady," Zubaida pleaded as she pulled the covers over Rashida. "I'm feeling really sorry for Ibrahim's mother. She's a wonderful lady, and we've never seen anything bad about her."

"Wars have their victims, Zubaida," Rashida replied, "and most of them are innocent."

CHAPTER THREE

Ibrahim summoned the entire household: his mother, her mother, the slave girls, and the servants. Zubaida was afraid.

"My Lady," she told Rashida. "He must know that his mother's been crying. What's he going to do to us?"

"Nothing. What have we done, girl? Use your mind! He wants to talk about Yusuf ibn Ayyub, the guest who never leaves this house."

The slave girl shuddered and closed her eyelids.

"Be careful, Zubaida!" Rashida told her. "Forget about that love of yours."

"I wouldn't dare, my Lady. He's an amir's nephew. How can I be in love with him when I'm nothing? Who's going to look at my dark skin when all sorts of foreign girls are available?'

"Men are never satisfied with just one shade or type of woman," Rashida responded with a laugh.

"My Lady, there's my Lady Kauthar..."

"My mother's not like other women. In fact, she's all women put together. Anyone who knows my mother can't forget her or fall in love with any other woman. But she's just one."

"You're like her, my Lady."

"That's quite enough flattery! Come on, we don't want to be late for Ibrahim. Zubaida, I wonder if we'll be able to detect the sadness in his expression today. Was he really in love with Sayyida? I'd sincerely hope he was."

"We've never encountered any evil in him, my Lady," Zubaida muttered as she looked at Rashida.

"What did you say?"

"That his expression will always be sad."

"That's better. Has Jawwad tried to get a glimpse of me?"

"Yes, several times," Zubaida replied, looking all around her. "But he hasn't managed it."

Rashida smiled contentedly.

Ibrahim's mother sat in the lounge; she was clasping her hands and looking depressed. Beside her sat his two sisters, frowning, and his brothers. Husain looked impatiently all around him. Ibrahim came in, carrying a sword in its scabbard. He gave them all a silent stare.

"The entire city of Alexandria is going to fight alongside Nur ad-din Zengi," he told them firmly, "along with his men in Egypt, Asad ad-din Shirkuh and Yusuf ibn Ayyub. There'll be no quarter given the Minister Shawar or the Crusaders. If they enter a village, they'll burn it down and humiliate its inhabitants. Anyone who offers the Crusaders help is an enemy."

"We hear and obey, Brother," his brothers said.

"What do you have to say?" Ibrahim asked, looking at Husain.

"I'm afraid of destruction and war," Husain mumbled.

"War's on the way; there's no avoiding it. We can either confront it courageously or hide in our houses like women. Alexandrians don't hide, nor do they fear the path of truth."

"Brother—"

"Don't interrupt me!"

"*Brother,*" Husain repeated, suppressing his anger.

"Real men defend without hesitation. The Crusaders are in Egypt. What do you want us to do? Wait till they besmirch our honour and kill our children as they've done in Jerusalem? I want to hear it from you."

Their eyes met. Rashida looked at Husain, hiding a smile.

"I hear and obey, Brother," Husain said.

Ibrahim gave a nod and looked around him.

"Discord seems to arrive with the ravens to teach one brother how to keep another brother's evil hidden. Who has brought the discord here, I wonder, and how has it entered our house?"

For a moment, he looked around. Then he stared at Rashida.

"Come over here, Cousin," he told her gently. "You're under my protection."

She gave him a dubious look.

"Don't be scared," he said. "Why should you be scared? Stand here in front of me."

She walked steadily toward him while looking at Zubaida, whose eyes were wide open in shock. She stood in front of him, and he gave her a smile. Raising his hand, he slapped her hard on the cheek.

She fell to the floor with a shriek. Her mother shrieked as well, and his mother put her hand over her mouth to stop herself from crying out, too. All the women shivered.

"How dare you!" she said, her cheek burning and tears falling nonstop. "If my father were still alive, you'd—"

He grabbed hold of her hair, and she shrieked again.

"If your father were alive," he said, "he'd kill you or tell me to do so."

"Ibrahim," her mother said. "you've no right to hit my daughter. She's done nothing."

"Rashida's mother," Ibrahim responded with due deliberation. "your daughter's not properly trained yet. She needs training, and a lot of it."

Her mother gaped.

"Members of Ibrahim the Sicilian's family," he continued, looking at her. "Rashida is here under my protection. She's not going to speak to anyone, leave her room, or purchase anything without permission. Everyone leave the room now. Only Rashida and her mother will stay."

He looked at his mother, and she came over.

"My son," she said gently. "this isn't right. Your father and uncle... The girl's young. Even if you want to teach her, do it gently."

"Leave, Mother," he said, looking at Rashida. "We'll discuss everything later. Go on."

"Brother," Husain asked angrily, "why such cruelty? She's a sister."

"I'll leave the affection to you, Husain," he said sarcastically. "We'll talk tomorrow."

No sooner had they all left than Rashida stood up, still unable to take in what had just happened.

"You'll pay for this," she stuttered. "I swear you will. Who do you think you are? I'll complain to the judge today, now....I'll complain to the judge. You've taken my money, and now you hit me and keep me locked up."

"Let's complain to the judge together," he said quietly, sitting down. "Mother of all girls, noble and pure lady, daughter of the Sicilian, Armenian, and halva-maker! So, what exactly happened between you and the wheat-porter?"

"How dare you? she asked, her mouth agape in shock. "I'm ʿAbd al-Wadud's daughter. How—"

"Bring in the flour-seller," Ibrahim yelled to his men.

"Put your face veil on," he told her.

She put the veil on with a trembling hand. Jawwad came in, his hands tied and his head bowed. Ibrahim drew his sword.

"I'll slay him now," he told her. "and then you. What do you think?"

"You're out of your mind!" she yelled.

"What happened between the two of you?"

"Nothing," she replied at once. "I swear to you, nothing happened."

He looked at Jawwad, then raised his hand and slapped him.

"Do you want to die?" he asked, grabbing Jawwad by the lapels.

"I beg you to believe me, my Lord."

"I'm not your lord. I'm going to leave you here till I've finished talking to my cousin.. Then I'll know whether I'm going to kill you today or let you leave the city forever."

He ordered the guards to take him out. Kauthar looked on in utter amazement, not understanding a thing.

"Take your face veil off, Rashida, and look at me!"

"This is all because of your beloved," Rashida replied bitterly.

"How on earth did you imagine for a single second, Cousin," Ibrahim asked her, "that you could tell that story and that anyone would believe it? Do you realise? If the jinn forced me to have sex with the female devil herself, I'd do it. But if they forced me to have sex with you, I'd choose hellfire forevermore. If you keep saying that you have to be married to Jawwad to avoid a scandal, then there must be a scandal. Who's the poor wretch, I wonder, who's fallen victim to you?"

"You realise that you're physically stronger than me," she told him in a slippery tone. "Otherwise, I'd make you pay the price for what you've just said."

He signalled to the door, and two huge women came in.

"I want to check," he told them. "She never tells the truth. If the wheat-porter has taken her virginity, they'll have to be married."

"Have you gone mad?" she shrieked in his face.

"Your daughter says she's lost her honour," he said, looking at her mother. "That's what she told Sayyida's mother. She swore not to tell anyone. But she forgot that Ibrahim always finds out; he finds out everything. Once she's confessed, Kauthar, mother of Rashida, what do you think we should do? Shall we go to the judge, which is what she wants?"

Kauthar put her hand over her mouth and looked at her daughter.

"She's still young," she said. "Maybe..."

"Maybe she wasn't lying. Why did she insist on being married to the wheat-porter? Because he was in love with her. If she was really that keen, then I'll marry her to him. But we need to check first. If she's lost her honour, then she deserves a hundred lashes. If she pretended that I'd had sex with her, she deserves eighty. We'll see."

"Ibrahim," Rashida said at once, staring at the two women. "I was lying. The wheat-porter hasn't touched me. It's your fault; you took my money. You've kept me a prisoner here and separated me from my fiancé. I wanted you to have a taste of the same bitter cup, that's all. Ibrahim..."

He did not respond, but he signalled to the two women, then to her mother.

"I'll wait here until they've checked while your mother watches," he told her.

Rashida grabbed his hand and clasped it.

"Don't do this to me," she said.

"I haven't done anything."

"You're the devil, not me," she said, squeezing his hand tightly. "You pretend to be so idealistic, and yet you hate me, my mother, and my father. I realise it's because we're rich and better than you. You're out to steal my money and..."

The two women took her out of the room, still shrieking and complaining.

"This will confirm your innocence, my daughter," her mother told her. "Why are you so angry?"

A while later, the mother and the two women came out again.

"Didn't I tell you?" her mother said. "that my daughter's the purest girl in the entire country? An untouched virgin."

"In that case," Ibrahim responded with a smile, "it's eighty lashes. Where is she?"

Rashida came back in.

"I swear," she said, wiping away her tears, "I'm going to kill you myself."

"Do you want him that much? Why do you want the wheat-porter? Or is it that you want any man?"

"I love him," she replied, looking straight at him.

He lifted his hand to slap her again, but then lowered it.

"That's slave girl talk," he said. "No cousin of mine should say such things. That kind of love is for singing girls and slave girls. How can you be so bold?"

"Why don't you just throw me out," she asked, hugging herself. "Let me go back to my own district?"

"That I can't do. If you really love him, then I'll let you be married to him. But he'll never be in charge of my uncle's and ancestors' stores."

"Do you hear, Mother?" she said, looking at her mother. "He wants our money, that's all."

"My son," her mother suggested shyly. "If you were married to her—"

"O my God!" Rashida yelled, slapping her own face. "What are you saying? I'm saying that I love Jawwad, and you're asking me to be married to the devil incarnate."

"Rashida's mother," Ibrahim responded firmly, "it's impossible for me to be married to your daughter. I must reject her as a pious believer must reject sin. What Rashida has done and said only serves to confirm her hatred and internal illness. I don't have the time to think about her future now. At this point, all I'd ask you to do is to keep her evil intentions in check. That said, I swear to you that, if she does something else, if she provokes some dispute between me and my brothers, if she so much as says a bad word about me, or if she dares do anything, she'll never set eyes on Jawwad for the rest of her life. I'll kill him, and I'll keep her here in prison till she dies. Do you hear me, Rashida?"

"Yes, I hear you, Cousin," Rashida replied, looking straight at him.

"Will you follow my instructions?"

"How can I trust your word after what you've done to me?"

"You don't have a choice. You have to trust my word."

"No, I have total discretion."

"Do you really want eighty lashes?" he asked her. "Or will you obey my instructions?"

"I prefer the eighty lashes."

"But you're going to obey my instructions," he responded, his gaze still fixed on hers.

"Poor Sayyida is heartbroken," she told him defiantly. "You'll never be married to her, Cousin. Her family will never agree, even though it's been proved that you didn't do anything."

Her brazen comment stunned him.

"I hereby promise you," he said, "that I'm going to be married to her. You'll be at the ceremony."

The tension inside the room grew. Husain looked around the room and saw that frustration was the primary emotion. Should he abandon everything so as to be rid of his brother's domination, or should he stay in the bosom of the family, one that had often treated him so generously? Did he dare say 'no' in front of his brother? Should he tell him that he was certain that the end was coming with the Syrian army? Should he defy Ibrahim?

Ibrahim stole a glance at his brother and tried to gauge how rebellious and angry Husain really was.

"Go ahead and talk," Ibrahim said gently. "I'm listening."

"I don't dare say anything, Brother," Husain replied resentfully. "You don't listen to me. You're always right."

"You dare to criticise me, so go ahead and speak. What did Rashida say to you to kindle such hatred?"

"I don't want to be married to `A'isha," he replied, avoiding Ibrahim's stare.

"Do you want another girl?"

"No, but I don't want her."

"What don't you like about her? Have you seen her?"

"You chose her, not me," he replied, stomping the floor with his foot.

"Fine!" Ibrahim replied gently with a smile. "I'll cancel the engagement."

"Don't you do it!"

Ibrahim looked at him in confusion.

"I'll do it," Husain said.

"Fine, you do it! `A'isha's very beautiful. I'll marry her to `Ali, who works with us."

"Why are you the one to marry her off?" Husain asked nervously. "Why have you chosen her? What's her relationship with us? You don't control the whole of humanity, as though you're the caliph."

"Husain," Ibrahim told him firmly.

"Forgive me, Brother! Sorrows keep piling up, and I can't stand it anymore. I can't stand having Yusuf ibn Ayyub and the Syrian army here."

"Do you prefer the Crusader army?"

"I prefer the Fatimid army. That's our army."

"It's Minister Shawar's army, not ours."

"Your sister Shafiqa's husband is one of them—Aftakin. You know him and them, too."

"Yes, I know him, but I don't know all of them. Some of them are loyal, but others are working for Minister Shawar, without thinking about the consequences. If you don't trust the Syrian army, how is it that the Caliph Al-`Adid himself does trust them?"

"What have we to do with power and caliphs? All our lives, we've been halva-makers. I have no wish to hurl myself into perdition. Neither myself, nor my mother, nor—"

"You've no wish," Ibrahim replied firmly. "So, what exactly do you wish? You're going to follow my orders and mine alone. I've listened to you. All you can say is 'how,' and 'what.' I haven't made any decision or done anything new. If you want to rebel, then you have to build something, too; destruction isn't the end. What are you planning to do when the Crusaders enter Alexandria? How are you going to protect your mother and sister?"

"If you don't ally yourself with Yusuf, they'll never enter the city."

Silence prevailed.

"What is it you want?" Ibrahim asked bluntly. "Money? You keep talking about marriage, wars, and the army, when all I can see in your expressions is a boy's craving for halva, no more."

"I'm not greedy, Brother," Husain replied angrily. "Even if I have asked about my money."

"You've put Rashida between yourself and your brother. Can you see yourself? Do you remember your father's will? Do you really want to divide up the inheritance and lose all prestige?"

"What you've given me isn't enough."

"I've given you your due."

Husain gasped.

"Yes, my Mother's son, I've given you your due," Ibrahim went on, keeping his fury in check. "Don't let this situation tear our family apart. Greed has no place in the Sicilian's household. We're a family clan, the way our father wanted. If you want to complain about me, then let's postpone it till the wars are over. Rashida's brought evil upon us; there's nothing good in her heart. If she managed to kindle strife among the men in the halva factory, what can she do with the brothers? Make sure you don't believe her."

"But you're not giving her her due. It's her money."

"I'm doing that as well, but she's not good at handling money; she divides rather than collects. The person who can reconcile hearts, my brother, is the one to make decisions. Anyone who merely follows their own desires needs to stay in the house and kitchen, making halva for women, not for sultans and caliphs. Let's put our disagreement aside and remember what our father told us. You're my brother."

"Come over here!" Ibrahim said, stretching out his hand. "Take my hand and promise me that we'll stay united in the face of the Crusaders, the Fatimid army, the Syrian forces, and Yusuf ibn Ayyub as well."

Husain gulped in confusion, then stretched out his hand.

"We'll drown together," he replied.

"Be optimistic. We have truth on our side."

Rashida's very existence was like grief, poverty, locusts, and lice, all rolled into one. If only Ibrahim could rip her off his clothes and rid himself of her intrigues and evil intentions! Closing his eyes, he remembered Sayyida's words. She told him that she believed him, and that he was her lord and master. He was all she had. She did not trust Rashida and was well aware of her plots. However, getting rid of locusts might also mean losing a few, or even all, of the plants as well. He found himself mounting his horse and heading for Giza. He left at dusk, hoping to get there quickly and return before the fighting started. He wanted to visit Bahnas, the Pyramid Witch. He knew about her; his father had told him about her veneration and respect for the ancients. No one knew what her faith was, but she was someone possessed of both trust and vision, to be found in every time and place. Each member of her family trained her successor, and each girl learned the language and knowledge of the ancients. Today, he needed her. Husain's words had penetrated to his very heart; his brother had never dared confront him before. With Husain losing confidence in his elder brother, that was just the beginning. It would not be long before the Sicilian's family was at an end.

When he arrived, he asked the Witch for permission to enter, and she gave it. He entered and offered greetings to the ancients. He knew what she liked and wanted. He had brought the kind of pastry she liked and the maulid bride halva. He put them down in front of her.

"I have need of you, Bahnas," he said.

She was looking at an old piece of cloth. When she looked up, her eyes gleamed with the light of knowledge, while her black hair was draped across her forehead.

"The halva-maker," she said, "son of the Sicilian, Armenian, and Egyptian. How are you, Ibrahim? You haven't come here for years. You forget about Bahnas and only remember her when there's a crisis."

"A girl's brought destruction down on us," Ibrahim said, sitting down. "In fact, there's destruction all around us, and she only makes it worse. Everything in the pastwas easier to deal with than what's to come. The Crusaders are a mammoth disaster. They're different from anything our ancestors have encountered. I don't know if I can live with the kind of catastrophe that's coming in different guises, like so many devils. Rashida—"

"It's time for courage," she responded with a smile. "That's when human beings decide to confront the devils of heaven and earth on their own—with no hesitation and no misgivings, tossing all caution into the ocean depths and just clinging to the lightning gleam. That's exactly what I said to your grandfather, Ibrahim."

"Egypt," he retorted bitterly. "That's what I'm concentrating on, and I'm desperately hoping that it won't be my misfortune to see it defeated. That's an obvious disaster, Bahnas."

"That's an obvious disaster," she repeated. "I've just said that it's time for courage."

"If you're talking about me, then—"

"No, I'm not talking about you," she interrupted.

"Then who are you talking about?" he asked, giving her a baffled look. "Who's the one with courage? Yusuf ibn Ayyub?"

"You've come here because of troubles and intrigue," Bahnas said with a smile as she stood up. "All because of a girl, isn't that right?"

"Yes, that's right. Rashida."

"It was her I was talking about," she said as she left for the desert.

"Bahnas, what do you mean?" he asked, his mouth agape.

"Bahnas never explains what she's saying, halva-maker. Come back to see me a little later. Don't forget to send my greetings to Yusuf ibn Ayyub. He'll come."

CHAPTER FOUR

The men gathered in the 'Attarin Mosque under the marble slab commemorating Badr al-Jamali, the Supreme Master, Sword of Islam, and Helper of the Imam.

"Police are filling the city," Ibrahim said, "and the Crusaders are at the gates."

"Muslim men," Yusuf ibn Ayyub told them in muted tones, "Crusaders are not to be trusted. It's not right for us to resort to the West and cross the seas because we can't solve our own problems. What's the weakness that has afflicted the Muslim peoples? Today, the Crusaders may be helping Shawar and consolidating his rule, but tomorrow they'll overthrow him. Ambition is just like the adventurous horse, saddled with self-love, that plunges recklessly into the desert wastes. The danger here lies in our own fractiousness, not with the Crusaders."

People looked at him, and some of them asked who he was. Some people said he was not as strong as Turkish soldiers, while others pointed out that he was not Arab. How could a Kurd rival Turks when it came to fighting? People whispered that his family was from Dvin, a city close to Badr al-Jamali's hometown, but he was not a Mamluk like Badr al-Jamali. He had been born in Iraq and lived in Syria. For an Army Commander, his shyness was peculiar and his gentle talk even more so. He was not more than twenty-seven years old.

Ibrahim listened to him.

"Yusuf ibn Ayyub has come here to help us," he said. "Alexandrians bow down to no one but God. Pride is blended into their limbs, and all blood is honourable. In us, he will discover a means of support that has often come to reconcile hearts, like Badr al-Jamali."

Yusuf looked at the marble tablet and then went over to Ibrahim.

"My brother," he told Ibrahim. "don't compare me with the great Minister. I'm simply a servant of God, while he was the Supreme Master."

"You're Sunni, and he was Shi'i."

"How trivial and cruel our caliphate is!" Yusuf replied immediately. "Once the Crusaders have wiped out all trace of us, perhaps we'll come to realise that such disputes are a poisoned dagger for which there's no cure and from which there's no escape. I've come here with my uncle upon orders from your Caliph, Al-'Adid. He's asked us to help him counter the aggression and machinations of Minister Shawar."

Police spies were observing this meeting, and they brought news back to Shawar. Alexandrians adhered to the Shafi'i school of law. And as the years went by—in fact, ever since the times of 'Amr ibn al-'As—it had proved impossible to control them. If Shawar could not break them today, he had no hope of remaining in power. With his own army and that of the Crusaders, he would be able to defeat Nur ad-din and his men and this youngster whom his uncle had left in Alexandria to urge its inhabitants to rebel. Shawar would teach the Alexandrians a lesson first, and then he'd have time to deal with the youngster and his uncle.

Whiffs of revolt filled the air, stirring both anticipation and caution. The men all agreed that the first step in gaining control of the city involved fighting the city police and then expelling all of Shawar's men. With Ibrahim at their head, the men decided to gather the city's women into the houses, to place a man outside to protect them, and then to go out and fight Shawar's men, who were concentrated by Alexandria's city gates. The women from every ten homes were gathered together in a single house. Ibrahim opened his own house to Sayyida and her family, her brothers, and all her neighbours. The women all gathered there. He decided that his brother Husain would stay there to protect the house with his weapon, while he and Yusuf ibn Ayyub would go to fight Shawar's forces outside the city gate.

Rashida rushed over to Ibrahim's two sisters, who both loathed her. There was a lengthy history between Ibrahim's mother and Kauthar, Rashida's mother, all of it involving jealousy and hatred. Ibrahim's two sisters clearly did not like her, but she would still do her best. One of Ibrahim's sisters, Shafiqa, was married to a Turkish soldier in the Fatimid army named

Aftakin; Kamila, the other sister, was married to Sufyan, who was working with Ibrahim. Rashida started with Shafiqa. She showered her with gifts and then told her that her brother, Ibrahim, would soon be fighting her husband and maybe even killing him. Her husband was the Turkish soldier in the army under the control of Minister Shawar. For that reason, her husband had become an enemy for Ibrahim, who was now siding with the Syrian army.

"Ibrahim's not just my brother," Shafiqa responded firmly. "He's my father as well. If I have to make a choice, then I'll choose my brother."

"I'd like you to think of your children," Rashida told her, pursing her lips, "not just yourself."

"May God do good!" Shafiqa replied after a pause. "My brother would never hurt me. He's the one who married me to the soldier and brought me up after our father had died."

Rashida let out a sigh, annoyed but still somewhat hopeful. Turning to Kamila, she asked why her husband was working with Ibrahim, her brother, if she had some rights to the inheritance. Why had the household bowed down to Ibrahim, as though he were the Imam, even though he was a typically ambitious man and walked just like everyone else?

Discord is both adaptable and vicious; it can slink its way into your veins even if it does not reach the outer limbs. Rashida was well aware of that. She allowed herself a smile as she noticedtiny threads of doubt in Shafiqa's expression and sorrow in Kamila's eyes. She went back to her room in triumph.

"My brother," Rashida pleaded with Husain, as she faked tears, "he's not letting me eat."

He gave her a shocked look.

"He's brought his beloved to live with us after he's humiliated me," she said. "What he's doing is going to destroy the Sicilian's family. Believe me!"

"Calm down, Cousin!"

"Here, take what you want," he said, pulling some money out of his pocket.

"You're a wonderful brother!" she said. "Defend me, please! He's beaten me and kept me locked up. I want to see Jawwad!"

"I can't do that, Rashida," he responded in shock.

"Give me my rights! You're the one who can do it."

"Only Ibrahim has that right."

"Our grandfather never sanctioned that, nor did Jawhar the Sicilian or Badr al-Jamali."

Even so, Husain arranged a meeting with Jawwad, who was hiding in one of the deserted houses by the port. Husain went with her.

"I'll stay with you while you meet him," he told her.

"You're the best brother in the whole world," she told him joyfully.

"Jawwad," she asked him, quivering with joy, "what's the tyrant done to you?"

"My Lady," he replied, glancing all around him, "no one can keep us apart."

"You're going to steal all his money," she whispered with a smile so that Husain couldn't hear.

Jawwad gaped.

"You're stealing all his money," she went on, "because it belongs to me. You'll give it to me."

"He'll flay me alive."

"He won't be able to. War's at the gates. He won't be here all the time. Give me the money."

"Will you be married to me after?"

"Do you need to ask, man? Why do you suppose I've endured all this hardship?"

"My Lady..."

"The day after tomorrow, you'll give me all the money in the factory treasury, as well as all the flour and all the sugar. He's busy now, and there are only one or two guards in front of the factory."

"I'll do my best."

"If you try to betray me, you realise that I can have you put in prison. Isn't that right? Get me the money the day after tomorrow. I'll come here to meet you."

"My Lady, there's no cure for love, and betrayal has no part in it."

She then looked at Husain and wiped away a non-existent tear.

"Come on, Cousin," she said with a smile.

On the way back, Husain kept trying to find out what kind of agreement she had made with Jawwad, but without success. He had started to feel uneasy, because his usual trust for Rashida had disappeared. Who was to know: these were times when everything was deceit and chaos. Minister against Caliph, Caliph asking for help from the Syrian army, and Minister asking the Crusaders to help him. He remained silent, but she could feel his suspicions.

"Do you trust me, Husain?" she asked bluntly.

"I don't know," he replied, looking straight at her.

"Do you agree with me," she asked, "that your brother's a tyrant?"

"He's my brother," Husain replied. "He's the only person I've known since my father died."

"But God orders us to speak the truth even if it's about a relative."

"Don't you dare hurt him. Jawwad's not right for you. You're the Sicilian's daughter."

"Love doesn't recognise such distinctions. He has neither homeland nor hue."

"I didn't realise you were so fond of poets!"

"What you've done with me today cements our friendship," she told him, stretching out her hand and stroking his shoulder. "You're a brother and support. God has sent you to me. I mean, I'm an orphan, alone and oppressed. You've seen him hit me and lock me up. Even my own father never did that. Why does time humiliate me so, I wonder?"

"Yes, I've seen him. I can swear that I've never see him mistreat anyone that way."

"It's in times of power and strife that the truths about humanity emerge. Today, Ibrahim has a lot of power, and it's wartime. I need your protection."

"But how are you going to protect me?" Husain asked.

"You'll find out, but not now. Still, I can promise you, Cousin, that this weak girl will protect you. She'll support you and do everything possible to give you what you deserve."

It turned out that stealing from the stores was not as easy as she had expected. Yes, Jawwad had gone inside, but he had not come out. The guard had arrested him, as though he had been expecting him to come, and thrown him into a cellar inside the factory overlooking the sea. The guard told him that he was awaiting orders from Ibrahim upon the man's return. Jawwad did not come to their arranged meeting-place, nor did he get either money or halva. Rashida waited anxiously for him and opened the window, expecting to receive some good news. Instead, she saw something deeply disturbing: Ibrahim.

He opened the door to her room. She let out a scream and opened her eyes wide, not believing his brazen conduct. The slave girl sitting on the floor beside Rashida bowed.

"Leave us on our own," he told the girl angrily.

"You know this isn't right," Rashida yelled. "You barge your way into my room! What do you want?"

"You've no modesty or manners, Rashida. Don't pretend to be something you're not, Cousin, and don't be baffled or surprised. Send your slave girl away. I need to talk to you."

Zubaida left, head bowed, and closed the door.

"Are you going to hit me again?" she asked, not believing her own eyes.

He grabbed her hand and sat her down in front of him. He then let her hand go disdainfully.

"You've claimed that I've committed debauchery, you've turned my brothers against me one after the other, and my own sister now looks at me with suspicion. Now, Husain has rebelled against me even though he's my favorite and the one brother who's closest to my heart. You've put a wedge between me and all the people I love, and now you've tried to steal my money. What crime won't you commit, Rashida? Theft, lies, hypocrisy, intrigues... what else?"

She stared straight back at him, and for a while they just looked at each other.

"You're the one who started the evil," she eventually stuttered. "There I was, settled with my mother in Fustat and planning to be married to the man I had chosen, and along you came and destroyed all my dreams."

"To be married to the man you wanted?" he repeated. "Did I break your heart by keeping you and the wheat-porter apart?"

"Yes, you did," she replied at once.

He smiled, lowered his head for a moment, then looked at her again.

"I can remember you, Rashida," he said, "when you were just a girl. Even then, you were a flirt and had all the determination of a cloud arriving just before a major storm. If you wanted something and did not get it, then you were ready to tear down the entire household. I can still remember you as a girl when your mother wouldn't let you eat the maulid-bride halva before the maulid date itself. You would throw it on the floor, stomp it with your feet, scream, burst into tears, and dig your foot into the ground. You asked for another one, and your mother immediately gave you one. You ate it angrily, having given your parents a lesson in obeying Rashida's orders. At the time, my uncle, who was the sole beneficiary of the inheritance—the one who carried the Sicilian family name in Fustat and Cairo—told us that we didn't want her to die like her brothers. So, let her fool around as she wants, let her scream, demand, tyrannise, and squander money. There's only one Rashida, and we all have to chase after her lead. Do you remember that, Rashida?"

"If you really do remember me," she replied defiantly, "then you knew I'd fight."

He did not respond. Instead, he stared at the wall.

"Yes, I was expecting you to fight," he reflected. "What's surprised me, Cousin, is the extent to which I have no idea what you're fighting for. Was it the doll-halva you couldn't have, or the fact that you weren't allowed to eat it before the maulid festival? And this time, I've no idea what you're fighting for, either. This time..."

He suddenly moved close to her face and looked into her eyes, as though to penetrate all the way to her heart.

"Rashida," he said, "this is a war unlike any other. No doll-halva can substitute for it, nor will crushing it underfoot restore life to one's arteries. Do you understand me, cousin?"

"No, I don't," she replied in confusion, as she swallowed hard.

"Oh yes, you do understand, and so have I from the very beginning. You'll never get what you want."

"You don't know me," she responded, angry and dissatisfied, "and you've no idea what it is I want."

"Oh yes, I do know you and what you want," he told her gently as he moved closer. "I also know what you fear in your heart, and what it is that extracts so much discord from it. I assure you that I do know, and that achieving all your dreams is impossible."

His words upset her, and she made no reply.

She heard the despairing shouts of the policemen as they ran down the streets, and then a scream from the women, followed by the sound of beatings and sword fights. Ibrahim's mother yelled at the top of her voice to everyone inside the house that they should gather in one room and hide there until the fighting in the streets was over. She grabbed Rashida's hand and snuffed out the candles. The women stayed there, the silence broken only by their terrified breathing.

"Mother," Sayyida said, clutching at her mother,. "when's Ibrahim going to come?"

"Go on," Rashida told her, pursing her lips, "cry like a woman!"

Sayyida buried her head as the sound of men's steps came closer.

"What are they going to do with us?" she asked, as she clutched her mother's shoulder as hard as she could.

Kauthar and Ibrahim's mother, Laila, started to recite verses from the Qur'an. His two sisters held on to their mother, as though every girl was returning to her mother's womb, and the hour had arrived or nearly so.

The Chief of Police's decisions were in an attempt to stay alive, and that involved both cruelty and despair. Together with Shawar's men, he had devised various ruses and maneuvers. In these conflicts, crushing men and humiliating women were the first steps towards success. He would arrest the men, crucify some, sever the limbs of others, and put still others in prison. But it was even more important to humiliate the women, and that could only be achieved by exploiting weakness and compulsion. He was not bothered about women's honor, and toying with that idea might do more harm than good. For that very reason, his only solution was whipping and public disgrace. He would choose an old or young woman from every household, whether sick or well, and flay her in front of her family until she begged for mercy and was close to death; but she was not to die. He would then crucify her by the front door of the house for several days to make clear how impotent every man and woman in Alexandria actually was. She would die of thirst right in front of her family and its menfolk. The Caliph's police needed to be in Shawar's hands and under his command. What the people of Alexandria had done had not happened for a hundred years or more. This was a noble cause, as significant as the Abbasid Caliph in Baghdad or even more.

Screams arose and hope died. The strongest men were busy fighting alongside the soldiers in West Alexandria. Only the weaker men were left, along with those who wanted to fight with Shawar and were afraid of his treachery. Accounts of whippings and death circulated. Every house locked its doors, hoping to be safe. Squads of soldiers made their way through the quarters of `Attarin, Kom Wa`la, and Al-Bab al-Akhdar. The arched wooden doors could not withstand the soldiers' brutal hands. When all doors were locked, clashing colours began to emerge. Amid the silence, brightly coloured houses almost surrendered to the sea's waves; whether that day or the next, they were bound to do so. Their life in the city was on the block. The sea will always win, but instances of courage will force the waves to bend a little, out of respect or perhaps sympathy for them all. No house was higher than three stories, and no house was without its firmly locked wooden windows to repel winter's ice and the winds that came with the waves night and day.

"I'll go and find out what the soldiers are doing," Husain said, heading for the door. "I'll talk to them."

"I beg you, don't!" his mother told him, clasping his hand. "Isn't it enough that your three brothers have all gone off to war? Stay here and don't move."

Giving her a confused look, he tried to pull his hand away, but she almost dug her nails into his hand and held tight, as though it would be her final plea on this earth.

"Kill me then before they kill you!" she told him.

Even before she could finish, the police were with them. Brandishing swords and whips, they broke down the door and entered the room—ten men circled the room, carrying lamps so they could see who was hiding there. They swept the whole room and surveyed everyone in it.

"The orders of Minister Shawar are that the people of Alexandria are to be punished," the troop's commander now told them. "Anyone and everyone who rebels, betrays, or offers assistance to the army of Nur ad-din Zengi, who has come here to raid this country, all will pay the price. Come."

"Brother," Husain asked quietly. "What do women have to do with this war?"

"They're paying the price of your brothers' stupidity. Are you willing to pay that price?"

"No, Husain, no!" his mother cried out. "I'll pay the price. Just tell me, Son, what is it you want."

"Because the police are merciful, we won't kill everyone in the household. But we are going to teach Alexandrians a lesson: betrayal and rebellion are crimes that disgrace those who commit them. So, choose from your number a slave girl or girl to be flayed and crucified by the front door. You have an hour to choose, and, if you don't, then I'll flay and crucify all the women in the household, as I've just done with your neighbours."

"That's impossible," Husain said, his mouth agape in shock. "I beg you to have mercy on the women. Take me."

"No, you're here to witness what will happen," the commander interrupted, "and to tell your brothers about it. Or do you prefer us to take your women as prisoners and use them as slave girls? Come on, choose one of yours."

"Take me," Ibrahim's mother responded immediately. "I'm old. I'm no use to anyone."

The soldier grabbed her arm to take her outside the house, but Husain stood between them.

"Don't touch my mother," he said.

The soldier punched him on the jaw so hard that he collapsed and fell groaning to the floor.

"Go on," Rashida said, looking at Sayyida. "You go. Save your mother-in-law to beyou're your fiancé's mother. Show Ibrahim how courageous you are, go on."

"He'll kill me," Sayyida said, staring at Rashida in shock, then hugging her own mother. "Didn't I tell you that Ibrahim hadn't done anything? She lied. She's as spiteful as infidels."

"You're right," her mother replied, taking a step back.

As Sayyida moved away from her mother, Kauthar looked over at Zubaida.

"You, my girl," she said. "You can tolerate whipping. Go on."

Zubaida shivered, but she also realised that Kauthar's command had to be obeyed. She looked all around her.

"You're the slave girl," Sayyida's mother told her. "You have to be sacrificed for the sake of the women under whose protection you've been living. Go on, my girl."

"Come with me," the commander said, looking at Zubaida.

Zubaida stood up, shivering, and looked all around her.

"I'm obeying the order," she said, "I have to obey the order."

At that, she collapsed in a faint. The soldier looked down at her and checked her pulse.

"Her heart's weak," he said. "She'll die before she can be crucified or the whipping's over. She's not suitable."

The soldier grabbed Ibrahim's mother again.

"Mother, no!" Husain yelled.

"Come on," Rashida said, looking at Sayyida, "sacrifice yourself for your lover's sake!"

"Where are you, Father?" Sayyida shrieked, crying loudly. "Where are you, Ibrahim?"

"Take me instead of the women," Husain pleaded.

"So, then, we're making the choice," the commander said. "We'll take all the women."

The commander looked at Shafiqa and Kamila hugging their children. He was on the point of grabbing Shafiqa when he signalled to his men to grab Sayyida, her mother, and Kauthar. The soldiers went over to take them outside the room. But before he could grab Rashida, she let out a yell.

"Me!" she shouted. "Don't take all the women. I'll come with you."

There was a shocked silence. Kauthar's eyes opened wide.

"My only daughter!" she said.

Sayyida smiled, but said nothing. Her mother let out a sigh of relief. Ibrahim's mother looked down. Before Husain could say anything, the soldier grabbed Rashida.

"Come on," he told her.

Husain tried to stop him, but Rashida went willingly with the soldier. She had no idea what awaited her, nor why she had said and decided what she had. She closed her eyes so as not to see the sunlight. She looked at the soldiers constructing the wooden frame so they could flay and crucify her for a day or more. Looking to the end of the street, she could see a girl crucified who seemed to be dead; in fact, she was certainly dead. Blood was oozing unimpeded from her mouth, eyes were closed in surrender, and life was short.

All the women in the household followed Rashida out of the house. They were all in shock and anxious, grateful for having escaped a fire that was, burning hot.

"Leave her," Husain yelled. "Since when are Egyptian women flayed? Leave her!"

The soldier put a sword to his neck, and Husain went silent. His hands and feet were bound, and he was thrown to the ground. The commander now looked at everyone gathered around Rashida.

"This is the fate of everyone who betrays the Minister and Fatimid army," he said, "all those who aid the enemy and conspire with the forces of Nur ad-din. I don't want to hear any shrieks or screams from the other women. Only *her* screams. I want them to echo all the way to Cairo, to all of Egypt. People in Fustat will hear them and learn the fate of Alexandria. People in Damiyetta and Balbis will hear them, and they will bow down in respect for the Minister and the army. Ibrahim the traitor will hear them, and he will realise that he's incapable of protecting even his own family's womenfolk. The Alexandria police now control the city and its inhabitants. Learn your lesson, Alexandrians! Rebellion inevitably leads to defeat. Once we've finished flaying her, we'll leave her tied to the frame and crucified till we have mercy on her after two or three days. Or not. That is the Minister's decision. Anyone who moves close to her or even tries to give her a drink of water will be killed.

"My only daughter, Rashida!" Kauthar screamed, begging for help. "Take me instead."

The soldier slapped her, and she fell to the ground. Meanwhile, Rashida's thoughts were not focused on what the commander was saying. Instead, they travelled to the halva factory. As a little girl, she used to wallow in the honey, and her father would chide her. Even so, she always asked him why honey stuck to the body, but water did not. He did not know the answer. She would swallow a bit of honey, then some water. He used to stop her going into the factory, but she never obeyed orders. She would go again, and he could not punish her; all his life, he could not do it. No one would punish Rashida. She was a heavenly miracle, God's gift to Kauthar and himself. Why had she dared to sacrifice herself? Had she? Was she afraid for her mother, or had the sight of children clinging to their mother really upset her? Since when had she thought about others? He was going to punish all the household's women. Her mother might die, and, who knows, so might other mothers as well, leaving behind a lot of orphans. There was Sayyida, self-centred and stupid, staying alive while she, Rashida was going to die, and all because Ibrahim had wanted Sayyida to stay in Alexandria during the war. So let him die, and her as well, and all the others who were after her money. She opened her mouth to tell the commander that she did not want to die or be tortured. She had not meant to sacrifice herself for anyone, and...

The whip's lash came like a judgment, sudden and brutal. She did not scream, but merely let out a sigh as fire scorched her back. More lashes followed. At first, she started counting and anticipating them. But then she could no longer concentrate. Closing her eyes, she could see the glimmer of crimson flooding over everything. She let out a suppressed groan, and blood fell from her lips where she had bitten her tongue in pain and then her lips as well. She wanted to say that she did not care about anyone, and that they should leave her alone and kill everyone in the household. She wanted to beg him to end her life. She had not realised before that the human body could hurt this much, erasing memory and crushing the will. What was strange was that, after forty lashes, she no longer felt any pain. She did not know whether she had become accustomed to it or had lost consciousness. But, when the soldier poured water over her face, she tried to moisten her lips; all she wanted was a bit of water, no more.

"Water!" she begged, closing her eyes tight.

What if Ibrahim found out now that she was prepared to leave him all her money for the sake of a drink of water? Would he be happy for her to die? Did he know he was the winner? She would not think about him, but instead about all the interlinked halva-flakes, with no first or last. The nice thing about halva was that it was like construction, starting with simple materials, but then emerging from the oven like a bride fully decorated for her husband. It was as though the tedious routine of blending things together with such perfection and accuracy would always lead to spectacular creations and a kind of spiritual beauty. Had the soldier stopped lashing her? He must have done. She could no longer hear any noise around her or move her neck. Closing her eyes, she was begging passers-by to give her a drink of water, but they seemed to be as cowardly as mice faced with flames that made you even thirstier and dried up the veins.

"Untie my hands," Husain pleaded, looking at his mother. "She's going to die."

"I can't do that, Son," she replied, looking at the soldier brandishing his sword.

"This is what happens," Sayyida told her mother, "to a woman who makes false claims of sexual abuse against a man. She deserves it."

"You're right," her mother replied. "I don't know why I believed her."

A lot of blood flowed. Kamila told her children to close their eyes. Everyone gathered around to wait for the end, the way an old man will wait without hope for his absent son to come. The groans were non-stop and almost deafened Husain.

"She's going to die," he pleaded with his mother.

Kauthar wept silently, as though she had given up hope. She went over to the soldier.

"Please, Son," she begged, "give her a drink of water. Think of me as your mother."

"I can't," he replied, without even looking at her. "Police Chief's orders."

When she insisted, he snapped, "Stop talking. Or else I'll cut her head off right in front of you."

Two days later, women were slapping their cheeks in both sorrow and impotence. Husain heard the sound of horses' hooves. His brother must be coming.

"Ibrahim!" he yelled, looking straight ahead.

The soldier grabbed his spear to strike the newcomer, but Ibrahim's arrow went straight to his heart. Arrows from Ibrahim and his men rained down and finished off all the men surrounding the house. Ibrahim and his men had finally arrived. He hurried over to the place where Rashida was crucified and started untying her without looking at anyone.

"Get me a drink of water," he told one of his soldiers.

Sayyida rushed over to him and started talking non-stop.

"The soldiers humiliated us, Ibrahim," she said. "They almost killed us.

They started whipping us. I realised that I was going to die. Do you hear me, Ibrahim? Is my father fine? I was scared without you, really scared..."

He did not look at her. He carried Rashida inside the house. Looking at her face, he could not tell whether or not she was still alive. He poured water over her face, leaned her head on his arm, and tried putting some water in her mouth.

"Try to drink," he kept saying. "Do you hear me? Open your eyes. If you can hear me, open your eyes..."

She tried opening her eyes, but could not do it.

"You're fine," he said in relief. "Thank God! Have a drink."

He opened her mouth and put some water in it.

"Try to swallow," he said.

Husain was standing in front of him, trying to convey his sense of sorrow.

"We won't find a doctor now," Ibrahim said, as though not listening to him. "The soldiers will be back. Leave the house and collect the men."

"Collect them how?" Husain asked in confusion.

"They've all come back. Tell their officers that Ibrahim needs to address all the men and shaikhs."

"Has Yusuf come back with you? He's the cause..."

"No, he's not the cause," Ibrahim replied, looking at Rashida. "The minister's the cause. Don't let humiliation cloud your vision like a handful of dust."

Kauthar put her head on her daughter's chest.

"My daughter," she said, weeping and sighing, "my beloved girl."

He looked at her filthy clothes, soiled with piss and blood, and then ran his hand over her forehead and soaking hair.

"Rashida," he asked anxiously, "can you hear me?"

"I'm dying," she muttered. "I want some water. Death, pain..."

He grabbed a piece of white cloth, dampened it with water, and started wiping the blood and sweat off her face.

"You're going to the room with Shafiqa and Kamila," he told her. "You'll wash and go to sleep. You'll be fine. Drink some water."

"Ibrahim," Sayyida said, giving him a shocked look, "leave her to your sister. This isn't right."

He ignored her and put some more water in Rashida's mouth. With difficulty, she managed to swallow it. Again, he wiped her forehead and hair.

"The soldiers have gone," he told her. "You're all right now. Do you hear? Open your eyes...come on!"

She tried opening her eyes again, but could not manage it.

"When you take her clothes off," he told Shafiqa, "be very careful. We need to treat the wounds with herbs and water. I'll wait till you tell me in person how she's doing. If she dies, I will hold you personally responsible."

She nodded in agreement. Rashida was still resting her head on his arm, her eyes shut.

"Can you hear me?" he asked moving closer.

"Mother," she said in a muted tone.

"Who's talking to you? Who am I?"

"I know your voice," she replied, trying to open her eyes again. "You're..."

"Who am I? Open your eyes!"

She found it hard to open her eyes. When she managed it, she stared at him as though not actually seeing him. Her eyes glazed over.

"You were incredibly brave today," he told her softly, still rubbing her hair and face with his hand. "If that continues and you can stand the pain, I'll be very proud of you, Sicilian's daughter."

"Ibrahim," she whispered, "the tyrant!"

"In person!" he replied, much relieved.

He carried her to the room, then left. He lingered by the door, listening to his brother, his heart aflame with anger. After a while, he went back into the room, where she was groaning and muttering some unintelligible words. He went over, sat down in front of her bed, and held her hand.

"Rashida," he said, rubbing her hand to get the circulation moving, "remember that you're the Sicilian's daughter, of my blood. I'll never take orders from anyone who hurts my family. The people who did this will pay dearly. Rest assured about that."

As he looked all around him, he was feeling confused and very sympathetic.

"I want something to drink," she said, trying to move.

"Drink slowly," he said, handing her some water.

How was it possible for a girl with such dynamism to act like a puppy that has just lost its mother and then been abused and nearly killed by a nasty child? Her wrongdoing had spread far and wide, but then it had disappeared like water in the desert.

"I want my father," she kept saying, tears rolling down her cheeks. "Where's my father?"

"She needs you, Aunt," he told her mother.

Kauthar went over to her.

"I'm afraid that, if I even touch her," Kauthar said hesitantly, "she'll die. Is she going to die?"

Rashida moaned and screamed, so Ibrahim took her mother out of the room. Ibrahim went over to her without even thinking, sat down on her bed, and cradled her head in his arms.

"You're fine," he whispered. "I promise you that this won't ever happen again. It's my fault. Forgive me!"

She tried to lift her head, but could not do it. She rested her head on his chest.

"Your father would be so proud of you today, daughter of the Supreme Master and Sicilian," he told her sweetly, running his hand through her hair. "Your courage is like that of your grandfather and grandmother. Do you remember the story about Jawhar, son of Husain, son of Jawhar, when he courageously confronted Al-Hakim bi-Amr Allah, fearing neither death nor torture? Today, you remind me of him."

"Tell me," she replied, clutching her stomach.

Looking around him, he could see the disapproving looks in his sisters' eyes and the confusion in his mother's. When he tried to move, she clung to him.

"I'm going to die," she said. "So much pain, hunger, and thirst. You…"

"What am I?" he asked, putting his hand over her ear.

"Are you going to tell me the story?"

"You know about Jawhar's courage," he replied, swallowing hard, "and then Badr al-Jamali's, the man who faced up to famine and saved Egypt. Now comes Rashida, who's saved the entire Sicilian household."

She smiled and closed her eyes, her head still resting on his chest.

"Is Rashida dead?" she asked.

"No, she's not," he responded immediately, holding her shoulders. "She's still with us. She's going to eat and drink something now, and then go to sleep."

She did not respond.

"Can you hear me?" he whispered anxiously.

"Yes, I can," she muttered. "This pain is unending. Will you tell them to stop?"

"Yes, I will."

She took a deep breath on his chest, then moved her hand feebly, putting it over his heart.

"Stay here with me," she asked.

"I'm here with you," he replied, running his hand over her shoulder.

She could see her father on the day when she had wandered around Fustat. She had called out to him, but the whole world had seemed strange and dark. Tears had fallen from her eyes, but then she had collided with the huge expanse of her father's chest. Even though she was no more than five years old, she could still remember her meandering, his chest, and her own tears. Now here was another chest like her father's, just as solid and broad, its edges embracing all of life. She sighed into Ibrahim's chest.

"That's my father's scent," she whispered.

"It's part of you and me," he replied, running his hand over her shoulder again.

After a while, she fell asleep. He got up slowly, doing his best to control his sympathy and affection. He left the room.

"Look after her till I get back," he told the women firmly. "When she wakes up, she'll need to eat. Shafiqa and Kamila, she's your responsibility, the two of you."

"Poor Rashida," they both said. "But Brother, what happened...whatever happened..."

Kamila did not complete her sentence; she did not dare. Even so, she repeated to Sayyida that Rashida was a she-devil out to dominate and bewitch Ibrahim.

Sayyida kept her eye on him, worried about the way he was treating Rashida and wanting him to reassure her. But he did not even look at her. Instead, he gathered his men, anticipating the policemen's punishment for being so bold as to rescue Rashida and kill the soldiers.

"We're defending honour and households," he shouted to his brothers, unsheathing swords. "Minister Shawar's police force has to be defeated in Alexandria. If it's not, then we'll all die in shame."

Salim and Sadiq both left with Ibrahim, but Husain stopped and looked at him.

"Peace is a better idea, Brother," Husain said. "The consequences of war are dire. Our rebellion and defiance are entirely responsible for what has happened. If—"

"If you're not man enough," Ibrahim interrupted, "then stay here with the women. Don't say another word so I don't kill you."

Husain gave his elder brother a chiding look, but said nothing.

"Ibrahim's angry, Son," his mother said. "Your elder brother's like a father to you now. You have to obey his instructions."

"My brother's going to finish off our entire family," he replied, looking straight at her. "I don't trust him, and I no longer feel any love for him."

"That's the way Rashida has influenced you," she said, her mouth agape. "She's a devil who sows discord and destruction."

"She's the only one of us who knows how he really is and who's now paid the price for his actions."

With that, he hurried out of the room and headed for his father's halva factory. He saw the men preparing for battle. From afar, he spotted Ibrahim moving as swiftly, angrily, and cautiously as a lion enveloped by flames. He went from house to house, from the Thousand Pillar Mosque to the `Attarin

Mosque, yelling to every shaikh and young man to pick up weapons and defend his womenfolk. One after another, the men listened to him, and they all found themselves surrounded by police. Chaos covered the sands and reached as far as the sea itself—an arrow fired, another hitting a child, a policeman's sword thrust into a shaikh's chest, a fisherman's spear stuck in the Police Chief's back.

The war has started, Husain thought, and Ibrahim, yes Ibrahim, was the one who had kindled it. He was the cause of all the destruction to come, he and his friend from Syria, Yusuf ibn Ayyub. Where was he now? People were saying that he was training soldiers around the 'Attarin Mosque. Do you hear and see it all, Badr al-Jamali? Minister of Sword and Pen, Supreme Master? Did you expect the Alexandrians to train to use weapons around your mosque, and —to be trained by a Kurd? Don't they say, Badr, that he has come from a country near yours? Have you heard of him? I, Husain, can tell you about him. He is the one who encouraged my brother to rebel, threatening an unprecedented danger from the north, like a plague of locusts that consumes the entire harvest and leaves nothing alive. We know nothing about him and pay him no heed. We were living in peace and security, far removed from government conspiracies. We Alexandrians have nothing to do with rulers. During festivals we go out, greet the Caliph, and sell halva. We look forward to festivals and holidays the way children look forward to the return of a father who has been traveling for many years. We were living in peace. Ministers changed. One would be nasty and demand taxes that we paid; another would change a policy, and it would stop. A minister might want to humiliate us, so we would submit, not out of respect, but rather because we simply wanted to live in peace. Now, here comes my brother Ibrahim, thinking that he can change the entire world! If Adam himself could not stop his two sons fighting, then will Ibrahim the halva-maker be able to put a stop to tyranny in the country, hold back the dangerous Crusaders, and restore justice in the world? How naïve are you, Brother? You have already transcended those limits. Naivete's limits involve wanting a virgin wife untouched by anyone but you. But wanting to control your destiny and seeking justice in a world based on tyranny, that has taken you beyond the limits of safety, Brother.

The screams now intensified, as women lost husbands and sons. You want to take revenge on the police? Don't you realise that vengeance is all perdition, and that spilled blood can never to restored to the veins?

He heard someone banging on the factory door. All the men had already gone out to fight. He tried opening the door for Jawwad, but could not do it.

"Save me, by the Lord of the Kaaba!" Jawwad pleaded. "I haven't done anything. Save me!"

Husain looked around him, trying to find a piece of iron to break open the door. He told Jawwad to move away from the door, then lunged at it with an iron bar. It did not break. He tried again, Ibrahim's image constantly beside him. Had Husain come there to hide? That is what Ibrahim would think, but actually, he had not come to hide. He just did not like wars and could not stand the sight of blood—of innards splattered on the roads and limbs scattered like so many pieces of bread on a feast day.

He was winning against the door. When Jawwad emerged, Husain looked at him, out of breath.

"Who imprisoned you inside there?" he asked Jawwad.

"Your brother did," he replied. "I haven't done anything. All I want is to be married to Rashida. Does someone like me deserve to die of hunger and thirst? Let me go."

"I believe you," Husain told him. "Leave here and don't come back to Alexandria, or else he'll kill you."

Jawwad departed, tottering as he walked and calling out his thanks to Husain.

The screams were still audible over the sound of the sea's waves. The fighting between the police and Alexandrians was still going on, the noise clearly audible.

Husain burst into tears; he had no idea why. Was it because he had lost the brother who used to hold his hand when he was young? Ibrahim had played with Husain and walked through the streets with him. He was the brother who had taught him how to swim, ride horses, and make halva. Or was it because the sight of Rashida, suspended between life and death, had shaken him to the very core? She had groaned and pleaded, but he had been fettered and weak. Ibrahim must be thinking that he was a coward. Ibrahim was the cause. He would never remember the joyous moments they had experienced as young boys. He would always remember the sight of Rashida, and that was Ibrahim's fault. Tomorrow, his mother was going to die, and so would all his brothers. Ibrahim, his brother, was no longer a brother. He had befriended the Kurd, and that Kurd was now closer to him than his own brother. Fine, he would not think about it. He would cry; that at least brought some relief. When he left this place, would he find out, he wondered, who had died and who was still alive? Would he ever see his mother again? He wanted to see her at least once in order to ask her forgiveness. Sometimes, he would lose his nerve and defy her just to confirm his own identity. Yet she was always like tent poles he could lean on, withstanding strong winds and destiny's tempests alongside him. How I love you, Ibrahim's mother, even if I have never told you so.

He took the rest of the kunafa and started eating it as he dried his eyes. A day went by, then another. His father...what had he looked like? Was he like Ibrahim? He hoped not. He was a compassionate father, that much was certain. Less innocent perhaps, but gentler. Why was it that, whenever his father's image loomed in his memory, it was Ibrahim's face that he saw?

A terrifying silence prevailed. There was no more fighting in the streets. Maybe everyone in Alexandria was dead. Yes, they had died. Why did his heart break over Ibrahim? He was more worried about him than about his mother, Salim, Sadiq, and his two sisters. He really wanted to go to him now, to hug him, and cry. If he was dead, would he hear him? He would ask him for forgiveness; after all, he had not done anything. He would ask that the two of them go back to the way they had been in the distant past, to plunge into the depths of the sea and search for conch and pearls. Whoever found the first shell would emerge happy to tell the other.

"Brother," he would tell Ibrahim eagerly, eyes gleaming as he clutched his shell, "you're the one who always finds the best shells."

Was Ibrahim now dead, he wondered, before he could congratulate him? Would he be able to ask that they both plunge into the sea again and look for shells? That day was all he desired. If he was going to die at that very moment, then let him search for a single, perfect shining shell, just as love concealed inside the heart never shifts.

This silence was harder to take than the clash of swords and whinnying of wounded horses. He felt his way cautiously, slowly opened the door, and looked out into the street. The sun was shining, and the police had disappeared. He noticed the corpses of police in the roadways. He hesitated, but then went out and, looking all around him, started walking slowly. He was not holding his sword; he could not do it and did not like killing. He noticed one of the men picking up corpses for burial.

"What's happened, Brother?" he asked gently.

"The Alexandrians have beaten the police," the man replied, eyes gleaming with a strange kind of joy. "The city belongs to its people once again."

"What do you mean?" Husain asked, not understanding. "What are you going to do with the corpses?"

"We'll bury them, Brother. Even enemy corpses need to be buried. Do you know Ibrahim the halva-maker? He's the real hero, our saviour. That man's a tribute to the whole of Alexandria!"

"Yes, I do know him," Husain said angrily. "But aren't you worried about Shawar's reaction, for instance?"

"The Alexandrians have managed to defeat the entire police force all on their own," the man responded enthusiastically. "This is our city. Why should I worry about that traitorous minister? Listen, Brother, he's a minister who asked the Crusaders to help him. Anyone who does that can't be trusted. The Crusaders are like weasels; they can change their colours and then attack one day or the next. The halva-maker, Ibrahim, son of the Sicilian, is a great man. Come with me to the `Attarin Mosque so you can shake his hand."

"I don't want to shake his hand," Husain replied angrily. "Don't you realise that this is the end of the city? Starting wars and killing the police is just the first spark in a fire that's going to consume us all."

CHAPTER FIVE

No sooner did Ibrahim enter his mother's room than she gave him a big hug, then turned to her two sons, Salim and Sadiq, and greeted them, too.

"We were fighting as well, Mother," they both said. "But it's Ibrahim who's getting all the kisses and greetings."

"You're all my children," she told them warily.

"Husain hasn't come back yet?" Ibrahim asked with a smile.

"No. I'm worried about him."

"He's fine. Don't be alarmed."

"I'm afraid they've taken him prisoner, or he's—"

"I'll find him today," Ibrahim interrupted her. "I promise you."

She prayed for him, then stroked his shoulder.

"Are the women well?" he asked, looking over at the women's quarters.

"Yes, Son, they're all well."

"How is Rashida?"

"The wounds are still painful. Some of them have turned septic. I don't know what to do with her."

"What has the doctor said?"

"We haven't found one."

"I sent one here," he replied angrily, "before I went off to fight Shawar's men."

"He never came, Ibrahim."

He looked at his brother and told him to bring the doctor. He then asked Zubaida to tell her mistress that he wished to see her.

"Open your eyes, my lady," Zubaida told Rashida, as she covered her back. "My Lord Ibrahim wants to see you."

She tried to move, but it was no use. Ever since she had been flayed by the soldier a week earlier, she had been sleeping on her stomach. She was eating a little and drinking a lot. She was in constant pain. All her visions and memories were confused. Her mother kept talking to her and encouraging her to eat. She put some herbs on the wounds, but they did nothing. The world seemed like wheat inside a sieve: it was shaken, and then everything vanished save the stones and sand.

She was not aware when he came into her room. He didn't hesitate to remove the cover from her back and inspect the wounds. He looked all over her back, examining every wound left by the whip. He focused on a deep wound in her lower back that was still oozing blood and pus. When he put his hand on it, she groaned.

"It needs time," he said with a frown. "Be patient. It needs to be cleaned. Forgive me. You should have been seen by a doctor."

He ran his fingers lightly over the edge of the wound, and she closed her eyes. The wound was more to the heart than to the body.

"What you did was truly heroic," he told her. "It is something neither I nor anyone else expected."

"I regret doing it," she said with a mixture of sorrow and sarcasm. "I swear to you that, after the first lash and as I hung there, Cousin, I would have sacrificed the entire family, including my mother."

"I understand," Ibrahim replied with a smile. "Pain will always weaken and humiliate people. But you're always proud."

She tried to move. She glanced at the sheet covering her, then at him, and was shocked by the flimsy clothes she was wearing.

"I want to clean your wound," he told her, as he stood up to leave. "I'll let you choose something appropriate, but I'm going to tear open the place where the wound is, so don't wear your most expensive clothes."

Once he had left the room, she called for Zubaida.

"That was Ibrahim, wasn't it?" she asked wearily.

"Yes, my lady."

"He said I'm always proud. I heard him say it. He said I'm courageous—strange words."

"He was looking at your wounds as though they were inside his own heart," the slave girl replied in confusion. "He was worried and anxious. Oh, my Lady, if only you'd seen him. He checked your whole back the way doctors do, then he ran his hands—"

"Quiet!" Rashida snapped. "I don't want to know. It seems I'm not well. I'm hearing strange words, and peculiar things are happening to me. Bring me my clothes."

The slave girl brought her some clothes from which to choose. After looking at all of them, she selected the prettiest and most expensive. The slave girl gave her a dubious look.

"My Lady," she said, "he asked you to wear something cheap."

"I never do what my cousin tells me," she replied. "He has no authority over me. Tell me, Zubaida, this is all like a dream. Did Ibrahim embrace me a week ago and tell me stories? Or did I dream it?"

"Yes, he did, my Lady," Zubaida replied. "He ran his hand through your hair as though you were his little daughter."

Her eyes glazed over.

"What did I do?" she asked with a frown.

"You let your head fall onto his chest as though he were your father."

"When you're ill," she stammered, "miracles can happen. It's as if his chest were as stolid as my own father's, offering reassurance to those who rested their heads in its folds. But Ibrahim's not like that. He's not as kind as my father, nor as merciful. In his hands, there can be no serenity."

"I don't understand, my Lady," Zubaida responded in confusion. "Forgive me."

There was a knock on the door, and she opened it. Rashida tried to sit up, but the pain made that impossible.

"Give me some kohl, quickly," she told Zubaida.

But, before she could take it, Ibrahim had come into the room. Their eyes met.

"Sleep on your stomach as you've been doing before," he told her firmly. "I want to clean that wound before the doctor comes."

"Let's wait for the doctor," she replied.

"Come on," he insisted, looking at the slave girl. "Help her lie on her stomach. There's no time to lose. Maybe he won't come under such circumstances."

Rashida opened her mouth to object, but after a look at his expression, she did what he wanted.

"Don't hurt me the way the soldier with the whip did," she pleaded. "Are you going to open the wound with a knife, Ibrahim?"

"I can't believe that Rashida is begging me not to hurt her," he replied, taking out a knife. "Tell me how you came to decide to sacrifice yourself for the sake of the entire household."

She tried turning towards him, but he stopped her.

"I was standing there, strong and defiant, in front of the soldiers," she said.

"They entered the house and said they were going to choose just one woman, one..."

She screamed and tried to move. Zubaida held her down as best she could. She cursed him and the day she had first seen him. He told the slave girl to shut her up.

"If you do that," she pleaded, "I swear that I'll kill you with my own hands. What are you doing? Do you plan to slaughter me, to flay my flesh again?"

"I've used the knife to open up the wound," he replied calmly, squeezing the wound to remove the pus mixed with blood. Now I'm going to clean it. You're being very brave. You remember, don't you: Rashida never begs or gets scared."

"Please stop," she pleaded, as the pain became unbearable. "I'd rather die."

"Sometimes, just an hour's pain is better than a lifetime of putrid wounds. Tell me when it was you started hating me so much."

"I don't remember. Ever since I was born. Now, I hate you even more. If I could, I'd tear you apart, stick the knife in your guts, take out your liver, and cut it into pieces."

She screamed again as he used the knife to open up another wound.

"What would you do with my liver after you'd cut it up?" he asked.

Rashida tried to get up, but Zubaida held her down. Rashida threatened her, then started to curse, swear, and scream at the top of her voice. Then she pleaded and started crying. tears fell, and the groans never stopped.

"Jawwad's tried to steal my factories," Ibrahim told her. "Could it be, Cousin, that you asked him to steal them from your own cousin? What should I do, and how should I punish you?"

She let out another loud groan as she tried to sit up.

"Stop!" she cried. "This is shameful. What you're doing to me is shameful. It would be better for me to die. The pain's unbearable."

She resisted as hard as she could and managed to escape Zubaida's grip. She put her hand on his stomach.

"Ibrahim," she begged, "please don't keep hurting me. Let me be, I beg you. I can't stand the pain."

The slave girl opened her eyes, but she could not say anything. Rashida was in so much pain, she did not realise that her naked breasts were pressed against her cousin's chest, and that her arms wrapped around his waist did not conceal anything in the darkness. But Ibrahim knew it; he was aware that the body clinging to him did not belong to a girl, but to a woman teeming with sexuality. His own chest, he realised, was pounding, and his mind was distracted. With a frown, he did his best to recall why he had come and who she was.

Hand raised, he paused for a moment, then ran it over her hair.

"The wound has to be cleaned," he told her gently. "You're brave, so you can tolerate it. If you died, who'd get your money? Me and Sayyida. Is that what you want?"

He tried to push her away, but she clung to him and, albeit unconsciously, kept her semi-naked body close to his. Zubaida looked at her in amazement, but found no words. Ibrahim reluctantly grabbed her shoulders, trying to push her away, but he stopped.

He let go of her shoulders, and she moved closer still.

"I've been in a lot of pain," she told him, "and the thirst! That's the worst of all. Don't leave me without any water again. Promise me, Ibrahim, that you won't leave me with no water."

As she closed her eyes, her pain blended with another frightening sensation. She could smell his scent inside her soul.

He raised his hand again to push her away, but she buried her head in his chest. He ran his hand over her ears and hair, then dug his fingers into her hair. He looked at her.

"There's just one wound left," he told her feebly.

"It's one that's hard to get rid of," she replied clearly.

"You'll be able to tolerate just one wound," he whispered, moving close to her ear.

Without realising it, he kept his mouth close to her ear and breathed slowly, trying to reassemble his distracted will. Where was his mind now? Why was his heart pounding and why were flames scorching his insides? Could it be that he really desired this female jinn, the cause of all humanity's suffering?

She gasped and shifted her position, searching for something to cover her body. Once she had done that, she closed her eyes.

"Where on earth has your mind gone, Rashida?" she muttered. "Where's your common sense?"

He sat up, worried thatshe might notice his shaking hand and quivering voice.

"We can wait for the doctor," he told her. "I'll go and get him."

"No!" she replied firmly. "You clean the wound."

He looked at the coverlet, not forgetting what it concealed.

"Come on," he told Zubaida. "There's just one wound left. Hold her down."

Rashida screamed and resisted, but finally Zubaida managed to control her. Rashida lay on her stomach. She fell silent and closed her eyes as she awaited the stab in her heart. He brought the knife close to the final wound. He shook his head as though he wanted to rouse himself from the effects of a glass of wine he had drunk unintentionally. As he stuck the knife in, she bit her lips till they bled. The taste of blood in her mouth calmed her heart. She wept silently. When he had finished, she did not look at him, but buried her head in the pillow.

He told Zubaida to get some bandages for the wounds and bound them tightly himself.

"I promise you that, given time, the pain will recede," he told Rashida. "It always does. Come on. Rashida never cries; she only hatches schemes."

She turned toward him and wiped away her tears.

"It's your beloved Sayyida who's always crying," she replied menacingly. "She's a coward who wouldn't sacrifice herself for anyone, including her own mother!"

"There's some wisdom in a bit of cowardice. Courageous women are not fit for marriage."

"Here's to your cowardly wife, Cousin!" she retorted, giving him a hateful look.

"What happened with Jawwad was at your urging," he said, looking straight at her. "I was expecting it. I don't know why I can expect anything from you."

"Maybe because you hate me as much as I hate you."

He glared at her, and there was a tense silence. The attraction was as painful as a whiplash. When had it started, and how had it burst into flame? She had no idea. He moved closer to her without explanation or question. When he put his hands on either side of her face, her strength crumbled, and her hand almost surrendered to the pain. However, he grabbed hold of it before her shoulder fell back on to the bed. He held onto her shoulder with both his hands and wiped away a tear that glistened on her neck.

"Zubaida," he said, "bring me some water so I can wash her face."

Rashida opened her mouth to object, even though she did not really want to stop him. He took the bowl of water and, with no warning, threw all of it on her face. She opened her mouth to breathe, and some of the water went down her throat. Grabbing a piece of cloth, he started wiping her face.

"If you'd obey my orders," he told her, "it would be better for you, and you'd achieve your every dream. But you're recalcitrant, rebellious, and bad."

"I'm just like you, Ibrahim," she replied, closing her eyes so that he would not wipe them with the rag. "Aren't you recalcitrant too, and rebelling against the Minister?"

"Yes, I'm rebelling against the Minister. But, unlike you, I'm not rebelling against the men in my family. You're a girl, just remember that!"

"And, if it weren't for me, "she replied forcefully, "none of the women in the household would still be alive."

"That's true," he replied reluctantly, turning pale. "Our grandfather used to say that courage at a crucial moment was the summit of generosity and nobility."

"Stop!" she said.

"I will," he said, moving closer and wiping her mouth.

She opened her eyes.

"You're going to be fine," he told her confidently. "A couple of days, no more, then the pain will fade."

"I'll be fine for sure," she replied angrily. "Just as long as I never have to set eyes on you again."

He looked at her lips, which were still bleeding steadily. He took the cloth and held it against her lower lip.

"Hold it there for a while," he said. "Nothing scares you, and no consequences make you reconsider. You amaze me, Rashida. Our war isn't over, just remember that. Today, I wish you to have a blessing."

Ibrahim. If only he knew! She had been eight years old when she decided that she would be married to him. She could remember the day. She had been playing with his sister and brother, and her mother had told her that, now that she was older, she had to stop playing and joining in the cousins' games. And it was not just games. He was always there in the background, standing still and aloof like the mast of a ship. His glow would hover all around him like a lighthouse at dawn. Ever since she had become aware of his name and lineage, she had seen no one else; when her girlish body had turned into that of a young woman, she had dreamed of no one else. At night, he would visit her in her dreams, give her endless embraces, and drown her in kisses. Then what? Her imagination could think of nothing else. The kisses had managed to drown out the darkness of night and help make the succession of days tolerable. She was just eight when she had rushed over to him.

"Why aren't you playing with Shafiqa and Kamila?" he had asked her, staring at her in amazement.

"Because I'm going to be married to you," she replied resolutely.

Maybe he had laughed. At the time, he was twenty and she was eight.

"Rashida," he told her. "Go and play with them."

"Don't poke fun at me," she replied seriously. "Women are married at an age like mine. I'm going to tell my father that I want to be married to you."

"But no girl will ever dare do such a thing," he replied, as though talking to a child that had lost its way. "If she's from a decent family, she'll wait till her father chooses a husband for her."

"But you're my cousin," she protested. "You have to be married to me. Are you going to refuse?"

Maybe it was her brazen approach that had surprised and even shocked him.

"Rashida," he told her unequivocally, "this conversation is utterly inappropriate. I thought you were a good girl. Good girls don't think that way. Stop talking about it. Go on, go and play."

"But I'm not a little girl."

"Go away, Rashida!" he told her angrily. "Don't speak like this again."

"You just don't want me. But my father's going to make you be married to me. He does everything I ask him. I'm going to be married to you."

He stood up and headed for the door.

"Come outside," he told her. "I know Rashida's a good girl. But the Rashida who was here a few moments ago was possessed by the devil."

He had not understood; clearly, he had not understood. No devil was possessing her. Rather, she detected part of her own self in him. That had all been part of a past, but now, she knew him better—he was ambitious and tyrannical. Denying your own heart was an unforgiveable sin. If he were to do anything or commit any crime other than that one, she could forgive him. But days and months went by, all of them spent longing for him while he kept rejecting her. As a result, she came to loathe him as much as she loved him. She constructed city walls around her heart. If he wanted to torture her for the rest of her life, then let him suffer along with her. If he rejected an unparalleled passion, then he would get none, and no wife would ever enter his life and assuage his thirst. Now she was more wary of him. From the lower neck, it was always easier to get access to the throat and grasp the soul.

Tears glistened in her eyes, but they did not fall.

"Tell me what you saw," she ordered Zubaida.

Zubaida gave her a confused look.

"I mean," Rashida went on, still lying on her stomach, "when he looked at my wounds and back."

The slave girl did not respond.

"You don't want to lie," Rashida went on. "You never saw anything. He was just like a doctor, wasn't he? His body didn't quiver or show any desire."

"You're very beautiful, my Lady," Zubaida replied, swallowing hard. "But the wounds..."

"They've disfigured my back, haven't they?"

"Given time, they'll disappear."

"He needs to disappear. Why hasn't he died in this war?"

CHAPTER SIX

He could not sleep. He was no longer thinking about the Crusaders, the Minister, or even Sayyida, the ideal, obedient wife. It was Rashida who occupied his thoughts. He would see her every moment, and his body would shudder, an unsettling feeling of inebriation coursing through his limbs. He would see her reach out to hug him spontaneously, begging him to stop the pain. He could almost envision himself running his hands over her body, the shadow of her bosom and curves of her waist visible through the torn garment. Was he in the grip of a satanic desire, or was it something else? He had no idea. He despised Rashida as he did serpents and scorpion; she was the very last girl in the world he could desire. How he blamed and despised his own body. It would have to obey him, as it had in the past. Ah, Rashida! He closed his eyes regretfully, as her hands that had clasped his waist passed over the calm, settled waters of the Nile like hurricanes. Fine, Rashida! You can toy with the body any way you like, Cousin, but the heart is far removed from your dreams. For several months now, he had been seeing her as she'd been when she was eight: a spoiled, bored, nasty child. He had been pushing her aside, like a child with whom he had no desire to chat, nor indulge in her lower level of thinking. But then, that same woman had appeared in front of him as someone of spectacular and unexpected beauty. While he was using his knife to open the infected wounds, the passion inside his own heart had burst out, and love had started toying with the doughnuts and halva. Ah, halva-maker's daughter, how do I withstand your despotism and lies? He did his best to recall little Rashida, who he had tried to avoid. How he detested her bored attitude, her nagging, and her sense that humans in general were slaves to her will. How much he wanted to forget her. Sayyida was prettier, more sophisticated, calmer, and...

He rubbed his eyes as he tossed and turned, moving right and left. He sat up. Wartimes were like changing seasons, roiling the peaceful heart and stirring anxieties in stable souls. In his dreams, he heard the voice of Qais, reciting his poetry about his cousin:

I adored Laila, young and innocent,

The shape of her breasts as yet invisible to others,

A tiny pair. As we tend our lambs, would that

We did not age, nor did the lambs.

He sprang out of bed, washed his face, and cursed his body.

"You traitor, stop being so stupid. That evil woman has rattled you and is out to destroy you. Just look at Sayyida's angelic face and think about her. She's a woman who will obey your every command and listen hopefully and admiringly to your every word. Just think about Sayyida and her innate modesty. She'll never burden the sorrowful heart or sting the limbs."

Yes, indeed, there was Sayyida. However, it was Rashida's body that lingered in his imagination. This was not love. It was sheer lust, the kind a man feels for a dancer or slave girl. True love is pure and beautiful, bringing out the loveliest aspects of the heart.

Once his mind had been reassured by those words, he relaxed and went to sleep.

After just a few days, Rashida's wounds closed their doors, as though her cousin's knife were capable of anything. She started moving around eagerly. In her uncle's house, there was an underground passage that led to the sea, as though it was difficult to breathe without the salty seawater and the waves that would incite rebellion and resistance. She was going to follow in his footsteps down the passage. She was planning to find out everything about him, his heart's secrets and his soul's weaknesses—not because she desired him, no. but rather because he was enemy number one. Still, she had to be cautious. The heart would never offer to help its owner. She went into the narrow, crumbling passage, at the end of which light blended with cascading droplets of water that moved in and out according to their desires and inclinations. Ibrahim took off his coat, trousers, and shirt. She closed her eyes, then opened them again as he plunged straight into the waves and did not float on the surface. She could not remember the touch of salt water on her skin. In the past, she had played with other children, splashing each other in fun and in the hope of success. Today, people were saying that women should not swim in salt water for fun. If she wanted to learn something about waves, then she could watch them without getting too close or touching them. She put her feet close to the edge and stuck them into the water. The waves struck her chest, and she gasped at the cold water and the sight of the spume that always lingered on the horizon. She sat down courageously to wait for the waves to come one after another, and let out a suppressed cry every time a wave hit her. Lowering her head, she rested it confidently on the water's surface. When it covered her entire face, she started laughing and wiping the water away, awaiting the next assault.

He was swimming so far out that she forgot he was there. Then she realised he had been watching her for some time. Eventually she heard his voice.

"Have you had enough?"

"No, I haven't finished yet."

She cupped her hands over her forehead to shield her eyes and looked at him, maybe for the first time. This time, bashfulness did not win. She had often imagined the way he looked. She ran her eyes over his powerful, tawny arms, his shoulders and chest. As she closed her eyes, she was imagining herself, settled here by his lungs for the rest of her days.

"You're not shy, are you?" he chided her.

"You're the one who brought me here," she replied as she stared at him.

"No, you've been trailing me. Why did you come? What is it you want?"

"I want what you want, Cousin," she responded angrily.

"No, Rashida," he said. "We've nothing in common. That'll never happen."

She scooped up some water and threw it angrily in his face.

"Whoever said that I wanted that to happen?" she retorted.

He may have been as surprised by her spontaneous response as she was by his. He moved the water in her direction and then hurled it in her face as hard as he could. She screamed and surrendered to the waves. The waves swept at her feet when she was not looking. He put his hands around her waist, carried her out, and pushed her to the sea floor. The world turned white, joy blended with destruction. She screamed and rose up, looking for him all around her. Once she found him, she put her arms around his neck.

"If you're planning to drown me," she told him, "then you're going to drown too!"

He grabbed her arms to push her away.

"Is it appropriate for a woman of such spontaneity to carry the future of the halva-maker's family on her shoulders?" he asked.

He let her push him and allowed himself to lay down on the sand.

"So, you're well again, Rashida," he said. "You've just proved that."

"If you let me go back to Cairo," she said, dumping water on him, "you'll never see me again. But you won't. Are you in love with me, Cousin? Have you loved me your whole life?"

"You're out of your mind!" he replied.

She seemed to have woken him up, or almost. He looked around for his clothes. He found them spread out on a rock and put them on, as she shamelessly looked on.

"I'll marry you off to someone who deserves you," he told her. "I wonder who might that be, Rashida? Someone who's committed all kinds of atrocities, put barriers between hearts, annoyed his parents, and cut off all mercy. Someone whose life is full of enough crime to deserve you."

"You..."

"That'll never happen. I've told you."

"I used to say you're a tyrant, and I've never said I want you as a husband. Where's your dream taken you? You're the very last man on earth I would think about."

"Come with me," he told her, taking her hand. "Make sure you don't come here on your own. Sometimes, the waves can be very powerful. Today they've been gentle, but tomorrow, Cousin, they might snatch you away, just like the world itself."

Whether deliberately or just on the spur of the moment, she grabbed his hand. He lay down beside her, and she rested her head on his chest without saying a word. Today, she was fully conscious. For the first time and maybe the last—who knows—her imagination had turned into reality.

He put his arms around her waist and pulled her even closer.

He moved his mouth closer... Did he? Did he move his mouth closer to hers, or did it just seem that way? She closed her eyes, and her heart pounded.

"Like pounding waves," he whispered.

He kissed her head slowly and ran his lips over her forehead, then her eyes, and then her cheek. For just a moment, his lips paused over her chin, then moved on to her neck, his breaths faltering at the very source of hers. The air inside his chest was hurting her even more than the lashes from the whip.

"The waves are always pounding," he whispered, as he buried his face in her neck.

She clasped her fingers tightly and whispered his name. Moments like these flashed by like rainclouds. After a few moments, he moved away and closed his eyes. Then he leapt to his feet, squeezing her hand before he let it go.

"That didn't happen," he said, head lowered. "Let's forget what's happened today. It's my fault. Forgive me! I wasn't using my mind. Sometimes..."

"I know what you're going to say, Cousin," she interrupted.

For just a moment, he stared at her, as though he had no idea what he was doing or why his body was acting with a spontaneity that was beyond comprehension.

"The wheat-porter's not good enough for you," he said, turning towards her. "I can't understand what you admire about him."

"His humility," she replied without thinking.

He gave a triumphant smile and moved closer.

"Cousin," he told her, putting a finger on her chin, "he won't be giving way to you. Once you're married to him, you'll become his servant."

"You don't know me, Cousin," she replied with a smile.

"Oh yes, I do. And I know him, too. Just as soon as he owns you—"

"Needless to say," she interrupted, "he'll never own me."

He stared at her in amazement.

"Furoon was our grandmother," she went on. "You know her story. She was married to a man against her will, and he never touched her. She went back to Badr al-Jamali. Girls are capable of doing things that men cannot accomplish."

He laughed and sat down on the sand.

"Did you imagine he was going to leave you alone without touching you? How naïve can you be? He'll force you, and you'll be his prisoner. He'll make free with all your money."

"No, he won't," she insisted. "He's promised me. I've taken documents from him before the judge. If he's married to me, he'll be selling himself to me. He's acknowledged that he has a huge debt to me; with those documents, he will obey my every instruction. If not, I'll have him put in prison. Love can work wonders."

He stared at her as though he did not believe what she was saying.

"Were you to be married to him just so that he would stand in front of me without touching you or without you even desiring him? Just so that he would have to obey your orders and spend the rest of his life in debt to you? What can I say? Cousin, the wheat-porter does indeed deserve you."

He walked away with a shrug. Her wiles were enough to nullify all thought.

Yet his tension and anxiety only increased. He became impatient and despised himself above all. When he went back to the house, he looked for Shafiqa, but could not find her. He realised that Rashida had convinced her to go back to her husband in Cairo without asking his permission or getting his approval. Shafiqa had sacrificed her brother for her husband's sake.

Rashida was humming some tunes she had learned from her grandmother as a girl, words of love spoken by the poet Tamim ibn al-Mu`izz li-din Allah. She had decided to make some sweet date halva. Meanwhile, her mother kept an eye on her, as though she had her doubts about her daughter's heart and intentions. She took a portion of baby carrots, dates, milk, and honey, and put them all in a pot over a baking pit with a moderate fire, stirring them so they would all blend together, like lovers making love. She then added a little ginger and chunks of semolina bread to thicken the mixture and poured in some sesame oil. She put her finger in the pot to make sure it was the right texture, then sucked her finger.

"It's wonderful, Mother!" she announced eagerly. "No one can make halva as well as Rashida!"

She did not notice him come in, but she could see the fire in his eyes.

"Why?" he shouted, right in her face. "What do I have to do to put an end to your evil ways? It's the devil who's giving you lessons, Rashida. My sister, my brother, and who else? Whose heart are you turning against me?"

She opened her mouth.

"Don't tell me that I'm keeping you prisoner," he went on, "and don't say you want to go back to Fustat. Don't you dare accuse me of taking your money and stopping you from being married to the man you love. You don't love Jawwad, and you never have."

Their eyes met. She was not afraid of him. She met his disapproving look with one of her own, noticing that there were threads of despair mingled with his fury.

"What's the story?" he went on. "What brought you here, and why did you enter my life? You've put a wedge between me and the people I love, everyone I love. It's as though you've come as a curse from the ancients or to take revenge on me. Is that what you want, Rashida? I wonder, do you want to humiliate me or maybe even see me dead?"

Her heart started pounding, but she did not respond.

"Why don't you answer?" he asked angrily. "If I let you go back to Fustat and returned all your money, I wonder what would happen. Would you leave me alone? Or would you keep on tracking me and seek out everyone who is out to destroy me, one after the other?"

"Your dearly beloved Sayyida still wants you. I haven't put a wedge between the two of you. But you don't want her. You never did."

He opened his eyes wide in shock.

"Your sister has to obey her husband," she went on. "and keep her marriage safe for the sake of her sons. No brother has precedence over a sister's husband, Cousin. Or have I been wrong? Even though the Fatimid and Syrian armies are at war with each other, your sister's a wife, and she has no part in a conflict between peoples. You've encouraged her to speak the truth in front of you. No one dares oppose you. I'm the only one who does. Shafiqa loves her husband, Aftakin. Her place is with him."

"You're not lacking when it comes to daring, Rashida," he replied quietly. "I only wish that I didn't have to set eyes on you for the rest of my life, although I realise that's impossible."

For the first time, those words brought tears to her eyes. She lowered her head and was unable to respond.

"What's the matter with you, Rashida?" her mother asked. "I've told you this man's hopeless. He's as spiteful as his mother."

Rashida clasped her throat as the tears overwhelmed her breathing. With a sigh, she swallowed all the moans of a life gone by and another to come.

The city had defeated Minister Shawar. The police had run away in shame. The men lifted up Ibrahim, and he became both hero and Commander.

Shaikhs and religious scholars clustered around him, some of them delighted, others unhappy about his crushing victory. Since when could a man from Alexandria liberate the city from the Minister's forces? How were they supposed to coexist in such a troubled situation? Should they be happy or worried? Shawar's men were no longer to be found in the city. So now what? Who would be in charge? Wouldn't thieves now emerge from their lairs and start attacking women? Wouldn't it have been better for the police to stay, even if they killed a girl or assaulted three women? At the very least, the population at large would be fine...

Some shaikhs and notables started whispering such things. Merchants were upset by the love that people showed for the young halva-maker. Whenever they had a crisis or felt baffled about something, they would go and ask him for help. It was as though he were the city's governor. The whole thing was dangerous. If a rebel could be the city's governor, then the entire world would be turned upside down, and they would have no idea who was good and who was bad. A familiar system of government was preferable to liberty's surprises and the shock of victory.

In fact, people became even more confused. The Crusader army was defeated at Al-Ashmunein by Asad ad-din Shirkuh, along with his nephew, Salah ad-din Yusuf ibn Ayyub. The possibility of the Syrian army entering Cairo was now confirmed, but Asad ad-din hesitated. Cairo was the capital city of the Ubaidi Fatimids, and it housed the entire Fatimid army. He did not know whether the inhabitants would support or oppose him. Alexandria was different: the people there were friends and community. Yusuf ibn Ayyub had made some firm contacts there, and people knew and respected him. Asad ad-din headed for Alexandria, and its inhabitants opened the city gates to him, hung decorations, and made halva.

Asad ad-din left Salah ad-din Yusuf ibn Ayyub in charge of things in the city and went back to Upper Egypt to fight the Crusaders, well aware that they were being resupplied and that their numbers would be increasing by thousands.

Ibrahim accompanied Salah ad-din Yusuf ibn Ayyub and announced that Alexandrians now needed a warrior, and he was a halva-maker. He'd had to fight, but he preferred to remain a halva-maker. He told them that he had learned from his great-grandfather, Jawhar, son of Husain, son of Jawhar the Sicilian, that, just like doing good deeds, heroism loses its effectiveness if it is disseminated among people. If the hero remains unknown, his impact on people at all levels is that much greater. Ibrahim said that he wanted to lend his support to the young soldier, Yusuf ibn Ayyub, and to have him take over the running of Alexandria's affairs. The Crusaders were bound to come.

Ibrahim was right. The Crusaders besieged Alexandria, and King Amaury [Amalric] was bolstered by the arrival of fifteen hundred horsemen. Men in Alexandria headed for the city walls to protect them against the Crusaders, but the siege was bound to test the people's stamina.

Water was scarce, and food cost as much as emeralds. Anyone owning a bottle of water or a jar for washing might write poems about it, as though it were a gazelle in the desert. Everything changed. Even fishing was rare. Fishermen could not go out, and there were no men around to do the fishing. They were all with Ibrahim and Yusuf ibn Ayyub, fighting against Shawar's men and the Crusaders who had besieged Alexandria. Ibrahim the halva-maker's house had been turned into a wasteland—every family had its hideout and weapons; every tent had its guard and shaikh. Rashida retreated to her room along with her mother and her slave girl, Zubaida, and she only rarely left it. She avoided encountering Sayyida and her mother. Ibrahim's mother and sister both took refuge in Sayyida's and her mother's room, where they chatted and talked for many long hours. Rashida realised that they were talking about her, saying how evil, deceitful, and ambitious she was. She asked Zubaida to spy on them. She did, and came back to tell her how they were plotting to get rid of her. They were as eager for her departure as she herself was. They were trying to come up with a way to convince Ibrahim to let her be married to Jawwad or go back to Fustat.

"I hope they succeed," Zubaida said casually.

Rashida looked into the slave girl's eyes, filled as they were with longing and anxiety.

"Zubaida," she asked, "do you really love the Commander so much?"

"My Lady," Zubaida replied in despair, "how can a slave girl devote her entire life to passion? It's not for someone like me to have hopes or dreams. If he didn't reject my origins, he'd certainly object to my colour."

"You're beautiful, Zubaida," Rashida said, giving her an affectionate look.

"Please, my lady, don't tease my heart with dreams. Men don't like black women."

"It's the colour worn by the Abbasid caliphs, Zubaida. The man's Yusuf ibn Ayyub, who's loyal to his caliph. Men like all colours, and women are not satisfied with just one."

"Caliphs can wear black by day and take it off when they go to sleep. I can't get rid of my skin-color, however hard I try."

"Don't say that. I swear that you're beautiful. Islam doesn't make distinctions, just as the heart sees only what the soul dictates."

"Islam doesn't make distinctions, but Muslims do. Men are totally influenced by beauty."

"Your every word is about influence, as though..."

"Despair trains and educates the heart. Oh, my Lady, the woes of desperate love! There is nothing so cruel! There is mercy even in the death of loved ones."

Rashida looked at her, then lowered her head.

"Don't talk to me about despair," she told Zubaida. "I only like discussing power and courage."

Now, tears came pouring from Zubaida's eyes. Rashida reached out and hugged the slave girl.

"Don't cry," she said. "Trust that God is with you, and He will not let you down."

Zubaida first smiled, then looked at Rashida in surprise.

"My Lady," she said.

"Love, Zubaida, is like death," Rashida went on. "It doesn't make distinctions between Arabs and non-Arabs, black and white, master and servant. You're just like a sister to me."

"But I'm a slave girl."

"From today on, you're like a sister."

"I don't deserve such an honour."

"One day, I'll set you free. I promise."

"No, don't do that. I've no other home. You're my only family."

"For people, days are dynasties. Just remember that. As my great-grandfather used to say: 'Every era has its own regime and men.'"

"He wasn't talking about women, my Lady. No era treats them fairly, and no time gives them their just deserts."

At night, Rashida recalled what Zubaida had told her about Sayyida and her mother and about Ibrahim's mother and sister; how they all loathed her and regarded her as a greater evil than the devil. At midnight, she was still tossing and turning. When she got out of bed, her throat felt strangely dry. She repeated Zubaida's words to herself: 'Oh, my Lady, the woes of desperate love! There is nothing so cruel!' And as she repeated the words, her throat felt even drier, so that she almost choked. She grabbed a bottle of water and took a drink, just a sip, as Ibrahim had instructed her. But Ibrahim was no one to tell her what to do and not to do, so she drank two sips, then three, trying all the while to block out Zubaida's words, but without success. Clasping her throat, without hesitation or thought she now drank the entire bottle. By the time she finished, the sips of water had nearly suffocated her. She cleared her throat and closed her eyes. Zubaida's words gradually faded away, and her thirst was quenched.

Next morning, when Zubaida checked on the water as she did every day, she discovered that her mistress had drunk her whole week's supply in a single night. She was shocked. She told Kauthar, then left the room and went to Ibrahim's mother's room to tell her what had happened. Ibrahim's mother put her hand over her heart, then rushed to tell Sayyida, her mother, and Ibrahim's sister. They all discussed things amongst themselves.

"We must help her," Ibrahim's mother said. "She's going to die of thirst."

But the rest of the women decided that Rashida had done it out of sheer greed and malice; she wanted the whole family to starve and die of thirst. If she needed help, then it should come from her own mother, not them. Each of them took a water bottle and hid it where no one could find it. Life was now as hard as a sinner entering paradise. Rashida did not ask anyone for water. She did her best to stay inside her bedroom so she would not feel thirsty. At night, her mother let her have a sip, and Kauthar asked her to have more, but she refused. Zubaida took her own bottle and handed it to her mistress.

"It's for you, my Lady," she said.

"No," Rashida replied firmly. "My mother's given me water. Keep it!"

Two days later, Rashida started to feel exhausted, but she did not grumble or complain to anyone. But then Sayyida shouted at the top of her voice that the water bowl she had been keeping had been destroyed. Someone had come into her room, drunk it all, and destroyed the bowl so as to kill her. She knew full well who had done it, and who nursed a hellish malice inside her, namely Rashida. Sayyida burst into tears and went to see first her mother, then Ibrahim's mother, to tell everyone in the house what had happened. The slave girls all offered her their own water, and she took the bottle off one of them, drank from it, and told her to leave it with her. This slave girl could share a bottle with another slave girl, Zubaida perhaps. Rashida objected, roused herself from her exhaustion, and rejected Sayyida's pronouncements. Not only that, but she threatened to destroy every water bottle in the house if they forced Zubaida to give half her share to another slave girl. Sayyida stood firm and accused Rashida of theft. Ibrahim's mother stood impotently between the two of them, not knowing what to do. She tried sending her son a message saying that the house was on fire, there was not enough water, and the food had run out.

"We're all waiting for Ibrahim to come," she wrote in despair.

"We're not going to wait for him," Rashida said. "He has no control over me. My slave girl's not going to share water with Sayyida's."

She then told Zubaida to go into her room and stay there with the water. She threatened to hit anyone who came near the room and to destroy all their bottles. Sayyida and her mother both screamed that such an outrage would not last long; Rashida was the one who had destroyed the bottle, drunk all the water, and then lorded it over them both with her usual insane cruelty. They both decided to take over the kitchen and regulate all the food. Ibrahim's mother could do nothing, but Ibrahim's sister, Kamila, came to their aid and realised that they were both right. Rashida was ruthless and evil. They stopped her from entering the kitchen, stood defiantly right in front of her, and told her that she had to obey the house rules. If she wanted to eat, then she would have to obey their rules. Rashida refused and started grumbling, but Zubaida went to see Sayyida's slave girl and gave her half of the water. She asked to take food for herself, her mistress, and Kauthar. They gave her some. The women all agreed that Sayyida should be in charge of the kitchen; she would divide up the food. Two days later, they also agreed that Sayyida should be responsible for the water as well. They gave her all the water and asked her to exert control over Rashida and all of them, because they sometimes drank more than necessary. Rashida kept a cane in her room and refused to join the other women, but her mother agreed and handed all the water over to Sayyida. Her mother told her that peace was always the best plan, but Rashida still refused. Even Zubaida seemed to give up on her. Now Rashida had food and water only on Sayyida's terms. As far as Rashida was concerned, it would be better to die of starvation. She left the house to look for fishermen, but she found the entire city asleep and exhausted. A month, then two months had passed. The siege had intensified, and people were dying of hunger and disease.

But in fact, Sayyida was not being fair. She would choose the best cuts of meat for herself first and then her mother. She would cut up the rest according to her affectionate feelings for the people around her. She drank a lot if she felt like it, without imposing any limits on herself. Even so, she had the impression that she was being more just than the entire Muslim judiciary; she was the person most qualified to run the household. Every time Rashida objected, the slave girls would raise the canes in her face, and she would retreat.

When Ibrahim entered the house, Sayyida gave him a loving look.

"Thank God, you're safe!" she said.

He gave Sayyida a smile and looked for his mother. He kissed her hand.

"Husain hasn't shown up yet?" he asked.

"No, Son," his mother replied fearfully. "I'm worried about him."

"He'll come, don't worry. I want to understand and confirm what's happened in my absence. I've no more than an hour, then I have to go back."

She asked him about his brothers, and he told her they were fine. When he sat down, Sayyida told him everything that had happened: how Rashida had smashed her water bottle, drunk all the water, and dominated the household. She burst into tears and told him how vicious Rashida had been. She went on to beg him to rescue her from Rashida's beatings and humiliation. He listened in silence and then demanded to see Rashida. They searched the house for her, but did not find her.

"She goes out sometimes," his mother said. "Then she comes back."

"I told women not to go out, Mother," he said angrily.

"No one can control Rashida, not even her own mother."

Ibrahim was furious as he waited for Rashida to return. She opened the door and came in. Her lips looked blanched and dry from thirst. He remained sitting where he was, surrounded by all her enemies. She looked first at Sayyida, who was smiling in triumph; then at Zubaida, with her sorrowful eyes, not daring to ask about the commander Yusuf ibn Ayyub; then at her own mother, who cared only about living; and then finally at Ibrahim's mother and the slave girls.

"If it weren't for the siege, I was planning to leave," she said firmly, looking all around her. "I'm not going to stay here with Sayyida in charge."

"Tell him you stole the water," Sayyida chimed in at once. "Why don't you tell him?"

Ibrahim stayed silent as he watched the two of them spar.

"I didn't steal anything," Rashida replied firmly. "You did it so you could rule over me inside the house. You're the only cursed, evil woman in this household!"

"Do you hear her?" Sayyida asked Ibrahim, tearing up. "That's the way she's been treating me ever since you left, or even worse."

"We're on the brink of a catastrophe," Ibrahim told them in a calm, measured tone. "The Crusaders are at the gates of Alexandira, and the women in Ibrahim's household are squabbling over food and water!"

Sayyida opened her mouth.

"I don't want to hear another word," Ibrahim went on. "We're going to rearrange everything."

"But Sayyida's never going to be in charge," Rashida chimed in immediately. "I don't trust her."

"You'll do exactly what I tell you," he told her, giving her a furious look.

He ordered the boy who was with him to distribute the food and water. Rashida took her share and quickly proceeded to take several large gulps of water, then wiped her mouth.

"Do you see?" Sayyida said. "She'll finish all the water in less than two days, and then she'll use the reserves that you've brought. I can keep back those reserves as I've been doing for the household up till now. They're all with me. Ibrahim's mother, say something."

Ibrahim's mother and sister and even the slave girls all acknowledged that Sayyida was the best person to have control of the reserves of food and drink. Her decisions were reasonable; she did not follow her own inclinations, and, above all, she was not as bold and impetuous as Rashida. He looked at Kauthar, but she did not say anything. Rashida kept her thoughts to herself, realising in despair what the decision was going to be even before Ibrahim pronounced it. Sayyida burst into tears, sat at his feet, and gave him a look of passionate longing.

"I'm following your instructions," she whispered. "I have no one but you."

He looked at Rashida, whose eyes looked powerful and defiant, but who otherwise seemed exhausted.

"Did it happen that you drank all the water?" he asked her.

"Yes, it did," she replied, trying to sound strong, although her voice was filled with exhaustion. "But I didn't steal anything."

"Why did you drink it all?" he asked, still looking straight at her.

A single tear welled up, but it did not fall. With unfathomable sorrow, she wiped it away.

"I don't know," she replied.

"Rashida's lying!" all the women yelled at once. "She's a tyrant. She tells lies about everyone. Remember what she's done before and the claims she made against you, my brother Ibrahim! We're all here to tell you that she's a thief, that's all!"

Rashida lowered her head, but did not react. Whom should she attack? Everyone? Why defend herself when she knew what he thought of her?

Her slave girl came over and gave her a sympathetic look.

He gestured to all the women to stop talking.

"You!" Rashida said, glaring at the women in fury.

"Shut up!" Ibrahim snapped. "I don't want to hear a single sound!"

"Put the extra food and drink in Rashida's room" he said, looking at the boy who had accompanied him.

There ensued a terrible silence, filled with shock and incomprehension. Rashida's eyes registered the same bafflement as Sayyida's.

"But Rashida's stolen and destroyed—" Sayyida started.

"But for her," he interrupted her firmly, "everyone in the house would be dead. This is an age that requires courage."

Rashida managed to suppress a smile of pleasure that encompassed the entire world. She placed her hand over her heart to avoid saying the words that had been floating all around. Ibrahim heard the protests and grumbling.

"This is my decision," he said assertively, "and she's under my protection. I'll personally punish anyone who hurts or strikes her. If the surplus food and water is stolen, I'll know for sure that she's not the thief, but somebody else, one of you women. Anyone except my own mother, of course."

"Brother," Ibrahim's sister told him, "we have encountered only good with Sayyida and evil with Rashida. What has this war done to affect you this way?"

"No one may argue with me about my decisions," he shot back.

With that, he stood up and headed for the door. When Rashida called after him, he turned round and looked at her.

"There's something I need to tell you," she stuttered. "If you'll allow me, in private."

His mother's eyes opened wide in shock, and Sayyida put her hand over her mouth as she exchanged glances with her sister.

"Fine," he replied, looking all around him, "but be quick about it!'"

She went back into the room, with him behind her. She closed the door.

"Don't close the door," he said immediately.

"You can't be married to Sayyida," she told him thoughtlessly. "I won't allow it."

He opened the door with a smile.

"Is that what you wanted to tell me, Cousin?" he asked her. "I'll be married to whomever I choose."

"Why are you never fair with me?" she asked, giving him a longing look. "Tell me the truth!"

"Because you never lie," he replied firmly.

She opened her mouth to say something, but he had opened the door and left before she could.

All the household's women were standing on the other side of the door. He glared at them all, then headed for the front door.

Sayyida followed.

"You don't love me anymore," she whispered. "That she-devil's bewitched you."

He stared at her, but said nothing.

"Rashida's an evil woman," Sayyida yelled at the top of her voice. "She claimed to have had sex with her cousin, and she wasn't lying. She seduced him, Aunt. She's the one responsible."

Rashida rushed over to the window to see Ibrahim pass by.

"Did you hear what he said?" she asked Zubaida.

"Yes, I did, my Lady."

"Why did he do that?'

"Nobody knows, my Lady."

"I'm afraid."

"Afraid of what?"

"Of desire."

Is it possible for a mother to give birth to a daughter and not know her? Kauthar looked at her daughter as though seeing her for the very first time. It seems we only get to know each other well when famine intensifies and there is not enough water. People who seem generous fail to give, while those who appear stingy give gratis. Those who previously have avoided the swords of fate now confidently open their arms wide to time's perfidy, and the allegedly courageous hide themselves in the gloomiest of vaults. Good is not good, nor is evil absolutely evil. When times are hard, light does not always mean daytime, nor darkness night. Realities are revealed, and times transformed. Where are you now, Jawhar the Sicilian, to witness times uprooted and grandsons so transformed? Come here now, Badr al-Jamali! People say that your power was unrivaled. Speechless, you climbed the Muqattam Hills, pursuing dominance the way wild beasts do in fables. And yet you would always get there, even if you lost all your limbs. Come here, Grandfather, to see your granddaughter, Rashida, counting her spoils and distributing them to foes before friends, making just decisions, and not listening to slander or succumbing to her own desires. Rashida was someone who toyed with mankind's destinies, played with intrigue and conflict, and laughed at other people's tears. Now, she wanted everyone in the household to live as though they were all waiting for Ibrahim, to testify to her just actions and knowledge. Was she trying to confirm something for him, one wondered, or for herself?

Her mother examined her carefully, looking at her gleaming eyes and lively expression. Emptiness had no effect on her, nor did war frighten her.

"Are you missing Jawwad, Rashida?" her mother asked as she moved closer.

"I can't remember him anymore, Mother," Rashida replied, looking at her mother as if to suggest that she could not recall that name. "That's all in the past."

"Don't pin all your hopes on your cousin," her mother told her gently. "You've loathed each other for ages and ages."

"Why should I pin my hopes on him? Rashida asked in surprise. "I don't obey him on principle. All I want is for him to give me my rights, no more, no less."

"Love has no leadership or commander," her mother replied with a knowing smile. "Even the Supreme Master stands helpless when faced with its swords, unsure whether to surrender or die a martyr. You're always strong. Don't let love weaken you. You're all I have left, and I need you as a support."

"I am your support," Rashida responded firmly. "Love has no hold over me, nor will swords strike me. Rest assured: We'll get our rights, and then we'll leave."

Sayyida did not trust Rashida's intentions, nor did the other women in the household, except for Rashida's mother and her slave girl. They all kept an eye out for trickery at any moment. They all hoped that she would lose her nerve and start behaving the way she had in the past. Then they could tell Ibrahim when he came back. Sayyida shared her worries with her mother, about the way Ibrahim's attitude to her had changed. Her mother reassured her, pointing out that, in wartime, men will often lose their common sense for a while, but, once the war is over, it comes back. There was no comparison between Sayyida and Rashida. Sayyida was the daughter of a decent man and woman; also, there was no hostility between her and Ibrahim, and no long history of hatred. Men chose women whom their mothers loved, and Ibrahim's mother loved and wanted Sayyida. She feared Rashida as much as she feared worm-infested rats. Sayyida did her best to slip into the place where Rashida was hiding the food and water, but Zubaida woke up and called out for help. Sayyida ran away as fast as she could; she tried, and tried again, but without success. In this war, fate was with Rashida.

The Syrian army's victories suggested the end was nigh. Asad ad-din Shirkuh had attacked Shawar's army in the south, crossing the Nile to the western bank and the camp in Giza. He had offered Shawar a pact against the Crusaders, but Shawar had responded that these newcomers were nothing compared to the Franks, who were the way forward.

Then at Al-Ashmunein, Asad ad-din, along with his nephew Yusuf ibn Ayyub, had defeated both Shawar and the Crusaders. Together, they marched toward Fayyum, triumphed together, and crossed the desert parallel to the Delta till they reached Alexandria. Then Asad ad-din Shirkuh departed for Qus and left Salah ad-din to make for Alexandria. The siege of Alexandria lasted for four months.

People hoped the siege was slackening. Indeed, it was beginning to do so. The Crusaders' strategy involved a combination of initiative and cruelty. When they were defeated by Shirkuh's army, they started fighting with a desperate barbarity. The Crusader King, `Amauri, who was governing Jerusalem, was acquainted with Alexandria, and knew Egypt even before he visited it. He made an agreement with Shawar that he would pay Almaric money for life-long protection. Most important was that Crusader knights would stand guard over Cairo's gates and Egypt. Almaric accepted the terms of the agreement with the Fatimid Minister Shawar, namely that the Crusader knights would stay to defend Cairo's gates even if the King himself left the country. Shawar would give the King thirty-thousand dinars every year from Egypt's annual revenue of a hundred thousand dinars. This agreement was both a dream and prize. Cairo, defended by Crusader knights, was something the King had longed for all his life.

The dream was now almost accomplished. But then Shirkuh arrived with his army and defeated the armies of Shawar and the Crusaders at the battle of Al-Ashmunein. In some ways, the defeat worked to the benefit of the Crusaders. Minister Shawar was now even more desperate, clinging to one final hope. He was ready to hand over the whole of Egypt as long as he could still be its Minister. As far as he was concerned, the Alexandrians were corrupt and treasonous; they deserved to be killed. They had cooperated with Salah ad-din and opened the city gates to the Syrian army. Ibrahim, son of the Sicilian, needed to be slain and hung on the Bab Zuweila gate in Cairo that his grandfather, Badr al-Jamali, had constructed. Shawar himself would make sure that happened. The reputation of the Egyptian from Alexandria had now reached the Minister and the Crusader King, Amalric. But no matter: Minister Shawar could handle that particular problem within a month, no more.

Men lingered in tents in front of the gates, preferring to give water to their wives, daughters, and sons, the elderly and sick. Some Crusader arrows managed to penetrate as far as the tents of men lingering behind the gates. Men died, one after the other, and, after a month, Crusader tactics shifted. Some of them fell sick. The plague started with chronic stomach pains, vomiting, and dehydration. They would be dead within the week. When one man after another died, Amalric ordered the corpses to be tossed on the tents of the Alexandrians. He ordered strong, powerful men who were good at projecting to throw the corpses as hard and high as they could into the city center. Plague made its way into the tents, and men were worried about the possibility of its spread. They preferred to stay inside their tents, not to visit their homes, and not even to give their children any food.

Yet King Amalric was not satisfied. He started hurling live sick men, initially using weapons to hurl any sick horsemen into the city. At first, the Alexandrians thought they had come into the city to fight them, so they mixed with them and were infected. After a while, they realised that the number of infected bodies had increased, and the disease had spread...

Only in the midst of the epidemic did Yusuf ibn Ayyub Salah ad-din move the men's camp. He had seen slow death and lived with it: the lack of water, the groans of terminal suffering. He had gone to war before, but had never witnessed such abject misery. A slow, lingering death was much worse than death in war, and more debilitating, too. Ibrahim raised his hands to the heavens and prayed devoutly to God, earnestly wishing that the armies of Shawar and the Crusaders would go away before the Alexandrians all died. But the pestilence continued. Salim came rushing over to see him, clutching his stomach in pain.

"Did you go near the Franks," Yusuf asked in shock, "the corpses of the horsemen?"

"No, I didn't," he replied weakly.

"Take him into my tent," Yusuf told his men.

"I'm afraid I might give you the plague."

"Take him into my tent," Yusuf said again. "We'll face this pestilence together."

Ibrahim passed his time between hope and suffering. When hope blossoms amid so much death, the soul is split in two. He wanted to catch the disease himself. Salim was scared and wept; his whole body shook.

"You're not going to die," Ibrahim told him, holding his hand.

"There are no doctors in this city."

"I'm here with you. Drink some water; you'll feel better."

When Sadiq tried to come closer, Ibrahim sent him away. He alone stayed with his brother, recalling how the young boy would run along the shore with him, asking about pearls, and collecting strange stones and multi-coloured shells. The two of them would burst into joyous laughter whenever they found a long shell gleaming with bright colours or a fish in its death throes. But, when we recall children's laughter in the midst of death, it turns into something bitter, like the memory of pleasant rivers when beset by drought. Salim closed his eyes and looked resigned and assured.

"My brother!" Ibrahim mouthed to himself, suppressing a scream.

He put his hand on his brother's chest, then kissed his forehead.

"I'm the one who should have died," he whispered. "Why am I still alive, and you're dead? You're the youngest, the kindest, the...

"Death's ordained for all of us," Yusuf said, stroking Ibrahim's shoulder. "We're doing our best to save the city. Are you feeling exhausted? Tell me the truth."

"I'm feeling fine. That's what's upsetting me."

"I don't understand."

"I'm alive, and he's dead. Is there any agony worse than that?"

Yusuf stared at him in silence.

The Crusaders pounded the gates of Alexandria with ballistas. Some horsemen made their way inside, fighting, hurling spears, and then leaving again. The Egyptians engaged the Crusaders, and impaled corpses were littered everywhere. Ibrahim went out to fight, hurling himself toward imminent destruction, praying for death. Today, he was going to die. When he did, his mother would be annoyed and sad, but she would remember that she still had Sadiq and Husain. But, if he went back to the house and said that he had lost his brother Salim, she would accuse him of being just like

Yusuf's brothers. Oh Laila, oh Mother of Ibrahim! How I fear your looks and remember your tears when you embraced twenty-year-old me following my father's death.

"You're my main support now," she had said at the time. "Take care of your brothers, Ibrahim!"

Now, here I am, totally failing to protect my brother and homeland!

"Sadiq!" Ibrahim yelled at the top of his voice, tugging at his brother's head.

"I'm here with you," Sadiq replied. "Why are you shouting like that?"

"Go to your mother," Ibrahim told him firmly, "and tell her what's happening."

"I can't."

"You must go, and don't come back here. There's death all around us. Your mother needs you."

"Am I not a man just like you?" Sadiq replied angrily. "We have to keep fighting and not surrender to the Crusaders."

For a while, Ibrahim said nothing.

"Protecting your mother's a worthy cause," he said. "Go back to the house."

"That's not going to happen." Sadiq shot back.

He heard the sound of death; it had its own particular sound, which he recognised today, one that blended with a piercing stench, but amounted to nothing in particular, like jumbled laughter and confusing times. Opening his eyes, he stared straight ahead.

He saw Yusuf fighting the Crusader horsemen, who were sidling their way in through the gates. Hurling his spear, he hit one or more of the horsemen. Then he heard the sound and smelled the smell. Had a spear thrown by the Crusader hit him in the chest? In his chest, or his brother's?

"You need to die today, Ibrahim, you puny weakling!" he yelled at the top of his voice. "Today you have to die!"

He kept on yelling, because that spear had not hit him in the chest. It had hit his brother Sadiq.

He bent over and, for the first time, sank to the ground. Yusuf looked at him with the kind of sorrow he had never felt in his life before.

"If only I'd never witnessed such sorrow," he said. "If only I'd never come to this country to witness such sorrow."

"I'm still alive, Yusuf," Ibrahim told him, giving him a somewhat baffled look. "I'm still alive, aren't I?"

"Yes, Ibrahim," Yusuf replied, tears falling, "you're still alive."

"I thought the arrow had pierced the heart. It did, so why am I still alive?"

Yes, death has its own particular stench. It never leaves either mouth or breath, especially when it is mixed with despair and shame. Perhaps it is like jasmine, mixed with ambergris and sweet basil, a mellow scent sweet to the taste, like Ramadan doughnuts stuffed full of cheese. He knew death and was used to it, but the despair he was feeling was ripping his guts apart. He heard screams all around him. Before long, his mother would be screaming, too. Now, two of her sons were dead.

He covered his head with his hands and did not feel Shaikh Zaidun's hand patting his shoulder.

"It's God's will," Shaikh Zaidun said. "The cause is not the goal. There's no avoiding the final decision."

Yusuf ibn Ayyub wept as he remembered his two friends, who were closer to him than Ibrahim. They had run along the beach together and played. Today, they were fading away like dust.

He was crying because his sense of wrongdoing was outweighing his reason for being there. He was the cause of it all, and his presence was responsible for the destruction of both the city and its people. He had come to save it, and had drowned. He had come to rouse it, but had killed it instead. He had come to help, but had sunk the boat. He had not saved the city's people, nor had God shown him any mercy.

"Be easy on yourself, my son," Shaikh Zaidun said, turning to look at him. "Wrongdoing involves error, and death is an inescapable reality."

Yusuf looked over at Ibrahim, and their eyes met. He did not know what was going through Ibrahim's mind, and he did not want to find out. In moments of despair, the heart will spit out all its fears, along with all the greenery buried deep down, with its foul stench and clusters of insects.

"If I asked you to forgive me, you'd never do it," Yusuf said. "If I told you it wasn't my plan, you wouldn't believe me. Today, Shawar's won. This is a country I don't know. I can no longer remember why I've come here. Today, I'll swear to you that I'm leaving, and I'll never come back here again as long as I live. Everything I've witnessed in battle is one thing, but what I've seen in Alexandria these past months is something entirely different. You didn't need these horrors and catastrophes. The true Commander will always acknowledge defeat and learn from loss. Nothing deserves such loss and impotence. My place is not with wars, Alexandria, or Egypt. Today I've said farewell to my friends and young men. I'm convinced that I'm still strong..."

Ibrahim did not respond.

"This siege must be broken today, not tomorrow," Yusuf declared in a determined voice as he stood up. "I hereby swear to you that I'll not leave this city till I've been able to assure its residents' security."

Ibrahim did not hear him. He had gone out of the city walls...on his own.

He did not cry; he was not going to cry over Salim or Sadiq. Ever since their deaths, he had wanted to die, and the feeling had not left him. At night, he talked to the King of Death. He would go out of the city and fire at the Crusaders, all the while pleading with the King to slay him. Grabbing his sword, he would make his way through the ranks of soldiers, asking them to put an end to this agony.

"How is it," he would ask the King at night, "that you leave me and can't be bothered with me? Don't you see me right here in front of you? I call on you to come and get me before I return to my house. After all this, I can't face my nights any longer. Not my life, either. Why have you let me live? I'm the eldest of them, the one who asked them to resist, who... You're not even listening. You don't follow orders. You come only when He gives the orders. O Lord, put an end to this agony. I can stand it no longer!"

A whole month passed with Ibrahim hurling himself into the fray and returning home safe and sound. A whole month when the people of Alexandria were dying of hunger and thirst, disease was wracking people's bodies, and despair was lodged in their bellies. Another month, and he would only be able to repeat his mother's name to himself. Another day of conflict would be inconceivable. He had to die before that happened.

Every day, he could see the sorrow in Yusuf ibn Ayyub's eyes, and he listened as Yusuf read aloud his letters to his uncle, begging him to bring the siege to an end.

Asad ad-din Shirkuh sent a letter to Shawar, telling him that what was happening was a crime against the Muslim community. He asked Shawar to cooperate with him in opposing the Crusaders. Shawar did not respond. Instead, he insisted, as he had done before, that the Franks were not the problem; they were the way forward.

Asad ad-din Shirkuh was still camped by Birkat al-Habash in the Fustat region. He moved closer to Cairo, but did not enter the city or surrender.

While Nur ad-din's army in Syria was putting heavy pressure on the Crusader King, the siege of Alexandria led to much destruction and death. King Amalric sent letters to Asad ad-din Shirkuh in which he stated that he was prepared to leave Egypt if the Syrian army did the same. He wanted peace and would give Asad ad-din Shirkuh fifty thousand dinars. If Salah ad-din stayed in Alexandria and Asad ad-din stayed in Upper Egypt, then he, King Amalric, would also stay in Egypt. Four months later, Salah ad-din sent a letter to his uncle saying that 'God does not charge any soul except to its capacity.' He told his uncle that, ever since he had been born, he had never witnessed such agony and death. Alexandrians had suffered enough. They should accept King Amalric's offer. The King would leave, and so would they, provided that Shawar would swear in front of all of them not to take revenge on the Alexandrians for rising up against him. If Shawar did that, they would come back and finish him off. He told his uncle that what he had seen in Egypt was hard to take in and bloodied the very heart, and that it was enough to make even rocks cry. No suffering could come close to what he had witnessed, and they needed to lighten the burden on the people of Alexandria.

His uncle, Asad ad-din Shirkuh, listened to him. The two sides agreed to withdraw. Asad ad-din Shirkuh made it a condition that King Amalric leave Egypt and that Minister Shawar would not punish the people who had cooperated with him, especially the Alexandrians. However, the Crusaders still left their horsemen at the Cairo gates and took thirty thousand dinars from Shawar. The Crusader King departed, but his eye was still on Cairo, the city fortified with stone gates. One of his own men was currently standing guard over it, and on the morrow, it would be his.

Salah ad-din was still deeply distressed by everything he had lived through and witnessed. The laughter shared by the three friends echoed in the heavens, adored by the planets and joining in conversation with the stars: Sadiq, Salim, and Yusuf ibn Ayyub. At dawn, they had all plunged into the sea at Alexandria. The entire world was theirs, part of the winter waves and autumn storms. Two friends had died. Then three, then four. Now, Ibrahim was no longer the same person, and Yusuf ibn Ayyub was not the young man who had revelled with his youthful companions.

The women all sat there, fearing what was to come. There they sat in front of their houses, waiting for the arrival of the family's corpses: a wounded mother, a widow, a girl who had just lost her brother, an orphan facing the big, wide world. Rashida leaned her chin against a hand, as she observed Ibrahim's mother's despair with a certain sympathy. She realised that Ibrahim's mother could not stand her; she would never willingly listen to any reassuring words Rashida might offer. Sayyida kept stroking Ibrahim's mother's shoulder and telling her that she felt optimistic. Ibrahim would come back today, along with Sadiq, Salim, her father, and Husain. Husain was bound to reappear, and everything would go back to the way it had been before the Crusaders invaded Egypt, Nur ad-din's army arrived from Syria, and the black cloud named Rashida had descended on them. Today, the world would return to the way it should be.

They all spotted the spectre of the men in the distance, dragging their swords as though their arms had gone limp. They were teary-eyed, their hearts rent asunder and split open like the moon on Judgment Day. Rashida saw Ibrahim and heaved a sigh of relief. Nothing apart from him mattered; her heart swelled. Where are you now, Rashida, and to what do you aspire? Have you lost your mind? That man has taken all your money. You are the one who has led his own sister and brother to rebel against him. He will never forget that offense; men never do, and especially not Ibrahim. There is neither mercy nor sentiment in his heart. For him, the heart is in service to the mind, and the interests of halva supersede all others, including his own desires and wishes. That is the very tyranny that has dominated the family for years; never listening to anyone or talking to anyone but himself.

There he was...the love of her life, from her weaning right up to today. So then, today she would confront that disloyal heart that was approaching from afar with filthy, torn clothes, an untrimmed beard, and dragging his sword as though today were the end. She even felt sorry for him, and, along with that sorrow, there was love. Maybe a lot of love. Now was the moment to confront that very heart. Closing her eyes, she said his name. He came over. Whenever he did, dawn drew close and turned into a rainbow. This time, as he drew close, his mother stood up shaking, and rushed over to him, weeping and embracing him.

"Your brothers will criticise me," she said. "But you're precious, my Son. Let them do it!"

She turned round to look for her other two sons to hug them as well and listen to their usual complaints. She could hear them now before they even spoke.

"You only love Ibrahim," they would say. "As long as he's fine, the world's fine, too. You've other sons as well, Ibrahim's mother. Here we are...Mother, Mother!"

"Where are your brothers, Ibrahim?" she asked anxiously.

He looked at her, but said nothing. Rashida was stunned, and she put her hand over her mouth in anticipation of what was coming. Then Ibrahim's sister let out a shriek loud enough to reach the very heavens. Ibrahim gestured to her to stop, but the screams continued, scream after scream. Sayyida's father had died, and so had her brother. Rashida kept her hand over her mouth as she watched the despair and weakness in Ibrahim's mother's expression. She was neither crying nor screaming. Instead, she kept asking her son the same questions: "Where's Salim? Where's Sadiq?"

"They're living and thriving with God," Ibrahim replied, his voice cracking in sorrow, "in eternal paradise." She stared at him as though she did not understand, then asked the same questions again. She started talking to herself, and had a lot to say:

"Did you kill them, or did I? You're the one I love the most and really worry about. They knew that, so they died. They knew it and died. I believed in you; they were both entrusted to your care, and you hurled them to perdition for the sake of the Syrian army. You've killed them so that you can grab what's rightfully theirs. Now all the halva factories are Ibrahim's, Ibrahim the greedy who wants everything for himself. Young Husain was afraid of him and ran away. He's the one who has killed his brothers. My son...dead. Ibrahim, son of the Sicilian, has died today. Where are your brothers? Bring me your brothers, and I'll forgive you; I swear I will. I also forgive you for the unbearable flames that are searing my heart. Bring me your sister, Husain, Salim, and Sadiq. You've discriminated among your brothers, Ibrahim. So, head of the family, Man, bring me your brothers. Where are they?"

He had no idea what to do and remained silent. Summoning all her strength, she slammed a fist into his chest.

"Why haven't you died?" she asked. "You're the cause of all these catastrophes. Sayyida, bring the Qur'an, bring it quickly..."

Sayyida rushed out to look for the only copy of the Qur'an in Ibrahim's house. It was large and heavy, and her slave girl helped her carry it in. She put it down in front of Ibrahim's mother. Ibrahim's mother now held the Qur'an, kissed it, and put her hand to her forehead.

"I swear on this copy of the Qur'an and by the Lord of the World that, on this day, my son Ibrahim has died. For as long as I live, I will never speak to him or look at his face again, till he either brings me his four brothers and sisters, or he dies. And, even if he does die, I will not offer any prayers for him. Today, my son has died. I don't want any tears or lamentations. The rest of my children are alive and thriving."

"Ibrahim's mother," Sayyida told her gently, "seek refuge with God from the Devil!"

"He's the only devil here," his mother replied, kissing this copy of the Qur'an. "Take me far away from him, my daughter. I've just sworn an oath."

Ibrahim remained silent, a stony gaze in his eyes as though he had indeed died, but not been resurrected. He stayed in the same dark spot between paradise and hellfire.

When swords sucked his blood, it was a mercy. When he heard the Syrian army's decision to leave Egypt and his heart tumbled into the depths of the pit, that was still a triumph. But, at the moment when his own mother announced his death, that was the final defeat. This was Ibrahim's mother, a lady who would never scream, groan, complain, or get angry with anyone. With her sagacity and forgiveness, she was like the very angels. And yet today she had decided to slay without the slightest hesitation or thought. After fifty years of silence, she had finally spoken and used her words to kill with absolute precision, leaving no trace on the walls or the mosque pillars—a neat killing, just like those of the most savage of commanders. What should he say to his mother now? Ever since he was born, she had kept a close eye on him with loving admiration, but tonight she was closing her eyes so as not to see him. She had locked her heart and pulled her soul as far from him as possible. The days to come were all darkness, and the defeat had not yet started. Shawar had promised Yusuf ibn Ayyub that he would never take revenge. He had also told the Crusader Franks that he would not take revenge on the people of Alexandria; he would leave them in peace. Ibrahim had made no promises to the Minister. He knew him well; he had never actually met him, but nevertheless he knew him better than anyone. From that day, the people of Alexandria would come to know the true meaning of defeat and humiliation. Punishment would start, and Shawar would toy with their memories. Alexandrians would have to forget that they had succeeded in putting an end to Shawar's police force, and that they had rebelled and fought like trained soldiers. Anyone seeking justice would feel they deserved everything that Shawar could throw at him. Those who dared to hope would face perdition and crumble before armed attack. He had not learned; his father had not trained him well. If only his father had taught him to stay away from rulers; that power belonged to the strong, not the just. How stupid he felt today! Even though Yusuf ibn Ayyub might believe Shawar's promises, he, Ibrahim, knew otherwise.

He left his room and his house and wandered around the Alexandria streets. Here was Kum an-Nadura and the `Attarin Mosque. The streets looked neglected, as though it were a deserted city. Every man was staying at home, and the silence that prevailed was that of helpless defeat. He could almost hear the muted cries of women lamenting those they had lost or would be losing. How could Alexandria look so dark in broad daylight? How could the sun close its doors in sorrow over what had happened and would happen? Husain, where are you, Brother? Who decided to spurn you, your mother or your brother?

"Husain," he yelled at the top of his voice, "come here! Your mother needs you."

He now headed for the halva factory to look for the safe. It was deserted, the doors wide open, and the men either dead or wounded. He put his hand over his heart and called as loud as he could for Sufyan, his sister's husband, whom he had asked to guard the factory in his absence. Sufyan came running from the far side of the city, closely followed by a sense of failure.

"Jawwad's stolen the money in the safe," he told Ibrahim in a frantic tone.

Ibrahim looked at him and then turned and looked around him. How had he missed Shawar's soldiers surrounding the factory in mere seconds, as though they were lizards?

"Where's the money?" one of the soldiers demanded.

"I was about to ask the very same question," Ibrahim responded bitterly.

"The wheat porter's stolen it," Sufyan said, looking at the soldiers. "Forgive me, Brother. There was nothing I could do. I was afraid. I needed to get food and look after my children. It's not my fault."

Ibrahim remained silent. He looked at the soldiers all around him, wondering whether they were going to arrest him that day or the next. What were they waiting for? He rushed back to his house, closely followed by the soldiers. He opened the door, called for Rashida, and went into his room.

He told her what had happened.

"I swear I didn't tell him to do that," she replied immediately. "Yes, I'd asked him to do it in the past, but then you put him in prison. Ever since then, I've been loyal to you."

"You've been loyal ever since then?" Ibrahim asked bitterly. "Should I be celebrating?"

"By God," she told him frankly, "I've never loved him, and he's never touched me. I was only going to be married to him to protect myself from the greed of the men around me."

"Enough talk!" he told her with a wave of his hand.

The ensuing silence was loaded with words, and their heartbeats raced. She looked around her. The soft light made his face appear like the ancients, as though it were carved of red stone, and his eyes looked red, too. Summoning all her courage, she moved closer. Breathing slowly, she confronted her heart for the first time. No other man on earth could so tear her heart to shreds, extract grudges from the very depths of night, and leave a hollow feeling in her soul. Only his embers could burn her like this; only he could light up the rest of her life. Oh Ibrahim, if only you knew, if only you realised that blood had flowed out of the heart in search of you! Why does the heart so long for you during times of defeat? Why does it so wish to forgive you all mistakes?

"Ibrahim," she said, putting her hand on his shoulder.

He did not respond. She could not tell whether or not he was even aware of her presence. So much the better. All the heart's feelings would pour out even if he did not hear. Actually, it would be better for him not to hear. She moved closer, put her arms around his back, rested her chin there, and breathed in his scent, something that had stayed with her for long nights ever since she was a child. Closing her eyes, she kept her eyelids tight shut. The tears clustered together, like cows at sunset waiting to return to their shed, one behind the other. They were just about to fall, but they didn't. No one opened the gate for them. Bodily pain is easy to tolerate when faced with the overwhelming presence of a soul that longs for another, but cannot reach it. She bit her lips until they bled. Did he realise she was there, she wondered. Was there any crime worse than denying that he loved her, and trampling on that passion like a field of grass? If you realised your fault and offense, Ibrahim, you would want to die. With death comes mercy, whereas your requital is neverending torture, a flaying of the soul.

After a while, he turned slowly towards her, although she could not tell whether he was aware of her presence. He sat up and pulled her arm toward him. She threw herself into his arms, and he hugged her so tightly that her chest melded with his. Her blood floated with his, their breaths mingled, and the whole earth shook.

"What are you doing here?" he stuttered, pulling her so close that she almost choked.

"I don't know," she whispered.

"You need to go back to your room. Go on..."

"Tell me you're all right," she said, putting her arms round his neck. "You're a part of me."

"Are you out of your mind?" he asked, pushing her away in shock. "What are you doing, and what did you want?"

She tried to stop the tears falling, but now they did, in spite of her. She stood up and wiped them away nervously.

She headed for the door, opened it, and left.

Time and time again, he tried to talk to his mother, but she neither responded nor even looked at him. Standing in front of her, he was simply a mote in the air that she could not see. She had closed her soul to his existence. He was sure that he was not dead yet, but he had entered hellfire before her very eyes. He was also certain that pain could sometimes bring a degree of consolation that he did not yet feel. He had hurled his two brothers to perdition; it was all his fault, intentionally or not. Even the noblest of intentions can lead to a bottomless pit. He held Sufyan's head.

"You, my sister's husband," he said in a loud voice. "I don't know whether or not you've betrayed me and stolen money from the factory. But we no longer have anything, anything at all. I want you to confirm your loyalty to my sister and the rest of us."

Sufyan gave him a shocked look.

"You're to take my mother and sister, your children, Sayyida, her mother, and all the household's slave girls, and you'll travel to Syria by night...today!"

"My brother, Shawar's soldiers are outside our door."

"They have not been ordered to arrest us. They'll let you go. You're not the ones they want."

"Then come with us, Ibrahim."

"I beg you, my brother," Kamila added, "come with us."

Ibrahim looked at his mother, who was staring silently at nothing in particular.

"Mother," he asked her, "do you want me to come with you?"

She did not reply.

"If I stay, I'm going to die," he said. "Do you want me to be killed?"

Again, she did not respond. He stroked her shoulder, and she shuddered as though she had just been bitten by a snake. He withdrew his hand.

"I'm not going to leave my country and homeland," he said. "This is the Sicilian's house. One day, we'll all come back here, and Husain will, too. Come on, there's not much time. Gather up the rest of your belongings and head for Syria. Quickly. Shawar won't be able to stop you, and, if he were to try, Yusuf ibn Ayyub would stop him."

"What about Rashida?" Sayyida asked, looking all around her. "Is she going to stay here with you?"

Rashida lowered her head, her sorrow stretching all the way to the borders of Sicily and Armenia. If only Sayyida realised how defeated she felt. Rashida held back her tears. Ibrahim could do whatever he liked with her; he had killed people, and that was the end of it.

He did not respond to her question.

"Are you going to forget me?" Sayyida asked, looking straight at him.

"You need to forget me," he replied firmly. "Don't tie yourself to a defeated soldier. You deserve better. I might die here, be imprisoned, or lose my memory. Nobody knows. Live your life, get married, and have children."

Rashida's eyes opened wide, not sure whether to be happy or sad.

"I'll have to try," Sayyida replied quietly. "I don't know if I'll be able."

"Yes, you can, Sayyida," he replied, looking at her. "You deserve better."

Later, he watched the camels that carried the luggage that belonged to his mother, sister, Sayyida, her mother, and the slave girls as they moved further and further away. Then, he relaxed.

He saw Rashida frowning as she sat on her own inside her room. He closed his eyes and took a deep breath. He had never been a coward, so he would confront his own heart courageously. He would face up to her boldness, her stupidity, and her aggression. He went in and closed the door.

He spoke her name, but she did not respond.

"Rashida, why don't you answer? Can't you hear me?"

She turned around, but said nothing. He lifted his hand to put it on her shoulder, but did not do it.

"I don't want you to think I hate you," he said suddenly, "or that—"

"You can hate me as much as you like," she replied firmly. "I hate you as well."

"I want you to understand," he told her patiently. "Sometimes you behave brashly, in a way that's not appropriate for the daughter of the Sicilian. Sometimes, it debilitates me, or maybe the weakness has been lurking for some time."

"You kissed me on the sand," she responded angrily. "You did it, Cousin. I didn't curse you. I'm not the ideal person who never makes mistakes as you claim to be. Don't you dare say you didn't deceive me and..."

She searched for the words, but did not know what to say.

Their eyes met, and he waited for her to say something.

"Why do you deceive me and...?" she asked.

He looked at her lips.

"What do you want with me, Cousin?" she asked him.

"You're right, Rashida."

His surrender shocked her. He had never done that before.

"Right about what?" she asked. She added, sadly, "You shun me like the plague."

"No, I want you as though you're all the world's property."

Her eyes opened wide, and she almost stopped breathing.

"You avoid me..." she said.

"Because you've a fixed place inside me."

"You treat me as though I'm nothing."

"Maybe because you're everything. I don't know."

"You're playing with words to take revenge on me."

"If I did that, I'd be scattering the vestiges of my own soul. I can't do that."

"You're deceiving me now. I'm the cause of all your troubles."

"Only you have ever realised the extent of those troubles, the heavy weight of passion, and the body's shame from up close."

"Don't do this to me. If you want to take revenge, then go ahead, but don't destroy my soul."

"I've tried taking revenge on myself, but I've failed."

"So, where does this path lead?"

"If I knew, I'd tell you. At this moment, I just want to embrace you."

She hesitated, then moved away. He held her arm and pulled her carefully toward him.

"I know," he said. "I understand that you don't trust me, and I don't trust you either. But the world around us has fallen apart. We're the only ones left. No, I won't forgive you; maybe I never will."

"Sayyida won't be very happy with you now, will she? Oh dear, she'll never be happy."

"Nobody's happy with me, Cousin. I'm not even happy with myself. Come into my arms."

"Why?"

"Then the world will be in balance."

"Only for a few seconds."

"That's why I want to have you in my arms. I realise that time's short and days are numbered."

"Don't deceive me, I beg you."

"There's no deceit in the soul; the only certainty lies in its existence. Everything else is perdition and doubt."

When he left the room, she was trying to tell herself that what had just happened between the two of them was not simply her imagination.

She had no idea if what had happened an hour earlier was real. But how could happiness and pleasure come together in the midst of defeat? She did not know. He had embraced her gently and cautiously, then left the room, telling her that he would come back in a while.

He had not spoken of love. Yet she realised that he loved her and wanted her. Was that not enough? He had not satisfied her. Even so, he had talked about the soul; she did not know why, and perhaps he did not either. Why had he used such words? They were pleasant enough. If they had a body, then the heart was bound to follow.

"What's the matter with you?" she asked, noticing her slave girl's sad expression.

"My Lord Yusuf's gone to Syria," she muttered. "I'll never see him again as long as I live."

"Would you prefer to go to Syria or to stay here with me?"

"Even if I went to Syria, how could a slave girl expect to see the Lord of the Worlds? My Lady, staying with you guarantees my safety."

"But we don't need safety as much as pleasure."

Ibrahim came back and asked her to come to his room.

She sat down in front of him, hugging herself. She did her best to collect the remaining fragments of her heart. If he realised that her heart yearned and would submit to him, then it would all be over for her. For just a moment, he stared through the wood-framed window.

"I've never witnessed anything like your kind of evil before," he said, without even looking at her.

She was used to his nasty comments and was not bothered by them. She did not respond.

"I haven't witnessed your courage either, Cousin," he went on. "It's as if you were born to fight. A hard heart, and a will of stone, like the Pyramids. Time cannot erase them, and winds cannot subdue them."

"Is that supposed to be a compliment or criticism?"

He looked at her, and their eyes met.

"Shawar defeated the Syrian army," he said, "and Asad ad-din Shirkuh's gone back to Syria, along with Yusuf ibn Ayyub. Shawar can't be trusted, nor can the Crusaders. Vengeance is on its way."

She swallowed hard. She had no idea why he was talking to her like this; he had never done so before.

"What the Sicilian built has to be protected," he said. "But I'm not sure it will last. Husain has rebelled against me, and it's your fault. Should I punish you today because you turned my brother's heart against me?"

"If you had a heart, then his heart wouldn't have been turned against you," she responded dryly.

He nodded, as though agreeing with her.

"I've no idea where Husain has gone," he went on. "My other brothers are dead, and my sister has chosen to follow her husband with your encouragement. The rest of my family's gone to Syria. You and I, we're all that's left of the Sicilian's family."

He sat down in front of her and moved a bit closer. Her guts rumbled and her limbs quivered.

"I don't run away," he said.

"I know," she replied clearly.

"You don't run away, either."

"No, I don't."

"Rashida," he told her in a gentle tone, the origins and motivations of which he did not know, "the Sicilian's factories and stores are all in danger."

"But the city's still standing. The Sicilian is not simply the halva-maker's grandson; he's also the Army Commander who built Cairo, and Badr al-Jamali, the Supreme Master, who saved Egypt from starvation. We're grandchildren of the ancients and of people who chose Egypt as their homeland."

"The halva-maker and Commander both have their own structures and memorials. I'm not capable of saving the city, but I can preserve the vestiges of halva-making, even if it involves parlaying with the worst of foes. That vestige is crucial to me, and the memory must be preserved."

"Who is this worst of foes, Cousin?" she asked, repeating his words.

"You know the answer," he said, looking straight at her. "You..."

She pursed her lips to stop herself from bursting into tears in front of him.

"You used to say I was everything," she said.

"In my heart, yes," he replied firmly. "But you're not a friend. Rashida. You're what's left of the halva-maker. You can preserve the tradition."

Her eyes opened wide in surprise. She had no idea what he meant.

"When an army commander is defeated," he went on, "he changes strategy and rereads his documents. Maybe he didn't see the whole picture or maybe he was so furious that his vision was impaired. If a powerful enemy turns into a friend, then the army can be reconstructed. You need to go back to Cairo and Fustat and try to—"

"You want to give me my rights?" she asked, putting her hand over her heart.

"I want you to take over all the factories your father deeded to you. Not because it's your right, but rather because you're the only person who can manage and preserve them. When you're far from here, we can save our grandfather."

"And what about you?"

"No, I haven't lost my mind. I'm trying to reconcile people's hearts. If only you knew how much harder that is. Do your best to take charge of things the way you've always dreamed of doing. I'm giving you the chance to prove that you can do it. If you succeed, I won't interfere in any matters concerning your factories for the rest of my life."

As she absorbed what he was saying, she remained silent, not sure whether she was happy to be moving far away from him or sad about the passionate feelings that she'd never experienced before.

"If you stir up trouble, then you'll be putting an end to what's left," he told her. "Just remember your father and grandfather, and recall who you are. Promise me you'll behave like the Sicilian's daughter, and I'll send men with you and give you total freedom."

"You want me to leave?" she choked.

"Isn't that what you've wanted from the outset?" he asked. "When you leave today, you're more powerful and knowledgeable. Trust your own abilities, Rashida. Within every pile of dirt, there's always a pure emerald and a fiery ruby."

"Are you criticising or praising me?"

"I don't know," he replied, giving her a smile. "I'll also give you all the money in the safe here. You're going to leave as soon as possible. Tonight. Tell people that you've run away from me and you're against my ideas. Tell them I'd forced you to stay here. Blame me and curse me as hard as you can—it won't matter. But take care of the heritage. The whole of Alexandria realises that you hate being here and I've made you stay despite your wishes. Shawar's spies will let him know that your story is true. You've escaped from me, and what's happened is not your fault. To the contrary, you're an enemy of Ibrahim and long to kill him. Convince everyone around you that this is the real situation."

"You want me to convince them that I loathe you and want you to die?"

He looked at her and moved closer.

"Tell them," he told her gently, "that you've never hated anyone as much as you hate me. You hate the very sound of my voice and my breaths."

When he held her hand, she shuddered. He moved his lips close to her forehead and gave her a tentative kiss.

"Did you but know it," she replied, closing her eyes, "you're a curse on me. You're a disease I've had ever since I was young."

"What's strange," he told her, moving away with a smile, "is that I would always imagine myself smothering you in kisses at the very moment when I was hitting or flaying you. I would drive the image away and tell myself that Ibrahim never does wrong or follows his basic instincts. It was just that hatred can sometimes seem like exile or passion, no more."

Swallowing hard, she clasped her hands.

He went over to the drawer, opened it, took out the money and gold. Then he put all of it in her hands.

"That's everything I have," he told her.

"I'll take good care of it," she replied, her heart almost bursting out of her chest.

"I know." he replied with a smile.

"When will you come to take it back?"

"How can I know?" he replied with a shrug. "If I knew, I wouldn't have given you all of it. If I'm still alive, I'll come back."

"Then what?"

"Then you'll give me my rightful share and keep yours."

She bit down on her lips. She wanted him to say a lot more, but he did not.

She opened her hands, and the gold slipped through her fingers.

"I told you to take care of it," he told her in surprise, "and here you are letting it slip from your hands!"

She ignored him and moved closer, summoning all her courage. She could smell his breath on her chest. She kissed his cheek without saying a word, then moved slowly back.

She could tell from his expression that he was affected by her gesture, but she could not be sure whether it was shock or something else.

"Rashida," he told her, "here you are, behaving thoughtlessly."

She bent down to pick up the gold, doing her best not to look at him, fully aware that she was blushing and feeling hot. He got down on his knees, took her hand, and placed it on his chest. She plunged right into the blaze without a second thought. He kissed her cheek slowly, then moved to her lips, where he discovered traces of passion and the heat of expectation.

"This is pure madness," he whispered, his lips brushing hers. "It shouldn't happen."

She had no idea how to taste his lips and inhale his scent to keep it with her for the rest of her life. Should she push him away or hold him even tighter? Should she respond to his unkind words, or loosen the reins for her desperate limbs? Cupping his hands around her face, he gave her a different kind of kiss, one that made its way into the very depths of her soul. She tried moving away, shocked by how profoundly she was affected, but realising that the feeling had been there for a long time. Why should she be so shocked at the hold it had on her when it had been there forever? Her entire world was turned upside down, and it plunged her into spaces she had never seen before and introduced her to a selection of halva that was all pistachio, musk, and the scent of fresh, brightly coloured roses. How could dates be twisted and shaped in the hands and come out soft, perfect, and delicious, like the fruits of paradise? And how could flour cover every space and then be turned into crisp flakes of sugar, honey, and grains of wheat?

Ah, Ibrahim, your love, and what you're doing to the heart! If only you realised how much I've suffered and how much I've sought to punish as well! She put her hand on his chest to push him away. If this kiss continued, she would lose her life; that much was certain. He seemed to be waking up after a long sleep. Maybe he hesitated, but then he put her head on his chest and left it there without saying a word.

"Now what?" she asked, clasping his arms. "Are you going to leave me?"

He opened his mouth.

"Just make sure you don't apologise, or—"

"You were just ten years old," he answered with a smile, resting his cheek against her hair, "when you asked to be married to me."

"No, I was eight. Do you still remember?"

"How can I forget? I'd never seen such brazen behaviour from a child."

"I wasn't a child."

"You've changed, Rashida, but you're just as bold as I remember."

She felt like hitting him. If only he would say the words she wanted to hear, if only...

"If I'm still alive," he told her firmly, "then we'll have to be married."

"Why?" she asked with a sigh, as she looped her arms around his neck.

"I've said we need to be married. That's enough."

"Yes, that's enough," she repeated, wiping away a tear.

She moved away slowly and sought refuge in picking up the gold and dinars scattered all around her.

"Go back to your room, Rashida," he told her. "I'll bring it all to you in a while."

She looked at him in surprise, not understanding why he had changed so suddenly. Did he really want her, she wondered. Perhaps he was tired of having her around without kissing her and fusing her with himself. Had her imagination run wild today? She would never think... She left him and went back to her room, the traces of his kisses still lighting up what was left of the days.

After a moment, he grabbed her hand and pulled her out of the room.

"Rashida hates Ibrahim, don't forget!" he told her as he stared into her eyes. "If they tell you that Ibrahim's dead, don't react. In fact, look happy in front of them. If they tell you that Ibrahim's being tortured in prison, tell them that that's what he deserves and worse. Rashida, you're this family's hope; saving the Sicilian is in your hands. Do you hear me? Put aside all your feelings. The real commander neither loves nor hates; he rids himself of all personal desires."

"Do you intend to stay alive?" she whispered, looking straight at him.

"Do I intend to stay alive?" he responded sadly. "I don't know. It's not important. Don't ask such questions."

"You're going to leave here," he told her, holding her hand. "Think only of the Sicilian. Think of your grandfather, Jawhar the Sicilian, and of Badr al-Jamali, and the halva-maker. Your ancestors are all expecting you to help them. That's my only request."

She nodded, while her slave girl looked on in confusion.

He gave a bitter smile, then opened his arms.

"Just once more," he told her as he pulled her closer. "Afterwards, you'll remember that Ibrahim's your enemy. When you pass through the gates of Alexandria, Shawar's soldiers will question you. You'll have to convince them to let you go. All my life, that's the only demand I've ever made of you."

"I love you," she said, hugging him tightly. "Maybe you'll never believe me.

I swear to you that I've never loved anyone else ever since the day I was born."

If those words of hers had any effect on him, he did not show it.

"Don't say those things again," he told her, stroking her hair. "Just remember that they'll be telling you that Ibrahim's being tortured, that he's dead, destroyed, crucified, hung on Cairo's city gates. They'll say he deserved it. You're going to seek refuge with Minister Shawar from your cousin's tyranny."

"I'll do everything you want," she said, kissing his chest.

His strength gave way, and his will disintegrated. He hugged her as though the entire world was in her hands and victory lay in her eyes. Bodies and chests clung to each other.

"Maybe we could be married now," he said. "Then you could leave. Shall I be married to you now? We can spend half a day, a couple of hours, one hour, one single moment, together. If I died, I would have savoured your love in this world."

"Let's get married now!" she replied, putting her arms around him and holding him tight.

"How can you say you hate me when you're my wife?"

"Let's get married, Ibrahim!"

"Make sure you're not so bold and naïve with men!" he said, suddenly and aggressively. "Stay away from them, and don't ever have any dealings with them. Do you understand? I shall know, and, if I find out..."

He moved away from her and looked around in despair. He opened the door.

"Come on," he told one of his men. "It's a long way. Summon the other men!"

She stared at him, breathing hard. He seemed impatient and looked annoyed. Misery penetrated deep. He looked at her, then closed his eyes.

He could imagine her in his arms, subject to his will, part of his property, shuddering with passion, her insides pulsing with longing. He looked at her again. She was deliberately sitting far from him; her arms were limp, and for the first time she looked humiliated. She stole a glance in his direction; their eyes met and embraced, exchanging passion and yearning. With her eyes closed, her breathing changed. It was only today that she was realising the raw power of passion and force of affection. Her entire body shuddered in a way that she could not describe, because she had never had such feelings before and had no idea of their significance. Nevertheless, it managed to shock her; it was as though desire and passion had joined forces against her.

Zubaida sat on the floor, looking at the pair of them, and sobbed silently because passion is supposed to bring lovers together, whether they realise it or not. It brings together those with no hope, and those anticipating deliverance.

Ibrahim heard voices outside the door, and a man came rushing in.

"Shawar's soldiers have occupied the city," he said.

Ibrahim stood up as though in a daze and looked at Rashida.

"Come on, Rashida," he insisted, "we've no time left. I want you to leave as soon as possible."

She stood up and went over to him, as though she were asking, begging him, to extinguish a fire that had burst into flames, and to be gentle with a heart that was now forever shattered. He held her hand and squeezed it hard. He closed his eyes, and she did the same. In his imagination, he saw her once again, sighing in her love for him, drowning in his kisses. He snatched a strand from her heart and kept it inside his own. She too could feel him in her imagination, tasting his kisses on her mouth, quenching her thirst and soaking her veins.

He pushed her away and looked at Zubaida.

"Protect her if you can," he said. "Don't leave her."

He pushed Rashida out of the house.

"I've now left a girl alone in the midst of danger," he said, "but she's more ferocious that any soldier. Don't disappoint me. Just remember Bahnas's words: 'Courage is a moment when man, on his own, chooses to butt against the demons of heaven and earth. There is neither hesitation nor misgiving. He casts all caution into the river's depths and cleaves solely to lightning's flash.' I've loved you for your courage."

She stopped in confusion and opened her mouth.

"What did you say?"

"On your way!" he responded.

BOOK TWO

For the pain of separation my heart has no salve,

Am I to live, I wonder, for the day of reunion?

Tala'i ' al-Amri, Fatimid poet

CHAPTER SEVEN

Ibrahim was arrested just two days later. As he expected and assumed, Shawar was not to be trusted. All Ibrahim could hope for was a mercifully swift death here on his home turf. He would never run away; he would be the one to choose, to wait for whatever the days to come would pour on him, to see how the scabs would come off his wounds, and the guts from his body. He had to endure. The body was a prison, and so was the world. That was what his grandfather, Badr al-Jamali, had once said. In the midst of all his prestige and triumphs, his body had let him down and his tongue had stopped speaking. The soldier thrust Ibrahim into the prison, with curses and oaths aimed first at him and then at his parents. Ibrahim remained silent, realising that courage at that point resided in silence. The soldier would be expecting him to scream in pain, but he was not going to grant the man that victory. His expression was stony, or even vicious.

"So," the soldier asked him maliciously, "where are Salah ad-din and his uncle Shirkuh now? They came here with big plans and left in failure. They've left you to an unknown fate, you traitor! I've heard that your own mother has disowned you. Of course she has! You've brought shame on them. Say something, or have you lost the ability to speak? Are you listening? Are you learning? Do you pledge allegiance to your Minister, Egyptian?"

Ibrahim's mind was swimming in seven seas, some stormy, others calm. Some were as blue as night, while others were as blue as the sky at dawn. O Laila, Ibrahim's mother! How cruel and unkind you are! Have you really disowned me today, Ibrahim's mother, have you killed me? You made a man of me, ever since I was a child. You made a cavalier out of halva and consumed it in seconds. I was your heart, and you've trampled me with your feet and crushed my soul! If only you had realised who I am from the outset; a weak body, Mother, a halva-maker. I am no army commander, nor am I knowledgeable about the inner working of things. God did not create me with Moses's magic or Solomon's abilities. How proud was your smile, Ibrahim's mother, when you took me in your arms when I was five years old and whispered in my ear!

"Little man," you said, "you're the knight and the hope. You're my man, the rest of my life."

You placed an unbearable burden on me, Laila. When that took me far away and my camel finally knelt, you simply withdrew, as though you had never loved me or shown any mercy. How can I protect my brothers, Laila? How can I do battle with time? If my grandfather, the Supreme Master, could not stop his own son from turning traitor, then how can you expect me to keep my brothers alive, as though I were the great provider and deterrent? Maybe I was right. In fractious times, justice won't prevail, and people with noble ideas will not stand firm. So let them all go to hell; I don't care. I've tried and failed. It all happened. You can tell them, Laila, that your son Ibrahim killed his brothers because of his own stupidity, principles, and love of charity and justice. Tell them that your son Ibrahim pushed the Sicilian's family into the abyss and put an end to those who were left. Tell them, too, that you killed Ibrahim on the day he came back to us. But he's weak, woman, neither dead nor alive. Ibrahim's dead, Laila. Don't be scared or sad. Either today or tomorrow, the body will surrender, but the soul has already departed the body; that's the end of the matter.

If only Laila would leave his memory alone! Today he could see his mother, but not with weak eyes, a bent back, and hands raised to the heavens as though addressing or appealing to fate. Instead, she was standing tall, with her hair black and eyes full of life, eagerly recounting the story of the Alexandrian in times of success and plenty.

"Do you know, Ibrahim," she told him, "that there once was a king like no other? He arrived after a period of tyranny. Can you believe that Egyptians were paying taxes for the earth's salt and the sea's fish? Then the king arrived; they say his name was Ahmad ibn Tulun. But the success came from here, from this very city. Alexandria rebelled, even though time itself had gone to sleep and was reclining on the clouds. The blood of Alexandria is blended with nobility; it will never tolerate injustice or permit it to last. The fisherman rebelled, and the tyrant killed him, but then the fisherman's son arrived and took his revenge. They say his name was Anas. He was married to a beautiful girl and set his sights on his city and on vengeance. He struck brutally. They severed his limbs and threw him in prison. He emerged victorious and expelled the foreigner. My grandfather told me the story. In

Alexandria, we always remember the glorious days of our forebears. It was a time like no other: dinars were made of pure gold, well-being was universal, and the world shone bright. Winds were abashed and scared of Egyptians, no vessels sank, and no tyrannical monarch could seize any vessel he wanted. After hardship comes relief, my son. Remember the fisherman and his story. They put him in prison and tortured him."

He smiled in sorrow. Where are you today, Laila? Have you really disowned me? What kind of love is this, one that, like the worship of God, sits on a fence: if I'm successful, you love me; if I'm not, you shun me. What kind of mother are you?"

He used his finger to write Rashida's name on the prison wall. What would she do, he wondered. Could he know for sure that she wouldn't be married to someone else? Could he believe his heart even when it contradicted the mind? Was he in love with his cousin? Had he forgiven her? Was it no longer her body that he craved, but her soul? He would never deceive his own heart, which was part of his soul whether he liked it or not. He had no idea when or how she had managed to infiltrate his inner self and smother him with her heart. He could see her in front of him all the time, sometimes laughing maliciously, and, at others, screaming in pain. He was not going to argue with his mind. If he did, it might well inject some ideas and doubts that would remind him that he actually hated her and despised her actions. No, he would not be accessing his mind; it was enough for his heart to be with her. Approaching her calmly, it had found solace. Was that not enough?

When Shawar descended the narrow prison staircase, the stench of torture and restraint was so foul he had to hold his nose.

"I want him to be awake," he shouted. "I don't want him broken by torture or humiliated by deprivation and maltreatment."

Ibrahim the halva-maker. Your grandfather was the Minister Badr al-Jamali, Supreme Master and Army Commander. Your great-grandfather was Jawhar the Sicilian, conqueror of Egypt and builder of Cairo. Now you're standing before Shawar, Army Commander and Minister of the Fatimid Caliph, Al-`Adid!

It was no dream: Minister Shawar had indeed demanded to meet Ibrahim, the halva-maker's son. He wanted to see him and speak with him. Shawar arrived, surrounded by his guards and accompanied by his son, Al-Kamil.

Ibrahim looked at him without saying a word.

"Do you realise, traitorous halva-maker, that your grandfather was my ideal and teacher. I learned from him. I'm not talking about Jawhar the Sicilian, but rather Badr al-Jamali. He could dispose of his enemies efficiently and slay anyone who stood in his way without mercy. How many men did he flay and crucify? How many limbs did he sever? Now, time presents us with his grandson, who stands here in front of Shawar, the army commander, someone who has adopted his grandfather as a father-figure and model. Isn't that a crime, Ibrahim?"

Ibrahim remained silent.

No matter. You realise what an enormous crime it is. You're going to beg and ask for mercy. That's what Abu Taher did with your grandfather, Badr al-Jamali, before Badr didn't hesitate to flay him alive. This is an era that doesn't allow you the time to examine actions and contemplate souls. It's a time of intrigue, greed, and betrayal. You're a traitor. You've betrayed the Fatimid army for the sake of the Syrian army, all the while proclaiming the word *justice*, and speaking of the peril lurking in the role played by the Crusader Franks, even though they're the way forward, not the peril. If it weren't for them, that shy young friend of yours, Yusuf ibn Ayyub, who's no good at fighting, would have occupied your country. Do you realise that, or are you misguided? They're all after Egypt. The Crusaders, the Syrian army, Nur ad-din, and his young Commander, Yusuf ibn Ayyub—they all want to feudalise the soldiers so as to snuff out the fire of blood ties in their veins and ignite the flames of conflict. There are no angels on earth, man! If I were your grandfather, I'd flay you. He killed his own son when he betrayed his father. I've come here to see you and tell you that your courage is polluted by delusion and your daring is besmirched by treason. Your destiny is everlasting defeat. If I ripped out your eyes, I would spare you the sight of your torture; if I severed your limbs, prison could turn into a spacious paradise. But let's leave your eyes in the gloom, longing for the light you can't find; and let's leave your limbs in chains, dreaming of running bur unable even to stand. O Badr al-Jamali, just come and gaze on the treason of your grandson, Ibrahim!

Come here so I can tell you that your son, Ja'far al-Muzaffar, has left his palace in Cairo to join the halva-maker's factories, and that his grandson deserves to be killed just as much as your own son, Al-Awhad. Shall I kill him today, and will that make you happy, Supreme Master? The caution in your own career is matched only by the humiliation in that of your grandson; your courage is paralleled only by your grandson's stupidity; and your guardianship of the country stands in vivid contrast to his betrayal of its Minister. Now speak. I'm listening."

"I've nothing to say. Let it be as God wills."

"No, say something. Your courage may perhaps save you from the whipping. A quick death will be less painful."

For a while, silence prevailed.

"The Crusaders aren't the way forward," Ibrahim said. "If they enter Egypt, that'll be the end, as it was in Jerusalem and the Syrian cities they've entered."

"They've left, you idiot!"

"With a promise to return. This is a war about land and treasure, not about belief and a Lord. They haven't left. They're camped by the gates that my grandfather, Badr al-Jamali, built. The gates to your capital, Cairo."

Why was he talking? He had no idea. Where were the words coming from? This year, even courage was manifesting itself in the month of Ba'una!

"It's clear," Shawar commented dryly, "that this tongue of Ibrahim's needs to be cut out."

He turned to his son, Al-Kamil.

"I want you to use your sword to pierce Ibrahim's thigh," he told him. "Don't hit a vein. I don't want him to die. Just skin his thigh."

"Father," Al-Kamil said, swallowing hard. "You asked him to speak."

"Silence. Just do what you're told."

"To God alone belongs the power and might," Al-Kamil muttered to himself. "O Lord, I beg You, don't make me. Cut out my tongue or rob me of speech!"

Hesitantly, Al-Kamil took a sword and held it over Ibrahim's thigh. He dug into the leg without touching the vein. Sweat poured off Ibrahim, and he let out a loud groan of pain that emerged from deep inside him. He saw his great-grandmother Sundus as a girl amid the flames. How had her face and part of her body been burned? He could feel her now. How evil fire is, and how shocking are the pains over which we have no control! He had no idea why he was remembering Rashida now—Rashida, who had steadfastly endured everything. Why couldn't he do the same? Was his cousin stronger than him? Amid all his agonies, he smiled as though he had lost his mind. Al-Kamil stopped and looked at his father.

"That's enough," he said. "Or else he'll die."

"I thought I saw him smile. Is he out of his mind?"

"Father, mercy is a mark of great men."

"Al-Kamil," Shawar told him firmly, "I want you to finish what you've started. When I visit him tomorrow, I want him to be completely flayed. Hang his flesh up. I want to see it burn in the flames. I want to rid the earth of his body."

"As you command, Father," Al-Kamil said, swallowing hard. "But the promise we made to—"

"Promises bind only the defeated," he interrupted his son. "Victors pay them no attention. I'll see him tomorrow."

"As you command, my lord and father!"

CHAPTER EIGHT

Rashida expected her confrontation with `Abd al-Tawwab to be like going toe to toe with a savage beast. She did not like him, but still, she needed him. What got on her nerves was the way all the workers listened to him, not her, even though she was the business's owner.

She sat down in front of him. "Ibrahim has asked me to take over the running of the stores and this factory in Fustat."

"My daughter," he replied assertively. "Ibrahim's in prison. I'm just like your father. I'll take charge of everything on your behalf. That'll be better. You can stay in your house, safely protected like a hidden pearl. We're all at your service."

"You're my right hand," she told him, doing her best to control her temper. "But the stores belong to me. My father wanted me to be in charge, and so does my cousin."

"My lady," he replied by way of challenge. "The workers will never listen to a girl as long as there's a competent man to run the factory. I've been doing it the whole of the past year."

"You're right, Uncle," she replied with a phony smile. "The men will take orders from a girl only when the good man, who was brought up here as a child, orders them to obey me. You can pass along that order."

"They'll never agree," he shot back.

"Uncle," she told him, "you're like my father now. Jawwad's run away, and I will be married only to Ibrahim."

"Ibrahim's in Shawar's prison. Nobody comes out of his prison alive."

"I can't manage without you, Uncle," she told him, holding back a tear, "nor do I want to. Let's just assume that the men decide not to obey me. Then

I'll be forced to cut out part of my own heart and dispense with the services of a man whom I now consider like my own father. Let's assume that I did that, and the men still refused to carry out my instructions. I'd have to look for other workers who would never be as qualified or loyal. You could then watch as the Sicilian's factory and stores collapsed."

"But you're not going to do that, my daughter," he replied, pursing his lips. "You don't hate your grandfather that much."

"Rest assured," she replied. "I won't make any decision without consulting you. I can't manage this factory without you. But, as my grandfather used to say, 'every era has its own regime and men.'"

"Yes, your grandfather was right. He was talking about *men*, however, not women and girls. In any age, the only place for girls is the house."

She let out a sigh as she tried to think about her love for Ibrahim and, at the same time, to control her own sense of commitment.

"I belive I saw my grandfather, Jawhar the Sicilian, in a dream," she told him. "He told me that, in truth, he meant that every era has its own regime and women; the word 'man' was meant to cover humanity as a whole. I'm not sure whether that was a vision or what. So, now, Uncle `Abd al-Tawwab. Yesterday, I had a visit from the owner of the halva stores in Cairo. He wants to buy all the stores. I told him that I'd think about it."

"No girl the same age as my own daughters is going to make such a decision," he insisted.

"Would you prefer to have Ash-Shumuli, the owner of the halva stores in Cairo, make decisions?"

"I'll leave the factory today."

"I'm not making threats, Uncle," she replied. "But I'm tired of arguments. If I sold the factory to Ash-Shumuli, then all the arguments would be settled. With me, you'll be preserving your status, and with Ash-Shumuli, you'd go back to being a minor halva-maker in a major factory. What is it you want?"

"I'll leave the factory today."

"Think about it, Uncle. Don't make any hasty decisions. I'll never be able to do without you."

With a shrug, he grumbled and muttered to himself, then left. Three days later, he came back and said that he would stay, on the condition that they make decisions together. As she reluctantly agreed, she prayed to God to give her patience.

The cautious truce between `Abd al-Tawwab and Rashida was even more difficult to maintain than the one between Nur ad-din and Shawar. She would keep track of him, and he of her. She would spy on him, and he on her. Sometimes, she would make a decision that would fence the men in, give her control, and show her authority—and then he would challenge her, just because he could. A month later, Jawwad showed up, full of passion. No sooner did he set eyes on her than he fell to the ground and swore that he had not betrayed her.

She gave him an expressionless stare and looked all around her, fully aware that `Abd al-Tawwab was spying on her and anticipating what would come next.

"You stole all of Ibrahim's money," she said decisively.

"I've come here," he replied, "hoping to please you and be married to you."

"You stole it!" she repeated.

"You're the one who asked me to do it," he replied quietly. "I did it for you."

"Where's the money?"

"My Lady," he replied, looking all around him. "I didn't do it on my own. I was helped by his sister's husband Sufyan, his assistant and right hand."

"I don't believe you."

"Believe me! I stole the money and gave it to him to keep in a safe place until the war and siege were over. We agreed to bury it in the cemetery in Kum Diqqa. We buried it together, and, just one day later, it disappeared. I rushed to find him, but he had run away to Syria. I swear I'm telling the truth. And I swear that I want you."

"Let's forget the past, Jawwad. Be gone!"

"Now you want me to go," he retorted, "when you promised to be married to me if I stole the money? You were just waiting for a signal from your cousin to toss me into the cesspool! Is that to be my fate, halva-maker's daughter?"

"Be on your way!" she responded firmly.

"Oh, Rashida. Haven't you learned not to toy with people as though they're just halva-dolls?"

"Don't you dare say my name without 'my Lady'!"

"Didn't your father bring you up properly, girl?" he said, standing up and grabbing her wrist. "Now you think the wheat-porter doesn't suit you! After I've wasted my entire life?"

"Don't threaten me," she replied, fighting him off as best she could. "Nobody threatens Rashida. Get out and don't come back."

He took a knife out of his pocket and raised it. `Abd al-Tawwab came rushing over, struggled with him, and grabbed the knife.

"Lady Rashida has told you to leave," he said. "Or do you want me to call all the factory workers?"

Jawwad took his knife and left the factory.

"You've saved my life, Uncle," Rashida said with a smile.

"You're my daughter," he replied with a proud smile.

For some reason, the relationship between the two of them went more smoothly after this incident. It became more like the relationship between Salah ad-din Yusuf ibn Ayyub and his uncle, rather than the one between

Nur ad-din and Shawar.

Once again, Jawwad disappeared. At night, she felt somewhat guilty. He was right: she had toyed with him and with other people as well. At the time, all she had seen was her own interests and her despair at her cousin. She realised that she had been a frivolous girl. She regretted that and dearly hoped that her punishment would not involve being deprived of her cousin for the rest of her life—even though, without a doubt, that was something she fully deserved.

Now, she started working hard, day and night. She really wanted to re-establish the relationship between the Sicilian's factory and the palaces in Cairo, both east and west. She made many varieties of halva and sent samples as gifts to the amirs of Cairo. Let her experiment with sweets! Today, she was going to create a new kind, just as her grandfather had devised the maulid doll and horse and cavalier. She asked her mother and Zubaida to help her.

She took sugar, honey, almonds, and sesame oil and divided them up into equal portions. After pounding the almonds, she put them, along with the sugar, over the fir with the sesame oil until it boiled down and the almonds were roasted. Then she added honey, covered it all in sugar, mixed it all, and baked it again in sesame oil. Finally, she added expensive saffron soaked in rosewater and musk, and put all of it in bowls.

"What do you think?" she asked her mother.

Her mother tasted it with her finger and let out a sigh.

"Like halva from paradise itself," she said. "Honey, musk, and almonds…"

"We'll give them as a gift to the Caliph Imam and amirs of Cairo," Rashida said proudly. "But we need to come up with a name for them. This halva is the creation of Rashida, daughter of the Sicilian, Armenian, and Egyptian."

"Call it 'courage halva,'" her mother suggested.

"No one will taste it with that name, Mother," Rashida replied with a smile. "They'll be worried about the obligations of courage. Let's call it 'revelation halva.' Rashida's the first woman to manage factories on her own.

Her competence and authority have been revealed."

She started distributing the revelation halva.

The Minister's amirs started coming to her factory, all of them looking for the new halva. Soon, a guest arrived whom she had never seen before, although he had been following her ever since he had first tasted the halva. He asked to meet the Sicilian's daughter who was in charge of the factories in Fustat. Donning her face-veil, she went out. Feeling somewhat anxious, she took ʿAbd al-Tawwab with her.

She stopped and looked at the visitor. She could scarcely believe her eyes. It was Al-Kamil, Minister Shawar's son, a young man in the prime of life.

"Will you take your face veil off, my Lady?" he asked with a gentle smile.

"That's not proper, my Lord," she replied.

"Send the men away," he said, looking all around him.

"My Lord," she responded hesitantly.

"I've come to see you with an important secret."

She asked ʿAbd al-Tawwab to wait outside. She gripped her shoulders with both hands, scared that he might be bringing bad news about her cousin.

"I'm listening," she said.

"The heart has neither commander nor minister," he said. "You've taken possession of my heart, my Lady. Decide as you will. I'll be married to you, and you'll command the whole of Egypt."

She gave him a stunned look, but said nothing.

"I look at you and watch you every single day," he went on. "It's as if the halva stores are your soul. What would you do if you lost them? What if I protected you from every kind of trickster and helped you without infringing on your freedom? Ever since I've tasted the revelation halva, I've been searching for the halva-maker. They directed me to you, and you've become my goal and great hope."

She did not respond.

"Don't say anything," he hurried on. "Just think about it. Our marriage will rest on the halva factories in Fustat and all Egypt. Think about it and ask other people. To show my good intentions, Rashida, I'll give you a dowry twice as large as your current savings."

"There are lots of girls in Egypt, my Lord. I thought you had come to bring me news about my cousin. He's in Shawar's prison."

"He's never coming back," Al-Kamil replied firmly.

Her heart sank, and she clutched her stomach.

"He's still alive," she shuttered. "I want him to be alive, my Lord. He's of my own flesh and blood. We may have had our disagreements, but to me he's like a brother and father. I was hoping you'd intercede..."

"I personally stabbed his thigh," he said.

Looking into her eyes, he could see the terror in her pupils and the commotion in her breathing. She could not help but let out a sob, and her eyes glazed over.

"But he's not dead?" she managed to ask in a subdued tone. "Is that right?"

"Are you concerned about him?" he asked, his gaze focused on her eyes.

"He's my own flesh and blood, my Lord," she replied, trying to sound as strong as possible.

He did not respond.

She gasped again, as though she had just swallowed a poisonous snake. She let out another sob and was unable to speak.

"You love him, don't you?" Al-Kamil asked. "Ever since I first saw you, I've had that feeling. Your eyes gleam when you talk about him and your heart races as it asks for more."

She put her hand on the store wall so as not to collapse.

"No, my Lord, forgive me," she pleaded. "Death always affects me badly, and he's my flesh and blood. But he's not dead. I realise that. He's escaped, hasn't he?"

Without warning, she burst into tears.

"If I say I love you," he said, putting his hand on her shoulder, "would you believe me? I can't love anyone else, even if I have all the women on earth at my disposal."

She did not hear him.

"Ibrahim!" she whispered as she removed his hand.

"My father's out to become Badr al-Jamali," he said abruptly. "That's his primary focus. He calls himself 'Army Commander.' But not everyone who becomes king is 'two-horned' Alexander, nor is everyone who has control of the country's storehouses Joseph. Do you need anything from me?"

She shook her head, devoutly wishing that he would leave her alone and go. Without another word, he left. She collapsed to the floor, heaving dry sobs. Then she ran to the shrine of Sayyida Ruqayya and sat down in front of it.

"My Lady," she said, "you understand me and know my heart. Please intercede for me or speak about me! O Lord, do not be angry with me. I was following my heart's desires. Forgive me! O Lord, do not take him away from me. I can't live without him. When he was in front of me, I hated him. O Lord, I've loved him ever since I was born. It's your wish, I realise. If you take him away from me, I won't be angry. He is Your possession, but I promise You that I'll improve and fight all the evil pent up inside me. I promise You! Will you give him back to me? No, don't say that Rashida's spoiled, doesn't like to lose, or lend her toys to strangers. Will you give him back to me?

"From this day onwards, I'll be kind to the weak and forgive everyone's mistakes. Will you give him back to me? O Lord, promise me that You will. My lady, you're a woman; you know, you understand. `Ali ibn Abi Talib's own daughter, do you hear me? O Lord, will you give him back to me?

"I'll ask politely, yes, that's what I'll do. I'll dispense with coquetry, war, and conspiracy. I'm Rashida, daughter of Al-Jamali the Armenian and Jawhar the Sicilian, Egyptian daughter of both. She loves You. Even in the midst of foul battle, I loved You. My heart has never stopped loving You. My lady, tell my Lord that I love Him. O Lord, will you give him back to me? You are gentle, forgiving, kind. Be kind to me! Use Your gentleness to overcome Your desire for vengeance. O Lord of the Universe, give him back to me!

"Here, I am asking politely. I will accept Your judgment, when You pardon and forgive..."

With that, she burst into uncontrollable tears.

She rushed over to Ibrahim's sister's house in Cairo and asked about him.

His sister told her that his mother would soon be coming back from Syria. Nobody knew anything about Ibrahim, but Husain had returned. Soon they would all be together again, but Ibrahim... She asked her husband Aftakin to tell her about her brother's fate.

"No one comes out of Shawar's prison alive," he told her gloomily.

CHAPTER NINE

Al-Kamil knew everything that had happened to Ibrahim.

Closing his eyes, Ibrahim surrendered. Death would be coming at last; so he should thank the Minister. How he had longed to tell his mother, Laila, that he was dead. For him to stay alive was a crime that would be paid for in flesh, separating skin from blood. Once his soul was safely in the Creator's hands, he wanted to return to the earth for a while, to listen to Laila and see what she would say. Would she be sad? He was disturbed by the thought that she would never be sad. She might even be glad to be rid of the person who had killed her two sons. Ah me, the tyranny of loved ones and betrayal of the heart! I've been wronged, Laila, wronged, and I'm still alive!

"Aren't you listening?" Al-Kamil yelled.

"No, I'm not."

"But the torture's stopped, hasn't it? Isn't it over?"

"Kill me quickly, and I'll be grateful for the rest of my days."

"I've been telling you to escape," Al-Kamil said, looking all around him. "I've opened the door for you. Leave. Come on, put these clothes on, cover your face, and leave quickly. I'll put the mutilated corpse of a dead prisoner in your place."

"Your father will kill you if he finds out," Ibrahim told him in shock. "Kill me, and you'll be safe."

"I'll never kill you."

"Why do you and the Monarch of Death hate me so much?" Ibrahim asked.

"Maybe the torture's made you lose your mind," Al-Kamil replied, looking straight at him. "Get out of here!"

A man dumped him in the Sinai desert and left him some food and water. The world still looked odd, and all his eyes could see was love of impotence. The suffering was real enough, and the distance was clear. For him, there would be no return to Egypt. The waves rose, sucked in the rebellious waters, and created conflict in the depths. Ah, for Alexandria! In spite of all the whippings, it still lingered inside the heart.

He lay on the desert sand.

A shaikh handed him some water. Opening his eyes, he could see the man's long, white beard, but he could not make out his features.

"Who are you?"

"I'm the one who saved your life and mind from the decay inside Shawar's prison."

"Are you an ascetic believer or a man of war?"

"I know and understand things that you don't. I've seen things that you haven't and lived through times that you haven't. I've dedicated myself to peace."

"Is peace a man to whom you can dedicate yourself?"

"He's the saviour, Ibrahim."

"Why has he saved me? I thought the man who saved me was Al-Kamil, Shawar's son."

"He had you brought here. From here on, I will take charge of things. You've a goal, Ibrahim; you were created for that purpose. With me, everything will be revealed."

Ibrahim turned his head away, as though he were trying to push away his dreams. This shaikh was a dream; that much was certain. But he was not disappearing...

"Shaikh," he asked suspiciously, "what are you doing in the desert? Do you worship in the wilderness, I wonder? Are you searching for those, like me, who have gone astray?"

"I'm here," he replied in a mellow tone, "to rescue souls and humanity. If need be, I'd kill in order to save souls. The difference between me and armies is that I kill for the sake of peace, whereas armies kill out of greed and stupidity."

"What have you seen?" the shaikh asked, stretching out his hand. "Do you know anything about the spread of peoples and gatherings of clans? Do you understand the meaning of internecine feuds and the wars between Dahis and Ghabra'? The pre-Islamic era was one of mercy, if you compare it with these times of ours. Iraq, where the Caliph resides, has been encircled by the Crusader Franks who are invading from Syria. Jerusalem has fallen into their hands. While the Crusaders were aiming at the entire community, the Caliph in Baghdad asked a Turkish king for help against the Seljuq monarch. That started a war that lasted for years. Fighters are dying, and then they gauge success by the Basus War. Can you believe it? Muslim fighting Muslim and conspiring against him. The Crusaders are simply waiting for caliphs to fall, one after another. When it comes to the Caliph in Egypt, you know more about his weaknesses than I do. He asks Nur ad-din Zengi for help, while being so scared for his own rule than he can't put an end to Minister Shawar. How can the Caliph rule Egypt? Can't it be done by one man? If you feel like crying, then come with me to the land of the Arabs. There, you'll see humiliation after prestige, ignorance after knowledge, and unrest after peace."

Ibrahim looked at him without saying a word. What he was saying was true; he himself had lived through and witnessed all of it.

"You're going to Syria with me," the shaikh continued, pacing across the desert. "From there, we'll go to Baghdad, and you can observe and judge for yourself."

"How do you know my name, Shaikh?"

"I've heard your name. Shawar's scared of you."

"He's humiliated me. In his hands, I was like an orphan at a villain's dining table."

"Anyone who humiliates his foe is afraid of him. You're coming with me to the citadel where only the people of paradise live."

"Where is that?"

"On a distant mountain in Persia, where intrigues don't reach.

"This is death's fortress on the mountaintop. Here is punishment for sinners and release for the tortured. Here is a single path; those who traverse it can circle the slope. It is security. But no army can reach us, and no monarch can control our difficult path. Come no, Ibrahim, let's savour the wind of paradise, where the good person is just one who is alive, who triumphs, who masters. Take a deep breath and sit atop the mountain. Here, everything opposed to us is feeble and trivial, just like mankind. Here are people who have come to know God and His purpose, and have worked for the good.

"You're going to taste food better than anything you have ever tasted. Tell me, Ibrahim, which elements give halva the rapture of eternity?"

"Saffron and musk."

"Good news, Brother. You're not one of us, but, when you come to know us, you'll become one of us. Yes, our ancestors were inimical to us, but from evil, good can be created."

"I don't understand anything."

"You will only when you've tasted our halva. Give him some halva, my son."

He looked at the tray of halva. The sweets looked like doughnuts, but they were a greenish yellow.

"What's inside it?" he asked as he took one.

"Ibrahim, you're dead. We've taken you out of the hands of Shawar, where you were flayed to death. Are you scared to take some halva from the hands of Muslims?"

"What's the green that gives it this colour?" he asked, bringing it close to his mouth.

"Paradise plants."

"I don't know what you mean."

"Taste it first, brother, then decide."

He put one of them in his mouth. It tasted either like sugared mulukhiyya or salted saffron; he wasn't sure which. He took one after another. His breathing slowed and settled down. His mind kept pausing between different regions—sometimes in Egypt; at others, on the long road to the fortress. He saw things he had never seen before. His eyes closed, he plunged into the cold, extremely cold, sesame oil, which mingled with the sea spume. Now his breathing was calm, ready to face any pain. The memory of his mother who had renounced him faded into the distance, as did that of his beloved, the flame of his passion which he had no time to extinguish, and of his brothers. Ah, the perfidy and rejection of brothers! Fortress of punishment and life, come here into my embrace! I will stay here, though all mankind may turn away, lord of people and solitary monarch.

"Ibrahim," his companion asked, "who's more powerful, you or Shawar?"

"I am."

"Shawar's going to die. You'll kill himself yourself."

"That's my only desire."

"Then eat the herbs of paradise and hope. They are plants that give you strength. How are you going to kill him? You need to practice using a spear."

"I'll do it today."

"We'll kill Shawar and rid humanity of his tyranny. If you killed him during a war, you'd be doing it to lots of others besides. But if you assassinate just him like a rat, then he'll die alone, and you'll save humanity as a whole. Yes, Ibrahim, you'll be saving humanity as a whole and liberating Jerusalem from the Crusader kings. Listen. Are you listening?"

"Yes, I'm listening."

"You're going to kill Shawar."

"Yes, I am. Of course I am."

"Have some halva, Brother. Can you feel paradise?"

"I'm worried about my mind. I don't know where I am."

"You haven't drunk wine before. Is that right?"

"Never."

"Even Yusuf ibn Ayyub used to drink wine with your brothers in Alexandria. Then, they say that he totally abandoned all pleasure out of regret for going to Alexandria. You're the best of men. You savour paradise to discover what awaits you. But you also realise that you're willing to sacrifice yourself; you'll kill Shawar, but you understand that you'll die as well."

"I'm willing to die if it will save people from the Minister's evil ways."

"That's the man of the fortress. Men here willingly sacrifice themselves for the good of everyone. Shawar will die, then Nur ad-din, then Asad ad-din Shurkuh, then Yusuf ibn Ayyub, and then the Abbasid Caliph. Once they're all dead, we can liberate Jerusalem."

Ibrahim did not hear that last sentence. He was soaring through the heavens on the wings of the Phoenix, with the fresh wind buffeting his face and tickling his insides. Here, the wind was like no other. As the bird transported him through the heavens, he collided with the clouds and was transformed between its wings into white-haired halva, which he could eat without ever feeling sated.

When he woke up, the bird had disappeared and the white halva along with it. He looked all around him in despair. What was the use of the magic cure if it disappeared within hours? How was death a benefit if it was followed by punishment? Why was everything so confused in his mind? Who had rescued him: Jalal ad-din, the ascetic Sufi shaikh, or Al-Kamil, Shawar's son, who had been born amid the denizens of evil and injustice?

Where did the truth lie? How could the ascetic shaikh advocate killing, even if it was to save mankind? He tried to remember what he had heard the day before, to recall his mother and the whipping, but it was his mother's face that prevailed, staring at him angrily, as though he were his brothers' killer and disowning him. Then it was Rashida's face, her eyes brimming with life. These were times of sheer madness. If he really loved his cousin's waywardness and mischief more than Sayyida's intelligence and calm demeanour, then he had to be mad. In fact, more than anything else he loved Rashida's courage and defiance. He adored the passion that would almost leap out of her eyes and the alert posture that poured from her very soul. What he loved about her was the knight's bravery and the ascetic's sense of justice. How could his own mother's eyes deliver a pain so acute that neither fire nor water could extinguish it? Even whipping was easier to bear.

Then the Syrian army came to Alexandria, accompanied by Yusuf ibn Ayyub. He had become a brother and companion. Had Ibrahim been misled? Inside his mind, heads shook, then expanded and fragmented. The Fatimid army was not Egypt's army; it had no Egyptian soldiers. People said that Ahmad ibn Tulun had inducted Egyptians into his army, but nobody followed his lead. Even so, was it not stupid for Ibrahim to confront the Fatimid army, the armed forces of the Imam and Caliph who was ruler of his country? What did he expect? Had he not hurled his own brothers into perdition? Why did he trust the word of Yusuf ibn Ayyub, the young man who as yet had no experience of combat" Why had not Shirkuh brought his army to save the people of Alexandria? It had not been possible, and, for that reason, it was time to acknowledge weakness and error. Now that he was fully aware, he really needed that green halva. You have made a mistake, Ibrahim. You have climbed the political ladder when you are just a halva-maker. You have not kept an account, nor have you protected men and women. You have been wrong, man! Neither the Syrian nor the Fatimid army are worth it! Let all armies be dissolved! Let Ibrahim's brothers come back to life! Let the grief and despair over the past be revealed! Whipping is easier to bear that its consequences!

Jalal ad-din offered him some halva mixed with magic and rapture, but he refused, saying that he was sick. He looked at the idols all around him and wanted to destroy them. All of humanity is idols, and all the ornament we desire is for oblivion.

"What's the matter with you?" Jalal ad-din asked anxiously. "You're not the same Ibrahim who flew through the clouds yesterday."

"I am the same person," he replied. "But flying in the sky and then dropping to the very depths of the earth is troubling, and it takes away one's sense of equilibrium. I'm sick."

"You remember what we agreed on yesterday, don't you?" Jalal ad-din asked, giving him an anxious look. "You're going to kill Shawar."

"Yes, that's right."

"To save mankind from his evil ways, even if you die as well. You're someone who's saved thousands. How many men have died in the war between Shawar, Asad ad-din Shirkuh, and Yusuf ibn Ayyub? Many. What do you think about the events in Alexandria? Did Yusuf ibn Ayyub mislead you? Did he hurl your family into perdition?"

"Yes, he did," Ibrahim replied without even thinking.

"Have a taste of paradise," Jalal ad-din said, handing him some more halva.

"I've lost the way," Ibrahim replied, taking some with a hesitant hand.

"No," Jalal ad-din insisted, "you've found it. Yusuf ibn Ayyub, known as Salah ad-din, is Minister Shawar, who is Nur ad-din, who is Shirkuh, who is the Abbasid Caliph, who is the Crusaders. They're all one and the same. Do you hear me?"

"No, I don't," Ibrahim replied, chewing on some halva and closing his eyes. "Tell me again."

Jalal ad-din repeated what he had just said.

"Salah ad-din isn't Shawar," he replied uneasily, "and the Crusaders aren't the Syrian army."

"They're all the same. Greed is their downfall. Some of them don pious garb. They're even more dangerous and inflict more damage."

Closing his eyes, Ibrahim left the world. Doors were opened and, after a while, the greenery of paradise appeared.

"Shaikh," he asked after a pause, "why are you wearing Sufi garb? It's as though you're dressed in the robes of piety."

"Come to your senses, Ibrahim. You're at death's fortress. Those who enter here never leave. That's the destiny you chose when you came with me. I'm Shaikh Jalal ad-din. The devil's giving you the impression that I'm not him."

"You want me to kill Shawar?" Ibrahim asked, giving him a long, hard stare.

The shaikh smiled and lowered his head, running his fingers over his long white beard.

"You can't kill Shawar," he replied. "He's expecting you to kill him. We're all prepared to sacrifice ourselves, but we always succeed in the task at hand. You must leave it to others to kill Shawar. Leave it to someone Shawar doesn't suspect or fear."

"The Minister's not afraid of me."

"To the contrary, he's not afraid of other people. We all recognise heart, fear, and the tender core inside the heart, Salah ad-din Yusuf ibn Ayyub."

"What is it you want of me?"

"You're his friend."

"That's all past."

"He'll never forget what you did for him."

"I want to die. Are you killing that halva? Everything that's sweet is being slain."

"For people like you, death's a blessing."

"God has left me alive and taken everything away. Why has He left me alive?"

"To kill Salah ad-din."

"Who?" Ibrahim asked, his mouth agape in amazement.

"Hasn't God demanded of us that we rid ourselves of everything we love for His sake? Is he closer to you than your own family, your mother, and your brother? Hasn't God said in His book that close family includes enemies, even your wife and son? For His sake, dispense with people."

Ibrahim was in another world. He was tired of running and needed a deep sleep.

"You're the best of men," Jalal ad-din said with a smile. "Don't worry; death is nigh."

"Don't worry," Ibrahim repeated. "Nigh..."

He started thinking about words he might use to counter Jalal ad-din. He planned what he was going to say.

"You're playing with words," he told Jalal ad-din as soon as he entered the room. "You're deluding people, not giving guidance."

"Ibrahim, don't be so bold with the shaikh."

"Renunciation is an ascent. There's no evil, no greed, no killing, and no treachery. Relatives can be a foe if they lead you to do what angers God. The greatest losers of all are those who go astray in their lives, thinking all the while that they are doing good deeds. People just like you. What you are doing is much worse than what any infidel might do, with a weightier impact on the believer and an even more severe set of consequences."

"I see that you're attacking me now, even though I'm the one who's saved you. Think about it. Yusuf ibn Ayyub killed your brothers during a completely useless war, and then left."

"You're deluding people," Ibrahim replied in shock. "This isn't guidance. It was the Crusaders who killed my brothers."

"And who started this entire war?"

"The Minister."

"I understand. Rulers' greed is the cause. We're dreaming of a community unlike any other, one with no cliques and no wars between Muslims."

"You're claiming to be right," Ibrahim responded. "The ascetic spends his entire life on a quest for the truth, certain all the while that he'll find just some of it, no more."

"I'm your teacher, Shaikh Jalal ad-din."

"You say that you know," Ibrahim told him, "and yet Sufis do not know; they strive. For great people, modesty is both start and finish."

"If you desire to be closely tied to the Creator, then you must face Him with a sincere heart. Such a heart neither hates nor boasts, nor does it divide people. It recalls that they are all of His creation. He is the One and Only, and so we need to be as one with Him. How can the ascetic designate himself a judge? Isn't that some kind of polytheism?"

"I have compartmentalised people and made them into different sects, like Moses's Pharaoh. In God's creation, the Sufi sees both miracle and wisdom; he bows in awe before His every creation, both big and small. He makes no distinction based on sect, colour, or creed, nor does he pass judgment on criminals and tyrants. The Sufi strives to achieve the ultimate goal, desiring and longing only for Him, the One who is his only aspiration and goal. He questions no one else and refuses to acknowledge monarchs other than Him. You long for power and land; you imagine that you know how to protect them. The Sufi's only aspiration is to strive toward Him and around Him. Let me leave. I have no room for hatred. Like the plague, hatred gnaws at the guts and weakens the body."

"It seems you don't even hate the person who stabbed your thigh."

"I pity him his anger. I want to help people who need it, but I've neither knowledge nor authority. I always recall that we do not possess either. That's what my shaikh, Abu Taher the Sunni, taught me in Alexandria."

"I'm impressed by the way you argue," Shaikh Jalal ad-din responded with a smile, as he rubbed Ibrahim's shoulder. "You're arguing because, deep down, you realise that I'm right. Everyone in Alexandria is putting the burden of blame on you for the deaths, whereas the blame really belongs with the young man who has no experience with combat, Yusuf ibn Ayyub, and not the halva-maker. Don't let your delusion finish you off. I'm going to give you till tomorrow morning to change your mind, or else I'll kill you at noon."

"I've already told you," Ibrahim yelled at the top of his voice, "that I welcome death. Where is it?"

"Tomorrow, you'll be pleading and asking for forgiveness. You'll only ever eat the fruits of paradise when you enter it."

Ibrahim did not respond.

For a moment, Jalal ad-din looked at him, then he left, denying him any food or drink.

After several days, Ibrahim bit down on his lips to taste the moisture of his own blood. He started hallucinating and plunged into a new abyss.

In front of him, he saw a shaikh like no other. His beard was pure white, and his clothes were translucent, as though not intended to cover what lay below. This was a shaikh unlike any he had ever known. Closing his eyes, he devoutly hoped that the spectre of this shaikh would stay with him. A sense of peace flowed through his veins like rosewater, its scent that of musk, and its colour saffron. He heard the lovely voice.

"Greetings to you, Ibrahim!"

"Who are you?"

"Don't ask. Be patient about things you don't know. When you return, contact Yusuf ibn Ayyub. He needs you more than you need him. Ever since he visited your city, he's been wracked by guilt."

"He's sworn never to return to Egypt."

"Breaking an oath and fasting for three days is better that following your own whims. Each one of us has a role to play and a mission. We've no choice; it's a charge from God. When the mission's over, you'll go back to him, and he'll ask you about it. Do you understand?"

"No, I don't."

"Do you own things?"

"No, I don't."

"Doesn't everyone who comes to Egypt have their cravings?"

"For treasure and land."

"What did your grandfather do?"

"Which one?"

"The first and second."

"Preserve the land and treasure."

"Do you remember which sect they belonged to?"

"That doesn't concern me."

"Why doesn't it bother you that you're Sunni and they were both Shi`i?"

"Those are human divisions, but God knows things we don't."

"That's an excellent response. God knows things we don't. Does He divide up paradise amongst His servants, I wonder. This one's for the rich, and that one's for the poor. This is for the Baghdad Caliph, and that one's for the Fatimid. Is He going to give space to non-Muslims?"

"It's God's own paradise, and it's a major sin to ask questions about it. You enter at His will. But He is just, and He has commanded us to deal fairly."

"Another excellent answer. Go back to your home."

"Nobody wants me."

"But they all need you."

"Are you a dream?"

"Or the only truth."

"I'm in a strange place. They keep distorting their message, and I don't understand their intentions. But I'm scared of them."

"The person with a sincere heart is never afraid. Believers have an intense love of God."

Opening his eyes, he put his hand over his heart, as though he wanted to preserve such beauty and halva. In front of him, he could see the cavalier on his halva horse, decked out in his finest glory. After a short while, he was going to eat it. He longed for halva and the cavalier. The time was between twilight and darkness, between dream and reality. He was eating part of a gigantic bird made of honey and sugar, its wings extending all the way to the heavens. It called on him to return, but he refused.

"I'm the one who made you," he told it.

"He wanted you to make me," the bird answered from afar, its voice coarse. "You have no choice, halva-maker. Do your duty before you taste any halva."

The man appeared before him with his white beard and fixed gaze, as though Ibrahim had known him for years.

"I've come to you, halva-maker," the man said in a coarse voice, "because you called me. Listen to me and do what I say. It's an order, not a request. Before you claim to know something, you need to differentiate good from bad."

"It's the same white beard."

"But I am not Jalal ad-din. Not every shaikh is sinless, nor is every one knowledgeable. The knowledgeable person is someone who is aware of his own ignorance. Al-Jilani says that the believer is a stranger to the world, and the knowledgeable person is a stranger to all but the Lord.

"The Sufi, Ibrahim, is someone who has rid himself of the world, not someone who wants to design it as he likes. 'Do not be with anything. Rather, be with the Creator of things, the One who is something unlike anything else.'"

"That's a quote from Al-Jilani. Which shaikh are you talking about?"

"Tell Yusuf ibn Ayyub," the shaikh said with a smile as he nodded, "that we met on the day he visited me in secret in Iraq. I gave him the glad tidings that he would have a great victory if his intentions were pure and his heart was reformed."

As Ibrahim woke from his dream, he gave a deep sigh and shuddered. In his dream, had he really been visited by Shaikh 'Abd al-Qadir al-Jilani, the Crown of all Sages, who had taught his sayings to his own shaikh in Alexandria?

'Do not be with anything. Rather be with the Creator of things, the One who is something unlike anything else.'

'The believer is a stranger to the world, and the knowledgeable person is a stranger to all but the Lord.'

Those were the words of Al-Jilani himself. Now *there* was certainty. God wanted that he not be one of the ignorant. He stood up and prayed.

"To God alone belongs the power and strength," he repeated.

When he woke up, his spirit was afloat, swimming in tranquillity like that of his encounter and a buoyancy associated with a bodiless soul. Smiling to himself, he summoned the guard and asked to talk to Shaikh Jalal ad-din. He asked him for some water.

"I'll do whatever you want," he told the Shaikh.

"You're lying."

"In either case, I'm dead."

"You're prepared to sacrifice yourself. There's a difference between that and being dead."

"And, if I don't do what you want?"

"I'll kill you myself," the Shaikh replied aggressively. "But not before I've ripped off your skin for three months. Every single day, you'll long to die, but it won't happen. I'll gouge out your eyes, then your ears, and then sever your limbs."

"I'll do whatever you want," Ibrahim interrupted him. "But make my killing quick."

"When you kill the man who claims to be 'the Righteousness of the Faith,' the one called Salah ad-din, then I'll kill you quickly. They say he's merciful. If you're just saying that to get out of here, then you need to realise that anyone who's seen the fortress of death, spoken to Rashid ad-din Sinan, and not remained loyal to him, will never live to speak about what he's seen."

"I know. You're the Assassins, self-sacrificers. I'm aware of that."

Ibrahim recovered his health, took his poisoned sword with him, and headed for Damascus to look for Salah ad-din Yusuf Ibn Ayyub, his fellow soldier and friend from times of weakness.

When Salah ad-din Yusuf ibn Ayyub was told who was at the door, he told him to come in. He did not search him or discover the poisoned sword concealed in his cloak.

Ibrahim looked at Salah ad-din, his friend Yusuf. The young man's appearance had changed: he was no longer dressed in silk, and his eyes no longer flashed with the liveliness of youth and hope. No sooner did he set eyes on Ibrahim than he grabbed hold of his hands.

"Ibrahim!" he said, eagerly. "Praise be to God that you're well!"

"Dismiss your soldiers," Ibrahim replied with a bitter smile. "I need to talk to you on your own."

Salah ad-din gave him a confused look, dismissed his guards, and sat down.

"What's going on?" he asked.

Ibrahim took out the sword.

"I've come here to kill you with this poisoned sword," he said.

Salah ad-din seemed unaffected. He simply smiled and stayed seated.

"Who wants to kill me, I wonder," he said. "Shawar or the Crusader King?"

"Why look for an enemy outside your own house? He's around you all the time; you see him and know him. Don't imagine the Crusaders are the enemy. Who was it who brought the Crusaders to Egypt? Egypt's Minister. Who's trying to kill you here in Syria?"

"The Assassins," Salah ad-din replied, after staring at Ibrahim for a moment.

"Precisely, the self-sacrificers."

"Have you become one of them?"

"They're invading the ranks, posing as shaikhs in mosques, monks in churches, and soldiers in Sinan's army. They won't leave you alive."

"So then, you're not one of them."

"I won't be staying alive for long."

"Here, take the sword and hang onto it," Ibrahim told him, handing him the sword. "Keep it to remind yourself that you're always in danger. I'm going back to my homeland."

"Brother," Yusuf replied emotionally, "I'll send a guard with you. I'm afraid they'll kill you."

"If my time is up, they'll kill me. The Assassins are always with you and around you; they're the number one danger. They want to be in charge like everyone else, but they're not afraid to die. That's what's most dangerous about them."

"Our lives are in God's hands. I swear to you, brother, that I've no desire to govern. My only aspiration is to gather people together around the concept of equality. But these are times with neither colour nor scent."

"Yusuf," Ibrahim went on, "I've come to see you about something else."

"What's that?"

"It's as though I saw him. Where is he? Is he in your council?"

"Whom did you see?"

"Our Lord `Abd al-Qadir al-Jilani. That's his name, but I don't know him. Where is he?"

Salah ad-din stared at him with mixture of confusion and shock.

"I myself visited Our Lord `Abd al-Qadir al-Jilani in Iraq some years ago."

"In that case, what I saw was real," Ibrahim replied in relief. "It was not just a confused dream. He seemed to be giving me a message for you, Yusuf. I've no idea why he's charged me."

"Brother," Yusuf replied, "you've just reminded me of my shame and weakness. I've been wanting to forget and to spend the rest of my life in withdrawal."

"But Yusuf, he told me that it was a command."

"What was?"

"He said that you need to bestow therapy on people."

"But I have no therapy to bestow. I'm no doctor. In spite of myself, I'm a soldier."

"But that's what he told me. He's ordering you to cure people. He says that the Prophet said that treating people is a charitable deed. In a dream, he told me: 'Tell Salah ad-din to give to them, treat them kindly, be friendly with them, and soften his approach to them.'"

"Brother," Salah ad-din Yusuf Ibn Ayyub replied with a smile, "I'm neither king nor sultan. If I couldn't protect you and your family, then how can you be asking me to do all that?"

"I'm not the one asking; it's our Lord `Abd al-Qadir al-Jilani. I'm just bringing you a message that I don't understand."

"How are you, Ibrahim?" Salah ad-din asked him, checking him over. "How did you escape from Shawar's prison?"

"You're asking me how I am," Ibrahim replied with a smile. "It's as though you're wondering if torture has made me lose my mind."

"No, I'm trying to find out what torture you've had to bear."

"It was painful, but the fortress of death was even more so."

"With Nizar's followers?" Salah ad-din asked. "The Assassins? You went to their fortress? You're right. They'll never let you stay alive."

"If I'd been born in a different era and among different people," Ibrahim replied thoughtfully, "I might well have had more luck. I wonder, will we ever again witness days like those of the ancient kings? Of Ahmad ibn Tulun? The building of the Great Pyramid, or `Amr ibn al-`As? Will our children witness a world and era different from ours, one where humanity will be like the carefully aligned structure of the crenulations in Ahmad ibn Tulun's mosque? Will our sons ever witness the prestige like that of the ancients and on territory that stretches as far as Mesopotamia, with no barriers and no interlopers? Will the Kingdom of Jerusalem come to an end, as though it had never existed? Will the Crusader Franks disappear, as though they had never invaded and built themselves fortresses on our lands? If only I'd been born at some other time; I would have accepted suffering with open arms. Yusuf, the Assassins have been around forever, and they'll stay. They're just like worms, feeding only on dirt and refuse. Take care of yourself!"

"What did you see?"

"I can't possibly describe it."

"Maybe you're not well."

"No, I'm fine. My mind wasn't working the way it is today. I've brought you a message from `Abd al-Qadir al-Jilani."

"I've often admired him, Ibrahim. He's my shaikh and teacher, even though I haven't met him in years. But he can't be sending me any message."

"Why not?"

"Because, Brother, he died years ago. You need some rest. Stay here in Damascus with me. You'll be safe here."

"He's died," Ibrahim replied, giving him a lengthy stare. "The shaikh is dead. You want me to stay here?"

"Yes, Brother."

"But I'm just like fish that never leave the sea. I won't leave my city. Listen, Salah ad-din, Police Chief of Damascus. This is a message from the shaikh, even if he is dead."

"I would much prefer it to be some confused dream. I don't own the world and have no desire to become a ruler."

"He's chosen you precisely because you're not ambitious."

"Stay here with me."

"Who said you're going to stay here?"

"I've sworn not to go back to Egypt," he insisted. "The shame, suffering, and death that you've witnessed is enough to last for two lifetimes."

"When it comes to homeland, rule, and death, Yusuf, we don't have any choice. You've lied to me, and that doesn't become intelligent people."

Yusuf stared at him, not understanding.

"In the dream," Ibrahim went on, "'Abd al-Qadir al-Jilani told me that you had visited him in Iraq in disguise. You imbibed knowledge at his hands, and he gave you news of a great victory."

"How did you find that out?" Yusuf asked, his face turning pale.

"He was trying to make it clear to you, but you didn't want to understand."

"He and I are the only ones who know about that."

"Now you know the message and the charge, Brother. You don't need me anymore. Till we meet again, Yusuf, whether in this narrow world or in the hereafter!"

"If you leave me today," Yusuf said after a moment's reflection, "you're going to die. They're waiting for you outside. Ibrahim, let me accuse you of trying to kill me and put you in my prison for a few days. Then you can escape. I'll never reveal the name of the person who tried to kill me."

"Do that if you want," Ibrahim replied confidently. "However, I've been to the fortress of death. Anyone who's witnessed what happens there is bound to die. I'll be dead in either case.

BOOK THREE

564 AH / 1169 CE

Still I see all the people as one,

And the entire land as one country

Tamim ibn al-Mu`izz li-din Allah, Fatimid poet

CHAPTER TEN

Husain was settled in Bilbeis, but his heart was not. He had been married there and had had a son, whom he had named Ibrahim. When his wife asked him why he had given his son the name of the brother he had disowned, he had replied that, while he had disowned his brother's actions, he had not disowned the past that united them or the womb that had borne them both, nourishing them with both food and blood. While he may have disowned Ibrahim for his domineering, he had not disowned the young man who had helped bring him up, running along the shore with him and steadfastly and patiently teaching him how to swim. His wife stared at him, not understanding, and started nursing her son. He was now working for another halva-maker, even though he had previously been the owner of factories and stores. But now, he was happier; that much was certain. He had rid himself of his brother's dominance and oppression. Even if the current owner treated him badly, he was not his own brother. As long as he was far from Ibrahim's heavy-handedness, he could willingly tolerate such humiliation. He alone had been married, and now had decided to live here on his own. Soon, he was planning to open a halva store in his own name and later a factory. He would be better than Ibrahim; yes, needless to say, he would. He had not inherited all the prestige and success, but he was creating that now. Even his mother was happy, welcoming him as though he were her only son. Indeed, these days, he was her only son. He would never deny that. He had been thrilled when he learned that his mother had disowned Ibrahim. Now she was his mother alone. She would look into his eyes and concern herself with him. Ibrahim's magic no longer dominated her feelings. Now, the world could smile. Without Ibrahim, the whole world was on an even keel. His heart did not catch fire every time he heard Ibrahim's name, even when it was his wife calling for their young son.

Shawar was a shrewd, powerful minister. Like his grandfather, Badr al-Jamali. He deserved the title Commander of the Armed Forces. That is what Husain told himself. He had heard the rumours, but he was not going to believe them, just as Shawar himself had not. People were saying that Amalric, King of Jerusalem, had moved his army to Ashkelon! Even if he had done so, he obviously was not planning to enter Egypt. There was a pact between him and Shawar. Shawar had adhered to all the conditions, retaining a Crusader guard at Cairo's gates. Even when they mistreated Egyptians, he had looked the other way. Amalric was certainly aware who was his friend and who his foe. Needless to say, he would not invade the country of a friend when the Fatimid army had made a pact with him. Amalric's enemy in Syria was Nur ad-din Mahmud, along with his general, Asad ad-din Shirkuh, and his nephew, Salah ad-din Yusuf ibn Ayyub. Shawar was a loyal friend. False accusations would never work. Shawar sent one of his amirs to Amalric to find out what was happening, but the Amir did not return. People said that Amalric offered him estates and money. Shawar then sent another amir with a letter expressing his affection for the Crusader King; he stated that he regarded the King as a friend and had not broken the pact. King Amalric sent an affectionate letter back, promising that he would not break the pact. He explained what was happening. He was only moving his troops because another Frankish force was arriving from the north, by sea, and planning an attack on Egypt. He was just protecting his friend, no more. He was putting the army close by and under his command. The entire Crusader army would be under the command of the Army Commander, Minister Shawar. However, Shawar would have to pay more money; moving troops had costs in gold and more. Shawar had to pay. Shawar responded that he was willing to pay whatever the King of Jerusalem, his loyal friend, demanded. Amalric sent him an affectionate reply with his best wishes. Thus, the entire matter ended.

But the rumours did not stop. They said that the Crusader King was coming to Egypt soon and was at the gates of Bilbeis.

That was utter nonsense, according to Husain himself.

Humanity slept, and Husain dreamed of a factory to produce halva, making kunafa by hand and drowning it in honey. People went on saying that the Crusader army was heading for the Delta. Utter rubbish! Traitorous rumours, no more. At dawn on Friday, he got up to pray, then heard shouts. Later, he could not recall exactly what happened, but men's voices had been silenced, and all he heard was the groans of women. Every woman on earth was screaming, weeping, and lamenting the pointless loss of life. The clanging of swords never left his hearing, as steel met steel. He rushed out, searching for his wife. He bumped into her and grabbed her arm. He was about to open the door, but she stopped him.

"The Franks!" she shrieked.

"What nonsense are you talking?!"

"The Crusaders are in Bilbeis! The Franks are killing everyone in the city."

He was about to open the door, but she stood in front of him.

"Don't do it," she said. "Don't move."

"I'm not a coward."

"Protect me and your child. Don't move."

But, before he could move, soldiers knocked down the wooden door to his house and rushed inside. They shoved Husain, and he lost his balance, falling to the ground. A soldier hit him on the head with the hilt of his sword; he almost lost consciousness and was unable to move. But he could still see, and he would never forget the scene as long as he lived—if only he had been able to do so. His hands and feet were paralyzed, but his mind was still working—if only it too had exploded or burst into flames. He watched as the sword pierced his wife's belly and emerged from her back. He saw the soldier grab his baby boy as though he were a dirty bit of food full of worms and threw him to the floor as hard as he could. The baby stopped breathing. They then rushed inside the house looking for spoils. When they did not find any, they dragged Husain away and took him prisoner.

Shawar now confirmed, without a doubt, that the Crusaders had invaded Egypt and would be entering Fustat and Cairo within a few hours. These were not suspicions or rumours. It was all confirmed when he heard that Bilbeis no longer had any men left. When the Crusaders had entered the town, they had arrested every young man and taken them away as merchandise to their country. They had slain every old man, child, and woman. They had terrorised people, but they had not left anyone alive to tell what they had witnessed. The splotches of blood spread all the way to Fustat and filled ditches and water canals. Shawar was stunned, his son Al-Kamil was distressed, and the

Caliph Al-'Adid asked Nur ad-din for help. He sent him some women's hair, and told him that Egypt would be finished before Nur ad-din could bring help from Syria.

When Husain woke up, he found himself in a boat at night, with his hands and feet bound. He started sobbing uncontrollably. The soldier heard him.

"Egyptians cry like women!" he said in broken Arabic. "Stop crying, slave!"

Husain could not stop, nor could he work out where he was going. Then he heard one prisoner talking to another.

"This imprisonment will never end," he said. "The way they do things, we're going to be prisoners for forty years or more. We'll never see our country again for the rest of our lives, nor what's left of our families. We're bound to be humiliated."

He saw his little son in front of him, at the moment when the soldier threw him to the floor; there had been no blood, and the boy had not cried out. What a sweet and wonderful boy he had been! He was not going to give the soldier the satisfaction of seeing him humiliated or feeling his pain. Ibrahim, my dear son, can you ever forgive me?

"How can we kill ourselves?" he asked in a tearful voice.

"There are no knives or swords here," the prisoner next to him replied.

"If we plunged into the depths of the river."

"You'll never be able to reach it from where you are."

"I'll crawl."

"Maybe..."

"I'll achieve death by crawling. I'm not going to stay a prisoner of the Crusaders."

He heard a guffaw, although he did not know where it came from. It deafened his ears. He was afraid he was losing his mind. For a few seconds, his heart paid no heed, and everything was confused. He could not remember what had brought him here and where his wife was.

"Fatima," he yelled suddenly, "I told you to open the door! I can fight the Crusaders, woman!"

There was laughter, and the gigantic mouth swallowed him, then spat him out. More laughter, and now blood spilled out. Still more laughter. It threw his wife's corpse down in front of him and laughed harder. He saw his brothers' corpses, and it laughed some more. As the laughter grew louder, it deafened him. He yelled for help, hoping they would hit his head with a hammer so he would lose consciousness. The mouth kept on laughing.

CHAPTER ELEVEN

When Rashida heard the news, she collapsed. Husain must have been killed. No one knew anything about him or his family. The King of the Crusader Franks was marching towards Cairo. The men all sat around her, their heads bowed.

"War's bound to come," `Abd al-Tawwab said.

"What war, Uncle?" Rashida asked bitterly. "Where's the army? If the Crusader King managed to enter Bilbeis in just three days and was confronted by only a few men, the people of Bilbeis can't have had any weapons or have been trained to fight."

"Ever since the Minister made a pact with the Crusader King," `Abd al-Tawwab responded, "the country has been rife with treason."

She remained silent and leaned her chin against her hand. She was doing her best to control the tears that always loomed on the horizon whenever she remembered a love that had not been fulfilled and a man who had taken possession of her heart. Then he had been forced to leave. Preserving the halva-maker's factory was what would gladden Ibrahim, his grandfather, as well as her family. She would defend it with everything she had. She stood up and told the men to store their weapons. The Crusaders may have entered Bilbeis, but they would never enter Cairo and Fustat. The men gave her confused looks.

"What are you saying, my daughter?" `Abd al-Tawwab asked. "Do you want halva-factory workers to fight the Crusader King in person?"

"When thieves invade your house, Uncle," she replied angrily, "you have no choice but to confront them, even if it's only with a kitchen knife and pillow."

"She's lost her mind," he mumbled to himself. "This is an end, controlled by women."

"If the men won't fight, then I will," she proclaimed. "I'll defend my money and my business just as anyone in power would."

The men remained silent. So, gathering all the money she owned, she slipped out at dawn. Looking all around her, she clambered up the Muqattam Hills, panting. She felt she could hear him, or even see him, as she felt his hand patting her shoulder—Badr al-Jamali. Can you hear me, Grandfather? Do you know how bitter defeat and powerlessness can be? Are you aware of passionate love and the certainty of distance? Every lord and commander must realise that passion's flood is part of resolve, and separation's burning embers can elevate the heart. Ah, my Grandfather! If only you knew the humiliation I've seen—a heavy burden that's almost broken my back!

She kept looking all around her to make sure that the place was deserted. She reached her goal, the Juyushi Shrine, her grandfather Badr al-Jamali's mosque. It was here that he had communed alone with his Lord, and his own humiliation and weakness had shown themselves.

Ah, my all and my family...

Humiliated and broken,

All I have to offer is my soul. Take it!

The soul is the endeavour of the destitute."

As she slowly opened the door, she could feel the angels waiting for her—or that is how it seemed to her. She was prepared for them to be there.

"O Lord," she whispered as she prostrated herself. "Last time, I asked You for certain things. I want to change them. Human beings are remarkable: their hopes change with the vicissitudes of time. Let's forget all my previous requests. Today, I want peace for Egypt, and that's enough."

Leaving the mosque, she took an axe out of her coat and started digging behind the mosque. She put everything she owned in the hole and covered it with sand and rocks. She sat on it and looked up at the stars in the sky. I wonder, what did you see here, Grandfather? Did you speak to the stars every day? Are you pleased with me? I swear that I've changed. I'm doing my best to confront myself as much as I can. God is merciful and forgiving, but human beings are not. When we meet, Grandfather, don't blame me or grumble about my actions. By God, among your grandchildren you won't find anyone more courageous and steadfast than Rashida.

As she hurried back down, daylight almost gave her excursion away. She was close to the shop when she spotted him: Al-Kamil, son and deputy of Minister Shawar. She let out a gasp as she stared at him.

"Where were you?" he asked in surprise.

"The Cru...sa...ders," she stuttered.

"They're close to Egypt and Cairo. I've come because I want you with me."

She stared at him, not understanding what he meant.

"I'm going to protect you," he went on. "The Crusaders will never reach the Minister's house."

"Who's going to protect the Egyptian people?" she asked forcefully. "Who'll protect my grandfather's factory? For me, that's more important than anything else."

"If I promised to keep it safe," he asked firmly, "would you be married to me?"

"You're not going to be married to me, and you know it."

"Because your love fires your heart," he interrupted. "But you have to give in. Whoever loves 'is humble and submissive about everything.'"

"My Lord," she replied, swallowing hard, "you deserve someone better than me."

"If only I could manage to see anyone else. I'll protect you from everything else."

"You're the noblest of men," she responded kindly. "Leave me with my family. I can't abandon the ones I love."

"Where are they? The only loved one you have, Rashida, is your mother, and she can come with us, along with your slave girl."

"They're all around me, my Lord, even if you can't actually see them."

Their eyes met.

"You have a feeling," Al-Kamil continued. "Or actually, you're certain that he's still alive. Your cousin."

"Someone drowning will always clutch at straws, my Lord."

"What's coming is going to be much worse than you could imagine What's already happened has not prepared your heart to even conceive it."

"I realise that."

"Fine. If you won't come with me, I'll still stay near you to guard and protect you. One day, you'll realise how powerful love is and how much the lover suffers."

Back at the house, she used her fingers to block her ears so she could not hear her mother's sobs and pleas and the slave girl's grumblings and tears.

"Let's escape, Rashida!" her mother blurted.

"This is our country," she replied. "If Ibrahim did not run away, even though he knew he would be tortured and killed in Shawar's prison, do you really expect me to run away?"

"Let's escape, my daughter. I can't stand the thought of seeing you dead."

"It's all predestined fate."

Soldiers sounded the trumpet, and the noise came out loud and harsh. They delivered their message in a quivering tone, full of despair.

"The Crusader King has reached the edge of Fustat and Cairo," they announced. "He's encamped by the Birkat al-Habash, people of Egypt. The Army Commander, Shawar ibn Mujir as-Sa`di, will defend the country, people of Egypt. He commands you to evacuate Fustat within three hours. The Crusaders will not enter Cairo. Within three hours, Fustat will be burned. Anyone with children, money, or gold should take it and leave. Today, Cairo's gates will be open to welcome the people of Fustat. The Crusader King has camped close to you, and the Army Commander, Protector of Muslims, will keep the Egyptian people safe."

Rashida laughed out loud at those last words, so much so that her mother thought Rashida had lost her mind.

"Did you hear, Rashida?" she asked her daughter. "We have to leave Fustat, my daughter. It's going to be burned."

"Which Commander burns his own city?"

"He's burning it so it won't fall into Crusader hands the way Bilbeis did."

"Then he can burn us along with it. I'll never leave Fustat and my father's factory and store."

Her mother wailed and called out to the men.

"My daughter's lost her mind!" she shouted at the top of her voice. "ʿAbd al-Tawwab,..."

"Mother," Rashida said firmly. "You'll go to Cairo. I'm staying here. I'm not going to leave my father's factory."

Covering up her face, she headed for the factory and sat down in front of it, like the Sphinx in front of the Great Pyramid. No one could budge her. A strange connection had linked this family to fire, ever since their great-grandmother Sundus had been burned in the halva-maker's fire. The agonies of fire blended with the sweet taste of sugar, and the world assumed a different shape and colour. Grey blended with red, then black was poured over the leaves. At that point, all sight was erased and vision cut off.

CHAPTER TWELVE

When sleep is the preferable faculty, you know you are in hell. Husain closed his eyes as sleep toyed with him, playing with what was left of his mind. Sometimes, it would come close and embrace him, but, at others, it would chide him for his cowardice and ignorance, blaming him for still being alive. He opened his eyes to look up at the stars in the sky, but could not see any. He closed his eyes, then opened them again. He edged himself to the side of the boat.

"I can't see, Mother!" he yelled as loudly as possible. "All I see is darkness."

"You coward! Now you're shouting for your mother!"

He did not know whether that voice came from within him or without. When Husain was to go to the land of the Franks, or to Muslim lands occupied by the Franks, they would be changing his name, identity, colour, and language. If he lost his mind now, that would be better. They might decide to beat him to death. Woe to the fates and defeat! Every time the Crusaders entered a city in Syria, he would tell himself that they could not possibly enter Egypt. Whenever they slew the inhabitants of a port, he would feel pity and purse his lips.

"What a terrible misfortune for them!" he would say. "But we're in Egypt, far removed from the Crusaders and in a safe haven."

But there were no such havens safe from the Crusaders, and no chance of sleep while they were in Syria. Had they entered Cairo today? he wondered. Had they slain his mother and two sisters?

"Ah Ibrahim, if only you realised how much I hate you! I hate you because you were right. I hate you because you showed me my own weakness. Are you laughing now? I've died and risen again. Are you looking down on me from on high and chiding me?"

"Are you chiding me, Brother?" he yelled.

The soldiers stared at him. Then they went back to sleep, muttering that he had lost his mind.

He heard whisperings and confirmed that he had indeed lost his mind.

"Listen, boy. I'm blaming you, stupid! Do you still remember how to swim, or have you forgotten everything I taught you?"

"Stay away," he said, closing his eyes. "Don't come here!"

All he knew was that a hand emerged from the water and pulled him downwards. He fell into the river's depths. The soldiers awoke to the sound of the splash. They had a lot to say and clustered around. They said that he had killed himself. He had wanted to do that from the very start. That was better; he had lost his mind and was no good for work or even for torture. The boat continued on its way. Water filled his eyes, mouth, and ears. He tried to float, but his hands and feet were bound. So, let him sink to the very bottom, probe the river's depths, and dispel the world's concerns. He had no idea when he would lose consciousness and the agony would stop. He was young and had always been able to stay under water for longer than Ibrahim. Whenever they had played together and plunged into the water, Ibrahim had always been the first to get out.

"There's something Husain can do better than Ibrahim," he used to say.

The same hand grabbed his and started fiddling with the lock and opening it with a nail. It then headed with a peculiar speed for his feet and untied them as well.

"You can float now," a commanding voice said. "The boat's gone."

He coughed and spluttered, then succumbed to a fit of both hacking coughs and confusion. When he looked at the face swimming beside him and saw its eyes and nose in the night's light, he saw himself, or rather, features similar to his own.

"Ibrahim," he said in a clogged voice.

Ibrahim pulled Husain's hands towards an island in the middle of the water. Once Ibrahim's feet touched ground, he started to pant. He did not look at his brother, but spat out water as he leaned against a rock on the island.

"I thought you'd forgotten how to swim," Ibrahim said. "But at least you've remembered that much."

Husain said nothing, but allowed his brother to take his hand and clamber up the rock onto the small island. When Ibrahim let go, Husain sank to the ground, still heaving and crying nonstop.

"Stop weeping like a woman!" Ibrahim told him. "I've been looking for you. Ever since the Crusaders entered Bilbeis, I've been searching for you. I was hoping you were one of the prisoners."

Covering his face with his hands, Husain kept on weeping. Ibrahim went over to him and gave him a hug.

"Stop weeping," he said. "Your mother needs you."

"Brother," Husain replied. "They killed my wife and son before my very eyes."

"That's how the Crusaders behave."

"Brother..."

"Death's a fate that comes either with them or without them. Get a hold of yourself! Don't let our enemies gloat!"

"You're the one who's come here to gloat, Cousin," Husain said. "You've rescued me because you're better. Ibrahim knows everything. He controls everything. He—"

"Stop your nonsense," Ibrahim interrupted. "Be strong."

"I don't love you. I never have."

"I'm not bothered about love, Cousin. You need to behave like the son of the Sicilian and Supreme Master. Your mother needs you."

"You..."

"Don't worry about me."

"You..."

"Escaped from a certain death at the hands of either the Crusaders or the Assassins. As far as I'm concerned, they're both the same. Or it may have been Shawar's doing."

"Do you really know yourself, Brother?" Husain asked, after looking at him for a moment. "I'm now going to tell you about yourself. No one's allowed to argue with either you or the Imam or to object to any decision that the two of you make. Ever since I was born, Ibrahim, you've been my mother's imam. Everything you do is right; you've grown up with that delusion. The only thing you know how to do is to give orders to everyone around you. All of us inside the house have to wait to hear Ibrahim's instructions. You're not even like the Caliph Al-'Adid. He doesn't have full control of the government. Maybe you inherited the notion that there's only one person in charge from our grandfather, the Supreme Master. Throughout your entire life, we've been less than you. You rise and hover over our heads like an eagle, while we quake in fear and longing. Do you even realise how great our tragedy really is? You're always right, even when it involves your whims and weaknesses. You never ask for advice or listen."

"Have you finished?" Ibrahim asked.

"I just want you to know yourself."

"Everything you've said is right, Brother," Ibrahim replied. "The notion of good has dominated my thinking, and I've forced existence to conform to my principles. I've been shunned by my brother, my mother, and even my beloved. No, I'm not used to modesty or to having my orders challenged by anyone. But, since I'm always right, you need to obey my commands!"

Husain let out a cry of sheer despair.

Moving Rashida was even harder than moving the ancient statues and Alexandrian columns. Shaikh 'Abd al-Tawwab was forced to carry her with the men, while she went on biting his hand and screaming at him. He meanwhile was muttering every single curse that he knew. He was dragging her out of Fustat as the flames drew ever closer.

"My father's factory," she kept yelling. "This is my city. I'll never leave it. Let me be burned along with it! Why are you burning the city, Shawar, you coward? Defend it, don't burn it down! Do you hear me, Shawar?"

`Abd al-Tawwab covered her mouth, and she bit him again. He would have thrown her to the ground if her mother had not begged him to get to Cairo with her daughter and slave girl. `Abd al-Tawwab entered the city through Bab an-Nasr and headed for the house that belonged to Ibrahim's mother and her two daughters. Ibrahim's mother did not want to receive them or to set eyes on Rashida again, but, at Shafiqa's insistence, she reluctantly agreed. They put Rashida in a room and locked the door. She banged on it until her hands bled. Then she sank to the floor and covered her face. By now, the smell of smoke had reached all the way to Cairo. This was no ordinary fire.

Minister Shawar poured twenty thousand bottles of oil over Fustat and used ten thousand torches to set in ablaze. He wanted to reduce it to ashes, and ashes do not burn. It was all supposed to be consolation for the Minister. No one would benefit from those ashes: not the Crusader King, not Egyptians, and not Syrian soldiers.

Shafiqa was getting more and more worried about her husband.

"I devoutly hope the Crusaders don't kill him," she said. "I also want the war to come to an end. Aftakin deserves the best."

Kamila gave her a sad look, not knowing whether or not her husband deserved the best. She had heard Jawwad talking about how he had helped kidnap her brother. Should she believe the wheat porter or her own husband? She always believed Ibrahim; he never lied. But he was not there. With her husband, she was now like a halva doll, living with him but without any feelings. He could approach her, but never possess her.

Shouts arose, and Crusader soldiers surrounded Bab ash-Sharqiyya, a gate that her grandfather had built, as though he had realised what the future would hold and was aware of the dangers. She wiped away her tears, then gave her mother a disapproving and somewhat shocked look.

"Don't you miss Ibrahim? she asked.

"No, I don't," she replied firmly.

"What about Husain?"

"He's fine."

"But Bilbeis isn't. He's there, Mother."

"If he's dead," she replied after a pause, "at least it won't be his own brother who's killed him, the way his brother killed my two other sons."

"Mama!"

"I don't like having Kauthar's daughter here. I also don't want Kauthar and her damned slave girl."

"It's wartime, Mother. Your sense of mercy always used to outweigh your anger."

"Mercy can go to hell! Everything left can go to hell! They're all the same."

"I wonder, are you sadder to lose your two sons or Ibrahim?"

"He's dead. I told you that."

"They say Shawar had him tortured, but then he fled to Syria. He was whipped."

"Stop!" she said. "You're one of your brother Ibrahim's siblings. Your heart's full of hatred. If you thought I'd feel pity for him, you were wrong. I told you, he's dead."

"Maybe he really did die, Mother."

"That would be a blessing. Enough about him. I want Rashida to leave this house, or else I will. Make up your mind."

"Mother, it's as if..."

"As if I'm not your mother. Throw her to the Crusaders! I want them to crush her after they've cracked her ribs open and soiled her honour."

Shafiqa gasped and left the room. Looking all around her, she saw the mountains draw close, then collapse. The sturdy gates were melting away like sugar in a glass of water. As she closed her eyes, she had no idea whether the Crusaders were going to leave anyone alive. Maybe they were bound to wipe out both this relic and ill-starred family.

At night there came a powerful knock at the door. Once Sufyan had confirmed the name of the person knocking, he opened the door. It was Al-Kamil, son and deputy of the Minister, who had come to the house of the Sicilian in Cairo. Sufyan was astonished to see him, surrounded as he was by his guards.

"I've come because I want to rescue you all," he insisted. "You're to come with me and take refuge in my father's palace."

All the women were gathered in a room, except for Rashida; no one opened the door to her room in case she might do something. Jawwad came out and looked at Al-Kamil without saying a word.

"You're all halva-makers, men and women," Al-Kamil said.

"May God bless you, my Lord!" Sufyan replied.

"Where is she?" Al-Kamil asked. "Where's Rashida?"

Sufyan told him what had happened.

"What you've done is fine," Al-Kamil replied. "Come on, gather up your things, quickly now. We don't know what's going to happen tomorrow."

"But Rashida..."

"We'll force her to come."

With a nod, Sufyan went over to his wife. She had started collecting her things and was making sure to protect her children. That was the most important thing. Kauthar banged on her daughter's door.

"Rashida," she said. "We're leaving with the Deputy Minister. We've been rescued."

"I'll only ever leave in order to save my factory in Fustat," Rashida yelled from behind the door.

"My daughter, ask God to forgive you and not bring down his judgement upon you!"

They dragged her and Ibrahim's mother out of their rooms. Ibrahim's mother gave her a hateful stare, but Rashida directed her attention at Al-Kamil.

"Wouldn't it be better to fight," she insisted, "rather than die?"

"We are fighting," he replied with a smile. "We men, that is. But not you. Come with me now."

Before he ordered his men to move, Ibrahim's mother looked at the door. Her heart leapt and shuddered. She knew the man standing by the door. How often had she embraced his eyes and fondled his cheeks as a little boy! She had never loved anyone as much as she had loved him. And never hated anyone else as much, either. Her son, Husain. He seemed older and looked skinny. His hair was turning white. Life had passed by between night and day, a year or two...

Husain came in through the open door and looked around. He stared at his mother, who was nailed to the floor.

"How are you, Mother?" he asked as he held her hand to kiss it.

She pulled her hand away.

Meanwhile, Rashida's eyes were hoping and scared of that hope, while her heart was holding a silent conversation. Then she saw him: Ibrahim. She held her mother's hand to avoid hurling herself into his arms in front of everyone or losing consciousness. Ibrahim's eyes met Al-Kamil's. The two men stood facing each other in silence.

"Thank God you're safe," Al-Kamil said eventually. "I was about to take your household to a safe location."

Breaths quickened and feelings churned, differing in the same way that the language and inclinations of imams do. One sister in tears was longing for her brother, while the other sister was feeling guilty and ashamed, because she had abandoned him for her husband's sake. She was crying, too. Ibrahim's mother was standing there like a statue, displaying neither sorrow nor joy. She was simply furious, even more furious because of the wave of gentleness that had invaded her heart and the sense of intimacy and ease that her eye was feeling. She disavowed it all and struck her heart with a stone.

Rashida meanwhile stared at him in silence, plunged into sweet waters with heavy waves. Her heart was all astir and her guts swung violently between hope and fear. She kept looking at him without saying a word. From her babyhood till that day, she had been with him. He was alive; that was what she had wanted and what had kept her alive. She looked back at Al-Kamil.

"My Lord," Ibrahim said, "we're profoundly grateful for your generous spirit, and I can never forget your kindness towards me. And yet I'm surprised that you should want to rescue my own family."

"There's someone here," Al-Kamil said frankly, looking at Rashida, "about whom I'm particularly concerned, because of the Crusaders' well-known cruelty."

Ibrahim raised his eyebrows, feeling confused and a little threatened. He looked over at Rashida, and their eyes met. She teared up, recalling the pain of separation and defeat and a sense of shame, because she had not been able to preserve the heritage.

Ibrahim did his best to keep his emotions in check. He would not lose his nerve, even when his own mother greeted him with a cold stare and his beloved was on the point of leaving with Al-Kamil.

Her eyes were half closed, and she could not stop herself going over to him in search of his aura. Ibrahim did not notice her; he was busy talking to Al-Kamil, more shocked by his presence than by the Crusaders.

"My Lord," he announced firmly. "I'm grateful for the protection you've offered, but now I've returned with my brother, and I'll personally take charge of my family's protection."

"I didn't come to get your opinion, Ibrahim," Al-Kamil responded with equal determination. "I'm protecting my own interests here."

"My Lord," Ibrahim told him threateningly, "nothing in our household is your concern. It's my mother, my sister, my cousin, and my betrothed.

"It's what you deserve, you killer," his mother muttered with a bitter smile.

"I'm surprised, Ibrahim, that you've forgotten that I saved your life. If I were in your shoes, I would be showing a bit of gratitude."

"I'm grateful indeed, my Lord, but I make my own decisions about what concerns me."

"I'm not talking to you. I intend to take Rashida and her mother away from here, whether you like it or not."

Rashida cried out.

"You're not going anywhere," Ibrahim told her, before she could say anything. "If you intend to take her, you'll have to kill me first, and then your rescue of me will have been for nothing. My men and I will fight, and Rashida's not leaving."

Rashida moved even closer, until she was only a single step away. She found his hand and clasped it. He wrapped his fingers around her hand.

"Leave, my Lord," Ibrahim said to Al-Kamil. "If we need your protection, I will come to you in person. I thank you for everything. We're not going to fight each other with the Crusaders at the gates of Cairo and Fustat on fire."

When he noticed Rashida's hand clasping her cousin's, Al-Kamil hesitated.

In front of everyone, she put her arms around Ibrahim's neck.

"You're alive, Cousin," she cried. "How I've missed you!"

"Yes, I'm alive," he replied, putting his arm around her waist. "Did you think I wasn't?"

"If Rashida dies," Al-Kamil said, giving them both a sad glance, "you'll be responsible..."

Ibrahim was shocked and tried to keep his jealousy in check. Looking at Al-Kamil, he pushed Rashida away, but still kept hold of her hand.

"I'm impressed by your concern for the Egyptian people," he said.

Al-Kamil turned away and ordered his men to leave the house. He stopped and looked at Rashida.

"Cover your face, Rashida, now!" Ibrahim told her. "Don't go out with your face uncovered, even if the Crusader King comes in."

She opened her mouth to object or say something, but his eyes silenced her. She was still holding his hand, and he moved closer. She was about to greet him with defeat. She had not managed to preserve the heritage, nor had she been able to confront the Crusaders, the Minister, conspiracies, and intrigues.

Once Al-Kamil had left, Ibrahim turned to his mother.

"How are you, Ibrahim's mother?" he asked.

She almost lost her balance and had to clutch at Husain's hand.

"Take me to my room," she said.

Ibrahim's two sisters fell weeping into his arms. Sufyan patted his shoulder in welcome. Eyes collapsed in defeat, and the world narrowed. Between one city on fire and another that would soon be, they had become refugees in their own country.

He did not try to let go of her hand, nor did she let go of his. She placed her other hand over her heart to warm it; it would submit to no one else.

She tightened her grip on his hand as he looked at her.

"How did you manage to win the heart of the Minister's son?" he asked her. "I thought I asked you to take care of the factory, not to make a collection of men's hearts."

She clasped her own hand so as not to embrace him again.

"I didn't look after the factory, Ibrahim," she said, as though she had not heard his question. "I've failed you."

"I'm talking about the Deputy Minister, Rashida," he said, moving closer as his passionate feelings surged forward like an army, "not about the factory."

She was anxious not to lose the little mental control she had left.

"Ibrahim" she pleaded.

Ibrahim summoned Husain and told him to bring a shaikh to marry him to his cousin right now.

Husain's eyes widened.

"The crusaders will be inside our house before..."

"Listen to me!" Ibrahim told him. "There are some things that can't be delayed."

Rashida blushed and lowered her eyes. Husain gave her a quizzical stare.

"Brother," he said.

"Go now! She'll be my wife within the hour..."

"My brother," Husain responded shyly. "Don't force her, I beg you."

Ibrahim and Rashida looked at each other.

"Am I forcing you, Rashida?" he asked her firmly. "Or are you willing?"

"I'm willing, Cousin," she stuttered.

"Rashida," Husain said as he looked at her. "It's Ibrahim. Have you lost your mind?"

"I know," she replied after a moment's hesitation. "It's Ibrahim. I want no one else."

Husain now withdrew, incredulous, and went to look for a shaikh.

She stayed in her room, contemplating events he didn't know about and a defeat, the full extent of which he did not realise. She really wanted to tell him about it, weep, and fall asleep in his arms. She realised she was enveloped in hatred. She had failed both to gain people's affection and to repair what she had corrupted. She moved closer to the door to listen to what was being said outside, then opened it slowly to look into people's eyes and hearts.

"He's come here to marry that she-devil!" Nafisa, his brother's wife, was saying to Ibrahim's mother. "And that after he's killed my husband—the very same scorpion who's stung you!"

"I have no son," Ibrahim's mother replied indifferently. "Let him do whatever he likes."

"We've war inside the house," his sister Kamila said sheepishly to her husband. "Does he really mean to be married to her?"

"He'll do what he wants," Sufyan replied.

"I don't agree. Nobody here trusts Rashida. Remember what she's done in the past."

"Prison and torture must have affected his mind," Sufyan replied in despair.

Kauthar gave the door a gentle push.

"What are you going to do, Rashida?" she asked.

"Ibrahim's come back, Mother," she replied, her eyes full of affection.

"I thought you hated him!"

When she remained silent, her mother gave a shrug and left the room. A moment later, Ibrahim returned. She closed her eyes, and then opened them again as Ibrahim's wife. Sitting in the yard, she looked around her and saw the threatening and hateful looks in their eyes, even Husain's.

"You've betrayed us all, Cousin," he told her as he moved closer.

She made no reply. She did not understand what Ibrahim was planning to do. Was he going to take her away from that house? Or was he going to insert her in such a hate-filled atmosphere? Having been married to her, was he now going to go to war without first enjoying a single night of sex with her?

As she followed him with her gaze, she kept doing her best to rouse herself, not knowing whether it was actually a nightmare or rather a heavenly dream.

Ibrahim stood up and went over to his mother. He tried to hold her hand, but she pulled it away.

"Is this the right time to get married, Brother?" his sister chided him. "Your brother Husain's wife and son have both just died."

He ignored her and looked at Husain.

"In a few hours, you and Sufyan are coming with me," Ibrahim told him.

"You'll never take my son," his mother screamed. "Go and die by yourself."

"I've done my best to die, Ibrahim's mother," he replied bitterly. "But I haven't managed it yet."

"You're not going to kill my only remaining son."

"You're right," he said, looking straight at her. "Husain will stay with you."

"You're treating me like a child," Husain said, giving him an angry stare. "I'm not going to wait here till the Crusaders slaughter my mother before my very eyes."

Ibrahim looked at Rashida.

"Go to your room," he told her.

As she slowly stood, hate-filled eyes followed her. She was hoping to spend every single moment of her life with him, but she did not want to add to the hatred all around her. She left the door open, sat on her bed, and sadly rested her chin on her hand. She realised that he would be leaving, but he did not. Instead, he came into her room and shut the door. Now all eyes were riveted on that door. All the women sat down around the room.

"Sister," Husain said, "this isn't right. We're leaving him alone with his wife."

"We're sitting here, brother. Should we leave her our house?"

"That nasty little snake rules him now," his brother's wife said. "She's asking him to kill you, too, so that the two of them can be in charge of everything."

"There's nothing left to be in charge of," Husain replied.

They were all expecting sighs, screams maybe, and even arguments. They kept blowing hatred all around the house, the way soldiers blew the trumpet to broadcast the burning of Fustat. He realised it, and so did she.

He looked at her without saying a word.

"They're all around us," she said in a blend of passion and sorrow.

"There's no one around us."

"They're listening and waiting, Ibrahim."

"I don't feel them."

He moved closer, sat down in front of her, and cupped his hands around her face.

"So," he asked her, "what's your story with the Minister's son?"

"I swear there's absolutely nothing between us," she replied immediately. "How could—"

"If he took you with him," Ibrahim went on, putting his finger over her mouth, "he'd protect you. If he were married to you, you'd be guaranteed a husband who would stay alive for at least a while. Moreover, I'm not that noble or good. I want you, and I need to put out the flame that's been burning for two years or more. If I die, I don't want you to be married to anyone else or to forget me. Today, I need to make sure that you'll never forget me. How can I be sure?"

He pulled her head to his chest and embraced her until their two chests and hearts were linked. Breaths expanded and overflowed. This was an embrace, a passion like no other. It shocked and scared her, and she focused her entire resolve on her hands.

"How can I possibly forget you?" she asked between breaths. "I've been praying to God every single day and pleading with Him day and night. I swear that I'll follow all your instructions and do anything to keep you with me."

His hands enveloped body and soul and left no spot unyielding. Her body's pulses extended to her eyes and ears until life as a whole was united in a single moment, a gesture, a man. She was scared of her own self and surprised by his overpowering strength. She tried to move away, but he held her tight.

"Do you love me, Cousin?" he asked her as he kissed her lips.

"By God," she replied. "As you well know, all my life I've never set eyes on anyone but you."

She held his hand to stop it from roaming all over her body.

"I know," he replied. "Forgive me! I'm not feeling kind or patient today."

She did not understand what he meant. She was not bothered about his patience and kindness as much as she feared his power and dominance.

He said he wanted to make sure that she would not forget him, and he did so. He plunged her into the sea, then brought her up again to face the waves on the surface. Her heart was collapsing and rolling in the sand. Sometimes, the sand was scattered all around her eyes, so that it distorted the water's true colour; at other times, it plunged ahead, pushing aside any and all obstacles. She suppressed all her screams and sighs, well aware that the others stood outside the room. Even so, she whispered his name a lot and begged him not to leave her. She clung to him like someone drowning, then left him like someone already drowned. "I've lost everything," she told him amid the fiery flames of passion. "I couldn't hold on to my father's factory and stores."

"You tried, and that's enough."

"Ibrahim..."

"Keep saying my name! I want your voice to be the last thing I hear. Come here!"

She buried her head in his chest and forgot the entire world. The room was no longer in Cairo or the house. They were both being transported on a magic carpet, hovering around paradise, sniffing its scent, and eating the fruit of its trees.

"I needed to have my fill of you," he told her, stroking her hair. "I didn't realise that it would be impossible. As my thirst increases year after year, I desire you even more. Forgive me my despair and uncouth behaviour today."

She did not understand what he meant. Her mind was now besotted; past and future had both been erased. His behaviour was certainly crude, and his defeat was truly terrifying, enough to trouble even Rashida, who had stood defiant in front of Shawar's soldiers.

She put her hand on his thigh and ran her fingers over the spot where he had been tortured. Leaning over, she kissed his thigh.

"If only I could remove all your pain!" she said.

"I've already dissolved it," he replied forcefully as he kissed her, "along with the honey in your mouth."

Those were the only words of love she had ever heard him say. She needed no others.

She looked at the bulging, recalcitrant skin that refused to leave the spot on his thigh.

"How life has maimed and degraded us, Ibrahim," she said. "Both you and me! Bodily injuries are less harmful."

"After suffering so much," he replied, as though talking to himself, "for a while I'd lost my way. I've been wandering like a babe in the woods. But God wanted to rescue me. There's no degradation in bodily torture, Rashida. Your spirit is still strong even though the wounds may have left some scars."

He placed his hands around her head and gave the spot over her heart a passionate kiss.

"Now I can love you again," he told her. "The way you deserve...or as I wish. You deserve my entire self, Cousin."

"Love me as you wish," she replied, not knowing what he meant.

"For the first time ever, you're not defying me!" he told her with a laugh.

After a long time, he tried to get up, albeit reluctantly.

"I'm proud of you, Rashida," he said. "You took care of your grandfather's factory the way men would, or actually even better than any of them."

"Stay with me for a while," she pleaded, holding his hand.

He hugged her hard and once again plunged into the intoxicating world of pleasure and rapture. Then he heard a knock on the door.

"Ibrahim," his brother said. "If you want to go to the Cairo walls, we must leave now. Or do you want me to go alone?"

He got up and put his clothes on. She was semi-conscious, but still soaring in a dream world. He kissed her head and left.

When he left, she closed her eyes. She heard her mother knock on the door.

"I'm going to sleep for a while," she said.

As she pulled the bedcovers up to her neck, she looked back over the events of that particular day and all the other days in her life. Now he was hers, the one she had dreamed about ever since she was eight years old. He was hers. She smiled and ran her fingers over her neck and lips. How often had she imagined that day and that twilight! And yet she had never anticipated such passion or the fire that spread through her limbs. She buried her head in the pillow. How many times had she hovered around him, sometimes pestering him, others actually aggravating him, all so that he would notice that she was there. How often had she conspired against him and exploited those around her in order to take her revenge on him, all on the assumption that he neither knew nor understood. For a few moments, he had been hers, and she his. When she pronounced his name, it was a blend of a lifelong affection and all the sufferings of a loving heart.

"What's the matter with you?" he had said. "Are you sorry to be married to a man who's going to die?"

"No," she replied, her eyes closed. "I'm reminding myself that you're inside me. That's unforgettable. Don't you forget it, Cousin of mine!"

He took her in his arms, and she settled on top of him.

"Here you are, giving me orders again," he said jokingly. "I'm the husband and commander here! You've promised to obey all my instructions. Don't you remember?"

She did not respond either yes or no. She hadn't realised that love involved months with changes in touch: thunder and lightning, rain and wind, cold and heat, wasteland and havens of bliss. She thought love consisted of kisses and hugs, but passion had left signs of its tempests all over her body. In the first instance, she had been shocked by his desire and dominance; in the second, by his gentleness and deliberation; and in the third, by his perfection, confidence, and giving nature. In each case, he had shocked her, troubled her, and kept her awake. He had settled inside her breast like a flaming star. As she remembered it all, she smiled. And, for the first time in two years, she fell into a deep sleep.

All around Kawthar, there was talk about her daughter's malice and inappropriate behaviour. Kawthar had no idea how to respond; Rashida's passionate love for her cousin had surprised her. They all banged hard on Rashida's door and asked her to help them. Raising her head, she gave them all a contemptuous look.

"You must treat me with respect," she told them proudly. "I'm Ibrahim's wife. Don't forget it!"

She left her room to look for some water. No sooner had she left than Kamila gave Nafisa a nod and went inside.

"I swear to you that she's a tart," she said. "She's seduced him and other men too. He's abandoned the sweet family daughter for her sake. I swear that she had sex with the wheat porter before she did with him."

"These days," Nafisa commented sadly, "only tarts win."

They started searching her room and opening her cupboards.

"You're going to find things that she's made for him," Nafisa said. "He'll hate them, that's for sure!"

Nafisa went over to their bed and was shocked by what she saw. Their eyes met and then focused on the spot of blood on the sheet.

"That's no proof," Kamila said. "She may have kept her virginity to deceive him."

"You're right," Nafisa replied.

They both looked at the door of the room where Rashida was standing, hands on hips, giving them a defiant stare.

"Have you both finished your search?" she asked with a smile.

Kamila hesitated, then looked at Nafisa.

"Evil never wins, Rashida," Nafisa told her spitefully.

"There's no evil in me," Rashida responded confidently. "But you two can only see what's right in front of you. I wonder, is it because I can ask, order, refuse, venture, defend, work, and think that I'm so rich compared with the two of you?"

"Yes," Kamila replied. "And you can plot, obey men, and bend them all to your will. You've also driven away the girl my brother loves in order to be married to him yourself. You're exposed, just like the halva you've been making. Now we know the truth about you."

"That's all past and gone," Rashida interrupted her. "Today, you have two choices: you and Nafisa can defy me, and, as you well know, I never forgive or renounce my rights; or you can both make a truce with me and raise the standards of peace. Then we can all work for the benefit of this household. The choice is yours, so think about it. Rashida never loses and is never scared. She'll take her revenge on anyone who tries to harm her, whereas those who make peace win the prize."

"My brother never follows his own desires," Kamila commented derisively. "No woman can ever dominate him, Rashida."

Rashida smiled in triumph, her hand still firmly planted on her hip.

"If only you'd heard him yesterday," she said. "He was swearing to do whatever I wanted and carry out anything I asked for. Did you hear him? You were standing by the door, so you must have heard him."

"Debauchery knows no limits," Kamila muttered, pursing her lips.

"Did you say something, Cousin?" Rashida asked. "We've agreed that there'll be peace in Ibrahim and Rashida's household. Ibrahim and Rashida are now one; his secret and heart are both with me."

"She's taken over," Nafisa whispered in Kamila's ear. "Now she's in charge.

Make peace with her."

Rashida moved away from the door so they could both leave. She gave a triumphant smile.

As they departed in shame, they realised they had lost. Surrender was the safest bet.

CHAPTER THIRTEEN

As Ibrahim stood addressing his men at the Barqiyya Gate, the Crusaders kept cursing and threatening as they pounded it with ballistas and hurled fireballs at the inhabitants. Ibrahim knew the scenario well. He had seen and lived it two years earlier. After two months, Cairo surrendered with the loss of half of its inhabitants and the utter exhaustion of those who remained. After several months, the Crusaders had entered the city and slaughtered women and children; neither Muslim, Christian, nor Jew had escaped, just as had happened before in Bilbeis. Men were to be taken prisoner; for any man, killing was a mercy; humiliation and shame were a torture that would last a lifetime.

"He's talking to you about Bilbeis and what happened to him there," Ibrahim said. "I'm talking about Alexandria, imprisonment, and the Minister's torture. At this point, Egypt has no Minister. Now, its future is in your hands. You're either going to save it or be destroyed the way Jerusalem and Bilbeis have been. Instead of defending Fustat, Shawar set it on fire, and all because his army is not like ours. We must resist; we can't live with weakness. We'll fight on our own, and, if we fall and Egypt falls, then the entire land of Islam falls with us. They know that, and so they're only going to come out when they're certain that they've lost. We're going to defend this city with everything we've got. So let's defeat the Crusaders and forget about a Minister who's sold his own country and allied himself with the enemy. Time is not on our side. We must defeat the Crusaders."

Jawwad now emerged from the crowd.

"So the halva-maker's going to defeat the Crusaders!" he said mockingly. "Who are you? Are you out to finish off the people of Cairo the way you did the Alexandrians? Who are you? What do we have to fight with?"

There were mutterings, and people hesitated.

"I'm going to fight," Ibrahim yelled. "You can stay here with the women."

"No one knows who you really are the way I do," Jawwad went on, moving closer. "No one else knows how ambitious you are!"

Ibrahim turned away, never losing his nerve. Husain went up to him.

"Do you want me to throw him out of Cairo?" he asked Ibrahim.

"No, don't bother about him."

"Today, I'm obeying you because you're right," Husain said. "But, once the war's over, I'm leaving."

"I know."

"Aren't you going to ask me to stay?"

"No. Do what you want."

"Yes, I will."

The fighting in Cairo was not like the earlier fighting in Alexandria. Egyptians rid themselves of despair; in confronting death, there was no longer a choice between courage or surrender. If it came to surrendering, then it would involve death, not defeat. They filled urns with oil, clambered up the wall of the Barqiyya gate, and poured the burning oil down on the soldiers. They shot fireballs into the air. The Crusaders responded with ballistas. Some of them slunk inside the city and killed people indiscriminately, concentrating on women rather than men. The populace surrounded these intruders, killed them all, and tossed the corpses off the walls. The people collected all the city's garbage, animal droppings, and refuse and threw all that down on the Crusader soldiers. They moved away from the gate, but kept firing ballistas, well aware that, either that day or the next, they were going to win. The gate would be destroyed, and behind it the city was waiting: Cairo. They had heard about its splendid palaces, the gold plating its trees, and the bags of emeralds that Badr al-Jamali had left behind at the time of his death. Where had they gone? Minister Shawar must have them now, or else the Caliph Al-`Adid.

This was a gate that had been built by a Sicilian general whose country was not far from theirs. But he had settled in Egypt and adopted it as his homeland. People said his name was Jawhar the Sicilian. King Amalric had taught his soldiers the history of the East. Their victory and the key to understanding its people lay in history. People also said that another general from Armenia had built another gate alongside the Barqiyya Gate after extending the size of Cairo. He had built it of stone, settled in Egypt, and adopted it as his homeland. King Amalric decided that destroying this gate would be a triumph to be recorded in history. History would state that the Crusader King had defeated both Badr al-Jamali the Armenian and Jawhar the Sicilian. He had defeated those who had adopted Egypt as a homeland because he knew and valued his own homeland. King Amalric gave orders that the gate was to be destroyed, even if it required the help of foreign mercenaries. He would ask the northerners to help demolish this particular gate.

"In just a few days," Husain told Ibrahim in a panic, "the Crusaders will push their way into Cairo. You realise that."

"They've had enough time," Ibrahim replied. "But they haven't succeeded yet."

"I can see that. But even though Bilbeis was fortified, they still opened the gates. We're not a properly organised army, Brother."

"But we're still defending everything we own. No army can ever be stronger than one that's defending itself."

"Shawar's army has disappeared. He's keeping it close to defend himself."

"Of course! What did you expect, Husain?"

When he looked in front of him, he saw Aftakin the Turk, his sister Shafiqa's husband. He had not set eyes on him for over two years, ever since he had demanded that his wife obey him and leave her brother's house.

"Thank God you're safe, Ibrahim!" Aftakin said awkwardly.

"Where's the Egyptian army, Brother-in-law?" Ibrahim asked forcefully.

"These are dark and deluded times."

"I'm asking you about the army, not about time."

"Minister Shawar, the Army Command..."

"In the whole `Ubaidi era," Ibrahim interrupted him, "Egypt has had only two Army Commanders: my grandparents, Jawhar and Badr. Shawar's a traitor."

"Don't say that."

"But he is a traitor. He disappears and surrounds himself with soldiers."

"He's agreed to have the Syrian army help, and to the Caliph's request that Asad ad-din Shirkuh and Salah ad-din return to Egypt."

"That agreement's no longer in his hands, Brother-in-law. He's not keeping it."

"Till they get here..."

"You've come to see me. Why?"

Their eyes met.

"I wonder," Ibrahim went on, "are you disobeying your Minister's orders? Are you going to fight with us, Aftakin?"

"If the Crusaders get into Cairo, it's all over."

"Why aren't you like Shawar, waiting for the Syrian army to arrive?"

"I've told you," Aftakin replied, looking all around him. "Shawar's agreed. I didn't say he's happy about it or that the Syrian army is on its way."

"Have you brought me a letter?"

"No, I've come as a fighter."

"Welcome!" Ibrahim replied, holding out his hand.

"There's one thing I want you to know," he went on bitterly. "So that you'll act wisely."

"What's that?"

"If Minister Shawar had a choice between having the Crusaders enter Cairo or letting the Syrian army in..."

"He'd choose the Crusaders," Ibrahim replied without even thinking. "I realize that."

"How do you know?"

"Because he's chosen them before."

"He didn't realise they were going to invade; he thought they were just there to offer protection."

"Anyone who keeps Crusader soldiers by the gates of his city to protect it is a traitor, Brother!"

"Don't criticise the Minister in my presence. We're going to fight and leave other issues to the people in charge."

That night, some of Amalric's soldiers tried to scale the gate, but the Egyptians had coated it in sesame oil, so they slid down and failed to get inside. Then Egyptian soldiers, armed with swords and knives, slunk out of Bab al-Nasr and Bab al-Futuh, headed for the Barqiyya Gate, and hid there. At this point, an old woman emerged with some doughnuts, saying in Arabic that she wanted the Crusaders to come; she much preferred them to Minister Shawar. The soldiers did not believe her. Taking some halva, she put it in her mouth. That gave the soldiers some encouragement. They took a doughnut and told her to eat it. When she did so, they grabbed the halva from her and ate it all. She told them that she would bring doughnuts every day. They found nothing worrying about that. The next day, they told her again to eat, and she did. They chose one or two for her to eat. She did so, and then they ate the rest. As she moved her hands, she told them that she wanted to show them Egypt's treasures.

She signalled to them to follow her. They were in a quandary and hesitated. Fifty soldiers went with her, and she took them out into the desert. She told them to start digging; when they did, they found emeralds. They raised a hue and cry, and the news spread rapidly. More and more soldiers went out to look for emeralds, leaving only a small platoon by the gate.

The Egyptians hidden by Bab al-Nasr now emerged and headed for the Crusader soldiers still left near Bab al-Bahr. The fighting that ensued was on equal terms—about a thousand Egyptian troops against a thousand Crusader soldiers in Amalric's army who were still stationed by the gate. After several hours of fighting, the Egyptians had taken a hundred prisoners and killed five hundred. The rest fled toward the sea.

There was general chaos. When the news reached Amalric, he was furious. He decided to punish all the soldiers who had left their post to search for emeralds, although no one had found any. The rumour spread in the Crusader camp that ancient sorceresses were helping the Egyptians. Legend had it that a witch lived in the Pyramids and came out at night to heap curses on men. That was what had struck them.

Amalric was not totally convinced by the witch story, but he was still worried and concerned that his army had been unexpectedly defeated by a group of untrained fighters. The siege lasted for a long time, but Cairo did not surrender. His soldiers were weary; they had not found any treasure, nor had they secured a victory.

It was now time to talk to Shawar. Amalric sent for him, and the messenger came back with gifts. He told Amalric that Shawar was still honouring his pledge, but he was asking Amalric to leave Egypt now and come back again when he, Shawar, was fully in control. Amalric was not at all happy with this message. He demanded money, and Shawar responded by giving him forty thousand dinars, stating that that was all he had at his disposal. That did not satisfy Amalric. He had entered Egypt. What would happen if he left without wresting it from the Ubaidis? If Egypt was safely in his hands, he would have control of the East. He had no plans to return.

News now spread that Asad ad-din Shirkuh's army was heading for Egypt. Nur ad-din Zengi had told him to fight the Crusaders in Egypt so it would not fall into King Amalric's hands. But so far, there was no sign of this army.

Amalric had no plans to leave Cairo unless it was in his hands.

Ibrahim began to toss and turn in his sleep. He was worried about Rashida. She totally possessed him, but he could not find solace in her embrace. He would be thinking about her when he was fighting or even when he was hatching conspiracies. Every single moment, he remembered her quivering lips and passionate glances. His pulse would quicken, and sorrow would score his heart. Why had time decided that he would have to spend his entire life fighting his desires? Why did he not leave everything and return to her embrace? He let out an angry sigh.

He sensed someone spying on him. It was Jawwad.

He felt for his dagger, then pretended to be asleep. Jawwad slunk into his tent and raised his sword with a quivering hand. He was about to strike Ibrahim, but Ibrahim moved quickly. Before he could grab his dagger, he heard Jawwad groaning, an arrow stuck in his shoulder. He dropped the sword. Ibrahim looked straight in front of him; it was Husain.

"Ibrahim," Husain said with a proud smile. "Tell your mother that Husain has saved your life, just as you did his."

"Husain's the bravest of men!" Ibrahim replied, patting Husain's shoulder.

That may have been the first time that Husain had ever heard any words of praise from his brother. How effective such words were in cooling the flames in the heart!

They seized Jawwad and tied him up.

"Do what you want!" Jawwad said, giving Ibrahim a hateful stare. "You've forced her to be married to you. You and she are both toying with me. Go ahead and kill me! Do what you want. But you're a dead man, either today or tomorrow!"

"Who asked you to kill me?" Ibrahim asked.

"I wanted to kill you."

"No, you couldn't do that. They're reckless enough to do anything, right?"

"Al-Kamil, Shawar's son," Jawwad replied, looking straight at him. "He's the one who deserves Rashida."

"Don't even say her name," Ibrahim responded, giving him a slap on the face. "Keep him in prison till we've decided what to do with him."

He went to his mother's house in Cairo. He'd made up his mind: he would not let Rashida out of his sight.

Laila refused to even look at him. She kept moving rhythmically—her back, then her shoulders, then her hand, banging it against the bed as though she was begging her Lord to help her oppose him and put an end to the endless suffering.

"Mother," he said gently.

"They're saying that Jawwad tried to kill you. If only he'd succeeded!"

"Don't worry; someone else will manage it. It's fate, something that can't be advanced or postponed for a single hour. If only I could stop fate, I would. But you've charged me with something I can't bear."

She remained silent.

"Mother, you began by charging me with something I couldn't bear, and then you've held me accountable for something that's out of my hands. With Joseph, his brothers were out to kill him, but God changed their plans and made them throw him in the pit. Was I supposed to save my brothers? Did I mean to kill them? I swear to you that I've suffered over their loss, just as I have suffered over the loss of my mother, even when you're still alive."

Her eyes quivered, and she looked away.

"Leave me," she said.

"Not till I've told you about the wrong you've done."

"You've come here to blame me."

"No, I've come here to blame part of my own self. Don't be so unkind,

Mother. You've done so my entire life, but don't abandon me like an orphan when you're still alive and breathing. Don't burden me with something I can't bear."

"If you've finished, leave!"

"I can't balance your affection with the way you distance yourself from me and my own need for your love."

Her eyelids flickered, and tears welled up, but she kept them in check.

He kept his eyes on her, hoping to see any sign of happiness or mercy. But there was none.

"I'll leave you in peace."

He went in search of his wife and found her making halva with his sister and sister-in-law. It was as though they had been friends for years. They were listening to her as she gave instructions, told them to stop, prodded them and urged them on as though she were head of the household and an army commander. He allowed himself a smile. Did he trust Rashida? he wondered. Just her?

When she noticed he was there, she gave him a loving look.

"My brother," Kamila said, "thank God you're safe!"

With his eyes on his wife, he asked how all of them were, including his mother. Then he stood up and told Rashida angrily to get everything ready so she could leave with him.

"To go where?" she asked him, confused. "I want to go with you, but...I need to understand. You haven't spoken to me for several days and I haven't—"

"Don't argue with me, Rashida," he interrupted.

He grabbed her hand and took her into the room.

"Don't you dare argue with me in front of my family," he told her.

"Fine then," she replied, resting her head on his shoulder, "I'll argue with you when we're alone. Why didn't you come here yesterday, or the day before? Every single day?"

He put his arm around her back and rubbed his cheek against her neck.

"Let's go!" he said.

"Tell me what's going on!" she said.

"I'm afraid Al-Kamil's going to kidnap you."

"He wouldn't do that. If you knew him, you'd know how honest he is."

He moved away and gave her a jealous look.

"I've no desire to know him," he said. "Nor do I want you to know him, either. Come on!"

He pulled her outside the house.

"I haven't taken all my things," she protested.

"You won't be needing them."

"Ibrahim!"

"Enough talk! We're at war. I want you to stay with me all the time."

She suppressed a smile.

"I wonder, Cousin," she said. "Have you missed me, or are you jealous?"

"Neither one nor the other," he replied, putting her on his horse. "But I want to have my wife by my side. Will you confirm this arrangement with me for the rest of the day?"

With that, he threw her into his tent, pushed her to the ground, and gave her a passionate kiss.

"Why don't you ever tell me how much you adore me, desire me, and have been in love with me since you were a boy?" she asked coquettishly. "Tell me you've been resisting that love all your life, but you've failed. You've..."

He shut her mouth with kisses. Once she had recovered from love's frenzied embrace, she put her head on his chest.

"I've more courage than you, Ibrahim," she said. "I can say out loud that I've never loved anyone else."

"It's risky for you to be here," he told her, as though he did not really wish to talk. "I've no idea what I'm doing or why I've brought you here. It's as though I'd rather have you die with me than leave you for someone else. I've lost my mind. I've been struck by your curse, Rashida. I've never been this selfish. I used to help my brothers and my mother. My mother..."

"You'll find out. You need time to understand, Ibrahim. Don't think she doesn't love you. She loves you just as much as she regrets what's gone. She isn't just angry with you, but also over what she's lost.

"In your company, I've become more selfish and vicious. Ibrahim the idealist has disappeared; now there's just a wild beast inside me."

"In your company, I've become angrier and more desirous. There's a wild beast inside me, too."

"Here's to our life together, Rashida!"

From behind the tent flap, she listened to the army's plans. She spotted Jawwad in chains and stared at him for a while. In the past, she had agreed to a token marriage with him, one based on her retaining everything. Had total despair overwhelmed her, or was she furious with a man who had no real feelings for her?

She heard her husband say that they would either kill the traitor or make use of him by sending his head to Amalric so that the Crusader King would realise they had uncovered his plans and would keep on fighting until he left Egypt.

"Ibrahim!"

He turned towards the sound of her voice and dismissed the men. He entered their tent.

"Don't call me when I'm with the men!" he told her angrily.

"I just wanted to say—"

"I don't want to hear your opinions!"

She almost exploded at him, but she managed to stay silent as she turned away. He was on the point of leaving, but then he came back inside.

"Fine," he said, "what is it you want?"

"Nothing."

"Rashida," he told her angrily. "We're at war."

"I've a plan."

"What plan?"

"You wanted to take advantage of Jawwad's capture. Send him alive to Amalric with a letter. Say that you're going to surrender."

"How can we trust Jawwad?" he asked, looking straight at her. "He's a traitor."

She moved closer with a smile and held his hand.

"Yes, he's a traitor," she replied. "Send him with the letter and pull the men back inside Cairo."

For just a moment, he looked down.

"Rashida," he said.

"Yes, that's what I was thinking about."

"What kind of mind do you have?"

"A woman's mind, Cousin."

"The cleverest woman I've ever set eyes on."

"Is that praise?"

"The most courageous and beautiful woman."

"The most beautiful...?"

"By God, I've never set eyes on anyone so beautiful."

He gave her a powerful kiss.

"Jawwad will take a letter to King Amalric," he said, with Rashida still in his arms. "It will say that we're withdrawing. He'll think that we actually plan to resume the assault, because that's what we'll be doing as far as Jawwad's concerned. But, when he goes to see the King, he won't tell him about the letter, and, because he's a traitor, even though we've made him a promise, he'll tell the King exactly what he's seen here, namely that we're ready to attack. At that point, he'll pound the gate with ballistas and weaponry and dispatch his men inside the city walls. But it'll be utterly futile to pound the gate because our men will have hidden themselves and withdrawn. He'll be crushing his troops psychologically and running out of weapons. When some of his soldiers slink their way inside Cairo, we'll meet them in every street and alley. But it won't be behind the wall that he finds an army; it'll be in every single nook and cranny inside the city. Once he's run out of ammunition and his men realise that they've fallen into a trap—"

"He'll leave."

"How can you know that?"

"The Crusader King knows full well that Cairo is a fortified city, Cousin," Rashida stated with certainty. "It's not fortified with gates, but rather with men, and women before the men."

"I love you."

"What did you just say?"

"Nothing. Get some sleep."

Everything happened exactly as Rashida had predicted

Crusader soldiers slunk into the city, fully expecting to plunge their swords into a hundred or more people inside, while the rest of them stayed at the ready outside the gate. That gate was never going to be destroyed. The soldiers used various gates to slink into the city at night. They might spot a vendor going into his own house or a man searching for his family inside Cairo. However, the Crusader soldiers did not find an army waiting for them inside Cairo. As they wandered their way through the alleyways, they found themselves isolated as they confronted men and women. A man or woman emerged from every single house with a dagger or axe. They killed a hundred soldiers, collected the corpses, and tossed them down on the King, who was waiting outside the Barqiyya Gate.

"Here are your corpses back," Ibrahim wrote to him in a letter. "Alexandrians have their principles: they always return the gifts they receive!"

The King erupted in fury. He almost killed all his soldiers. He slaughtered Jawwad.

"There's worse to come," he yelled without thinking or the slightest hesitation. "Corpses will bring the plague. There's no point in staying here."

"My Lord," his Commanding General said, giving him a sorrowful look, "it was your dream to enter Cairo."

"And it didn't happen. Come on, we'll go back to the sea-shore, then on to Ashkelon and Jerusalem."

"My Lord, people will say that the Crusader King's been defeated."

"I don't care what people say."

"They'll say it wasn't an army involved; he was defeated by the city's inhabitants. That's..."

"Nur ad-din's army, commanded by Asad ad-din Shirkuh and his nephew, Yusuf ibn Ayyub, is on its way to Egypt," Amalric interrupted. "Tell them that the Crusader King has left so as not to start another war with Nur ad-din."

"But Nur ad-din hasn't arrived yet. If we enter Cairo before he gets here—"

"That's impossible," Amalric said firmly.

"How can the strongest possible army...?"

"Collect your property and soldiers, General," Amalric interrupted him. "This war's over."

Before the army left, it still fired ballistas at the gate and fireballs at the tents of the fighters behind the gate. When Ibrahim heard the bang of explosions all around him, he looked round. Forgetting about everything else, he rushed to the flap of his own tent. He shouted Rashida's name as loudly as he could. She was waiting for him, shivering as she looked through the tent's opening. No sooner did he set eyes on her than he pulled her toward him and gave her a hug. She could hear his heart pounding. She put her arms around his neck, surprised by his spontaneous response.

"I'm fine," she told him.

She was deeply touched by his response.

"Are you worried about me, Ibrahim?" she asked him gently.

"I want you to be far away from here," he replied with a frown. "But then again, I don't want to leave you far away. What am I supposed to do?"

"The Crusaders will leave," she replied with certainty. "That's the way defeated armies behave."

"Rashida...!" he threatened.

"Be patient!"

"It would be better for you to leave the tent."

"Be patient... Just for a bit."

CHAPTER FOURTEEN

With Rashida in his arms, Ibrahim breathed easy. He even smiled. Salah ad-din Yusuf ibn Ayyub had sworn that he would not return to Egypt, but then Nur ad-din and his uncle Shirkuh had forced him to do just that. He would have to fast for three days. He had come after the Crusaders had given up the idea of entering Egypt and Cairo. The Crusader army was now going back the way it had come. No, this time he would not be witnessing a slow death; the only failures would involve the defeat of the greedy and ambitious. Of all people, Ibrahim knew what defeat actually meant. People told themselves that victory involved killing the enemy, seizing their land, and taking their women prisoner. But no. Victory meant making the enemy realise how weak they were and how meagre their power actually was, no matter how many prisoners they took and how much territory they occupied. The Crusaders had been weak and had given up; that was what was needed. But this would not be the last time. The land had its own treasure and magic. The Crusaders would be back, and they would have to learn how weak they really were, whether they stayed or left. Oh, Ibn Ayyub, nerve-wracking days and major trials lie ahead!

"Isn't it strange," Ibrahim told his wife, "that the Sicilian built the Barqiyya wall, then the Armenian added to it and constructed a larger wall of stone, and then the Kurd arrives in Egypt to find that the wall has protected the city and kept the enemy out? Now he's going to add to it even more."

"Who are you talking about, Ibrahim? Yusuf?'

"Yes, Yusuf."

"Yusuf's come with his uncle. He doesn't have an army or a plan. He's the Junior Commander and is the least ambitious of them all."

"This world gives only to those who neither expect nor desire."

"What about Minister Shawar?"

"Intentions emerge from actions."

"What's the Kurd doing about the Barqiyya Gate?"

"He has to be thinking about it; that is, when he has enough power and influence."

"Ibrahim, how is the Kurd going to be able to take command of Turkish and Arab troops?"

"We're all one and the same before God—neither Kurd, Sicilian, nor Armenian. The soil changes colours every season, and yet it still produces the same flowers, even if the colours are different. It always borders sweet waters even though the temperature may vary. Till now, we've no idea of Yusuf's potential or the extent of his capabilities."

"Do you like him, Ibrahim?"

"I know him well. Our longstanding friendship has been accompanied by death and sorrow."

"Go to see him and give him a gift."

He sat up and looked at her, not understanding what she meant.

"Give him Zubaida as a gift from me!" she told him enthusiastically.

"What are you saying? He's an ascetic. He wears wool and has stopped drinking."

"But Cousin, this is something that God has declared legitimate! The ascetic does not have to deny himself what God has declared legal! She's my servant-girl, and I want to make her a gift from me to him. He may manumit her or give her to his wife as a servant. He can do what he likes."

"You're cunning," he said, giving her a lengthy stare. "I don't trust you!"

"Have I ever confounded you before?"

"What kind of mind do you have! What's your plan?"

"She's in love with him. He kept her close out of kindness even if she saw him only once a year. Being in his household will make her very happy."

"You bring hearts closer together. Do you sympathise with lovers?" "

"She's like a sister to me. I well know what desperate love is like."

"We'll do what you want," he agreed, after looking down for a moment. "I'll take her with me when I go to see him and give her to him as a gift."

Zubaida could hardly contain herself. She bent down and kissed Rashida's foot, her tears flowing freely.

"Come on," Rashida told her, as she lifted her up again. "Get yourself ready to go with Ibrahim."

The Caliph vested Shirkuh, Yusuf ibn Ayyub's uncle, by appointing him to the ministry. Now Egypt had two Ministers: Shawar and Shirkuh. Shawar did not object; in fact, he welcomed Shirkuh as someone who could finally bring relief after so much hardship. He invited Shirkuh, Yusuf, and some generals to a banquet at his house in Cairo. Men spread out to pass on the news that the army of Nur ad-din the saviour and his courageous generals had arrived. Shawar seemed to be thinking shrewdly, realising full well that, for him to remain in power, he would have to rely on Nur ad-din's protection. For that very reason, he offered to share power rather than lose all authority. He therefore shared it all with Shirkuh and his powerful army. Meanwhile, the Fatimid army had rebelled against itself and was no longer loyal. The army that, in the past, had managed to conquer countries and ports could now no longer stop Crusader raids or even defend the Ubaidi capital city. Shawar needed Shirkuh's men.

"Father," his son Al-Kamil told him, "you've behaved wisely."

"Your father always behaves that way, my son."

"My Lord's fully aware of where the danger lies."

"Your Lord and father is always fully aware of that. Today, I want to welcome Nur ad-din's generals. I want Shirkuh to feel that Egypt is his country. His presence here brings stability."

"I knew the Crusaders were not to be trusted. They offer no protection, Father."

"Today I know that as well," Shawar said resignedly. "They've taken their entire garrison away."

Zubaida's eyes were searching for him. As soon as she spotted him, she blinked nervously and closed her eyes for a moment. Opening them again, she listened to what Ibrahim was saying to Yusuf Ibn Ayyub Salah ad-din, the man she loved, although she realised she could never win him. The two men exchanged greetings, and Yusuf shared all his news with Ibrahim. Ibrahim then brought Zubaida over.

"Forgive me, Brother," Ibrahim told Yusuf somewhat hesitantly. "Sometimes women will behave spontaneously and carelessly. But my wife has insisted that I give you this servant girl as a gift from her."

Ibrahim then told Zubaida to lower her veil, and she did so, her eyes begging Yusuf to kiss her. For just a moment, Yusuf stared at Ibrahim.

"It's Zubaida, isn't it?" he asked gently.

She swallowed hard, then bent down and kissed his hand.

"Your servant, if you'll have me," she said.

He pushed her away and took her hand to lift her up.

"I remember you," he said.

"Your wife's gift is hereby accepted," he told Ibrahim with a smile.

Her heart almost leapt out of her ribs. She bent down and covered her face as though she were crying. He looked at her in amazement.

"Do you prefer to go back to your mistress?" he asked her. "If you do, I'll send you back to her or set you free now. Tell me which..."

"No, no," she interrupted him in a barely audible voice. "My heart was almost stopping for sheer joy! I've never had anything I really wanted. And now, I've been given an honour I don't deserve. Just keep me with you, my Lord. I ask for nothing more. I can serve your wife."

He looked surprised, and perhaps a bit affectionate. Then he controlled himself and gave Ibrahim a serious look.

"Today we're going to see Shawar," he said. "Do you want to come with us? You have a history with him and a desire for revenge, I realise, but that's the way of the world. We torture each other, and then we sit down to dinner together. Some of us have to bear the burden of a brother's death, while others only bother about booty. Come with us! You have just cause to talk to Shawar."

For a moment, Ibrahim said nothing.

"Can I have a meeting with Shawar?" he asked. "I want to see him alone. Can you arrange such a meeting, my Lord? I'd be grateful to you for the rest of my days."

"I don't understand what you mean."

"Today, we're dining with him. If you let me meet him before that, I'll be grateful. You can send a guard with me and tell him that you've sanctioned the meeting."

"Why do you want to meet him alone?"

"That's between the two of us, my Lord. That meeting's your gift to me."

"Fine, Ibrahim, you'll have what you wish. Go to see him today with a guard."

After Shawar's guards had checked him, they allowed him to enter the Minister's quarters. Shawar sat there and gave Ibrahim a contemptuous and somewhat hateful look.

"Minister," Ibrahim told him, "I've come here to share with you the glad tidings that the Crusaders have left Egypt."

Shawar did not respond.

"I wonder," Ibrahim went on, looking all around him. "Do you still imagine, Minister, that you're the Army Commander?"

"If I give the order to my guards," Shawar responded angrily, "they'll kill you now. The entire army is under my command. My son owes me because he hasn't killed you."

"Tell your guards to leave us alone. The Army Commander doesn't need anyone to protect him."

"You slave…"

"No, you should say 'you Egyptian.'"

"The Minister's not afraid of anything."

With that, he told the guards to leave.

"One day, I flayed your skin," he said, moving closer to Ibrahim. "and then Al-Kamil saved you."

He grabbed Ibrahim's hand and punched him hard on the jaw.

"Shawar's still Army Commander," he said. "I still control the entire Fatimid army. No one can dismiss me or harm me. Even if you've trained with the Assassins in the Fortress of Death, Ibrahim. Oh yes, I know everything about you."

Ibrahim moved close to him, put his hand over Shawar's mouth, and banged his head swiftly and powerfully against the floor. The Minister emitted some suppressed groans, but Ibrahim kept on banging his head on the floor.

"Listen, Shawar," he kept saying, "anyone who aspires to be like Badr al-Jamali has to be just as great. I know you, even if no one else does. I realize your intentions, even if your son, who's from your own stock, does not. Do you know why? It's because I've been tortured by you. Your heart's now in my clutches. Do you realise that anyone who's been tortured by someone has total control of them, just as Abel controlled Cain and made him powerless? Listen to me, as you're about to die. Are you listening to me?"

Shawar closed his eyes and entered another world. Ibrahim kept banging his head on the floor till the guards came in and grabbed him. Some of them made up their minds to kill Ibrahim on the spot, while others decided to postpone the decision until they had consulted the Caliph. Ibrahim closed his eyes and remembered Jawhar, son of Husain the Sicilian. Today, he had imitated him. He had wanted to be as courageous as his grandfather, but he had no idea whether or not it would all end in death.

Today was the dinner. Today. The guards searched for their Commander, but he was dead. They threw Ibrahim to the ground and beat him till he lost consciousness. But they did not kill him. These days, you had to be cautious. No one knew precisely what loyalty entailed or who would be in charge the next day.

The news shocked Salah ad-din. All his plans had been trashed; there would be no banquet today. He needed to see Ibrahim as soon as possible. He must have lost his mind. He was bound to die. Even the Caliph had remained silent when he heard the news; he may have been thinking of a way to get rid of Shawar's killer. Al-Kamil was furious at the man who had killed his father and robbed him of his beloved. He wanted to kill Ibrahim right away, but the soldiers did not listen. With his soldiers, he rushed to Rashida, but he did not find her; she had followed her husband's advice and gone to Alexandria, just as his grandfather had once done with his wife. No matter. He would go after her, but not until he had killed her traitorous, murdering husband.

Salah ad-din hurried to see Ibrahim in prison. He chided and blamed Ibrahim, who listened silently. Salah ad-din looked at the bruises and scars all over Ibrahim's body.

"If the Caliph Al-'Adid decided to have you killed," he asked, "how can I stop it? Tell me, Brother."

"I've saved your life today," Ibrahim replied calmly.

"What are you saying?"

"I'm saying, Yusuf, that I've saved your life."

"Are you out of your mind?"

"Shawar sees a model of power in my grandfather."

"You mean in Badr al-Jamali."

"I mean Badr al-Jamali the Armenian, the Army Commander."

"You've started raving. The beating's affected your mind. Did they hit you on the head?"

"Badr al-Jamali isn't your enemy, Yusuf. He's a great leader."

"Yes, he is. There's no doubt about that."

"Shawar aspired to be as great. He adopted the same title, Army Commander, but how can someone so feeble aspire to greatness? How can such a despicable person yearn for what's in such a noble hand?"

"Are you going to boast about your grandfather all day?!"

"In the past, when Badr al-Jamali came to Egypt, he prepared a big dinner for all the Turkish generals, and killed them all afterwards."

Yusuf stared at him. Then he began to understand.

"Did you have your doubts about Shawar's intentions?"

"No, my Lord, I had no doubts; in fact, I was absolutely certain. He planned to kill you all during the banquet this evening. He was trying to imitate Badr al-Jamali, but he was like the donkey carrying scripture: he did not understand Badr al-Jamali or realise his goals."

"What proof do you have?"

"I don't need any."

"No! Mere surmise is wrong."

"I wonder: did you really believe that Shawar was happy to have you around and was an enemy of the Crusaders?"

"Ibrahim!"

"I've a friend in Shawar's army."

"A spy."

"No, a friend. He made it simple for me to kill him yesterday. He told me about a letter that Shawar sent to Amalric, the Crusader King."

"What letter?"

"A letter that asked the King to enter Egypt by way of Damietta. Yusuf, Minister Shawar asked the Crusader King to enter Egypt. He promised to make it easy for them, provided that they share power with him. Now, Kurd, that's the man who invited you to dinner. If I'd told you, you might have killed him, and his soldiers would have killed you. Either your uncle or the Caliph would have blamed you. But Ibrahim's just an Egyptian halva-maker. Maybe they're thinking that his motive is revenge, nothing more."

Yusuf ibn Ayyub gave him a stunned look and then stood up without a word. He went to see his uncle and then the Caliph Al-`Adid. He confirmed the letter's contents and ordered Ibrahim freed. Ibrahim had saved his life and Egypt, too, in a gesture of unprecedented courage. If he had told Salah ad-din before, Shawar might well have escaped or asked the Crusaders for help. Instead, he had risked his own life to save Yusuf or Egypt—maybe for Egypt's sake. The Caliph ordered Al-Kamil to be killed as well; he did not want to leave any trace of Shawar's progeny in Egypt. He then made Asad ad-din Shirkuh, Salah ad-din's uncle, Minister of Egypt, Minister of Sword and Pen.

The strange thing is that Ibrahim asked for permission to kill Al-Kamil himself. He told Yusuf ibn Ayyub Salad ad-din that Al-Kamil had tried to kill him before, and he wanted to have his revenge. Salah ad-din agreed to let Ibrahim undertake to kill Al-Kamil.

Ibrahim entered Al-Kamil's cell and sat down in front of him.

"Get out of here," he told Al-Kamil calmly. "There's a horse waiting to take you to Syria, then to any country you like."

Al-Kamil gaped in amazement.

"You saved my life once," Ibrahim said.

"And now you're returning the favour."

"Yes, I am."

"What about Jawwad's claim that I wanted to kill you?"

"I didn't believe him. You're not a traitor. You're a good worker for an evil man. Now go in peace."

"The Caliph will punish you."

"I'll bring him some phony blood. I'll tell him I killed you, then buried you. Now leave!"

"You—"

"I'm a man, and so are you. You didn't hurt me, so why should I hurt you?"

"Rashida..."

"You could have forced her while I was away, but you didn't. I've just told you you're a decent man. Leave before it's too late. People will say that Al-Kamil's dead."

"If you knew I was innocent, why didn't you defend me before the Caliph?"

"Because in times of war and treachery, no one's listening. It's easier and much safer to let you escape."

Al-Kamil left. Ibrahim sacrificed a sheep and spread its blood around the cell.

CHAPTER FIFTEEN

Ibrahim went back to Alexandria, where he had left his wife, his sister Kamila, her husband Sufyan, his brother's wife Nafisa, his own mother, and Rashida's. He had made up his mind to rebuild the stores in Alexandria first, then the ones in Fustat, and then Cairo.

Every night, Rashida was waiting for his embrace and would settle down only when she was on his chest. However, she was well aware that her husband and cousin did not trust her, even though he adored her. In her past, he could detect cunning, malice, slickness, and reckless behaviour. She had never imagined that she would need to take his opinion into account. Setting a goal and achieving it was all she had bothered about. She desired him, loved him, and knew no other. She had won him and now owned him; or that was how it seemed to her. And yet, a woman never owns a man who does not trust her. She frowned and waited for him. When he came back, and they both plunged into the fiery flames of passion, she rested her head on his chest.

"What's the matter with you?" he asked. "Your mind's not with me."

She kissed his chest and ran her hand over his heart to feel it beating.

"Do you trust me, Ibrahim?" she asked. "I mean, you gave me everything before you left. Was that a courageous gesture, or a sign that you trust me?"

He did not respond, and that troubled her.

"A husband must trust his wife," she insisted. "You've told me that I'm the most courageous woman you've ever met. That's what you said."

"What about you, Rashida," he replied, holding her hand and kissing its fingers. "Do you trust me?"

"Of course!" she replied, without even thinking.

"You're lying! All the time, you keep watching me and thinking about what I'm going to do. I can see that there are things you keep hidden from me."

"Those words shock me," she replied, swallowing hard.

"Because they're true."

"I wanted us to keep each other informed."

"That's what I wanted, too. You're clever, but you're not cleverer than me. Just remember that."

"It's true, yes," she went on bitterly. "I'm a bit scared, because in the past..."

"Yes indeed, in the past," he interrupted her, sitting up. "The past makes trust difficult, doesn't it?"

It was as if he'd cornered her in a ditch with no way out.

"So where do we start?" she asked in desperation.

"What is it you want?" he asked, looking straight at her. "If it's trust you want, then it needs two hands. I have one and you have another. If you want to control me, that's never going to happen. What's yours is yours, Rashida, and what's mine is mine."

"We should share everything," she replied immediately.

"Since when have women shared everything with men?"

"Women aren't all the same," she replied angrily. "I want to start working with you in the stores again, either in Alexandria or Cairo."

She was in her fifth month of pregnancy.

"Are you crazy?" he said immediately.

"After I've given birth, of course," she replied, "after a while. My mother and yours can take care of our baby."

He remained silent.

"You'll be with me," she went on enthusiastically. "I'll only work with you. I'll supervise the halva-making. I've done it successfully before. If Shawar hadn't set fire to Fustat..."

"That's never going to happen," he told her firmly.

She pursed her lips, then stood up and stared at him.

"That's because you only ever see yourself," she said with a listless calm. "You never hear anyone else. You took a big risk in giving me everything; it wasn't trust. Ibrahim knows everything. Ibrahim's the only one to decide. Ibrahim's always right. But I'm never going to give in to you, Cousin, nor will I yield like everyone else."

He looked down for a moment.

"This isn't war, Rashida," he said. "Life involves sharing."

"But it isn't sharing where you're concerned," she replied, sitting down in front of him. "It's a single decision made by you. If you just gave me a chance..."

"Your property's yours," he told her firmly. "I'll never touch it."

"I'm not talking about property, Cousin," she replied. "I'm talking about the heart. Let me probe its depths and tend my passion there."

"You've a fine line in talk!"

She held his hand and kissed it.

"Let me work with you," she said. "Husain's going to work with you, isn't he? What do you say I work with him at the new store you're going to open in Alexandria, and you be in charge of the old one? I'll be working with your brother, not on my own."

"I'll think about it," he replied hesitant.

"Don't take your heart away from me. You know I love you."

"I know, but I don't know what love means to you."

"You... you're everything I desire."

"I'm not some commodity you can save up money to buy!"

She looked all around her, headed into his arms, and gave him a hug.

"Fine," she said. "I'm hiding something from you."

"So am I," he replied with a grin.

"You tell me, then I'll tell you."

"No, you tell me first, then I'll tell you."

"Let's both talk at once."

But there was silence.

"Give me your hand," he told her with a laugh. "Come on, let's wait till trust takes root in our veins. That needs time."

He agreed that, three days a week, she could go with Husain to the new store. They did not have much money, and it was halva sales that kept the household and new store afloat. However, Husain had never liked making halva or working in the store. He would leave work and wander the streets, looking for what he wanted. Rashida kept it all hidden from her husband because, if he found out that Rashida was solely responsible for the store, he might well punish Husain and stop her going there.

One day, when her husband returned, he sat her down beside him and talked to her like a friend. She smiled, proud and somewhat hopeful.

"The Caliph Al-'Adid has made Salah ad-din Minister following the death of his uncle, Shirkuh," Ibrahim told her. "The Caliph has dubbed him 'the Victorious King.'"

Nursing her little daughter, Rashida looked at her husband, expecting to hear more. He went on to tell her patiently that, three months after Shirkuh had taken on the job as Minister of Sword and Pen, he had died. The Caliph Al-`Adid had thought about appointing one of the Turkish generals as Minister, or else one of the Syrian generals who had come with Shirkuh's army. The secretary came in with three names. The Caliph looked down for a moment, then made a snap decision. He would make a different appointment as minister. He wanted someone who was unthreatening, ascetic, and young; someone with no men clustered around him and no army under his command. The Caliph wanted someone he could order around and with whom he could restore his ancestors' suzerainty that had gradually dwindled ever since Badr al-Jamali had occupied the post as Minister of Sword and Pen. There was a young man not yet thirty years old who was accompanying his uncle and had no authority or troops under his command. He was Kurdish, so no Arabs would ever listen to him, and no Turkish soldiers would trust his abilities with either a spear or horse. Salah ad-din Yusuf ibn Ayyub ibn Shadi ibn Marwan ibn Ya`qub ad-Duwaini. Salah ad-din agreed immediately, and the Caliph Al-`Adid dubbed him 'the Victorious King.'"

"Salah ad-din isn't that simple, Ibrahim," Rashida said, looking into his eyes. "He's not a pushover, either. How stolid is the ascetic who's learned from Al-Jilani, and how stubborn someone who has both prudence and purpose! The Caliph doesn't realise what kind of heart he's chosen and what soul he's given authority to and dubbed victorious."

"Yusuf ibn Ayyub Salah ad-din is a trustworthy person."

"I'm not talking about trust. I'm talking about prudence and purpose."

"We need someone who'll bring security back to the streets so we can begin again."

"Begin from where, Cousin?"

"From where we left off, Rashida. One day I'll tell you."

"Tell me what?"

"What happened in the past."

"Why won't you tell me today?"

"The time's not right. We're between dynasties, eras, and wars. My hand's a ghoul that's trying to toss us into the fire."

"Didn't the ghoul die?"

"No, but its boy did."

"I want to tell you that I managed to save some money and gold from the fire."

"I know."

"How do you know?"

"I know you. But we won't talk about that now. We'll eagerly rebuild what's been destroyed. Can you guess the very first decision made by 'the Victorious King'?"

"What?"

"To open up Cairo to the general public."

"To poor Egyptians?"

"All Egyptians. Cairo's gates are open for the riffraff, the poor, Sufis, and even madmen."

"That's good, what he's done!"

"He didn't consult the Caliph when he made the decision, Rashida."

Their eyes met, and she understood what he meant to say.

"God is doing good for us and Egypt," she said.

A few months later, Ibrahim heard news of Husain's situation. He went into a rage and returned to the house. He called his brother and wife in and spoke angrily to them both, issuing threats. For a moment, Husain lowered his head.

"Maybe if you gave us a chance," Rashida said, "then we wouldn't tell lies."

"Lying's in your blood," Ibrahim responded furiously. "How can your rid yourself of something that's second nature?"

Rashida swallowed hard, went to her room, and closed the door.

"Rashida's not responsible for this, Brother," Husain said. "I'm the one who made the decision."

"Without asking me first?"

"Yes, Brother, without asking you first," Husain replied firmly. "In fact, it's two decisions. The first is that I don't want to be a halva-maker. I've started to learn about medicine."

"And what's the second?" Ibrahim asked defiantly.

"I'm going to be married to Nafisa, my brother's wife," he replied. "Strangers shouldn't take care of our own flesh and blood. If I'm not married to her, some other stranger will be."

Ibrahim looked at him.

"Is that what she wants?" he asked.

Husain said nothing.

"That's a major sacrifice," Ibrahim said.

"It's what our brother deserves, Ibrahim. We should take care of his wife and children."

There was still more silence.

"Maybe you've been better than me all along," Ibrahim went on. "Do what you like. I'll bless whatever you do."

"How am I better than you?" Husain asked, looking straight at him.

"I swear you're better than me," Ibrahim replied. "I realise that you are fulfilling your obligations and deep down don't really want to be married to Nafisa. Perhaps I'm incapable of being so giving."

Their eyes met, and they both felt as though they were covered by a hand, the way they'd felt when they were playing together and searching for shells and pearls on the seabed.

Husain left.

When he opened the door to his wife's room, she closed her eyes and pretended to be asleep. He pulled back the sheet.

"You lied to me, Rashida," he said, not accustomed to apologising or expressing regret.

She did not open her eyes.

"I know you're awake," he said, shaking her.

"In which case," she responded dryly, "you realise I don't want to talk."

He picked her up, hugged her, and kissed her cheeks.

"Maybe I was a bit too unkind," he said hesitantly. "I didn't mean it when I said that you lied all the time. I know how often you do it, and I'm fully aware that you devote the utmost effort for this family's sake. I value that."

She pushed him away.

"That's the trust we're missing," she replied bitterly. "It may well be missing forever."

"No," he replied, clasping her hand. "I want to tell you about another decision."

"I don't want to know," she responded, looking away.

He wrapped his arms around her back and kissed her hair. Her heart pulsed with longing, and she was afraid her body was giving away. He slowly kissed her neck.

"How I long for you every day," he said, "every single hour. I can never have enough..."

"We were talking about trust," she replied, doing her best to remind herself why she was feeling so sad.

His wet kisses covered her shoulder.

"I don't remember," he replied as though he had not heard her. "Come to me!"

He pulled her toward him and gave her a passionate kiss on the lips.

"Trust, Ibrahim!" she whispered.

But she melted into his kisses and caresses. She kept going in circles, no longer able to see the way.

"I haven't forgiven you," she told him later, as she went to sleep on his chest.

Eyes closed, he held her hand and kissed it.

"Your temper is much nicer than your forgiveness," he said.

"You said you'd made a decision."

"If you accept my decision," he told her, still kissing her hand, "you can run the new store on your own."

Before he could even finish, she had leapt out of bed with a joy that stretched far beyond the seas.

"I agree, and I love you!" she shouted, putting her arms around his neck.

"You're strangling me!"

"Because I love you so much."

CHAPTER SIXTEEN

Salah ad-din summoned him suddenly, and with an unexpected request. He told Ibrahim that he wanted to pay a visit to the Pyramid Witch. He had heard about the magic of the ancients, but he did not believe it. He realised that everything was in God's hands, but he had dreamed about her; it was as though she were asking to meet him. Ibrahim took him to see Bahnas in disguise.

When Yusuf ibn Ayyub went in to see her, he looked at her huge eyes and was riveted to the spot.

"Welcome, Kurd!" Bahnas said. "Give your greetings to the kings of old."

"Sister, they—"

"You're too intelligent to pass judgment on them and too just to claim that you have knowledge of the unseen. You will never separate belief from unbelief, because you've learned from your shaikh to be in control of your own self. And that's enough."

"Do you know my shaikh?"

"I know you and everything about you."

"You are a genuine witch."

"That's the way people describe those who have learned. Even though such knowledge is right in front of us, we close our hearts to it. Give your greetings so I can speak to you. Thank them for preserving the land and gold."

"Greetings to those who have fought for this land," he said calmly, "and thanks for preserving the land and gold."

She smiled and looked at him with her black eyes. He gave an involuntary shudder.

"Make your passion pure," she told him, "and your goals specific."

"Your words..." he stuttered.

"Yusuf," she went on, "Al-Jilani is unlike any other shaikh. He differentiates truth from falsehood and good from evil. This land does not make its rulers belong to separate sects. It has bestowed its gifts on Christians, Muslims, Jews—those who've worshipped the Lord in their own way and based on their own knowledge, and those who've done their best to apply justice in the midst of iniquity. Act justly, and the land will reveal itself to you like a bride. Rule unjustly or rapaciously, and you'll see it flee like angels from devils."

"I've come to tell you...that I'm weak."

"Your trials are commensurate with your abilities."

"I realise that my abilities are limited. The burden of care is like the sun, traversing the heavens to reach the loftiest star. I can neither fight it nor ignore it. So give me advice...

"You've understood your weakness, man, so you've been saved. You've learned the extent of your shortcomings, so your arms have reached beyond the very moons. You've been given a commission; people in such a position have no choice. If they give up, they fail; if they hesitate, they wander aimlessly around the tent ropes like a child who has only just learned to walk the day before. Do you understand the words of your shaikh, Al-Jilani?"

"How do you know him?"

"He's part of me, as I am of him."

"I thought you knew the magic of the ancients."

"I also know the magic of the words of the wise."

"Witch..."

"Call me Bahnas. Now we've become family and friends. With that, you can set out on your commission. Yusuf, don't preserve land and treasure just here. Use your sword to envelop many lands. Make sure you bear in mind that you're empowering Muslims. Who are the Crusaders slaughtering?"

"All humanity."

"So, you've come to help humanity as a whole. He who averts iniquity is conducting repairs. He who defends the covetous sees his trace vanish from the surface of the earth. Things begin here. From here, you will make your way to the places where iniquity and greed prevail and remember that you have come to reunite what greed and malice have torn apart. Our ancestors have taught us that unity among people is a powerful force. But for the unity of north and south, Egypt would not have existed. North and South, Yusuf, East and West. The world awaits you. You're beginning, and others are finishing. That's the way of the world in which life alternates: some of us leave traces, while others perish with no beloved and no achievements. Those who do leave traces are memorialised in stone, the earth's soil, and the Pyramid walls."

Ibrahim gave his brother Husain an expectant look. This particular Friday was not like others. The Caliph Al-`Adid was on his deathbed, and Nur ad-din did not trust Salah ad-din. He was afraid that Salah ad-din might take exclusive control of Egypt. He insisted that Salah ad-din dedicate the Friday sermon to the Abbasid Caliph, mention the Rightly Guided Caliphs in it, and return the call to prayer to its old format. Nur ad-din insisted, and Salah ad-din agreed. So the sermon was delivered by the foreign shaikh from a far distant land, Shams ad-din Muhammad ibn Abi l-Qada', in a coarse voice in which he prayed for the Abbasid Caliph. The Egyptians neither objected nor rejoiced; they simply accepted the order without really caring. Salad ad-din was conducting himself well, with no greed in his heart and no hatred controlling his actions. He was humble in the face of wrongdoing and would open his heart to the poor and weak. One day, he worried about the way Minister Shawar was oppressing the people of Alexandria, and on another, he cancelled tax payments for the citizens of Bilbeis for forty years after the death and humiliation they had experienced at the hands of the Crusaders. His goal was to eliminate injustice, exchanging one state for another and one Caliph for another. Egypt was under the Kurd's control, and he wanted it for himself because it was the heart and world of the state. Now, the Fatimid dynasty, the Ubaidis, was at an end.

During the Friday prayers, Salah ad-din recited some lines of poetry:

"I see myself and my people divided into sects,

Even though kinships united us in principles.

Strange then that, wherever I look, my family

Is one, yet men all around me are in cliques.

"Those are Abu Firas al-Hamdani's words," he said, "and I repeat them for you today, now that the sermon once again mentions a single caliph, the Abbasid Caliph, and Friday is again a day of gathering. I want Egyptians to know that Salah ad-din will not rule people on the basis of any one creed or belief. Time requires that we come together and be united. To God Almighty belongs the power, both before and after."

When the prayers were over, Salah ad-din went with his Minister, Baha' ad-din Qaraqush, to the Ahmad ibn Tulun Mosque and walked around the pillars, looking up at the crenulations in the sky.

"You did all this before me, Ahmad," he said. "You kept Egypt for yourself, but now times have changed. If only you could see that your concerns were less severe than mine and your dream, one that seemed so impossible at the time, was actually more feasible than mine. Did you but know that the Crusaders have settled here and been our neighbours for a hundred years and maybe more! How can I motivate a people who have stood still for a century? Not only that, but I have no strategy or authority to bring hearts together and to unify bodies. A time will come when I'll form an army unlike any other, with men from every Muslim land, men who won't let commerce distract them from mentioning the name of God. But that'll just be a few moments in time, Ibn Tulun. Life's only in the balance for moments, no longer. That army won't last long. The glorious reputation fostered by monarchs is just a series of stories and fairy-tales to amuse children. Like us, they dream in a world that's constantly breaking apart and kindling discord. So, Ibn Tulun. I wonder, are you looking down from on high and cackling at my dream or my aspirations? Answer me, Ibn Tulun!"

The situation in Egypt changed, as did the Caliph's affiliation. The halva-maker started to worry. The festival halva had been devised by the Fatimids. What would its fate be in Salah ad-din's Egypt? Ibrahim could not sleep at night, and his wife was aware of it. She calmed his fears, even though she realised he was actually right. When Salah ad-din got rid of the entire Fatimid army and left Aftakin, it was really time to worry for Shafiqa's jobless husband.

"Go and talk to him," Rashida told her husband.

"He'll tell me," Ibrahim replied firmly, "that I need him, now he's become Egypt's ruler."

"But you've saved his life twice or more," she said.

Ibrahim did not respond. She was determined and did not wait for him to approve. Along with Shafiqa, Ibrahim's sister, she went to see Zubaida.

Cairo was no longer the city that Rashida knew. How can cities change overnight? Now, the city gates could not stop the general public, the riffraff and vagrants, from entering. People poured into the city through the open gates, looking to left and right as though they had entered the gates of paradise by mistake and were now chasing its fruits—apples and grapes— and searching for houris. Vagrants made their way into the Ubaidi palaces, came out with bottles and lamps, and hurried away with bits of gold. They were eating leftover kunafa and basandud cake, then dancing in the palace gardens. Only rulers and the wealthy had ever lived here--the walls and magic. Now times had changed, and all the palaces were open to the public. The people who once lived there had abandoned them. The people could gulp down all the caliphs' halva and make a pile of money and silver. But then what? The next day, they would still be vagrants and hooligans. What was going to happen the next day? Would the Crusaders enter Cairo? Would 'the Victorious King' treat them justly? Now, the Al-Azhar Mosque was just standing there like an elephant in the desert wastes, with no shaikhs, no prayers, and no worshippers.

Rashida did not know whether she preferred this Cairo or the one she had known in the past. But that past was not coming back. Her great-grandfather had said it, the city was inherited by generations: each era has its dynasty and its men. Once the populace had left the palaces and the land was secure and calm again, people would need to do some thinking. Time can deceive and humiliate. That much, she had learned from her journey. Today, she had come to meet her servant girl, or the woman who had been her servant-girl.

She looked at Zubaida, who was nursing her baby. He had black hair and a round face like his father. His skin was a blend of brown and white. It was like the Nile mud at flood stage, a blackish sludge oozing with richness.

"Can I hold him?" Rashida asked, holding out her hand.

"Of course, my Lady!" Zubaida replied as she gladly handed the baby to her.

"Don't make fun of me, Zubaida," Rashida said. "You're the lady now."

"No, my Lady," she replied with a smile, "I'm just a baby's mother."

"You've won the man you've loved all your life," Rashid said.

"I'm still asking myself," Zubaida said, giving Rashida an affectionate look, "why he wanted me in his bed. What did he see in me?"

"He saw a beautiful woman whom he loved."

"Me, beautiful?"

"As musk and moon combined, like grains of sand on sacred Mount Sinai. He knows the true value of love. He's not the usual kind of man."

"If I live out my entire life," Zubaida said, closing her eyes, "I'll repay you as much as I can. You're the cause of this. I can never forget that."

Rashida looked at Shafiqa.

"Zubaida," Rashida said hesitantly. "You're my sister, as you've always been. Your son, ʿAla ad-din Shadi, is as beautiful as you are. May God bless him for you and guide Salah ad-din's heart for you and him."

"All I want is to live in peace and to see that no worries bother him. But they're constantly with him."

"Are you happy with him?"

"I used to dream of being close to him. God who gives to whom He wills has given me an angel. When he's with me, the sun shines."

"If you used to feel any affection for me, Zubaida, then please help me."

"Ask me whatever you wish."

"Shafiqa, Ibrahim's sister and the wife of Aftakin, the Turkish general, is in terrible shape, as is her husband. You know that The Victorious Monarch Salah ad-din has got rid of the Fatimid army and put in its place a new army consisting of Mamluk, Turkish, Syrian Arab, and Egyptian troops. Those new soldiers have taken over the property and houses of Fatimid army personnel. Salah ad-din has not raised any objections. I'd like you to intercede with Salah ad-din on Aftakin's behalf so that he can get his house and money back."

Zubaida gave her a worried look.

"I don't think he'll agree," she said. "I can promise you, my Lady, that he's not using the money for himself or his household. You can see our house and my clothes. But he needs the money to raise the army. War's continually at the gates, and the Crusaders show no mercy."

"I realize that, but I'd like him to make an exception for Aftakin. I know him; he's a good man."

"I'll try, but don't be annoyed with me if I can't change his mind."

"I understand, Zubaida."

Rashida stood up. Zubaida held her hand and clasped it tightly.

"Don't blame me, my Lady and sister," she said, her voice pained. "I want to help, but I don't want to make him angry. I'll do my best."

But Zubaida realised that he would never agree, and he did not. His decision covered the entire Fatimid army, and he would make no exceptions for friends or their brothers.

Ibrahim watched his wife from afar, and he saw the tyrannical hold she had over everyone in his household, sometimes using threats, at other times, promises. He no longer knew who was in charge. Sometimes, he would smile at the extent of her abilities and defiance. His sister Shafiqa now obeyed all Rashida's instructions; Rashida was her guide and counsellor. His sister Kamila was afraid of Rashida's temper, and Nafisa was bullied by her. She did her best to reduce Nafisa's position in the family, but she felt sorry for her children and gave them lots of presents.

"Rashida can never relax," he told her one day, "unless she's controlling everybody."

"Rashida can't control Ibrahim," she responded with a smile.

"If she managed to control her husband," he chided her, "that would be the end of Ibrahim."

"If he talked to her," she replied, "she might be able to give him advice."

"Don't let your minor victories blind you and give you illusions," he scoffed, holding her chin. "No one controls Ibrahim. How old are you, Rashida?"

With a smile she kissed the fingers that were touching her chin.

"I don't want that, Cousin, or dream of it," she whispered. "All I want is your trust."

Ibrahim was increasingly aggravated by the decisions of Salah ad-din Yusuf ibn Ayyub. The Victorious King had ordered the cancellation of all Fatimid customs. He did not like the maulid halva, the bride halva, or the cavalier on horseback. He did not approve of Egyptians observing Shi`ite festivals, or that was the way he saw it. He did not want to remind them of times past. The people were divided, and that was dangerous. Ibrahim would have to confront him. What he did not realise was that Egyptians were not fussed about customs that the Ubaidis had foisted on them when the caliphs were living behind the walls in their city of Cairo. They had never mixed with the Egyptians or allowed them to enter the city. Eventually, Badr al-Jamali had allowed wealthy Egyptians to build in Cairo. But he had not opened the city to the general population and the poor. Today, Cairo had expanded and comprised Egypt as a whole. Did Egyptians not appreciate the difference?

"I'm going to see him," Ibrahim told his wife.

"Wait a while," Rashida replied hesitantly, "and be prudent. This isn't the same Yusuf with whom you used to stroll along the seashore, Ibrahim. This is 'the Victorious King.'"

But he had made up his mind, and he did not have to wait long at Salah ad-din's door.

The guards let him in. No sooner did Salah ad-din set eyes on him than he greeted him warmly.

"Ibrahim," he said, "I've missed you. Why haven't you come to visit me?"

"I know how busy you are, and I've no desire to get close to rulers. Doesn't your own shaikh, ʿAbd al-qadir al-Jilani, tell us: 'Everyone you rely on is your God; everyone you fear and beg from is your God; everyone you consider for either detriment or benefit, without realising that the truth lies in His hands, that person is your God. Purge your hearts of anyone but Him. Detriment and benefit come solely through Him. You are in His house and His guests'? Those are your own shaikh's words, my Lord. They provide his definition of the most profound unbelief."

Their eyes met.

"Have you come here to remind me of his sayings, I wonder, Brother?" Salah ad-din responded seriously. "Or is it something more personal?"

"But we're friends and brothers," he went on. "If you've come to remind me of the shaikh's sayings, I haven't forgotten them. If you've come to blame me for something, you're a brother, someone I'll listen to with a heart that's open to your anger."

"My lord, Victorious King, I've come to make a request, something I don't like doing. It might be advice from a brother or a request."

"Ibrahim, don't worry about making your request. But forgive me if I can't help your sister's husband. I want to be just, but, if I were to treat one soldier in the Fatimid army differently from the others because he's related to a friend of mine, I'd be doing myself wrong."

"I see that, my Lord. But I still think you're treating them cruelly, even though—"

"You're saying that?" Salah ad-din interrupted him. "That army fought with the Crusaders, Brother!"

"Then they stopped."

Their eyes met.

"I hold my army to account," Salah ad-din said firmly, "and deal harshly with any hesitation. Any soldier who runs away from encounters with the Crusaders has his body torn apart by me bit by bit. When an army is fighting the Crusaders, there's no room for cowardice in the ranks."

"Badr al-Jamali," Ibrahim muttered.

"What did you say?"

"You remind me of him."

"Who?"

"It doesn't matter. All soldiers fight for feudal rights, my Lord, and for gifts, even if their hearts are sound and they want Muslims to win. Fatimid soldiers are just like the soldiers in the Syrian army."

"You didn't understand what I'm saying. When I take my army out to the field of battle, I have to know that the men defending my land are loyal to God and not the Devil. If men change as much as rulers do, then they're no use as soldiers. You don't need me to explain that to you. As your great-grandfather put it, 'Every era has its own regime and men.'"

"You know of my great-grandfather?"

"Yes, I do."

"You regard him as your enemy because he was an Ubaidi general."

"I regard him as a general who deserves respect. If I regarded him as an enemy, I wouldn't have fortified a gate that he built. He built the Barqiyya Gate, and I'm fortifying it. Any monarch who destroys things that other rulers have built is a failure and is cursed till the Day of Resurrection."

"But allow me, my Lord..."

"Have I touched a single building?"

"You're destroying ideas."

"When Egypt's Minister makes a deal with the Crusaders, when the Crusaders enter Cairo once or twice, when the Caliph is too weak to fight his Minister or the Crusaders, you realise that the time has come for a new era. Ahmad ibn Tulun did it earlier and made Egypt independent of the Abbasid Caliph, so as to elevate its status. Do you see me destroying any monuments? The Al-Azhar Mosque is still there, and so is the Mosque of Al-Hakim bi-Amr Allah, the wall of your Sicilian ancestor. The lofty walls built by your grandfather, Badr al-Jamali, are still standing. I'm supporting them all, not destroying them. Even so, this is a different era, and there's no time for conciliatory gestures."

"My Lord..."

"I'll remind you, Ibrahim, of your grandfather's history. When Badr al-Jamali took over Egypt, he gathered all the Turkish generals and slaughtered them in his house. Do you remember? The only people I've killed have been people who have rebelled or started a war. That's what Badr al-Jamali did, and he became the hero of heroes because he saved the Egyptian people from famine and corruption. Today, Egyptians are surrounded on all sides by Crusaders. Do you want me to take pity on the Ubaidi soldiers and forgive their treason for a single day? That's never going to happen. If it had happened, I would have been wronging the people of Egypt and Syria and everyone who longs for a different era and a time of strength."

"What has the era got to do with maulid and bride-halva, my Lord? If Egyptians eat halva, are the Crusaders going to enter Egypt? Isn't it the halva-maker who's protected Cairo?"

"I know that you've protected Cairo," Salah ad-din said with a smile of understanding, "and you've saved my life once or twice. I realise that. But it's time for Egyptians to get rid of heresies and associate themselves with the saints. Halva symbolises the Ubaidis. In the cavalier, they envision the Fatimid caliph on horseback. The bride halva is his wife. What's the Ubaidi caliph done for us? I felt sorry for him, and I won't deny that I had some warm feelings for him. But that era's over. Anything that reminds Egyptians of it is dissent."

"You know that's not the way it is."

"I'm afraid of civil unrest, and that's even worse than killing. Listen to me, Ibrahim. I don't want halva for festivals shaped like a caliph or for celebrations of birthdays of the Prophet's family. In Islam, people are judged according to their actions. Only with God's permission can anyone intercede for another; 'a day when wealth and children will only benefit those who come to God with a clean heart'." (Qur'an, Sura 26 [The Poets], v. 88)

"Allow me to disagree with you, my Lord. The Egyptian people value Salah ad-din and realise that these are dangerous times. However, they've also valued their freedom and festivals since time immemorial. I don't know what harm it will do the ruler if they eat halva and enjoy the festival celebrations. As God says in the Qur'an: 'Who has forbidden the ornaments of God and the good things of His bounty?'" [Sura 7 [Al-A'raf], v. 32).

"I'm not forbidding bounty and ornaments, Ibrahim."

"No, you're depriving children of their fun, and for no reason."

"Ibrahim!"

"I realise that I've overstepped the mark, but I've learned from my ancestors that there's triumph in beauty and making halva is just as creative as designing buildings. If you haven't destroyed Ubaidi mosques and walls, then don't destroy a craft that an Egyptian devised for his wife one day because, after she was burned by fire, she could not see beauty in anything. Out of her pain, he wanted to extract something to soothe her heart. There's a great deal of faith in that story. God the Creator made us out of clay; He values the human creator."

"Does halva dissolve in the mouth, leaving nothing behind?"

"Like the world, my Lord, it dissolves in the mouth, leaving nothing behind. However, in moments of beauty, a certain solace can be found from ugliness, greed, and pain. Moments of beauty in the eyes of children—as they dream of the cavalier and bride—also deserve our attention. When a child falls asleep with the cavalier halva before him, it reminds him that the dream may be real; horse and sword are not impossibilities. If the child can be convinced of that, then we've won."

"Ibrahim!"

"If The Victorious King will reverse his decision, it will be a sign of genuine greatness. I know you to be a modest person who dislikes arrogant behaviour. Egyptians really value happiness because they have so little of it; they relish moments of pleasure because they're like the cavaliers, my Lord; they bring dreams and power, then vanish."

"I thought you came here to argue with me about your business and stores, but you've managed to touch my heart with your words."

"I see you as someone with worries and ambitions. The two always go together."

"And I see you as someone possessing knowledge and insight. It's as though you were a shaikh, Sufi, or architect."

"Like shaikhs, I can see majesty in the beauty of man's creations; and, like an architect, even if my monuments should vanish, the memory of them will survive. Like compact buildings, memory will never disappear, however hard we may try."

"Your wish is granted, Ibrahim. The Victorious King will reverse his decision, on condition that you come to see him more often."

As he left Salah ad-din, he was feeling more relaxed and at ease about

Egypt's and Syria's futures. Here was a king like no other. He wore raw wool and listened to people with all the humility of Sufis and ancient soothsayers. Out of respect, Salah ad-din instructed his personal guard to escort Ibrahim back to his house. The guard walked silently beside him. Ibrahim was thinking: His wife would be delighted by the decision, but what about his mother? She had started exchanging greetings with him every morning and looking for him every day. His sister and her husband would be flooded with halva, and that would soothe their hearts. From the mountaintop, the world looked weak; we sport and play in it. However, it brings wafts of paradise along with embers of hell. In it, we taste both heaven and hell and crave assurance. Assurance. Why was the guard bothering him? Why was he filling the air with treachery? He abruptly turned to face the guard who was walking slowly behind him. The guard seemed to be putting his hand in his pocket, then changing his mind, and hesitating. Their eyes met, and Ibrahim turned away. He slowed his pace, fully on guard. They walked on for a while.

"My Lord," the guard eventually asked, "why aren't you riding a horse? Why are you returning to your house in Cairo on foot? Or are you going back to Alexandria?"

Ibrahim looked at him as he walked at a measured pace between the streets' square stones.

"I like walking," he replied. "What about you? When did you come to serve The Victorious King?"

"A long time ago, when he was still in Syria. He trusts me."

"Of course!"

What happened next was like a dream. Death can draw near and move away; it can flirt and desire; it can change plans and leave. The guard raised his sword, intending to plunge it in Ibrahim's back while he was talking. Ibrahim sensed it and bent over, so that the sword sliced his shoulder. He hurled himself at the guard and grabbed the hand holding the sword hard, pressing it to the ground. Taking a dagger out of his pocket, he plunged it into the guard's heart.

"Who are you?" he demanded.

"The King's guard," the man replied with a groan.

"Liar."

He grabbed the man's shoulders and hurled him to the ground.

"It was Rashid ad-din Sinan who sent you here, wasn't it? Are you an Assassin? Were you planning to kill me or Salah ad-din?"

The man managed to raise two fingers, eyes still defiant, and died.

Ibrahim looked at the wound on his shoulder, well aware that the sword's blade had been poisoned. He rushed to the first house on the street to get help. He needed someone to open the wound and remove the blood as soon as possible.

Closing his eyes, he fell into a deep sleep, or else he saw in front of him a large open space. From the middle of it, his cousin's eyes emerged. She was weeping. Was she actually weeping?

"How did you get here, Rashida?" he asked in a weak voice.

"I'm always around you," she replied firmly.

He smiled and fell back asleep.

"Is he alive?" she asked Husain in a panic. "Is he going to live?"

"God willing," Husain replied.

"Go to Salah ad-din," Ibrahim said weakly, "and tell him that the Assassins have infiltrated his ranks. He must be careful."

Ibrahim's wife rushed to see Layla, his mother, and told her in a panic that Ibrahim was hovering between life and death. The Assassins had tried to kill him, and it seemed they would succeed. Kamila shrieked, and Shafiqa groaned. They rushed over to Rashida and begged her to let them see their brother. Yet Rashida stopped them entering his room and told them that only his mother could go in. Layla lowered her eyes and said nothing. Rashida clasped her shoulder.

"If only you could see Ibrahim, Aunt!" Rashida told her. "Sweat's pouring off his forehead, and his lips are as white as the clouds in the sky. His soul is calmly making its way to its Creator. He's calling your name; he keeps saying 'my Mother'..."

His mother clung to the wall, still not responding.

"Aunt," Rashida said, "don't smash every single bag of halva because you've lost the bridal one. That's what I used to do as a child. But I stopped doing it when I realised that there's little enough time. It's the love around us that brings it all together. Go in and say farewell to your son."

"I have no son," his mother replied in a quiet, tearful voice.

"Yes, you do have a son," Rashida replied decisively, "and he's not a king. He doesn't make decisions between life and death."

"You're lying. He's not dying."

"Yes, he is. I've seen his wound for myself."

His mother lowered her eyes.

"Ibrahim!" she said suddenly, as though she had just woken up. "Where is he? Take me to see him!"

She went into her son's room and ran her shaking fingers over his face, as though she were rediscovering him. When she called out his name, he opened his eyes and looked at her.

"The Assassins are out to kill me," he told her in a weak voice. "But they haven't succeeded. I wonder, Mother, if I'd let them kill me, would that have soothed your heart?"

As she stared at him, her eyes were full of weakness. She swallowed hard as she looked at his bandaged shoulder.

"You haven't said 'mother' to me for ages," she choked, her hands shaking even more.

"You were my eternal companion, Mother!"

"And you were the prop and wall I could lean on!"

He held her hand and kissed it.

"If you abandoned me because you were blaming me for death, then there's nothing I can do. If you abandoned me because you were afraid of losing me, then there's nothing I can do about that either. If you realised how weak I am, you'd be able to forgive me for a sin I didn't commit."

"Ibrahim can do anything," she repeated to herself.

"He was a boy who couldn't do anything," he went on affectionately. "Then he became a man standing alone in the midst of Crusaders, ministers, and kings. He's a halva-maker, that's all."

She looked around the room and spotted the maulid halva he had made.

"All your life," she joked in between her tears, "you've been no good at making halva. Just look at its sagging face and misshapen body. Ibrahim, what are those colours you've smeared on it? They make no sense."

He moved closer and used his hand to wipe away her tears.

"So what am I?" he asked.

"You're...heart and soul."

He pulled her toward him and put her small head on his chest. Grabbing his shoulders and repeating his name, she burst into tears.

"My son," she sobbed, "the heart sympathises like an ancient wall; if only it would collapse or disappear. If I've given you an unbearable burden, I've done the same thing to myself."

"Our time in this world is short, Mother. Don't deprive me of an affection I've long enjoyed."

"If only you knew how I've deprived myself of an affection I had enjoyed ever since you were born."

He kissed her head and looked at her tear-stained face. His wife now slunk into the room, picked up another bridal halva, and put it in front of her mother-in-law.

"Look at this one," Rashida said. "I've just made it. Give me a fair verdict. Who makes the best halva in this house?"

She looked at the halva, then at her son.

"Ibrahim's good at everything," she replied confidently.

"I asked you to make a fair decision," Rashida said with a sigh. "There's no justice in this world of ours."

Rashida looked at her husband and noticed the happiness in his eyes, maybe for the first time for ages. She was reassured, and so was he. He smiled at her, and she smiled back, then left the room, pretending to be upset and muttering that she was always treated unfairly in that household.

CHAPTER SEVENTEEN

Like death, trust has its appointed time; it is a postponed decree. She watched him as he addressed his men with a quiet confidence. He was the love of her life, the dream of innocent times. He allowed her free rein in matters of commerce. They decided not to be partners; that would destroy their relationship. She would make halva and trade independently; he would do the same with his stores. But he left it to her to organise everything. He gave her encouragement and listened to her. He admired her intelligence, but he did not forget the tricks she had played in the past, nor was he particularly happy about the sudden bursts of energy she would display. He was worried about his own fate and that of his family. For her part, amid all the love she felt, she never forgot that there had been a time when he had seized all her money to spite her; or that is what she thought. Love blended with aspiration; caution remained alert along with all the passion. Who knew: maybe she would die the next day, and he would be married again to Sayyida or someone else. One day, she woke from their love-making, kissing his back.

"If I die, Ibrahim," she said, "I don't want you to be married to anyone else."

With a smile, he buried his head in the pillow without saying a word.

"Can I be sure you won't be married to anyone else?" she asked threateningly.

"If I live," he replied, looking at her and pulling her toward him, "you can be sure I won't be married to anyone else."

"Did you love Sayyida?"

"I don't remember the past," he told her, putting his hands around her face.

"You preferred her to me."

He grabbed her, held her close, and gave her a passionate kiss.

"Your eyes have all the sweetness of sugarcane and honey," he told her after a while. "Where did you get such coquetry?"

She smiled.

"There are times," he told her, as he kissed her eyes, "when I want total control of your mind. I realise that that's impossible. Do you trust me, Rashida?"

"No," she replied without hesitation.

"Even so, you've sacrificed everything for my sake."

"How about you, Ibrahim?" she asked defiantly, running her hand over his beard, "do you trust me?"

"No," he replied without hesitation.

"Even so, you've chosen me and treated me fairly. For my sake, you've fought people and your own mind."

"What do you say, should we share information with each other?" he asked, embracing her. "What'll happen? I'm afraid of treachery, and so are you. Do you know why we don't communicate? It's because, when treachery originates in the heart, it destroys the soul. My passionate love for you is equal to my caution about what's left of my mind."

"We're playing a game," she replied, holding his hand and kissing it. "This world's a game, a sport. Some of us trust others. My own soul is inside yours."

"The soul!" he responded in disbelief. "Leave it alone; it belongs to our Lord God. It's the heart we should trust. It's the source of peace and security."

"I want to tell you a secret," she told him, closing her eyes and holding his hand.

"Don't talk."

"If I told it to you," she asked, "would you tell me yours, too?"

"Once we've shared secrets, what'll we do for the rest of our lives?"

"Make up new secrets to share."

"I swear, I've never met a woman like you all my life," he responded with a laugh. "You've taken over both heart and mind. My body shivers only for you, Cousin."

"And I swear that, ever since I was born, I've never loved anyone so much as you."

"And now..."

"And now..."

"Tomorrow," she told him decisively, "I want to go with you to our grandfather's mosque."

"Badr al-Jamali?"

"Exactly. We'll climb the mountain together. There's a secret I want to tell you about."

"Not before I share one with you."

They climbed the mountain together, their eyes riveted on the mosque. Here, their grandfather had been isolated with his Lord, and here Badr al-Jamali had been honest with himself.

Ibrahim stood in front of the mosque and looked at her for a moment. She did not understand what his look meant. Slowly, he opened the door. He lit the lamp, and the yellow light was reflected on his face.

"Where did you hide the money, Rashida?" he whispered.

"Beside the mosque," she replied. She was afraid without knowing why.

Closing his eyes, he could hear the Qur'an on the horizon, as soft and serene as love and tranquillity.

"Bring it here," he told her.

"Won't you come with me?"

"No, I'll wait for you here."

As she went out of the door, she kept turning to look at him. Then she grabbed the pickaxe and started digging at the spot where she had buried the money, gold, and jewellery. She hoped that nobody else had found it and that he would come to realise how courageous and intelligent she had been. She found the money intact; no one had touched it. She breathed a sigh of relief. When she went back into the mosque, she found him praying. She waited, then put everything down in front of him. He looked at it, then stood up quietly and went outside. She was surprised.

"Ibrahim," she asked him, "are you annoyed with me?"

"No," he replied. "Be patient for a moment. Don't move."

She heard the sound of the pickaxe and focused her attention on the gentle light from the lamp, as gentle as love itself. After a while, he put his hand on her shoulder to have her look at him. She did so and opened her eyes in sheer amazement. He was holding a huge basket with jewellery and money in it.

"This is the money that Jawwad stole," he told her calmly. "It's everything we own, everything that did not fall into Shawar's hands."

Her voice left her, and she looked at him, expecting to hear more.

"When you sent Jawwad to rob the factory, I arrested him and kept him prisoner inside the factory. My brother Husain got away. Do you remember?"

"Yes, I do," she choked.

"After that, I sensed that Shawar was going to take revenge. The Syrian army left after Shawar had pledged never to punish the people of Alexandria. I realised that Shawar would rob us of everything we owned. That's why I wanted you to go to Fustat, so that Shawar's wrath would not fall on you as well."

"I don't understand. Jawwad came back and stole everything."

"Yes, he did, with encouragement from Sufyan. I assumed that Jawwad would never leave. Like all thieves who don't succeed, he would hover around the place. I agreed with my brother-in-law, Sufyan, that he should encourage Jawwad to steal and agree to divide the loot with him. The two of them stole everything and hid it together at Kom ad-Dikka. However, a few hours later, Sufyan went back, took it all, and escaped with it to this spot, at the mosque of your grandfather and mine, Badr al-Jamali. He buried it here, according to my instructions. Jawwad squabbled with him and almost killed him. He told my sister and made threats, but Sufyan never breathed a word. Amid all this treachery, there still are some loyal souls."

"You...you're the one who asked Sufyan to help Jawwad steal your money, and then bury it here, in exactly the same place! How...?"

"There are times," he told her, cupping his hands around her face, "when sinking a boat preserves it from a monarch who's seizing all boats by force. I had to think how to keep our inheritance safe."

"Why here?"

"Forefathers always guard inheritance. That's what the Pyramid Witch said."

"My God, how do you know the Pyramid Witch, Ibrahim?"

"I met her with my grandfather years ago. All his life, my grandfather provided her with the sugar cakes she liked. My father did the same for the witch who replaced her. Forefathers have power, Rashida."

"Indeed, they do," she replied, her voice heavy with dread.

"What's strange, Cousin," he went on, "is that my soul and heart are part of yours. What both worries and delights me is your intelligence and courage, along with my realisation that you can preserve the heritage even though you're a woman."

"Ibrahim."

"I've given up and acknowledge defeat. I'll let you take charge of everything. I'm going to let you control your own wealth and part of mine, too. We'll rebuild the stores in Cairo and Alexandria. But you'll be in charge of the Alexandria stores, Cousin. I won't interfere."

"People will say you've let your wife walk through the markets and talk to men."

"And I'll respond that I've been married to a woman like no other. She's faced down the Minister and the Crusaders with more courage than men. But your store in Cairo will be there, and you'll chose the person to take charge of it."

"Sufyan. He's loyal. And Aftakin."

"Will the Turkish soldier agree to take charge of a halva factory?"

"Halva, my dear wife and Cousin, is what makes wars bearable and life as sweet as sugar. That's what we've learned."

He placed his hands around her face, then looked over at the plaque his grandfather had left. He read it aloud:

"In the name of God, the merciful, the compassionate. God's mosques are peopled only by those who believe in God and the Day of Resurrection, who perform the prayers, give alms, and fear none but God. The construction of this mosque was ordered by the Noble Lord, Army Commander, Sword of Islam, Supporter of the Imam, Chief Judge of Muslims, Guide of Missionaries for Believers, Abu an-Najm Badr al-Mustansiri, upon his entry to the port of Alexandria and witness of this old mosque in ruins. With his sound belief and loyalty, he determined to rebuild it as a compliment to God Almighty, that in the month of Rabi` Awwal, 477 AH."

With that, Ibrahim extinguished the lamp and looked to the horizon, waiting for dawn to emerge over the mountain.

"From up here," Ibrahim whispered, "he surveyed Egypt and gave witness to it. He may have thought it was all within his grasp. Stretch your arm out from here; all wishes are minor, and all problems and trials are trivial. From up here, the world looks like the proverbial 'eye of the needle.' (Qur'an, Sura 7 [Al-A'raf], v. 40) I wonder, when the world withdraws, does the soul come closer? Tell me, Cousin."

Rashida stretched out her arm, then clasped her hand.

"It wriggles in our arms, then flees with perfect ease like motes in the air. It's as though we can neither possess it nor seize it. He knew that, Ibrahim."

"Who did?"

"Our grandfather, in fact all our forebears."

"Did he want to seize it from his place up here, I wonder. When it rises, you can see clearly; it blots out everything below. From here, Badr al-Jamali could see the courtyard of Ahmad ibn Tulun's mosque, gleaming like the earth, and its structures, like the pillars of life itself, dependent on deeds and intentions."

He looked at her for a moment. Her expression shone with an unassuming comfort.

"I trust you, Rashida," he told her firmly. "If I let myself be ruled by caution, then I sacrifice the union of your soul and mine when I really need it."

"You're telling me this after three years of marriage."

"You can praise God that it's only three, Cousin. Men don't trust their wives even after thirty years of married life."

"Nor do women," she replied with a laugh. "But I do trust you because you're a halva-maker. They never cheat."

"Don't ask me for too much, the way my mother did."

"Maybe you've realised your own strength. I've certainly realised how stalwart your heart is. Someone with strength knows how to love, to give, and to trust. The Assassins didn't kill you or Salah ad-din. Today, they're aware of their own weakness. They won't try killing you again."

"I admire your certainty and self-confidence," he replied with a smile.

He focused his gaze on the horizon below the mountain top. He spotted a man standing with his arms open wide to confront the winds with his heart and to fight time with his gaze. He was saddling his filly with a will of iron, gold, and a whole pile of emeralds. Ibrahim looked at his wife.

"Can you see that man on the horizon?" he asked. "Take a look..."

She put her hand on her forehead as though she were expecting to see something that her eyes could not take in. Then she felt relieved.

"It's Yusuf ibn Ayyub Salah ad-din," she said.

"He's planning to build his Citadel here at the base of the hills. From here, he can see our grandfather's mosque and Ibn Tulun's minaret. I can hear his heart beating, Rashida, and understand his worries and hardships."

The Victorious King, Yusuf ibn Ayyub Salah ad-din, was indeed standing there at the site of his Citadel. Amid the Al-Muqattam wilderness, he looked weak. Those hills, with their veins of gushing blood, never dried. Each vein comprised longing, desire, an ending firmly linked to a beginning, and a frustration that seeped out of its enduring folds. There, people claimed that the sands could heal the sick. Those who were buried there would be close to the coals of paradise. Hope for a carefree life and merciful death would be there. Egyptians were always eager to guarantee the life to come before worrying about this world, as though eternity controlled the spirit and could inspire iniquity and devotion.

Yusuf ibn Ayyub allowed himself a smile. First, they had built the Pyramids, immortalising the living and leaving the dead to their Lord. Then they had buried their dead on the mountain, so as to guarantee them paradise. Death baffled them; they were used to stability, but then along came death and shook up that same stability. It reminded them that there is no such thing as stability on earth. They built for stability, and the structure remained, while the builder disappeared, or almost. The builder might survive, as his name would be remembered, and his image and soul reflected.

"Ahmad ibn Tulun, why is it that you still survive, even after so much time has passed? Your greatness is all around me and your purpose is buried deep within me. I know you and I know your trials. Jawhar the Sicilian, your gate bears witness to ambition and greatness. Army Commander, you have left behind a whole army of halva-makers! And you, Badr al-Jamali, when I see you, I will beat you once or twice; who knows, I may even try to kill you. I will then stand respectfully before you and pronounce your title, 'Supreme Master,' fully convinced of its appropriateness. You belonged to a different sect and lived in a less cruel age, although it was still full of death and contempt. If only you had known! Here I stand, confronting the Seljuqs, the Zengis, the Ubaidis, the Assassins, and the Crusaders. Ah me, the Crusaders! How they slunk into our fragmented land and used their swords to draw our future in blood while we played at our own wars. You lost your son, Badr al-Jamali, and I also lost my son in war. You're no better than me, Army Commander. If I ever met you, I might consider you an enemy, but the fear in my heart is never-ending. I have learned that the heart always tells the truth, and the world is a pure heart. In a world unlike this one, we'll meet and enjoy a meal together in peace. Till then, I shall endure, patient and satisfied."

Salah ad-din Yusuf ibn Ayyub ran out of words and gazed straight ahead.

He appeared on the distant horizon amid the howling wind. Then the rain started pouring, and her image was erased by the rain, wind, and all the stars. He had seen her once before and recognised her. She had remained inside him ever since he'd offered his greetings to the ancients who had preserved land and gold. Bahnas, the Pyramid Witch. Every three decades or so, she would be reborn, her birthday falling at the time of the flood of the blessed Nile. People were in awe of her and did not dare infringe on her space. Bahnas appeared on the horizon. His whole body trembled, and he fell to the ground looking at the hills. He heard the sweet, powerful voice say: "Make your passion pure and your goal your primary focus."

CAIRO 2016 CE / 1437 AH

`Amm `Abdo stopped speaking. There were tears in my eyes, and I forgot why I had met him and listened to his stories.

"Go back home, Daughter," he told her me with warm understanding. "Come here tomorrow to see the wooden horse I inherited from my great-grandfather. You need some time to really understand..."

"That story," I choked. "It's full of pain and majesty. Thank you, ʿAmm ʿAbdo!"

"Do you remember? You came because you wanted me to make halva so as to make your daughter happy. Fatimid halva. At the time, I told you that that particular halva is only any good if it's a mix, just like Egypt itself. Every time strangers add something to it, it blends in with the flour and gives its taste a wonderful flavour and colour."

"That's right! I thank you once again for remembering. Now let me return home; it's almost dawn. Tomorrow, I'll come back to see the wooden horse."

I left ʿAmm ʿAbdo's store and looked around me at the narrow street that had suddenly turned into a deep expanse that no eyes could encompass.

At dawn, I met them all. They were now a group of friends. Whenever my pain grew worse, I would go with them; whenever my own tears ignored me, I would follow in their footsteps. When we met, all differences, all wars, and all conflicts would vanish. All that remained would be the story, with all its purity of passion and splendour of dreams. I no longer see armies marching ahead in cautious anticipation or screams of despair and terror. The taste of halva prevails. I have witnessed the maulid doll at the very height of its beauty, just as sweet as a grandmother with a pure heart, as lovely as Sundus, glistening like Furoon in her passion, as persistent as Rashida. I raised my hand to greet Jawhar the Sicilian in front of Cairo's gates; I have told him about ʿAmm ʿAbdo and the taste of doughnuts. I have told him that he was speaking the truth when he said: "Every era has its own regime and men." Then I went on my own way, my eyes fixed on the Al-Muqattam Hills. I saw him looking down on me, as though to remind me of a companionship that had lasted a year or two, one that had never ended and never would. It was the Supreme Master and Army Commander.

"Badr, Armenian, I know you and understand why you chose to be alone in worship and prayer."

"In relationships with God," I told myself, but not him, "there is rest, savour, patience, anger, knowledge, and ignorance. Should you not be serene, then you will never hear His voice, nor will His light shine for you. You will walk alone in your world, like Satan after defiance. You will be angry and ask Him why He does not respond, offer help, and communicate. You will never realise that you have not opened up to let Him in. If you do not do that, do not complain. He will only manifest Himself to those who face Him with a pure heart and contented spirit. You knew all that, Badr. Forgive me if I do not address you as 'Supreme Master.' We have been companions forever, and such companionship has no need of titles. How can you have remained loyal to your love all this time? What kind of scenario did you construct, and whom did you mourn at night in the desert wastes? Ah, those desert wastes, when they fuse into a vacuum with beloveds trembling all around us, then vanish just like joy! As you well know, Badr, just part of a day is all of it. You realise that Jawhar was never scared of you, nor did he tremble before your might. In fact, in you, he saw his own craft and might. You remember Jawhar, Badr, don't you? Forgive me for going on like this, but it was your family with the halva doll. It consumed you even while you imagined that you were the one providing it. Do you know all that? At first, it was just a halva doll, but eventually, it became a bride lingering in your breast and stoking the flames of passion."

Then I looked around and saw it, the Citadel that Yusuf ibn Ayyub Salah ad-din never saw completed. O Lord of your army, as you anticipated, no such army was ever gathered, like a flash of heavenly nectar that strikes a single spirit, then disappears for thousands of years. Your name still prompts more sorrow than joy. You realised that hopeful moments are brief, just a small part of a single day.

I grabbed the chunks of hot doughnut and plunged my hand into the honey. It felt hard, fine, fresh, and alive, just like the free spirit. I put one in my mouth, then looked down at the mosque's open courtyard and colonnades, wide enough for every single indigent and seeker. Ahmad ibn Tulun, friend and companion, just like Badr, Yusuf, and Jawhar. They would all be meeting at the banquet table and talking about her, the treasure, and Bahnas, the Pyramid Witch. Why did you leave us? I looked for you, but could not find you. Was it despair? How I miss your lively disposition, your laughter, your learning, and your conviction. I also miss your passion, your fidelity, and your kindness.

As I looked around me, I saw him standing tall: Sultan Hasan. He came to say that the pledge was a debt and the promise had to be fulfilled. They all approached, and I could almost feel their spirits all around me: in the crenulations on the walls, in the minaret atop the mountain, in the Citadel's protective wall, in the lofty building that almost touched the sky. They were all with me and around me, laying the foundations of unity and chatting in a peaceful serenity. They all knew me, and I knew them. Now they had become a group of colleagues and a whole life, and I would often pay them a visit. The best thing about them was that they were all closely tied to history in all its awesome stature. The gaps between them weren't wide. If they had all conversed with each other through buildings, perhaps they realised that a time would come when I would need their warmth and friendship, when the world would oppress me and give me grief.

There was a tear in my eye, and then light appeared and spread.

I looked at the maulid doll and held it at a distance, so I could see it more clearly. Then I saw it blend with the minaret and Citadel in the gentle light of dawn. I saw lamps lit, stretching as far as the horizon, and heard paeans of praise in multiple voices. There is devotion in beauty and creativity in halva. How often has a sultan in love with this lower world come to this land of ours and only left it as an ascetic believer bowing before God alone on the mountain! Where are you, halva-maker?

ON THE MARGINS OF HISTORY

Unifying the community was the hardest task facing Salah ad-din the Ayyubid. He had fought in Syria for two years or more and made pacts with the General, using either threats or promises. Eventually, he became ruler of Egypt and Syria and founded the Ayyubid dynasty. He spent the majority of his ruling years at war.

Salah ad-din the Ayyubid recaptured the Kingdom of Jerusalem from the

Crusaders after they had occupied it for some two years. After the Battle of Hittin in 1187 CE, he liberated most of the territory occupied by the Crusaders. When he died six years later, the danger caused by the Crusaders throughout his life was not at an end. Ending the Crusader threat would take another hundred years.

Salah ad-din was known for his tolerance in dealing with Christians and Jews. Even his war against the Fatimids was not so much about religious sects as it was about one dynasty replacing another. Afterwards, the Shi'ites of Aleppo made a pact with him. In general, it was his interest in Sufism and his studies with 'Abd al-qadir al-Jilani that were major factors in his personality. They made him extremely ascetic, tolerant, and appreciative of all faiths and different opinions.

Salah ad-din the Ayyubid never destroyed a single monument in Egypt. The Mosque of Al-Hakim bi-Amr Allah is still standing, and, even before that, there was the Al-Azhar Mosque. In fact, he bolstered Cairo's walls and expanded the city's limits. But he never witnessed the magnificence of his Citadel; he died before it was completed.

The Crusades started in 1095 CE and the Muslims did not completely recapture Jerusalem until the arrival of the Mamluks in Egypt and Syria. The Crusaders recaptured the city years after Salah ad-din's death in 1228, but the Muslims still hoped to regain the city after Salah ad-din managed to pierce the barrier of fear. In 1291, the Mamluk Sultan, Al-Ashraf Khalil ibn Qala'un, arrived and conquered Acre. With that, the Crusader presence in Jerusalem came to an end.

Salah ad-din the Ayyubid was the first to build schools in Cairo that did not carry his name. Before that, schools would always bear the name of the sultan or king. Traces of Salah ad-din are still to be seen in Cairo and other cities.

Salah ad-din had a son, 'Ala' ad-din Shadi, by 'a boy's mother'—in other words, by a slave girl.

The nuptials of Lady Farida's daughter included many types of halva, including, of course, lots and lots of doughnuts. But something exciting happened. Some of the cooks added chocolate to the doughnuts. Lady

Farida and her daughter objected and claimed that the cooks had distorted the beauty of history and profundity of the past; the cooks, they said, had no idea about heritage. However, the guests ate only the chocolate doughnuts. Lady Farida sighed in despair and looked at her daughter.

"Badr al-Jamali used to speak to Ahmad ibn Tulun," she said. "'Forgive me, friend,' he'd tell him. 'We meet each other in the quarter where sorrow and love of Egypt unite!'"

THE END

LIST OF CHARACTERS (in order of appearance)

BOOK ONE

Jalal ad-din as-Suyuti (1445-1505): a prolific writer, he was a major Egyptian historian and jurist

Salah ad-din al-Ayyubi (1137-93): 'Saladin,' a Sunni Muslim of Kurdish origins, he fought the Crusaders and became ruler of Egypt and Syria, founding the Ayyubid dynasty.

Jawhar the Sicilian (d. 992): a general who commanded the Shiite Fatimid army in its conquest of the Maghreb (960) and Egypt (969) on behalf of the Caliph, Al-Mu`izz li-Din Allah. He initiated the construction of the city of Cairo.

Al-Hakim bi-Amr Allah (965-1021): the sixth Fatimid Caliph, one of the most controversial figures in Islamic history, in that his tyrannical acts (he may well have been schizophrenic) are offset in historical accounts by his status as a divinely inspired ruler, particularly to Shii and Druze communities.

Badr al-Jamali (c. 1006-94): of Armenian origin, he was a prominent minister for the Fatimid Caliphate, particularly during the Caliphate of Al-Mustansir bi-Allah.

Jawhar ibn Husayn ibn Jawhar: son of Husain ibn Jawhar

Husayn ibn Jawhar: son of Jawhar the Sicilian

Sundus: wife of Jawhar, son of Husain ibn Jawhar

Lamya' bint Hamdoon: wife of Husain ibn Jawhar

Mas`ood ibn Thabit: a general in the Fatimid army

Al-Mu`izz li-Din Allah (932-75): the fourth Fatimid Caliph. It was during his reign that the Fatimids moved from Tunisia to Egypt.

`Abdallah, the halva-maker

Mariam: the halva-maker's wife

BOOK TWO

Furoon: youngest daughter of `Ali, son of `Abdallah the halva-maker

`Ali, son of `Abdallah the halva-maker

Badr ibn `Abdallah al-Jamali: Governor of Damascus, husband of Furoon

Susie: Badr's sister

Hafsa: wife of Furoon's brother

`Azeeza: Furoon's mother

Ibn Hamdan: minister to the Fatimid Caliph, enemy of Badr al-Jamali

Shareef Abu Taher; rival of Badr in Syria

Al-Mustansir, Fatimid Caliph

Jamal ad-daula ibn `Ammar: purchaser and trainer of the young Badr al-Jamali

Sha`baan: eldest son of Badr al-Jamali by Amina Khatun

`Abd al-wahhab: Badr's mentor, secretary, and counsellor

Asad ad-daula Idalkiz: Turkish general in Egypt

Sulaiman al-Luwati: Badr's host in Damietta

Rasad: mother of Al-Mustansir, the Fatimid Caliph

Hamza: Furoon's first husband

`Amer, son of Hamza: diehard opponent of Badr al-Jamali

Ahmad al-Awlad: middle son of Badr al-Jamali by Amina Khatun

Muhammad al-Afdal: youngest son of Badr al-Jamali by Amina Khatun

Ja`far: the possessed inhabitant of the Muqattam Hills

Tutush; Seljuq Governor of Syria

Atsiz: Turkish mercenary commander

`Aziza: mistreated Egyptian wife who becomes an admirer and a friend of Furoon

Mas`ood: young man sent from Syria to subvert the intentions of Ahmad al-Awhad, Badr al-Jamali's eldest surviving son

BOOK THREE

Ibrahim: son of `Abd al-Hamid

Yusuf ibn Ayyub: Salah ad-din, generally known as Saladin

`Abd al-Hamid: Ibrahim's father, grandson of Jawhar, son of Husain, son of Jawhar the Sicilian

`Abd al-Wadud: elder grandson of Jawhar, son of Husain, son of Jawhar the Sicilian, and husband of Kauthar

Rashida: daughter of `Abd al-Wadud and Kauthar

Laila: mother of Ibrahim

Kauthar: wife of `Abd al-Wadud and mother of Rashida

Shafiqa: Ibrahim's sister, wife of Aftakin, Turkish soldier

Kamila: Ibrahim's sister, married to Sufyan

Husain: Ibrahim's younger, recalcitrant brother

Zubaida: Rashida's servant and later Salah ad-din's wife

Al-Mustansir: Fatimid Caliph (d. 1094)

Al-`Adid; Fatimid Caliph (d. 1171)

Shawar ibn Mujir as-Sa`di: duplicitous minister of Egypt who ordered the burning of Fustat

King Amaury (Almaric): Crusader King of Jerusalem who invaded Egypt

A LIST OF FATIMID HALVA

Al-Basandud: "There was an array of basandud cakes stuck to each other in hollow circles that made it difficult to be satisfied with just one or to separate one from the other. The smell of almonds and pistachio blended in with the powerful colours that decorated them."

Al-Khushkananaj: "Khushkananaj sweet-cakes had been placed one on top of the other, like new moons high in the sky. I have no idea why they did not fall over or collapse. Cream had been mixed with sugar, almonds, and pistachio."

Al-Fanayid: "They were made of sugar, eggs, rose petals, and almonds. They would melt in your fingers before you could even get them into your mouth.

An-Needa: "Needa is a sweet found only in Cairo. They do not make it in Fustat; they are not allowed to do so. But here it was, inside his store. I could almost smell it: wheat with cream and sugar, blended with all the delicate care of palace fountains."

`Asabi' Zainab: the main ingredients are flour, semolina, oil, sugar, yeast, and rosewater.

Al-`Alaliq li-Ashkal al-hayawanat wa-al-wurud: halva shaped like flowers, people, and animals.

Halwa al-`ajwa: "He would rub the date-paste in his hands, then add almonds and sesame seeds, soaking them in saffron, adding poppy seeds and sugar, and coating them in musk and rose water."

Laqimat al-qadi: "Lighting the fire, he would put some sesame oil in a bowl and toss the judge's morsels into it. Adding corn starch and peeled and crushed pistachio to the mixture, he would mould them into dinar shapes. Once he had finished, he would sprinkle cloves, saffron, aloes, and musk on the individual pieces."

Halwa al-`ajwa: "I grind pistachios and almonds with sugar. Then I'll add ground dates and rose water. And then, there comes the amir of all spices. There can be no halva without saffron; it gives both colour and vigour to halva as a whole."

Al-Qata'if: "Sugar and wheat are blended. Apply wheat dough to a blend of sugar, pistachio, and almonds. You blend the sugar with bees' honey, pistachio, and hazelnut, then add musk, smoke the mixture in aloes and ambergris, and insert it all into the doughnuts. You boil them in sesame oil. Sesame oil: made from sesame seeds.

Al-Halwa al-wardiyya: "She cut the rose petals and put the rose in a bowl full of water. Adding some starch, she left it to boil, expecting eventually to add some musk and sesame oil. Once it had turned bright red, she added sesame oil and sat by the bowl while it cooled."

Al-Kunafa: "She got some semolina, mixed it in her hands, then used her fingers to mix it with butter. After adding honey, she rolled the mix into disc shapes and put them to one side. Now she took some flour, doused it in sesame oil and water, and made that too into discs, trimmed their edges, and baked them."

Halwa al-khabis: "She took a portion of baby carrots, of dates, milk, and honey, and put them all in a pot over a baking pit with a moderate fire, stirring them so they would all blend like lovers making love. She then added a little ginger and chunks of semolina bread to thicken the mixture and poured in some sesame oil."

Halwa al-makshufa: "She took sugar, honey, almonds, and sesame oil, and divided them up into equal portions. After pounding the almonds, she put them, along with the sugar, over the fire with the sesame oil till it all boiled and the almonds were roasted. Then she added honey, covered it all in sugar, mixed it all, and baked it again in sesame oil. Now, she added expensive saffron soaked in rose water and musk and put them all in bowls."

The most important things that distinguish Fatimid-era halva are musk, saffron, and sugar, carefully blended with flour and sesame oil. It is a kind of halva that only works when all the ingredients are properly blended.

EGYPT: DYNASTIC CHART

Islamic conquest of Egypt: `Amr ibn al-`As: 20 AH, 641 CE

Umayyads: 41-132 AH, 662-750 CE

`Abbasids: 132-656 AH, 750-1258 CE

Tulunids: 254-292 AH, 868-904 CE

Ikhshidids: 323-358 AH, 934-968 CE

Fatimids: 358-567 AH, 969-1171 CE

Ayyubids: 567-648 AH, 1174-1250 CE

Bahri Mamluks: 648-784 AH, 1250-1382 CE

Burji Mamluks: 784-923 AH, 1382-1517 CE

TIMELINE

958: Jawhar ibn `Abdallah (d. 992), of Croatian and Sicilian origins, is sent by the fourth Ubaidi Caliph, Al-Mu`izz li-Din Allah, to restore control over West Africa

969: Jawhar leads Ubaidi forces to Egypt via Alexandria and begins the foundation of Cairo

970: city of Misr al-Qahira (Cairo) founded by Fatimid Caliph, Al-Mu`izz.

972: the Al-Azhar Mosque is established

973: Fatimid Caliphate established in Cairo

996-1021: reign of Fatimid Caliph, Al-Hakim bi-Amr Allah

c. 1006-94: life of Badr al-Jamali

1009: Al-Hakim orders the destruction of the Church of the Holy Sepulchre in Jerusalem

1021: The Caliph Al-Hakim "disappears" while star-gazing in the Muqattam Hills, probably assassinated on orders from his half-sister, Sitt al-Mulk

1036-94: reign of Fatimid Caliph Al-Mustansir bi-Allah

1063: Badr al-Jamali appointed military Governor of Damascus

1065-72: severe famine in Egypt; Turkish forces, led by Nasir ad-dawla Ibn Hamdan, ravage the country

1068: Abu Taher leads a rebellion against Badr al-Jamali in Syria; Badr's son, Sha`baan, is killed

1073: Al-Mustansir invites Badr to bring his troops to Egypt; he arrives via Damietta

1074: established in Cairo, Badr assassinates all the major Turkish commanders; he becomes the de facto ruler of Egypt

1076: Badr brings the whole of Egypt under central control, encourages immigration into Egypt, and divides the country into 23 provinces

1080s: refortification of Cairo and construction of the city gates: Bab al-Futuh and Bab an-Nasr

1092: Badr has a second wall built around Cairo, including the Bab Zuweila

1085: death of Al-Awhad, Badr al-Jamali's son

1094: death of Badr al-Jamali; he is succeeded by his son, Al-Afdal

1137-03: life of Yusuf ibn Ayyub, Salah ad-din (Saladin)

1160-71: reign of Fatimid Caliph Al-`Adid

1164: Nur ad-din Zengi, Governor of Aleppo, Syria, sends Asad ad-Din Shirkuh and his nephew, Yusuf ibn Ayyub Salah ad-din (Saladin), to Egypt to reinstall and support Shawar, minister to the Caliph Al-`Adid

1164-68: Shawar reneges on his agreements, and a power struggle ensues between Shirkuh and Shawar, during which Shawar seeks the support of Crusader King Amaury (Almaric) of Jerusalem

1167: Shirkuh leaves Salah ad-din to defend Alexandria, which is subjected to a lengthy siege by the combined forces of Shawar and the Crusaders

1168: Crusader King Amaury (Almaric) of Jerusalem attacks Egypt, sacks the city of Bilbeis, and marches towards Fustat; Shawar orders the destruction of Fustat by fire

1169: Nur ad-din orders Shirkuh to return to Egypt, and he joins with Salah ad-din to recapture Cairo from the Crusaders; Salah ad-din arrests

Shawar, and he is executed on orders from the Caliph Al-`Adid; Shirkuh is appointed minister, but dies shortly afterwards; Salad-din replaces him

1171-1254 Ayyubid dynasty in Egypt, founded by Salah ad-din following his abolition of the Fatimid Caliphate

THE HALVA-MAKER: AFTERWORD

Why do we read historical fiction? For one thing, it promises an entry into the past that is richer and more textured than straightforward history, which is obliged to stick to the facts—or, at least, to preface speculation with a responsible disclaimer...For a few hours the boundaries of time and mortality, geography and class are erased.

Sophia Pinkham, "*The Freedom of Historical Fiction*," New York Review of Books, Vol. LXIX no. 4 (March 10, 2022), 13.

Of all the encounters and confrontations between medieval Europe and the world of Islam, the Crusades must surely offer historians one of the most cogent rationales for the implementation of Oscar Wilde's sage advice: "the one thing we owe to history is to rewrite it." Recent studies in English, such as those of Carole Hillenbrand, The Crusades: Islamic Perspectives (1999), and Paul Cobb, The Race for Paradise (2014), already offer strong correctives to the distortions and falsehoods of Christian myth-making over the course of many centuries. However, for me at least, it is the television series, The Crusades (1995), that reveals in detail the true extent of that one-sided approach to the historical record. The host of the series is none other than Terry Jones, a member of the Monty Python comedy troupe, but also an Oxford-educated medieval historian. Following in the tracks of various European rulers and their relatives who responded to Pope Urban II's initial call for "holy war" in 1098, Jones traverses Europe. He visits the Jewish cemetery in Germany where victims of Crusader pogroms are buried, and crosses the Bosphorus at Istanbul, where—as Constantinople—the Orthodox Patriarch ordered the city's gates closed in the face of such an unruly horde. Once on the Asian side, Jones dons heavy chain-mail for the trek southwards, pauses at the Syrian town of Ma`arrat an-Nu`man where the historical record describes Crusaders resorting to cannibalism as they eat local babies roasted on spits, and finally reaches Jerusalem. By the time Jones's travels and the series are at an end, barely a single Crusader myth is left standing.

Reem Bassiouney's three-part novel, *The Halva-Maker* (in Arabic, *Al-*

Halwani, 2022) contributes through the medium of fiction to this different interpretation of the historical record, in that its third segment, entitled 'The Kurd,' is set during the final years of the Fatimid Caliphate in Egypt and the attempts by Amaury (Almaric), Crusader King of Jerusalem, to take advantage of the weaknesses of the Egyptian regime. A central figure—the 'Kurd' of the section's title—is Yusuf ibn Ayyub, known as Salah ad-din (Saladin), who is sent by Nur ad-din Zengi, the governor of Aleppo, Syria, to oust the Crusaders. In 1171, Saladin brings the caliphate of Al-`Adid and the Fatimids to a close, restores Egypt to Sunni Islam, and assumes the sultanate himself, giving his name to the dynasty that follows (Ayyubids). However, before those events are recounted, *The Halva-Maker* devotes the first two sections of its trilogy structure to the foundation and development of the Fatimid dynasty.

The entire novel opens with an introductory section set in 2016 in which a female narrator goes to see `Amm `Abdo, 'the halva man,' who many people consider to be either crazy or possessed. He insists that the narrator try some of his halva and then proceeds to link the production of these renowned sweets to the history of Egypt and some of its most famous historical figures, especially during the Shi`ite Fatimid era. The narrator is initially incredulous, but is gradually convinced that this highly unusual character does indeed have a great deal to impart to anyone who is prepared to listen to his accounts of the past. Thus does the trilogy of stories begin, and indeed thus does it end with the conclusion of the third section.

Following this introduction, the first section of the novel, entitled 'the Sicilian,' offers retrospective comments on the career of Jawhar, who hailed originally from Sicily, but became the commanding general in the army of the Ubaidi Shi`ite dynasty, based originally at Al-Mahdiyya on the coast of Tunisia. In 969 CE he led the army eastwards to Egypt, and in 973 the Fatimid Caliphate was established in the newly built city of Cairo (named after Fatima, the daughter of the Prophet Muhammad and daughter of `Ali ibn Abi Talib, the Prophet's cousin and founding figure of Shi`ite Islam). Jawhar set about constructing the new city, to the north of Fustat, the earliest Muslim capital in Egypt, and the ruins of the city of Ahmad ibn Tulun, of which only the great mosque survived. Fatimid Cairo, now the "old city" of the contemporary city, sits beneath the Muqattam Hills, and its primary monument remains the Al-Azhar Mosque, originally a

Shi`ite shrine, but today a major center of Sunni worship and scholarship. However, the narrative tells us how Jawhar's family also brought to the new city of Cairo a particular skill, one that gives the novel its title and is reflected in `Amm `Abdo's introduction: the making of different varieties of halva (the well-known sweet whose name derives from the Arabic adjective for sweet, "hulw"). As one generation followed another, the matchless skill of the family members in making the various categories of sweet is regularly recorded in the narrative, often including specific details of the ingredients involved and the various stages in their preparation—duly reflected in the listing at the conclusion of the narrative.

This summary of Jawhar the Sicilian's life and achievements constitutes an accurate reflection of the historical record, but Reem Bassiouney's proven talents as a historical novelist are reflected in the fact that, in this first section of the novel, the details of his life are not narrated directly, but instead take the form of a lengthy retrospect dated 1019 CE. They involve the similarly named Jawhar, son of Husain, the son of Jawhar the Sicilian. Times have changed; as Jawhar the grandson puts it: "Oh, my grandfather, if only you could witness these times today: the populace in revolt and the loss of prestige!" The Fatimid Caliph is now Al-Hakim bi-Amr Allah, one of Egypt's and Islam's most renowned and controversial figures. Jawhar's father, Husain, son of Jawhar the Sicilian, has been killed by order of the Caliph, his family has had to take up residence in Fustat to the south of the closed city of Cairo, and his son, Jawhar, is now in the complicated process of seeking re-instatement in the Caliph's esteem while still countering the resentment that his mother and other family members feel at his apparent readiness to forget the past, one that he himself is constantly recalling.

As is the case with all Reem Bassiouney's historical novels, the narrative also introduces its readers to a series of remarkable female characters whose lives and loves are intertwined with the public careers of their spouses and relatives. In the case of Jawhar, son of Husain, it is his wife, Sundus, formerly—the narrative informs us—a teenage beauty, but, her body and face now cruelly scarred by burns from a fire, a powerful and often troubling presence in his life. Initially shunned by her husband, she has spent an entire year in the darkened company of Bahnas, the Pyramid Witch, a frequent source of wisdom and advice for characters in this novel, as in others by this author. While Sundus emerges from that experience with both wisdom and resolve, her husband has decided to ally himself with the Caliph Al-Hakim and describes in appalling detail his own participation in the fire and destruction that the Caliph has ordered wreaked on the Egyptian people in Fustat because of a perceived insult. Inevitably however, as his attachment to Sundus and his awareness of her inner beauty and sagacity grows, so too does a realization of his own folly in following the wayward orders of Al-Hakim bi-Amr Allah, the very same Caliph who has killed his father. The consequences of that folly become clear when the tables are turned. Al-Hakim's general, Mas`ood, manages to persuade the people of Fustat, who have now lost their homes to fire and their women and children to the attacking soldiers, that Jawhar alone was responsible for the attack on Fustat. Expelled from Cairo and returning to Fustat with his wife, Sundus, Jawhar is savagely attacked by its inhabitants and is only rescued by a local halva-maker, `Abdallah, whose halva-store in Fustat has been destroyed. In another twist to the novel's halva-theme, `Abdallah tells Jawhar how his father came to know Jawhar the Sicilian, Jawhar's grandfather, and goes on to provide yet more information about the earliest days of the Ubaidi regime, the foundation of Cairo and the Al-Azhar Mosque, and the establishment of the Fatimid Caliphate.

Like the vast majority of the Egyptian population, Jawhar now has to steer his way through the often incomprehensible vagaries and whims of Al-Hakim's caliphate. Exiled from Cairo and his palace (where his mother, Lamya', still resides), then readmitted; deprived of his army rank, then reinstated, Jawhar joins `Abdallah as they search for their families. As he himself expresses it: "I was tired of rulers and commanders, the changing moods of people, the destruction of the soul, and my prolonged absence from my own wife, the only woman I ever loved." Jawhar discovers his wife, Sundus, secluded in his Cairo palace, but `Abdallah's wife, Mariam, captured by Al-Hakim's general, Mas`ood, has resisted his advances and been killed. Jawhar kills Mas`ood in a sword-duel and rescues `Abdallah's son, and the group takes refuge at a sea-side house in Alexandria. When the star-gazing Caliph Al-Hakim does not return from one of his nocturnal excursions into the Muqattam Hills and is replaced as Caliph by his son, Jawhar's identity is discovered and he is invited back to Cairo. However, he is now closely involved in halva-making. Dismissing references to his illustrious ancestors and their achievements, he declines the invitation.

As the novel's title makes clear, halva-making is to provide a linkage throughout its three sections. As the narrative itself tells us: "Ever since the start of the Sicilian family's era, their passion for halva had involved them in the governance of Egypt and linked them to the rulers in marriage." As its first section concludes, the introduction's female narrator (mentioned earlier) returns to ask ʾAmm ʾAbdo for some halva for her daughter's upcoming wedding. At the same time, she inquires as to the eventual fate of Jawhar, son of Husain, and then requests a further narrative about Salah ad-din (Saladin). However, ʾAmm ʾAbdo tells her that, before that story can be told, the linkage of generations needs next to include the story of "the Armenian," the second part of the novel.

The narrative opens in the Syrian city of Damascus, to which some of ʾAbdallah the halva-maker's family members have fled in order to escape the increasing chaos and continuing drought that are making life in Egypt so unbearable. It emerges that ʾAli, ʾAbdallah's son, has taken the advice of Ibn Hamdan, Turkish army commander and minister in Egypt, to leave the country and seek refuge with Badr al-Jamali, the Governor of Damascus, an arrangement that allows each local ruler to be aware of the other's policies and intrigues. Once again, the reader is introduced to a female figure who is to play a major role in the narrative: Furoon, youngest granddaughter of Jawhar son of Husain and Sundus. Ignoring her elder sisters' scorn, she has made some maulid halva for the Amir. Setting eyes on Badr for the first time, she falls instantly in love with the handsome Armenian who has welcomed her family to his residence. However, little does Furoon realize at the time that, while Badr has been lending his distant support to the weak Fatimid Caliph, Al-Mustansir, in Egypt, her own father, ʾAli, has colluded with Ibn Hamdan who, as we read in the novel, "was responsible for all the disasters plaguing Egypt: he had laid siege to its people and imposed heavy taxes on them in order to pay for his soldiers and their retinue." Not only that, but his intentions are to return the country's allegiance to Sunni Islam and the Abbasid Caliphate.

However, in spite of the chaotic and disastrous situation in Egypt and the sectarian antagonisms provoked by the ruling cliques in both Syria and Egypt, it is on the personal level that this second section proceeds. If Furoon is immediately attracted to Badr, the sentiment is rapidly reciprocated. He is initially entranced by the beauty and apparent innocence of the eighteen year-old girl, but he soon discovers that not only is she aware of the broader dimensions of the current political situation, but also quite prepared to pose pertinent questions and comment on his responses with a disarming frankness. As the narrative informs readers about Badr's childhood seizure as a mamluk along with his sister, the ruthless rigor of his military training at the hands of his master, Jamal ad-Daula, Governor of Tripoli, and his eventual manumission, it becomes clear that he is emotionally ill-equipped to withstand and cope with the personality with which Furoon confronts him. A crisis in the relationship rapidly develops when ʿAli rejects Badr's request to be married to his daughter, announces his intention to marry her to Amir Hamza, an associate of Shareef Abu Taher Haidar, one of Badr's main rivals in Syria, and moves his family out of the Governor's palace.

However, circumstances now cause a brutal interruption to the romance. Badr, still the loyal Shiʿite Governor of Damascus on behalf of the Fatimid Caliph, finds himself embroiled in a civil war in Syria involving other Shiʿite contenders for power and Turkish Seljuq forces. Not only is his palace in Damascus and part of the city itself set ablaze, but his son, Shaʿbaan, is killed. His now divorced wife, Amina Khatun, Shaʿbaan's mother, curses him for his arrogance, but she too has to join the family and Badr's retainers as they flee the burning city. Furoon meanwhile, still yearning for Badr, has been forcibly married by her father ʿAli to Amir Hamza, but has been resisting his advances by invoking the curse of the jinn in order to keep him at bay.

The process of rekindling the passionate relationship that has been so brutally severed by external events becomes one part of Badr's relentless pursuit of revenge against his enemies. They are systematically cut down, including Amir Hamza, whose womenfolk, including Furoon, find themselves confronting Badr's wrath before being sold cheaply as slave-girls in the local market. It is one of Badr's men who buys Furoon, leading to a climactic encounter during which Badr's assertion of complete authority meets its match in the telling impact of Furoon's beauty and muted determination. As the passionate relationship is resumed and residual family complications are debated and resolved, Badr receives a letter from the Fatimid Caliph in Cairo asking him to come to Egypt and help resolve the country's continuing crisis. A new phase in Badr's career is about to begin.

Badr's journey to Egypt, accompanied by his army, dates to the year 1073-4, and marks the beginning of his rise to power, eventually becoming the de facto ruler of the country and acquiring thereby an impressive list of titles, culminating in his designation as "As-Sayyid al-Ajall," which I translate as "supreme master." Badr already has a general awareness of the dire conditions faced by the Egyptian people even before his departure from Syria, and a stop in the Nile delta city of Damietta provides him with further details concerning the influence of the Caliph's mother in decision-making. However, nothing can prepare him for the shocking scenes that he witnesses during an initial walking tour of the environs of Cairo with a local pauper, with people searching garbage on the street for something to eat and teenage girls prostituting themselves in public. Badr has the chance to admire the Ibn Tulun Mosque, but the horrifying experience he has witnessed makes clear to him the sheer magnitude of the task that now confronts him. Carefully but relentlessly, Badr eliminates all the power-bases that have brought Egypt to its knees, browbeating the weakened Caliph into accepting his strategies. The inevitable bloodshed traumatizes Furoon, and she often arouses his ire by suggesting that more moderate and sympathetic approaches to his opponents might pay dividends. However, she too succumbs to the perceived necessities of the situation and, above all, to her love for her husband. In the midst of all the turmoil, she bears him a son, Ja`far, so named after the ascetic sage whose advice he often seeks, climbing to the top of the Muqattam Hills where the so-called madman lives in seclusion.

Cairo, the city built by Jawhar the Sicilian, long closed to all but the Fatimid caliphs and their retainers, is now opened to all Egyptians, no matter what their religious affiliation. As Badr's policies improve the lives of Egyptians, former pockets of power in both Upper and Lower Egypt rebel and are put down. Already Army Commander and Chief Judge, the Caliph now appoints Badr as "Minister of Sword and Pen." Badr is now, to all intents and purposes, ruler of Egypt.

While Badr continues to exert his authority with ruthless efficiency, his wife follows her own instincts by making donations of food, clothing, and money to Egypt's poor and by offering Qur'an classes to women in the Ahmad ibn Tulun Mosque. However, it is the latter function that is to prove devastatingly fatal. The family of her former husband, Hamza, whom Badr has killed, are still out for revenge, and it is a woman hired for that purpose who stabs Furoon with a poisoned knife as she is about to enter the mosque. As if that is not enough, Al-Awhad Ahmad, one of Badr's sons from his previous marriage, whom he has appointed Governor of Alexandria in the expectation that he will be his father's successor, and whose rebellion against Badr has been put down after a siege of the city, determines to kill his father. The arrow misses its target, but wounds Badr's hand. Defiant to the last, Al-Awhad dies, or is killed, in prison.

Badr forces himself to continue his functions as de facto ruler of Egypt, strengthening Cairo's walls and gates, for example. And yet, his final years are punctuated by sorrow and loss, something that is immediately evident to Bahnas, the Pyramid Witch, when he pays her a visit. He has long grieved the death of his son, Sha`baan, killed in battle in Syria, but now he mourns not only his beloved wife, Furoon, but also his problematic but still loved son, Al-Awhad Ahmad. From such a burden of grief he seeks whatever solace he can find at the isolated spot on top of the Muqattam Hills, where, as already noted, he has often sought advice from Ja`far, the sage 'madman.' It is in such isolation from the world's cares and tribulations that Badr seeks consolation in prayer, and it is there that he follows Ja`far's advice by constructing his own monument, the unique structure known as the Juyushi (armies) Mosque. Entering the building, he can indulge in his own prayers and pleas to God. Standing by the entrance, he can look down on the Fatimid city of Cairo immediately below, and, in the distance, see the Pyramids on the Giza plateau to the west and the Mosque of Ahmad ibn Tulun to the south, all of them enduring monuments to the various phases in Egypt's lengthy history. And, if his son named "the one" (Al-Awhad) is now dead, another son named "the preferable" (Al-Afdal) is to be his successor as Minister to the Fatimid Caliph.

When the novel's narrator has asked `Amm `Abdo at the outset to tell her about Salah ad-din, he has informed her that other accounts need to be told first. At that point in the novel's narration, she may well not have realized quite how lengthy and detailed would be his narratives devoted to Jawhar the Sicilian and Badr the Armenian, the novel's first two sections. But, with the third section, we finally reach the focus of her initial request, Yusuf ibn Ayyub, renowned as Salah ad-din (Saladin). Even so, we are also immediately introduced to another character who is to play a major role in the narrative that follows: Ibrahim, descendant of Badr al-Jamali through his marriage to Furoon, who lives in Alexandria and maintains the family tradition of halva-making.

The year is 1164 CE, and Salah ad-din has joined his uncle, the Kurdish general, Asad ad-din Shirkuh ibn Shadhi, in traveling to Egypt on orders from Nur ad-din Zengi, the Governor of Aleppo in Syria, in order to support the Fatimid Caliph, Al-`Adid, and to counter the schemes of his increasingly powerful Minister, Shawar, who has been seeking support from the Crusaders. Knowing of Ibrahim's significant role in the city of Alexandria, Salah ad-din asks him to mobilize its citizens. In a gesture that is to prove of utmost significance for the course of the novel's third section, he also inquires about Ibrahim's female cousin, Rashida. Ibrahim describes her as "a trial for all of us"—an opinion seemingly justified by the account of intra-family strife that follows. Rashida's intrigues against Ibrahim know no bounds: she sows doubt and discord about him among the female members of the household, and expresses her support for Minister Shawar in his confrontation with the Fatimid Caliph. Inevitably, Ibrahim learns about her intrigues. Summoning the entire family to a meeting, he slaps her to the ground and excoriates her for her lies and machinations. Alexandria and the family, he informs them, will stand with the Fatimid Caliph and Salah ad-din against Shawar and the Crusaders. However, while Ibrahim takes his men out to fight, the local police who are supporting Shawar, decide to make Alexandria's womenfolk a lesson for those who dare oppose the minister. Rashida opts to be the woman of the family to be flayed. When Ibrahim returns to the horrific scene that has ensued, everything is changed. Rashida, in excruciating pain after being flayed to within an inch of her life, is now the major focus of his concern and admiration, much to the consternation of Sayyida, his supposed fiancée.

Two narratives are now interwoven: the general situation in Alexandria and Egypt on the one hand, and, on the other, the equally confrontational situation involving the women from different branches of the family inside Ibrahim's household. Ibrahim's forces manage to defeat the police, and he is declared a hero in Alexandria, where he and Salah ad-din are now in control. The city is besieged by the Crusaders, and that leads to an immediate crisis of food and water. The situation becomes even worse when the city is hit by the plague. Eventually a truce is declared, the siege is lifted, and the Syrian forces withdraw. However, two of Ibrahim's brothers are killed. The external situation is echoed inside the family home where the women have been arguing over the distribution of precious water. The changed situation between the two cousins is made abundantly clear when an infuriated Ibrahim solves the dispute by assigning the distribution of food and water to Rashida. When Ibrahim finally returns home without his two brothers, the family is devastated, and his own mother declares him dead along with his slain brothers. It is only now that, faced with conflict and disruption on all fronts, Ibrahim and Rashida come to realize how much they love each other, a realization not made easier by their clashing personalities. Because of the continuing danger from Shawar's machinations, Ibrahim dispatches the entire family to Syria. While Rashida remains in Egypt, she too leaves Alexandria, but to return to Cairo in order to preserve and manage the family's halva business.

While Ibrahim is arrested and languishes in Shawar's prison, Rashida sets about reviving the halva-making business. Her life becomes more complicated when, among the amirs who flock to taste her newly devised halva, is Al-Kamil, Shawar's son, who declares his love for her. It is the same Al-Kamil who engineers Ibrahim's escape from prison, leaving him alone in the Sinai Desert. Ibrahim is taken to the "Fortress of Death" in Syria where Rashid ad-din Sinan and his Assassins reside. He listens as a shaikh justifies the need to kill Salah ad-din. Apparently acceding to those demands, Ibrahim takes a poisoned sword with him to Damascus, but, when he meets his old friend, Salah ad-din, again, it is to warn him about the imminent danger that threatens them both and the region in general--a prediction that is to prove all too accurate, as the narrative will soon relate...

One member of the family, Ibrahim's youngest brother, Husain, has disapproved of his brother's activities and involvement in conflict and has long since disappeared. It emerges that he has moved to the Delta town of Bilbeis, where he has married, had a son (named Ibrahim), and is working for a halva-maker. Family and conflict combine yet again, in that Bilbeis is the town that is brutally attacked by the Crusader forces of King Amaury, breaking a truce agreed to with Shawar. Husain's wife and son are killed, and Husain is taken prisoner and put on a boat. As it makes its way up the river towards the sea, an unseen hand grabs him and pulls him into the river, unties his fetters, and guides him to land. His rescuer is the person who taught him how to swim as a child, his own brother, Ibrahim.

Back in Cairo, Shawar decides to prevent the invading Crusaders from capturing Fustat by burning it to the ground. Determined to preserve her factory and store, Rashida refuses the general order to evacuate to Cairo.

Screaming and cursing, she has to be carried to the Cairo home of Ibrahim's mother and sisters, where she is, needless to say, hardly a welcome guest. Shawar's son, Al-Kamil, arrives to take the family to his palace, but, before he can do that and in a climactic moment, Husain, the long-lost son enters the room, followed by his rescuer, Ibrahim himself. Ibrahim instructs Al-Kamil to leave, and then, faced with a sea of hostile glares, announces that he will be married to Rashida then and there. There is just enough time for a passionate union of minds and bodies, but then Ibrahim and Husain rush away to confront the Crusaders. When there follows a stalemate at the city gates, it is Rashida who suggests an alternative strategy, one that involves the citizens of Cairo in urban warfare. With mounting Crusader losses and news of an approaching Syrian army, the Crusader King decides to leave Egypt and withdraws to Ashkelon.

Salah ad-din now returns. With the departure of the Crusaders and Ibrahim's killing of Shawar, the Caliph is able to appoint first Shirkuh and then Salah ad-din as minister of Egypt. Salah ad-din gradually takes over full control of the country: he abolishes the Fatimid caliphate, restores allegiance to the Sunni caliphate in Baghdad, and forms his own multi-ethnic and – sectarian army. It is when he proscribes the manufacture of halva-types associated with the Fatimids that Ibrahim feels compelled to pay his old friend, the de facto ruler of Egypt, a visit. After a lengthy discussion, Salah ad-din is finally persuaded that Egyptians may still enjoy those and other types of halva and sends Ibrahim home with an escort of one of his own guards. That guard turns out to be an Assassin plant ordered to kill both Salah ad-din and Ibrahim, and Ibrahim is grievously wounded. However, he survives the attack and, as an additional benefit, is acknowledged by his mother as her still beloved son.

Ibrahim and Rashida have come to the realization that, while passionate love holds them together, the crucial element of mutual trust is not there. Rashida finally confides to her beloved husband that she has a secret, one that requires that they climb the Muqattam Hills to the shrine built by their joint grandfather, Badr. There she digs up the treasure in gold and money that she has had buried. Leaving her in front of the mosque, Ibrahim goes off and returns with the rest of the family's treasure also buried there. As they look down from the heights, they spot the distant figure of Salah ad-din, planning the Citadel that he is going to build on a promontory beneath the Al-Muqattam Hills and contemplating the various monuments that have been constructed by Egyptian rulers of past ages.

Reem Bassiouney's novel, *The Halva-Maker*, provides its readers with accurate historical details about three periods in the Ubaidi Shi`ite Fatimid Caliphate in Egypt—those of Jawhar 'the Sicilian,' Badr 'the Armenian,' and Salah ad-din, 'the Kurd.' It does indeed offer its readers, as the epigraph that I cited at the beginning of this Afterword suggests, a "richer and more textured" entry into the past. A particular feature of her works of historical fiction is also the insertion into the narrative of significant, strong-minded female characters—in this case, Sundus, Furoon, and Rashida—who not only supervise the making of halva and experiment with new varieties, but also have a profound influence on their husbands and families. As the novel's title suggests, halva is to be a prominent feature in the narrative. As if to underline that fact, the author provides an Appendix, in which the fourteen different types of halva are listed, along with a short description of their preparation. In spite of the delicious varieties listed there, my own particular favorite remains kunafa.

In conclusion, I would like to thank Dararab for publishing Reem Bassiouney's prize-winning historical novel. I owe a particular debt of gratitude to Marcia Lynx Quayle, who has applied her habitual editorial skills to the translated text, rendering it that much more accessible to readers of English.

ROGER ALLEN

August 2022

Reem Bassiouney

Author

Dr Reem Bassiouney, an award-winning author and a professor of Sociolinguistics, was born in Alexandria, Egypt (1973). She has authored seven academic books and eleven novels. Her works have been best-sellers in the Arab World. Seven of her novels have been translated into other languages. She obtained her MPhil and DPHIL in linguistics from Oxford University. She is a professor of Linguistics at the American University in Cairo. Before that, she was an associate professor at Georgetown University in the US.

Dr Bassiouney is the winner of the Sheikh Zaid Award (2024) for her novel, "The Halva Maker, The Trilogy of The Fatimids." She also won the National Prize for Excellence in Literature (2022) from the Egyptian Ministry of Culture. Bassiouney was awarded the prestigious Naguib Mahfouz Award (2020) from Egypt's Supreme Council for Culture for "Sons of the People," making her the first woman to win this prize. "Sons of the People" has also been nominated for the Dublin Literary Award by Bibliotheca Alexandria. Dr. Bassiouney was granted the King Fahd Literature Award (2010) for "The Pistachio Seller." She also won the 2009 Sawiris Foundation Literary Prize for "Professor Hanaa."

Roger Allen

Translator

In June 2011 Roger Allen retired from his position as the Sascha Jane Patterson Harvie Professor of Social Thought and Comparative Ethics in the School of Arts & Sciences at the University of Pennsylvania, where he also served as Professor of Arabic and Comparative Literature in the Department of Near Eastern Languages & Civilizations. He served as President of the Middle East Studies Association of North America (MESA) for the year 20092010-. He is Honorary President of the Banipal Trust and Sub-editor of the Encyclopedia of Islam 3rd edition for modern Arabic literature. He is a 2020 winner of the Lifetime Achievement Award of the Shaikh Hamad Award for Translation and International Understanding (Qatar).

Among his numerous published studies on Arabic literature are: The Arabic Novel: an historical and critical introduction (2nd edition 1995, 2nd Arabic edition 1998), and The Arabic Literary Heritage in 1998 (and in abbreviated paperback form in 2000, as Introduction to Arabic Literature; Arabic translation, Cairo, 2003).

He has translated a number of fictional works by modern Arab writers, including the Egyptian Nobel Laureate, Naguib Mahfouz: a collection of short stories, God's World (1973), and the novels, Autumn Quail, Mirrors, Karnak Café, Khan al-Khalili, and One Hour Left. He has also translated novels and short stories by a number of other Arab authors, including Jabra Ibrahim Jabra, Yusuf Idris, `Abd al-rahman Munif, Mayy Telmissany, Halim Barakat, BenSalim Himmich, Ahmad al-Tawfiq, and Hanan al-Shaykh.

Since retirement, he has published a number of translations: the first complete edition of the original episodes of Muhammad al-Muwaylihi's Hadith `Isa ibn Hisham (What `Isa ibn Hisham Told Us, 2 vols., [Library of Arabic Literature series], New York: New York University Press, 2015); a novel (The Elusive Fox) and short-story collection (Monarch of the Square) by the Moroccan author, Muhammad Zifzaf (with Mbarek Sryfi); `Abd al-karim Ghallab's novel, Dafan-na al-madi (We Have Buried the Past, London: Haus Publishing, 2018); Naguib Mahfouz's newly discovered collection of narratives (untitled in the original, The Quarter, (London: Saqi Books, 2019); Ameen Rihani's travelogue, The Heart of Lebanon (Syracuse University Press, 2021); and three historical novels by Reem Bassiouney: Fountain of the Drowning, (Diwan Publishers, Cairo, 2021); Sons of the People, (Syracuse University Press, 2022); and Al-Qata'i, (Georgetown University Press, 2023).